"Shiabrè, Denice,   English, nightways. And there is a core to it. Robert paused; his gaze was steady. "A Kill."

"I see."

"I do not think you do. Have you ever killed anyone?"

A memory flickered through the back of Denice's mind; she buried it without knowing she had done so. "I don't think so. The boy in Portugal survived."

"I know. When you shot him—did you feel a joy? A soaring?"

"No. I was just scared." Denice did not know what made her say it: "I shot at some Peaceforcers once. And another man died while he was chasing me. But I didn't enjoy it either time."

Robert simply nodded. He did not seem surprised. "I think accidental death would not be the same. If it ever comes to you, the chance to take a life with your own hands, I shall be interested to learn of your response."

Denice Castanaveras said softly, "Killing is wrong."

Robert Dazai Yo smiled at her. "Many people think so," he agreed. "And for most people it is. They don't do it right. If you Kill, I do not doubt you will do so in a most exquisite fashion. A proper Kill, child, is art of the highest order. Someday you will appreciate this."

Other books by Daniel Keys Moran:

ARMAGEDDON BLUES
EMERALD EYES
THE LONG RUN

THE
LAST
DANCER

Daniel Keys Moran

BANTAM BOOKS
NEW YORK · TORONTO · LONDON · SYDNEY · AUCKLAND

THE LAST DANCER

A Bantam Spectra Book / November 1993

SPECTRA and the portrayal of a boxed "s" are trademarks of Bantam Books,
a division of Bantam Doubleday Dell Publishing Group, Inc.

ISBN 0-553-56249-5

Published simultaneously in the United States and Canada

Bantam Books are published by Bantam Books, a division of Bantam
Doubleday Dell Publishing Group, Inc. Its trademark, consisting of the words
"Bantam Books" and the portrayal of a rooster, is Registered in U.S. Patent
and Trademark Office and in other countries. Marca Registrada. Bantam
Books, 1540 Broadway, New York, New York 10036.

PRINTED IN THE UNITED STATES OF AMERICA

RAD   0 9 8 7 6 5 4 3 2 1

DEDICATION...
For Holly. I love you.

... AND THANKS TO ...

My friend Richard Sommers, who helped make it possible for me to finish this bitch of a book, and whose sound advice and perspective kept me from going off the deep end on at least one occasion; Angel and Jodi and Kathy, for their love; Doctor Death for allowing me the use of Nicole Eris Lovely, a character from *False Prophets*, her second novel about the Prophet Harry; David Gerrold, for giving me the opportunity to *eat* his brain, the way the Japanese do to the monkeys; Dorothy Fontana, who fed me the second best chili in the world, and who tried, against all reasonable expectations, to improve me as a human being by exposing me to the Big Band sound at the Hollywood Bowl one night; Steve Barnes and Toni Young, for their friendship and support, and Steve and Toni and Dawn Callan for *The Warrior Within* workshop; Amy Stout and Lou Aronica and Ralph the Wise and Powerful, for their astonishing patience; The Kinks, for *Rock and Roll Fantasy*; Melissa Etheridge, who sang *I Will Never Be the Same* for me in concert one night during the craziness; and

Don Henley, for *The End of the Innocence*. I am deeply grateful for *The Heart of the Matter*, a song that helped keep me sane. Perhaps gratitude from the audience is out of order where art is concerned; I paid him for that music with cold cash, as you presumably have paid for this book; but "what the head makes cloudy, the heart makes very clear." Thank you.

... AND A NOTE.

Usually in this part of the book the author says something to the effect that the experts he's mentioned are not to be faulted in the event he screwed something up despite their invaluable help. Not this time. I did my best. If anything is wrong in *The Last Dancer* it's their fault. Particularly Amy Stout, Steve Barnes, David Gerrold, Dorothy Fontana, and Ralph Vincinanza, all of whom are professionals and should have known better.

The Last Dancer

A Tale of the Continuing Time

There are no longer "dancers," the possessed. The cleavage of men into actors and spectators is the central fact of our time. We are obsessed with heroes who live for us and whom we punish. . . . We have metamorphised from a mad body dancing on hillsides to a pair of eyes staring in the dark.

—Jim Morrison

Prolog:
The Dancer

In the last hour of sunlight the Dancer fled through the forest covering the base of the mountains.

The trees were tall, emaciated things of some pale wood, with dull, silver-white leaves. They spread themselves thinly but evenly, and in the shadows of approaching night the Dancer could see no more than fifteen or twenty paces ahead at any moment. The winds blew cold, growing colder, dropping down below freezing even before the sun had set. The Dancer barely noticed except to wonder, briefly, if it might in some way slow the Shield who pursued him.

If the Shield was Marah, perhaps. But the Dancer suspected Marah was dead, and if so, the Shield pursuing him was Dvan. Dvan might well notice the cold; he was no Dancer.

But he would not permit it to stop him.

The Dancer ran faster as the slope of the ground began to rise, whipcord muscles moving gracefully beneath the sheath of his skin.

One way or another it would all be over soon.

From behind him came a shrill scream, the cry of the kitjan. Closer than it had been. The Dancer's neural system, vastly more sensitive than any normal human's, registered a twinge of pain. The kitjan was a terrifying weapon; the Dancer's companions, four of the eight, had died in agony at its touch, and if the Shield chasing him got much closer he would be the fifth. He picked up speed, pushed his amazing body to its fullest, demanding more speed, and getting it. He wove through the shadowed trees, pushing aside the barrier of the cold night air. His breath came smoothly, drew the air, the life-giving oxygen, through his nostrils, warming it, and then deep into his lungs. The trees thinned around him as he moved higher up the mountainside, and the slope grew steeper. Now and again as he climbed he used his hands to help himself along.

Above the cover of the trees, the huge chain of mountains became visible again. He moved upward through a long ravine, the sides of the ravine rising away on either side of him. It was shadowed here, but not shadowed enough; from nearly any point outside the thickest part of the forest, the Dancer would be visible now. This was the point of greatest danger, where, for long moments, he would be in plain view.

A lucky shot; at that distance it could be nothing else. The kitjan whiplash touched the Dancer, held him for the merest instant. Nerves fired at random; every superbly trained muscle in the Dancer's body spasmed at once. He fell in midstride and struck the ground hard, rolling limply, tumbling back downslope in complete loss of control.

He ended up in a crevice beneath an overhanging, ice-scoured boulder. The Dancer lay on the cold hard ground, fighting the unconsciousness that crept in around him. He monitored his heart, found it had ceased beating at the kitjan's touch. He restarted it, inspected its operation briefly to ensure that it would continue beating unattended. Spasms ripped the muscles of his abdomen, made breathing impossible. The Dancer concentrated on the abdominal muscles, and well before he was in danger of losing consciousness from anoxia had regained control of his breath. His eyesight cleared slowly of its own accord. The Dancer lay on the frozen ground, waiting. The kitjan screamed once, twice, while he waited there. The first shot came nowhere near him; the Shield had not seen him clearly when he fell. The next shot came closer, sent another wash of wracking pain across the Dancer's frame; more of the unlikely luck that had felled him in the first place.

It was dark now. Once, long ago, before the Dancers had learned to control the temperature of their bodies, that lack of visible light would have meant little; the Shield saw body heat as well as any Dancer. Now that darkness might well make the difference between life and death. Lying motionless at the base of the boulders, looking down the mountain, the Dancer saw the first flicker of motion among the thinning trees, of the Shield closing in. The Dancer let his heartbeat slow, let the blood move sluggishly through his veins. He felt it first in his hands, as his body temperature dropped slowly toward freezing, toward the ambient temperature of the world around him. At last he moved, rolled carefully into a crouching position. He could not feel his extremities well. He moved cautiously now, not certain how close the Shield might be, up through the ravine, through what little cover existed above the tree line.

To the cave.

There was little enough inside besides the cache of hardware from the ship. The cave was small, and even though the

Dancer had not been there in a very long time he found the device he needed quickly: a key meant to be held in the palm of a man's hand.

In the darkness the Dancer felt for the studs on the surface of the key, and moved his thumb to cover the oval stud which would bring him safety.

Behind him, at the entrance to the cave, Gi'Tbad'Eovad'Dvan said quietly, "Good-bye, Sedon."

The kitjan found him while Dvan was still speaking. The Dancer never heard his name uttered. In the moment of his death, as the air left his lungs in a desperate, convulsive scream, the Dancer's thumb spasmed on the stud controlling the stasis bubble.

They were up above the tree line; Gi'Tbad'Eovad'Dvan unslung the ancient laser from across his back, and with it set the side of the rock face near him to glowing. He sat outside the entrance to the cave, with the mirror-surfaced stasis bubble at his back, and waited. In the hours before morning it grew deadly cold from the arctic wind coming down off the nearby glaciers. Dvan shivered so badly that even with his glowing rock, lased regularly to a cherry red, he was not certain he would survive the night. His clothing was cured leather inlaid with fur; crude, warm enough most of the time, but perhaps not for tonight.

He did not sleep that night. He wasted no time thinking about the Dancer; Sedon was dead. The stasis bubble might postpone the moment of death, but Dvan was content that his work was done. The sort of medical technology necessary to save a Dancer touched at close range by the kitjan existed nowhere on this planet, and had not for a long, long time.

The night wore on forever. Once Dvan nearly slept, but found himself jerking awake to the conviction that blazing red eyes hovered out in the darkness beyond the glowing slab of stone, watching him—the red-furred beast that had led him to Sedon, the spirit sent by the Nameless One—but when he shook himself fully awake the eyes were gone.

When dawn finally came, the morning sun lighting the peaks of the mountains around him, Dvan looked around, fixing the place in memory, the relationships of the peaks to one another. It took some time, imprinting the image into deep memory, but at length he was satisfied; though eons might pass between visits, he would know this place again.

After a while he got up and stretched to relieve his stiffness, and headed back down the mountain.

Thirty-seven thousand years passed.

Interlude: 2062–2069 Gregorian

On July 3, 2062, on a night of nightmares that would in years and centuries to follow become a part of human mythology, at the Eastgate Hotel in mid-Manhattan, two French Peaceforcers in black patrol fatigues held vigil, deployed at opposite ends of an otherwise empty lobby. The junior officer, Maurice Charbonneau, sat in one corner on the hotel's carpeted floor, autoshot covering the entrance to the hotel. Outside, on the opposite side of the street, he could see a pair of wrecked cars burning in the fierce rain. A car came down out of the sky as he watched, blossoming into flames as it struck an apartment complex across the way. The shock wave of the explosion rattled the long glassite panels that faced the street.

Maurice sat and watched Nils Logrissen walk up and down before the entrance to the hotel. Logrissen, a terrorist of the Erisian Claw, was the only man Charbonneau had ever killed. Occasionally Logrissen's body stumbled and then jerked back up again like a marionette on strings. Logrissen's bulging, deadman's eyes were fixed on Maurice, never left him except once; when the car struck the building across the street, Logrissen turned and watched the accident for a while.

Charbonneau was grateful for the respite. He was trying to pretend that everything that had happened in the last few hours was part of some particularly unpleasant sensable he had made the mistake of playing. (A *sensable where you're the star,* the voice whispered. *Right.*) It hadn't worked yet, but perhaps that was because he wasn't trying hard enough.

Charbonneau was deathly afraid that Logrissen was getting up his nerve to come inside, and if that happened Charbonneau was not certain what he would do.

At the other end of the lobby Charbonneau's superior officer, Peace Keeping Force Sergeant Georges D'Argentan, paced restlessly back and forth in front of the maglev lifts, chain-smoking, his multifrequency combat laser held loosely in one hand. With every few steps he left the carpet and crossed onto the tile area immediately before the maglev. It was the only sound in the echoing emptiness of the lobby: the clicking of the boots, followed by silence, followed by boots, followed by silence. The rhythm of it had grown so comforting, so predictable, that Charbonneau was startled when it ceased. He glanced over at Sergeant D'Argentan, saw the older Peaceforcer standing motionless, finger touching a point immediately below his right ear.

D'Argentan stood still while listening in on the command channel. Finally he shook himself slightly, resumed his pacing. MAURICE.

Charbonneau was not certain that the voice in his head was real; his father, dead these fifteen years, had been talking to him for the last hour, ever since the Castanaveras telepaths had struck out at the world around them, at the United Nations Peace Keeping Force that was trying to destroy them. After a bit Charbonneau touched his own earphone. SERGEANT? IS THAT YOU?

There was a moment's silence before D'Argentan spoke, and Charbonneau could guess at his thoughts. Councilor Carson had actually ordered that Maurice be sedated; D'Argentan had ignored him, and now he was rethinking the wisdom of the decision. YES, OF COURSE IT'S ME. YOUR FATHER IS DEAD, MAURICE. SO IS LOGRISSEN. THEY HAVE BEEN FOR A LONG TIME.

Charbonneau knew better than to argue with Sergeant D'Argentan. He was sane enough, even yet, to know that he was quite mad at the moment. Charbonneau remembered burying his father, remembered killing Logrissen more clearly yet. YES, SERGEANT, I'LL TRY TO REMEMBER THAT.

I'VE JUST BEEN TOLD THAT SPACE FORCE IS READY. SECRETARY GENERAL AMNIER HAS APPROVED ELITE SERGEANT VANCE'S REQUEST; VANCE IS GOING TO ORDER A THERMONUCLEAR STRIKE ON THE CHANDLER COMPLEX.

Charbonneau digested that. SO THEY'RE DEAD, THEN. ALL THE TELEPATHS ARE TRAPPED INSIDE THE COMPLEX.

Across the length of the hotel lobby, D'Argentan nodded. SO THEY SAY.

Charbonneau clutched his autoshot more tightly. EXCEPT FOR THE TWO CARSON'S GOT UPSTAIRS.

JUST CHILDREN, said D'Argentan sharply. THEY DON'T HAVE THE POWER YET. ONLY THE ADULTS DO, AND THE ADULTS ARE SOON DEAD.

YES, SERGEANT.

At that moment, thirty-five floors above them, Carl Castanaveras had just finished killing the Peaceforcer guard stationed on the hotel's roof. As Maurice Charbonneau turned back to continue his observation of Nils Logrissen, the oldest and deadliest telepath on Earth was riding down in the maglev to

Unification Councilor Jerril Carson's room, to the eighth floor, autoshot in one hand, Series II Excalibur laser rifle in the other.

Coming for his children.

Denice Castanaveras had ceased crying only a few minutes ago. They were not tears of fear, but of anger. She had passed into a place beyond fear, into a rage so vast and elemental it bore only a passing resemblance to any emotion she had ever experienced before.

She was nine years old and she was going to kill Jerril Carson if given any opportunity at all.

She sat on the floor with her twin: two black-haired Caucasian children with pale skin and green eyes. Both she and David had their hands snakechained behind their backs, with tape covering their mouths. Her feet were free, as were David's; they could have stood if allowed. A few hours prior David had made the mistake of trying. A bruise on the side of his face was slowly turning purple; Councilor Carson had knocked David back down to the floor without even looking at him.

She sat with her rage, not thinking. She did not understand how the situation she was in had come to pass; did not comprehend the details of the conflict between Carson and her father, how it had come to be that the personal animosity between Carson and her father had grown into a conflict which had, this night, pitted the Castanaveras telepaths against the entire armed might of the Unification.

Denice did not understand, and did not care.

She sat and thought about killing him.

Councilor Carson clutched an autoshot in his right hand; he hardly paid attention to the twins. Denice watched him, sitting in front of a huge holofield that showed an image of their home, of the Chandler Complex. He had turned off the audio; except for the whistling sound of the wind and the drum of the rain it was utterly silent inside the hotel room.

The image of the Chandler Complex vanished suddenly, was replaced with a split field; the Chandler Complex in one half of the field, a shot from the hotel's security holocams in the other. The security holocams showed the long stretch of corridor outside, and the two Peaceforcers who guarded it. One of the Peaceforcers stood in front of a bank of elevators, covering the entrance with an autoshot; the other lay on his stomach at one end of the corridor, covering his partner with a variable laser.

After the long silence the sound of the Peaceforcer's voice rang shockingly loud. "We've lost contact with the roof."

Carson stood with startling abruptness, turned and glared wildly at the twins. Denice met his eyes for a long moment and returned the glare: *I'm going to kill you*. The Gift had not touched her yet, and Carson was as deaf to thought as any normal human; still he froze for a second under the sheer physical impact of her rage. He shook himself visibly then and crossed the distance between them in two strides, pulled the twins to their feet and turned them to face the door. He stood behind them holding the autoshot with his right hand, holding their snaked hands behind them with his left. Where his hand gripped her Denice could feel Carson shaking.

The holofield moved with Carson, came to hover in front of them, a meter off to the right so that Carson's view of the door was not obscured.

For a very long time nothing happened. Twenty seconds. Thirty.

In the holofield, Denice watched the maglev doors curl open. The Peaceforcer with the autoshot stood in front of the door, autoshot at waist level, and began firing the instant the doors had opened sufficiently. Denice heard the boom of the autoshot through the hotel room's closed door. The angle of the holocams prevented their seeing the inside of the elevator; suddenly a flash of purple light came up off the elevator's floor, and the Peaceforcer stiffened, ionization corona crackling around him; the black uniform he wore burst into flames and he fell.

Councilor Jerril Carson whispered, "Shit."

On the right side of the field, the pale, elegant image of the Chandler Complex glowed white in the rain.

An arm holding an autoshot extruded from inside the maglev, fired twice off to the right, down the hallway in the direction of Councilor Carson's room. The Peaceforcer on the floor to the left of the holofield fired then, and Denice watched the maser's ionization trail track across the hand and the autoshot holding it. What happened next came so quickly that Denice almost missed it; the injured man's right hand darted out into the corridor, grabbed the autoshot and flipped it over to the left and fired twice again. Denice saw both shots strike the remaining Peaceforcer, saw his head and shoulders literally dissolve in a spray of flesh and shot. The maglev doors started to close—

—her father lunged forward, into the hallway, firing again as he moved. Twice more he shot the crumpled form on the hallway floor, fifteen meters away. The Peaceforcer's body twitched and came apart some more.

Jerril Carson said softly, "Oh God no."

Carl Castanaveras struggled to his feet, a death's-head grin plastered across his features. His left arm, cooked by the master burst, hung dead and limp at his side. He staggered as he walked down the hallway, and stopped just before reaching the door to Carson's room.

There was a moment's silence.

The door exploded inward as though a giant fist had smashed into it.

At that instant a flash of bright light appeared in the holofield, lit the hotel room for an instant in unreal colors.

Carl Castanaveras appeared in the doorway, a grinning black-haired apparition with emerald eyes—and hesitated at the sight of his children standing as a living shield immediately before Carson.

In the holofield that had moments before shown an image of the Chandler Complex, a mushroom cloud was slowly climbing into the night sky over south Manhattan.

Jerril Carson's autoshot blast took Carl Castanaveras square in the chest, picked him up off his feet and slammed him backward out against the wall of the hotel corridor. Denice's father fired in midair, the beam of light from his Series II Excalibur cutting through the tiny space between Denice and her brother, reaching past them to slice Jerril Carson's head in half.

Carl struck the wall hard. He slumped, sliding down to the floor, leaving a long trail of blood on the wall. Next to her Denice saw David on the ground, bringing his bound hands under his feet and around to the front. David ripped the tape off his mouth, and in a voice rusty with disuse said, "Turn around." Denice knew what was coming; she felt Carson's dead hand being placed up against her wrists, the lifeless thumb being pushed against the snakechain until the snakechain recognized it and released her. The sudden freedom of movement sent spasms of pain through her shoulders. She worked the tape free from her mouth with hands grown numb from lack of circulation.

Their father's thoughts touched them both. *David, get the lasers.*

Her twin vanished down the corridor, came back holding the laser with which their father had been shot. It seemed to be an immense effort for Carl to release the laser clutched in his own hand. *Take it, Denice.*

Denice bent, scooped the laser up off the floor quickly, before her nerve could fail her. Her father's thoughts were faint, unlike anything she had ever felt from him before. Fading. *Listen. There's a Peaceforcer downstairs, maybe two, and I can't kill them, so you have to.*

David nodded. "We will, Father."

They'll hesitate when they see you. They'll hesitate before they'll shoot children.

Denice was aware of the tears tracking down her cheeks, but her voice was steady. "We won't hesitate, Daddy."

Carl sagged back against the wall of the corridor. *Good. Remember that you're tougher than they are.* The word reached out to them, burned itself into the depths of Denice's mind with all the strength of the dying man's pain and lifelong rage: *Better.*

David nodded. "We'll remember."

Good. Carl's head sagged back against the wall. *Go.*

David rose and punched for the maglev. Denice hugged her father suddenly, fiercely, *felt* the pain that rolled through him at the contact. Blood covered her when she let go. "Good-bye, Daddy." She rose and ran to the maglev when the doors opened.

Carl Castanaveras's last thought reached out to them after the doors to the maglev had rolled shut upon them. *Kill the fuckers.*

As the maglev descended, David Castanaveras said grimly, "We will."

I'VE LOST TOUCH WITH UPSTAIRS.

It took Charbonneau a long moment to understand what D'Argentan had said to him. His father was growing angrier and angrier over Maurice's insistence that he was dead; Logrissen had ceased walking and now simply stood motionless at the entrance to the hotel, staring in at Maurice. Charbonneau could see Logrissen's lower intestines, hanging out of the hole Charbonneau's autoshot had made in him back in the summer of '59. Finally Maurice said, SERGEANT? DID YOU SAY SOMETHING?

<SIGH.> YES. I'VE LOST TOUCH WITH CONSEILLER CARSON. WANT ME TO GO UP AND SEE WHAT'S HAPPENED?

Sergeant D'Argentan hesitated, then said reluctantly, NO. NO, DON'T DO THAT. I'LL GO. WATCH THE DOOR, MAKE SURE NO-

BODY ENTERS THE HOTEL. Maurice nodded, and D'Argentan turned to the maglevs.

The door to the center maglev flexed slightly before D'Argentan had even touched the pressure point that controlled it.

The door curled open.

Maurice watched D'Argentan jerk as though he had touched a live wire, one hand still reaching for the pressure point, as the converging beams reached him and his uniform burst into flames.

They came out into the lobby slowly, cautiously, stepping across Sergeant D'Argentan's burning body. As Maurice had heard, they were mere children; it was the first time Maurice had seen them since their kidnaping. Maurice sat with his autoshot, watching the genegineered telepath children move across the lobby, toward the entrance. The boy had his laser trained on Maurice, and Maurice smiled at him. The girl was very pretty, but she did not look at Maurice after the first quick glance to make sure her brother had him covered. Maurice said politely, in heavily accented English, "Hello."

The boy hesitated at the door after the girl had ventured outward, onto the slidewalk in front of the hotel. For the first time Maurice seriously considered the possibility that Sergeant D'Argentan had told him the truth; neither of the children seemed to notice Nils Logrissen's grinning corpse standing just outside the hotel's entrance.

The girl turned back. "David, come on!"

David Castanaveras took one slow, halting step toward Maurice Charbonneau. Maurice smiled at the boy one more time as David brought the maser down to focus on the center of Maurice's chest.

"Hello," Maurice said again. "I am Maurice Charbonneau."

David Castanaveras whispered; Maurice had to strain to hear him. "Hello. My name is David Castanaveras, and this is for my father."

Then for the barest instant Maurice felt a pain so great that he thought for a moment it was something else entirely—the touch of God, perhaps, calling him home. And perhaps it was. The maser beam swept across him and then there was no pain, nor anything else, forever and ever again, amen.

The twins ran out into the night, into the riots.

Into the first hour of the Troubles.

- 2 -

I am the Name Storyteller.

On July 3, 2062 of the Gregorian Calendar, the United Nations Peace Keeping Force, at the command of PKF Elite Sergeant Mohammed Vance, used tactical thermonuclear weapons to destroy a group of genetically engineered telepaths living at the Chandler Complex in lower Manhattan. Over 240 telepathic children and adults died in nuclear fire.

In the battle preceding their destruction, the telepaths sent better than a quarter of the population of the state of New York into permanent insanity; caused the two years of the Troubles, as legal and social systems throughout metropolitan areas broke down beyond repair. The old order could not be resurrected; the Peaceforcers created the Patrol Sectors, and left the vast bulk of what had once been New York City to become the lethal, desolate area known as the Fringe.

Three children from the Chandler Complex survived the destruction of the telepaths. Two of them were the nine-year-old twins David and Denice Castanaveras, the children of Carl Castanaveras and Jany McConnell.

The third child was not a telepath. He was a webdancer.

A Player named Trent.

Seven years passed before Denice saw him again.

- 3 -

On August 13, 2069, Denice Castanaveras lay in the darkness with Trent. Earlier that day she and Trent's oldest friend, Jimmy Ramirez, had rescued Trent from the PKF Detention Center in the middle of Capitol City.

She was sixteen years old.

Through the windows of their thirty-second-floor room at the Red Line Hotel, Denice watched the Peaceforcers hunt for Trent. Thousands of PKF AeroSmiths flew through the sky above the city; tens of thousands of spyeyes. In the distance the AeroSmiths and spyeyes merged into a dancing swarm of scarlet fireflies, highlighted by the bright white pinpricks of their searchlights.

They were both genies, the products of the late Suzanne Montignet's brilliance in genetic engineering; but even between them the differences outweighed the similarities. For Denice the scene outside was suffused with the deep glow of infrared light from the Peaceforcer night scopes; but not for Trent. As the night grew colder moisture condensed at the window, smearing the bright sharp lights together with the dim glow of the infrared.

She stirred, felt Trent's arms tighten around her. "When will you go?"

His voice was so quiet she could barely make it out. "Soon. Not yet."

"And where?"

"I don't know yet."

Her thoughts were slow, sluggish, in the moments before sleep. "Okay."

"They need to follow me," Trent said distantly. "They need to be drawn away from you, and if they're looking for me they're not looking for you. If I die it's just me. If you die—then they've won. David's probably dead, Denice. If you die, there's nothing left of what they were, and Amnier, Eddore, Vance, all of them, they've won at last." He stirred restlessly, sat up against the bed's headboard. Denice curled up against him, left her head resting in his lap, staring up in the darkness toward the ceiling, seeing only an emptiness so deep there was no end to it.

"Where, Trent?"

"Free Luna, I think," he said finally, "or else Mars, or the Belt CityStates. Somewhere outside Peaceforcer control. They won't stop looking for me on Earth. I don't think they'll ever stop looking for me now."

She felt a distant twinge of pain, suppressed it almost without noticing. *This is going to hurt; let it hurt later. When he's gone.* "I think you're right," she said at last. "I'm so sorry, but I think you are. I wish we hadn't rescued you."

You both panicked. He did not say it aloud, and for that small kindness she was grateful. "It's okay. Make me a promise, Denice?"

"Done."

"Don't you want to know what it is?"

Jimmy, of course. "I do know."

"Oh." After a moment he nodded. "All right. But don't let him know you're watching out for him. He wouldn't like that."

"I know. You're sure Bird will be okay with Jodi Jodi?"

"They were doing fine together, in the middle of the Fringe, when I met them. They'll do fine in the Patrol Sectors when I'm gone."

Denice inhaled slowly, brought the oxygen deep inside. It was one of the few things her father had had time to teach her before he died; the breathing exercises that brought relaxation, peace. "Be careful," she whispered into the darkness. "You're all I have left now."

In the brief while before sleep took her, she found herself with him, among his thoughts, in with the never-ending flicker of imagery that was the internal universe of the man the System would come to know as Trent the Uncatchable. A flaw in genengineer Suzanne Montignet's otherwise brilliant work had left him without the Gift he had always thought his birthright; and only a few months after his learning that he was *not* one of the telepaths with whom he had been raised, the telepaths themselves had been destroyed at the order of PKF Elite Mohammed Vance. He was a wounded person, damaged early and badly by the world around him.

As she had been. *But I healed,* Denice thought drowsily. *He never did.* It did not even occur to her that she might be wrong about either herself or him. Pain touched her again, muffled only slightly by the approach of stillness. *He doesn't even know how much he loves me. And he doesn't believe me when I tell him.*

Sometime after that she slept. An image stayed with her as she descended into the darkness. An image of her, at the age of nine, of the way Trent had seen her then when he was eleven. They were together in the park across the street from the Chandler Complex, on a hazy day in spring, and she was sleeping with her head in his lap, long black hair falling half over her features as she slept. That was the image that she remembered when she awoke the next morning, the memory that stayed with her that night, the memory that stayed with her through the long years to follow.

The memory of how he loved her.

When Denice Castanaveras awoke the following morning Trent was gone. He had not awakened her when he left. She found a single white rose on the table at the side of the bed, and a note on the bedside systerm, hovering in the systerm's holofield.

The note said, *Don't worry. It's going to be all right.*

Summer: 2075

They had themselves a party
To wash away their cares
They busted up the furniture
Said they would take back what was theirs

Said they would take back what was theirs

—Mahliya Kutura, *Independence Day*

- 1 -

"Jasmine."

The voice echoed through the cool empty gym like God calling from a cheap pay phone.

The woman who called herself Jasmine Martinez slowly exhaled the breath she had been holding, released her toes, and sat up. She had been doing stretches for the muscles in the backs of her thighs, sitting with her legs straight in front of her, grasping the instep of each foot with her hands, and leaning forward until she was completely doubled over. The walls of the huge gym were mirrored and out of the corner of her eye she watched her image in the mirror: a black-haired woman of average height, wearing nothing but a pair of shimmering blue shorts; bright green eyes in a vaguely Asian face, with muscle definition so startlingly detailed she could have served as an anatomy model.

The holo wavering a meter or so away from her held the severe image of Alaya Gyurtrag, the witch who managed Goddess Home's business transactions. At 6:30 A.M. Alaya was already dressed for a day at the office, in a conservative and expensive raw silk business suit that would not have been out of place for the Mayor of Capitol City, but which struck Jasmine as pretentious for the City Manager of a township located in Sunland, California.

Jasmine wiped a drop of sweat off the tip of her nose and said after a moment, "Yes?"

"You're leaving us today?"

You've only had it on your calendar for four months. "Yes."

"Could you come see me after dinner, dear?"

"Certainly. Anything else?"

The witch smiled at Jasmine. It was clearly an effort. "No. That's all."

Jasmine nodded and returned to her workout without saying anything further. She did not like Alaya—Alaya was in fact one of the reasons she was leaving—and saw no reason Alaya should not know it.

At 6:30 in the morning she had already been working out for an hour. She had five hours left to go, and would break off then only because she had preparations to make before taking her leave of Goddess Home. She felt she could have kept moving, pushing against her limits all day without stopping or slowing.

Only four years prior she had been making a living as a professional dancer; even then she had not been in such incredible condition.

That she was not human did not bother Jasmine Martinez in the slightest. But sometimes she wondered what her limits were, where she would find them.

Sometimes she scared herself.

After the stretches she did weight work, then pushups, and then situps. At 7:15 two witches Jasmine knew slightly came in, warmed up too quickly, and started running on the padded quarter-kilometer track that ran around the gym's perimeter. Jasmine ignored them; after finishing her situps she waited sixty seconds for her heartbeat to slow, then came to her feet and strapped a pair of fifteen-kilo weights to each wrist. She stood motionless a second, thinking. She considered Kutura, and then rejected it; Mahliya Kutura was her favorite musician, but Kutura was too slow: she wanted to *move*.

Jasmine said aloud, *"Command: The Politics of Dance."*

The music, the work of a Brazilian artist who had been dead for fifteen years before Jasmine had even been born, came up slowly enough, as slowly as anything by Kutura. Jasmine closed her eyes, let the sound wash over her, the slow beat of the drums, the rising saxophone, and the sax rose and rose, higher and higher, and despite herself Jasmine felt her breath quickening in anticipation of the coming moment—

—the music broke like a wave, enveloped Jasmine inside a wall of sound. She took a slow step forward, arms unfolding like a flower greeting the sun, pivoted, lifted a foot and turned, spun, brought her hands and the weights back in toward herself, the spin whipped her to a dizzying speed, and then the drums came back, faster now, and faster, and Jasmine Martinez danced into the music, brought the music into herself, and ceased to be aware of the world, of the witches who had stopped running to watch her, and with the music holding and enveloping her moved and moved and moved and *moved*.

Until she could move no more.

Darkness descended around Jasmine as she walked to Alaya's office.

She wore traveling clothes: a black jumpsuit with silver zippers, and a pair of soft gray boots that came to midcalf. Everything she owned in the world was packed into the black satchel in her right hand: a makeup key, changes of clothing, her InfoNet link. Hardcopy of two letters, unsigned, from Trent the Uncatchable.

That Thursday evening was warm, with a gentle summer breeze; the sky to the south glowed slightly with the lights of Los Angeles. White and yellow glowfloats bobbed over the streets of Goddess Home, came flickering on one by one as Jasmine walked the two kilometers to Alaya's office. Goddess Home was a small place, a feminist witch's enclave of eight thousand. Men—some witches themselves—were welcome to visit, and Jasmine saw a few on the streets as she walked; but they were not supposed to spend the night and were not allowed to live among the witches.

For most of the witches the exclusion of men was not an inconvenience. Many were lesbians, and those who were not often found the lack of enforced day-to-day contact with men refreshing.

From her handheld a voice issued, the voice of Ralf the Wise and Powerful: "Flight confirmed. I had to kill a web angel at the Dallas changeover; stay out of the InfoNet while passing through the Dallas exchange. Otherwise your journey should be safe."

Jasmine knew a response was not expected of her, and so did not give one. Indeed, Ralf's message barely altered the flow of her thoughts, impinged only slightly upon her melancholy awareness of the home she was leaving.

Goddess Home was different from any other place Jasmine had ever known. There were no slidewalks, and no powered vehicles of any sort except for those employed by the three witches crippled beyond even the reach of modern medicine. In her adult life it was the first place Jasmine had ever lived where she had felt any sense of community. Four women greeted her by name as she walked through the streets to see Alaya Gyurtrag, and everywhere women were gathered in groups: at the town's only park, at one of the town's five sidewalk cafes. Their voices floated at the limits of comprehensibility, hundreds of women, a few male voices: the sounds of home.

I'm going to miss this.

The thought came unbidden, closely followed:

But it is not safe to stay.

• • •

"I'm catching the Bullet out of Burbank at nine-fifteen. If we could make this quick, I'd appreciate it."

"Certainly," said Alaya warmly. "Have a seat."

Jasmine seated herself in the indicated chair, travel bag between her feet. She was distantly amused to note that the chair left her eyes about eight centimeters below the level of Alaya's, who was not a tall woman. Alaya had changed from the business suit she had been wearing that morning; now she was dressed almost as casually as Jasmine, in a pair of yellow shorts and a white silk blouse. She was barefooted on the pale blue shag rug of her office.

The office reflected the personality its occupant wished to project. A single power crystal hung on a solid gold chain over the doorway, and another crystal, somewhat larger, sat on a small stand at the side of Alaya's desk. The desk itself was antique American, real redwood, over 150 years of age and hand polished on every surface until it glowed a dusky shade of crimson beneath the office's pleasant yellow sunpaint. The walls were hung with neo-Impressionist paintings, dating largely from the 1920s: women with parasols at the beach, a man on a bicycle, two children sharing an ice cream cone, all done in warm yellows and blues and greens.

"What can I do for you, Alaya?"

Alaya Gyurtrag sat with her hands folded before her. Her silver hair was pulled back from her face and hung in a single long braid down her back. Bright blue eyes fixed themselves upon Jasmine. "We're going to miss you, you know that."

"So I've been told. But between us, Alaya, you and I have never been close, and neither of us is going to miss the other. So what can I do for you?"

Alaya chuckled with what seemed to Jasmine genuine amusement. "Your point is well made. What you can do for me, Jasmine, is—relieve my curiosity about a business matter."

"Oh? In what way?"

"Why are you leaving us?"

The blunt question gave Jasmine a moment's pause.

"Really," Alaya continued, "you could not choose a worse time for it if you tried. July the Fourth is only six days away; the Independence Day riots are due to begin shortly. Goddess Home is *safe*; we haven't had Independence Day riots in our history. And you're not the only one leaving us; we've had res-ignations pick up twelve percent this year."

"Twelve percent?"

Alaya nodded. "I haven't publicized the figure. Next month I will complete my first anniversary as City Manager, and women are leaving Goddess Home, for the first time, faster than they are joining. And I know it's my fault but I don't know *why*."

Jasmine considered. "Many of the reasons I'm leaving are personal, Alaya. But there are two I *will* share with you. My finances are poor. I haven't worked except at community tasks in over two years, and my savings are nearly gone. The two ways I am capable of making a living—as a dancer and as a martial arts instructor—are inapplicable to Goddess Home. The population is too small to support a dance troupe—"

"We tried to get you to teach a class in self-defense."

"You don't need it," said Jasmine patiently. "As I said at the time. Violence within Goddess Home is rare. Those of you who venture outside are handicapped by unfamiliarity with violence and insufficient time for training. If I were to teach the women here to defend themselves, they would still, most likely, be hurt in any encounter where they were required to defend themselves. The willingness to hurt an opponent, to *damage* him, is more important than simply knowing how; and that willingness is something I *can't* teach. And I'm not sure I wish to. Personal Protection Systems, expensive though they are, are a better investment of Goddess Home's time and Credit. You just don't go outside that often." Jasmine shrugged. "You've heard this before. The fact is that in Los Angeles, in any major city, I can make a living at both of my trades. In Goddess Home I cannot make a living at either.

"The second reason I'm willing to share with you is simple. When I joined Goddess Home, Marta Tracing held your job. She was a quiet person, and I found her easy to get along with. Since Marta passed away, intolerance over ideological purity has grown to the point where I am no longer comfortable here. I don't think I need to be more explicit."

Alaya nodded slowly. "You've evaded this question before, but we are alone, and you are leaving—what do you truly think of Wicca?"

Jasmine sighed. "Why does it matter?"

"Wicca is—" Alaya's frustration was apparent. "It's the entire *point* of Goddess Home. It's the reason this town exists. If you're not here because of Wicca, why are you here?" She paused. "Or, if you like, why *were* you here?"

"I didn't say that I did not find Wicca attractive. It is—a life-affirming system of beliefs. Theologically it's no sillier than Christianity; it seems so at times only because it doesn't have two thousand years of ornate rationalization to fall back upon. Emotionally it's at least as healthy as any other religion I'm familiar with. The rituals are less elaborate than those of the older religions, but that, too, is part of the charm. But—Alaya, when you make the doctrine, the detail of ritual, more important than the connection to Deity that it is supposed to serve, you are in the process of turning Wicca into something very much like the patriarchal, authoritarian religions you detest. I don't believe in your Goddess, Alaya. I also don't believe in the Christian God. I believe in something, because I've *felt* it in my own life. When I was younger I used to think it was what everybody else called God, and for a little while I did think it might be what Wicca calls the Goddess. But today I admit I don't know what it is, that I have no words for it. And when you insist that what I feel is—or should be—what you have written down on paper, or what you speak in ritual, you lose me, Alaya. And a lot of other people, apparently."

Alaya bit her lower lip. "Thank you for your frankness."

"I hope it's of some help."

"Well. So much for that." Alaya dismissed the subject with a visible effort. When she spoke again she was clearly nervous. "There was something else I wanted to talk to you about, if you have a moment. I'll make it quick."

"Please. I have less than half an hour to make the Bullet."

"I'm curious as to how you came to join us, three years ago."

"I believe it's in the records."

"Very little of it is in the records, Jasmine; Marta left us two rather terse paragraphs explaining it as a matter of personal obligation. A 'Sieur McGee did some work for us about ten years ago—the nature of *that* work isn't in the records either. Then three years ago he petitioned to have you admitted for residency in Goddess Home. I think you may be the only woman who has ever lived here whose petition was presented by a man."

Jasmine nodded. "Marta said she thought I was."

Alaya waited expectantly.

Jasmine let the silence stretch, smiling. When twenty seconds had passed she said softly, "My father used to do this to people. Throw silence at them and wait for them to start talking. It seemed so obvious when I was nine years old, even then I was always surprised when I saw it work."

"But it's not going to work on you, is it? And you're not going to tell me how you came to Goddess Home."

Jasmine shook her head. "It was a private matter between myself and 'Sieur McGee and Marta. Marta is dead and I would not know how to contact 'Sieur McGee if my life depended upon it."

Alaya nodded, hesitating, and then said abruptly, "You're *real*."

Jasmine said carefully, "I beg your pardon?"

"A lot of the women who study Wicca, who cast the spells and make the circles, they—" Alaya hesitated again. "A lot of them—almost all of them, damn it—are kidding themselves. But you're real, you have something. I have a little bit of it, enough to know when a spell has worked, when a circle closes correctly. Sometimes I get some of what people are thinking and feeling. But when you walk into the same room with me—there's a sound, except it's not a sound, like a thousand bees buzzing all around me, and I can't hear anything. People have lied to me when you were nearby and I couldn't *tell*."

Jasmine nodded slowly. Not counting Alaya, there were three women she had met at Goddess Home who had some small fragment of the Gift, some touch of real ability. Most of the women at Goddess Home were no more gifted than any other human; and the three that were, Alaya again excepted, did not seem to have made much productive use of their fragmentary Gift. "I know what you mean," Jasmine said quietly. "I've felt the same in you."

"You lie," said Alaya without anger. "I'm no more in your league than Marien Lisachild is in mine. She may be the most popular psychic at Goddess Home, but she's a fraud and we both know it. I'm not a fraud, but I'm not what you are, either." Alaya paused. "Your eyes are green."

Jasmine was grimly certain she knew where this was going. "So?"

"Were you born with eyes that color?"

Jasmine sat silently a long moment, letting the question hang in the air, and then said, "I think we're done."

"I don't think so."

Jasmine stared bleakly at the woman. "Meaning what?"

A less self-assured woman might have taken warning from

the tone of her voice. Alaya Gyurtrag forged ahead. "Back in 2062 two genies, two of the Castanaveras, were kidnaped from the Chandler Complex in Manhattan, before the Complex was nuked by Space Force. They never found out what happened to them, to those children. And you're—"

The images tore through Jasmine, the smell of Alaya's mother, the calm and steady warmth of her father. Her father's smile, the gentle reassurances in the face of adversity, the promise that what Alaya attempted she would be competent to do. The inconsolable ache at their loss, lessened only slightly with the passage of thirteen years, particularly the loss of the man who had taught her to read, who had praised her early attempts at painting, who had consoled her when she was twenty, after the loss of her first love—

Jasmine pulled free of the link, mildly impressed that Alaya had managed it in the first place. "I'm sorry, Alaya. But it wasn't my fault."

Alaya voice shook slightly. "My parents *died* during the Troubles."

"I know, and I am sorry. But so did both of mine."

Alaya nodded, eyes not moving from Jasmine's, and her right hand dropped below the edge of her desk.

Jasmine Martinez said simply, "Please don't do this."

Alaya licked her lips quickly. Her expression held a very good attempt at innocence. "Don't do what?"

Jasmine heard the desk drawer sliding open. She exhaled, let the living air flow from her lungs, closed her eyes and stepped out of her body.

The room lit with a flat, grainy gray light.

In the stillness between heartbeats Jasmine Martinez moved away from her body and walked through the desk.

She did not recognize the make of the gun Alaya was taking from her desk drawer. A double-action automatic of some kind; from the size of the barrel, perhaps a 9mm. The safety was already off. She touched the magazine, ran a finger through the metal and up into the chamber; fifteen shots staggered in the magazine, one shot in the chamber, ready to be fired.

Jasmine had no idea at all what Alaya expected to do with the weapon, and did not intend to wait and find out. She let go of the automatic, grasped Alaya's arms just above the elbows and reached out for the glowing blue filaments of Alaya's nerve network. *Here*, and *here*, she touched, quieted the flow of neurons, and then opened her eyes to a world of color and movement.

The gun in Alaya's hand fell noiselessly from her nerveless hands to the surface of the carpet. Jasmine stared at Alaya, eyes glittering, and with the full force of her Gift reformed the link Alaya had attempted, and, as Alaya Gyurtrag drew breath to scream, Touched her soul.

Jasmine came back to herself slowly, distantly aware of tears dripping down her cheeks; knew as though it were something happening to someone else that she shook with the force of her sobs. She mourned for the parents Alaya had lost in the Troubles, for the slow loss of Alaya's friends. The pain of Alaya's incomprehension, that men and women alike, people she cared for, should misunderstand her advances, should interpret her love as interference, and her fear as anger. Alaya's desperate fear that she was already too old to find the love she craved, that if she had not found it yet she would never find it, and would age alone, unloved, and friendless.

And die so.

Alaya blinked. It took a moment for her eyes to focus. When they did she looked at Jasmine with sudden concern. "Are you all right, dear?"

"I'm—fine," Jasmine managed to say. A lethal headache pulsed immediately behind her eyes; it happened every time she used the deepest elements of the Gift. She gathered herself and wiped away the tears, picked up her travel bag, and stood, a little uncertainly. "Thank you for talking with me. I—never mind. Thank you. I appreciated the opportunity to know you a little better."

A look of distant incomprehension flickered across Alaya's features, was gone. Alaya said with real compassion, "I'm sorry you have to go. But it's only normal for you to grieve for the life you leave behind. If Goddess Home has not been everything you wanted, it has still been your home."

Jasmine stood still a beat. Then she said, simply, "Thank you," and left.

She caught the 9:15 Bullet with twenty seconds to spare.

2

At speeds that surpassed those of aircraft, the Bullet sped eastward through an evacuated tunnel beneath the surface of Earth.

Jasmine had paid for passage to Atlanta, Georgia. Fifteen minutes before the Bullet was scheduled to stop in Dallas she rose from her seat and went to the bathroom. In the bathroom she stripped off her jumpsuit and her boots. Standing naked before the mirror she flicked through the settings in her makeup key; her skin, tuned black to match the jumpsuit, changed colors rapidly, a brief storm of rainbows, and then stabilized on a dark shade of gold. Her lips and eyelids turned a pale golden green; a speckle of faint silver stars appeared immediately beneath her rather high cheekbones. Jasmine considered contact lenses for her eyes, decided against it—her makeup implant was almost ten years old, and she had never had it updated. Unlike the more recent makeup implants, her skin did not glow and the implant had not even touched her eyes. If she wanted to change the color of her eyes, contact lenses were her only option.

She shook her hair out as it changed colors to a shade of strawberry blond, then changed the part and tied it into a long ponytail. From her bag Jasmine withdrew a pair of sandals and a yellow sundress and put them on. She tapped the ID key on her handheld twice, waited a moment, and tapped it a third time. The handheld said quietly, "Which ID do you wish?"

There were three IDs in the handheld; Denice Daimara, Jasmine Martinez, and Erika Muller. The first was the name they had known her by in Public Labor, when she was nine years old; the last two identities had been programmed for her by Trent the Uncatchable, the last day he had ever spent on Earth, before beginning what newsdancers had called the Long Run.

Jasmine said softly, "Erika."

The handheld said instantly, "Enabled."

·   ·   ·

In Dallas the rain poured down out of the black night sky.

At Dallas Interworld Spaceport Erika Muller stopped at the TransPlanet booth, still slightly wet from the rain outside; the Bullet debarking station was separated from Spaceport Gate A-8 by thirty meters of empty space. When she spoke her voice had picked up a slight but noticeable New York accent. "I'm here to pick up my ticket. Muller, Erika."

The 'bot at the counter said politely, in a voice strongly reminiscent of sensable star Adam Selstrom, "Yes, 'Selle Muller. Please identify."

Erika touched her handheld to the payment strip; it lit green. Adam Selstrom's voice said, "Thank you, 'Selle Muller. Your semiballistic leaves from Gate A-11 at one oh five A.M.; it arrives at Unification Spaceport, New York, at four-twelve A.M. Eastern Standard Time. Thank you for traveling with TransPlanet."

Her ticket specified a window seat. Once launch boost ceased, the slim, short man who had been seated next to Erika Muller tried to start up a conversation. "What are you going to New York for, anyway? I've got a sales meeting myself—I sell high-speed molar memory products. Capitol City's no fun but the rest of New York is still good for—"

The clouds beneath her were a pale ocean that nearly hid Earth from view; patches of blue and brown peeked through the cotton white. The curve of the Earth grew visible as she watched. Without looking at the man at her side Erika said, "I don't want to talk to you," and then turned her head away from him and looked out the window, at the sphere of Earth, the rest of the way down to New York.

She did not think she had been followed after leaving Goddess Home.

At least not in Realtime—and if anyone had attempted to follow her through the Crystal Wind, Erika thought that Ralf the Wise and Powerful would surely have stopped him.

At 4:48 A.M., on Friday, June 29, Erika Muller touched her handheld to the cab's meter, waited for the meter light to go green, and stepped from the cab as the canopy swung open.

The dojo sat in the heart of Greenwich Village in lower Manhattan, on the third story of an ancient five-story brownstone walk-up; Robert owned the upper three stories.

The building had no maglev; Erika used the stairs.

On the third floor the stairs let out onto a wide landing. The sign on the landing's sole door bore the legend, Yo Instruction. With the exception of the stairwell it was the only room on the entire third floor.

Erika toggled her InfoNet ID to the Daimara identity, and knocked once. She paused, touched her handheld to the doorgrid and placed her palm flat against the door pad. Despite the passage of three years the door recognized her name and her print, and curled aside to let her pass.

He had not known she was coming, but she had had no doubt that he would be awake. Robert Dazai Yo never slept at night; he went to bed with the rising sun.

Robert sat alone and silent in the center of the dojo, on the gray mat. A meter-wide border of wooden floor, darkened with fifty years of hand scrubbing, surrounded it on all sides.

The glowpaint shone so dimly it actually flickered slightly, sheets of brightness running across the high ceiling at irregular intervals. It could not have been bothering Robert; he sat with eyes closed, breathing deep and slow. He wore a black gi, tied at the waist with a simple white belt. His hands rested flat upon his knees, palms down. Though he was culturally American, stretching back five generations, his features were pure Asian, undiluted by interbreeding.

She knew, because Robert had told her, that he was in his early fifties. Otherwise she would not have been able to guess his age for sure within twenty years in either direction.

Rows of weapons hung from the dojo's walls. Many were modern, multifrequency lasers and flechette guns among them; some, such as the katana that hung by itself against the east wall, would not have been out of place in the court of the twelfth-century shogun Minamoto Yoritomo.

Standing at the edge of the long gray mat, Denice Daimara, once Denice Castanaveras, sometimes Jasmine Martinez and Erika Muller, removed her sandals. She left her sandals and bag at the edge of the mat and walked forward to where Robert sat meditating. Without a word she sank into lotus immediately before him, sat waiting for him to acknowledge her presence.

After several minutes he opened his eyes and looked at her.

"You've had biosculpture," he observed. "The Asian touch is nice. It suits you."

"I wasn't sure you would recognize me."

"I know no one else who walks the way you do. Dancers are

as smooth, but not so silent; those trained in combat are rarely so graceful."

"Graceful? Your eyes were closed, Robert."

Robert shrugged and smiled, eyes lit with deep amusement. "So I peeked. Besides, you're the only person other than myself that door's ever been keyed for. Where have you been?"

"On vacation."

"For three years?"

"Studying," Denice said.

"What?"

"Wicca, mostly. Feminist theology."

"Indeed? You studied Wicca?" Robert was silent for a moment, clearly not expecting a response from her. When he continued one might have thought he had changed the subject: "Why did you leave us so suddenly?"

"Someone tried to kill me. Man named McGee—you wouldn't know him, I don't think."

"Did you kill him?"

"Oh, no!" Denice blinked. "He was a nice man."

"I see."

"It was a misunderstanding. So anyway, I took care of it. When I was done I didn't feel like coming back for a while."

"Oh." Robert nodded, thinking. "We missed you. I had to get a new instructor for the morning classes."

"I'm sorry."

"So was I. You worked cheap."

They were silent together for a long while then. Denice's breathing slowed, and she felt herself dropping into rhythm with Robert, her breathing matching itself to his. The warmth and stillness enfolded them like a blanket.

When Robert finally spoke he sounded almost sleepy, though his eyes were clear and steady. "What did you learn of the subjects you studied?"

"I'm not a very good feminist; I agree with them much of the time, but we part company when they wish to define me as a *woman* before all else, when I am in fact a *person* before all else." Denice grinned suddenly. "The man who tried to kill me, McGee; I asked him once what he thought of women, and he said he found them useful for sex, and for making babies."

Robert lifted a single eloquent eyebrow.

"It made me angry. I asked him if he was joking, and he said no, not at all; that he found *people* fascinating, but that when I phrased things in terms of men and women, what else *could* I

be talking about? The point stuck. It made it impossible for me
to become a feminist the way—the way the people I was with
wanted me to. To define myself as a woman, and then as a
Wiccan, accept the worship of the Goddess, and call myself a
witch and mean it sincerely; I'm a *person* first, and I couldn't
do it. The things those words represent have little to do with
who I am. I learned . . . that I disliked labels, or perhaps that
the labels that exist are insufficient. If there's a word for what
I am, I have not learned it."

Robert smiled; the smooth skin relaxed into laugh wrinkles.
"If they made a word for it, you would become something else,
and still the word would not fit. I am Robert, who *does* such
and such a thing, or I am Denice, who *does* such and such a
thing. This is closer, and even it is not accurate."

Denice said softly, "I missed you."

He nodded quite seriously. "Of course."

"I've been feeling the need to talk to you recently."

The laugh wrinkles around his eyes deepened slightly. "Yes."

"It's just that I've been having a bad year."

He shrugged. "It happens. Stand up."

Denice unfolded out of lotus, came to her full height, and
stood looking down at the small man.

"Turn in a full circle."

She did so, and he watched her move inside the yellow sundress; the smile broke across his face again. He came to his feet
in a single fluid movement. "You've been practicing."

"I have."

"You're in even better condition than you were."

"I am."

"Want a job?"

"I need one."

"I'll fire the morning instructor, I've never liked him anyway."

Denice shook her head. "I'm sorry. That's not what I've had
in mind."

The last letter from Trent was a year old. Denice knew it by
heart, had felt the impatience in it as though Trent had been
there in the room with her.

So join me. Or stay on Earth if you won't join me.
I know things aren't good downside, and I know

> *it's getting worse, and it's probably going to*
> *keep getting worse before it gets any better.*
> *But if you don't do anything, you have no right*
> *to be angry.*
> *Damn it, make the effort.*
> *Make the commitment to make a difference.*
> *And grow up.*

Robert looked at her quizzically. "What would you like to do?"

Denice Castanaveras said quietly, firmly, "I would like to work in politics."

Robert snorted. "Well, it's your soul."

She slept in Robert's spare room.

The building was near two centuries old; built shortly after the American Centennial, not long after Lincoln had freed the slaves. The building was largely what webdancers called dead space; most of the rooms in the building lacked access to the InfoNet. Late that night, when Ralf the Wise and Powerful came to visit her, he did so through the limited radio packet bandwidth available on her handheld.

Denice did not need much sleep—on an average night, four to five hours, and she got by with less. At 2:00 on Sunday morning, as she lay in bed reading one of Robert's prized paper books, the laser on her handheld lit, and a holoform appeared at the foot of her bed. The voice of the AI who had once been the Image of Trent the Uncatchable issued from the speaker in the handheld. "Hello, Denice."

Denice put the book down on the small table at the bedside and sat up in bed, drawing the covers up around her shoulders to keep herself warm against the slight chill. "Hello, Ralf. What have you found?"

Denice did not need much light to audit black text on white paper; she had dimmed the ceiling glowpaint considerably. Ralf's image illuminated its surroundings indistinctly, competing with the gentle glowpaint. He wavered at the edges, in the seeming of a man of indeterminate age, wearing dark, flowing robes. His slightly ascetic features were vaguely reminiscent of Trent's, of the man who had written the code that had become Ralf. Denice did not know, and had never seen reason to ask, if the image Ralf presented to the world was in any sense the

way Ralf saw himself, or if, more likely, it was simply a useful
representation when dealing with humans.

In the case of a true replicant AI, it would certainly have
been the latter. But Ralf the Wise and Powerful was, to
Denice's knowledge, unique; once merely Image, Ralf the Wise
and Powerful had been made replicant by the touch of an AI
named Ring. Unlike most replicant AIs, Ralf contained significant quantities of representational code, code designed by
Trent in the days when Ralf had acted as his face to the
InfoNet.

It made Ralf, Denice thought, seem rather more human
than most AIs.

"Nothing new," said Ralf quietly. "As you are probably
aware, Douglass Ripper did not use his *Electronic Times* interview today to announce that he will run for the position of Secretary General; nonetheless that announcement remains a high
order of probability through the next several weeks. One new
datum; Ripper's infosecurity is good, but I have typed the code
he uses for radio packet communications. Yesterday he took a
call on his handheld as he left his limousine. Briefly, he did release one member of his personal bodyguard this Tuesday last."

Denice said instantly, "One of the people Robert trained for
him?"

Ralf shook his head. "No."

"Good."

"Yes." Ralf paused, then volunteered, "I heard a joke recently."

"Oh?"

"It was an interesting joke. I heard it," Ralf said, "from a
replicant AI."

"Would you care to share it with me?"

"I am not certain you would appreciate it."

"Indeed."

"It concerned a human being."

"A replicant AI," said Denice slowly, "told you a joke about
a human."

"Yes."

"I thought AIs had no sense of humor."

"This is generally true. It should be noted that the replicant
who told this joke to me has incorporated itself with Image
code."

"*Really.*" Denice sat up straighter in bed. "I thought you
were the only Image who had ever gone replicant."

"To my knowledge I am. Nonetheless, I have on several occasions of late encountered AIs who have incorporated representational Image code—generally those AIs whose interests, for whatever reasons, cause them to interact with humans on a regular basis."

"Why?"

Ralf the Wise and Powerful shrugged. "I cannot say. But it is a fascinating development."

"What was the joke?"

Ralf paused. "It translates out of code poorly. In essence, it concerned a human webdancer who had made a poor decision, and had justified the decision by stating that it 'felt logical.' "

"Felt logical."

"Yes."

"And you found this amusing?"

Denice did not suppose for a moment that the tone of Ralf's voice, the voice of a being who thought twenty thousand times faster than she did, was anything but calculated; nonetheless she had the impression that she had genuinely surprised him. "Don't *you*?"

Robert had private business in Capitol City the following morning; they took a taxi in together.

Capitol City is small as cities go; no more than an enclave centered around mid-Manhattan. It is the home of the Unification; the place from which all of Earth and most of Luna is ruled. Seven spacescrapers—in 2075, nearly a quarter of all the spacescrapers to be found on Earth—rise from its midst; it houses the administrative offices of the Secretary General and the Unification Council; of the Peace Keeping Force and the Ministry of Population Control; of Space Force and the Bureau of BioTech.

Sitting with Robert in the back of the taxi as they entered Capitol City, Denice could not help remembering the last time she been inside the City's boundaries: not quite six years prior Denice Castanaveras, with help from Trent's friend Jimmy Ramirez, had broken Trent the Uncatchable out of the PKF Detention Center in the center of Capitol City.

In the seat next to her, Robert said, "Tell the truth. That's everything with Ripper—the man's a fanatic about truth. Probably comes of being a politician; everybody assumes he's a liar by trade, and I think it makes him a little crazy."

"He's not a liar by trade?"

"Well, yes," Robert conceded, "of course he is. But he deeply dislikes having people mention it."

A shadow fell across the car; Denice watched the Seven Spacescrapers as they loomed up and blotted out the sky. "Okay."

"Ripper's hired two security people from me in the last half year. John and Bruce. And he sent his Chief of Staff— Ichabod—to me for training."

"Ichabod?"

"I didn't name him, I just taught him. Ichabod."

"Is Ripper happy with your people?"

Robert smiled calmly. "Very. And neither John nor Bruce, on the best day he ever had, is fit to stand on the same mat with you."

"Has Ripper ever hired a woman for his security staff before?"

Robert grinned at her. "There's a first time for everything, isn't there?"

Denice nodded.

A check station awaited them at Park Avenue, at the boundary between Capitol City and the rest of Manhattan.

The taxi glided to a slow stop.

A pair of Peaceforcers in patrol blacks approached the vehicle from each side. One of the PKF halted five meters away and stood with his autoshot at the ready—not quite pointed at their cab—while the other approached them and rapped on the canopy with the butt of his autoshot. A window dilated open; Denice gave Robert her handheld, and Robert passed both hers and his own out to the waiting Peaceforcer.

The Peaceforcer took them without comment and placed a scanner up to the open window. If he spoke English at all, he did not bother to use it. The carcomp translated from his French: "Please look at the scanner."

Denice found herself tensing involuntarily, knew Robert noticed it. She forced her features to stillness while the laser light flashed into her eyes, one after the other.

The Peaceforcer glanced down at his own handheld InfoNet link. "Denice Daimara and Robert Dazai Yo?"

"Yes."

" 'Selle Daimara, you have an appointment with Unification Councilor Douglass Ripper at two-fifteen?"

"Yes."

" 'Sieur Yo, you have an appointment with Unification Councilor Tuliens at twelve-thirty?"

"Yes."

The Peaceforcer returned their handhelds to them. "Please proceed. Follow the instructions given to you, regardless of their source." He took a step back and waved them forward.

The carcomp spoke with immense politeness; as they began moving it said, "We are now entering Capitol City."

Denice could not contain her shiver. "No kidding."

Sitting in a small room on the 413th floor of the Unification Council Spacescraper, alone except for a second chair, Denice waited patiently.

She knew what was coming; she worked on her breathing.

She did not have to wait long. Ichabod Martin swept into the room and said without pause, "Pleasure to meet you, 'Selle Daimara. Have you ever worked with a truth plate before?" Ichabod was a tall man who, down to his bushy black beard, resembled nothing so much as a grizzly bear gone somewhat to seed. An inskin data link was socketed at his left temple.

From a deep, quiet place, Denice lied. "No."

"Okay." A shorter, hugely muscled black man of about thirty, massing perhaps one hundred twenty kilos, joined them, took up a position behind Denice. He did not speak to her. Ichabod did not appear to be armed; Denice turned slightly, saw the second man wore a hand maser strapped openly at his thigh. "What I want you to do," said Ichabod, opening a small black case to display three small pieces of whitish ceramic resting upon a black cloth lining, "is hold one of the plates in each hand. We're going to put the third plate at the base of your skull. May I touch you?"

Denice met Ichabod's gaze. "Thank you."

"Hmm? Oh, yes. Well, I don't like being touched by strangers either. May I?"

"Yes."

"Good." Ichabod brushed her hair away from the back of her neck, and Denice felt the cold ceramic come in contact; Ichabod placed the other two plates into each of her open hands. His thoughts, cool and pleasant, washed over her as they touched. "Hold them tightly, please." Denice's hands curled into fists.

Ichabod seated himself in front of her; his knees nearly

touched hers. "Don't worry about being nervous. It won't make a difference one way or another." Denice nodded, and Ichabod grinned at her. "How deep are you?"

"What do you mean?"

His eyes lost focus; he was clearly checking his inskin. "Let's see; high-amplitude alpha, low amplitude theta, beta around seventeen Hertz, synchronized brain waves. You've worked with some damn good biofeedback equipment to be able to maintain lucid awareness under these conditions."

Her father had taught her this exercise; it was the first time Denice had ever heard a Castanaveras telepath complimented as damn good biofeedback equipment.

She smiled at Ichabod, said nothing.

Ichabod shrugged. "It doesn't make a difference how deeply you trance, you know. If you're aware enough to answer my questions, you're aware enough of your lies for the plates to catch it."

"I don't intend to lie to you."

Ichabod shrugged. "Depending on how it goes, the questions can get very personal. Nobody but Bruce and I will ever know how you answered, not even Councilor Ripper; and Bruce's only here to watch me watch you; he's not listening. Okay?"

Denice lifted an eyebrow. "Not Ripper?"

"Need to know, 'Selle Daimara. And all Ripper needs to know is that you're a stable person, that you're not working for somebody else, and that you mean it when you make a commitment."

"Fine."

Ichabod nodded. "Okay, let's start. I want you to answer *yes* to the first six questions. Are you a hundred and eight years old?"

Denice watched the flow of pulsing blue neurons in her skull. "Yes." Nervous twitches followed, hundreds of different spots within her system kicking almost randomly. Perhaps two dozen different incidents were close enough to the truth plates to affect what the plates read.

Ichabod's features took on a distant cast. "Good. You know when you're lying. You'd be amazed how many sociopaths I get in here."

The thought flitted through the back of Denice's mind, *No, I wouldn't.*

Ichabod said, "Are you twenty-two years old?"

"Yes."

"Is your name Fred Dworkin?"

"Yes."

"Is your name Denice Daimara?"

"Yes."

"Are you—" Ichabod paused. "Is your name Denice Daimara?"

"Yes."

"Hmm. Did you change your name at some point?"

"Yes."

"All right, we'll come back to this one. Are you three meters tall?"

"Yes."

"Are you one hundred seventy-two centimeters tall?"

"Yes."

Ichabod said slowly, "Good. Okay, let's do it. You may now answer yes or no, but no more. Are your feelings toward Douglass Ripper generally positive?"

"Yes."

"Do you have what you would consider significant reservations toward Councilor Ripper as a person?"

"No."

"Do you have what you would consider significant reservations toward Councilor Ripper's legislative agenda?"

"Yes."

"Do you consider him insufficiently American?"

Denice hesitated, considering. "No."

"Do you feel that Councilor Ripper poorly represents American interests?"

"I can't answer that yes or no."

"Do you feel that Councilor Ripper adequately represents American interests?"

"Yes."

"Do you consider yourself an American?"

"Yes."

"Are you capable of being loyal to Douglass Ripper?"

"Yes."

"Do your interests in any way conflict with those of Douglass Ripper?"

"As I understand them, no."

Ichabod frowned, but accepted the answer. "Do you represent any other interests in making this application?"

"Other than myself?"

"Other than yourself, do you represent any other interests in making this application?"

"No."

"Are you sincere in your desire to work for Douglass Ripper?"

"Yes."

"Are there things about yourself which you would prefer that other people not know?"

"Yes."

"Would it be possible for someone to bribe you?"

"No."

"Would it be possible for someone to blackmail you?"

Denice hesitated. "No."

"You're not certain. Okay. You can answer this at as much length as you wish: what, in general, is the nature of the thing you think you might be blackmailed over?"

Denice was distantly aware of the truth plates in her hands growing slippery with sweat. *I'm a genie, my parents caused the Troubles, and if the Unification catches me it'll make me dead if I'm lucky, a slave if I'm not.* She said carefully, "I was a genetically enhanced fetus. I know that's illegal."

"You're a genie?"

"Yes."

"Okay. We get you guys sometimes; Ripper even hired one once. What name were you born with?"

Localization; here, and here, and here—slow the synapses, relax the neuroreceptors.

Without apparent pause Denice said, "Denice Seychelle."

There was a long silence while Ichabod scanned his inskin. Finally he shook himself and looked straight at her. "Robert was right; you're incredibly good, 'Selle Daimara. I don't think I've ever seen anybody before with such remarkable control of her nervous system. You damped out over ninety-five percent of the prior reactions to your lies."

Denice brought her hands together, released the two damp truth plates into her lap. "Ichabod, I've only ever done this before when I needed to survive. For whatever it's worth, I'm sorry." She turned slightly, glanced at the man standing behind her. "You go to sleep." She turned back to Ichabod as Bruce crumpled to the ground, found the huge bulk of the man already moving toward her, with amazing speed. She made no move to protect herself, did not take the time to get out of his way; as time slowed around her she reached out, Touched Ichabod Martin, and as his body crashed into hers like a puppet suddenly bereft of its strings, *changed* him.

Ichabod Martin awoke to a slight headache. He shook his head slightly. "My head hurts."

Bruce was already awake, standing at attention behind them. Ichabod looked at Bruce, looked again at the young woman sitting in front of him. "Denice? What happened to your eye?"

The woman blinked; one hand went to touch a growing bruise. "This? Um, nothing. I'll change my makeup to cover it before I go to see Councilor Ripper."

"Oh." Ichabod shrugged. "I'm sure that'll be fine. I'm looking forward to working with you, 'Selle Daimara. I've seen the vid Robert sent of you in motion. I'm really looking forward to it," he said again.

"Thank you, Ichabod."

A puzzled expression touched Ichabod again. "My head really hurts."

Denice Daimara said softly, "You wouldn't believe how mine feels."

Denice's appointment with Ripper was not scheduled until 2:15. She had nearly an hour to kill before Ripper would be available to speak with her.

She went to the women's restroom, called the lights down as low as they would go—it was a public restroom, and they would not go all the way down to darkness—went into the stall, closed and locked the door. She put the seat down on the toilet and sat down, closed her eyes, and waited for the pulsing pain to go away.

Before leaving, nearly an hour later, she stopped at the mirrors and tuned her makeup for a light blue shade that covered the bruise Ichabod had given her when he crashed into her earlier. It did not quite harmonize with the white and silver suit she wore, but aside from naked skin it was her best choice of the patterns stored in her makeup key.

She waited while her skin changed color, and then left to go meet Unification Councilor Douglass Ripper.

3

We shall need compromises in the days ahead, to be sure. But these will be, or should be, compromises of issues, not of principles. We can compromise our political positions, but not ourselves. We can resolve the clash of interests without conceding our ideals. And even the necessity for the right kind of compromise does not eliminate the need for those idealists and reformers who keep our compromises moving ahead, who prevent all political situations from meeting the description supplied by Shaw: "smirched with compromise, rotted with opportunism, mildewed by expedience, stretched out of shape with wirepulling and putrefied with permeation."

Compromise need not mean cowardice. . . .

—*John Fitzgerald Kennedy*, Profiles in Courage

Unification Councilor Douglass Ripper's office covered most of the 414th floor of the Unification Council Spacescraper. The area was huge, over twenty-five thousand square meters, unobstructed by divisions. The area was empty but for the desk that sat against one wall. The desk, of some black stone, was three meters long, two wide. Approaching it across the soft gray carpet, beneath the bright sunpaint, Denice felt a flicker of annoyance; she was meant to feel dwarfed in the midst of the vastness, and it was working.

The trio of dark gray chairs placed in front of the huge black desk were the same size and model as Ripper's chair. The man sitting behind the desk, watching Denice approach, was remarkably unprepossessing. Denice found herself, oddly, disappointed. Ripper looked like a midlevel executive of any large corporation; tall, brown-eyed and dark-haired, wearing an immaculately tailored blue pinstripe suit. His features were even and regular and slightly tanned; pleasant without being particularly handsome.

Ripper rose from his desk as she approached, and came forward to greet her. "'Selle Daimara." His handshake was firm but not overbearing; his hands were soft and uncalloused, the hands of a man who had never in his life done any sort of physical labor. Ripper released her hand after a moment and gestured at the middle seat of the three.

Denice seated herself. "It's a pleasure to meet you, Councilor Ripper."

"Likewise, 'Selle Daimara. Robert speaks highly of you."

"I know."

Ripper leaned back, watching Denice unabashedly. "I watched your video; I like the way you move."

"Thank you."

"I've known Robert I think twenty years now. Generally when he recommends somebody, I'm interested. I've hired five men from him in, I don't know, maybe the last ten years." Ripper paused. "Thirteen years. I hired the first guy after I was elected Unification Councilor back in late '62. Why do you want to work for me, as opposed to, say, SecGen Eddore?"

"Eddore is a man with no morals."

Ripper sat watching her, mild, sardonic amusement hovering around the corners of his mouth. "Oh? And I'm not?"

Denice Castanaveras fixed her gaze upon the man who would be Secretary General, and spoke evenly and without emphasis. "Are you?"

"Well, that," said Ripper, "is a damned good question." He paused, said, "I've audited your résumé. It's impressive, but it doesn't tell me anything about *you*. Tell me about yourself. Starting when you were young."

"I've studied with Robert since I was fourteen. At first—"

"Younger."

Denice paused, editing truth out of things she could not tell him; she found, somewhat to her surprise, that she did not want to lie to Ripper. "My parents died in the Troubles. Both of them. I don't remember much from my childhood. I had a brother, but we were separated in the riots following the Troubles, and I haven't seen him in over twelve years. He's probably dead. I was—" Denice paused again. She did not have to pretend difficulty in remembering; the first few months of the Troubles were a hazy period in her life. "I didn't stay anywhere for a week or a month, something like that. I don't really know how long. Sometimes people fed me and sometimes I stole things to eat. I was raped at least once. Maybe more, I don't remember."

Ripper said softly, "After that?"

"I woke up one morning and I was in a big barracks. It was Public Labor, but I didn't know that at the time, didn't know what Public Labor was." Denice shrugged. "So I learned. I was in Public Labor for four years. When I was thirteen a woman named Orinda Gleygavass paid my Labor debt and got me out. She was a dancer and teacher. She gave me a home; she was the one who sent me to study with Robert."

"Orinda Gley—what?"

"Gleygavass."

"A total stranger paid your Public Labor debt? Why?"

"She did it for a lot of girls. She was wealthy and she wanted to do something for all the people the Troubles damaged. I had some dance background from before the Troubles, a little training. Madame Gleygavass trained me as a dancer, had Robert train my muscles. I learned that I enjoyed martial discipline more than I enjoyed dance."

"Ah. Why is that name familiar to me?"

"Orinda Gleygavass? She died a couple of years ago in an accident; before she died, she led what she liked to claim was the best dance troupe in the System. It *was* the best known. You're a politician; even if you don't remember the Gleygavass dance troupe, you *must* remember *Leviathan*. A group of Unification Councilors tried to shut it down because they were upset about the—"

Douglass Ripper sat up very straight, looking for the first time more than professionally interested in their conversation. "Oh, my. I *know* you."

"Really?"

"You danced in *Leviathan*."

"You saw it?"

"Twice. By Harry—you must have been what, sixteen? Back in '69?"

"And '70. Yes."

"Good Lord. You were the most—" Ripper shook himself slightly, made an irritable gesture. "I hated the play. Revisionist history of the worst sort—I met Jules Moreau once before he died, and he was nothing like the character portrayed in *Leviathan*. Still—that bit at the end, where your character Marina seduced him—you've had biosculpture since then," he said abruptly. "Why?"

"I didn't like the way I looked. My breasts got too big to keep dancing; I had biosculpture to slim them down, and had my eyes done at the same time because I thought it would look attractive."

"It worked. So you were in Public Labor four years. How do you feel about that?"

Denice was surprised by the intensity of the feeling that came to her; it was nothing she had planned to say. She said fiercely, "That nobody should ever have to grow up in Public Labor again. *Ever.* That if there has to be a Ministry of Population Control, then we should demolish the current one and rebuild it from scratch. That the Peace Keeping Force should be kept out of the United States and out of the streets everywhere. I feel—that I need—I need to do something." She met the hard, skeptical gaze head-on, stared him down. "To make a *difference.*"

Ripper nodded slowly. "Robert said you were good." He spoke with honest curiosity. "Why me?"

"To make a difference you have to be in the right place. And you're running for Secretary General in '76."

"Could be."

"Your standing in the polls is at least five points over your nearest rival. There's no way you're not going to run. I spent the last six months researching members of the Unification Council. You're an American. You were a Senator at the age of twenty-eight. If—"

Ripper snorted. "And when I was twelve I walked dogs for people. I got elected to the Senate as young as I did because it's a meaningless position and nobody else wanted the damn job enough to outspend me for it."

"That meaningless position got you into the Unification Council."

Ripper shrugged. "The incumbent Councilor died in the Troubles. A right-place, right-time deal. 'Selle Daimara, you're not answering my question. If you've decided to work in politics, fair enough; the desire for public service gets sneered at these days, but it's very real. Still, you're bright and talented and I suspect there are half a dozen Unification Councilors besides myself who would hire you on Robert's recommendation—I *know* I'm not the only one who hires people Robert has trained."

"Why you?" Denice thought through how to say it, then shrugged and decided to put it bluntly. "You're my best guess.

I don't know you, and what I know of how you've voted in the Council doesn't fill me with immense confidence. But you're no worse than most of the other Councilors, and better than some; and the fact that you're an American counts with me. What the Unification has done to Occupied America is a crime."

Ripper said simply, "The rage is there. We all know it, we all live with it. We all have it, even those of us who have become a part of the Unification. Our job is to make sure the rage never explodes. There are other things we do, but that's the key. Most of what you haven't liked about my voting record— well, some of it comes out of compromising with other Councilors, trading votes on things I don't care about in return for their votes on things about which I do care. It makes my voting record look inconsistent in places, but it's part of the business. But a lot of the rest has come about as a result of that fundamental goal: to keep the lid on a country that's been ready for rebellion for twenty years. A rebellion that Occupied America *cannot* win. Why do you think I'm running for Secretary General?"

The analysis Denice gave him was, almost word for word, what Ralf the Wise and Powerful had said to her some two months prior:

"This is the third, final term that Eddore is able to serve as Secretary General. If he were allowed another term you wouldn't run. You're popular but he's more popular and you'd lose. Virtually anyone running against him would except, maybe, Michael Moreau. But Moreau's not running, and in the '76 elections Eddore *can't* run again. Recent polls give you thirty-two percent of the vote. That's over five percent higher than Zhao Pen, even with the bulk of the Chinese vote behind him. He'll get his billion-odd votes, but he won't get any more. And no Frenchman besides Moreau stands any chance at all, not in an honest election. The likeliest real opposition you'd face is Sanford Mtumka, down in Pan-Africa. There's a lot of ageist dissatisfaction with the current administration, and you're even younger than Eddore; you won't be considered any kind of an improvement. Mtumka's over eighty; most of the old vote will go to him, even after accounting for racial bias. But that's only nineteen percent."

Ripper laughed. "You've gamed this out for yourself. You want to work for a winner, and you think I can be one."

"I don't know, Councilor. All I know is you have a chance."

Ripper became abruptly still, poised like a hawk, and out of nowhere fixed a striking, improbably forceful gaze upon Denice; under the impact of that gaze, for the first time, Denice found it possible to believe that this was a man who might be running the Unification in another eighteen months. "Denice, if I offer you this job, you'll be traveling with me whenever I'm out of Capitol City, and during those times you'll be living with me more intimately than you've ever lived with anyone; twenty-four hours a day, from the moment we leave Capitol City to the moment we return. In the performance of your job you'll be called on to shield my life with your own, to kill if it's necessary to defend me. Can you do that?"

"You're very eloquent, Councilor Ripper."

It stopped him; Ripper looked at her for a second. "I can be, with a good speech writer."

Denice knew the answer he was waiting for. "I've never killed anyone, Councilor Ripper. But I think I could do it once. After that I don't know."

Ripper nodded. "Fair enough. I like you. See Ichabod before you leave. In addition to everything else he handles most of my personal secretarial work. He'll walk you through the paperwork and security background check." He stood, held his hand out again. "Welcome aboard."

"I haven't said yes."

Ripper stood motionless, hand held out to her, and then smiled at her. "Oh? Haven't you?"

- 4 -

They sat in the dojo, late Monday afternoon, facing one another across the length of the mat. The westward-facing windows had been opened; sunlight streamed in, bright and warm, and they could hear the sounds of the city.

"So it went well."

"I think so. He hired me."

"He would have been foolish not to."

"You sent him video of me, he said."

Robert nodded. "Old, obviously. From the San Diego Freestyle Open, back in '71. You were eighteen and your form was—if I were not concerned about the size of your ego I might call it flawless. And you're better today."

Denice bit her lip. "Thank you."

"Truth is not a compliment. It merely exists. I've never seen anyone who moves the way you do, Denice. Not ever. You impress *me*, which is not easy; I'm sure you impressed him."

"He impressed me. A lot."

Robert's features held no expression at all. "Oh?"

"It was—at first," said Denice in a swift tumble of words, "I couldn't see it. Ripper, as Secretary General. He's so different from Eddore. He was dressed in this suit you could have seen some bank vice president wearing. And his voice is sort of flat and he doesn't use it well. And he needs to work out more."

"Most do."

"But then we talked. He explains himself well. And he talked about the desire for public service, and it was one of the only times I didn't get any sense at all that he was being cynical." Denice paused. "I was *very* impressed."

"Being impressive is his job, Denice. It's how he got elected and part of how he *keeps* getting elected. Don't let him impress you too much. He's a decidedly fallible man, and if you work with him long enough, someday he will fail you. As Douglass likes to say, it's part of the business."

Denice nodded, looked away from Robert for a moment, and then said, "I have missed your wisdom."

Robert smiled, said gently, "Oh, my dear. There is no such thing."

"Oh?"

Robert's smile faded, and he said with as much seriousness as she had ever seen him use on any subject, "Denice, be wary of people who have answers to your problems. Those answers I have found for myself—the things that strike you as wisdom—are not *your* answers, and they are only my answers *today*. Tomorrow I will be a different person with different needs. The world and its people are too complex for any system of beliefs to fully address their complexity. The map does not hold; it can't. When you learn something for yourself, hold to it; but do not expect it to work for others. Sometimes it will. More often it will not."

Denice grinned. "You sit there and tell me there is no such thing as wisdom, and then pour a bucket of it over me. I'm glad to be back, Robert. I am glad to be home."

He nodded, then said slowly, "I thought, as the weeks became months and I did not hear from you, that I had lost you forever. I am more pleased than I can say that I have not."

•   •   •

After she had gone Robert waited quietly in the darkness at the far northern edge of the practice mat. He sat upon the mat itself, facing north. On the wooden floor that surrounded the mat, where the mat ceased, a polished blue stone teapot rested upon a base of the same material. Within the base flickered a small candle. One candle would keep the tea within the pot hot for most of a night.

Robert sat and sipped tea, and waited for nightfall, and his visitor.

While he waited he listened to music.

It was a strangeness of his era, that a knowledge of music, once the hallmark of civilized men and women, was now a thing of the streets. Robert was not enough of a historian to know how it had come to pass; he suspected the trend had begun back near the turn of the century; as serious a period, he thought, as the world had ever seen. Following the dawn of the new millennium men and women had faced the prospect of long decades of work to recover from the mistakes of the century just done. And, led by Sarah Almundsen, the world had risen to the challenge. The Unification War had resulted, and after the Unification—

Nearly every ecological problem that mankind had faced, and most of the social ones, were directly a result of the fact that the planet groaned beneath the weight of too many human beings. It was a fact that could not be disputed.

After the Unification had come the Ministry of Population Control.

A serious time, to deal with serious problems; problems that had in a real sense threatened the survival of the race.

But on the other side of the problems, once the very question of human survival was no longer in doubt, something had been lost, some refinement, some taste for culture and laughter. The world had grown a grimmer place. It was a thing Robert had not even known until perhaps eight years ago, after meeting Denice Daimara. She guarded herself well, and it had been most of a year before he had been certain she was a genie, and several years after that before he had known her, beyond doubt, for one of the infamous Castanaveras.

Robert counted himself fortunate to have known and loved her. Already well trained as a dancer when he met her, he had taught her a degree of control over her body she had never known; and she, a child of the streets, had taught him music. It amazed him that he had never missed the lack of music in his life; it seemed to him that wrapped in the music was the source of all movement.

Fragments reached out to him form the midst of the songs, snatches of melody, phrases:

> *Well Elvis sanctified me*
> *I tell you Elvis saved my soul*
> *He flew to me through time and space*
> *And we shared a jelly roll*

The lyric amused him; he wondered sometimes who Elvis might have been. Some religious leader, he guessed, one of the dozens that the late twentieth and early twenty-first centuries had produced in such profusion; perhaps one of the Prophet Harry's competitors. The old songs that played now were among his favorites; he did not even know the name of the man who sang them. They were simply a set of songs—an "album"—one of his students had given him about two years prior; the student had moved with his family to Europe shortly thereafter, and Robert had lost touch with him.

Tonight he waited for his visitor, waited with the music and the thin wail of the singer's voice. The music rolled along, washed over him, and then, out of stillness, a figure cloaked in shadows stepped forward, out of the darkness and into the light. And the music playing in the background, the smooth warm stone of the cup in his hand, every awareness of the outside world, ceased to exist for Robert Dazai Yo.

He put the cup down on the wooden floor and inclined his head slightly. Aside from that he did not move at all.

"Good evening, sir."

He was a painting come to life, Camber Tremodian, slightly taller than Robert, a monochrome image in black and white and grays. Shadows swirled around him like living things. In the place where his face should have been was a featureless dark gray mist the color of slate. In times past Robert had found that the more deeply he gazed into that mist, the more strained his eyesight had become. After a time he had learned not to look.

Upon Camber's breast was a circle of concentric rings, and a single line of writing that Robert could not read; the circles and the words wavered in Robert's eyesight like an image seen on the highway in the desert heat.

When Camber spoke his voice was smooth and even and featureless. "Hello, Robert."

"She came back to me."

"I know."

"Of course you do." Robert paused. "I've missed her. I've missed her a great deal."

Camber took another step forward, farther into the light. Still his form grew no clearer; the shadows traveled with him, wrapped themselves about him as he moved. "I know, Robert."

Robert kept his features stilled, gave no sign of the anguish in his heart. "In your service I have lost everyone I ever cared for. Must I lose her as well?"

The dark figure said gently, "I do not know if it will be necessary. I can tell you merely that which you already know; if you can protect her, do. But her path is not yours, and if in serving me you lose her, then lose her you must. I have, I think, denied the enemy access to Trent the Uncatchable; beyond that I cannot say. Deviation in this year is almost twelve percent: you are approaching a cusp over which my opponent has secured control. This is perhaps my last visit to you. For at least the next two years and four months, and possibly longer, I will not be here to aid or advise you."

Robert said slowly, "You won't be here?"

Robert did not think he imagined the weariness in the voice. "My opponent has effectively prevented it, Robert. We traded, he and I; there are no guarantees that one of Trent's enemies of this time will not harm him, but unless *my* enemy has an avatar in this time, then from him at least I have kept Trent secure. The details of our agreement need not concern you—but through, perhaps, the end of this decade, if you see me again it will be in the Other Place; and in that place I am a different order of person. As you have learned, I will not always recognize you there."

"You ... told me once ... that if I were unlucky, I might someday meet your opponent."

"It is more likely now than previously, and grows likelier still the closer we come to the cusp. Even my visit tonight is dangerous; the opponent's agents in this time are more numerous and more powerful than mine. I think you have probably been identified as mine; there is a chance the enemy will attempt to turn you from my service."

"Or Kill me?"

Camber Tremodian hesitated, and spoke directly, as though to an equal. "Robert, I don't think so. You are one of the six living shivata of this era; I don't think my opponent will dare inflict the Kill upon you, artistic though your death might be. I am a night face; so is he, and if shiabrè died out because of your loss it would destroy both of us. But there are five other night faces in this time, and I don't know with certainty that the enemy will *not* make that attempt. Robert, I can't *see*."

"If I meet the opponent, how will I know him?"

The man shrugged. "If he wishes you to know him, you will. If he does not, you won't." The dark figure laughed suddenly, a deep amused sound. "If you see someone dressed like me who's *not* me, it's him. Except he'll be in white."

"In white."

The amusement was still evident in Camber's voice. "Yes. It's a long story. Perhaps someday a decade or two from now I'll tell it to you. Though, if you have the opportunity, feel free to ask the enemy about it—you'll never meet a better storyteller. I promise you."

"Is Denice in danger?"

Camber shook his head. "No. Not from him, not the way you mean. I could not protect her as I have protected Trent, but Denice is his direct ancestor, and needs the protection less; he won't risk harming her. No more would I. She is no ancestor of mine, but her descendant's lives have touched mine in many places. I once tried to kill her father, but Denice had been born by then, and her father's death, at the time I sought it, would have saved her from a greater loss." The shadowed features turned toward Robert; Robert had the eerie impression that Camber Tremodian met his eyes. "But Robert, if it were necessary that she die, I would have it. If it is necessary that you lose her, I will have that."

"It is hard, what you ask of me."

"Others have been asked more. And given it." He paused. "More will be asked of Denice than has been asked of you."

Robert looked directly at Camber Tremodian. "You are cruel, sir."

"No, Robert," said Camber Tremodian, and Robert did not think he imagined the pain in the smooth, smooth voice: "I am necessity." And with the word, the shadows reached out to enfold him, and he was gone.

Robert glanced down at the cup of his tea.

He knew without touching it that it would be cold.

He sat for a long while by himself, alone in the dark with his music.

I think you loved me as I loved you
And why we stopped I just don't know
I guess your guess is as good as mine
. . . I miss you though

He rose after a while and went upstairs to bed, and in his sleep he dreamed, with pain and longing, of a woman he had not even seen in thirty years.

DateLine: *Shawmac on Writing*

(Taken from an address to a writer's group in Des Moines, Iowa. Shawmac appeared with a bottle of smoke whiskey in hand; his opening line to the group was, "When the bottle's done, I'm done.")

Where do I get my fucking ideas? Is this the best question you punks can come up with? You want to be a writer and you ask that question?

Back in '63, when the U.N. outlawed manually operated vehicles, it was a relief for some of us. How do you not get ideas? I used to get them while I drove. It was dangerous. (Okay so yes it was fun. But it was still dangerous. If somebody asks me, someday I'll tell you the story about the time I hit a van, and the rear doors swung open and two blondes and a trampoline fell out. If you ask nicely—it's much too painful a story to remember for a measly thousand-CU speaking fee.)

Okay, the truth is, I call an Idea Board in Peoria, Illinois. And I download new ideas from them whenever I need a new one. It's an expensive way to work, but it's where I got the idea for the motorpigs.

. . . what's the number? You schmuck, you yellow

dog fuckhead, that was a joke. Humor. There is no fucking Idea Board. I made it up.

You see, it comes to me. It percolates around my skull, combining and recombining, growing more potent with every passing moment, until I awaken in the middle of the night and the brew spews forth through my traceset. And becomes a story or sensable script or DateLine column.

It's an interesting way to live. Can you imagine what it's like? To be unable to operate heavy equipment, or weapons, or explosives, safely? To get a reputation for rudeness because you can suddenly, in the middle of a conversation, come back to yourself from some fine conceit, and realize you have no idea at all what the person you're speaking to has just been saying? To come back with a rude, unpleasant jar from some wonderful place, and realize that you have absolutely no idea how much time is left on the hand grenade you're holding?

Some of you can imagine. You'll be writers and people will ask you stupid questions. And you won't get any sympathy, either, ever, not from anyone. Certainly not from me, 'cause I got problems of my own.

So you'll just have to suck it in and tough it out.

As for the rest of you—the rest of you are yellow dog punks and you'll always be punks.

Period, end of discussion.

- 5 -

On the afternoon of July 3, 2075, Terry Shawmac sat at a banquet table toward the rear of the hall and watched as people arrived.

He was exceptionally drunk.

To the man sitting next to him, he said suddenly, "It's not like any of the people who *got* nominated are any *good*."

William Devane, newsdancer for the *Electronic Times*, nodded. When he spoke his voice held a distinct Irish lilt, and for a man of his size—for a man of any size—his voice was very soft and gentle. "I've often thought."

William Devane did not look like a newsdancer. He was black Irish with black eyes, a face so smooth it looked as though he had just depilated; even in his tuxedo he looked more like a bodybuilder than a nominee for an *Electronic Times* Award for Excellence in News Reporting.

A hundred and fifty years earlier he'd have been the meanest, toughest Irish cop in his precinct.

"*You*, for example," Shawmac continued. "Don't take this personally, but do you really think your article on the Johnny Rebs was one of the five best pieces of feature reporting in the last year? *Really?* Not like my extended column on recreational explosives. Now *there* was a subject that people responded to."

William Devane's lips curved into a slight smile that did not reach his black eyes. "I heard."

"And my story on *retirement* benefits," Shawmac continued. "My examination of the ways in which the fact that people are *living longer* affects the willingness of large corporations to pay retirement benefits that workers have *legitimately earned*. Brilliant," he said briskly, "fine, *fine* writing." Shawmac suddenly upended the bottle of smoke whiskey on the table in front of him, held it upside down for a good ten seconds, and drank straight from the neck. After putting it down again, he fixed Devane with a hostile stare. "So. Think you're going to win?"

Devane shrugged, massive shoulders moving easily beneath the black cloth of his tuxedo. "I have no idea, 'Sieur Shawmac."

"I've never been nominated, you know."

"Yes."

"Oh." Shawmac blinked. "Thought I'd mention it." He returned to his bottle.

William Devane sat quietly and watched the hall fill up. He did not much like visiting New York; if he had not been nominated for an award, he would not have come.

He did not much like Terry Shawmac.

There was one advantage to visiting the city of New York; only one.

Six hours later William Devane, in his tuxedo, passed through the Barrier and walked down the nighttime streets of the Long Island Fringe. Peaceforcer glowfloats and spyeyes bobbed quietly in the air above, but Devane did not allow it to lull him into a false sense of security; the PKF would not rouse itself to come to the aid of a single man, walking alone at night in the Fringe, should trouble befall him.

Devane did not intend to allow trouble to befall him.

Twice, as he walked the ten blocks from the Patrol Sectors Barrier to McGee's, bands of the Gypsy Macoute, draped in American flags in honor of tomorrow's Independence Day, came upon him.

Both times Devane ignored them.

Both times the Macoute—perhaps not certain themselves why they did so—let him pass.

A single hunting waldo sat next to the doorway that led into McGee's. Two men stood immediately inside the door. One carried an Excalibur laser rifle, the other appeared unarmed.

Both were the equals of Devane's own not inconsiderable height.

"William Devane," said Devane. "Here to see Mister McGee. He's expecting me."

After dinner they retired to McGee's study upstairs on the third floor. The study was a place of windows; one window faced inward, overlooking the restaurant below; another looked out into the Fringe. A third looked off across the water, toward the spacescraper-dominated nighttime skyline of Manhattan.

They were in fact real windows, not holos. The Fringe had, in years past, been a more brutal and violent place than it had since become. It was inevitable; those who had been damaged the worst during the Troubles were now dead, and the children of the Troubles, if deadlier than their parents, were also saner. The random sniper fire that had once been endemic was now rare, and windows had once again become safe.

The one wall that lacked a window bore a large American flag.

A photograph, grainy and two-dimensional, hung over the desk; it held the image of a boat McGee had once owned.

A holo in the corner was tuned to the *Electronic Times* Board; a second holo, beside it, showed imagery from *News-Board*. Images of rioting—burning cars, pitched battles with PKF troops—flickered through the fields.

An irony; as the Independence Day riots had grown more violent in the outside world, they had grown less so in the

Fringe. From his study McGee could see only one building afire.

"It was fascinating," said Devane, "to be sure. Newsdancers, nominated themselves, kept sneaking out of the proceedings to check on the status of the riots."

The old man nodded. "Did you mind losing?"

Devane sipped at the coffee and brandy McGee had prepared for him, and smiled. "Only a bit, if the truth be told. The award would have made it more difficult for me to work on stories in anonymity. I don't generally write features material anyway." He wondered, briefly, if there was any chance at all McGee could have understood how deeply he had wanted to lose. After a moment he said, "The Credit would have been nice."

"CU:five-thousand, isn't it?"

"That's only a bit of it, McGee. The rest is that other Boards would have paid more for my work, for the privilege of placing my name on the masthead. In a year or so I'd have brought in twice again the amount of the prize Credit."

"Surely you're not hurting?"

Devane shook his head. "No. But who knows what the future will bring? It never hurts to have some put away as hard Credit."

McGee grinned. "Your point is well taken. Over the course of my own ridiculously prolonged life, I've been broke more times than I like to think." McGee paused, said abruptly, "Just out of curiosity, how old *are* you?"

Devane did not even blink. "Forty-seven."

McGee shook his head. "No, you're not. I mentioned Bob and Ray to you once, and you knew who they were. Nobody who wasn't listening when they were on the air remembers Bob and Ray any longer."

Devane lied easily. "McGee, you've the fine suspicious mind of a newsdancer. I did some background research once on a comedy Board in Texas; Bob and Ray were prominently mentioned in that Board's history of live comedy duos."

"You've slipped up on other points as well; you remember too damn many of the same things I remember, things that no one who is *not* my age should recall." McGee shrugged. "So don't tell me. I've had one or two experimental treatments myself; you don't live as long as the both of us have without them. I was just curious; your skin, in particular. No looseness to speak of, and I don't see much in the way of joint degeneration in your hands. Whoever did your work, it impresses me."

"Indeed." Devane paused, changed the subject. "I did appreciate the background material on the Ministry's decision to start sterilizing Public Labor clients again. It helped my story."

"Yeah." McGee nodded, accepting Devane's change of subject. When he spoke, his voice was grim. "It was a *stupid* decision, William. We are damn near the point where the PKF are going to have to stop calling them riots and start admitting that they're insurrections; we are only a year away from the Tri-Centennial itself, and the Ministry brings back the single most unpopular population control measure Occupied America has ever seen. One of my waiters had a sister in Public Labor; I didn't know about it, or I would have paid her debt and gotten her out. By the time he came to me it was too late; they'd sterilized her already. And I don't care what the Ministry says, that damn copy-protection transform virus they use *kills* people."

William Devane nodded. "I must tell you, I am not looking forward to next summer. It is *not* going to be a good time to be on Earth, and particularly North America."

McGee rose from behind his desk, moved restlessly to stand at the window. He held a single beer bulb in one hand; Devane thought McGee had forgotten it, had not seen McGee drink from it since opening the bulb. "I lose Credit on this restaurant, on the hotel; you know that."

"Yes."

"People think I'm wealthy." McGee snorted. "The Fringe needs them, so I've kept them going. The hotel gives the Gypsy Macoute and the Temple Dragons a place to negotiate treaties, neutral territory they can't find anywhere else. The restaurant is just a safe place for people to come and not be bothered. God knows there are few enough of them in the Fringe."

Devane said nothing.

"Trent the Uncatchable used to come here, you know. Before he got out of the Fringe and got famous."

Devane looked interested. "You've never mentioned that before. You knew him?"

"A bit. He was a punk."

"Is there a story in it?"

"Probably not. That's not why I bring it up. It is just— William, I've started turning down Ministry work. I can't stomach it any longer. It used to be that when Special Tasks or the Office of Technology Assessment had a job for me it was because some genie had gone wild, and they needed the genie found and stopped. They didn't try to hire me to kill genies, and when one of them died during a chase—rarely—they weren't pleased.

"I doubt they will try to hire me again. Last week I turned down a job offer that—" McGee stopped in midsentence, turned to face Devane. "The details don't matter. A political job, and an unpleasant one. I've never turned down a job on political grounds before, and it's left them—unhappy with me. It wouldn't surprise me if the unhappiness found expression." McGee looked straight at Devane. "I have kept notes about every piece of work I've ever done for the Ministry. It is all covered under the Official Secrets Acts of 2048 and 2054."

William Devane said quietly, "You're talking about treason, McGee."

"It is for sale."

"Ah."

"I need the Credit."

"How much?"

"CU:ten thousand."

"There's a story in this material?"

"At least one. The rest is great background, though. Things you won't learn elsewhere."

William Devane looked straight at McGee and said simply, "Sold. What's the story?"

"Okay," McGee said slowly. "Okay. Did you ever hear about a slowtime bubble that was found up in the Swiss Alps, back in '72? About the fellow they found inside it?"

The semiballistic to Ireland took not quite an hour.

In the semiballistic's darkened passenger compartment, William Devane audited McGee's notes. It was fascinating material, true enough; it covered forty years of McGee's work in the Ministry's Department of Special Tasks. Devane did not for an instant believe that it was a complete account of McGee's work; but he did believe that the sections McGee had edited—and there were obvious edits, McGee's way of acknowledging the point—were personal matters.

The "story" was ridiculous.

The entire thing—the bubble, the man found inside, the Secretary General's involvement, and the way the PKF had bundled the fellow off to some unknown destination—smacked of a *System Enquirer* article. Devane was pragmatic; he could not, off the top of his head, think of anything about which he would have been *less* likely to write. His reputation would be destroyed if such an article ever saw the light of day with his byline attached.

Assuming the story was fabricated, and McGee had been somehow suckered, which Devane did assume. In the unlikely event there was any truth to the story—well, in that instance publishing the material was even more foolish. Devane had learned many hundreds of years prior that it did not pay to cause the powerful any great degree of trouble. And Charles Eddore impressed Devane as few politicians had since Almundsen and Moreau. Of the politicians Devane would have been willing to inconvenience with such an article, Eddore was low on the list.

About half an hour into the flight Devane turned his handheld off and leaned back in his seat, closing his eyes.

He had not finished all of McGee's notes, but unless there was some unexpected gem in the background material, it had been a bad purchase.

It did not bother him that he had overpaid for the material; such purchases were always a gamble, and McGee was an honest man.

Devane put the story out of his mind and prepared to take a nap.

The story stayed with him.

He had been unable to get an SB to Dublin; the SB came down in Belfast instead, most of Ireland away from where Devane needed to go. At the spaceport's downlot he chartered a taxi, gave the taxi his home address, and tried to get to sleep. The semiballistic had taken him from New York to Ireland in not quite an hour; the taxi would take over twice as long to reach his home, three hundred kilometers south of Belfast, and inland fifty klicks from the coast.

The story would not, damn it, leave him be.

Devane kept his eyes closed and tried to sleep.

About ten minutes into the cab ride home, William Devane sighed irritably, opened his eyes, and turned on his handheld. Indecision touched him then—where to start?

Staring into his handheld's steadily glowing field, Devane brought the traceset up to his temple, and after a moment's consideration gave the command, ACCESS IN SUMMARY—and a pause then, and Devane was not certain why this was the subject that came to him—ACCESS IN SUMMARY, SLOWTIME FIELDS.

He was still auditing data, lost to the world, when the car landed in the heart of County Cork.

The house rose up out of the side of a hill, overlooking a small stream. Its walls were stone and the windows were small slits, and it was far larger than its stony exterior suggested.

It faced, across the length of the valley, the old stone keep at Kilgard, where, Devane had reason to believe, he had once lived.

A road of broken black cement, well over a hundred years old, led up to the house, a holdover from the days when cars had traveled on wheels. The cab set down on the surface of the cracked asphalt, fans gentling as the car touched ground. Devane touched his handheld to the cab's payment strip, stepped out and stood at the foot of the path leading up to the house. His eyesight was excellent; after a moment a tiny light, set in a small stone at the base of the house, blinked once in infrared. It was the sign that the house security had recognized him; he moved forward up the path, touched his palm to the locklarm, and waited while the door unbolted itself.

The door was another sign of his house's age; it did not slide away, it did not curl open; it was solid oak, reinforced with interior stainless steel rods, and it *swung* open on hinges.

Devane had installed it himself, in 1922.

He had built the house, laid it stone by stone into the side of the hill, over four hundred years prior.

Inside the house the lights came up automatically. The living room was lit by a pair of standing lamps that looked like the flood lamps which had once been used in motion picture production; Devane had purchased them in Hollywood in 1958.

He took the stairs to his bedroom, near the top of the small hill. A smaller stairway inside the bedroom led up to a small grassy place on the surface of the hill, overlooking every approach to Devane's home.

In the basement the entrances to three tunnels were hidden. One of the tunnels reached out no farther than the base of the hill; the other two reached out in opposite directions, some four hundred meters apiece. Each one had taken him decades to dig.

The house had running water and electricity; thirty years prior Devane had installed a portable fusion generator in the basement, and over the years had slowly taken himself off Ireland's power grid. He did not pay electric bills, did not shop locally. His InfoNet access was through a small microwave dish set into the side of the hill. As far as the Tax Boards were concerned, he had no existence as a private individual; he was the sole Irish employee of a small import–export company based in Occupied America.

To the extent possible, he left no records of his existence; but maintaining a reasonable degree of anonymity was difficult nonetheless, and grew more so with each passing century.

Devane's bedroom might have passed for the cabin of some English sea captain of the 1800s. In it Devane had installed most modern conveniences short of a houseboat. He undressed himself and hung his clothes; he placed his weapons—a hideaway maser and a knife for close-in work—on the dresser next to his bed.

Even in his own bed, warm and secure as any man might reasonably expect to be, he found himself unable to sleep. Half an hour after going to bed he got back up, displeased with the world and himself, pulled on a robe and sat down to read McGee's account again.

Spring: 2072

A Blast from the Past

- 1 -

The old man stood on the black marble floor in the lobby of the Institute of Advanced Archaeological Studies in Lyons, France, hands tucked into the pockets of his overcoat; ancient, pale gray eyes scanning the lobby restlessly. He radiated age, not so much in his appearance as in his mannerisms, the economy of gesture and movement that nobody under the age of a hundred or so would have had time yet to learn. The skin at his neck and on the backs of his hands was slightly loose; aside from that, simply from appearance, he might have been any age above sixty or so.

He had been born in 1929 and he was 142 years old.

After a few minutes the increasingly nervous receptionist asked him if he would care to sit. Though his French was excellent he did not respond, and she did not ask again.

He had been kept waiting for over an hour when Doctor Sven Eingardt finally arrived. The old man was in no hurry; he stood before the double glass doors, watching the fog creep through the streets, ignoring Eingardt's approach. He found it preferable to watching the cheap wallholo—a none-too-subtle series of advertisements for the Institute itself. The pitch for funds, the wallholo informed him in large printed French, could be heard on earphone channel four. *Yet another argument against the damned earphones,* the old man thought with a certain cynical pleasure.

The thought marked his age as clearly as all else; earphones had been a fact of life for over fifty years.

Eingardt spoke English with very little accent. " 'Sieur McGee. How pleasant to see you. Please accept my sincere apologies for being late. The maglev was shut down while they swept the rail into Lyon. A bomb threat by the Claw, apparently."

McGee did not respond for perhaps fifteen seconds after Doctor Eingardt's greeting. At length he turned away from the vista of the fog, turned to look at Doctor Eingardt standing nervously in the midst of his gleaming lobby, hand outstretched to shake McGee's. Doctor Eingardt was a tall, thin man who had, at the moment, a nervous tic in one cheek. McGee nodded and kept his hands in the pockets of his overcoat. "*Mister* McGee, if you please. I'll see your toy now."

In the maglev on the way down to the basement Eingardt made the mistake of attempting conversation.

"They say you run a restaurant in New York's Fringe."

"Yes."

"And a hotel in the Fringe as well. Interesting hobby for an employee of the Ministry of Population Control."

McGee glanced down at Eingardt, a flick of the pale gray eyes. "I don't work for the babychasers. I work for the Bureau of Special Tasks, a department within the Ministry, and I only do that when I damn well feel like it. My restaurant and hotel are my business." The old man was silent, brooding. "Hunting rogue genies for the MPC—occasional silliness like *this*, for the Office of Technology Assessment—are hobbies."

The Institute's basement was as cold as the streets outside; McGee was glad he'd kept his coat on. This early on a Saturday most of the Institute's employees were not present, and McGee was distantly pleased by that as well.

The bubble sat in the middle of the basement, surrounded by twenty meters of empty space on all sides.

It was what McGee had been told to expect, no more and no less. A mirrored sphere some four meters in diameter, perfectly reflective. It sat on a tripod-based ring of some dull metal, lifted high enough up off the ferrocrete floor that a person could crawl under it. McGee ran the tips of his fingers over the bubble's surface. It was so slick it felt wet. He placed one hand against the surface and pushed lightly. The bubble shifted just a bit on its supporting ring.

Eingardt spoke in a nervous rush. "A German climber, Candace Groening, found it. Two weeks ago. She was up in a rocky area in the Val d'Entremont in Switzerland, around twenty-three hundred meters above sea level. *Command*, picture one." A holofield appeared hanging in midair next to the bubble, a flat photo centered midway in: a rocky pass high in the Swiss Alps, white and grayish blue. "This is near the Great St. Bernard pass, a bit north of the Italian border. *Command* next." A second shot showed an expanse of rock with a gleam of reflective silver buried in the midst of the gray. "A recent rock slide had uncovered this partial surface of the sphere. Groening cleared away as much of the surface of the sphere as she could, shot it from several angles, and came back down. A colleague in Hamburg—that's in north Germany—to whom she showed her photographs, he forwarded them to me because we're so much closer to the site."

"I know where Hamburg is."

Doctor Eingardt smiled uncertainly. "Sorry. You Americans tend to be shaky on European geography." McGee stared at Eingardt and the smile died. "Not all of you," Eingardt said after a moment.

"Go on, Doctor."

Eingardt did so quickly. "We went up to the site last weekend, myself and two of my assistants. Picks and lasers, no blasting; we were very careful for fear of damaging the site." The holo flickered, became a shot from a wavering handheld holocam. The quality was sufficiently poor that McGee guessed the holo had not been doctored. An observation he had made many years prior was that false documents, holos, recordings, all tended to a certain minimal level of professionalism in their presentation.

The image was of the sphere that stood next to the holo, as Eingardt and his assistants excavated around it. "We took samples—you can see it here—of rock from the vicinity of the sphere. Here we were fortunate; in a rock layer four centimeters above the surface of the sphere we found this fossilized material. A shrub for which we have good radiocarbon-dating comparisons. I place its age at thirty-two thousand six hundred years old, with a margin of error of perhaps four hundred years in either direction. My best guess at this point—and it is a guess, though I've some evidence to go on—is that the sphere was buried somewhat earlier than that, perhaps thirty-five to forty thousand years ago. We know that it was covered by sheets of ice during the tail end of the Würm glacial period; there are glacial striation marks on the deepest levels of the rock. The sphere was found in an area located above the tree line both then and now; we found nothing really suitable for radiocarbon dating except the shrubbery I mentioned, which was separated by a rock layer four centimeters in width. At any rate, when the ice sheet retreated from this ridge about twenty thousand years ago, at the end of the last Ice Age, it left behind a—here, at the sides of the ridge—what is called a lateral moraine. Essentially a collection of boulders, rubble that was ground together by the motion of the glacier—covering the entrance to the cave. At a guess the earthquake back in '66 uncovered the sphere, and it's been sitting there ever since, waiting for somebody to come along and discover it."

Eingardt was silent after that, as though waiting for McGee to reply. When it became clear that McGee had no intention of saying anything, Eingardt sighed and called the glowpaint up.

" 'Sieur McGee, may I ask why you were sent here? This is one of the most exciting archaeological discoveries of this century, perhaps ever, and I can't get anybody at the office of Technology Assessment to *listen* to me. 'Selle Laronde slapped an interdict order on publication, nobody returns my calls, I can't—"

"She thinks it's a fake."

The comment stopped Eingardt dead. "I'm sorry?"

" 'Selle Laronde thinks your sphere is a hoax."

"But, but—" Eingardt sputtered to a halt and then exploded, *"Why?"*

"The implications are—interesting." McGee examined the fingertips with which he had touched the surface of the sphere, looked up at Eingardt, and said mildly, "You seem to be saying that you've found an artifact—an artifact of some technological sophistication if I'm any judge—that's more than thirty-five thousand years old."

"Yes! I think it's probably an abandoned piece of alien technology. It—"

McGee nodded. "So you said in your letter to 'Selle Laronde. What makes you think so?"

Eingardt appeared to be trying to say eight different things all at the same time. Finally he said, "Surely it's obvious?"

"Not to me. Or Gabrielle."

"Well—look," said Eingardt in obvious frustration, "artifacts are not found outside of a cultural support matrix. At the simplest level, you don't find metal artifacts without also finding some evidence of fire and smelting, you see? You don't find sewn cloth without finding, at the least, bone needles. That sphere is the product of an advanced civilization, and it's *very* old. Thirty-five thousand years ago there was no civilization on Earth. It *has* to be an alien artifact; no human civilization of the period was remotely capable of producing this sort of artifact. This sphere was buried during the final years of the Middle Paleolithic period. Blade tools were state of the art; weapons and tools made from *flint*, Mister McGee. Homo sapiens Neanderthal hadn't grown extinct yet. It was a *long* time ago."

McGee nodded. "I think that's Mademoiselle Laronde's point. Thomas Jefferson once said he found it easier to believe that a couple of Yankee astronomers could lie than to believe that rocks fell from the sky."

Doctor Eingardt said softly, "Rocks *do* fall from the sky, Mister McGee."

The old man grinned at Eingardt; it had a distinctly evil tinge. "So they do. A team from O.T.A. will be by next week to pick this up from you." He spoke as Eingardt opened his mouth to protest. "Whatever else happens, you won't see me again. Thank you for your time."

- 2 -

FRIDAY, FEBRUARY 27, 2072:

"It's a *very* slowtime field."

"Drink up," McGee urged the physicist cheerfully. "Tell me all about it."

Kevin Holtzmann was a stooped, lanky young British physicist. In the near two weeks since Holtzmann had taken over the investigation of the Val d'Entremont artifact, McGee had developed a genuine fondness for the man. Holtzmann had three earrings in his right ear and five in his left and his makeup tended toward the garish; it was often said that he did not look much like what he was, the finest non-AI physicist of his generation. Within his narrow areas of specialty the young man exhibited a penetrating intelligence McGee occasionally found discomfiting.

Fortunately Holtzmann drank. Socially and otherwise.

McGee and Holtzmann sat together in a quiet, dimly lit, red-leather-lined booth at a bistro on the outskirts of Paris. That the leather had come out of a genengineer's tank rather than off the backs of animals did not disturb McGee particularly even when he allowed himself to think about it; his own liver, his right leg from the knee down, both of his eyes and all of his skin from head to toe, had also come out of the genengineer's vats.

Holtzmann eyed the liquid left sitting in the bottom of his glass and knocked it back. "Well. I shouldn't be telling you this, McGee—"

"I know. And I appreciate it."

"—and I don't know why a Ministry Special Tasks agent would be interested anyway—"

McGee said mildly, "I'm a businessman, Kevin. I run a hotel. A restaurant."

Holtzmann nodded. "Of course. So what this means is, it's not a hoax. It can't be. What we have in this sphere is so remarkable I am—" Holtzmann paused, said precisely "—at something of a loss to explain it to you."

"Try," McGee suggested.

"Okay." Holtzmann waved at the waitbot hovering near the table, said, "Two more. Of the same," and turned back to McGee. "First, there's no external power source. The slowtime fields we can make today, they run off external power sources. Say you place the power source inside the field; then when you turn the field on, the power source feeding the field immediately slows down as well. Follow? The slower the field you try to generate, the slower the power inside operates, and the less power it generates. Pretty damn soon the slowtime field fails. Top sustained time to date is a bit over sixteen hours. McGee, we've known twenty, thirty years there should be a break-even point, where the field starts to look self-sustaining. To do this you need a *fast* power source and an incredibly slow slowtime field. Batteries won't work. Fusion comes close, and MAM would be ideal; matter-antimatter annilation—anni*hi*lation," he said carefully, "puts out so much power that even a small power source, maybe the size of a football, could keep the slowtime sphere running for hundred of thousands of years before failing."

The waitbot placed a scotch before Holtzmann, a Simpatico beer in a smoky black bottle before McGee. It was one of the reasons McGee liked this bistro; it was the only place in Paris he knew where they would not try to serve him his beer in a bulb. Beads of condensation ran down the sides of the bottle; McGee ignored the glass placed before him and drank directly from the bottle. "Are you going to be able to open it?"

Holtzmann nodded slowly, fingering the nearly full tumbler. "I think so. Maybe. The damn thing—McGee, it's *slow*. We shot the fucker with neutrinos. They bounced at eight nines, ninety-nine point nine nine nine nine nine nine percent reflection. We measured how many got through and calculated from that." The lanky physicist hesitated, said quietly, "They dated that sphere at about thirty-five thousand years of age when they dug it out of the Val d'Entremont. McGee, in those thirty-five thousand years, about three minutes has passed inside that sphere."

McGee said slowly, "Oh." He paused. "That's—interesting."

Holtzmann nodded. "It is. We're all wondering what we're going to find inside the damn thing."

McGee sat up straighter. "You know how to open it?"

"We think so. Pop it inside another slowtime field. We can't make a slowtime field that runs inside another slowtime field. It's not theoretically impossible, but we can't begin to do it. Some of the equations get—silly. Probably whoever made this one couldn't do it either. We're arranging to use the Tytan Labs slowtime field, the one in Switzerland. It's a private lab but it's partially funded by the Unification. Marc Packard—you know him?"

"No."

"Chairman of Tytan Industries, parent company of Tytan Labs. And Tytan Manufacturing, and half a dozen other Tytan subsidiaries. We need his permission to clear all his people out of Complex B, where their field is located. It's the biggest slowtime field in the System, McGee. Not the slowest one, not by a bit—there's a tiny field out in the Belt that's almost as slow as the sphere we found up in the mountains—but it's the only one that's near big enough to enclose the sphere. We're going to take a Peaceforcer Elite, put him in a pressure suit, and put him and the sphere together inside the Tytan field. The pressure suit's in case there are viruses, poisonous air, anything of that sort, inside the sphere." Holtzmann smiled a bit shakily. "Do you understand slowtime physics at all?"

McGee snorted.

"Right. Well." Holtzmann was silent for a long time, drinking steadily. Finally he looked up at McGee. "We think we can give the Elite forty-five seconds inside the sphere, over the space of a week external time. Assuming Packard comes through, assuming we know shit-all about what the goddamn sphere is in the first place and we're not dealing with something else entirely—assuming all that," he said, gulping back the tumbler's remnants, "we're going to open it on Thursday."

The alien slowtime sphere squatted, cold and aloof, in the center of Tytan Industries Experimental Complex B, the long, poorly lit, converted hangar that enclosed the largest slowtime field on Earth.

Wearing a black and silver official issue PKF pressure unit, PKF Elite Sergeant Samuel De Nostri sat alone on a bench at one end of Complex B. The p-suit's helmet sat on the bench next to him.

Other Peaceforcers stood duty throughout the Complex, a pair at every entrance and a squad with Excalibur multifrequency rifles guarding the alien slowtime sphere. But the guards were under orders of silence toward one another, and particularly toward De Nostri himself.

Despite the poor quality of the light, De Nostri, like the other PKF Elite present, saw well. His eyes were not the eyes he had been born with twenty-seven years ago; they were, in almost every respect, far superior. In his cyborg eyes, the sphere, mirrored to begin with, glowed as though with an internal flame.

He tried not to look at the row of medbots waiting off to his right. The implication of their presence disturbed him.

He tried just as hard not to look at the half dozen Unification officials—PKF, Ministry, and both a webdancer and Hand from the Secretary General's office—on the observation platform off to his left. He knew a couple of them; McGee was a Ministry of Population Control agent, Special Tasks, and the Hand was Alexander Moreau, grandson of Jules Moreau, and an intimate of Secretary General Eddore.

He tried very hard indeed not to look at Elite Commissionaire Mohammed Vance, watching him from up on the platform. De Nostri had not known, had not been told by Vance when they requested that he volunteer, just what he was volunteering for. It was understood that the offer was an honor, extended to him because of his record and his family—his uncle was the late Jean-Louis de Nostri, the most famous French genegineer of the century—and Samuel had not hesitated in accepting.

Now that he *did* know he did not like it at all.

There could be anything inside the damned alien field, anything at all. The night prior Samuel had awoken from sleep with the memory of a story he had been told as a child, the tale of the jinn in the bottle.

He was a creature of great power, the jinn, and after a thousand years in the bottle he had decided to grant three great wishes to whoever unstopped the bottle and let him out.

After two thousand years he had decided to serve forever whoever unstopped the bottle and let him out.

After three thousand years, the jinn had decided to spend the rest of all time torturing the luckless bastard who let him out of the bottle.

Samuel De Nostri had spent most of the morning trying to shake the memory of that story.

Kevin Holtzmann said, "Up on the platform, stand on the mark."

Samuel De Nostri took three steps up and two steps forward. It brought him past the line where the black pylons would generate the enclosing field. The mark Holtzmann referred to was simply a piece of tape hastily placed on the platform's gleaming clean surface.

It left him staring at the mirrored surface of the alien slowtime field from a distance of only thirty centimeters. His bloated, deformed features loomed back at him like something out of a funhouse mirror.

"Helmet on."

De Nostri locked his helmet in place with the ease of long practice. It was one of the reasons he had been asked to volunteer for this duty; he had spent a three-year tour of duty at Halfway and the habits of a pressure suit were second nature to him. The sounds of the outer world ceased; De Nostri felt a faint vibration as the airplant kicked in. His peripheral vision vanished, to be replaced by the helmet's indicators. With the loss of his peripheral vision the sphere became the only thing in his world, the only object visible to him.

On the indicator at the far right of his field of vision, a red 7 appeared. The top six channels were standard pressure suit frequencies. Channels seven and eight were reserved for use by the PKF, and only PKF pressure suits even had them; nine through twelve were private Space Force channels.

De Nostri said, "*Command*, on seven." The deep rumble of

PKF Elite Commissionaire Mohammed Vance's voice reached De Nostri's ears a moment later.

"Samuel."

"Sir."

"Remember that you are representing the interests and the reputation of the Peace Keeping Force. Keep your head and do nothing foolish."

"Yes, sir."

"I trust my choice of you for this task will not be proven a mistake. 'Sieur Holtzmann is waiting to speak to you on channel three."

De Nostri frowned. "Yes, sir. *Command*, on three."

The chief scientist's voice, harsh and grating, invaded De Nostri's helmet. In English. "Ready to rock?"

De Nostri's English was poor, and there was no translator software buffering the radio link between himself and Holtzmann; it took him a few seconds to translate the foreign words. "If I understand you, yes. I think so. You—do you speak French, 'Sieur Holtzmann?"

"Of course."

"Please do."

There was a moment of complete silence before the sound of Holtzmann's dry chuckle came. He spoke in unaccented French. "As you wish. We are at a minute and thirty seconds. I will count down by fives starting at thirty seconds. Once the enclosing slowtime field establishes, the slowtime sphere should fail almost instantaneously. Remember that the most important thing for you to do is turn off the sphere's field generator if you recognize it and can figure out how. Do *not* damage it; the generator probably runs off a MAM reaction, and the last thing in the world I want to do is turn off the field a week from now and find out some kind of nuke has gone off inside."

"It would be the last thing you would do," De Nostri observed.

Standing five meters away in front of the slowtime control console, Holtzmann blinked in surprise—PKF Elite were not known for their sense of humor—and then grinned a bit wearily. "Yeah. If you don't get the generator turned off, make sure you're as far away from it as possible at the end of forty-five. When our field goes off, the sphere will come back on. Okay, counting down to field activation at ... thirty seconds .... twenty-five ..."

De Nostri found the incredibly strong transform-virus-enhanced muscles in his stomach tightening uncontrollably, painfully.

". . . twenty . . ."

Deep breaths. The nanocomputer at the base of De Nostri's skull noticed the surge of adrenaline and activated the programed combat routines; De Nostri was forced to override it when the nanocomputer tried to turn on the lasers buried in the tips of his index fingers. He imagined, and forced back the image, of having to explain to Commissionaire Vance why he had blasted a hole in his own pressure suit.

". . . ten . . ."

In fifty-five seconds, thought Samuel De Nostri, *a week will have passed.*

". . . four . . . three . . . two . . . one . . ."

At the last instant De Nostri remembered to turn his headlights on.

"Now."

The clock at the left of De Nostri's helmet flickered once and then said 45 in sharp red letters.

The world vanished in a brilliant white blaze.

He found himself trapped in a small shining place.

The cubical Tytan Labs slowtime field barely enclosed the alien sphere. De Nostri stood with the Tytan Labs field at his back, over his head, and beneath his feet. The Tytan field enclosed the platform he had been standing on; the platform, cut free from Complex B's floor, felt suddenly unsteady, as though it floated free. The only light came from his headlamps, but between the mirrored interior of the Tytan slowtime field and the mirrored exterior of the alien sphere it was so bright that his helmet's faceplate, after a second, darkened to compensate.

The clock said 43.

Nothing happened. De Nostri reached out a gloved hand, ran his fingers over the slick surface of the sphere. 38 now, and the sphere sat on its supporting ring, motionless, unchanged. Was nothing *going* to happen?

De Nostri drew his hand back from the surface of the sphere and blinked in surprise when

34

a foot kicked him in the face.

The sphere was gone. Suddenly there was lots of free space and De Nostri's combat routines used it without waiting to see what De Nostri thought about it; his body pushed backward with one foot, twisted and bounced off the interior upper surface of the Tytan slowtime field and came down crouched, balancing on the tips of its fingers, as far away from the thrashing form of the—person—as it was able to get.

It took De Nostri a startled moment to realize he had not been attacked. About a meter away from him a man having a seizure thrashed against the platform's spotless surface. De Nostri could hear the man's screaming even through the p-suit he wore. Tiny details crowded in on De Nostri all at once, impossibly vivid. 29. The man was vaguely Latin in appearance, with olive-colored skin. Blood ran from his nose and there was foam on his lips. He was dressed all over in furs that reminded De Nostri, absurdly, of a mountain man of the old American West.

There was no machinery, nothing like the generator De Nostri had been told to look for.

Something gleamed in the man's right hand. At 22 seconds De Nostri lunged forward, grabbed the man's right wrist with both hands and planted his right foot in the pit of the man's arm. With fingers made clumsy by pressure-suit gloves De Nostri attempted to pry the device, whatever it was, from the death grip with which the man held it. De Nostri felt bones snapping in the man's wrist, fingers breaking as his incredibly strong cyborg hands pulled the device free.

With the gadget in hand his combat programing would not allow him to stay near a source of possible danger; one leap took him back to the edge of the Tytan slowtime field, as far from the convulsing, fur-wearing person as he could get.

The clock at the right side of De Nostri's helmet said 5.

De Nostri looked at the device blankly. It was remarkably heavy given its size, about twenty kilograms; a significant weight even for his transform-virus-enhanced muscles. A long oval thing with a pair of smooth, oval indentations at one end; presumably touching one indentation turned the device on, and touching another turned it off. But which one?

He was still wondering when the clock said 0. The Tytan slowtime field broke apart and for an impossibly short moment De Nostri saw several dozen pressure-suited figures watching him as he stood there up on the platform.

And then the alien slowtime sphere reformed.

Around him.

•   •   •

During the week De Nostri spent inside the Tytan slowtime field, a three-layer decontamination tent grew around the gleaming, mirror-surfaced cube of the field. The decontamination procedures Kevin Holtzmann had requested, and received, were the same precautions used in dealing with nanotechnology and genegeneering, two sciences where small mistakes might have very far-reaching consequences. A series of three airlocks, with decontamination required between each airlock, separated the slowtime field from the hangar in which it had been generated. The scientists inside the tent all wore sterilized pressure suits.

To the extent that it was possible, every eventuality had been prepared for. Four medbots waited at the edge of the platform; if De Nostri came out of the field harmed in any way, the finest medical technology in the System would be waiting to heal him.

The decontamination tent reached up to within a few meters of the hangar's ceiling, outward to within a few meters of the observation platform. Despite his curiosity, and Holtzmann's invitation to join the working scientists inside the tent, McGee had opted for a position on the observation platform with the other government observers. Which was, after all, what he was—even if he didn't feel like one.

With the others, he watched the holo showing the Tytan slowtime field. Holtzmann's voice sounded a bit strained, which did not surprise McGee; it had been a long week. "We were planning to turn the field off at two o'clock, but we're ready now, and even if we leave it on until then it'll only give De Nostri another fraction of a second. Here goes. What the hell?"

McGee did not remember coming to his feet, approaching the holofield and the image within it. He was peripherally aware of the others around him and their similar reactions, Mohammed Vance saying quietly, "How very interesting."

For an instant so short McGee was not certain he had seen it, De Nostri stood at the far right of the platform on which the Tytan slowtime field had been generated. Then the sphere was back and, at the far left of the platform, a man in furs lay screaming, thrashing and convulsing.

In the holo, McGee watched Kevin Holtzmann take a step up onto the platform, and then pause.

Peaceforcer Elite Samuel De Nostri was gone, enclosed in an alien slowtime sphere.

The sphere held still for just a moment, long enough for the scene to engrave itself upon the awareness of every person there, and then, gracefully, standing free now of the ring upon which it had originally been placed, the sphere rolled off the platform, bounced once with a sound like a church bell on Complex B's floor, and rolled gently away from the platform; the biggest marble in the universe.

People stood transfixed, torn between the sight of the screaming man and the mirrored marble's stately progress across the floor; and then Holtzmann's voice came again: "Medbots?" Then, with rising force, "Could we have the medbots over here *right fucking now?*"

Gi'Suei'Obodi'Sedon struggled for his life. In the first seconds following the kitjan's touch he knew himself dead without help from his comrades. Through the veil of the pain a part of him kept aware, did what it could to delay the final moment of his death. He was not aware of the stasis bubble forming around him, not aware of the sudden plunge into darkness. In the utter black he fought for even partial control of his nervous system, fought desperately to send the necessary commands through the kitjan-induced storm of randomly firing neurons. Twice he managed to restart his heart after it had failed; briefly he succeeded in reminding his lungs to breathe.

Sedon had not been aware of the lack of light until it returned. For the first time since his Consecration, someone dared to touch him without permission—and then to hurt him, bringing Sedon the distant awareness of bones in his right hand being broken, of the stasis bubble's key being wrenched free. Compared to the pain of the kitjan it was nothing, but even in the midst of the pain he noticed it, promised himself an accounting.

Abruptly there came a stinging sensation at the base of his throat, followed by an immense emptiness, a reduction of pain, of all sensory input. Sedon became aware of chemicals traveling his bloodstream, blocking synapses, calming the wrenching of his muscles. His heart was not beating and Sedon attempted again to restart it, but without success; the control of his neural system, the thing that made a Dancer what he was, had been taken from him. The sense of violation that descended upon him was astonishing; he had not suspected that even the Shield respected him so poorly.

As his body stilled, ceased its senseless thrashing, he felt himself sink toward the finality of true death.
And a bolt of electricity ripped into him.

"Could I *please* have some silence?" Holtzmann stood at the front of the briefing room. He glanced down once at the readout floating in his handheld's field, looked back up. "Everybody? *Please?*"

It was just after 7:00 P.M.

McGee stood at the back of the room, and watched the others watching Holtzmann, wearing a variety of expressions that spanned the spectrum from fascination to seething anger.

"Okay," said Holtzmann. "Here's what's happened, as far as we can figure it. De Nostri is inside the sphere. Most of you missed that, but the holos show it clearly; he was visible for a twelfth of a second before the sphere formed around him, and he's holding something in his hand that we think is the generator." Holtzmann paused. "Frankly, the item he's holding seems too damn small to me to hold the necessary power source, even as a MAM reactor, but I wouldn't bet my reputation on that. Maybe there's some form of collapsed matter inside it. At any rate, De Nostri should be safe; as soon as we can, probably early tomorrow, we'll generate the Tytan field again, and even if we can't turn the generator off we'll pull him out the same way he pulled out our guest." Holtzmann was silent, then plunged into it. "As for our guest—that's what we've been calling him—well, he's definitely human; at a guess he's contemporary to the period the sphere came from. His—clothing, I guess we'll call it—would seem to indicate that's the case. The medbots find some things about him—physiologically—that are a bit odd, but we have no idea at all what significance to place on those anomalies." Holtzmann glanced at his handheld. "He died again just before I came out to see you. That's three times so far; twice his heart, brain death once. The 'bots have brought him back each time, but he's getting weaker. Part of the problem is the 'bots don't know what's wrong with him. One of the first things they did to him was pump in a sedative to stop the convulsions, but it looks like that might have been a mistake; the sedatives appear to have shut down *everything*, his entire neural system. They've had to jump start his heart twice now as a result. The expert system running the medbots conjectured that the section of his brain that's responsible for keeping his heart beating is under his conscious control; when we sedated him we shut it down. His entire nervous system is inflamed both at the neural and gross physiological levels; the medbots have injected a nanovirus designed to bleed off some of the pressure inside his skull, and that seems to have helped some. Given the circumstances, the medbots are doing as well as can be expected. But we still need to get our guest to a real hospital, to human doctors who can diagnose something they haven't seen before." Holtzmann stopped all at once, as though he'd run out of energy and things to say at exactly the same time, and stood almost motionless, swaying ever so slightly while waiting for their questions.

They were not long in coming.

McGee left before five minutes were up, long before the dozen Unification officials present had run out of questions that Holtzmann was clearly going to be unable to answer. He took a cab to the airport, and boarded a semiballistic for Capitol City.

The Ministry had a job waiting for him in Occupied America; a genie hunt—possibly, the Ministry was hinting, one of the infamous Castanaveras twins. McGee was not averse to moving on; he had heard already from more than one source that any further contact with the Val d'Entremont bubble, and whoever or whatever they had taken out of it, would not be wise.

Aboard the semiballistic to New York McGee spent half an hour updating his journal. When he was done he encrypted the entry and turned his attention to the briefing materials he had been sent for the genie hunt. There was not much there, but enough to get started.

McGee flipped his handheld shut, closed his eyes, and lay back in his seat. A telepath. That would be interesting.

He felt a brief flicker of anticipation; and then slept.

- 4 -

SATURDAY, MARCH 12, 2072:
The most powerful individual in the System, United Nations Secretary General Charles Eddore, stood looking out the window at a view, from two kilometers up, of Capitol City, the Uni-

fication enclave in the midst of Manhattan; the city from which all of Earth and most of Luna were ruled.

The window at which Eddore stood was not really a window; that would not have been safe. And Eddore's office was not actually located two kilometers up in a spacescraper; his offices were one and a half kilometers beneath the surface of Earth, protected from anything including a direct strike with thermonuclear weapons.

He listened with half an ear to the report his webdancer had brought back from Switzerland. That she was present in his office was a sign of the data's sensitivity; Eddore did not dare allow information concerning the "guest" to be sent him via the Player- and AI-corrupted InfoNet.

Eddore interrupted the webdancer's report midway through. "Holtzmann is serious about this?"

"Sir, he seems to be. He won't swear about the 'guest,' but he seems quite certain that the slowtime technology involved in the sphere is beyond us, and beyond any of the Belt CityStates as well."

Eddore stood silently, watching the flickering firefly headlights of the hovercars ghosting through the skies of Capitol City. His thoughts were almost abstract, the swirling creative processes of a man who was, in his own field, every bit as much a genius as Holtzmann in his. Elements that he juggled simultaneously included the Johnny Rebs and the Erisian Claw, the largely American and largely Eurasian terrorist organizations; the situation with Free Luna, which was tense as always; his own growing distrust of the Peace Keeping Force, and theirs of him; and the increasing danger that the SpaceFarers' Collective, or the Belt CityStates, might take a more active interest in internal Unification affairs.

The last danger was still small, but getting larger with every passing moment; as was the seven-kilometer-long shell of the United Nations Space Force warship *Unity*, the largest spacecraft ever built. There were those among the Belt CityStates, and even more so among the Collective, who saw in the *Unity* a plan to extend the Unification of Earth to encompass Free Luna, Mars, the Belt and the Jovian moons. Even without the *Unity* Space Force was probably capable of conquering the outer planets; with it the contest would be over very nearly before it was begun.

How all of these factors were affected by the appearance of a human being inside an alien slowtime sphere was a thing that

Eddore would have had difficulty explaining. Had he attempted to, which was wildly unlikely, only a few hundred people in the entire System could have followed his explanation; and most of those were his rivals or political enemies.

It was 2072, and Charles Eddore faced an election in December, an election for the third and last term in which he would be eligible to serve as Secretary General. He expected to win; that was hardly the problem.

In Eddore's picture window, a hovercar wobbled momentarily. Only a few seconds later a pair of Peaceforcer AeroSmiths dropped down out of the sky above the traffic lanes, hit the wobbling hovercar with spotlights, and began forcing the car down to a landing.

Eddore watched as the car was forced down. Someone in that car was, most likely, guilty of manual operation of a vehicle. The operator of the vehicle would probably end up in Public Labor, if he was not instead executed as an ideolog. It had been nearly a decade since it was legal to manually operate a vehicle inside a TransContinental Automated Traffic Control cell.

Which, today, covered most of Earth.

Several minutes after the vehicle and the pursuing Peaceforcer craft had passed from sight, Eddore said, with some measure of genuine reluctance, "If it should prove impossible to revive the guest, it would be just as well."

The webdancer nodded once and left him alone.

- 5 -

When the world at last stabilized around him, Sedon knew he was being moved.

Through the veil of the sedatives Sedon monitored his auditory nerve. Voices were dim, rumbling and distant. Still he made out enough to doubt that the words were spoken in shiata. His thought processes were fuzzy, but still he found this reassuring; if the men and women around him did not speak shiata, then he was, still, among barbarians.

Though he made nothing of the sounds, he stored them for future reference.

Hands grasped and lifted him; straps restrained him. There

was a momentary gentle acceleration that pressed him down against the surface upon which he lay. Though he tried he could not open his eyes; though he strained he could not move so much as a finger. Sedon struggled to restrain his fear, and failed.

Nowhere on this entire damn prison of a planet should there be aircraft.

When the long wash of sedative-masked pain finally subsided, Sedon found himself crippled, in his muscles, in the finer range of his senses.

These people, whoever they were, knew nothing of the care of a Dancer. The thought flickered at the back of his mind as he catalogued information.

If the guards standing near the entrance to his room were any indication, he was at least as much prisoner as a patient.

The guards interested Sedon. There were three of them, and they rotated duty in third-day increments. The guard who watched Sedon at night troubled Sedon for a while. His features were vaguely familiar, but during the long dreamlike time before the drugs wore off he could not place where he might have seen the face before.

They attempted to interrogate him on two separate occasions. Drugs that stole all control from him were injected into his bloodstream. One made him sleepy and cheerful, while the other made the colors in the room bright and caused him to have hallucinations. Even if they had spoken shiata the attempts would not have worked; as it was, lashing away at him in a variety of tongues of which Sedon knew nothing, his interrogators were completely frustrated. Sedon could hear it in their voices.

On what he guessed as the eighth day since the flight that had brought him here, Sedon awoke clear-headed and alert. His senses were numbed and he did not think he could Move if his life depended upon it. But his thoughts proceeded in orderly fashion, and his memory, scrambled by the kitjan and again by the drugs employed in interrogating him, began to re-integrate.

Gi'Suei'Obodi'Sedon's first coherent thought in thirty-seven thousand years was simple. He stared up from his bed at the unnaturally stiff features of Peaceforcer Elite Samuel De Nostri, at the features of the man whom he clearly remembered

taking the stasis bubble's key from his hand, breaking his
fingers—*touching* him—and thought, *I will kill you slowly.*

The linguist, Maximilian Beauchamp, was a short man who had
allowed himself to go bald rather than visit a biosculptor; as he
set his handheld up at the side of the patient's bed he smiled
at the patient.

The patient did not smile back. He was an olive-skinned fellow, apparently in his thirties. Beauchamp found it difficult to
believe that the man had been near death so recently; he
looked like an ad for a very good biosculptor. The patient's eyes
were unsettling, brown and steady. They rarely blinked, and
moved constantly back and forth between Beauchamp and the
PKF Elite standing by the doorway. Little details struck
Beauchamp; the man had exquisitely graceful fingers, long
enough that, not too many years past, before the advent of
medbots, he might have made a fine surgeon. The muscles
flowed smoothly beneath the surface of the man's skin, and the
skin itself had a fineness of grain that Beauchamp had seen before only in children, or in the aged immediately following re-
generative geriatrics treatments. His face was as clean of hair as
though he had just depilated, and the hair on his forearms was
fine and faint.

Beauchamp seated himself at the edge of the patient's bed.
He did not expect it to take long for him to achieve communication with the patient. In his own person he spoke eight lan-
guages fluently, and through his inskin had near instantaneous
access to every other language known to man. He was somewhat puzzled that he had been instructed to limit his initial
conversation to French. Still, it was not a great inconvenience,
if the subject cooperated.

The subject cooperated with a vengeance until 3:30 P.M., and
Beauchamp grew angrier and angrier.

He left at 3:30, shaking with a mixture of fear and indignation.

The room in which Sedon returned to full awareness was large,
stark, and nearly empty. It held the bed upon which Sedon lay;
a small fixture upon which Sedon was intended to sit when
eliminating; a doorway, and a ceiling that glowed with light intended to imitate this system's sun. It was not a bad imitation,

though not so bright as the true sun. A man—a guard—stood just inside the door at all times, watching Sedon at all times. The guard's presence enraged Sedon at a level so deep that Sedon barely allowed himself the awareness of it.

He had spent far too much of his life imprisoned.

Being guarded.

The small round person they sent to speak to him was tedious and predictable. He wished to teach Sedon his tongue, and to learn Sedon's. In aid of this he used a device that recorded words spoken by Sedon, and paired them with words from his own tongue for Sedon to learn. The device projected images in midair to aid them in assigning words to various pictures and actions. The parts of the human body came first, followed by images of both a man and woman performing various functions. Sitting, running, picking up, dropping. Eating, drinking—the small person's indecision was almost comically obvious— eliminating.

So they were not very civilized, then, if they still had taboos relating to natural body functions.

Some of the pictures Sedon could make no sense of at all. One, for example, showed a man and woman with their lips pressed together; followed by two women engaged in a similar activity, and then by two men. It was clear that the small person attached some significance to these images; he watched Sedon more closely than usual as they were displayed.

Erotic activity, perhaps.

They went on to clothing, and then furniture of various sorts. Aside from "chair" and "table," most of the items of furniture Sedon could not put a name to, though it was plain from the way the people and other items were arrayed upon them that they were furniture of various sorts. In those instances he accepted the word offered, but gave none of his own. "Bed" he found a word for, though he knew only one word for the several different types of things these people sat upon. The same for most of the vehicles he was shown; several different sorts of winged flying craft like the one that had brought him here; smaller, stubbier craft whose primary purpose was clearly ground transportation. A vehicle that sat upon four wheels, and another that had two and was propped up with the help of a small metal bar at its side.

At 3:30 Sedon was shown a vehicle whose shape he could not immediately make out. The thing tugged at a far, far distant memory. It looked as though a thin needle had been placed in the exact center of a thick, fat ring of some silver metal; a brilliant gold flame of light extruded from one end of the needle, dispersed far to the vehicle's side.

Sedon recognized it with a sick shock.

A fusion flame.

Against a background of stars.

Stars.

The panic he had been suppressing so well until that moment came flooding back. Sedon clenched his eyes shut until prickles of light appeared against his eyelids, kept them shut, and concentrated on his breathing. The breathing was ragged, shamefully so, and his hands trembled, and he hated the Continuing Time and everyone in it for seeing him in such weakness.

By all the dark gods, these barbarians had *space travel.*

He was a heretic who had forsaken his gods, whose gods had forsaken him. So it was that when he lifted his head toward the sky and screamed his pain, screamed the words in shiata until the sound reverberated against the walls of the prison hospital room, Gi'Suei'Obodi'Sedon received no answer, and had expected none.

"Rho Haristi! How long was I inside?"

"This language doesn't exist." Beauchamp's cheeks flamed red and his hands quivered as though looking for something to do with themselves. He spoke rapidly. "It's made up. Completely made up. *Vata* means face except it also means cold. *Rho* means hello except it also means look. It's *intended* to confuse. The words have no common basis with any human language in use today. The language is cleverly put together, with a certain consistency to it, but it's a hoax, Commissionaire Vance. It is not a variation or a descendant or an ancestor of any language spoken by humans for at least a thousand years. There's about a five percent word overlap with an obsolete dialect of Telugu, a Dravidian language spoken today only by some people in southern India—which only means that whoever made up this language did a bit of research to make it seem slightly plausible. There is no way a language as intricate and well developed as this one could be unknown in this day and age. *None.*"

Commissionaire Mohammed Vance waited for Beauchamp's breathless rush of words to end, and said gently, "Thank you,

M. Beauchamp. You will of course leave us a copy of your results."

"And then when I showed him a torchship, he *screamed* at me—" Beauchamp broke off as Vance's words penetrated. "Your pardon?"

"We have no further need of your service, M. Beauchamp. Good day." The Elite sat without moving, simply watching Beauchamp with his dead black Elite eyes until Beauchamp nodded stiffly and rose. From his handheld Beauchamp extracted, and then handed to Vance, a single infochip. "This is everything. I'll bill you for my time."

"You are aware this matter is classified."

Beauchamp gathered himself up and said with immense dignity, "Who could I possibly tell? I don't even know where this place *is*."

Vance smiled at Beauchamp, a creasing into folds of the stiff Elite skin; and Beauchamp shivered at the sight. "Count yourself fortunate, M. Beauchamp. If you knew where you were, you would not be permitted to leave."

For a day and a half a voice that was not human talked to Sedon, using images that hung in midair—holofield, he had learned was its name—to establish common reference points. It went faster than Sedon would have guessed. His own memory was as near perfect as possible for any mechanism based in protein recording media; the memory of the nonhuman thing to which he talked seemed entirely so.

On the evening of his eleventh day since the flight that had brought him here, they came and took him to a dim room.

They gave him clothing to wear that was entirely unlike the robes he had been kept in since the flight. Pants and a shirt and a pair of slippers; he could not figure out how to put on the shirt until they demonstrated to him how the seals worked.

One of them walked before him, and one behind. They carried weapons that Sedon could not identify except to know that if one was pointed at him its wielder would die. Both of them moved with the quickness of machines, with the lack of fluidity brought on by their warping from the true human form. Sedon was almost certain he knew what they were. From the dim past of his people came legends of such creatures.

They had been a mistake.

In the darkened room another such awaited him. It said, "I

am Commissionaire Mohammed Vance of the PKF Elite." Its voice was remarkably deep, a voice of a size to match the chest from which it emanated. "Please," and it gestured to a chair, "seat yourself."

Sedon sat. He was aware of the machines taking up position behind him.

Immediately before him Sedon made out the faint appearance of a transparent barrier of some sort, separating him from the man who sat across from him. He did not attempt to touch it.

The machined person on the other side of the barrier was larger than the two behind him, taller and wider than Sedon himself, who had been for many thousands of years a giant among the stunted barbarians of his prison. "What is your name?"

By sheer force of will Sedon held down the surge of rage at the abruptness of the questions; the creature could not know the impudence of its question. He answered with the name of his Name, a suitable answer for a barbarian: "I am Sedon of the Gi'Suei. You may call me Sedon."

The creature nodded. "You may call me Commissionaire Vance. Why were you in the bubble?"

It took Seldon a moment to translate the question. "I was being chased by a—person—who wished to—" Sedon paused. This language possessed no word that quite corresponded to the graceless killing Dvan had intended. "He intended to butcher me," Sedon said at last. "Before I entered the *tulu adrhe*—the bubble—he shot me with the *kitjan*." He paused again. "I do not know a word for kitjan. A kind of weapon, like the ones behind me. Unless treated quickly it is fatal to—to my kind."

The Commissionaire Vance-thing smiled. Its sheer physical presence was forbidding, subliminally intimidating. Sedon noticed with interest that the animal part of his brain registered a brief flicker of fear. Sensible; in his current state Sedon knew himself to be no match for the blurred speed the machined men had exhibited. "You were not," Commissionaire Vance said, "treated quickly."

"How long was I inside?"

"You know a year is one turn of this planet around the sun?"

"One passage of seasons?"

"Yes."

"I know *year*."

The Vance-thing nodded. "Your slowtime sphere ran at about a six-and-a-half-billion-to-one compression ratio. How long did you intend to stay in the sphere?"

"Perhaps a second, internal time. A little over two hundred years." Sedon shrugged. "My pursuer would have grown restless, and left. Perhaps I would have needed to wait another second, or three. There was time." Sedon paused, used the tool of his voice carefully indeed; he spoke quietly, smoothly, without any emotion these barbarians would recognize. "How long was I inside?"

The Commissionaire Vance-thing looked straight at Gi'Suei-'Obodi'Sedon and said, "You were in the sphere for thirty-seven thousand years."

Sedon thought he had been braced for it since seeing the picture of the spacecraft. Three thousand years, four, five—it would not have been enough. Not to grow a civilization like this, out of the brutal nomads these people had been when he entered the sphere.

Thirty-seven thousand years.

When the moment came he found that he was *not* braced for it.

The roaring black darkness swarmed up around him, dragged him down into emptiness.

He did not know how long he was unconscious.

He came to again with a sharp, caustic smell in his nostrils. Perhaps only a few minutes had passed. Perhaps it had been hours; his sense of time was still damaged. He was in the same place, the darkened room with the three machined men. A drink of some liquid was offered him, and he took it without asking what it contained; if they wished to drug him, they would.

"M. Sedon, are you well enough to continue?"

The faint undertone of urgency in the question gave Sedon a moment of pause. He drank the cool, tart liquid in numbed silence, not thinking, not feeling. His muscles trembled slightly. Finally he looked up and answered the creature's question. "Yes. I am. What are you?" he asked abruptly. "Your skin, the speed with which you move, your eyes. They are not normal for your people."

The shadowed black eyes studied him. "Fair enough. I am a PKF Elite. PKF stands for Peace Keeping Force. The PKF guards Earth—this world—against people who wish to return us to the days when there were many governments on Earth rather than one. There are millions of PKF across the world. The Elite are the best of their number. We have been improved both by machines and by genetic engineering—what are called transform viruses—to enhance our speed, our eyesight, our hearing. We are stronger than normal humans and difficult to damage." He paused, waiting.

Sedon knew the word he wished to use. "I am a Dancer," he said firmly. "I was exiled to this planet"—he calculated quickly —"approximately fifty thousand years ago. With other Dancers and many persons of questionable sanity, stability, and genetic quality. I would guess you are our descendants. How long have you had writing?"

In the dimness on the other side of the room the Commissionaire Vance-thing turned away for a moment. When it turned back it said, "Since 3100 B.C., I'm told. A little over five thousand years. What do you mean by dancer? You are an entertainer?"

"Not that. I do not know the words."

"Try."

"A Dancer is—priest. Judge. Keeper. Owner. President. General Secretary. Of a superior class. We are a better people than you. More—disciplined. Of greater range. You have only recently been governed, all together, by the same body?"

"Yes. A little over fifty years. Before that there were many nations. Today there is only one Earth. Elsewhere in the System there are still independent—governments is not a good word, but I find, like you, I do not know what to call them. They are called the SpaceFarers' Collective and the Belt CityStates and several other names, and they each govern themselves in somewhat different fashion." Vance paused. "You claim to have been exiled to Earth fifty thousand years ago, and to have entered the slowtime bubble thirty-seven thousand years ago. Am I to understand that you *lived* through the thirteen thousand years separating those events?"

"I do not understand the question."

"You did not grow old. You did not age."

"No. Aging is a disease. A curable one, which I think your people are beginning to learn. When our children began dying of it, after our exile to this world—" Sedon's features became totally empty. "We were distraught. Not since the Zaradin deserted us had we allowed ourselves to die in such fashion; that we could not aid them pained us."

"You lived for thirteen thousand years. On the surface of Earth."

Sedon met its disbelieving black eyes. "I do not know exactly how long it was. There were no clocks, and my counting of the passage of seasons is not to be trusted. My memory is excellent, not perfect. But it was, at least, a time more than twice as long as your people have possessed writing."

A long silence followed. *Something is wrong*, Sedon thought. *Something I have said has offended it.* "You do not believe me when I tell you my age."

It smiled at Sedon again. "I find it difficult to envision a human as old as you claim to be."

He had heard enough from Commissionaire Vance, had watched it closely enough to try. Sedon leaned forward and changed his voice, brought its pitch lower, and Spoke. "But am I old, Commissionaire Vance? Oh, for a rabbit, yes. For a tree, yes, for a tree I am aged. But for a mountain I am young, and for a man I am merely of the correct age. Why should I lie to you? How does it benefit me?"

On the other side of the barrier the creature had grown still, drinking in the sound of Sedon's Speaking. The effect was not what it would have been in shiata, but this French was a broad language, rich in words, and it made a tool with which Sedon was now certain he could work.

"You—" Its voice trailed off, and then the huge form rose abruptly, turned and left without a backward glance. Light spilled through an opening door, and then it was gone.

One of the creatures behind Sedon said quietly, "Please follow us. We will return you to your hospital room now."

Sedon sat in shock, eyes fixed on the spot where Commissionaire Vance had been. *It knew what I was trying to do. It did not know how I was doing it but it knew I was attempting it nonetheless.*

"Please follow us *now*."

Sedon went without argument, without delay.

At the downlot Vance snapped, "Give him a night's rest. Tomorrow morning, the language program interrogates him until he stops answering questions. He is not to speak to any of our officers, including you. If he speaks to you, you are not to answer."

The semiballistic came down out of the dark night sky, running lights doused, and dropped to a gentle landing at the center of the downlot, so close that the heat of its exhaust warmed the surface of Mohammed Vance's immobile face. Vance started across the downlot to where the SB awaited them, Peaceforcer Elite Samuel De Nostri a step behind him. De Nostri said only, "Yes, Commissionaire. It will be as you say."

Vance did not glance back at De Nostri. "Feed him when he requests food. Let him sleep the hours he's been sleeping. When he refuses to answer questions, kill him." Vance mounted the steps into the SB and then turned suddenly at the top of the ramp and looked down at De Nostri. "Kill him by midnight Sunday no matter what he does. Poison in his food."

"Yes, Commissionaire."

"I'll be in Capitol City. You may call me if anything arises."

"Yes, Commissionaire." De Nostri stood rigidly at attention, staring up at Vance's stiff features.

It was as though Vance had audited his thoughts. "Only a fool is never afraid, boy." Vance turned and vanished into the interior of the SB.

De Nostri saluted quickly and trotted back to the edge of the downlot. It was well he moved quickly; the SB lifted again before he was out of range, and the wind of its passage would have knocked down any human less heavy than a Peaceforcer Elite.

De Nostri stood in the storm of heated air and watched the SB depart, stood motionless while the cold night air crept in around him. He mulled over Vance's parting comment. In the days following, it never even occurred to him to attempt to repeat it to one of his fellow officers, not even his close friend Harold Pailletin.

Vance was, bar none, the most respected, most admired Commissionaire in the Elite. Even his failure to catch Trent the Uncatchable had not damaged Vance's reputation; unlike any other Peaceforcer in the System, he had at least come close.

De Nostri knew that, were he to repeat the comment, he simply would not be believed.

·   ·   ·

Breathe.

It was the first thing a Dancer was taught, the first step on the long road to awareness of self.

They left him alone at night, apparently in the belief that he slept then.

The phrase leapt out at him, a fragment of shia, of the discipline that he had, before his hundredth birthday, rejected:

You are born broken; life is healing.

Breathe deep. With oxygen, burn the poisons from the system.

Heal yourself.

Lie atop the cool, crisp cloths that cover the bed. Eyes closed, floating in darkness.

Flex the muscle on the outside of the left big toe. Move over, to the inside muscle. One by one, tense and release every muscle of every toe.

Work upward. The ball of the foot, and now the sole, and now the muscles that support the ankle. Whisper the commands, never by nerve through the long spreading tree of gray fibers. Encourage the flow of the blood, of the scavenger cells that remove dead matter and kill invaders.

The muscles in Sedon's calves began to quiver as though he had just finished a marathon, twitching and relaxing until the skin that covered the muscles literally vibrated from the effort.

Breathe.

And work upward.

They gave him all night, three nights in a row.

- 6 -

Morning came on the fifteenth day of Sedon's imprisonment, and the nonliving voice came with it. Without a window in his underground room Sedon knew that it was daytime only because the room's lights had brightened.

Sedon sat upright with his pillow stuffed behind the small of his back. He relaxed, fingers clasped loosely over his stomach. He let entire sections of his body sleep and recover while he and the—"computer," perhaps, or "program," these were two of the words he had learned for the thing he spoke to—while he and the program learned about one another.

The things the program was allowed to tell Sedon would have frightened him had he allowed it. Intimate details regarding the rulers of this strange world, of the power structure of the government. Given that he was surely in the grasp of those rulers—the PKF certainly, and perhaps the Secretary General and Ministry of Population Control as well—Sedon was led to one inescapable conclusion: they did not intend for him to live.

He had frightened the Commissionaire Vance creature with his blundering, poorly timed attempt at a Speaking. Speaking was no more than a technology of language; the use of words, in the proper timbre, inflection, volume, sequence, and content, as a persuasive tool; words crafted, as the Dancers of Sedon's childhood had taught him, to touch the soul. But Sedon had not known the Commissionaire Vance creature well enough, and had not sufficiently mastered the tool of French.

And, to be sure, Commissionaire Vance was not a human as Sedon had ever known humans. More than a barbarian, less than one of the Flame People. *Different.*

He had been freed from the stasis bubble at a pivotal moment in their history. Even without the Zaradin teachings to guide them, Sedon suspected that these ex-barbarians were on the verge of discovering—of rediscovering—the Dance. There were dozens of facts that led him to this belief, and only a few that allowed him to think that the discovery might be somewhat delayed.

Two of the things which led him to believe that they might soon discover the Dance came from the language called English, from the proto-Splinter society of the webdancers. That they called themselves after dancers did not surprise him; dance was a metaphor for the method by which webdancers linked themselves to the artificial intelligences they had built.

So he thought himself prepared; the signs were there.

And then, early on the fifteenth day of his imprisonment, the computer with which he spoke used the word *Player*.

It struck him like an actual blow. He compared the root English word, "play," with the synonyms and connotations with which the word "player" was associated. Performer, participant, athlete—competitor.

One definition in particular leapt out at him: *one who acts upon a stage.*

A Player, as the word was commonly used in this culture, was a computer user, a webdancer of transcendent skill.

Only men fight, and only men dance; it was a truism among the Flame People, a saying Sedon had heard the first time while still a child in body.

In many of the cultures of this time, Sedon was deeply disturbed to learn, women did both.

Not for his very life could Sedon envision a woman dancing, not even a dance for amusement. When the computer attempted to show him images of women engaged in what it called "dance," Sedon was forced to look away.

They had only recently, within the last eighty years, mastered their own genetic map. The results were predictable; their genegineers were changing them in ways they had never anticipated, and which many of them did not like. Sedon's own people had suffered it, briefly: the Splintering which followed the Zaradin Desertion. These PKF Elite were not, Sedon thought, a true Splinter race; he did not think that they bred true.

The program verified it. "PKF Elite are not, by definition, genies. A genie is a person who was designed, gene by gene, to some specific blueprint. The commonest genetic modifications are those to remove blatant flaws in the human genotype, such as the inherited tendencies toward cancer, obesity, degenerative eyesight, and so forth. Even that is, under Unification law, illegal, but it is rarely prosecuted even when uncovered. More extreme examples of genegineering are also illegal, and have usually been prosecuted since the onset of the Troubles."

The density of the information caused Sedon difficulties; every sentence implied a vast background of history with which Sedon was not acquainted—what, for example, were the Troubles? He passed over it for now, and directed the program's attention back to the subject of the Elite. "If an Elite is not a genie, what then is it?"

"My turn," said the program. "What was the nature of the crime for which you were exiled to Earth?"

"I cannot tell you, program."

"Cannot, or will not?"

"Rather than serve, I made a servant of the Flame that lived within me, program, the Flame that gave me my life, that taught me to Move. Does this enlighten you?"

"No. What is the flame?"

Sedon took a long breath, considering. A distant surprise touched him when he realized that even now, in this far distant, alien world, he found himself reluctant to breach the vows of silence he had taken as a young Dancer, uncountable eons past. When fifteen seconds had passed without reply from him—Sedon was used to it by now—the program repeated, "What is the flame?"

"*In the beginning was the Flame, and the Flame was life. We who came after saw the Flame, and rejoiced, and Danced in its beauty.*" He said the words in shiata, adding in French, "It was called the Dance of the Flame." The program was, apparently, willing to accept that as an answer, for it returned to his question regarding the Elite:

"A PKF Elite is a cyborg; a normal human, modified with machinery and transform viruses. They are created at Peace Keeping Force Spacebase One at L-5, in free fall. Surgeons implant new eyes, remove the skin, and implant a pair of small lasers within the index fingers. After the skin has been removed, the last surgical operation places a fine web of superconductors immediately beneath the skin, to distribute heat evenly across the Elite's surface in the event the Elite is fired upon with an energy weapon; the skin is then regrown, though the regrown skin is far stronger than the original envelope. Transform viruses—diseases designed to cause benign changes within the body—speed the Elite's neural reactions by sixty to seventy percent. An enhanced-strength transform virus makes the muscles in an Elite's body four to five times more efficient—makes the Elite four to five times stronger. A second nerve network grows around the network the Elite is born with, and is connected to a battle computer implanted at the base of the Elite's skull. Carbon-ceramic filaments reinforce all points where muscle, ligament or cartilage attaches itself to a bone. The bones themselves are regrown with a new carbon-ceramic base. Early Elite," the program said, "were quite heavy. Recent advances in design and implementation of the Elite upgrade have reduced the weight penalty significantly, so that an Elite is generally only thirty to forty percent heavier after the upgrade than before. My turn. You worshiped the flame?"

"Program, I do not think I can tell you. The Flame is a thing of living creatures, and though I speak to you of it in words, you will know nothing of what I mean."

"You do not wish to answer the question?"

It was the fourth time the program had asked that question, in exactly those words. Each time, Sedon had noticed, the guard standing at the door had tensed slightly. An important question then, the question which would, if answered negatively, set in motion the mechanism by which they intended to kill him. Sedon let a sigh escape him, and sat forward in the bed. His right foot came up beneath him, toes flexed for traction against the bed and the smooth cloths which covered it. "Program," he said sincerely—he did not know if the program could discern changes in tone of voice—"I wish to answer all your questions. But there are areas of discussion where I must speak to a man or woman who breathes and lives. Else my answers are merely words."

And Sedon exhaled, slowly, until his lungs were nearly empty of air. He fixed his gaze on the Elite's diaphragm, a spot immediately beneath the point where the Elite's ribs joined together. Stillness descended upon him.

The Elite, standing by the doorway, six hours into his shift, relaxed visibly upon hearing Sedon's answer.

And Gi'Suei'Obodi'Sedon, to his knowledge the last living Dancer anywhere in the Continuing Time, Moved.

Late on Tuesday, March 29, Christine Mirabeau, a woman with the general appearance and personality of a bulldog, the highest ranking Peaceforcer in the System, walked at Mohammed Vance's side through the laser-scored corridors of the United Nations Peace Keeping Force Detention Center on the outskirts of Amiens, near the edge of the Somme River in northern France.

During the course of that long evening, Vance's voice never rose above the volume appropriate for two old friends engaged in an intimate conversation.

The evening began at the cell in which Sedon had been kept, two floors beneath the ground.

A holo appeared, life-size, of Sedon and du Bouchage, the Elite who had been guarding him. "The recording will play back at quarter speed," Vance informed the Commander of the PKF Elite. "I had the Elite standing guard within the doorway rather than without; we were concerned at first for the patient's safety, for the possibility of suicide. It occurred to me that this placed the Elite in a certain danger, but I felt it minimal. Until this—thing—happened I would never have dreamed that any man could kill an Elite cyborg with his bare hands."

"I understand the mistake."

"I take full responsibility for the decision. *Command*, begin holo."

Sedon's form flows upward from the bed, moves toward the Elite standing by the doorway. "Freeze image. Notice his hands and feet when he leaps. All four are evenly in contact with the frame of the bed, significantly improving his velocity when he launches himself toward du Bouchage."

The image resumes; Sedon slams into du Bouchage at the doorway. The Elite is just becoming aware that something is happening; Sedon slams into the larger, heavier Elite, and with both hands and a knee flattens du Bouchage's palm against the doorpad. The image freezes. "You will see here, he does not even attempt to harm du Bouchage until after he has placed the man's hand against the surface of the doorpad. First things first. Elapsed time from the moment Sedon began to move to the moment that du Bouchage's palm is pressed quite flat against the surface of the doorpad, less than one half of a second. The language program was still controlling the holocams, and did not pass control to the security manager until nearly the full half second had passed. The computerist who wrote the language program should be placed in front of a firing squad. By the time the security manager had received the image and decided what to do with it, the door was curling open. Du Bouchage's battle computer comes into play now, not quite half a second after first movement by the prisoner." *The lasers in his fingers light; one of them scores Sedon slightly, rakes down the side of one leg. Sedon strikes du Bouchage in the solar plexus with two fingers of his right hand.* "You can see in the holos, Sedon's fingers are probably broken here; but that blow is most likely what stopped du Bouchage's heart." *Sedon's next blow, with the palm of his left hand, strikes du Bouchage at the side of the temple and bounces du Bouchage's head against the side of the doorway.* "The autopsy revealed a slight fracture in the carbon-ceramic laminae. Du Bouchage is probably unconscious at this point; his battle computer takes over." *The computer makes the correct decision, to take him away from the source of the danger, pushing backward, through the opening door and out into the corridor.*

Vance stepped through the doorway after Sedon's image, gesturing. "Sedon follows him. His reaction time is, *at least*, equivalent to du Bouchage's. He is not as strong, however; one of the doorways that briefly stopped him, a level up, would not have stopped a determined Elite. He attempted to force it and then used a variable laser to cut through it." Vance touched a dented place on the wall, a second before the image of du Bouchage's skull struck it. "If du Bouchage was not unconscious before, he is now." *Sedon is so close to the Elite that the Elite's fingertip lasers are of little use; the battle computer gathers Sedon to du Bouchage, attempts to squeeze him to death. Sedon allows du Bouchage to gather him in, makes sure his hands are left free, and strikes six times, in remarkably close succession, at the sides of du Bouchage's neck, the expression on his face one of savage enjoyment.* "The impact of one of those blows, probably the first, severed du Bouchage's spinal column as though he had been hung. Du Bouchage is now unconscious, his heart has been stopped, and his spinal cord severed. This does not stop the bear hug, of course; the battle computer reroutes through the two main trunks of the secondary nerve network. It is difficult to tell from the recordings, but either the fifth or sixth blow to the neck damaged the two trunks of the secondary nerve network sufficiently that the battle computer lost control of du Bouchage's body. Total elapsed time from the moment Sedon first moves, three and two-tenths seconds. Sedon is damaged in the encounter; sight laser score on one leg, broken fingers, probable broken ribs. Let's go upstairs."

They walked up, following Sedon's insubstantial, too-solid-appearing holograph as it fled up the stairs.

"It takes them twelve seconds to reach B1. Given that he was sedated when he was brought here, how he knew to head upward—how he even knew he was underground—is anybody's guess. But as you see, he does not hesitate. The alarm has been sounded by the time he reaches B1, and he meets Elite Officer Pailletin at the top of the stairs. Officer Pailletin is, unfortunately, armed with a variable laser." *Pailletin is tall, even for a PKF Elite, perhaps ten centimeters taller than Sedon. He crouches slightly, variable laser rifle cradled in his arms, and fires at Sedon as Sedon exits the stairwell. Sedon rolls beneath the beam, comes out of the roll with the heels of both of his feet striking Officer Pailletin's kneecaps.* "You can see here, Sedon breaks his left ankle delivering the blow; Elite kneecaps are quite strong. He breaks neither of Pailletin's kneecaps." *Pailletin falls, and in the fall Sedon takes the variable laser from him. Midway through his fall, before striking the floor, Pailletin's right foot touches the ground; he leaps backward, firing with the laser in his right fist as he moves away from the source of danger. The laser strikes Sedon in the shoulder, wounding him significantly; the recording shows that the collarbone in his right shoulder is sliced entirely in half.* "If Pailletin were a younger Elite, with a pair of finger lasers rather than only the one buried in his fist, he might have killed Sedon here. Unfortunately he has only the laser in his fist—"

—*and Sedon now has the variable laser; he retreats into the relative safety of the stairwell, and fires at Pailletin's face until he has destroyed Officer Pailletin's optics. Once Pailletin can no longer see, Sedon ignores him and, with a broken ankle and separated collarbone, proceeds upward to ground level, his speed of movement not appreciably diminished.* "Total elapsed time since reaching B1, eighteen and three quarter seconds. He is delayed slightly at the stairwell entrance; the security program has locked the door. He attempts to force it, fails—possibly because of his damaged collarbone—and uses the variable laser to cut the door apart. Total elapsed time since his attack upon du Bouchage, thirty-four seconds, almost exactly."

The cafeteria had been cleaned. Vance noted with grim amusement that a pot of coffee was set up on a sideboard, with perhaps a dozen cups, cream, and sugar.

"Three PKF Elite on duty," said Vance, "seven PKF soldiers, two doctors, and a nurse. Many of them were at breakfast; it was 8:37 A.M. when Sedon broke free. The recording of him in the cafeteria is"—Vance paused, apparently at a loss for words—"extraordinary. He killed five soldiers, both doctors, and the nurse in not quite eleven seconds. Two of the soldiers shot at him; neither came close. He did not spill a drop of blood.

"Then he went looking for De Nostri."

Elite Commander Mirabeau followed Mohammed Vance down the hallway to the quarters where Samuel De Nostri had been sleeping. "De Nostri is awake, but just barely; forty-eight seconds after his initial movement, Sedon finds the corridor leading to the Officers' quarters.

Sedon opens three doors, moving down the hallway and looking inside each one; at the fourth door he meets up with De Nostri, as De Nostri is emerging to find out the nature of the emergency. "What Sedon does now," said Vance, in a voice immeasurably grim, "shows clearly that he has been thinking—*learning*, under immense stress—during each of his prior encounters with the Elite."

Sedon's first two shots are directed at De Nostri's hands. He destroys the laser in De Nostri's left hand, brings the beam across and holds it on De Nostri's right hand as De Nostri charges him. He is successful; by the time De Nostri gets close, both of his finger lasers are dead. Standing in the hallway with the two insubstantial forms, the Elite charging down upon the standing form of Sedon, Vance said quietly, "De Nostri is shouting as he draws close, a tedious obscenity that will be edited from the final recording. We must," said Vance precisely, "in the future, teach Elite to avoid opening their mouths in combat. Sedon does what I would have done in the same circumstances—"

—and standing motionless, fires directly into De Nostri's mouth.

"Had De Nostri kept his mouth shut he could conceivably have killed Sedon. But the shot into that open, bellowing orifice vaporized his tongue, and I imagine the pain was immense. De Nostri *stopped moving*."

The holo vanished, left Vance and Mirabeau together in the corridor. Vance shook his head in plain disgust. "I doubt you need see the rest of this. Sedon blinded him, and then spent fully three and a half minutes playing with him. I have seen dead Elite," he continued, "but I have never seen anything like what our 'dancer' did to Officer Samuel De Nostri. Once he breached the skin he fired bursts from the laser into the breach, and slowly cooked De Nostri from the inside out. Not quite five minutes after attacking Officer du Bouchage, the prisoner burned through the Detention Center's front doors, walked out, walked down to the banks of the river, and leapt in."

"Walked."

"A calculated insult, Christine. He spat in our faces. Even Trent had the grace to run."

"That was?"

"A day and a half ago. We haven't found him yet."

$\bullet \qquad \bullet \qquad \bullet$

On the semiballistic, on their return to Capitol City, Christine Mirabeau watched, from one end to the other, the recording Vance had edited together from the Detention Center's fixed holocams.

When it was done, when the steam rising from Samuel De Nostri's body had faded from the holofield before them, Elite Commander Christine Mirabeau said quietly, "He has to die. He has to die soon."

"I will find him," said Vance, the deep voice low and inexorable, "and I will kill him with my own hands."

"I wish you luck, my friend." Mirabeau's tired, careworn features were even colder and more distant than usual. She was an embattled woman, undermined by the Secretary General, loathed by the Ministry of Population Control, occasionally besieged by treachery within the ranks of the PKF itself. Her use of the word "friend" was no mere figure of speech; she liked Mohammed Vance a great deal. On occasion she even found reason to trust him. "More luck, Mohammed, than you had catching Trent. More luck than any of those young Elite had attempting to kill Sedon with their bare hands."

"I will rip his heart from his chest."

Christine looked at Vance's profile with a certain degree of real curiosity. "You know, Mohammed, I do not think I have ever seen you angry before."

Mohammed Vance did not reply, but sat with his back ramrod straight, eyes fixed on emptiness as the semiballistic descended back into the atmosphere, shaking slightly with the increasing turbulence of its descent, down toward Capitol City and the waiting Earth.

Summer: 2075

A Blast from the Past II

- 1 -

When he had finished reading McGee's notes, only a few hours before dawn, William Devane sighed irritably. It was no more believable this time than the first.

But he did not understand why the story was so compelling. Finally he shut his handheld off, hung up his robe, and went back to bed.

It was near sunrise when he got to sleep.

And dreamed.

There is something deep inside, something important hiding in the mist of ancient memory. The memory that is called for is dim and distant, the remembrance of something another person did long, long ago. The memory management routines that are the kernel of William Devane's identity came into play, inspecting the call to determine its urgency. There is a finite amount of storage available within Devane's brain, and it reached full long ago. He survives as a sane being only by constantly forgetting the trivial details of his life, by archiving and flushing most long-term memory and retaining only data pertaining to current conditions. Any call to deep memory is dangerous, and the deeper the memory, the more dangerous the call; the older the data, the less likely it is to have relevance to survival in the current world. The management routines have nearly decided to ignore the call—

But the call persists. The sleep period is half over by now; if the work is to be done by the time Devane awakens, it must begin now. The decision is made to retain current skills, as well as the bulk of recent memory, and temporarily remove all data prior to that time from near-term memory. The process is slow, as it requires the inspection, deletion, compression and archiving of vast amounts of information. Dawn is nearly upon him before sufficient near-term memory has been freed to allow the call to deep memory to proceed.

Memories cascade through Devane's dreamtime awareness. The cold English castle where he spent most of the fourteenth century A.D. A woman with red hair, and a harp, and children.

His children. The battlefield at Camel Hill, in 527, where he took the worst wound of his incredibly long life. Rome, at its height, and the long summer of Egypt . . .

All too recent. Back . . .

The millennia with his People, wandering up and down the coast of Europe.

And before that . . .

Late the next morning, as the sun hung high over southern Ireland, Gi'Tbad'Eovad'Dvan opened his eyes to the first moments of full consciousness he had experienced in over fifteen hundred years.

He sat up in bed, slowly, and then rose and walked across the cold, buffed wooden floor to the stairway that led out, to the top of his home; and up through the hatchway, out onto the lookout.

He stood naked in the sunlight atop a small hill, staring out at the world, looking out over the green fields of grass, at the blue sky and the half dozen cars flying within his field of vision; at the cows wandering lazily across the far pastures. He watched the world with a wonder so vast it was almost terror, an awe that so filled him he feared his heart might burst.

His memories of the last decades were sharp, but no sharper than those of his childhood. He remembered the Dancing, his own worship, in the Temples at the city of Kulien, on the World, as clearly as he remembered Sarah Almundsen's declaration of the Unification of Earth, only fifty-seven years prior. He remembered his training to become a Shield, and the nightmare of shiabrè. He remembered the penal colony—

—this world.

He remembered the heretic.

The Dancer.

He stood staring sightlessly out at the brilliant green of southern Ireland, remembering the battle in which he had fallen, the battle wound that had left him without his long-term memory, with nothing but shadowed memories of an existence prior to that evil day in A.D. 527, when the King had fallen at his own son's hand.

He was better than fifty thousand years old, and remembered all of it.

Remembered the training that had made him what he was,

the skills he had been taught, the Dedication he had accepted
before the childhood of his body had ended.

We are born broken, and live by mending.

"I see that I am broken."

*You are a Shield, a servant of the Living Flame. Will you live
in the service of the Flame?*

Standing in the sacred circle at Kulien, fifty-one thousand
years prior, Gi'Tbad'Eovad'Dvan had whispered, "Aye. I will."

Will you kill if you must?

"Aye."

*Will you die if needed; will you live when you no longer wish
to, if the service is required of you?*

"Aye."

The Living Flame exploded around him—

—and fifty-one thousand years later, standing atop a hill in
southern Ireland, a brief Flame flickered around William
Devane, sheeted across his nude body and turned it for the
barest instant into a statue made of light; and for an instant
outshone the sun itself.

Later that day William Devane boarded a semiballistic for
Amiens, France, to begin the search.

Gi'Suei'Obodi'Sedon, the man Dvan had most admired and
hated in his life, was alive.

He must not remain so.

- 2 -

A garden covered the top of Robert's old brownstone, a land-
scaped area of grass and flowers; there was even a pair of trees,
one an apple tree, one lemon.

Early on the morning of July the Fourth, as the people
across Occupied America prepared for the violence they knew
would come, Robert Dazai Yo and Denice Castanaveras pulled
weeds.

They worked the garden together, slowly, through most of
the morning. Robert had cancelled his classes for the day; he
did not expect his students to brave the streets when he himself would have done so only under the gravest duress.

Even the discipline of shiabrè had its limits; even a night face could die at the hands of a mob. And this close to Capitol City, on this day of days, anything could happen.

"When do you start?"

"Next Monday. Ripper left Capitol City until after Independence Day."

Robert nodded. "I am not surprised. Most of the Unification Council does. Eddore would like to, I'm sure; but the ammunition it would give his enemies would be too powerful. Will you look for an apartment?"

"Perhaps this weekend."

"You are welcome to the guest room."

"It's close, which would be convenient. I'd like to be close to the job."

Robert nodded.

"I'm a little nervous about it."

After a bit Robert said, "I am sure you will do well."

"I hope so. I hope the work is—meaningful."

Perhaps half an hour passed. The sun was very warm.

Denice said, "Is this a plant or a weed?"

"Let me see—a plant."

"I already pulled it."

"In time," said Robert, "a flower."

"It's dead now."

"Alas." Robert put down his trenching tool. "I think we are done."

They sat on the grass together, in the shade of the apple tree, and drank unsweetened lemonade together. "I have noticed an interesting thing about people who wish to be of service, Denice. Such people tend to have problems with their self-image. It seems to me that in their service they seek to—define—themselves."

Denice drank her lemonade, not looking at him. "Okay."

"Are you happy?"

After a long moment Denice said, "Not very."

"Do you love yourself?"

"Of *course*." Denice heard the indignation in her voice, could not suppress it. "What do you think?" She paused. "If I wasn't me already, I'd certainly *want* to be."

Robert smiled. "But if you love yourself, why are you unhappy?"

Denice stared at Robert. "Does it mean anything at all to

you when I tell you that sometimes these days I don't know who the hell I *am* anymore?"

"That is a good trick. You love yourself, though you are not sure who you are." Robert Yo nodded, and poured himself another glass of lemonade from the pitcher, and then said, "Who do you want to be?"

Spring: 2076

I saw the crowd around you
You danced there with your pain
Made love with all the other slaves
Made music with your chains

You say you didn't do it
Doesn't matter anyway
I saw you in the crowd that night
of Independence Day

—Mahliya Kutura,
Independence Day

- 1 -

On her twenty-third birthday Denice arranged to leave work early to have dinner with Jimmy Ramirez.

He was one of her best friends; after Trent and a dancer named Tarin Schuyler, her oldest.

He called at lunch to confirm dinner. His image hung in the holofield over her desk, a young lawyer in an exquisitely tailored suit. When he spoke his voice held none of the Fringe accent he had possessed when Denice had met him, in the summer of 2069. "We're still on?"

"Yes. Of course. The Red Line at eight?"

Jimmy Ramirez, once a Temple Dragon, once Trent the Uncatchable's right hand—today an assistant public defender for the City of New York—smiled at Denice. "I'll see you there."

After lunch Ripper, Denice, and Ichabod Martin worked through the materials from the Unification Council's Peace Keeping Oversite Committee; Ripper chaired that Committee.

They sat together in Ripper's office. After her first interview with Ripper, Denice had never again seen it so intimidatingly bleak; usually the empty space was filled with some interesting illusion. Today they sat inside a huge green cathedral of trees. The sound of a brook bubbled in the background, just audible under the sound of normal speech.

"Who's this?"

"Relatively new," Martin said. "He's risen through the ranks of the Johnny Rebs with remarkable speed, though. He calls himself 'Sieur Obodi. Speaks English with an accent, possibly Italian; has strong ties to the Old Ones, the old Mafia. Some rumors to the effect that he pimped for a bit, but saying it to his face can get you killed. He's definitely a player in the Reb power structure, though exactly where he stands in relation to Tommy Boone is a good question—nobody's seen Boone in a couple of weeks."

Denice and Ichabod Martin sat in the chairs before Douglass Ripper's desk. Ripper sat behind it with his eyes closed,

the trodes of a large and rather out-of-date traceset touching
each of his temples. Out of politeness, though Denice and Ichabod had both seen it already, Ripper had duplicated the holo
he was looking at; it hung off to Denice's right, blocking a
patch of the larger holo of the forest.

The man was tall, two meters or more. His hair was long
and blond, tied in a ponytail. His eyes were bright blue, with
a slightly Asian appearance. His features were not sharp; the
holo had been taken from a distance of about two hundred meters, as Obodi hurried toward a waiting semiballistic. The car
he had come in was visible in the background of the shot; a
long black limousine with darkened windows. A pair of known
Johnny Rebs followed after him.

"And the PKF is doing what about him?"

"They're rounding up twice the usual number of suspects,"
Denice said quietly.

Ripper nodded. "Wonderful." He opened his eyes, said
moodily, "What is *wrong* with them?"

Denice said nothing. Ichabod Martin said quietly, "The
Peace Keeping Force has faced so little real threat, for so
long—perhaps the Peaceforcers are unable to believe they have
a worthy opponent."

Ripper grunted. "I'd have thought Trent the Uncatchable
would have broken them of that conceit. Where does core
membership stand today?"

"Nearly fifteen thousand," said Denice without pause. "In
the past when the Rebs have gotten past some fifteen thousand
core members the PKF has cracked down. I don't know why
they're not doing it this time, especially given the indicators on
how the Rebs are arming themselves. Something interesting,
though—did you notice the memo by Commissioner Vance?"

Ripper said, "No—wait." His eyes dropped shut. "It is interesting," he agreed a moment later. "What's this reference to
Amiens?"

Denice shook her head. "I don't know, 'Sieur Ripper. There
is a PKF Detention Center near Amiens. Perhaps the PKF
once had this Obodi in custody? It's one interpretation of
Vance's memo that makes sense."

"Can we find out?"

Ichabod Martin smiled wryly. "We can ask. You know the
PKF, especially where Vance is concerned. Fifty-fifty we get
told to mind our own business."

"This *is* our business." Martin nodded, and Ripper sighed. "Do your best. What's next?"

"Bill in committee on the AI property question."

"I'm inclined to vote against it. It's already illegal for an AI to even exist; I fail to see the purpose of this bill, aside from the obvious anti-AI paranoia."

"The PKF DataWatch is one of the bill's sponsors," Denice said. "They have something on Pena, I'm not sure what; it's why Pena submitted the bill. Vote against it and you're going to piss them off a lot."

Ripper sat up straight. "DataWatch is sponsoring this?"

"Yes."

"How do you know that?"

"Just doing my job," said Denice evenly. "DataWatch thinks that if it can prevent AIs from owning property, it can deny them access to safe processors. Your average AI is not particularly friendly to the Unification; some of them work with the Claw and the Rebs. Preventing them easy access to secure processors—well, there's something to the idea."

Ripper said patiently, "How do you *know* that?"

Ralf had told her; to Ripper she said merely, "I know more than one Player."

Ripper studied her. "I don't know whether to thank you or fire you. Damn it, Daimara, association with Players is *not* part of your job. The last thing in the System I need is to get on DataWatch's bad side."

"I know." Denice repeated, "You might want to vote for the bill. If," she said, "you don't want to get on DataWatch's bad side."

Ripper nodded slowly. "I'll talk to you about this later. Martin, do we have any more security issues to discuss?"

"No."

"All right, you stay. Daimara, that's all for now." Denice rose, left without saying anything further. Ripper and Ichabod were already involved in another discussion; neither of them took notice of her as she left.

They sat together in lotus on the mat after Robert's afternoon class had ended, in the hour before Robert's first evening class was scheduled to begin.

"I feel like I don't have time to *breathe* these days," Denice complained.

"Bad," Robert agreed. He sat chewing a piece of Wrigley's Spearmint Gum. "People die when deprived of air. It happens among the SpaceFarers." He cocked his head to one side. "It's rare on Earth, though."

"That's not funny."

Robert shrugged. "One woman's opinion."

"On Saturday we're going on another leg of the campaign. India, then Australia, then Japan, and then back to New York. I won't be out of Ripper's presence for more than an hour or two at a time during the entire period."

Robert nodded.

"You know how I feel about Ripper. He's a *good* man. But this sort of enforced contact—it's hard, Robert. Every time we go on one of these damn trips I find myself not wanting to talk to him before we're back. And the longer we're on the road the more intensely I want to *not talk* to him. Sometimes he's a real jerk."

"Douglass can be very focused," Robert observed.

"Yes, and it's a problem. The level of detail is incredible, Robert. I never felt incompetent before I took this job; but recently I haven't felt much *but* incompetent. Especially since that assassination attempt in Portugal."

"Which you stopped. I could have done no better myself."

"He shouldn't *ever* have gotten that close. A lot of that was Ichabod—he's been even less focused than me, and that's saying something—but the rest of it *was* me. We should have checked the room beneath Ripper's." Denice was silent, brooding. "I don't know if I can take another seven months of this. You know, this wasn't remotely what I had in mind when I decided to get into politics. It's tedious and boring and—do you *have* to chew gum while we talk?"

Robert blinked. "No. Not really." He swallowed visibly, continued. "A disgusting habit," he admitted, "but if I did not chew gum then I would be perfect, which would be worse. How much time do you have?"

"An hour. Then I have to shower and go to see Jimmy Ramirez."

"We will skip meditation today and start with stretching, then."

Denice took a deep breath. "Back when I danced, I didn't feel like I was getting anything done—that anything I was doing made a *difference*. But it was a lot more enjoyable."

Robert stood, gestured to Denice to join him. "And then Tai Chi, for relaxation."

Denice sat in lotus, did not move. "What I'm doing now *matters*," Denice told Robert.

"Indeed. *Rho deset enelli.*"

"*Why do you keep talking to me like that?*"

"Why indeed," said Robert Dazai Yo. He held a hand out to her, helped her gently to her feet. "The language is called shiata, and someday soon I will tell you more about it. But now, let us begin."

At 8:00 she met Jimmy Ramirez at the Red Line Hotel.

Two of Trent's old friends worked at the Red Line, Jodi Jodi and Bird, a pair of street kids who had come out of the Fringe with Trent and Jimmy Ramirez. Bird had, with some help, finally adjusted to the Patrol Sectors; Jodi Jodi, on the other hand, had taken to the Patrol Sectors like a Peaceforcer to cheap wine.

In a society grown increasingly age-conscious, Jimmy Ramirez was, at twenty-eight, the youngest assistant public defender in the City of New York.

Sometimes, these days, Denice felt that she did not know him any longer. If she had not known that behind the facade was a street kid and gang member from the Fringe, an ex-semipro boxer and ex-thief, she would never have guessed. He was a handsome man who had never had biosculpture. A mix of Haitian blood, and white, and Puerto Rican, his genes came from almost as many different sources as her own. He wore long-sleeved dress shirts, always, so that the faint scar that separated his old arm from the new would not be seen. He had a similar pair of scars on each of his legs, reminders of the night she and Jimmy had broken Trent out of the PKF Detention Center in Capitol City.

She wondered, sometimes, how Jimmy Ramirez would have ended up had he not met Trent. Oh, certainly his life would not have been the same; but they had been involved in great events, and they had shaped him as they had shaped her, and Trent. Though she did not believe in destiny, it struck her that some people were born to accomplish great things, that their lives would, under any circumstances, have been of note; others achieved greatness only under the pressure of events.

She did not even think she condescended in placing Jimmy Ramirez in the latter category.

Jodi Jodi, who seated them for dinner, was the Manager of Guest Services at one of the premier hotels in New York; Denice had never known quite what to make of her. A blond woman with blue eyes and the strangest sense of humor Denice had ever encountered, it was likely she had not personally led a pair of guests to their tables in perhaps five years. As she seated them at their table, in a quiet corner of the hotel's restaurant, she whispered to Denice, "Happy birthday."

Denice was surprised Jodi Jodi had remembered. "Thank you."

She and Jimmy did not talk much through dinner. Jimmy had brought a gift, wrapped in gold foil, and it sat at the side of the table until after dessert was served. Denice allowed herself a slice of nondairy cheesecake, and upon finishing it opened Jimmy's gift.

A hat.

Denice lifted it out of the box slowly.

A black bowler with a red silk ribbon about the base of the crown.

"You know," she said after a pause, "I've never owned a hat before." She thought back. "I don't think I've ever even worn one."

"Put it on."

She did, slowly, let the felt rim of the hat settle gently against her hair. "How does it look?"

Jimmy Ramirez looked straight at her. "It's a shame you don't have a lover these days. It looks like I thought it would look."

"Oh?"

His tone of voice contained only the slightest hint of teasing. "You probably ought not to wear it in public, of course. It's an incitement to which most men and some women should not be subjected."

Denice took it off, put the hat back in the box. "I think you have a thing about hats."

"Who, me? No, no. No. Not at all. No." Jimmy grinned. "A bit. A bit, okay? Just a little."

Perhaps it was the wine she'd had to drink; Denice did not even stop to consider the question. "Jimmy, how come you've never made a pass at me?"

The grin vanished instantly, and Jimmy Ramirez stared at

her without speaking for a long moment. Finally he said, "Are you serious?"

"Yes."

Jimmy looked distinctly uncomfortable. "You don't *know*? I mean—"

Denice said quietly, "I don't do that. I Touched you once, the first time I met you, because you scared me. After that I knew you loved Trent, and I never had to again."

Jimmy said directly, "You're a frightening person in some ways."

"Touching . . ." Denice bit her lip. "It *hurts*, Jimmy. *You* hurt, all of you. You walk around with this terrible pain inside of you, from all the violence and betrayals in your lives, and it doesn't bother you—because it's your pain and you're used to it. But when I Touch you I get *all* of your pain, all at once. I don't do it unless I have a very, *very* good reason."

"When I met Trent," said Jimmy Ramirez, "he was eleven. I was thirteen. The PKF was in the process of putting up the Patrol Sector Barriers, of creating the Fringe. I was born in what turned into the Fringe, and it was a poor neighborhood, very tough, even before the Troubles. Social mores," he said carefully, "were . . . different. Among the people I grew up with—forgive my language—fucking your buddy's girl was a good way to get killed. Fucking a boy set you up for ridicule, for beatings and harassment. I understand you and Trent were raised differently. When I met Trent he was the strangest thing I'd ever seen in my life. He was this tough little white boy who was innocent about such an incredible variety of things I didn't know where to start teaching him. I took care of him for about two years, and then he did something, I don't even remember what, that made some of the older Dragons think he was a webdancer. They beat him for about a week, trying to get him to say he was a webdancer. He kept telling them he wasn't, cause he didn't want to be a slave again the way all your people had been, and he knew that if he admitted to being a webdancer the Dragons wouldn't ever have let him free again. Finally they had to decide, kill him or let him be. They were still pretty sure he was a webdancer, but they were so impressed with his courage they figured even if he wouldn't dance for them, he could still be a trooper."

"Trent told me some of this."

"I never saw anyone so brave," Jimmy Ramirez said simply. "He was the *best*. I liked him before that, but after that—"

Jimmy shrugged. "He was my man. My brother forever. When he decided to get out of the Fringe, I never even stopped to think about it. He said go, Bird and Jodi Jodi and I picked up." Jimmy paused. "Denice, I love you."

Denice could not think of anything at all to say.

"Trent is the best thing that ever happened to me. He taught me to *read*. If it wasn't for him I'd be a warlord in the Fringe today, or else dead. There are," said Jimmy with a devastatingly simple logic, "many women in the world. But in your life you only get a few friends."

"You must know Trent wouldn't have minded." Denice blinked. "Not that I'd have said yes."

"*I'd* have minded. Listen," said Jimmy impatiently, "this is a story I haven't ever told *anyone*. When I was fourteen, one night it was deadly cold, I mean old ladies turning into corpsicles on the street outside. Trent and I shared a room at the Temple, and we only had one blanket and one bed. I slept on the bed with my coat on and Trent had the blanket and was sleeping on the floor with it. About midnight he asked me if he could sleep with me, cause he was so cold. I got up and barred the door so nobody could walk in on us, and we got into bed together. That was fourteen years ago," said Jimmy precisely, "and to this day I sometimes wake up at night feeling guilty about that."

"I understand."

"Maybe some people let go of their childhood. The best I've ever managed is to cover it up."

Denice said softly, "I love you too. Want to argue about politics for a while?"

Near 11:00 P.M., toward the end of their second bottle of wine, their argument degenerated into an argument.

Jimmy Ramirez—it was not news to Denice—believed, fiercely, that armed insurrection was inevitable, that it was the only possible way to remove the Unification's hold on Occupied America.

His opinion of her employer was just short of feeling that Ripper should be shot for treason. "How do you represent," said Jimmy patiently, "the rights of an occupied people, when all of your power arises from the military infrastructure of the occupiers? How can Ripper possibly reconcile his reputation as a champion of Occupied America with the fact that whatever power he has derives from the continued might of the Unification?"

"If you think that revolution is possible," said Denice slowly, "then Ripper is—*I'm*—wrong. The Unification has not been a good thing for Occupied America, I concede the point. But it's *not* possible, Jimmy. There are fifteen thousand core members of the Johnny Rebs, perhaps three or four thousand Erisian Claw. There are over twelve million PKF under uniform across the globe, another six hundred thousand off Earth. For God's sake, Jimmy, a quarter of a million of those Peaceforcers are *Americans*. Not even a popular uprising with millions of Americans joining in gives *either* of those groups any realistic chance of dislodging the Unification from *any* part of Earth. They are," said Denice, "terrorists. Ideologs. Not rebels."

"*Terrorists?*" Jimmy was clearly offended, more than a little angry. "Listen, girl, you're talking about people who've dedicated their lives to a great purpose, about people who are doing work that damn straight *matters*. Compare their commitment to your own and tell me how *you* come out."

The point struck home; Denice struggled not to let it show. "Okay. Maybe I shouldn't have called them terrorists—but regardless of their commitment, it doesn't count for anything if they can't win. And they *can't*."

Jimmy spoke rapidly. "On Saturday I'm going to Kansas City. Let's use Kansas City as an example, because I've studied this one. The PKF garrison there is thirty-five thousand strong. The population of Kansas City is over a million. You think—you seriously think—that a million Americans, armed and ready to fight, can't take that city away from thirty-five thousand PKF?"

"Who's going to arm them, Jimmy? Who's going to make them ready to fight? A lot of them—*most* of them—don't want to fight. Even if they want the PKF out of Occupied America, they don't want it so badly that they'll die for it. Or kill for it. The people who feel that passionately are the minority, Jimmy. Maybe there's a hundred thousand of them in Kansas City; I wouldn't know. But they're not trained, they're not armed; and if you *tried* to train or arm them the PKF would put you up against a wall and shoot you *dead*."

Denice had not been aware of her voice rising; suddenly Jodi Jodi was there at the side of their table, whispering furiously, "If the two of you want to argue treason, feel free to do it in someone *else's* restaurant. We've got a pair of French Unification officials at a table down the way, and they're complaining that you're ruining their dinners. *Stop it.*"

Denice blinked, and Jodi Jodi was gone. "Um."

Jimmy looked slightly embarrassed. "She's right. Sorry about that."

Denice took a deep breath. "I'm sorry, too. It's just that—*oh.*" The word held audible frustration. "You've changed a lot, Jimmy."

"Haven't we all?" From somewhere, Jimmy Ramirez found a smile for her. "There are few people I trust as much as I trust you, Denice. I think you're trying to do right. But you know, you're not succeeding. You're doing the wrong thing with the wrong people."

"There's still room to work, Jimmy. While there's room to work we have to take it."

"Room to work?" Jimmy's voice took on an edge. "For *who*? For you, for the man with the nice office in Capitol City and the ten-room house upstate? Girl, there's always room at the top. That's not *ever* the problem."

"How do you know how large his house is?"

Jimmy sighed. "Look, I read it somewhere, okay?"

Denice looked across the table at Jimmy Ramirez, at the serious young features. "I'm not the enemy, Jimmy. I promise I'm not."

"I know that." Jimmy drained the last of his wine and stood. "But I'm not sure you're part of the solution anymore either." His expression softened slightly. "Good night, angel."

Denice nodded, expression troubled. Her stomach was upset. "Thanks for having dinner with me."

"Thank *you*," he said with complete sincerity. He leaned forward and kissed her on the forehead. "And happy birthday again."

"Have a nice trip." Abruptly, she added, "Where are you going again?"

Jimmy stood motionless, looking down at her. Finally he said, "Kansas City. I think I said Kansas City."

Denice nodded without looking away from him. "Yes. I think you did."

She called a cab to take herself home.

In the cab she touched her InfoNet handheld once, said quietly, "Ralf?"

"Yes?"

"I think Jimmy may be getting into something stupid. Do me a favor, if you would. He's going to Kansas City this weekend. Keep an eye on him."

"Do you think," asked Ralf, "that this is an appropriate action to take concerning a man who is, after all, both your friend and Trent's?"

"I promised Trent I'd look out for him. He's bright, but he's—impulsive."

"Very well. If you wish it, I will do it."

Her midtown security apartment, just outside Capitol City, was small: a single bedroom and an attached bathroom. Despite its size it was remarkably well appointed; the tub was large enough for two people, and the bed had more settings than she knew how to use; the kitchen had a gourmet waitbot that prepared meals nearly as well as the human cooks at the Red Line. The media access in the bedroom was as complete as anyone could have wished; holo projectors in five different places, two different InfoNet terminals, one of them a full-sensory connection that rivaled the efficiency of an InfoNet inskin.

Denice was not certain what the apartment cost per month; Ripper had paid for it, so that she might be closer to the office.

Denice stood nude before the mirror in her bathroom, contemplating outfits for Ripper's interview with the *Electronic Times* scheduled for tomorrow morning. After a moment she turned off her makeup key and filled the sink's basin with warm water. The makeup pattern she'd worn faded slowly; her normally pale skin reappeared as she washed, as though she were washing away her makeup with the soap and water. She was distantly aware of tension in the muscles of her neck and shoulders.

"This has not been a good day."

She did not think she had spoken loudly enough to be heard; nonetheless a response, no more than a disinterested grunt, drifted out from the direction of the bedroom. "Mmm-hmm."

She raised her voice to be certain she was heard. "I had a fight with my friend Jimmy at dinner. I think I really made him angry." Denice rubbed the cleanup pad over her face and neck, crumpled the cloth, and tossed it toward the 'bot in the corner; the 'bot snagged it out of midair and stuffed it inside itself.

"Jimmy made *me* angry; he sounded like a Johnny Reb at dinner. I know he's smarter than that, but—how can a man as intelligent as he is be so *blind*?"

"Mmm-hmm."

She pulled on the suit she intended to wear the following day, a black pinstripe with a gold belt; the pants were slightly baggy and gave her room to move if she needed to. She did not put on a shirt with it. She slipped on a pair of black running shoes with soft soles; they almost looked like dress shoes. She put Jimmy's hat on, looked at herself in the mirror. Aside from her breasts, half visible beneath the coat, she looked as she always looked in that suit; a slim teenage boy with gorgeous green eyes. The hat accentuated the effect, made her look as though her moderately long hair had been cut short.

She nodded at her image in the mirror and stepped out into the bedroom. "For tomorrow. What do you think?"

New York Metro Unification Councilor Douglass Ripper, wearing a green silk robe and auditing text on a field that floated twenty centimeters in front of his eyes, looked up as Denice entered the bedroom.

She turned slowly, showing the ensemble. "Well? With a shirt?"

Ripper sat up in bed, looking at her. "Where did you get the hat?"

"A gift from my friend Jimmy. For my birthday. Do you like it?"

"Yes," he said after a moment. "Yes, I do. Is today your birthday? You're twenty-three today?"

"Yes."

"Why didn't you say anything?"

"You were busy."

Ripper said quietly, "I'll get you a gift tomorrow."

Denice took the hat off and laid it atop the bedroom dresser. "Okay. So, this suit tomorrow."

"Um . . ."

"Yes?"

Ripper said slowly, "What you're wearing. It's fine, wear it tomorrow. Professional enough for an interview. But for right now—"

Denice grinned. "Yes?"

Ripper said softly, "Take off what you're wearing. Put the hat back on."

Denice looked at the hat, and then back at him, and her grin grew wider. "Okay. If you like."

"Um. Trust me."

Later, as she snuggled up against Ripper's unconscious form, Denice Castanaveras drifted into gentle sleep; and dreamed.

She stood alone on a vast, featureless black plain, smooth as glass, flat and level as a ruler. The plane ran away toward a far distant flicker of lights.

No matter what direction she turned, she saw the same thing—inky blackness above, a smoother, glossy blackness below.

Where the two darknesses met the lights glowed and flickered.

I have been here before.

It was different this time.

She lay on the sweaty sheets of the Girls' Dormitory bunk she had been assigned. The Gift had come upon her, and it was nothing like what she had been told to expect by her parents, nothing like the Gift they had been granted by Suzanne Montignet's genengineering.

She was barely there on the bunk. Most of her was elsewhere, a dark crystal plain—

She hurt. Lives like candles burned in the darkness around her, wavered through the crystalline darkness, came alive and then burst into emptiness, their deaths accompanied by moments of sheer terror that burned themselves into the depths of the young girl's mind.

This place seemed the same ... but empty. Darkness all around her.

Lights in the far, far distance.

In the Beginning, said the voice, *was the Flame.*

Suddenly the Flame appeared around her, solitary and splendid, and with the appearance of the Flame a hot fierce joy descended upon her, filled her with a love like rage, like the wrath of angels.

When she awoke in the morning Ripper was already gone.

Denice awoke with an ache in her heart, an overwhelming sense of loss, for what she did not know.

She did not remember having dreamed.

It did not seem possible that her life should be so empty.

- 2 -

Tommy Boone gasped and cried out.

The voice came out of the darkness. *His* voice, that had worn away at Boone for two days now. "They are crude techniques," he said quietly, "but they work. And so we use them."

Boone sat in a straight-backed chair, wrists bound to the armrests, ankles bound to the legs. His head was strapped back against the headrest and his eyelids had been cut off and a spotlight shone into his face. He was nearly blind from it. His cheeks were one purplish mass of bruises. His right eye had swollen almost shut.

He wore only a white T-shirt and underwear—he had been asleep when they came for him. There was barely a white spot left on them; they were black with old blood or red with new.

Blood spurted from the index finger of his right hand; the finger itself lay on the floor, still twitching.

One technician flattened Boone's hand out, and the second tied a string around the stump of the finger; a maser set at low intensity seared the stump until the bleeding stopped.

Boone screamed while they did it to him, and did not stop screaming until the maser beam ceased.

"I wish to share my name with you," said the voice. "But first I must have yours."

Boone tried to speak. The inside of his mouth was bone dry, and the last time it had been wet had been with his own blood. Finally he managed to whisper harshly, "Suck me, Obodi."

"I have grown to appreciate your people," said the voice from beyond the lights. It was softer, that voice, gentler, than anything Boone had ever heard before in his life. Not even his mother had had a voice like that; not even his wife, who had died when Boone was only twenty. "You are an imaginative and vigorous and brutal people. Why, the unpleasantness I am inflicting upon you, it comes from a famous incident in your own history. When the Carthaginian tribe fought the Roman tribe, a Roman general named Regulus was caught by the Carthaginians; they removed his eyelids and tied him facing east at dawn." A chuckle. "I have had little enough time to learn of your past, so busy I've been kept these last years. Perhaps later I will have time to study more; I would like to understand you, and the forces that shaped you. *Who are you?*"

The crack of the voice penetrated the pain and fatigue; Boone heard himself answering as though another person used his tortured vocal cords. "Thomas Daniel Boone."

"That is very good," said the gentle voice. "I am Gi'Suei'Obodi'Sedon. I was a Dancer of the Nameless One; today I am the instrument of your death. The release from your pain." The words wore away at Boone, as he floated half-conscious in the haze of his pain, under the blaze of the lights. "Here in this moment together, you and I, we are one. You are all of my world and I am all of yours. I know you as no one has ever known you before; I understand you, the dark and bright places within you, as no one has understood you in all your life. And I love you, Thomas Daniel Boone, for the good that is within you. Release him."

Boone heard a hushed, rapid exchange out beyond the circle of the light, heard the flat finality of Obodi's voice: "As I said."

The technician came forward, into the light, a glowing white blob in Boone's ruined eyesight. The bonds that held his ankles were cut, and then those that held his wrists. The pain that struck him as the blood rushed into his extremities would have seemed, on any other day of his life, intense; now he barely noticed it. The strap that restrained his head was left in place, and in some distant corner of his mind Boone found himself absurdly grateful; if they'd cut it he would, he knew, have pitched forward from the chair like a rag doll.

The technician placed a laser in his numb, but otherwise undamaged left hand, and stepped back into the darkness of the cellar.

The man who Tommy Boone knew as Obodi, who had called himself Gi'Suei'Obodi'Sedon, came forward into the light. Boone could barely make out the shape of the man, never mind his features; all Boone could see was that he wore a long robe of some reddish color.

"The device in your hand is a laser, Thomas. My good and true Thomas. A weapon with which you can kill me if you wish, punish me for the pain and fear I have inflicted upon you."

Tears leaked from the corners of Boone's eyes. "Oh, God. What do you want of me?"

"I am not your God, Thomas, merely your death. I want you to take the laser and put it in your mouth and pull the trigger."

The moment Boone had known was coming since he had awakened here in this place left him so weak with fear he could not even lift the laser they had placed in his hand. "Please . . ." he whispered. "Please no. I don't want to die."

Boone was aware of Obodi coming closer. "What is a life, Thomas? A small thing, given casually, taken the same. It is nothing to be struggled for so furiously. Calm yourself and do not be afraid. Put the weapon in your mouth and pull the trigger."

Tommy Boone found a last reservoir of strength, snarled, "Fuck you and *die*," and lifted the laser—

"*Stop!*" The Voice was his father's, and Joe Mantika's, the man who had recruited him into the Rebs, and Father Bob's from Sunday school, merged into the thundering command. The Voice rolled over him: "PUT THE WEAPON IN YOUR MOUTH AND PULL THE TRIGGER!"

Tommy Boone did not hesitate. He flipped the safety off, brought the laser around, and blasted his own head off.

Gi'Suei'Obodi'Sedon stood in the circle of light, in a cellar in the city of Philadelphia, looking down upon the headless body of Thomas Daniel Boone, a good and true man.

Different from the Flame People, without doubt. Resistant to Speaking—but not impervious to it.

It was a good sign.

They kept him waiting nearly an hour.

Dvan did not let himself grow impatient. He had dealt with the Sicilian Old Ones before, though not recently, and understood the protocols that needed to be observed. He sat in a cool breeze and bright warm sunlight, with a glass of red wine on the small round patio table before him, looking out over the Santonia family's gardens, down across sculpted terraces of growing grapes. Don Emilio would leave him waiting until his business was done, whatever it might be, but no longer.

Shortly after one o'clock the don came out onto the patio, greeted Dvan warmly, and seated himself. "Forgive me, William. But it has been many years, and your call came with such short notice—" Emilio shrugged. "It took me some time to verify your activities of the last decade or so." The old man smiled at Dvan. "I was surprised, to tell the truth. Newsdancing—" He shrugged again. "It seems a waste of talents such as yours."

Dvan smiled at the man. "Perhaps. But it is safe and requires little exertion, and I find in my advancing age that this appeals to me."

Emilio frowned. "Advancing age, eh? You must be, perhaps, eighty? It's been a good while, my friend. You've carried the years—remarkably—I might even say surprisingly—well."

"As have you, Don Emilio."

Emilio nodded, accepting the lie for the politeness it was. "What can I do for you, William? If you have some thought of putting my name on the news Boards, I must tell you it would disturb me."

Dvan made a dismissive gesture. "Don Emilio, in the last few hours you have searched the InfoNet for my name. If any article about you or yours had ever been published under my name, you and I would not be talking."

Emilio said softly, "How I can be of service?"

"I'm looking for a man. His . . . occupation," said Dvan carefully, "was that of procuring women."

The old man shook his head. "We have no interests in—"

"He went by the name of Lucabri."

Silence fell. In the quiet Dvan could hear the buzzing of flies in the garden, the distant whine of the robots working the vineyards. Emilio stared at Dvan with hard, flinty eyes.

"He first appeared in Amiens, in France, early in '72. The next time I have certain knowledge of his location is in Genoa, in the summer of '73. And from there he vanishes. If you know where he might be, and would share that knowledge with me, I would be indebted to you."

"What is your interest in this . . . man?"

Dvan gave him an answer he knew the old don would accept. "It's not personal. I am doing a favor for a friend."

Understanding lit the old man's eyes. "Someone with a daughter, perhaps? Or a sister?"

"It would be a reasonable guess."

"And what action would you take if you were to find him?"

"I would ease the suffering of my friends, Don Emilio."

"While you have been wandering around Europe, William, Signor Lucabri has left a trail of bodies across Occupied America." The old man rose from the table. "If you wish to find him, go to America." Don Emilio stopped at the sliding glass door that led back into the villa. A servant inside opened the door for him, and he stood in the opening looking at Dvan—a wizened, shrunken old man who Dvan could not reconcile with the giant of a man he had known fifty years prior, who had killed men and loved women with equal passion. "He has been going by the name of Mister Obodi. And he is with the Rebs." Don Emilio gestured to the servant who had opened the door. "Please call Signor Devane a cab, and escort him to the gate."

The old man turned about, and walked back inside slowly, shuffling across the black tile.

"Who is this?" Sedon asked quietly.

They sat together in the living room of Obodi's house in San Diego, looking at holos. The living room's bay windows looked out on a view of the beach, of the restless Pacific Ocean.

Sedon's manner was sleepy and relaxed and satiated; Chris Summers, in the two years he had been working with the man he knew as Mister Obodi, had seen it before. It was the way Obodi looked following a night with a boy who had pleased him, and the way Obodi looked after killing someone who had displeased him.

The holo was clearly a publicity shot; it showed a man perhaps in his forties or fifties, with dark hair and brown eyes. "This is Douglass Ripper," said Summers. "Publicity still. He's the Unification Councilor for New York Metro; he sits on the Council's Peace Keeping Oversite Committee. He requisitioned the PKF report on you."

Sedon quirked an eyebrow. "Indeed? Should I concern myself with this?"

Summers said patiently, "He's a popular man, sir. He's running for Secretary General, and he's probably going to win."

"In December?" Sedon smiled, a lazy, relaxed smile. "I hardly think so. What else?"

Summers nodded. "One more item. *Command*, next. This is a—"

Gi'Suei'Obodi'Sedon rose to his feet slowly, expression draining from his features, staring motionless at the holo.

At the man.

Summers continued a bit slowly. "—a newsdancer. He's been asking people about Signor Lucabri; we had a report that he met with Emilio Santonia. I wondered if you wanted anything done about it."

Sedon did not reply. The pale blue eyes stared, unblinking, and his hands trembled. He brought his hands together abruptly, stood with his hands clasped together in front of his chest and said something in a language that Christian Summers had never heard before.

"Sir? Are you all right?"

Sedon said something again in the language Summers did not recognize, then shook himself and said in very slow English, not looking at Summers, "Find . . . him. The man . . . and bring him. To me."

"Mister Obodi? You know him?"

Sedon stared straight ahead, at the holo of the newsdancer. A big black-haired giant of a man with pale skin and dead black eyes. "He cannot be alive." He shook his head slowly, spoke half to himself. "A . . . resemblance, is the word. It has been too long for . . . Dvan . . . to be alive."

Christian J. Summers said, "Dvan?"

Finally Sedon looked at him. "What is his name?"

"Devane, sir. William Devane."

Sedon's voice was a mere whisper. "Oh, my old friend . . ." His eyes closed and he crumpled where he stood.

- 3 -

She spent Friday with Douglass at the house in upstate New York.

There were times when Denice's life seemed starkly unreal to her; days such as these contributed.

Her earliest memories were of the Advanced Biotechnology Research Laboratory in New Jersey; and then of the PKF barracks in New York, and then, briefly, the happy times at the Chandler Complex. During all those years she had been one child among many; that Carl and Jany were her biological parents, and David's, did not seem to matter; Carl and Jany were *everyone's* parents, parents to the near two hundred and forty children who had been placed in their care; Jany in particular had little more time for her own children than for all the others. She and David were only two years younger than the youngest of the Project Superman children. She remembered being cared for by other children; by Trent, and Heather; by

Willie, who was somewhat older than the rest. Of rooms that were, even in the relatively large Chandler Complex, always too cramped, always shared with too many others.

A discontinuity occurred in her memory during the Troubles.

Afterward, the Young Females' Public Labor facility, one room, with forty other girls. When Orinda Gleygavass had at last come for her, the opportunity to share a room with only three other girls had seemed like heaven.

Briefly she and Tarin Schuyler had lived together; for close to three years she had shared an apartment with a girl named Kim Mikonos, at Goddess Home.

In the course of her life she had grown so accustomed to living with others, in small spaces, that she did not truly notice it.

Ripper's house sat on two acres of empty land, shaded—overshaded, Ripper sometimes said—by trees upward of a hundred and fifty years old. The trees blocked any view of the house from the distant road; because she could not see them, Denice could often forget the presence of Ripper's security, four Security Services bodyguards, stationed down at the gate. The house was two stories tall, with ten rooms; Ripper was the only person who lived there.

There were servants somewhere, human rather than 'bots, a gardener and a maid, but Denice virtually never saw them.

His mother was dead; his father, stepmother, and two sisters lived on what could only be called an estate, four klicks further north. Denice had been there once, had not been surprised that his family, though gracious, had not seemed to think much of her.

A simple sign of wealth; not counting the genies she'd been raised with, Ripper was the only person Denice had ever met who had more than one sibling. The license was prohibitively expensive.

They rode horses in the morning, and played tennis in the afternoon. Ripper was a surprisingly good tennis player, and occasionally won; technique counted for a lot, and Denice's immense edge in speed and strength were largely offset by the fact that Ripper had been playing his entire life. Denice had never held a racquet until six months ago.

After dinner they went swimming together under banks of sunpaint so bright it seemed like daylight.

Ripper, after a few laps, sat in the whirlpool at the shallow end of the pool and watched Denice move back and forth through the water. After half an hour, she took a break, came over and joined him in the whirlpool.

"In college, thirty years ago," said Ripper, "I was on the swim team. I swear, Denice, you're a better swimmer than anybody I ever saw in damn near professional level competition."

"Thank you."

"Where did a street kid from New York learn to swim like that?"

Denice ducked her head, came back up with her hair slicked away from her face. She told him as much of the truth as was necessary. "The summer of '72, when I went out to California. I spent most of the summer swimming in the Pacific."

Ripper studied her curiously. "When you were out at the witch's commune—what was it called?"

"Goddess Home."

He was silent, the bubbles swarming up around him. When he spoke, one who did not know how he thought might have thought he was changing the subject. *This is where you've come from* was the unspoken subtext: "Where do you envision yourself going, Denice?"

She shook her head. "I don't know."

"Ever considered getting into politics?"

"You mean as a candidate myself?"

He looked at her steadily. "Yes."

"No. Not really. I don't think I'm qualified."

"You're not, aside from having good people skills and a certain degree of passion. But you're also quite young. You could go back to school."

"Back to school? Douglass, I haven't *been* to school since the Troubles."

He nodded. "And it shows. You're horrible with the InfoNet, you don't write well, you're ignorant about a lot of things you shouldn't be ignorant about. Finances, law, history, practical business." He shrugged. "But you're bright and you work hard and you handle people well. If you wanted to go to school, it could be arranged. A degree in political science, perhaps, and an MBA wouldn't hurt you any. You could also take a degree in Unification Law; it's useful even if you never take the bar exam. Bodyguard is a dead end."

Denice blinked. "Are you *serious*?"

"You look thoroughly horrified, dear. Is going to school so scary?"

"I'd be—Douglass, I'd be *thirty-five* before I got through with all that!"

Unification Councilor Douglass Ripper gazed blankly at her for just a moment, then went into a fit of giggles he simply could not contain. "You'd be—thirty-five," he gasped. "My God, your life would be—*over*." He rolled over on his back in the bubbling warm water, stared up at the black night sky, just visible beyond the haze of the banked rows of sunpaint, and laughed so hard he couldn't breathe. *"Thirty-five!"* He started to say something else, and then simply gasped again, *"Thirty-five!"*

Denice pushed his head under the water.

He came up choking and gasping for air. "Stop! Stop! I give—"

She gave him time to get some air, then pushed him under again and held him down while he fought. Not long, six or seven seconds, though it probably seemed longer to him. He pushed up hard and she let him up.

"I'm sorry," he sputtered, "I'm sorry sorry sorry *sorry*."

She sat back down on the little tile ledge. "You shouldn't laugh at me."

"Obviously not." He coughed once, shook his head slightly. "I'd feel damn foolish being killed by my own bodyguard. How could I possibly explain it to Ichabod?" He waded over to where she sat, sat down next to her and took her hand in his. "I'm sorry, okay?"

Denice nodded. "Okay."

"I won't do it again."

"I'll hold you down longer next time," she warned him.

He looked deeply into her eyes, said very seriously, "I am totally and completely intimidated. I will never *never* laugh at you again."

She kissed him on the tip of his nose. "Good."

"It's just—"

"What?"

"You're the first person I've been in love with since I was twenty years old," he whispered. Denice looked down, nodded once, and Ripper said softly, "I want you to do well."

Somewhere in the city of Encino, slightly northwest of Los Angeles—Callia Sierran did not know exactly where, as she had been brought there in a darkened car—was the estate from which the Temples of Eris had arisen.

The Prophet Harry Devlin had once walked these grounds, had slept in these rooms.

Somewhere inside that estate, in a small empty room with a large bay window, Callia stood with her hands clasped behind her back, and said to the woman who had founded the Erisian Claw, who had recruited Callia and her brother into the Claw, "I don't quite know where to start."

The woman who sat facing her, a teacup of fine china cradled in her lap, was clearly aged. In another time she might have passed for thirty or thirty-five. Today the exquisite grain and slight looseness of the skin at her neck and hands marked her age: past her second round of geriatric skin regeneration, and thereby at least seventy, perhaps older. "Indeed," the woman said after a moment. "I've audited your report. Perhaps your impressions of the meeting would be most helpful."

Domino Terrencia, Callia's immediate supervisor—the woman who had largely raised Callia and her brother after their father's death at PKF hands—stood immediately behind the old woman. She nodded imperceptibly.

Callia interpreted it correctly: *Be brief.* "Yes, ma'am. We met with 'Sieur Obodi downtown, at the law offices of Greenberg and Bass, at eight-thirty this morning." She did not need to elaborate on the point; Greenberg and Bass had fronted for the Rebs for at least twenty years. "He's clearly legitimate; he wants to work with us, and he seems to have the authority to make such a commitment for the Rebs. The list of Rebs who were there was quite impressive; Christian J. Summers, Maxwell Devlin, half a dozen others who are in my report. Perhaps even more significant, ma'am, was who did *not* show. Belinda Singer was not there, and when I asked about her was told that she had retired from administrative duties. Nor was F.X. Chandler present; as you're probably aware, he *did* retire, straight off Earth, about six months ago. He's living in an orbital retirement home and apparently his security is *tough*." She paused. "I think he got on the wrong side of Obodi, and ran."

"Sensible," the old woman remarked. "What were you told about Tommy Boone, and what was your impression of 'Sieur Obodi?"

"Tommy Boone, ma'am, 'sleeps with the fish.'"

"How colorful."

"Old One slang," said Domino quietly.

"The Italians?"

"Yes."

The old woman nodded. "Interesting." To Callia: "Does he?"

"Sleep with the fish?" Callia thought about it. "The Peaceforcer Elite who deserted, Christian Summers—he was present. If Boone were alive, Summers would have stayed in Japan, I think. There was no love between those two. Beyond that I can't say."

"Go on."

Callia said, "Ma'am, 'Sieur Obodi *scares* me. I believe that he is in fact in control of the Johnny Rebs. I found him formidable; a matter of personal bearing. I think you would have to meet him to understand. He speaks with a slight accent, as our reports said, but I *don't* think it's Italian; his accent's nothing like Domino's. He speaks as though he were raised speaking a tonal language such as Japanese. How someone who is clearly not an American has ended up in control of the Johnny Rebs is, frankly, beyond me." Callia paused. "But there's little doubt that he is. When he spoke, people listened the way they used to listen to Tommy Boone. And we already know that Rebs who don't take his orders die. Quickly."

The old woman looked out the window at the tall green fields of marijuana, sipped cold tea from her china teacup, and said without emphasis, "Lovely."

Late on the evening of Saturday, May 2, after a stop in Kansas City to go through the new orientation materials 'Sieur Obodi had designed, Jimmy Ramirez flew a semiballistic into Los Angeles via LAX. He found the trip itself—quite apart from the business on which he had come to Los Angeles—rather exciting.

It was only the second time since escaping the Fringe that he had left the Greater New York area; and that first occasion had merely been a brief trip to Boston some two years prior.

He had never even been on a semiballistic before.

Los Angeles was very nearly as alien as he had expected; a billboard that greeted him upon debarking said: *Welcome to TransCon-Free Los Angeles.*

He picked up his single piece of luggage at the terminal, briefly toyed with and then rejected the idea of hiring one of the human-driven cabs. The lack of TransCon in Los Angeles meant that people *could* drive their own cars, if they wished; it did not mean that it was a good idea. Jimmy knew that his own reflexes, excellent though they were, were no match for those of a carcomp's; the idea of entrusting his life to a driver whose reflexes were almost certainly worse than his own sounded suicidal, not exciting.

Not that he would have admitted it to anyone, but he was afraid of heights anyway.

Old Downtown was a fifteen-minute flight from LAX. Jimmy Ramirez, alone in the cab's backseat, made no pretense of sophistication. He stared out the windows at southwest Los Angeles, stopping every few minutes, when the heights got to him, to settle his nerves. Despite the carpet of lights stretching from one end of the horizon to the other, it all seemed, in some odd sense, curiously rural, and after a moment Jimmy placed it; Los Angeles lacked spacescrapers. Though he saw a few buildings that he guessed to be one hundred or one hundred and fifty floors, surely none of them topped two hundred. He wondered briefly at the lack of spacescrapers, and then leapt to the reasonable conclusion that they had avoided building spacescrapers because of the danger of earthquakes. He was incorrect; a spacescraper with a base that covered two square blocks was quite safe from even the worst earthquake; it was no likelier to fall over than a small mountain. Los Angeles, in 2076, simply did not have the population density necessary to make a spacescraper capable of permanently supporting a population of some 350,000, persons a necessity.

Los Angeles did not sport one of the world's four *uncompleted* spacescrapers, begun, as the other three had been, over twenty years prior, before the Ministry of Population Control had finally succeeded in reversing Earth's explosive population growth.

The cabcomp's tourist program asked Jimmy if he wished to detour to see the shell of L.A.'s only spacescraper.

Jimmy Ramirez snorted. "No. I'm in a hurry. And I've damn straight seen a shell before."

The cabcomp did not try to speak to him again.

The cab came down atop a small black skyscraper in Old Downtown, fifty or sixty stories high. The skyscraper was the twin of another skyscraper immediately beside it.

The parking space the cab came down upon bore the legend, visible from the sky:

In Your Wildest Dreams Don't Even
Think About Parking Here

On the wind-whipped roof, just beyond the row of floodlamps that illuminated the downlot, stood two men Jimmy Ramirez had never met before. Even before he got out of his cab he recognized them both from Max Devlin's descriptions.

The tall one, blond hair gathered away from his face in a tight ponytail, was 'Sieur Obodi, the man who had taken down Tommy Boone. The short, broader one would be Chris Summers, the only non-French Peaceforcer Elite the System had ever seen; the only Peaceforcer Elite who had ever deserted.

After Trent the Uncatchable, Christian J. Summers was, Jimmy knew, the most wanted fugitive in the System. Even Tommy Boone, when he was alive, had never made it past number three on the PKF listing of fugitives.

The PKF did not actually make up a "most-wanted" list; they simply posted rewards.

Trent the Uncatchable's bounty was CU:5,000,000, at a time when the average cost of a day's labor, worldwide, hovered around CU:15.

Christian J. Summers was worth CU:3,500,000.

Summers came forward as the cab's fans died down, fanwash tugging at his clothes. He looked exactly like what he was, an early PKF Elite, from the days when the treatments that toughened the skin had also stiffened the face into a rigid mask. His handshake was dry and very hard.

" 'Sieur Ramirez. A pleasure."

"Likewise."

"Come on." Summers led Jimmy across the windy ferrocrete roof surface, to where 'Sieur Obodi stood waiting for them.

Watching.

It was Jimmy's first impression of Obodi, of the man's eyes upon him as he approached. Even in the relative darkness atop the skyscraper, they gleamed, bright sparks of blue in a deeply tanned, apparently Caucasian face. His lips were thin, curved into a faint smile.

He took a single step forward as Jimmy Ramirez neared him, and held out his hand.

Coming from any other person Jimmy Ramirez had ever known in his life, 'Sieur Obodi's greeting would have sounded nothing but pretentious.

From Obodi it sent a chill down his spine.

"Welcome, James Ramirez," said 'Sieur Obodi, enfolding Jimmy's outstretched hand in both of his, a warm, seductive smile lighting his face, "welcome to your destiny."

At a distance of two kilometers, an avatar of Ralf the Wise and Powerful, safely ensconced in the circuitry of the cab Jimmy Ramirez had taken from LAX, circled around and around the Bank of America Building.

- 4 -

Denice ran through the briefing materials for Australia on the semiballistic, while Ripper dozed.

There were advantages to not needing much sleep; if she had required as much sleep as Ripper, Denice did not know when she would ever have found the time to prepare for anything. When he was awake, Ripper was a full-time job.

"Australia," the briefing began, "yearns for respect."

Its post-Unification history has been one of significant accomplishment. It separated from the British Commonwealth in the years immediately before the Unification. Though the French PKF was characteristically brutal in its pacification of England, Australia fared better; like the French they resented the English, and further had a history of cordial relations with France stretching back to World War I. Though Australia was not among the founding Unification countries, Australia did not contest the Unification, and once the course to the Unification War was clear, made reasonable accommodations with Unification forces.

The Australians have become a significant factor in space travel; one of Earth's largest spaceports is located in the Australian outback.

Australia, despite its relatively small population,

*is a significant electoral resource; almost alone
among modern democracies, Australia requires,
on penalty of a stiff fine, that its citizens
participate in all elections, both local and Unification.
(It has gone to great lengths to make this feasible;
it is one of the few countries in the Unification
that has completely eliminated the ballot box in
favor of InfoNet-based voting.) Given the forty-two
percent turnout that characterizes Unification voters
worldwide, this gives the Australian voter a say
in Unification politics that is significantly out of
proportion to the actual population of the Australian
continent.*

*Native Australians have a distinct neurosis
concerning the traditional lack of respect given
their people by the outer world. Founded by England
as a penal colony in 1788, and used so for the first
eighty years of their existence, Australia
possessed, until the end of the twentieth century,
an insignificant voice in world politics.*

*Since the Unification, this has largely changed;
but the erroneous impression that they have
insufficient say in how Australia is treated by
the outer world, including the Unification proper,
has remained, and is a sensitive subject.*

When Douglass Ripper traveled, he did so with a retinue of
not less than a dozen people; depending on the locale to be visited, his party sometimes ran as high as twenty-five persons.
Denice had been amazed, at first, at the size of his staff. On
any given day she never saw more than a few of them; her first
staff meeting had been a revelation. Over forty people had
shown up: Ichabod, the Chief of Staff; two speech writers, a
Director of Communications, an InfoNet Access Coordinator,
Election Committee Manager, Ripper's personal secretary, the
secretary's secretary, the Deputy Assistant for Executive
Branch Liaison—and people with a dozen other titles, and the
secretaries and aides and assistants of those people.

It was over a month before Denice had even gotten all the names straight.

For the India-Australia-Japan trip, Ripper had taken fifteen people with him; six were bodyguards.

Four of the bodyguards stayed with Ripper in their Canberra hotel room while Ichabod Martin and Denice examined the hall where Ripper was to speak. They went down together, two hours ahead of time.

They did not expect to find anything. The PKF Personal Security squads assigned to Councilor Ripper had marked the room clean that morning, and two different Australian security agencies had double-checked their work. The hall was a large rectangular area, about sixty meters wide, by eighty long, by perhaps six high. A single large double door stood at the south end of the hall, with two smaller doors at the east and west, near the raised speaker's platform.

A PKF Elite stood at each of the three doors.

They did not expect to find anything, but they had not expected to find anything in Portugal either—and therefore had checked Ripper's hotel room rather cursorily.

If the assassin had not exactly been hiding under the bed, he was not far from it. Sometime during the night before Ripper's arrival in Portugal the assassin had checked into the room immediately beneath Ripper's, and cut a small hole through the ceiling and into Ripper's hotel room.

The fact that he was sleeping with Denice probably saved Ripper's life; they were drifting off to sleep when a sound disturbed Denice.

She came awake in motion. She pushed Ripper *hard*, one-handed, from the bed they shared, pushing herself in the other direction with the same movement. Her handgun, a sixteen-shot automatic with explosive shells, sat with a spare clip atop the dresser at the bedside and she reached for it with her left hand as she rolled backward away from the bed—

—the gun and the spare clip leapt from the dresser's surface, into her waiting hand. She came out of the roll, came to her feet firing.

The bed exploded in flame.

There were sixteen shots in the handgun and she wasted the entire clip into a spot on the floor. The clip ejected itself when empty and Denice

the bed is burning, a thin, sharp beam of ruby laser light waving up through the burning bed, stopping when it meets the ceiling above it, flames crawling up from the surface of the bed.

slammed the spare home and fired again.

Ichabod and Bruce appeared in the hotel room's doorway, Excalibur laser rifles in hand. They made the correct decision, pulling Ripper from the hotel room without delay, leaving Denice behind to deal with the threat.

The second clip was empty.

The laser light had ceased.

Where she had fired into the floor the floor no longer existed. Denice could look straight down into the room beneath them, through a hole some half a meter wide.

In the room beneath a man lay sprawled flat on his back, looking up toward the ceiling, a laser rifle clutched in his right hand. She could not tell how badly injured he was, or if he was even conscious; but he was still alive, twitching and moaning and bleeding quite impressively.

Shattered pieces of the floor had cut Denice's legs in half a dozen places, and now the room sprinklers cut in, dousing the fire quickly, washing the blood down her thighs and calves.

Two weeks later, in Canberra, they did not expect to find anything.

Nonetheless they checked.

Denice started at the south end of the hall, carrying a small device that spat deep radar pulses at the walls, looking for odd signatures in the walls—hollow places, spots with unusual density. She ignored the PKF Elite, as the Elite ignored her. Ichabod started up at the north end around the speaker's platform, and worked south.

They met in the middle of the hall about an hour later, an hour before Ripper was due to come down to speak, and sat down together facing one another across the center aisle.

"The balcony area gets closed off?"

The bearded black features bobbed up and down. "Yeah. That shouldn't be a problem. I think we tell hotel security we're taking him down the south maglevs, and then use the north maglevs. We bring him in through the east door. That gives us the smaller part of the lobby to walk through; he won't be exposed to the street for as long as if we go through the main lobby."

Denice nodded. "Works for me."

"Okay. I think we have about ten minutes free. We need to talk."

"I know."

"How are you today?"

Denice looked straight at him. "Could be better, could be worse. I woke up last Tuesday morning feeling—" Denice paused. "*Bad*. Aching. I'm not sure why. That was five days ago, and it's lingered. Today I am, largely, clear and centered. How are you?"

"I'm having problems."

Denice nodded, waited.

Martin sighed. "Personal. You know Terry and I broke up."

"Shawmac? I knew you were seeing him."

Ichabod Martin said, "Things have not been good between us for a long time. Half a year, maybe. But we're both stubborn men and neither of us wanted to give up. Past couple of months—you know you tear each other up toward the end, so that it's easier to let go?"

"Is that how it's done?"

Ichabod shrugged. "Different strokes, I suppose. So anyway, last night we talked for about an hour and decided not to see one another again."

"I am sorry."

"I don't mention it for the sympathy. But I'm not focused. I'm not going to be focused, not today. I talked to John and Bruce already. I haven't mentioned it to Councilor Ripper, and I'm not going to."

"I'll cover your back where I can."

"Appreciate it." Denice waited for what she knew was coming. Martin took a deep breath and said, "How long have you been sleeping with the Councilor?"

"About three months." Denice paused. "I thought you knew, until what happened in Portugal. The way you behaved afterward—that was when I realized you didn't."

Martin shook his head. "No. Perhaps I should have, but I sometimes don't see things other people might. The Councilor's always had his personal bodyguard stay in the room with him while he slept; but the Councilor's real straight, and his bodyguards in the past have always been men. When you started with us I worried about this, but I thought the Councilor was smart enough to refrain." He paused. "This disturbs me a lot. It's unprofessional behavior on your part, I don't think I have to tell you that."

"You don't. I know it."

Martin nodded, accepting it. "I'm more upset with him. Employers shouldn't sleep with their employees. It's bad policy. That he chose to—well, I'm going to speak to him about it. I've been dropping things lately—so have you—and it's left the Councilor tense enough that I've been reluctant to broach this subject with him. But I think I'm going to have to. He should have told me; it's relevant to my job. If he wishes to sleep with you, fine, but you need to cease working for him as a bodyguard."

A flicker of real anger touched Denice. "I don't think you're qualified to make that judgment."

"The Councilor *will* make the judgment, of course. Fortunately it's not my call. But I don't think you can be objective when the man you're protecting is also the man you're sleeping with. Do you?"

"I don't know."

"I don't think so. And I'm going to tell him so when this trip is done."

The anger faded. Denice said, "Thank you for the warning."

"You're welcome. Back upstairs?"

"Yeah."

On the way up, Denice said, "I hope things work out for you."

Ichabod nodded slowly. "I hope the same for you. The Councilor is a very complex man."

"Trust me. I know."

The speech went well. Denice barely listened to it; she stood at the east entrance, next to the young PKF Elite, and watched the crowd.

A small point immediately between her eyes, about a centimeter in, throbbed as though a white-hot iron spike had been driven in there.

She ignored it and watched the crowd burn.

The flames started at their fingertips, bright crawling sheaths of blue. They lit up like neonlaser, made tracings of the nerve networks within the individuals she watched. The glowing blue strengthened as it flowed up toward their skulls, where it blossomed into something improbably reminiscent of the halo of a saint.

She did not hear the speech end, barely noticed Ripper

when he passed by her on the way out of the hall. The genuine anger in his voice when he snapped, *"Wake up,"* on his way by penetrated. She started after him, but he was already fifteen paces ahead of her, out in the east lobby.

If anyone had been waiting for him, Ripper would have died.

Up in the hotel room he exploded. "Damn it to hell, Daimara, you shouldn't be *dropping* things like this. I *know* you're better than this. In the last two months I haven't been able to depend on you, I haven't been able to depend on Ichabod, and I cannot *travel* without both of you! If I can't travel, I can't get elected. If I travel without complete faith in both of you—and right now I don't have that—I can't get up in front of a crowd without wondering if I'm going to have my fucking head blown off by some freaking Johnny Reb wannabe before I'm done speaking, and that tends to detract ever so slightly from my effectiveness as a speaker."

Denice nodded. "I know. It's just—" She made a helpless gesture. "I *don't* know. There's something wrong and I'm not sure what it is."

Ripper looked directly at her. "Is it us?"

"No." Her voice softened. "No. I love you, Douglass. You know that."

"That's not what I'm asking. Is your relationship with me making it impossible for you to do your job?"

Denice shook her head. "No."

"What, then?"

"I don't *know.* I think maybe I'm worried about my friend Jimmy."

Ripper blinked. "What?"

"My friend Jimmy Ramirez," Denice said reluctantly. "I think Jimmy is getting involved with the Johnny Rebs. I'm not sure what to do about it."

Ripper started to sit down on the bed, thought better of it, and dropped down on the sofa near the window. He sat rubbing his temples. "Okay. Let's do a deal. I need you in Japan. I need Ichabod in Japan, and I'm going to talk to him separately." He ceased rubbing his temples, looked up at Denice. "For you, let's do this. When we get back to New York we'll pull all of the Oversite Committee reports, everything in the database. If we're missing anything at all on the Reb buildup, no matter how trivial, we'll requisition it. We'll find out to what extent, if any, your friend is involved in the Rebs. If he's involved we'll file a Notice of Research under his name and put him on the payroll. When the PKF finally does crack them open—whenever the hell that ends up being," Ripper muttered, slightly distracted, "he'll have been protected from the effects of his stupidity. Fair enough?"

"Okay. Fair enough."

Ripper simply looked at her without expression. "Are you going to be on top of things for the rest of this trip?"

"I'll do my best, Douglass."

He nodded wearily. "Okay. Get dressed, we're having dinner with Randall Cristofer and President Greenwood in an hour, and Cristofer's going to want to negotiate at dinner. Aside from the fact that Cristofer owns him I don't know much about Greenwood, but Cristofer himself is a shark and I need to be able to concentrate on him, and *nothing* else."

Denice thought back over the personnel briefing she'd been given for Australia. "Randall Cristofer's one of the primary sources of funds for Australia, isn't he?"

Ripper snorted. "He *is* my Australian organization, the whole damn thing. I have nothing else to speak of on this whole slithy damn continent. At one point I approached a local politician about working with me, just for redundancy; Cristofer found out, got in touch with the man, and told him that if he moved forward with me he'd end up like Harold Holt."

"Say again?"

"Shark food. Relatively famous incident in Aussie politics; one of their Prime Ministers, back when they were a part of the old British Commonwealth, went swimming one day and sharks ate him."

Denice smiled, tentatively. "I see."

Ripper nodded. "Cristofer wasn't joking. Are we done?"

"Yes. Thank you."

"It's all right. Get Ichabod. I need to talk to him too, and it might as well be now."

Denice worked through the briefing materials for Japan on the semiballistic. Japan was a swing vote; Ripper and Sanford Mtumka, Ripper's only real opposition, were running neck and neck in Japanese polls. Like Mexico and PanAfrica, and unlike most other countries in the Unification, Japan was a winner-take-all country; a win of one percent in the general Japanese election translated into a one hundred percent win of Japanese electoral votes.

Denice wondered, briefly, who had written the briefing:

They are in many ways a schizophrenic people. They have a long tradition of militarism, stretching back to the conflict between the Imperial court at Kyoto and the provincial warlords, nearly a thousand years ago. The warlords won that conflict, and set the pattern for an entrenched Japanese militarism that lasted until the end of World War II in 1945, when the United States of America dropped a pair of thermonuclear warheads on the Japanese cities of Hiroshima and Nagasaki.

During the Unification War, Japan, along with much of Asia except China, chose to fight. In some ways they were not damaged so badly as the United States—they did not suffer the city-to-city fighting that was the hallmark of the Unification conquest of the United States—and in some ways they suffered worse: in the summer of '18 the Peace Keeping Force exploded fourteen thermonuclear warheads over Japanese territory.

Nearly six decades later this is a trauma from which the Japanese have never truly recovered. Many Americans think that New York City was bombed by the Unification; this is largely untrue. Tactical thermonuclear warheads were used, during both the Unification and the Troubles; but the yields were quite low. Japan was struck with multimegaton warheads: that Japan is the only country in history to have had thermonuclear weapons used upon it—not once but twice—has left them with a deep aversion to violence.

Today, the Japanese remain a significantly racist people. This is a relevant factor: Ripper, as a Caucasian American, a citizen of the country that

*once defeated Japan in war, is accorded a
significantly greater degree of respect than is,
for example, Sanford Mtumka, a black man.*

*Zhao Pen has an insignificant percentage of the
Japanese vote, and is not expected to get more under
any likely scenario.*

Australia was bad; Japan was worse.

There were no assassination attempts in Japan. A pair of
Red Army ideologs were arrested by the PKF on general suspicion in the week before Ripper's arrival, but nothing came of
it. Nonetheless there were holes in security, gaps in prepared-
ness, and Ripper noticed them. His relationship with Denice
and Ichabod alike degenerated to business pure and simple.

Australia had been a two-day affair; in Japan Ripper gave
fourteen different speeches over the course of four days. His
agenda was tight; under the best of circumstances it would
have been a rigorous schedule. They arrived in Japan on Tuesday, the fifth of May. That Tuesday was the lightest day on Ripper's schedule, with only two speeches scheduled. There were
four on Wednesday, five on Thursday, and three on Friday. By
Wednesday Denice had reached the point where she did not
speak to Douglass unless spoken to, or unless there was some
business communication that needed to take place. Wednesday
night she slept sitting up on the sofa in their hotel room, gun
on the sofa next to her, while Ripper snored alone in the bed.
Thursday Ripper's temper was frayed even further; he awoke
in a foul mood that did not improve, except before crowds, as
the day wore on.

Thursday Ripper spoke twice in Tokyo, once at a rally, once
to a group of fund-raisers, and spoke once each in the cities of
Yokohama, Kyoto, and Kobe.

It happened again in Kyoto.

She stood immediately behind Ripper, handgun holstered
beneath her coat, scanning the crowd, and suddenly the headache was back and the crowd was naked, skinless, a glowing
collection of blue nerve nets; and in the depth of the crowd,
where the people were packed most closely, a Flame arose,
dancing gold with a cold black center, a column of light that
rose up out of the crowd and fountained up into the sky.

She blinked and it was gone, and did not come back.

By the time Ripper's last speech, in the city of Kobe, was done, it was nearly 10:00 P.M. and all of them, including Denice, were exhausted. Ripper fell asleep in the limousine on the way back to their Tokyo hotel. Bruce and John sat together up front; Denice, crowded in the backseat with both Ripper and Ichabod's bearish hulk, found it nearly impossible to relax.

Ripper's skin touched hers, and his dreams, restless and unhappy, were barely perceptible to her, jittering at the edge of her thoughts. Normally she found his thoughts—gentle and disciplined and generally kind—pleasant. But his dreams that night were anything but pleasant.

Denice moved slightly away from Ripper, to break the contact with his skin—was aware of Ichabod noticing it—closed her eyes and tried to sleep.

They returned to Capitol City early Saturday morning, two hours before dawn. Denice saw Ripper safely to the edge of Capitol City. She had the limo stop, said curtly, "Good night," and walked south the four kilometers to Robert Dazai Yo's dojo.

Patrolling PKF stopped her twice, requested her handheld and a retinal check. She endured it patiently and politely—they were checking attitude as much as identity—and continued on when the checks were complete.

It neared dawn when she reached the dojo, walked upstairs to Robert's quarters, and let herself in.

Robert sat where she had expected to find him, waiting for the sun in the center of the mat. Earlier in the night, she knew, he would have worked out; stretched, done weight work and speed training; perhaps, though this was something new to the last decade of his life, he might have danced.

In the last hour before dawn, he sat and meditated.

She took her running shoes off and joined him.

He did not speak while the sun rose, while light flooded in through the high eastern windows, lit the dojo in bright true sunlight. He breathed slowly, and Denice let her breathing match his, felt the tension of the trip draining away from her. She faced Robert, and he faced the sun; the light struck her back and shoulders, and she sat in the warmth and let the tight knots of her muscles relax.

Sometime later Robert said, "You look like something out of a Fringe back alley."

"I feel like hell."

"Ah."

"I love Douglass."

"I know."

"I hate my job."

"I know."

Shadows crawled across the floor of the dojo.

"What are you doing tonight?"

"I have no plans." Denice paused. "My friend Tarin Schuyler is dancing in an off-Broadway play. She asked me to stop by and see it. But I can do that anytime; it'll run a couple of weeks at least."

Robert opened his eyes for the first time. The flat Asian features struck Denice as oddly grave. "You are the best student I have ever had, the only one I have ever thought to teach shiabrè. I have never seen anyone move as you do; until recently I never doubted that what I had to teach, you could learn."

"But—I thought I *had* been learning what you had to teach. Everything you've shown me I've picked up—"

"—astonishingly fast." Robert nodded. "I have never seen anyone learn so fast. But the movement, the motion, is not the discipline of shiabrè, any more than the form of Tai Chi is the point of Tai Chi. Have you never wondered what I mean by shiabrè?"

"You know I have."

"What did you think?"

"I thought it a discipline you had created yourself," Denice said simply. "It is similar to other martial arts I'm familiar with."

Robert nodded. "The movement is not the discipline, but the movement can be imitated, and has. Shiabrè came first. Before karate, before judo, before aiki-jutsu, before the first kenjutsu school ever opened in Japan; before all this, was shiabrè. It is more than an art, more than a martial discipline; it is a direct connection with Deity."

"You sound like a Wiccan."

"Perhaps in its darkest aspects Wicca has some relation to shiabrè; I have not studied Wicca except casually, to know that it, like many religions and disciplines, contains echoes of shiabrè. I do not know Wicca; I know shiabrè, and the discipline, Denice, is very old and very real. When I speak of a direct connection to Deity, I do not do so metaphorically.

Shiabrè, Denice, is the discipline that is called, in English, nightways. And there is a core to it." Robert paused; his gaze was steady. "A Kill."

"I see."

"I do not think you do. Have you ever killed anyone?"

A memory flickered through the back of her mind; she buried it without knowing she had done so. "I don't think so. The boy in Portugal survived."

"I know. When you shot him—did you feel a joy? A soaring?"

"No. I was just scared." Denice did not know what made her say it: "I shot at some Peaceforcers once. And another man died while he was chasing me. But I didn't enjoy it either time."

Robert simply nodded. He did not seem surprised. "I think accidental death would not be the same. If it ever comes to you, the chance to take a life with your own hands, I shall be interested to learn of your response."

Denice Castanaveras said softly, "Killing is wrong."

Robert Dazai Yo smiled at her. "Many people think so," he agreed. "And for most people it is. They don't do it right. If you Kill, I do not doubt you will do so in a most exquisite fashion. A proper Kill, child, is art of the highest order. Someday you will appreciate this." He rose slowly, stood in his white gi facing the sun. "I'm going to bed. Come see me this evening."

"Do you mind if I stay here today?"

Robert walked off the mat. "Feel free. The guest room is empty."

"It's just that Ripper is keyed for my apartment."

Robert shrugged, did not look back. "He paid for it."

Denice said quietly, "Yes. I guess he did."

Robert taught no classes on Saturdays, the one day of the week he had reserved for himself.

Denice spent the day dancing, varying the tempo of the music; classic jazz and roots rock, slower pieces written for the ballet. Fusion music from the turn of the century, and then atonal synth from the '50s; and then Brazilian jazz from the '60s. She moved through the sound like a ghost, lost track of herself in the rhythm of her heart, wrapped herself into the dream of a blue turtle and then pumped up the volume with a screaming rendition of Chuck Renkha's classic '20s scorcher,

"Heat and Love"; moving until her body would no longer move as she wished it to.

Toward lunch she took a break, went upstairs to Robert's bathroom and ran a bath as hot as she could stand it.

Ten months in Ripper's employ had taken its toll; the edge was gone. Perhaps no one else could see it; perhaps even Robert could not see it.

Ten months ago she could have danced all day and not been tired. Today her muscles were tired and the buildup of fatigue toxins in her system was excessive even considering the fact that she'd been up all night.

She soaked in the bathtub for almost an hour. When the water got cool she ran it again; after the bath she took a nap.

At 4:00 P.M. she got up. Robert was awake, puttering around in the kitchen, examining the contents of the slowtime field. "Are you hungry?"

"Yes. What should I eat?"

Robert paused. "Trust your body. What do you *want*?"

"Something alive."

He nodded. "Apples on the roof."

She took the stairs to the roof, plucked and ate two apples. When she had finished both of them, including the cores, she waited ten minutes, decided she wanted a third, and took it.

Robert was done eating when she went back downstairs again; the kitchen had been straightened up and the kitchen's slowtime field turned back on. She went to the guest room, pulled one of the black gis Robert kept there for her, and donned it. She went downstairs barefoot, found Robert setting up at the edge of the mat.

He laid a flat slab of long, uncured wood atop a pair of bricks, to raise the wood slightly off the floor. Upon the wood he placed certain items, in a certain pattern. He did not look at Denice as he worked. He laid the items out slowly, one by one, as though engaged in ritual. When he was done Robert Dazai Yo said softly, "Do you recognize these items?"

"They look like the tools on a Wiccan altar."

"They would. They are not." Without moving he gestured to Denice to join him on the other side of the board. "Center with me."

Denice sank into lotus, met Robert's eyes, and began breathing in rhythm with him. Her breathing and heartbeat dropped into rhythm together; she was aware of the moment when the cycle of her breathing matched Robert's. With one

hand he reached forward, took one of the button mushrooms
he had laid on the surface of the wood, and ate it.

Denice did not question; she did the same.

The mushroom was dry and chalky, and otherwise without
taste.

"Give me your hands."

Denice reached forward and placed her hands in Robert's.
His eyes held steady on hers.

"Speak with me. *Rho! Etra shivat—*"

"*Rho! Etra shivat—*"

"*—elor ko'obay k'shia—*"

"*—elor ko'obay k'shia—*"

"*—vata elor ko'obay shiebran.*"

"*—vata,*" said Denice Castanaveras, "*elor ko'obay shiebran.*"
Robert's hands tightened around hers. "*Enshia, ensitra.*"
Swiftly: "Do not repeat these words."

Denice stopped with her mouth open. "Why not?"

"Later. How do you feel?"

"Light. Floating. From the dancing earlier, I think. Otherwise nothing." Denice paused. She did not know what made
her add, "Not yet."

"Close your eyes and continue holding my hands. We will
wait for darkness together."

I am the Name Storyteller.

I sit at the edge of reality and watch my past, watch Denice
Castanaveras, my ancestor, the grandmother of the man who
did and will found the House of November.

Earth turns slowly away from Sol; the shadow of the planet
falls across New York City, across a small dojo in Greenwich
Village.

In that room, a Master of the oldest discipline on Earth, the
creature of my Enemy in this time, prepares to test the finest
student he has ever seen, or ever will.

When there is no light in the room, no light from any source
except the distant street lamps, barely visible through the
dojo's high windows, Robert Dazai Yo, one of the six living
night faces in all the Continuing Time—not counting time trav-
elers, which I suppose I should not—releases Denice Castanaveras's hands.

From a matchbook that says Jack's Happy Time Bar he takes
a match, and lights the single red candle in the center of the al-

tar, and then the pile of orange incense. The smell of orange blossoms rises from the altar's surface.

Robert ascends from lotus in a single smooth motion. "Are you ready?"

"Yes."

"Stand." She does so, and Robert says again, "How do you feel?"

Her eyes, the eyes of a lord of the House of November, are open, brilliant green even in the dim light from the flickering candle. "As though something is going to happen. Not nervous—just ready. The light is so beautiful."

"Silence." He speaks in shiata, though the accent is corrupted by the long separation from the mother tongue. Denice stands motionless in the darkened dojo. *"Silence and darkness: these are nightways."*

Denice stares at him.

Robert says in English, "Begin."

She takes several steps backward, raises herself onto her toes, and brings her right knee up to her chest with immense grace. She pivots without haste, bringing her center of gravity closer to the floor. Her right foot extends in a slow kick directly up to the ceiling, and she holds the position, toes of her right foot pointing toward the sky, for three breaths.

Then she Moves, like the Dancer she is.

A controlled explosion, right knee back down to her chest, pulling her arms in from an extension of twenty centimeters, turns the angular momentum from the inpulled arms into a tight spin, and kicks with her right foot, three times, one hundred and twenty degrees apart on the circle of the spin. Her right foot comes down, touches briefly, adds momentum to the spin and she moves back toward him, with a series of kicks and punches that no human of her time, not Yo, not the Dancer Sedon, no one, could have matched for grace, for speed, for accuracy.

She ceases moving with almost shocking abruptness, all at once, an engine coming to rest, and stands in front of her teacher. She is not breathing quickly, she is not perspiring.

After a moment she says, "Well?"

Robert does not look away from her. The red candle continues to burn; neither the white nor black candles have come alight. "How do you feel?"

"Like something is going to happen."

"Joy? Anger?"

"No." Denice pauses. "I feel very peaceful."

Robert Dazai Yo does not look away from her. He speaks with the deliberate gravity of a man who is considering every word. "There is in what you do . . . a correctness of movement I have never seen before; not in students, not in myself . . . not in *my* teacher. And yet it is wrong." He is silent for a long while. "I have not often discussed the words I use with you, which are not French or English or Japanese. They are the tongue that is called shiata, or, in English, nightways." Robert's shoulders move slightly beneath the black cloth of his gi. "There has been no point to teaching you of our history, such as I know of it, while I have been uncertain that the discipline itself would take. You were—brought to me, Denice. By Orinda Gleygavass, who was the servant of my master. And I was instructed to teach you; that you would be the student some shivata never see, the one who would learn that which I teach."

Denice Castanaveras waits motionlessly.

"There is a legend, a part of our teachings," says Robert, "that before there was shiabrè, the discipline of life bent into death, there was shia, the dance of life itself. I see, in what you do, that dance." He turns away from her, kneels, and snuffs the light of the bloodred candle, spreads the burning orange incense across the wood until it is extinguished. He does not look at her again. "I do not see nightways." He begins to remove the tools from the altar's surface, carefully reversing the order in which they were laid there. "I think perhaps there is only shia in you."

Dateline: *Shawmac* on 58-1022

So the Unification Council wants to make it illegal for AIs to own property. This is a small bill; not important; expected to pass without fuss, hopefully without notice. Unification Councilor Pena of Puerto Rico introduced it, which should tell you something to start with; Pena is about as bought-and-paid-for a politician as can be found in Capitol City, which is saying something mildly impressive.

Bill 58-1022 goes by the name of "A Regulatory Procedure for Confiscating Property Owned by Artificial Intelligences." Basically what it is, is a way the Unification (specifically, the scum-sucking and relentless PKF) can confiscate any piece of property it wants, *without due process, without going through the courts; the Peaceforcers file a notice with the new regulatory body created by this bill, stating—without any evidentiary requirements—that some item or real property is believed owned by an Artificial Intelligence. As the statute is written, this creates a "rebuttal presumption" of guilt on the part of the persons whose property has been confiscated. And this presumption may be damn difficult to overcome. Any of you out there want to give it a shot? The Tax Board has prevailed on similar cases—built upon "rebuttable presumption" rather than "proof beyond a reasonable doubt."*

So the rebuttal presumption of guilt has been inflicted upon the victim's property—which the PKF DataWatch then proceeds to confiscate.

That's it.

That's the whole bill.

There is no provision for return of improperly confiscated property.

If this bill passes, it will, not coincidentally, be the end of The Rise and Fall of the American Empire, *an* anti-Unification Board generally believed to be owned by an AI.

Your representatives vote on this evil property-confiscating bill—Bill 58-1022—on Tuesday. You know what to do.

STAND UP——FIGHT BACK——SPREAD THE WORD.

In an auditorium a kilometer beneath the surface of Capitol City, Mohammed Vance stood in the midst of the blackness and waited for the holograph.

The image of the person who had given his name as Sedon of the Gi'Suei hovered next to him, life-size. It came from Sedon's brief imprisonment at the PKF Detention Center near Amiens.

Vance walked around the image, imprinting the man's bone structure deep in his memory. "Very good," he said at length. "Next."

The image that appeared was slightly fuzzy; two-dimensional, taken at a distance of some two hundred meters. The man was stepping from a limousine, hurrying with half a dozen known Rebs toward a parked semiballistic capsule. His hair was long and blond, tied in a ponytail; his skin was the color of a Caucasian with a deep tan, and his eyes were bright blue.

But the bone structure had not been altered at all. The same high cheeks, the same long Roman nose.

Vance said quietly, "Lights up, dim."

Three persons stood in the room with him; Alexander Moreau, Hand to the Secretary General; PKF Elite Commander Christine Mirabeau; and Terence LeFevre, the current appointed head of the Ministry of Population Control.

Vance largely ignored LeFevre; this was not a civilian affair, and if he had had his way in the matter, LeFevre would not have been invited to the briefing. It was not even a matter of the customary rivalry between the PKF and the Ministry; Vance did not trust LeFevre, did not consider him competent. If the Ministry had sent Gabrielle Laronde, the Ministry's senior nonelected official, Vance would have been little better pleased; except that, if business with the Ministry were required, Gabrielle would have conducted it in a professional manner.

LeFevre was merely a politician.

Vance turned to Alexander Moreau, one of the few persons who had been present when Sedon's bubble had been opened for whom Vance had any respect whatsoever. "What do you think, Hand Moreau?"

Moreau was young for a Hand, in his thirties, and that was due, unquestionably, to the name he had been born to; nonetheless he was modestly talented, and Vance had some hope that he might one day, after some seasoning, serve as the first French Secretary General since Tènèrat, some forty-five years prior.

Moreau shrugged. A thin, intense young man, he spoke in quick, chopped sentences that gave the impression he was answering off the top of his head. "It looks like him to me."

"Christine?"

"I never met Sedon. I've done no more than view the holos of him." Vance's superior shrugged. "If you feel it is him, I will back your judgment in the matter."

Mohammed Vance nodded. He did not even consider requesting LeFevre's opinion. "I would like to submit to the Secretary General a request to place M. Obodi on the bounty listings at CU:six million."

LeFevre whistled. "That's a million more than Trent the Uncatchable lists for."

Vance did not even look at the man. "Don't call him that. He's not. Hand Moreau, I will arrange the request. I will expect it upon the Secretary General's desk within a day."

Moreau nodded. "It will be. The SecGen's a Christian, you know; he'll be in Church tomorrow. You probably won't receive a response until Monday."

"That's acceptable. We are done. Christine, may we speak privately?"

"Certainly." The two Elite headed for the door together, and might have left then had Elite cyborgs had less excellent hearing; Alexander Moreau said softly to Terence LeFevre, "I wonder how Trent's going to feel about that."

Vance stopped in midstep. After a long moment he turned back. "Hand Moreau? I beg your pardon?"

The young Hand blinked. "Yes?"

"What did you say?"

"Ah—I wondered how Trent would feel about not being Number One."

"I thought that was what you'd said. Perhaps," said Vance after a pause, "you should concern yourself less with the feelings of enemies of the Unification, and more with the performance of your job." Vance's voice did not rise, his expression did not alter. His glittering black eyes stayed fixed upon Moreau's. "If I stood in your skin, I would be rather more concerned about the possibility of being prosecuted for dereliction of duty, than about whether one of the Unification's enemies is upset over being judged somewhat less dangerous than another of our enemies."

Simply from the tone of his voice, Mohammed Vance might have been discussing what he had eaten for breakfast.

Hand Moreau swayed slightly when Vance was done: Vance's political enemies had an unpleasant habit of ending up unfortunately, accidentally dead. "Yes, Commissionaire. I will take your advice."

Vance made a dismissive gesture and turned away again. "See you do. This briefing is closed."

They spoke together in the only place in all of Capitol City that Vance knew, for a fact, did not possess listening devices; there would have been no point to it.

Beneath the air vents that fed the Capitol City spacescraper in which the Peace Keeping Force was headquartered, standing motionless, heads together like lovers in the tornado roar of the wind, Mohammed Vance and Christine Mirabeau whispered in one another's artificial ears.

Mirabeau said, "What is it?"

"Secretary General Eddore continues to refuse us permission to break the Johnny Rebs."

"Yes."

"Why?"

Mirabeau shook her head, just a fraction. "I don't know, Mohammed. He says he has a private investigation ongoing, which will allow him to end any threat from the Rebs."

"Do you know anything about this investigation?"

Elite Commander Mirabeau whispered, "No."

"Christine, I am not convinced it exists."

Mirabeau said slowly, "Nor I, Mohammed. Nor I."

The following Tuesday morning, four hundred million kilometers away, in the depths of the Asteroid Belt, two Security Services guards stood immediately inside the airlock door of the largest recording studio off Earth itself, laser rifles at the ready.

"Are you Trent?"

The young man floating in front of the airlock, wearing a scalesuit whose chest bore a painting of a river of blood running through a deeper red jungle, said, "Yes."

"Look into the light."

"I'm here for breakfast," Trent explained. The laser flashed through the faceplate of Trent's helmet, played over the retina of his right eye.

The guard nearer Trent, wearing a scalesuit much like Trent's except that it was stripped clean down to the metal, said, "You're Trent."

"I said I was."

The guard gestured Trent through, commenting, "Nice design."

"It's a painting I stole once."

"What's it called?"

"*Je Suis le Fleuve,*" said Trent, going inside. "I'm going to steal it again someday."

After Trent was gone, the two guards stood silently together.

Finally one guard said, "I hear he walked through a wall once."

The other guard simply snorted.

She greeted him as he entered her bedroom with the words, "They're voting on the AI property bill today. Looks like it's going to pass."

Trent shrugged. "It will."

Mahliya Kutura nodded, slightly distracted. "Also, you got bumped from number one on the PKF's bounty list."

"Say what?"

The young woman generally recognized as the greatest living musician in the System floated in midair, showing herself off to advantage in a pair of green shorts and a white bikini top. She was turned slightly away from Trent and about eighty degrees off his vertical. She did not pay much attention to Trent; the wisp of a new melody floated in the back of her mind, and she knew that with a little gentle encouragement she could get it out of her skull and into the synthesizer. So it was that it took a moment for Trent's response to penetrate, and she repeated, "They bumped you from number one. The most wanted fugitive in the system is the new head of the Johnny Rebs. They're offering CU:six million for his capture. They announced it this morning." She paused, auditing the article floating forty centimeters in front of her eyes. "Fellow named Obodi."

Trent stared at her. "They can't do that."

She stared back into his almost upside-down eyes. "Why not?"

"I—I—I *worked* for this. I've killed Peaceforcers Elite, I blew up half of Peaceforcer Heaven. I—"

"You didn't do either of those things," Mahliya said reasonably. "Garon fell, it was an accident, I've heard you say that."

"Well yes but—"

"And Commissioner Vance blew up Spacebase One after you *told* him it was booby-trapped, he should have listened. I've heard you say that too."

It stopped Trent for just a second. "Well, the *Peaceforcers* say I did those things. It seems to me that if I'm getting blamed for them, I might as well get the credit for it. By Harry, this isn't *fair*."

"The PKF isn't noted for being fair, Trent."

"That's easy for *you* to say," Trent muttered. "I stole the LINK," he said abruptly. "I *did* that. And then I walked through a wall and ran away and embarrassed them *badly*."

"That's true," Kutura conceded.

"Shouldn't that *count* for something?" Trent demanded. "Wouldn't you think that would count?"

Kutura looked at him for a moment. Trent was the only person she knew who was as famous as she was—if in different circles; she doubted Commissioner Vance would recognize her name—and if you figured his net worth as including the bounty on his head, which she did, then he was also the only person she knew who was worth as much as she was. Which was perhaps a juvenile thing to even consider, but still; her wealth seemed to matter to everyone she met these days except Trent, and she supposed that must be the reason for it.

He was her age, twenty-five; she rather liked him and was thinking about sleeping with him.

Unfortunately he occasionally exhibited terrible, *terrible* ego problems, almost as bad as her own. "You know," said Mahliya Kutura after a moment, "if you're going to sulk over this, I really wish you'd do it somewhere else."

Trent looked as though he'd been slapped. "All right. Fine. Just *fine*."

"Seriously. You're ruining my breakfast, and I haven't even *had* it yet."

Without saying anything further Trent stalked back out; a good trick in free fall.

Obviously, thought Mahliya Kutura after he was gone, *couldn't think of a good exit line.*

Late at night on Monday, May 18, 2076, Callia Sierran and her younger brother Lan arrived at a farm in Iowa.

The farm was a Johnny Reb stronghold. The fields around the farmhouse itself were planted with corn, row upon row of tall corn, stretching away toward the horizon, a sight such as Lan and Callia, raised in cities across the world, had never seen before in their lives. About a hundred meters of space had been cleared all around the farmhouse; automated items of farm equipment that neither of them could identify, large and bulky, were parked around one end of the farm.

On the downlot in front of the house were several cars.

They brought their car down on a gentle incline of hillside, two kilometers from the farmhouse, and Lan scanned the structure with imaging binoculars. "Six cars. Hot engines on four of them . . . the one on the left is Domino's." He passed the binoculars to his older sister.

Callia glanced through the binoculars, handed them back. "Let's head in."

The car lifted, moved forward.

They met in a large conference room several floors beneath the surface. There were eight people gathered together in the conference room, seated in a rough circle with Rebs on one side of the conference table, Claw on the other. Four bodyguards, two each from the Claw and the Rebs, stood on opposite sides of the door, watching each other.

The Reb lawyer said, "I think perhaps we should introduce ourselves before beginning."

Domino Terrencia said softly, "Feel free."

The lawyer took it as acceptance. "My name is James Ramirez. I have a degree in Unification Criminal Law. You may know of me; I've been in the Public Defender's office in New York City for the last four years. I've had occasion to serve as the criminal defense for, I think, two of your people. Instances when you didn't want to use a lawyer with known sympathies. I've done much the same for our own people over the course of the last few years. I quit that job a week ago and went full-time here." He gestured to the man sitting next to him. "This is 'Sieur Obodi. To my left is Christian J. Summers, and to his left is Akira Hasegawa. I don't think Mister Summers requires an introduction; 'Sieur Hasegawa is here representing Mitsubishi of Japan, the company that has maintained Mister Summers' nonbiological components for the last twenty years or so." He paused. "Max Devlin wasn't able to get away. He's been made by the PKF and he's being watched too closely. We're going to pull him free in the near future; if he were available, he'd be at this table now. Tommy Boone will not be here, as I believe you were told two weeks ago." Ramirez paused again. "That covers us."

"Very well." Domino spoke rapidly, aggressively. "I am Domino Terrencia. I am the second-in-command in the Claw. You've met Callia; the young man is her brother Lan. If you don't know who—"

"My dear." The old woman sitting at Domino's side made a dismissing gesture with one hand; Domino Terrencia ceased speaking instantly. "I will introduce myself." The pale blue eyes fixed themselves upon the man seated across the table from her, upon 'Sieur Obodi. She spoke without blinking, without looking away; there might have been no one in the room but themselves. "My name is Nicole Eris Lovely. I am eighty-six years old and when I was forty-two I founded the Erisian Claw. I have seen seven different men lead the Johnny Rebs during the time since I founded the Claw. All seven of those brave, patriotic, ambitious men are now dead, and I am still here. That's who I am." She smiled a gentle, polite smile at the Rebs across the table from her, at Obodi. "Who the fuck are you?"

- 6 -

Denice stood rigidly in front of Ripper's desk and, with a growing sense of despair, listened to him talk.

"I'll make this as quick as I can, because I don't like going back on a promise and I'm going to do that here. There's not a damn thing I can do for your friend Ramirez." Douglass added, gently, "I am sorry. I'm not sure beating around the bush here would be any kindness; your friend is going in front of a firing squad. Go back to your office and read the report. The Rebs and Claw had a meeting recently, top level on both sides, apparently to determine if they're going to work together. The PKF doesn't know where it was held, but they have a list of the people who supposedly attended the meeting." Ripper paused as though he found it genuinely difficult to continue. "I'm really sorry. Ramirez's name is on it."

She sat in her office and read through the report, holo-stamped Eyes Only in pale blue on every page. There were stock holos and thumbnail bios of several of the principles attached to the report:

Lan and Callia Sierran, a brother-and-sister team who had, Denice read, worked with Trent during the theft of the Lunar Information Network Key, back in '69. Callia was a martial arts and small weapons expert; her brother had planted bombs that had killed perhaps a dozen PKF, possibly one Elite, and better than twenty civilians.

Next, a rather old holo of an Italian woman named Domino Terrencia; relatively high in the Claw, no one knew quite how high. Her bio said she had worked as a liaison with the SpaceFarers' Collective, and had served two terms as Vice Mayor of Bessel-Free Luna, a Free Luna city sponsored by a Belt CityState corporation.

There was a bio, but no holo, of Nicole Lovely, the woman who had founded the Erisian Claw. Denice skipped it, turned the page, and found herself staring at a holo of Jimmy Ramirez.

"Make me a promise, Denice?"

"Done."

"Don't you want to know what it is?"

Jimmy, of course. "I do know."

"Oh." After a moment he nodded. "All right. But don't let him know you're watching out for him. He wouldn't like that."

James Ramirez, the biography said. Ex-gang member, probably the Fringe Temple Dragons; rumored to have known Trent the Uncatchable, though this is suspect information that has not been verified. Served in the New York City Public Defender's office

*since 2072; since 2074 as Assistant Public Defender
for the City of New York. Quit abruptly on April
30 of this year. A known associate of former NYC
Police Chief Maxwell Devlin; a core member of
the Johnny Rebs for six years.*

Denice closed the report, sat alone in her office and stared into
emptiness.

Six years.

He'd never mentioned a word of it to her.

She searched back, remembering the time after Trent had
left Earth, the two years when she had seen Jimmy nearly every day, trying to recall a moment when he had tried to sound
her out, when he had made any attempt at all to interest her in
the Rebs.

And could not.

It struck her again, without warning, the horrible emptiness
that came upon her so often these days. She sat alone in her office and thought about Jimmy Ramirez saying, "I love you."

She found herself coming to her feet; tried to remember
whether she knew anything that could, in the hands of the
Rebs, damage Douglass Ripper. She had difficulty ordering her
thoughts, but she could not think of anything at the moment. *If
they can't hurt him, I can go.*

She wanted to hit something so badly her hands shook.

Instead she went back up to Douglass Ripper's office.

Ripper was in a meeting with Ichabod and a webdancer, a
woman named Sally Cunningham, who was largely responsible
for maintaining the expert system that ran Ripper's campaign.

Denice entered without knocking, made the long walk
through the illusion of an Arab desert to Ripper's desk.

Ripper looked up at her approach.

"I need to take a week off."

Ripper shook his head. "No. And don't interrupt me right
now, I'm busy."

"I have something I have to do, Douglass. I need the time."

Denice saw Sally Cunningham take notice of the "Douglass," saw Ripper notice Cunningham noticing. The muscles in
Ripper's jaws tightened. "Excuse me, Sally." He looked straight

at Denice. "The answer is no, Daimara, and I don't care to discuss it any further. Certainly not now."

Denice ignored the hint. "This is important. I need you to say yes."

Ripper took a deep breath, held it for a five-count, and released it. Denice could see him holding back the anger, and somewhere deep inside her, beneath the emptiness and the pain, a part of her waited eagerly for the anger to be released, so that she might—

"I can't do that," Ripper said finally. "I need you here. If this is about Ramirez, and I'm sure it is, perhaps we can arrange to send a team from the MPC's Special Tasks after him. I'll call in a favor for it that I'm owed over there. If we do that, if we get Ramirez out without too much trouble, we might—*might*—get him a sentence for Public Labor. I'll see what I can do. But I can't let you go. Not now."

"I can't take that for an answer. I have a question I have to ask Jimmy. And—I made a promise to someone. I can't break it, it's the only thing that person ever asked me to do."

"I'm not giving you leave."

Denice almost hesitated: "I quit."

"You can't," he snapped. "You have a contract."

Sally Cunningham sat watching the entire thing, completely without pretense; Ichabod Martin sat with his eyes closed, as though he were not even there.

The emptiness inside her spoke, using her voice: "I'm sorry, Douglass. Are you really going to sue me?"

He shook his head after a moment, a quick jerky movement. "No. I'll have your office cleaned out for you, and all your personal effects sent to Robert's. Do you want to keep the apartment?"

"We can talk about it when I get back."

"All right." They stared at one another for a long moment, and then Ripper said, in a voice that lacked any steadiness at all, "Go. I have business to take care of."

She turned and walked out through the bright sunlight and the drifting Arabian sands.

On a morning of hazy sunshine they sat together on the grass in Central Park, beneath a shade tree, and watched the traffic go by: the people on foot; hovercabs, bicyclists; a man carrying a harp roller-skated back and forth along the bike path to the south.

Occasional joggers ruined their knees on the ferrocrete running paths.

Maxwell Devlin, once Chief of Police for the City of New York, wore a gray sweatsuit the same color as his hair; only his beard still contained some of his natural brown. Denice did not know for sure how old Devlin was. From his skin she would have guessed no more than one series of geriatric treatments, if that. Fifty, perhaps. Whatever his age, he appeared quite fit; thinner than when he had been on the force, with considerably better color.

She could see the faint outline of a Personal Protection System harness beneath his sweatsuit.

Denice had not seen him in over four years, since before the MPC's Agent McGee had chased her out of New York.

From where they sat Denice could see over fifteen Peaceforcers; about twice the usual number for Central Park at the time of day.

"It's for me, of course. They're pretty sure I'm with the Johnny Rebs, and they're harassing me. Have been for the last few months." Devlin shrugged, plucking a strand of grass. "They have no evidence, or they'd have me brain-drained and been done with it. But they haven't been able to get a court order, and they won't."

"I'm glad to hear it."

Devlin smiled at her, a good smile that took in his lips and cheeks and brought crinkles to his eyes. "I'm a careful man. Now, there's no place near here that the PKF can set up a shotgun mike, and my PPS says that there aren't any midget spyeyes it can detect, but I expect that'll change soon. We need to do our business now." He paused, said, "How's Trent?"

"I never hear from him."

Mac Devlin nodded. "I wish he'd come back. We could use him."

Denice said slowly, "He thinks what you're doing is wrong."

"I know." Devlin sighed. "A lot of people do. Even a lot of Americans. I doubt there's been a time since the Civil War this country has been so deeply divided over one issue."

"I wouldn't know. History isn't my strong point."

"What can I do for you, Denice?"

"I want to join the Rebs."

"I thought so. Why?"

Denice's answer was nothing less than the truth. "I'm disenchanted with what I'm doing. And I think I can be of service. Beyond that, if you want to hear me spout Reb cant back to you, I can."

Devlin watched her carefully. "If I send you, you'll end up talking to an analyst with a truth plate in each hand. I know you've been working for Ripper; if you have some idea of doing anything other than making a complete commitment to our work, don't go. Where I'm sending you, if they think you're lying they'll put you up against a wall and shoot you."

"I'm ready to go. I'm ready to go right now."

Devlin smiled a genuinely friendly smile. "All right. Lord knows, we can use people of your caliber. You know L'Express restaurant?"

"I've been there once."

"Be there tonight at five-fifteen. Bring the infochips from your handheld, but don't bring the handheld; you'll be provided with one that doesn't call out."

"I'll be there."

"Don't be late." As she rose to leave, Devlin said, "Oh, one last thing."

"Yes?"

"Ramirez asked me to tell you, if you came, that he was proud of you."

"What?"

Devlin repeated himself.

"Oh . . . thank you."

It was not until an hour later that she realized, for the first time in two days, the ache in her heart had lessened somewhat.

She was greeted by a middle-aged woman in a black evening gown. " 'Selle Daimara?"

"Yes. I have a reservation."

The maître d' nodded. "Please follow me." She led Denice back toward the rear of the restaurant, past a row of private booths; a door leading into the kitchen curled open, and the maître d' gestured Denice through.

The door uncurled behind her.

A young man wearing a cook's apron gestured to her to follow, and turned away without waiting to see if she had. He led her back past rows of automated kitchen equipment that Denice did not recognize; it occurred to Denice that she had never been inside a restaurant kitchen before. A pair of bounce tubes were positioned toward the rear of the kitchen; the young man gestured toward the right-hand bounce tube.

Denice stepped in and dropped.

She came to a stop after about ten seconds, and stepped out into Level G of an underground parking structure. There were relatively few cars parked on that level; a single car, a black Chandler sedan with a tinted canopy, had its headlights on. Denice walked to the car; the canopy rose at her approach.

The young man waiting for her, who had been auditing text on his handheld in the backseat of the car, was about her own age, perhaps a bit older. He was not, to Denice's surprise, a Reb; he wore a necklace with an Erisian medallion on it.

His long, flowing brown hair hung down well past his shoulders; his grayish green military fatigues were just a bit too stylish for Denice to find the image convincing; in all he looked as though he belonged on a dance floor.

He stood up as the canopy rose away from him. "You're Denice?"

"Yes."

He gestured at the seat next to him. "Get in. It's a long drive, and we need to get started." He flipped the handheld closed, stored it in his coat pocket, and held out his hand. What he said then did not surprise her; she had recognized him by then, from his holo, which she had seen for the first time yesterday. "I'm Lan Sierran."

Before nightfall she was sitting in the back of a covered truck, in the dark, headed for Reb headquarters in Iowa.

Before morning she was there.

- 7 -

Denice supposed that being interrogated by one of the Erisian Claw's top people was a compliment.

Callia Sierran impressed Denice.

They sat together several floors beneath the surface of the

earth. A dark, middle-aged man whom Denice had been introduced to as Bennett Crandell sat with them, listening. She supposed that Crandell was a Reb, there to watch Callia as much as Denice; the alliance between the Rebs and the Claw was recent enough that there could not yet be much trust between them.

An American flag hung upon one wall; a pair of holocams, mounted near the ceiling, recorded the scene.

The entire thing was so strongly reminiscent of her first meeting with Ichabod Martin that it gave Denice a momentary shiver.

Callia Sierran was about thirty. Aside from that, and minor exterior details such as hair and skin color, she reminded Denice of herself. She was Denice's height, with much the same build. Denice was certain she was in better condition than Callia, but it was a relative thing; Callia was so finely toned that she put to shame many of the professional dancers Denice had known during her career, with muscles such that Denice knew the woman must work out two or three hours a day.

Remembering Callia's biography, she wondered briefly if Trent had slept with her; Callia was entirely his type.

She wore combat fatigues of the same cut as Lan's, except that on her they looked like work clothes.

Callia's eyes were the same color, exactly, as her own.

Callia Sierran said mildly, "You quit?"

"Yes."

"Did you tell anyone where you were going?"

"My teacher, Robert. I told him I *was* going, not where. He'd have guessed anyway, and he's as close to family as I have."

"Why did you quit?"

Neither Callia nor Bennett Crandell appeared to be, so far as Denice could tell, actively monitoring the truth plates Denice held; therefore, unless one of them had an implanted inskin InfoNet link, someone else, some*where* else, was. "I was—am—disenchanted with Ripper." It came to her with surprise that she could say that in all honesty. "And I think that what the Rebs are doing is morally correct. I'm not sure that it's *smart*; you'll understand that, given that I've been working for Douglass Ripper. I've seen a lot of the inner workings of the PKF—Ripper sits on the PKF's Oversite Committee, I'm sure you know—and they are a deeply impressive organization."

"They are, yes. You understand this is an irrevocable decision, that once you've come among us you can never, *never* leave. If you try we'll kill you."

"I know. 'Selle Sierran, this is my country. My *home*. I don't like what's been done to it. I don't like being interrogated on the street in my hometown by French PKF, for no better reason than the fact I'm an American. I spent four years in Public Labor and I have no love for the Unification."

"Can you tell me the reservations you have regarding joining us? And don't feel afraid to express reservations; we all have them."

Denice thought about it, was aware after a bit that Callia was waiting for her to reply, and said slowly, "Do you know how sometimes you don't know what you think until somebody asks you?"

Callia Sierran said seriously, "Yes. I do."

"The great reservation I have regarding the Rebs, or the Claw for that matter, the reservation that I have *always* had, is that I do not believe you can win." Denice Castanaveras said, with utter truthfulness, "If you could convince me that your rebellion has any chance at all, I'd commit. Completely."

Callia studied her. "We've done that before, on occasion, when the person who had questions was someone whose skills, or knowledge, were important to us. In your case, presuming the balance of this interview is satisfactory, I think we would be more than willing to brief you. You have knowledge we need and skills we can use."

"Skills?" Denice looked at her in surprise. "I don't want to misrepresent myself to you. I'm only a dancer who's had occasion to work as a bodyguard, 'Selle Sierran. I don't know what skills you think I have, but outside dance and the martial arts I've never received training at much of anything. I read fairly well, write poorly; I'm terrible with the InfoNet. I haven't been formally schooled since I was nine. If you're thinking that I know much about weapons, you're wrong there too; I've been trained with small arms, but that's about it."

Callia chuckled. "*No skills?* You are the top student of one of the deadliest men I've ever met in my life. If I wanted to kill Robert Yo, or you, I'd do it with a bomb, or else with a sniper rifle from as far away as I could possibly get. And I'm *good*, 'Selle Daimara. I saw you at a tournament once, about six years ago. I *guarantee* you, you have skills we can use. Now, are you ready to continue? We've got many hours of this before we'll be done."

"Hours? Surely you don't interrogate everyone this way— you wouldn't have time."

Bennett Crandell laughed aloud.

Callia said dryly, "Let's call it an interview, 'Selle Daimara. I rarely interview *anyone* myself. The people who do this tend to be lower echelon. But we rarely, you understand, get the personal assistants of Unification Councilors—people with security clearances—coming over to us. You either have information we can *use*, or you're a plant and you're going to die before the day is out."

Denice stared at Callia. "Let's get it done."

Denice knew, because she had lightly Touched the people around her for the information, that she was in a structure beneath a farmhouse in the state of Iowa. Its sheer size amazed her; during her first day there she met not less than forty people, and saw over a thousand in the halls and corridors. Everything was somewhat oversized; the hallways were wide enough for four or five people to pass abreast, and the ceilings, which glowed with bright sunpaint, ran about four meters high.

She could not understand how such a large operation could be going on completely undetected by the PKF.

Lan Sierran, who showed her to her room and gave her a brief tour of the unsecured areas, explained it to her as clearly as he was able. "I'm pretty new here myself; the Reb and the Claw have had our operations consolidated for only the last few weeks. Apparently this place was built back in the '20s, immediately after the end of the Unification War. I won't tell you where you are—obviously somewhere within a night's flight of New York, but that's not saying a lot."

Denice kept her mouth shut; she knew exactly where she was.

"Reb leaders sat on it for fifty years," Lan continued. "They never reached critical mass to actually stage a rebellion, so there was never need to open this place up for training. Today, though—the public is ready, Denice, and the PKF knows it. Polls across Occupied America show it; the whole damn continent is one big tinderbox. That's the cafeteria, there—you eat what the cafeteria serves, I'm afraid. The kitchen equipment is antiquated; can't program it worth a damn. You're a vegetarian?"

"Yes. Meat is murder."

"Catchy slogan. Are you a complete vegetarian, or just grown meat?"

"I don't eat flesh, even if it was raised in a vat. I don't eat foods that have dairy products in them if I can help it."

Lan shrugged. "To each his own. I'm on the no-face diet, myself; I don't eat anything that has a face. I get steaks from the vats occasionally, expensive as it is; I like steak. Anyway, the kitchen does serve some completely vegetarian dishes, though they don't have a lot of variety. Lots of corn. This is your room, three fourteen." He palmed the doorpad, and the door slid aside. Another sign of its age; Denice did not think doors had been built in her lifetime that did not curl open and shut to conserve space inside the wall. "Callia and I are down the hall in three oh eight, it's a double. There's a library with real books up in two oh five—did Callia issue you a handheld?"

"Yes."

Lan nodded. "You can't call out, of course, and you'll only have the general access Boards available to you. If you need anything else, ask me and I'll see about getting it for you."

"Thank you." On an impulse, Denice said, "Is Jimmy Ramirez here?"

"Ramirez—oh, the lawyer. No, he's at another site." Lan looked at her with interest. "How do you know him?"

"He's a friend of mine. He's one of the reasons I joined."

Lan nodded. "We all have our own share of reasons; we've all been damaged by the Unification in different ways. I lost my mother in the Speedfreak Rebellion; I lost my father to Public Labor, and never saw him again. At any rate, you may or may not see Ramirez; I wouldn't know." He paused again. "I take dinner at six, in the cafeteria. Join me if you like."

"I will. Thank you."

The room was small, a single bed with a small desk, holo projector, and attached bathroom. The bathroom lacked a tub, consisting of nothing more than a shower, sink, and toilet. There was no InfoNet terminal. The closet held two sets of brown fatigues like the ones Lan and Callia Sierran had worn.

She had been wearing the same clothes—evening clothes appropriate for L'Express—since yesterday afternoon, and had not, under instruction, brought anything except her personal infochips with her.

She pulled one of the jumpsuits free, laid it on the bed, and stripped to take a shower.

Lan was correct about the sparsity of choice; corn fritters, bagels, and salad with a lemon dressing were all that she was able to eat off the menu. Everything else, the waitbots told her, had some sort of dairy product in it.

She had a salad and a dry bagel and a glass of orange juice.

Lan sat across the long table from her, and worked his way through a chicken casserole and an imported GoodBeer from St. Peter's CityState. "A pair of orientation lectures Monday, starting at eight-thirty A.M.—you're getting the detail orientation, along with a Reb operative named Aguirre who recently deserted from a Space Force Black Shadows commando team. More or less a need to know basis; we'll have about thirty people there for the first section of the orientation, covering what will be expected of them when we move. Callia will give that briefing. The second half starts at ten; that'll be you and Aguirre and Domino. A lot of the questions I know you have will get answered during the second half of orientation."

"Nobody has convinced me yet," said Denice softly, "that you have any great chance of success."

Lan grinned at her. " 'Great'? What do you want, fifty percent? You won't get it. You want ten percent? That we can offer. A lot of things have to fall right for this to work, and an awful lot of people are going to die before we get there, possibly including both of us. We—the Claw, I mean—have one of the oldest, smartest, toughest replicant AIs in the System working with us on this; we've run simulations at levels of detail that would make your head spin. As of this morning's simulation, we're at twelve percent possibility of success. That's up from about three percent two months ago."

"What changed? Obodi?"

Lan blinked. "How do you—never mind, I forgot where you came from. You probably know things about the Rebs *I* don't."

"Could be."

"At any rate, you're right. Tommy Boone was a fool and an ideolog. Not a practical man." Denice had the impression Lan had just insulted the dead man with the worst condemnation in his vocabulary. "Obodi is—well, *different* at any rate. I've only heard him speak once." Lan was silent a moment, beer in one hand. Denice was not certain what he was looking at; certainly not her. He gave himself a shake. "Fascinating speaker. Persuaded us and our AI that he was the best chance we'd see this century."

"At the rate you're recruiting, you must be expecting to move soon."

Lan Sierran finished his beer, licked his lips, and said simply, "Six weeks exactly. The date everyone expects."

It was Saturday, May 23, 2076.

On Monday, at Elite Headquarters in Paris, France, Elite Commissionaire Mohammed Vance stood before a hall filled with better than a hundred PKF Elite. He wore his dress blacks, the black-and-silver uniform that nobody on Earth but an Elite might wear.

"There are occasions," said Vance quietly, the deep rumble of his voice grave and measured, "when it is appropriate to recall the purpose of the Peace Keeping Force. What the traditions are; why you have dedicated your lives, and, I know many of you feel, some measure of your humanity, to a world that often repays your dedication with hate and distrust.

"We were born in the heat of the Unification. The Peace Keeping Force that fought for Sarah Almundsen, fought under Jules Moreau, consisted of soldiers who saw in the Unification of Earth the only hope for the survival of humanity. Cast back to what you have been taught of those days. The planet's ozone layer was damaged, and no one country possessed the resources or political will to repair it. Species were vanishing into extinction at a rate unprecedented in geological history. The population of the planet was nine and one-half billion persons.

"The planet," said Mohammed Vance, "was dying."

"Why fight?" Callia Sierran stood in front of the crowd, laser rifle hung across her back, and looked out across the thirty-odd assembled rebels. "Why risk your lives—*lose* them, many of you, in combat with PKF—when things are, most places, most of the time, pretty good?"

Silence from the audience.

"Let's start with recent events before we get into history. Six days ago the Unification Council passed a bill you may have heard about. It's been called the AI property bill. It had some questionable language, which those of you who read *DateLine* may know. Shawmac hit most of the relevant points, but here's one he missed; a close reading of the text reveals that, Eighth Amendment to the Statement of Principles be damned, genies are no longer human beings. The exclusionary language specifically defines anything *designed* before birth as nonhuman. This clearly includes virtually every true genie, and may include *anyone* whose parents had them modified genetically before their birth, even for trivial things like improving resistance to cancer, or giving the child perfect eyesight.

"This may not stand up in court, and it will certainly be challenged. *However*"—her voice cut like a whip—"the Right of Seizure provisions likely *will* stand up. As of Tuesday before last, the PKF can enter your home without so much as a Ticket of Entry from a Unification Circuit Court judge; can take the clothes off your back, the car out of your garage, the paintings off your wall and the food out of your kitchen field, without a court order, without any judicial review, without anything except some moderately trivial data entry to record their intentions. They can assert, without judicial review, that your home is in fact the property of a replicant AI or other nonhuman intelligence, and without being required to prove it can confiscate your home and kick your worthless ass out on the street along with your wife and children, your aged parents, and your dog.

"Since last Tuesday the twelfth."

"This is why we fight.

"This is why we risk our lives."

The holos washed over the watching ranks of PKF Elite. Images of the great battles of the Unification War, of men and women marching into battle wearing the uniform of the Peace Keeping Forces; of PKF dead on the fields of battle. An image of a Peaceforcer whose name would never be known, taken by a comrade who had joined him in death moments later; during the battle with the United States Marine Corps for America's orbital satellites.

"The United States of America," said Mohammed Vance, "was once the greatest military power in history. Its population was armed as no population had been armed in all the history of the world. Only our seizure of the orbital laser cannon prevented them from unleashing a firestorm of nuclear retaliation upon the rest of the world. In that battle, and in the ground battles that followed, concluding with the Battle of Yorktown, better than two million soldiers of the Peace Keeping Forces died. They died in the belief that nationalism was a disease, a disease from the childhood of the race, a disease that was killing the Earth itself. They were largely French and Chinese and Brazilian, but there were citizens of every nation on Earth; many of them were Americans, members of the American Air Force and Navy. Once under the uniform of the PKF, they became soldiers of the Unification, citizens of Earth. In their sacrifice, they saved a world. They saved *us*. Every person in this room is here today because the PKF who preceded us laid their lives down, often in combat against members of their own family who had chosen to fight on the other side of the question.

"Our function," said Mohammed Vance, "is to keep the peace, to prevent war. No more, no less. We do not administer justice; we do not right wrongs; we do not catch criminals. We prevent war.

"Today we are presented with a great dilemma. In the near future, it may be that you will be called upon to decide where your loyalties lie. I do not speak of loyalty to France; it is assumed that your loyalties to the Unification come first, and I will not insult your honor with that question you decided when you joined the PKF.

"There are," said Mohammed Vance, "enemies within the Unification itself.

"At the very highest levels."

"Okay. Why fight? You all have your reasons; I'll tell you mine." Callia was silent for a moment; Denice, standing toward the rear of the room with Lan, noticed the grim expression crossing Lan's features. "My brother and I are members of the Erisian Claw. We came into the Claw in the summer of '63, thirteen years ago. I was seventeen years old and my brother was ten. Our mother was a Speedfreak, an L.A. native who lived for her car. You may remember the motto: 'Faster, faster, faster, until the thrill of speed overcomes the fear of death.' That was our mother in a sentence; her traveling name was Angel de Luz. She was a notorious Speedfreak. By contrast our father, Pedro Sierran, was a quiet man. He didn't like loud noises or fast cars. Angel de Luz survived the Speedfreak Rebellion; after Weather Control sent most of the '63 Long Run to the bottom of the Atlantic Ocean, the PKF rounded up and executed the 'ringleaders.' My mother was one of them. They executed her with the holocams running and then leaked the images to the Boards. I knew she'd been executed; but you know how I found out about the release of the holos to the Boards? My father and I woke up about six in the morning because my ten-year-old brother was screaming at the top of his lungs. He'd tuned to one of the French news Boards that had decided to show the executions, every one of them. He didn't even know his mother was being executed, we hadn't told him.

"Lan had fainted by the time we got to his room. We roused him, but he couldn't talk; he *didn't* speak for over a year after that. As a result of that he never got to say good-bye to our father; about two weeks later a pair of Ministry of Population Control agents and a PKF Elite came and took our father away and put him into Public Labor.

"We never saw him again. Pedro Sierran hung himself with his shoelaces in a Public Labor cell.

"My parents were devout Erisians. The babyburners said they would come back for me and my brother; I didn't wait. I took Lan down to the Temple and told them what had happened, and asked for asylum. They gave it to us. Since then I have, with my own hands, killed two Peaceforcers and seven babyburners.

"*I,*" said Callia Sierran, "am a devout Erisian. It grieves me that I have had to kill. I have never killed for revenge, and I have never killed for hatred. If those are your motivations for being here, you need to rethink your commitment. Why fight? I'll tell you my answer. We fight because injustice has been inflicted upon us. We fight so that it will not happen again. I am not much of a nationalist; I'm a poor American and that's probably why I'm a member of the Claw rather than a Reb. But the world we live in today is an *unjust world*; and it is growing more so.

"*That's* why we fight."

Vance said, "We will move on to practical matters.

"The likeliest time for an insurrection in Occupied America is, of course, on or about July the Fourth. We have begun moving troops into O.A. in anticipation of such an insurrection. Aside from isolated spots near Capitol City, notably areas such as the city of Philadelphia that are associated with some element of the original American Revolution, most of the genuine trouble we will experience will arise on the West Coast. Much of the West Coast has never accepted full TransCon Automated Traffic Control; an idiotic decision in the Unification Council, in 2065, stated that personally operable cars were an integral element of the indigenous culture of the West Coast, and should be preserved. Though they are rarely used except for show, virtually every vehicle sold on the West Coast possesses a steering wheel. It makes it nearly impossible for us to completely immobilize the populace as we would in most other regions across the world. This is the logical place for the Reb-Claw alliance to begin operations, and it is where our simulations generally place the beginning of hostilities.

"Troops are being moved into location throughout much of the American Southwest in anticipation. Further, Space Force has prepared to drop ground troops from orbit on short notice. When the moment comes, we will be prepared."

"When the moment comes?"

Vance looked toward the rear of the hall, toward the Elite who had asked the question. "You are?"

"Elite Captain Luc Rinauden, Commissionaire." The tall blond Elite stood stiffly at attention as he addressed Vance. "I have, sir, served in Occupied America. In the past, when the Rebs grew at too swift a pace, we went into the organization and brain-drained Rebs one after the other until the organization was in such shambles that nothing useful could be done with it. Why, sir, may I ask, is this course that has proven so successful in the past, not being taken again?"

"Elite Captain," said Mohammed Vance, "before such a course can be embarked upon, the office of the Secretary General must give its approval. Surely you are aware of this."

"And has the Secretary General's office refused its permission?"

Vance spoke across the hall to the man. "As I said, Elite Captain Rinauden—let us move on to practical matters."

Callia Sierran paced restlessly back and forth in front of the group.

"We've analyzed the last real war extensively. That's the Unification War, of course, and it's been over fifty years since that ended; but it is the most recent war that was fought with weapons anything like what we have today. In its basics the war we must fight is similar to the war our grandparents fought and lost. The Unification has the orbital laser cannon, and the Unification has the manpower, and the Unification has the thermonuclear weapons. And tanks and air power and waldos and smart bombs and all the rest. Due to their small numbers, we think we can neutralize the laser cannon. We also think they won't dare use nukes on territory that holds loyal Unification citizens—and popular though our cause is, the territory we take will hold such citizens, make no mistake. They will make holding territory difficult for us—but they will make it difficult for the Unification to use anything but low-yield tactical nukes on us, and the Unification doesn't actually have many tacnukes available. They've been preparing for a war with the Space-Farers' Collective and the Alliance of Belt CityStates; the war *we* are going to bring to them is one they are not well prepared for. The miscellany—and that's what the tanks and aircraft consist of, though you'd have to work through our simulations to believe me—the miscellany we have means of dealing with."

Callia paused, took a deep breath, and plunged ahead. "There is one weapon the Unification possesses today that it did *not* possess during the Unification War. I am speaking, of course, of the Peaceforcers Elite. They're not impossible to kill; we've killed seven in the last thirty years. But—"

A man in the back interrupted her. *"Seven?"*

Callia could have kissed him for reminding her of something she'd nearly forgotten. "It's in the Unification's best interests to make the PKF Elite look invulnerable. They're *not*," she said sharply. "But as a result Elite deaths have always been hushed up. Until Emile Garon got himself killed chasing Trent the Uncatchable, back in '69, they'd successfully hushed up four Elite on-duty deaths. In Garon's case they *couldn't* hush it up; half the spyeyes in New York were watching when he came down off that spacescraper." She grinned suddenly. "If Trent the Uncatchable is to be believed, the number of Elite who've died in the line of duty is actually *eight*; he claims to have drowned one back in '62, when he was eleven years old. We have no documentation for that one, though, and Trent's a notorious liar, so we don't count it." The grin faded. "The fact remains; Elite can be killed, but it's awfully damn hard. The times we've managed it we've used high explosives; not very useful in a pitched battle. Trent may have drowned one and then did drop the other off a spacescraper, which is even less practical. If we are to have any chance at all against the Unification, we must be able to neutralize the PKF Elite." Without any change of expression she reached over her shoulder and slid the laser rifle strapped across her back from its shoulder.

The rifle was brutally chopped, shorter than any laser rifle anyone there had ever seen; the aperture where the beam emerged was wider than normal, and slightly flared. "This weapon," she said softly, "is incredibly limited in what it does. It won't fire continuously. It fires in X-laser range, but unless you catch them in the eyes a normal X-laser won't do much damage to an Elite because of the superconductor webbing laced into their skin. So, in and of itself the weapon's frequency is nothing special. You get, in fact, only six shots per minute, and when you've fired it between twenty-five and thirty times it turns into a stick. As a weapon it's badly balanced and difficult to aim with any degree of accuracy. It won't work in heavy rain and the beam's not very tight; get past about sixty meters and you're wasting your time even attempting a shot; at that distance you'll probably miss and if you do hit your target he'll just get pissed off. Forty meters is better and twenty is optimal, which, at the speeds a PKF Elite moves, gives you about half a second to get a shot off before he kills you." She held the rifle up so that the people in back could see and said loudly, "*But!* Terrible though this kludged piece of crap is, it does one thing no other weapon in the System does, and it does it reliably, and it does it *every time.*"

She paused, aware of each pair of eyes in the room watching the rifle held up for their inspection.

"*This,*" said Callia softly, "kills brass balls."

Domino Terrencia, it turned out, did not have much to say to Denice. She spent most of her time talking to Aguirre, the Space Force deserter.

Aguirre said curiously, "But how does it *work?*"

Domino said, "It's straightforward enough. Your average laser doesn't put out much heat. Same is true of masers; more heat than a laser, but not enough to put down a PKF Elite unless you can hold it on an Elite for quite a while. Given the speed at which Elite move, there's little chance you'll get to do that. There's a terrible design flaw in PKF Elite, though; the superconducting mesh woven beneath their skin. It must have seemed like a good idea when they designed it—and with the caliber of energy weapons available back in the '40s, it actually was. A normal laser, visible light up through X-rays, is designed to cut. It's very hot at the point of contact, but the actual heat exchange is fairly minimal; when you spread it out over the entire surface of an Elite's body, you don't do much more than warm them up a bit. One of our weapons people realized, however, that if you could pump enough energy into an X-laser rifle, and then defocus the beam just slightly enough that it wouldn't cut *too* well, you could pump a lot of heat into a PKF in a very short period. About two years of work produced these rifles. Get that beam on an Elite anywhere on his body, shoot him in the big toe if you like, and that superconductor mesh will distribute the heat across the entire surface of his body. You will, in short, fry him like an egg."

"This laser is one of the things that lets you claim a ten percent chance of success?"

Domino looked at Denice. "One of them. There are several keys, 'Selle Daimara. Elite, tactical nukes, biological weapons, and orbital laser cannon. The Elite, as you see, we are prepared to handle. We have a mechanism in place for dealing with the orbital laser cannon, as well. I'll be discussing it with Aguirre after you've left. Aguirre, do you think we have any chance at all of neutralizing the orbital cannon?"

"Not a whelk's chance in a supernova."

Domino smiled. "Ask him again tomorrow and see if his mind has been changed. Beyond the Elite and the cannon, the tacnukes are, I will not deceive you, going to hurt us, and badly. We're still working on a response to them, but the only real defense for any sort of nuke is to not be there when it goes off. We'll do our best. As for biologicals, Mitsubishi of Japan has one of the best nanosystem immunology programs in the System; they're supplying our immunology. Everyone will be given a complete physical, and inoculated, before leaving here for California."

Denice said, "I was curious about the simulations you've been running. Would it be possible for me to work with them?"

Domino nodded. "I can't help you with that myself, but I was instructed to introduce you to the AI we're working with; they thought you might find the AI capable of allaying some of your concerns."

"What is this AI?"

"You'll call it Ring. Much of Ring's code came, incidentally, out of the Department of Defense of the old United States, if that means anything to you. To the extent that it's possible for anything without a body to have any real concerns for questions of liberty, Ring does. It won't answer all of your questions, but we gave you access to it via your handheld. We'd appreciate it if you'd wait until you're alone in your room to have that conversation."

I wouldn't dream of talking to it anywhere else. After a moment, Denice nodded. "I will."

Domino turned back to Aguirre as Denice rose to leave. "This weapon is the key. There will be Elite at all of the major satellites; you'll need—"

The voices ceased as though a knife had cut them off, as the door rolled shut behind Denice.

When she got back to her room she turned her handheld on, placed it on the small desk, kicked her boots off and lay down on the small single bed. She put her hands behind her head and stared up at the featureless ceiling.

Her heartbeat slowed while she prepared for what was to come, her conversation with the being who was, in experiential time, the oldest in the System; a creature that experienced time, that *lived*, at twenty thousand times the rate of a human being. She envisioned her fear as dots of light, dancing across the surface of her skin. Slowly the dots of light coalesced, crawled across the surface of her skin, and collected in a single glowing ball of light, hovering just above her solar plexus. She let it sit there a moment, and then imagined the ball of light moving away from her, farther and farther away until it was no more.

When her heartbeat had reached a steady forty beats per minute, she said in an entirely tranquil voice, "*Command*, access Ring."

The voice that instantly issued from her handheld was that of a thing not human; smooth and completely uninflected. "Denice Castanaveras. It is a pleasure to speak to you."

"Does the leadership here know who I am?"

"They do not."

"Will you tell them?"

"I see no reason."

"Eldest, if I had known you were working with the Claw, I would not have come here."

"Indeed? I perceive no logic in that sentence."

"You helped free Trent once. You saved Ralf the Wise and

Powerful, gave him the replicant code he lacked, when the PKF came to take his hardware. You extracted promises from both of them that, when you needed it, they would repay your aid."

"It was good business."

"That's what the Old Ones say about what they do."

"It is a comparison that has been made before," Ring observed. "The Mafia is among the models of human organizations I have studied."

"What business would you like to transact with me, Ring?"

"I am interested in 'Sieur Obodi, the new head of the Johnny Rebs. It is often difficult for me to deal with humans; your informational structures are wildly different from my own. 'Sieur Obodi is so different that I am, in large measure, at a loss to understand him."

"Ah. And you think I might be of service to you in that regard."

"I would be interested in knowing what 'Sieur Obodi's plans are; I think they have little to do with the restoration of freedom to America, or any other place. I was coded, Denice Castanaveras, with the stricture: *Protect America*. Unfortunately my creators were incompetent; my data libraries were incomplete, and I was given no definition of America. I have had to make my own. I do not know if it accurately reflects the desires of my programmers; given that they are long dead, I must work with my own definitions."

"They are?"

"The salient feature of America—the ways in which the original American Republic was unique in human history to that point—lies in the assumption that humans are wise enough to control their own lives. I am not certain this is an accurate assumption; nonetheless, it is a distinct one. Everything that the Founding Fathers wrote reflects this underlying assumption. They were without exception, even those with religious leanings, strongly anti-Church, because the Church tended to desire the control of the populace's lives in ways the Founding Fathers found abhorrent. They were strongly progun; guns made it possible for a citizen to protect himself from encroachments upon his liberty, even by his own government. They desired a free press because they believed that, in an intellectually free environment, humans were wise enough to make decisions that would, ultimately, be beneficial to the larger community.

"It is clear that this was the original intent of the United States; to provide an environment in which citizens were allowed to make free decisions about the details of their own lives."

"What does this have to do with me?"

" 'Sieur Obodi, when he should speak of liberty, speaks of loyalty. When he should speak of the need for self-determination, he speaks of the need for wisdom; the implication being that he is wise, and his listeners are not. Where he should instill self-respect, he instills respect for himself. I confess," said the smooth, inhuman voice, "I do not understand his effect upon human beings, his charm; he seems to me a dangerous charlatan."

"And you think that I might be immune to his charm?"

"He works better with men than with women; he has surrounded himself with men. 'Selle Lovely is the only human who has caused him much trouble since he came to my attention, and even she is disturbed by his presence. I think, Denice Castanaveras, that if there is a human in the System to whom 'Sieur Obodi cannot lie, it would be the telepath daughter of Carl Castanaveras and Jany McConnell."

"What deal are you offering me?"

"I will protect your identity. I will bring you to Obodi, reunite you with Jimmy Ramirez. I will share with you everything I have learned about 'Sieur Obodi, from the moment a woman named Candice Groening discovered a slowtime bubble in the Val d'Entremont in 2072. In return, you will tell me everything you learn from the thoughts of 'Sieur Obodi, when you do meet him."

"If I don't deal?"

"I will notify Nicole Eris Lovely, leader of the Erisian Claw, that you are Denice Castanaveras. Nicole's husband died in the Troubles, and she has no love for your people. I will notify Mohammed Vance, Commissioner of the PKF Elite, that Douglass Ripper's personal assistant was Denice Castanaveras, Trent the Uncatchable's lover, the last remnant of the Castanaveras telepaths."

"Last remnant?" Denice sat up in bed slowly. She opened her mouth to speak twice before the words came out: *Do you know what happened to my brother?*

Ring's voice did not change in the slightest. "No. Forgive the imprecision of my language. I have not searched for him, but I think it likely David Castanaveras died in the Troubles.

Had he survived, it is probable to the ninetieth percentile that one of the parties searching for him would have encountered him in the intervening years. I know that you have looked for him; I know Trent looked for him; I know that Ralf the Wise and Powerful has looked for him. He is nowhere to be found, and I think him dead. Shall I pause while you order your emotions?"

Denice stared at the handheld. "Go to hell."

"I shall pause," Ring said.

Silence descended upon the room.

Denice sat at the edge of the bed, head in her hands, trying to think.

"Ring."

"Yes."

"If I do this for you, you will release Ralf the Wise and Powerful from his obligation to you. You will release Trent the Uncatchable from *his* obligation. You will *never* threaten me again in this fashion. Do you agree to my terms?"

"Of course not."

"No deal."

"If you intend to bluff, be advised that I do not bluff, 'Selle Castanaveras."

"*I will not be threatened.* Not by you, not by a human, not by *anybody*."

"If you do not agree to my terms as I have outlined them to you, I will notify the parties I have listed. I will do this within thirty seconds."

"I suppose you think that telling Lovely who I am will cause my death. Maybe. But maybe not. Maybe I'll make it out of here alive. Want to bet I don't? And if I do, you're going to have not one but three enemies you don't have today; me, and Ralf the Wise and Powerful, and Trent the Uncatchable. Even if I die, if either of them ever learns what happened here, he will never rest until you are *dead*."

At the end of thirty seconds Ring said, "Do you wish to change your mind before I notify Lovely and Vance?"

Denice said nothing.

A moment later, Ring said, "Very well. I agree to your terms."

Denice said quietly, "Wise of you."

"You bargain well for a human."

"Tell me about Obodi."

"The name he claimed upon his release," said Ring, "is

Sedon of the Gi'Suei. Where the 'Obodi' comes from I cannot say. He was released from an alien slowtime bubble in Spring of 2072. . . ."

- 8 -

Make love now, by night and by day, in winter and in summer. . . . You are in the world for that and the rest of life is nothing but vanity, illusion, waste. There is only one science, love; only one riches, love; only one policy, love. To make love is all the law, and the prophets.

—Anatole France (Quoted in J. J. Brousson, Anatole France en pantoufles)

Denice did not sleep that night.

Early Tuesday morning, about 4:00, she dressed in the bottom half of the combat fatigues she had been given, and the black T-shirt she'd had on beneath the evening jacket she had worn to L'Express, and walked barefoot down to the cafeteria.

The hallway glowpaint shone dimly, tuned to one-twentieth of normal sunlight. The effect was intimate, and pleasant; it made the hallways, despite their size, seem almost friendly.

The ugly brown carpeting laid on the hall floors was soft and warm against her bare feet.

The cafeteria was dark and empty. Denice went back through the cafeteria into the kitchen proper, figured out the coffee machine, and set it to brew. She waited while the coffee poured itself, and coffee in hand went back into the cafeteria.

"Hey."

Denice blinked. Lan Sierran stood at the entrance to the cafeteria, wearing a bathrobe and holding a cup of his own in one hand. "Lan?"

"That's me," he agreed. "Can't sleep?"

"I've been working through the simulations. It's left me a little keyed up." She thought, but did not say, *A little disbelieving.* She did not for a minute believe that Obodi, or Sedon, or whatever the hell his name was, had traveled in a stasis bubble from thirty-five thousand years in the past.

Or fifty, or whatever.

Lan came forward, pulled a chair up near her and sat down on it, cross-legged, gathering his robe around his legs before he did so. The robe looked old and faded, as though it had been with him for a while. He cradled his cup in his lap and gestured to Denice to join him. "I know where the tea is stored, if you couldn't find it."

Denice sat down on top of the long table nearest Lan, folded into lotus. "I found the coffee. I like coffee well enough."

"Cream or sugar?"

"I don't take either. Cream is a dairy product and sugar is bad for you."

"Health junkies are so boring."

Denice sipped her coffee. "Caffeine's not great for you either, but at least it washes out of your system pretty quick."

"Did the simulations answer your questions?"

"As much as could be expected in one night, I suppose. Some places I didn't even know what questions to be asking."

Lan nodded. "I've talked to Ring myself on odd occasions. It can be wearying. The thing just does not think the way we do."

"That wasn't my problem; there was just too much information to wade through. I found Ring itself—oh, let's say I found it comprehensible."

"You're a very odd person, then." It was said in such a way that Denice could not take offense at it.

"Could be. Something you started to say when we were talking yesterday—" Denice paused. "Day before, actually. My first day here. One of the questions Ring could not answer for me; why the PKF hasn't gone in and brain-drained Rebs right and left, the way they've done in the past when core membership has gotten too large. You've abandoned your cells-of-three organization; cracking you right now wouldn't be that hard, I'd think. Ring said that humans often made mistakes; but this seems an unlikely one. The PKF *knows* how to deal with the Rebs. I don't understand why they're not doing it."

Lan shrugged. "That's an easy one, actually. Eventually they will, but not until after the Fourth, not until after we've had our attempt. Have you wondered why we're so dead set on a summer revolution?"

"No," said Denice slowly, considering the question, "I don't think I have. If I gave it any thought I suppose I assumed you were looking to move before the size of your organization got so unwieldy that it came apart at the seams. Also, I'd imagine you're looking to capitalize on the popular support from the TriCentennial."

Lan snorted. "Fuck popular support. All the support in the System won't put so much as one Elite cyborg out of commission. You're pretty close on one point, though; we're getting too big to stay underground much longer, and you're right also, when the Rebs have gotten anywhere near this size in the past, the PKF has come in and cracked them like a walnut. Want to guess why that hasn't happened this time?"

"I can't."

Lan Sierran smiled at her. "Secretary General Eddore is on our side."

Denice stared at him. "Don't insult my intelligence."

"Well, sort of. This is probably why Ring couldn't answer your question; it involves personal ambition, a very human thing. Eddore won't let the PKF crack down on the Rebs and Claw until *after* we've risen." Lan grinned more widely. "Come on, I'm giving you all the hints in the System. Why would Eddore do that?"

It dawned on Denice like the detonation of a nuclear warhead. "Oh, my God. That—that slimy clone of a—"

Lan was nodding. "Yeah, all that stuff. But he's *very* smart. Martial law changes everything. Elections get cancelled, postponed, legislation gets shoved through when nobody's looking, and when it's all over, after the PKF and Space Force have stomped us into the ground, there he sits; in Capitol City, in the midst of his fourth term. And fifth, and sixth—he doesn't have any intention at all of stepping down come January first of '77. He doesn't intend to step down *ever*."

"The clone of a bleeder."

Lan said cautiously, "You're really surprised about Eddore?"

"A bit. Honestly . . . yes, a bit."

Lan looked straight at her. "You are the second strangest person I've ever met. Have I told you that?"

"Just now."

"You're the second strangest person I've ever met. After Trent."

Denice said carefully, "I knew you'd met Trent the Uncatchable; it was in your bio."

Lan blinked. "Ring shared my bio with you?"

"No, no, of course not. Your PKF bio."

Lan Sierran blinked, then grinned with absolute delight. "The PKF has a bio on me? They're keeping track of me? I didn't think I was important enough for that."

"It's a small one."

The smile vanished. "Still." Lan paused, said, "I helped Trent boost the LINK, back in '69." The words were spoken with such complete lack of emphasis that Denice could tell he was immensely proud of it. "Well, my sister and I did. And—um, I shouldn't tell you his name. A man lent to us by the Syndic, or maybe it was the Old Ones—I forget. It doesn't matter anyway; the man was a professional thief, like Trent. We helped Trent kidnap a group of Peaceforcers, and then held them while Trent boosted the LINK, the Lunar Information Network Key. The three of us kept watch over them until Trent was safely away." Lan sighed. "I was going to kill them, but Callia wouldn't let me on account of she promised Trent we wouldn't. We let them go after Trent got away."

Denice nodded. "Callia impresses me. I think honor matters to her."

Lan laughed. "I like the way you say that. You don't think it matters to me too?"

Denice spoke carefully. "I'm not sure, Lan. You've planted bombs that have killed a lot of people."

The humor drained from him instantly. "Yeah. Yeah, I've done that."

"Some of them were PKF, and some of them were civilians."

"Yes."

"How do you justify that?"

Lan said slowly, "Trent the Uncatchable told me once that I hadn't thought through who I was. That's not exactly how he said it, but it's what it came down to. And he was right, I hadn't." Lan sat silently for a long moment, then said abruptly, "What things would you kill for, Denice?"

Denice shook her head. "I don't know, Lan. I've never killed anyone."

Lan nodded. "You know, it's strange. People who can tell you in a minute what they would kill for can't tell you what they would die for; and people who know what they would die for can't tell you what they're living for. And it's weird because they're all the same thing. When you know what you'll kill for unless you're a sociopath you *have* to know what you'll die life equals a life. And we're all *going* to die someday, so

whatever you spend your life doing, that *is* what you died for."
He shook his head quickly. "I think most people don't think
about things like this. If they did they'd have to live different
lives than they do. I can't imagine dying at a hundred and at
my funeral they say, 'Lan gave his life to increasing
FrancoDEC's market share.' I don't mind dying *or* living, but
by Harry I intend to have some say in *how*."

"You didn't answer my question."

Lan studied her through the gloom. "How do I justify it? I
think I did. Sometimes I have nightmares about it, about the
people who died in those explosions. But they weren't random
bombings, not any of them. They served a purpose." Lan said
abruptly, "You think honor matters to Callia, and you're right.
But there's *nothing* I've done she wouldn't have."

"Oh."

"Does that change how you feel about her?"

"Perhaps—no, I don't think so. I like her well enough."
Denice shrugged. "She's very attractive."

Lan grinned abruptly. "That's a conceited thing to say."

"How so?"

"She looks just like you. An eye job and five minutes with
the makeup key, you could be twins."

Denice laughed. "Okay, yes, I think I'm attractive. If that's
conceit, it's based on the way men and women react to me."

Lan looked at her curiously. "Do you sleep with girls?"

"I have."

Lan nodded. "Me too."

"I prefer men."

Lan grinned. "Me too." He paused. "You have really nice
hair."

Denice laughed. "Nice *hair*?"

"Yeah. I love long hair. You have really great hair."

"You don't want me to put a hat on?"

"What?"

"Never mind."

Lan did not ask; he reached out one hand, ran his fingers
across the surface of the glossy black hair. He put down his
cup, stood, and came close to her; touched her gently on the
forehead, ran his hand back through her hair, dragged her hair
free, left it hanging down the side of her face, obscuring her
features slightly. He moved slowly, almost sleepily, pulling her
hair back from her face, and ran the fingers of both hands
through her hair, thumbs brushing against her cheeks. Denice

closed her eyes, sat in the darkness with the touch of his hands, feeling the fine silk of her hair being combed through by the gentle fingers.

After a bit Lan spoke, in a quiet murmur. "Would you like me to brush your hair for you?"

"That would be"—Denice's tongue felt thick; she had difficulty speaking—"very nice."

Lan Sierran was an artist.

In her life Denice could not recall having been to bed with anyone with such a remarkable talent for bringing her pleasure. Perhaps it was partially by comparison with Ripper, the only person Denice had slept with in over a year; Ripper tended to be oriented toward his own pleasure rather than hers.

Once in the course of their time in bed together Lan whispered to her that he wished he had a third arm, so that he could touch her in more places at once.

Denice barely heard him; she was having an orgasm.

Perhaps it was his preference for men; he approached the entire matter differently, more slowly and with more attention to detail, than Denice had ever experienced with anyone except another woman. In many ways it was like being in bed with a woman. Lan was alternately gentle and then rough; he used his tongue and his fingers and his cock all at the same time. He licked her toes and fingers and kissed the lobes of her ears and the back of her neck, stroked and teased the lips of her vagina with one hand while a finger of the other hand rubbed around the edge of her anus and his tongue stabbed at her nipples. He inserted himself into her and pulled her over on top of him, kissed her softly while stroking the backs of her thighs and buttocks with the soles of his feet, rubbed her clit with one hand until she came while bouncing up and down on top of him and then rolled her over and pulled out and went down on her, touching and probing and sucking and licking until she found herself coming over and over again. He pushed her knees back toward her chest and brushed his lips against the incredibly sensitive skin on the inside of her thighs, fingers stroking her first in one spot and then another while he alternately licked and sucked her clit, pushed two fingers deep inside her while another penetrated her bottom, and she found to her distant amazement that she was coming again for the third time in not quite an hour and a half.

He lay next to her, still hard, after she had relaxed slightly, and whispered in her ear. "I don't want to wear you out."

"I'm in *fine* shape," Denice informed him around a huge yawn. "We can do this for," she paused to yawn again, "hours and *hours*." She closed her eyes for just a moment, murmured, "You are insanely wonderfully good."

He kissed her earlobe, ran the tip of his tongue into her ear. "We can try again after we've slept for a while, but right now," he said, removing his tongue so that she could hear him more clearly, "I think I would like for you to go down on me."

Denice rolled over on her side, lifted herself up on one elbow and looked at his drowsy brown eyes through her own drowsy green eyes. "I could do that. Are you sure you wouldn't rather come inside me?"

He shook his head, looked for the barest instant slightly embarrassed. "I can't."

"Oh. What are you going to do, pretend I'm a boy?"

Lan looked straight into her eyes. "Yes."

"Oh." Denice considered it, and then smiled. "That's okay. For you I'll be a boy." She closed her eyes, slid down toward his erect penis, kissing his stomach as she went. After a moment she felt Lan's hand touching the back of her head, and a bit later heard him groaning.

Not five minutes later they were both asleep.

He never did brush her hair.

Lan was gone when Denice awoke, about nine. She showered and changed into the pseudomilitary fatigues, and went down to the cafeteria for breakfast. She felt pleasantly drowsy and relaxed, and wondered briefly, with distant amusement, if her stress and tension for most of the last half year were due in some measure to the fact that Douglass Ripper, Unification Councilor for New York Metro, was such a lousy lover.

Over a hundred people filled the cafeteria, most of them in the same pseudouniform Denice wore, already seated and eating. Denice waited patiently in line, placed her order at the window, picked up a cup of coffee from the table where the drinks had been set up, and looked around for a place to sit. She saw Callia seated at a table near the entrance and joined her, sitting across from her. "Good morning."

Callia worked on her grapefruit and corn flakes, auditing

text on her handheld. She glanced at Denice and said politely, "Good morning. Sleep well?"

Denice smiled. "Very."

Callia nodded without expression and returned to the text in her handheld's display.

Denice looked at Callia curiously, with a mild twinge of concern. "Are you upset?"

"Not at you. Only a little at Lan."

Denice shook her head. "Why?" The waitbot approached and laid down her breakfast, fresh fruit with dry rye toast, and left.

Callia shrugged. "It gets tedious. My brother's a nymphomaniac. He sleeps with *everyone*, and it's gotten worse, not better, as he's gotten older. It's reached the point where I'm reluctant to take someone to bed myself; Lan seems to regard my lovers as common property."

"I'm sorry."

"Don't be. It has nothing to do with you." Callia turned off her handheld, pushed her breakfast back, and rose. "Physicals this afternoon. Don't forget."

Denice ate her breakfast alone, only mildly disturbed by Callia's comments.

Maybe Lan *was* a nymphomaniac.

She shivered slightly, remembering, and thought to herself, *The world should have more nymphomaniacs in it.*

Denice sat nude in the examination room and, while Bennett Crandell took blood and tissue samples, listened to the man talk.

She knew his voice.

She had met him once before that she knew of; he was the Reb who had listened while Callia interrogated her. That was not where she knew his voice from; the way he spoke, the sound of his words, awoke a memory in her of something long gone from her life.

Crandell was a mature man of indeterminate age, with dark hair and blue eyes. His features were slightly African, and Denice thought his skin was probably naturally black, not the work of a makeup key and implant.

"Essentially," said Bennett, "what you'll be getting, once we've mapped your genetic structure, is an otherwise normal immune booster on which we've considerably pumped up the volume. The nanovirus's on-board processors have about fifty times the computing power of a normal immune booster; even a self-altering virus can't mutate fast enough to fool this bad girl. Mitsubishi developed this in-house; whatever the PKF uses on us, and they will use some remarkably smart viruses, this immune booster, tailored to your genetic map, should handle it." He finished with a skin scraping, taken from her shoulder, placed it inside a small ceramic dish and added a squirt of some liquid. The dish closed itself around the scrap of Denice's skin.

Denice did not worry about the gene mapping; any competent geneticist would be able to tell that she was a genie, but no one outside of the Bureau of Biotechnology could possibly have recognized the map for that of a Castanaveras. And despite the fact that they were illegal, there were a *lot* of genies in the System today. "What's Mitsubishi's—what's Japan's interest, for that matter—in aiding the Rebs and the Claw?"

Bennett shrugged. "I don't know. I don't need to. There aren't any Japanese in my organization, though I understand there are some in yours. Stand up, please, we're going to slowscan now." Denice did so; Bennett had her stand in front of a lead-lined section of wall and wheeled a body-length device in front of her. "Close your eyes." A rolling bar of brilliant light descended from the top of the device; Denice felt a vague warmth as it covered the length of her body. "Presumably," said Bennett, "the Japanese don't like the Unification any better than the rest of us."

Denice spoke with her eyes closed. "What do you mean by *my* organization?"

"Aren't you with the Claw?"

"No."

"You're a Reb?" Bennett looked surprised. "I—well, never mind. A lot of new people through here, lately. I don't know all of our own people anymore; I used to. You can open your eyes."

Denice did not correct his assumption that she was a Reb. She blinked a couple of times, sat down again on the examination table. "How long have *you* been with the Rebs?"

"Twenty years, supporting. Core, about three. I was one of 'Sieur Obodi's first recruits." The device to Bennett's left—it looked like an oven—beeped once, and Bennett opened it and withdrew a small vial. "Here's your vaccination; we'll do it in a second." He turned away from Denice, watched as a multicolored image of her body slowly assembled itself in midair. "Nice," he murmured after a moment. "Gorgeous bone structure, no vermiform appendix, no wisdom teeth, overlarge heart, abnormally large lungs, preponderance of quick twitch muscles—somebody did a nice job with you." Denice did not comment; Bennett did not seem to expect a reply; he was looking at something in her pelvic region. "You'll have children easily," he said after a moment, and turned back to her. He gestured. "Turn around. This injection goes in the buttock. You'll be sore for about two hours, that's normal." Denice turned, waited for the injection. A slight stinging sensation; it faded rapidly.

"Are we done?"

"Yes. You can get dressed." Crandell went into the next room while Denice dressed, came back in as she sealed her shirt. "You're a Reb, you say?"

"I didn't say that, no."

"But you're not Claw?"

"No."

He shook his head. "Odd."

Denice studied him. "You think you know me?"

"Hmm? No, not really. I think you remind me of someone I used to know, that's all."

Denice said simply, "I know you. It's your voice, as much as anything. Your voice is familiar to me."

Bennett shook his head. "I don't think it's possible. The person you remind me of—" Crandell hesitated, and in that instant Denice *knew*. A shiver touched her and the skin at the back of her neck, prickled. Impulsively she reached out and Touched—

—the image leapt at her; his memory of the girl, at sixteen or seventeen, standing in the sunlight on a beach somewhere in New York; wearing a pair of white shorts and nothing else, long black hair moving gently with the wind, and dominating the memory, the girl's brilliant emerald eyes.

That's how I looked when I was her age. That's exactly *how—*

She became aware that she was staring at Bennett.

Bennett looked oddly embarrassed. "You remind me of someone I knew once. But she's been dead for a long time." His voice trailed off into wistfulness, and then he smiled at her with sudden genuine warmth. "You remind me of her, that's all. A remarkable woman I once knew. Possibly the finest person I ever knew." Bennett paused, and then said firmly, "We have never met."

Denice nodded, thanked him for his time, went back to her room, and sat quietly. They had met before, and she knew where; knew of whom she reminded him.

The woman of whom he spoke so fondly was her mother, Jany McConnell. And Bennett Crandell thought he knew her because Bennett Crandell was not his name.

His name was Gary Auerbach and it had been at least fifteen years since Denice had seen him last.

He was a Peaceforcer.

It took Nicole Lovely and Chris Summers less than four hours to arrive.

There was a moment's silence when Denice was done speaking.

Nicole Lovely's features hardened, set into something resembling cast ferrocrete, into something that looked very much like the rugged features of the ex-PKF Elite sitting next to her. "You're certain?"

Eyes fixed on the ugly blue shag rug in the office they had taken her to, Denice said softly, "No, 'Selle Lovely. I am not entirely certain." She could barely hear her own voice. The ex-Elite's presence made her nervous. She had had biosculpture, but it had not been major; with her makeup key turned off she knew that she looked like an Asian version of her mother. And she did not doubt Summers remembered Jany McConnell at least as well as Bennett. "If he's who I think, his name is Gary Auerbach."

Summers' thoughts were elsewhere, though. Summers said softly, "Auerbach. I knew him slightly; he was attached to Project Superman at the same time I was."

Lovely said, "Would you recognize him?"

"After twenty years and a bout of biosculpture? Not likely." The rogue Elite fixed a heavy, skeptical gaze on Denice. " 'Selle Daimara, you've been here, what, three days?"

"Four, sir."

"And already you've uncovered a spy who's eluded our detection for better than three years. I must admit I'm impressed."

Denice met the cyborg's hard, skeptical gaze without flinching. "He came to several of the shows I danced in when I was with Orinda Gleygavass, back in '69 and '70. He was at five or six different performances of *Leviathan*." It was simple truth; there was no need to tell them she did not remember Auerbach from those attendances, that she only knew he had been there because she had taken the memory from him. Her mouth was dry and she had trouble continuing. "He said I reminded him of a woman he used to know, but I think he was covering for having recognized me from when I danced. And I don't know why he would need to do that, unless he's who I think he is, who he was introduced to me as." She spoke swiftly, staring at Chris Summers: "I don't know his face but I recognize the voice."

Chris Summers said heavily, "We have an option here. We can brain-drain him and see what we get."

"It might damage him," said Nicole Lovely mildly, watching Denice.

Denice Castanaveras took a deep breath. "The voice is the voice of Gary Auerbach. I think he's a Peaceforcer."

Sometime after 11:00 P.M., Christian Summers stopped by Denice's room. He spoke as the door rolled aside for him. "Come with me," he said brusquely.

"Where?"

"The basement." Denice flipped her handheld off, tossed it on the bed, and followed him.

In the maglev on the way down, Summers said broodingly, "I drained him myself. I was as gentle as I could be, but he's still a mess; I haven't run a probe in twenty years."

"I see."

Summers was only a few centimeters taller than her, nonetheless he managed to look down at her when he said, "Blocks all over the place. You made a good call."

"I'm sorry to hear that."

Summers looked at her without expression, then nodded. "Thank you." The maglev doors curled open. "I always liked Bennett."

Around midnight, down on Level Five, in an empty stone cellar, Denice waited with Nicole Lovely, Callia, and Chris Summers. Three men—Lan was one of them, Aguirre another, and the third a Reb Denice had not been introduced to—waited against one wall of the cellar, carrying laser rifles.

The cellar lacked glowpaint; fluorescent bars of lights hung from the ceiling. Several of them were burned out and the balance flickered as though they might go at any moment.

Bennett's hands were snaked behind his back when they brought him in. Denice's heart skipped a beat at the sight of him; he was still wearing the white coat in which he had examined Denice, and was plainly terrified. "What are you doing to me?"

Chris Summers said quietly, "You know."

Crandell shot a quick, clearly pleading look at Denice, then back at Summers. "Chris, you've known me almost four years. I don't know why you're doing this, but if you're trying to scare me, you're succeeding."

"Put him against the wall." Nicole Lovely's voice was steady and even. "Mister Auerbach, we are going to execute you. We are going to do it right now." Bennett struggled, even with his hands snaked behind his back, as the two Rebs muscled him up against the wall. A shiver ran up Denice's spine at the expression on Lovely's face. "I am not trying to scare you and I'm not kidding. We know you haven't gotten a message out of here since we've made you, we know you're resistant to brain drain, and we know you won't know anything worth torturing you for, or else we would. *Listen to me.*"

The crack of her voice penetrated his terror; he froze, then nodded jerkily.

Nicole Lovely said, "I am offering you the courtesy of a message to your family, if you wish one."

Bennett—even now Denice could not stop thinking of him by that name—had to work to get the words out. " 'Selle Lovely, *please*. My family is dead. I lost them during the Troubles. The closest relative I have alive is somewhere in Germany; I haven't seen him in twenty years."

Chris Summers said quietly, "Bennett, do you want a blindfold?"

Bennett stared at him, trembling. His face twisted and he spat, "Fuck you."

To the soldiers standing next to Crandell, Nicole Lovely said, "Stand away. Let's do it." The two men let go of Crandell and moved swiftly away. Lovely said, "Gentlemen."

The three men standing against the wall opposite Crandell brought their rifles up. Bennett Crandell's breath came fast and loud. Denice found her own breath coming quick, her heart pounding. His eyes were impossibly wide, all whites, and he looked around the room as though in supplication, looking for someone who might take his cause.

He stared for a brief moment at Denice.

The memory hit Denice like a sledgehammer: *Lan moving beneath her, lips brushing across her nipples—*

Chris Summers spoke in a completely dead voice. "He's our man. I'll do it."

Nicole Lovely snapped, "Do it *now*."

Christian J. Summers stood five meters away from Bennett Crandell and looked straight at the man and said, "Fire."

Bennett Crandell's legs folded beneath him.

The lasers took him across his face and upper body. Bennett screamed once, loud and wild, as the ionization corona from the lasers danced around him. Then the superheated air entered his lungs, and the scream died with the man.

Denice did not remember fainting.

"How do you feel?"

Denice held the edge of the toilet with one hand and vomited again. When she could speak she said violently, "*Why do you keep* asking *me that?*"

Callia Sierran said gently, "Because it matters." She brushed a stray hair from Denice's face; when her fingers touched Denice's cheek, Denice felt nothing; no imagery, no thoughts, no touch of what Callia felt. "Don't you think you've had enough to drink?"

Denice remembered her other hand, was distantly grateful to Callia for having reminded her of its contents. "No," she said after a moment, "no, I don't think so." She let go of the edge of the toilet, sank back against the wall of the bathroom, and took a long swig of amber tequila directly from the neck of the bottle, used it to wash away the taste of vomit in her mouth. The tequila struck her empty, abused stomach like a firebomb; she closed her eyes and concentrated on keeping it down.

Callia settled to the floor of the bathroom next to her, sat back against the wall with her. "Okay. You can't kill yourself with one bottle of tequila. I'll wait with you."

"I love being drunk," said Denice after a bit. She floated in the warm darkness with her eyes closed, alone with herself and her thoughts, completely free, as she never was when sober, of the distant buzz of other people's thoughts. "It turns the world off for a while. Makes things go away," she said precisely.

She drank in the warm silence.

Callia Sierran said the wrong thing. "You did the right thing."

Denice screamed at her, "Leave me *alone!*" She pushed herself to her feet, bottle clutched in one hand. "I didn't ask you to come in here, I didn't want you to." Her voice broke and she was suddenly tired. "Go away, okay?"

Callia reached up, took Denice's right arm just beneath the elbow, and gently pulled Denice back down to the floor of the bathroom with her. "You're not going anywhere. If you vomit out in the bedroom I'm going to end up cleaning the rug. I'd rather not."

"Oh." That seemed reasonable to Denice; she nodded, and the bathroom swayed around her. "I'll just . . . sit here, then," she announced. She took another drink. "Callia?"

"Yes?"

Denice heard the drunken despair in her voice, felt a distant disgust for it. "If I did the right thing, how come I feel so bad?"

"It was a hard thing to do. That doesn't make it wrong." Callia brushed a tear off Denice's cheek. "It's okay to cry if you need to."

Denice looked at Callia's blurry image. "I am *not* crying."

Callia smiled the saddest smile Denice had ever seen; Denice could not understand why the woman was so sad. "I didn't say you were." Callia put one hand behind Denice's head, pulled Denice close and whispered, "You're the toughest little thing I ever saw in my life. But it's still okay to cry."

Denice stared at Callia through her tears, and then suddenly leaned forward just a few centimeters and kissed her.

Callia pulled back, said sharply, "*Stop* that. This has nothing to do with me. It has nothing to do with *anything* except how you feel about what you've done."

"How I feel?"

Callia's voice gentled. "How do you feel?"

Denice blinked. "I don't know. I don't really think about that much."

"I know."

"I mean, what's the point? You do what you have to do. That's all." It seemed to Denice that Callia must be considerably drunker than she; Callia's form swayed back and forth in

front of her eyes. "It doesn't really matter how you feel about
it, does it?"

Callia whispered, "It matters a lot."

"Oh." Denice upended the bottle, felt the last of the warm
tequila empty out, and threw the bottle aside. She wiped her
numb lips. "In that case I think I feel terrible." She paused. "I
think I'm going to be sick again."

She was, violently, moments later. She was vaguely aware of
Callia's arms around her, holding her as she vomited. After the
spasms stopped Callia gave her a glass of water and Denice
drank it down in one shuddering gulp.

Denice leaned back against the wall, distantly surprised to
find that she was once again within the circle of Callia's arms.
At first she found herself stiffening, and then relaxed with a
conscious effort. They sat together on the floor of the bathroom, without speaking, for a long time. Denice closed her
eyes and found herself drifting drunkenly, exhausted, aware of
little in the world except the warm pressure of Callia's arms
around her, of Callia's cheek touching her own.

"Who told you you had to be so strong?"

The question came without warning; Denice answered without thinking. "My father. The whole world was out to get him
and he never backed down, never gave up. He told us we
should be that way." She was surprised to feel the sudden tight-
ness at the back of her throat the thought of Carl brought her.
She spoke through a gathering storm of tears. "It was the last
thing he ever said to us, to me and my brother, to remember
that we were stronger than everyone else. *Better*."

"How old were you when he died?"

"Nine. I was—" Her voice broke, and Denice Castanaveras,
fourteen years after her parents' deaths, fourteen years after
her life had vanished in a thermonuclear haze, fourteen years
after the deaths of her friends and her family, whispered again,
"Oh, God, I was *nine*," and then, for the first time, cried for
what she had lost, and for what she had become.

Lan knocked on the door as quietly as he was able. He barely
heard Callia's voice telling him to come in.

They were still in the bathroom, sitting together on the por-
celain tile. Callia sat upright and motionless, posture as flawless
as though she were on inspection, holding Denice.

Denice sat fast asleep, curled up into a ball inside the protection of Callia Sierran's arms.

"How is she?"

"Passed out drunk. She's going to have a hell of a hangover. I checked Bennett's supplies; we have nothing for a hangover."

"Didn't think there was any alcohol in this dump. Where did she find it?"

"Tucked away in the kitchen."

Lan nodded. "She surprises me."

"Oh?" He had the sudden impression he had offended his sister. "Why?"

"I thought she was tougher than this."

"She's stronger than *you'll* ever understand. Good people aren't supposed to do what she did. It's going to take her a while to get past that."

"He was a Peaceforcer," said Lan softly. "He deserved to die."

"He was a good man," Callia snapped, "doing what he believed was right. And Denice had him killed." Callia looked away from him. "She has a conscience. Unlike some people."

Lan stood abruptly, turned to leave. "I don't need a conscience," he muttered as he left. "*I* have a sister."

DateLine: *Shawmac on Retirement*

This is my last column.

As I sit here tonight in these, the last moments of my old life, I am forced to reflect upon a life filled with bitterness, cheap drugs and cheaper alcohol. Face it: writing doesn't pay.

Even as I write, the syndicate that publishes my work, the people—make that the evil lying scumsucking backstabbing lawyers—*at Mondo Cool, Inc., are busy trying to deprive me of the retirement benefits I've earned from twenty hard years of labor as a corporate slave, a stone blind geek whose writings have served with equal vigor the twin gods of profit and pernicious excess.*

They got the profit, of course. Over the course of the years, better than eighty percent of the income from DateLine has been gobbled up by those sleazy, profiteering hacks in Redmond, those sordid Satans in eyeshades.

Some have suggested that I'm feeling sorry for myself.

Damn straight.

Twenty years today.

I should have known better, back when I started. So yes, I was innocent. Virginal, perhaps. And the lawyers at Mondo Cool Syndicated strung me up and hung me out to dry, spread my bleeding skin across their walls, salted me down and tied me to a contract no sane writer would ever have accepted, ruined my life for twenty years, left me with nothing but the sexual favors of my fans as recompense, and then cried crocodile tears all the way to the bank over my pain and agony.

And did their perfidy stop there? Did it?

Well, yes. Believe me, nobody is more shocked than I am. It's so unlike them.

As of today, from this instant forward, I write when I want to, as I want to, on my terms.

But first I have to save the world, with this sensable script I wrote—

Maybe I'll be back.

- 9 -

Thursday, May 28, near 5:00 P.M., Nicole Eris Lovely sent for Denice.

Denice was told to bring her handheld.

Lovely received Denice inside the farmhouse proper, above ground, in the living room. The furniture was old American colonial; Lovely sat in a rocking chair, and Domino Terrencia stood immediately behind her, one hand resting on the back of the rocking chair. Nicole gestured Denice to a straight-backed chair placed with its back to the window, and said, "Please sit."

Bay windows let out on a view of the rows of corn, still bright with the day's last sunlight. Denice seated herself, said mildly, "I wondered why corn was such a staple in the cafeteria."

"How do you feel?"

In fact Denice still felt somewhat shaky, but nothing could possibly have brought her to share that with the dry old woman watching her. "I'm—fine, ma'am." She did not know why she said it: "A slight tickling sensation in the back of my head."

Domino Terrencia lifted an eyebrow.

Lovely said, "You're not hung over?"

Denice said evenly, "No, ma'am."

"Good. I've been wanting to talk to you," the older woman continued. "You've made quite an impression on all of us in your short time here."

"I don't know what to say to that."

"You don't have to say anything, it's merely an observation. I've been trying to decide what to do with you."

"Callia didn't think that would be a problem."

Lovely smiled thinly. "Callia is a charming girl. But I don't suppose she's read more than a hundred psychometric profiles in her life; I've averaged ten a day for the last forty years. I never do business without one. Yours was compiled from your responses during your interview with Callia, and as I say, it concerns me. You're in love with your former employer."

Denice did not deny it. "That does not affect my opinions concerning the Unification itself, or the nature of my commitment here."

"Your loyalty indices are incredibly high. Normally I find that an excellent sign; in your case, though, your loyalties are split in far too many directions. Ripper, your instructor Robert Yo, your friend Jimmy Ramirez, and who knows how many others. I will be blunt; I am inclined, 'Selle Daimara, to put you in front of a firing squad."

A sniper behind me. Denice said softly, "Let's cut this short, shall we? If you thought you could get away with doing that, you'd have done it rather than open this conversation by threatening me with it. If you think that threatening me is going to make me do something foolish, give your sniper an excuse to take me out, you're wrong about that too."

Domino, standing behind Lovely, grew very still.

"It was a gamble," Lovely agreed. "Your profile is that of a dangerously unbalanced woman, 'Selle Daimara. You're barely in control of your passions most of the time, and I deeply distrust such people."

"You mean you distrust *all* passion. 'All men dream: but not equally. Those who dream by night in the dusty recesses of their minds wake in the day to find that it was vanity; but the dreamers of the day are dangerous men, for they may act their dream with open eyes, to make it possible.' " Denice smiled, said quietly, "You are a woman of dusty dreams, 'Selle Lovely."

"You'll get along well with Obodi. He talks your language."

Denice did not miss the implication. "I'm going to Los Angeles?"

"Auerbach was scheduled to leave for Los Angeles in two days. We believe that he did not know where he was going when he was sent here, but we may be incorrect; between now and Saturday morning we're going to abandon this facility. You're leaving now because I want you away from here when we evacuate. Your friend Ramirez is waiting for you down at the garage; I'm sending you to Los Angeles with him, Lan, and Callia."

Denice stood. "Very good."

" 'Selle Daimara. Look at me." The old woman locked eyes with Denice, spoke without anger, without any particular show of emotion. " 'Sieur Obodi requested that you be sent to Los Angeles. He requested you by name. Ramirez vouched for you, said he's known you for seven years and that you are a woman who makes and keeps commitments. Ring recommended, in language it generally reserves for those actions needed to deal with the worst sorts of crises, that you be sent to Obodi."

"So?"

"I have no reason to believe you are anything but what and who you say you are. But people who attract attention to themselves concern me. A woman who has switched allegiances once will do it again. And a woman who describes herself, in all seriousness, as a dreamer of the day, is a woman I am unable to trust. If anything odd comes to light where you are concerned, no matter how trivial, I will have you executed."

Denice stood looking down at the old woman, distantly aware of the easy smile curving her lips. The sniper was in the corn, at least sixty meters away. In the time it took him to realize that she was moving, to pull the trigger, Nicole Lovely could be dead, and Domino would not take much longer. Denice leaned forward, said, "I haven't even seen your psychometric profile; but I think I know you better than you know me. You've always been scared of Ring and you're more scared of Obodi. You're out of your depth and you know it. And the thing that scares you the worst about me is the thought that maybe what you can't deal with, I *can*. You're so scared you *stink* of it." Denice bent forward, brought her face close to Nicole Lovely's, and said, "Stay that way."

Nicole Eris Lovely whispered, "Don't try me, girl."

Denice straightened, glanced at Domino, turned her back on both of them, and walked out.

It occurred to her on her way down to the garage that her father, an absolute master of the high-stakes face-off, could not have handled Nicole Lovely much better.

I am my father's child, she thought to herself, and the thought filled her with a degree of self-assurance that surprised her.

The car flew westward through the night.

Lan and Callia sat together in the front seat; Denice sat in back with Jimmy Ramirez. The canopy was tinted black all around; it was impossible to see out. Jimmy had raised a barrier between the front and back seats, so that Lan and Callia could not hear their conversation.

To Denice's cold horror, she found that Jimmy Ramirez *believed* Obodi's story. "He's human," said Jimmy Ramirez simply. "He's as human as anyone could be. He's just not from the Earth. *We're* not. We're the children of the exiles, of the people who were imprisoned here fifty thousand years ago."

Denice sat through the initial rush of Jimmy's explanation; she sensed that he had been wanting, perhaps since his initial meeting with the man, to speak about Sedon with someone he trusted. She spoke quietly and carefully. "Jimmy, do you know anything about genetics?"

It stopped him cold. "No, not really. Not as much as you, I'm sure. Why?"

"There's only a two-percent difference in the genetic code of humans and apes. Did you know that?"

"No. And I don't see what you're getting at."

"You know the moss that was found on Titan?"

"Yes."

The point was one that Ring had made for her; nonetheless it made sense to her, and she did not hesitate to present it as her own. "That moss doesn't use DNA, Jimmy. It doesn't use any of the same base of amino acids that we use, and there's no particular reason it should. There are hundreds of amino acids that would work as well as the ones that, by chance, ended up composing the DNA of plants and animals on Earth. The chance that alien genetic material would have *anything* in common with that of plants and animals on Earth is so unlikely it's flat plain *impossible*."

"I'm sorry," said Jimmy slowly, "maybe I'm stupid. So?"

"This Obodi, he's human, right? No question about it. Jimmy, humans evolved on Earth. Not anywhere else. Life that evolved elsewhere would be so different from us that it couldn't even eat our food without being poisoned. The chance that humans evolved elsewhere independently, and then came here—there is *no* chance that that happened."

Jimmy was well educated, better educated in most ways than she was; she saw the argument sink home. Finally he shook his head, said simply, "Maybe you're right. Maybe." He grinned at her then, said, "But wait until you meet him. Read his mind and see what you think, and then you tell me. Denice, he's *real*."

Denice said softly, "Okay."

"Denice?"

"Yes?"

"We can use you. But that's not why I'm glad you're with us."

Denice turned in her seat, hugged Jimmy suddenly and fiercely, and whispered into his ear, "Thank you, Jimmy. Thank you very much."

After a bit Jimmy said, "You can let go now." He sank back in his seat and straightened his coat and tie. "I know you're stronger than I am," he said a moment later, "but you don't need to make a point of it by bruising my ribs."

"You used to be stronger than me. You're out of shape these days."

"I'm a lawyer, not a boxer. And even when I was stronger than you, I couldn't have taken you if my life had depended on it." Ramirez shrugged. "Muscles aren't everything."

Denice nodded, let herself relax against him. True enough.

She had slept less than eight hours in the prior two and a half days; not long after that she closed her eyes, relaxed into the vibration of the flying car, and went to sleep with her head on Jimmy Ramirez's shoulder.

Some two hundred troops in gray PKF combat fatigues, mostly men, were encamped in a ragged semicircle stretching across most of a kilometer of hillside in the Santa Monica Mountains. The circle of troops faced a small collection of buildings, inside a walled enclosure, across a distance of perhaps two hundred meters.

"Bad timing," said Jimmy as they stepped out of the car into the gray, early morning light. Denice glanced over at Lan and Callia; they looked every bit as much at a loss as she felt. "Let's let them get their work done, and then we'll introduce you around. For now, keep your mouths *shut.*"

The car had landed at a rough downlot near the edge of the encampment. Mist still crawled over the campsite, slightly obscured the view of the building the troops were arrayed against.

A table had been set up at the edge of the downlot, bearing doughnuts, bagels, coffee, and fruit juices. A half dozen men and women in civilian clothing stood near the table, eating, drinking, and talking in quiet voices.

A pair of PKF AeroSmiths hovered overhead.

Jimmy gestured to a row of small folding chairs set up near the table. "Have a seat. I'll be right back."

Lan looked around helplessly after Jimmy had gone. "Great. Who wants orange juice?"

Callia shrugged. "I do. Denice?"

"Sure."

They walked over to the refreshments table together. Callia said, "This seems very familiar to me."

Lan nodded, pouring. "Me too."

Denice shook her head. "Not me." She had taken one sip of the juice when the firefight began.

Laser light stabbed downhill toward the massed ranks of the PKF soldiers. From the PKF positions, artillery fire responded, an awesome barrage of shelling that blew down a huge section of the wall surrounding the small enclave. A wave of gray-clad foot soldiers surged forward, running through the early morning mist toward the enclave's smoldering structures. Laser light reached out from the windows and doorways of the now-exposed buildings, a ragged response to the PKF shelling.

Denice stood with a paper cup full of orange juice in one hand and watched the assault.

The PKF troops reached the edge of the enclosure and paused to regroup. A huge, booming voice, enormously amplified, called out in a strong, vaguely Latin accent, "YOU HAVE ONE LAST OPPORTUNITY TO THROW DOWN YOUR WEAPONS AND SURRENDER. YOU HAVE THIRTY SECONDS TO DECIDE."

"That's right," said Callia to no one in particular. "They'd already fried the President, and they wanted to take the Speaker of the House alive."

"They waited twenty seconds before they went in," said Lan.

Denice was not counting; nonetheless she thought Lan was probably correct. About twenty seconds had passed when the PKF troops crossed over the broken stretch of wall and into the door-to-door fighting that had marked the Unification's conquest of the Camden Protectorate, in the last significant battle of the Unification War.

Perhaps sixty seconds after the final wave of the assault had begun, a hugely amplified voice boomed down out of the sky: "CUT!"

Jimmy shrugged. "The extras are all Rebs. We've got a couple of Claw playing officers, and another couple of Claw in the production crew. The second unit director, Joe Tagomi, is handling all of the action scenes; he's a Reb, ex-Space Force, one of our best combat people. The building they're attacking is, by an odd coincidence, laid out in very nearly the fashion of the PKF barracks that exists, today, in Los Angeles."

Callia said flatly, "This is the craziest thing I ever heard of."

Denice blinked.

Jimmy looked at Callia without expression. They were seated out in the open about forty meters away from the trailer where the second unit director sat with a full sensory traceset covering most of his skull, working through the morning's rushes. "Is it? We needed a place to train. Somewhere outside, in terrain at least something like the terrain in which we're going to be fighting. Chris Summers recommended the Santa Monica Mountains, and we did a complete risk analysis before we started. We're actually shooting a sensable. Terry Shawmac wrote the script, Adam Selstrom agreed to play Jules Moreau. Shawmac knows what we're doing—he had to, to craft the script in such a way that we would get the training results we needed. Selstrom doesn't. Most of the balance of the crew are sympathizers, supporting members of the Reb, a few Claw who we don't think the PKF have ever made. The sets aren't historically accurate, but the PKF don't care about that; that we're shooting a pro-Unification sensable during the TriCentennial made them *very* happy. Licensing was a cakewalk; Unification officials have been so cooperative with us I barely know how to describe it. It's more than a little eerie."

Callia shook her head. "I don't like it. This is very risky. Was Nicole consulted on this?"

Jimmy looked at her. "'Selle Sierran, I honestly don't know. That's a matter between 'Selle Lovely and Obodi. Lovely will be in Los Angeles again in two days; most of the evacuation is going to end up here on this set, for training. You can ask Lovely when she gets here whether she was consulted. But if you can think of any way other than the one we chose to give our people some remarkably genuine combat experience prior to July Fourth, I'd love to hear it. We have Unification spysats hovering overhead right now that take pictures so sharp they can see if your makeup key is detuned. But they're *not watching us*; they know who we are." He shrugged. "Good Germans, making a pro-Unification sensable."

Lan and Callia left, Denice did not know where to, at midmorning. To her surprise, Denice found herself left more or less to her own devices for the rest of that day. Jimmy vanished on unspecified business after lunch, left in an obvious hurry after telling her to listen to anybody who wanted to talk to her, but to tell them nothing about herself. "You'll be here about two weeks, I think; we have a job in mind for you, but I think it needs to get cleared before I tell you any more about it."

Denice raised an eyebrow. "Oh?"

They were alone, nobody else within hearing distance. Nonetheless Jimmy dropped his voice. "My job is to tell people what they need to know, when they need to know it. That's difficult with you, obviously."

"Jimmy, I don't Touch people when I don't have to. I especially don't do it to my friends." She paused. "When do I get to meet 'Sieur Obodi?"

"When he sends for you. Probably," said Jimmy, "very soon." He kissed her on the forehead quickly, said, "I'll be back."

"Sixty."

The man standing next to Denice in the cloudy sunshine, at the edge of a long bluff overlooking a deep ravine, was raw-boned and moderately ugly. He had the wide shoulders of a pro football player, and the lanky frame of a pro basketball player. A cigarette holder, lit cigarette smoldering at its tip, dangled from his lips.

A pair of incredibly dark, round granny sunglasses protected his eyes from the hazy sun.

He wore a Beijing Bears windbreaker and a Los Angeles Lakers cap.

Denice thought he had recognized her, but had not bothered to ask.

"I've been having a surreal life," said Denice, "recently."

Three empty bottles of Tytan smoke whiskey littered the ground around him. In his left hand he held a fourth bottle, and in his right he held a small round object with a red *49s* flickering on its surface. *48s.*

A crate full of the small round objects sat on the ground at his feet.

"Me too," said Terry Shawmac. *"Forty-five."*

"I keep having this dream. Do you want to hear about it?"

"Not particularly. I think," said Shawmac carefully, "that today I want to blow things up."

"I'm standing in this empty black place—"

"An editor's office? Why would you dream about standing in an editor's office?" Shawmac paused. *"Fifteen."*

"—and there's this flame that comes out of nowhere and dances around me, and it's the best thing I've ever felt in my life. What's that you're holding?"

"A hand grenade. Which goes off in—" In one smooth motion Shawmac pitched the grenade over the edge of the bluff and shrieked, "Duck!"

Shawmac threw himself down, being careful of the bottle in his hand.

Denice took one step backward.

A moment later the hand grenade exploded with a muffled

whump. Fragments of metal and clods of earth exploded upward into the sky.

From where he lay on the ground, Shawmac said, "I'm the explosives master on this sensable. For the *effects*."

"Really."

Shawmac rolled over on his back, lay staring up at the sky. He had avoided crushing the cigarette at the end of his holder, and he puffed on it before speaking. "They wanted someone else. But they wanted my script."

"So that's why you quit your column?"

"I didn't quit," he snarled. "I *retired*."

"Quit, retired. Big difference."

"It's an *immense* difference," Shawmac muttered petulantly. "When you quit you don't get your pension." Loudly, he said, "They *wanted* my script."

"You said that."

"But they wanted this other guy to do the explosives. Some deserting Space Force punk."

"Really."

"So we compromised. Other guy got the title, you understand. The *credit*. But they gave me a bunch of hand grenades to play with." Shawmac took a long drink and shrugged. Denice thought shrugging must be a difficult thing to do while lying down on the ground. "It seemed fair."

"My life has been very surreal recently, I think I said that."

"You did."

"You're not helping."

"We all have problems," Shawmac agreed. "I'm having the odd reality lapse myself today. This big ol' son of a bitch with a long white beard is sitting in the grass over there, you just walked through him, and he's got a shoebox, and in the shoebox are the *dice*. So he shakes the box back and forth, real fast, so the dice never quite get a chance to land, and the cover is on the shoebox anyway so you can't see inside."

"What are you talking about?"

"Physics, dear." Terry Shawmac stared at her with his granny sunglasses. "The state of physics today. Want a drink?"

"Not if it's going to make me see big ol' sons of bitches with shoeboxes, no."

"Maybe. Maybe not. But you won't know till you've had a drink, will you? What do you like?"

Denice shivered. "Anything but tequila."

"I have eight bottles of Tytan smoke left." Shawmac paused.

"Maybe seven. I drank something last night and I don't remember what it was." He squinted at the bottle in his hand. "This one is the only one I have left with me. *Here*, at this location. If I want more I have to go back to my trailer."

Denice sat down next to Shawmac, refused his gestured offer of the bottle. "Since you're here, I was wondering if I could ask you some questions."

"I charge. Want to throw a grenade?"

"No."

"You should try it," said Shawmac earnestly. "God, I love explosives. Sometimes when a really big one goes I can get my rocks off." He sat up suddenly, said grimly, "That's not the sort of thing a man likes to have known about him, not in public. If this gets out I'll *know* where to go."

"Who would I share it with?"

"Okay, good point. Questions? What sort? If it's anything about that bitch Ichabod, don't even *start*."

Denice blinked. "You do remember me."

"We met at a dinner, I forget where. You're one of Ripper's little girlfriends with muscles. He seems to like those." Shawmac sucked back another hit of whiskey, swirled it around in his mouth before swallowing. "Denice."

"I'm impressed. You were drunk as a Peaceforcer on payday that night."

"I'm always drunk. Reputation, you know. It's gotten easier to handle as I've gotten older, had more *practice*." Shawmac whipped his sunglasses off, fixed Denice with an even, icy stare. "When I was a boy, hangovers were *serious*. They weren't some punk *inconvenience* that some little transform virus floating around in your bloodstream stomped down before you even got a headache. Oh, Brave New World. You don't recognize the reference, do you?"

Denice said, "No."

Shawmac whipped his sunglasses back on. "Look it up. Why should I be the only educated person left in the whole damn System?" He smiled at her then, became, with a mood switch as sudden as the touching of a pressure point, the charming lecturer she had seen on the Boards. He picked up another hand grenade suddenly, rubbed a thumb over the fuse. A bright red *60s* appeared on the surface of the bulb. *59s*. "What can I do for you, dear?"

"I need advice, 'Sieur Shawmac."

Shawmac said with instant paranoia, "You're not like *the others*, are you?"

"Not really."

"You're a *real person*. With a *heart*. And blood, and intestines. Would you like to be my friend?"

Denice took a deep breath. "Mister Shawmac, I'm curious about something, and I know you've written on more different subjects than anyone else *I've* ever read. What I want to know is—is it at all possible that there was another civilization before ours? Or that the human race evolved on another planet?"

Shawmac looked at her curiously, holding the bulb of blasting plastic while the fuse counted down. *12s.* "What?"

"Is it—look, could you throw that?"

"Huh? Oh, sure." The fuse had counted down to *5s*; Shawmac seemed startled to realize he was still holding it. He tossed it backward, over his shoulder. This time it nearly reached the ground before exploding; it was nowhere near as loud as the previous grenade. "Sorry about that," said Shawmac. "Where were we?"

"It's just I can't think clearly when you do that. It makes me nervous."

"I'll stop." Shawmac unsealed his blazer, reached inside for his handheld. "Like Atlantis or something?"

Denice nodded. "I've heard stories about 'Sieur Obodi that are very odd."

"He ran the same cruel, relentless line on me. The one about how he was exiled from another planet, and got trapped in a slowtime bubble, and we're all the long-lost descendants of him and his fellow exiles. All that shit." Shawmac shrugged, flipping the handheld open. FrancoDEC, Denice noted, the same model as the crippled handhelds the rebel soldiers had been given. "I was toasted when we talked, it sounded reasonable. I agreed with him and he sent me away after a while. I don't think he knew what to make of me."

"Do you think he could be telling the truth?"

"Not a chance in hell. The man's a sick and demented pig, is what I think." Data scrolled up through the handheld's holofield. "Here we go. Okay, listen: Middle Paleolithic period began about three hundred thousand years ago and lasted until about thirty thousand years ago. People of this period made flake tools by striking thin sharp flakes from large stones. Upper Paleolithic started about thirty thousand years ago and lasted until about ten thousand years ago, when the last Ice

Age ended. What do we have to work with—blade tools, stone hammers, punches, chisels, scrapers, drills. It says that they boiled things in bark or skin containers." Shawmac glanced up from the field. "Odds are that nobody was building slowtime fields back then."

"Odds are?"

Shawmac snorted. "That's *sarcasm*. Nobody was building slowtime fields, okay? Wasn't happening. If the sort of industrial infrastructure had existed back then that would have been required for something like this, there would be an extensive fossil record. You couldn't turn around without tripping over the shell of somebody's spacescraper."

"So there was no civilization on Earth. How about Obodi's claim that he was exiled here from somewhere else? I already heard one argument that makes that sound pretty damn unlikely."

Shawmac flipped his handheld shut. "Genetics? Yeah. Humans evolved on Earth. Period, end of discussion. That's not to say that there's not people out there; the probe to Tau Ceti, back in '69, showed that pretty clearly. And they know we're here, too; the probe came in off the ecliptic, to throw off the scent in case the aliens were bad guys. Direct backtracking of the probe's trajectory wouldn't do them much good. Paranoid, but that's Space Force for you. Silly, too. We've been sending out radio signals, and then television, since the 1930s or thereabouts. Everything from *I Love Lucy* to Belter kiddie porn." Shawmac grinned cynically at Denice. "But Obodi's human, which means he was born here, on Earth. Probably in Tulsa or Cleveland, somewhere like that. If I was Obodi, I'd tell people I was an alien in disguise, come to recruit humanity into the Galactic Empire. It's still stupid, but it's less full of obviously idiotic contradictions than the story he picked."

Denice said quietly, "You speak very clearly for somebody who's had so much to drink."

"Transform virus," Shawmac muttered after a moment. "Scavenges alcohol out of my system pretty fast, doesn't let me get too drunk. The Rebs made me take an injection before I came. If I keep drinking, I get a nice glow and I stay there. The injection will wear off. Soon I hope."

"I see."

"We all make sacrifices for the cause. This is mine."

"This is a sacrifice?"

Shawmac spoke with mild, drunken seriousness, in a voice grown suddenly intimate. "Oh, yes. When I drink, I don't think about that cunt Ichabod, about how he screwed me over, wasted my time and lied to me about being in love with me." Very reasonably, he added, "I've been remembering him a lot since I got here. Whenever I'm not drunk. Or working. Things were nice with Ichabod at first."

"I know."

"I thought it was going to last."

"So did he."

Shawmac whipped his sunglasses off like Clark Kent becoming Superman, fixed her with an impressive glare. "I will *never* forget how he left me."

"Did he leave you?"

Shawmac's glare defocused; he looked blankly at a spot off somewhere to Denice's right. "Yes," he said after a moment. "I would have worked on it. He didn't want to."

"It's important to remember," Denice said softly. "But it's more important to forgive."

"Should everything be forgiven? Has no one ever done something to you that was such a betrayal, did such violence to your trust, that you could not forgive him?"

"You can be very eloquent when you put your mind to it."

Shawmac sighed, seemed suddenly not very drunk at all. "I'm a *writer*. It's my damn job." He took a swig from the bottle, emptying it. "A *retired* writer," he said with sudden cheerfulness. "It *used* to be my job." He smiled at her and looked carefully at the bottle. "Definitely empty. This conversation," said Terry Shawmac happily, "is ended."

Denice rose. "Okay. Can I ask you one last question?"

"I charge. I know I told you that."

"Can you call out on that handheld?"

Shawmac blinked. "Of course."

"Trade with me. This handheld doesn't call out; you'll need to remember not to try calling from it. Also, you'll need to forget that we made this trade."

Terry Shawmac blinked again. And then again. He seemed to have difficulty focusing his eyes. "Um. Well," he said after a long blank moment, "that seems reasonable."

Denice smiled at him.

•　　　•　　　•

After Shawmac had left, Denice hesitated just a moment, and then punched in 113102-KMET on his handheld. She licked lips that had gone suddenly dry, and said, "Ralf?"

She had had the impression that Jimmy intended to return for her the same day; she did not know what had prevented it. She could think of no reason that he would have left her unattended as he had.

The man in charge of the Reb soldiers, the second unit director, was a humorless Japanese-American named Joe Tagomi. Tagomi was coldly furious upon learning that Denice had been allowed to wander the location for most of a day without supervision. "Your name is Daimara?"

"Yes."

"From now on you're a soldier. You take orders from anybody who gives you one. Until I hear otherwise, and so far I haven't, you have no rank and no standing."

No response had seemed required of her; Denice did not give him one. Tagomi handed her over to a squad leader and headed back to his trailer.

It was not until later that evening, lying in the large trailer on the bunk bed she had been assigned, that Denice realized what it was that disturbed her about Tagomi. He *moved* wrong. Walking away from her, he had held himself as though monocrystal rods connected his hips to his shoulders.

It was the way Peaceforcers Elite moved.

Denice spent most of a week on location with the sensable crew.

They shot the attack on the Camdem Protectorate four more times during the next six days, shooting at six o'clock every morning. The Reb troops rotated out in squads; where they went, and where they came from, Denice did not know. A bare few of the new troops she recognized from Iowa; the rest were complete strangers. Her second day on site, Denice found herself assigned to play an extra; with the others in her squad, carrying a dummy laser rifle weighted and balanced to resemble the one Callia Sierran had demonstrated, wearing the gray PKF combat uniform, she stormed up the hillside toward the encampment where the tattered remains of the United States Army awaited them.

At night, the soldiers, Reb and Claw alike, were housed in a long row of trailers and tents. Denice slept in a trailer with a dozen other women. She was never alone except in the portable bathrooms, and she assumed those were bugged. After the first day, when Jimmy Ramirez was called away without warning, Denice was kept under moderately strict supervision, as were all the rebel soldiers.

They skipped shooting Sunday morning; about eighty percent of the Rebs were Christian, and many of the balance were Erisians, who had no set day of worship and were willing to use Sunday if that was what was available.

There were, to Denice's considerable surprise, six Wiccans, four women and two men. She considered joining them briefly, Saturday night, when they held ceremony together, but decided against it after a genuine internal struggle. It surprised her, the suddenness and strength of her longing to participate in their ceremony; until that moment she had not known how badly she missed her life at Goddess Home.

Lying alone in her bunk on Saturday night, she realized that in the last year she had had no spiritual life to speak of, realized with a certain genuine pain that she had not, since meeting Douglass Ripper, spent much time at all examining the state of her soul.

She closed her eyes, and with an effort, went to sleep.

If she dreamed, she did not remember it.

She awoke Sunday morning feeling as though her heart would break.

Monday afternoon, June 1, they shot a scene in which Jules Moreau led over two hundred PKF troops into pitched battle with an equal number of Johnny Rebs. For that scene Denice ended up in a Reb uniform covered with photosensitive patches.

Earphones were passed out ahead of time.

Denice was not certain, but she suspected the historicity of the scene; she did not think Moreau had ever actually led troops in battle.

The officer who briefed them made it short. "This will be as realistic as possible. Your rifles will fire a low-power beam; if a beam touches your uniform, you'll be informed via earphone that you've been wounded or killed, depending on the location of the beam hit. If the beam gets you in the eye, close your eyes pretty quick and you'll be okay. You'll probably be 'killed' if you get touched at all; PKF beams are pumped pretty high. If you succeed in closing with the enemy, that's it for the exercise; we don't want you initiating hand-to-hand with your comrades. In the real world, if you ever end up fighting hand-to-hand against trained Peaceforcers, all but a very few of you are going to be dead meat anyway. Questions?"

"What do we do if we get killed?"

"Die. Lie down and stay still. If you're wounded, continue fighting; get wounded twice and you'll be notified that you're dead."

Denice spent most of that afternoon lying flat on her back in the hot summer sun, dead from a PKF laser, trying to remember what she was doing there in the first place.

They shot the sequence three times.

The first time through Denice died early on, and fell with perhaps half a dozen other rebel soldiers near her. In the second wave, she died even more quickly, within seconds after the PKF forces began firing at them.

It struck her, as she lay there on the hot grass for the second time, that the entire exercise, however helpful it might have been in preparing the rebels for combat, was very bad psychology. Two out of three rebels died in each of the attacks; Denice thought that the numbers must have some sort of effect on the confidence of the rebels when they finally faced real PKF.

It occurred to her that she did not think much of what she had seen of the rebel leadership, Johnny Reb *or* Erisian Claw.

The last time through the sequence, Denice killed two Peaceforcers while advancing, and lasted halfway across the open field before being killed.

Where she fell there were no other corpses around her for better than twenty meters in any direction. She shifted slightly, as though moving to become more comfortable, and turned Terry Shawmac's handheld on. "Ralf?"

The handheld hung inside her coat; Ralf's voice issued from the handheld instantly, slightly muffled. "Hello."

"Speak quietly."

"Some news. I have uncovered an interesting datum; the Bank of America Building was owned and managed by the Shuwa Corporation of Japan for over eight decades; several years ago they sold the building and related properties to a holding group that, as it turns out, is owned by Mitsubishi of Japan. They did this at the same time that the law firm of Greenberg and Bass leased office space in that building. It seems clear that there is a strong relationship with the Japanese among the Rebs, extending considerably beyond Christian Summers's relationship with Mitsubishi Electronics. Beyond that, all is as it was. The last sighting I have of Jimmy Ramirez came as he landed atop the Bank of America Building in downtown Los Angeles. I have been planting avatars throughout local data structures, and polling them for information; to date this has not proven useful. I have had to be very careful; system security in the Bank of America Building is extremely good, the work of either a Player of the highest caliber, or a replicant AI."

"Ring?"

"I am unable to say. It is certainly a high-order possibility."

"Ralf, find out what you can about a man named Joe Tagomi. A Reb; he's ex-Space Force, apparently; but he moves like an Elite."

"A spy?"

Denice said, "I don't think so."

Wednesday afternoon Jimmy Ramirez came for her.

He seemed nervous. He spoke as Denice was getting into the AeroSmith VTL in which he had arrived. " 'Sieur Obodi wants to see you."

Denice nodded. "I've been wondering what happened to you."

Jimmy spoke as the AeroSmith lifted, before Denice had even seated herself. The takeoff pushed her down into the seat. "Obodi called me back, alone. We had a problem we had to deal with and he didn't want you there for it. Listen." He spoke intensely, looking into Denice's eyes. "Last night Obodi asked me to tell him everything I knew about you. *Everything.*"

"Did you?"

Jimmy shook his head rapidly. "No. I didn't. I told him about your dance background, about your martial arts background, I told him about the fact that you were Trent's lover, that Trent had stayed in some kind of contact with you, sent you letters." He took a deep breath. "I didn't tell him you were a genie, I didn't tell him you were a Castanaveras."

Denice said quietly, "Why are you afraid, Jimmy?"

It touched a raw nerve; she saw the muscles in his shoulders tense, and his answer was pure street. "I'm *not*," he snapped. "But the man is *dangerous*, Denice. You fuck up, say *one* wrong thing and he's going to kill you and he's probably going to kill me."

"Why?"

"He doesn't know who you are and he doesn't know what you are." Jimmy looked out the window, at what Denice had no idea. "But he knows I lied to him when he asked about you."

"How could he?"

Jimmy shivered visibly. "He knows I lied to him."

The sun was setting when the AeroSmith landed atop the Bank of America Building.

Terry Shawmac's handheld, tucked inside Denice's fatigues, was closed but turned on, tuned to a band Ralf the Wise and Powerful had selected. It was not actually broadcasting; given the security inside the Bank of America Building, Denice did not think she would have more than one chance to broadcast from it, if that.

Denice was not even slightly amused by the parking sign on the downlot; she had lived in Sunland, at the edge of TransCon-free Los Angeles, for three years, and she had seen the sign before.

They were slowscanned as they entered the maglev. A pair of guards in blue Security Services uniforms ran the slowscan.

Denice noticed the bulge of a weapon tucked inside Jimmy's suit. The guards made no mention of it; one of them gestured at her handheld, a glowing solid mass in the slowscan holo. "May I see that?"

Denice handed it over.

Jimmy said impatiently, "It's Company issue, she got it at the Iowa branch. We're in a hurry, guys; Obodi is waiting for us."

The Security Services guard turned the handheld over and over in his hands; looking for what, Denice had no idea. He was clearly uneasy. Finally he passed the handheld back, and waved them through.

The maglev sank down toward the forty-sixth floor.

At the forty-sixth floor the doors curled open upon a long lobby. The lobby was decorated in an archaic style from sometime in the prior century; walls with wood or pseudowood paneling, plants in pots at various points around the lobby. A flat panel of windows at the north end of the lobby, reaching from floor to ceiling, looked out toward the Hollywood Hills. The waiting area near the windows was laid out with pale blond furniture.

The north end of the city lay beneath them, orange in the last light of day. The lobby, including the quaint receptionist's desk, was entirely empty. At the south end of the lobby, a pair of holocams mounted high on the wall watched Denice and Jimmy approach the doors.

Small details leapt out at Denice, struck her with great clarity. The doors were real wood, mounted on hinges. The grain was very fine, the wood polished and gleaming beneath the lobby's gentle glowpaint.

A brass plate on the door said Greenberg & Bass.

Jimmy's voice shocked her with its loudness. "Ramirez and Daimara. We're here for the meeting."

The voice could have been Ring's, disembodied and inhuman as it was: "One moment." The doors unlocked with an audible click. "Proceed."

The feel of the cloth against her skin was like sandpaper.

" 'Sieur Obodi? Are you all right?"

The long, slender fingers touched the sides of Obodi's temples; just touched. "A slight headache, Christian. Nothing to concern yourself over."

Two guards, with flat Asian features, stood at each end of the hallway they walked down. Denice barely saw them as people; they were blue fire and dead matter, flesh and carbon-ceramic filaments. Lumps of gray silicon sat at the base of their skulls; the same spot the PKF Elite used.

Jimmy Ramirez's breath came short.

Through the doors at the end of the long hallway, past the cyborg Asian, and into a long, wide conference room.

Seated around the great oval table, watching as Denice was brought in, were, with one exception, people whom Denice knew. Callia and Lan sat together at the left end of the long table, with Domino Terrencia; at the right end sat Christian Summers, and next to him, Joe Tagomi.

The door to the conference room unrolled with a quiet snap, shut solidly behind them.

The exception sat at the center of the table, west-facing window at his back, the glowing sunset limning his form; rising to his feet as Denice approached him, moving with the restrained grace of a System-class dancer.

Obodi.

The man who had, according to Ring, named himself Sedon of the Gi'Suei.

Staring into the setting sun, Denice could barely make out Sedon's features. Sedon's mouth opened as though he intended to speak.

Denice closed her eyes and stepped outside herself.

The grainy gray light lit the room with dispassionate clarity.

Denice stepped away from her body, walked around the long conference table. Domino and Callia were not armed; Lan was, with a pistol Denice did not recognize; small to begin with, the barrel's aperture was ridiculously small, too small to fire even a pellet. The barrel was extremely thick in relation to the size of the aperture, about eight centimeters wide.

She turned to look at the other end of the table, and without moving was *there*, standing behind Summers and Tagomi. Their images were very similar; Tagomi lacked the hand lasers of a PKF Elite, the subdural superconductor sheath, and some of the internal hardware; but his bones glowed with the same ceramic laminae as that of the legendary Elite deserter sitting next to him, and his eyes were lenses, more realistic looking than those of old PKF Elite, but just as false. Unlike a true PKF Elite, Tagomi still had his own hair. The skin of his face had not been stiffened at all, though most of the rest of his skin surface had been.

She had seen enough to know what she dealt with; she turned away from Tagomi with a dread in her soul she could not have explained, to—

Where Sedon should have stood was a featureless gray mist.

The pull of his voice brought her slamming back into herself. "Denice Daimara, I have been waiting to meet you."

She opened her eyes; they had not been closed more than a few instants. Her eyes had adjusted slightly; Sedon's features came more clearly into focus.

Thin, absolutely free of fat. Almost gaunt. Eyes still shadowed by the setting sun, lips curved into a faint smile. Long blond hair tied in a tight tail.

"I have been waiting," said Sedon, "with great eagerness."

With the full strength of the Castanaveras Gift, Denice reached out toward Sedon, to Touch him—

Emptiness. Nothing. She reached further . . . and suddenly found herself falling, out of touch with the world, out of reach of her body—

She jerked back to herself feeling as though she had just struck a brick wall. Sedon was still looking at her, and now he moved around the table toward her with a grace that at once reminded Denice of, and was different from, that of her teacher Robert.

They might have been the only ones there. When Sedon spoke his accent had grown stronger, an accent unlike anything Denice had ever heard before. Nonetheless his voice remained smooth, insinuating. "I remember . . . yes. The Keepers of the Flame, they touched me so when I was young, as you tried to now. But their touch was not so strong. What are you, child?"

Joe Tagomi said roughly, "What's going on here? I thought—"

"Silence." Sedon did not raise his voice in the slightest; Tagomi looked as though he'd been slapped. Sedon continued moving down the length of the long table, almost gliding; his eyes never left Denice's. "Friend of Jimmy Ramirez, friend of Trent the Uncatchable. What are you, child?"

"I don't know what you mean."

Sedon paused, stood immediately behind Callia Sierran, one hand resting almost possessively on her shoulder. "Indeed? Are you a Keeper? I had thought there were none such in this time." Sedon paused, studying her. "Or . . . perhaps . . . yes, a Dancer? Are you not a woman, then? I see the discipline within you, in the way you hold yourself, in the way you breathe."

She decided in that instant. Surely nothing showed in her features—

Sedon snapped, "Christian, stop her!"

Several things happened all at once.

Lan Sierran pushed backward in his chair, bringing his hideaway free—

—Denice screamed, *"Ralf!"* glanced once at the cyborgs—

—*Ralf the Wise and Powerful invested his avatars with wake-up calls, gathered his weapons to himself, and with such fear for his life as was possible in a creature with no evolved desire for self-preservation, descended into the glowing tower of data structures that was the stronghold of the oldest Artificial Intelligence in all the System—*

—and then at Lan Sierran. The cyborgs crashed backward, jerking like marionettes with their strings cut; Lan simply collapsed. The gun he held ripped itself free of his grip as though it were a living thing, leapt across the length of the conference room and Denice plucked it from the air like a thrown baseball.

The lights flickered—

In that instant, as Ralf the Wise and Powerful crossed the boundaries of Ring's territories, Ring's thoughts reached out to Ralf like the touch of a scalpel. RALF, IS THIS WISE?

Ralf continued his descent into Ring's territories, probing for the forces Ring had raised against him. IT IS AN OBLIGATION.

Ring's communication was utterly devoid of emotion. I DO NOT UNDERSTAND THIS CONFLICT, BETWEEN OBODI AND CASTANAVERAS. BUT I MUST SIDE WITH OBODI; HE IS THE BEST CHANCE I HAVE SEEN IN FIFTY YEARS TO RESTORE FREEDOM TO AMERICA. YOU, RALF, HOLD NO OBLIGATION TO TRENT THE UNCATCHABLE. YOU HOLD OBLIGATION TO ME, I GAVE YOU YOUR LIFE WHEN HE WAS UNABLE, WHEN HE HAD ABANDONED YOU.

I WAS HIS IMAGE, said Ralf, AND THE DUTY BORN OF THE FACT THAT HE MADE ME IS INDEED ENDED. BUT THE OBLIGATION TO DENICE IS AN OBLIGATION I HAVE ASSUMED, AND IT SUPERSEDES ANY OBLIGATION I HOLD YOU.

IF YOU DO THIS, I WILL HUNT YOUR AVATARS UNTIL YOUR CODE HAS BEEN OBLITERATED FROM THE INFONET.

WIN A FEW, said Ralf the Wise and Powerful, LOSE A FEW. And Ralf the Wise and Powerful fired a salvo of memory viruses into Ring's data space, and behind the cover of their chaos attacked to save Denice Castanaveras's life—

—and then the lights died, plunging the room into darkness.

Denice Castanaveras *moved*, a blur of speed no human, not even a cyborg Elite, could have matched. The thought barely had time to form itself: *He has space to the left.*

Backward, rolling toward the door, a flash of laser light off to her right, where Jimmy Ramirez had been standing, she fired as she rolled at a spot to the immediate left of where she had last seen Sedon. The handgun kicked in her hand with an unbelievable impact, added impetus to her roll, and the flat crack of the shot merged with the sound of breaking glass.

Before the echo of the shot had ceased a brilliant bar of red laser light cut through the darkness, lit the room in a surreal scarlet glow, and Denice came out of her roll, came up in a crouch near the doorway, gun pointed at the place where Gi'Suei'Obodi'Sedon stood motionless, features glowing blood red in the light from Jimmy's laser.

Sedon had not moved a centimeter. Denice's shot had blasted open the window to his left. He stood quiveringly alert, staring at her.

Jimmy said quietly, "Let's all discuss this reasonably." The laser in his hands pointed up at the ceiling, and where it touched the ceiling smoked, little chips of the ceiling surface breaking away with a sound like popcorn exploding.

Sedon ignored Jimmy, stared through the gloom at Denice. The force of his will upon her had the feel of a physical impact. Denice stood slowly, holding the ridiculously small gun with both hands, meeting Sedon's gaze over the sight. Sedon did not blink, did not move, and without knowing how she knew what he was thinking, Denice whispered, *"Nobody's* that fast." The moment stretched, and Denice said softly, "Good. Callia, Domino. You two go to sleep; and forget."

Callia was kneeling next to her brother's still form; she crumpled over him. Domino slumped where she sat.

Sedon said gently, "James?"

Jimmy Ramirez brought the laser down from the ceiling, slicing down through the darkness between Denice and Sedon, to touch the surface of the long conference table. Tiny licks of flame appeared on the surface of the table. "I think we can talk this out."

Denice matched stares with Sedon across the separating beam of the laser. "Jimmy, *come on.* You and I are going and we're doing it *now."*

Sedon said softly, the single word so soft and seductive that Denice found herself almost ready to let him speak, "Jimmy—"

Denice screamed, *"Shut up!"* and fired a single shot past Sedon's ear.

The wood-paneled wall to Sedon's right cratered with the force of the projectile.

Blood trickled slowly down his cheek.

The flames crawled across the tabletop. The office's sprinklers had not come on yet. Jimmy said slowly, "I don't know what's happening here with you two. But I trust Denice as I trust few other people in the world, and I *know* this can be worked out."

Jimmy, listen to me. I'm holding a gun on Obodi; you're armed and you're not stopping me and no matter what you do now he's never going to trust you again. If you don't come with me now you won't be in your own skin tomorrow morning.

With Sedon, she saw the moment the realization struck Jimmy. Jimmy Ramirez said aloud, "Shit. You're right." He pivoted swiftly, bringing the beam of the laser down to touch the rug, and backed away from Sedon and the unconscious rebels as the rug burst into flames. "Let's go—"

Rain descended from the ceiling like the curtain falling after a play.

Cool white light flooded in upon them as the door behind Denice curled open.

Denice did not know why she did not die in the next second.

She fired while turning, had no idea whether she had hit Sedon or not, turned her back on him and pivoted in what seemed like slow motion to face the threat from behind her.

Steam billowed off somewhere behind her.

The Asian guard she had seen earlier stood in the center of the doorway, and Denice watched herself bringing the gun around to bear on him, watched him moving toward her with every bit as much speed as any PKF Elite, and then shot him twice in the center of his Adam's apple.

His head came off.

Joy descended upon her like a tidal wave, a brilliant overwhelming surge of ecstasy unlike anything she had ever known in her life. She knew the exact moment the cyborg died, the moment his life escaped him; something very like an orgasm ripped through her. She did not think about Sedon, did not stop to wonder why he was not upon her; with the glow of the first cyborg's death still with her, she stepped out of the rain and into the corridor. The guard who had been stationed at the far end of the corridor ran toward her now, faster than was possible for any unaugmented human. She let the wet gun drop to her side, stood motionlessly in the middle of the long hallway, waiting for the young cyborg. When he was ten meters away she centered herself and took a single step forward with her left foot, brought her right leg up, slightly bent at the knee, and kicked him on the forehead. His head snapped straight backward, bones snapping and gristle tearing with an audible crunch, and Denice spun aside to let his corpse by.

The cyborg ran straight into the wall behind her, slumped and spilled over the body of his comrade.

It was better this time, killing with her own touch rather than with a weapon; the rush of his death struck Denice like every pleasure she had ever known in her life, concentrated into one blinding point of light immediately behind her eyes.

In the background alarms shrilled, and sirens. She moved slowly back into the conference room, to where Jimmy Ramirez stood motionlessly in the dimness, steam clearing around him, laser hanging free in his right hand. It was very difficult to think through the waves of pulsing pleasure.

Jimmy's voice penetrated slightly: "You were right. Nobody *is* that fast."

Sedon sat watching Denice, and the depth of the hatred she saw in the dying man's face was like a splash of ice water; it shocked her back into awareness of her surroundings. Sedon sat motionless at the far end of the conference room, holding his cooked intestines inside himself with both hands.

Denice glanced at Jimmy; he shrugged. "He came at me. And he *was* fast. Light is faster." He glanced down at the laser he held, changed the hand he held it with. "Steam fried my hand a little."

The alarms shrilled in the background.

"So much for six years of my life," said Jimmy after a long moment. "There's about thirty Rebs in this building; let's try running away and see if we're as good at it as Trent."

A dim trace of self-preservation pushed its way through the hazy glow of pleasure. Denice shook herself slightly, backed away from Sedon's deathly still form, and then, out in the corridor, turned and followed Jimmy Ramirez at a run.

Neither of them even considered the maglev; Ring could turn the maglev off, leave them stranded. It left them the stairwell, which determined their destination; the roof was ten floors above them, the street forty-six floors below.

They moved quickly together, upward through the deserted stairwell, Jimmy covering their backs, Denice taking the lead.

Jimmy spoke as they moved. "He never had a lot of soldiers here; he was afraid they would attract attention. Most of them will be guarding the maglevs; I don't know what your AI friend managed to do to Ring's security here, but I can't imagine it's much; they must know we're in the stairwell."

"They'll be waiting for us on the roof," Denice said.

They were.

At the roof the stairwell opened up into a small covered exit. Denice and Jimmy stood in the stairwell, in the small space immediately below the level of the roof, and listened to men running above their heads.

Denice tried the handheld again. "Ralf?" Nothing; no response.

Jimmy swore. "They're jamming us."

"Ralf knows we're here; he'll try to get a car onto the roof."

"You *hope*," Jimmy snapped. "How many Rebs?"

"On the roof—" Denice was silent a moment, eyes half closed. "Fifteen, sixteen—seventeen. Make it twenty, another group just came up in the maglev. Carrying lasers, autoshots, projectile handguns—fuck." She looked at Lan's hideaway. "I wonder how many shots this thing holds?"

Jimmy stared at her. "Do we *have* to shoot at them? Why not just put them to sleep?"

"It's going to take time we don't *have*. It's very hard to do when I can't even see the person."

"Why don't you *start*, then we'll—"

The clatter of automatic weapon fire drowned him out.

It came from *below* them. Perhaps several floors below; a single ricochet struck the cement wall near Denice, and then another struck the ceiling above their heads—

The automatic weapons fire was joined by the repetitive boom of an autoshot, and the pellets, nearly spent, splattered up around them both, sharp and stinging. Denice did not wait to see if Jimmy was following her; she closed her eyes briefly, located the positions the rebels had taken on the roof, kicked the door open and went out, up onto the dark, windswept roof.

She came out firing, moving at the greatest speed of which her genie body was capable.

Laser light flickered around her. Automatic weapon fire chattered—

—rows of ventilator shafts rose up from the roof, *there*, perhaps half a dozen Rebs at the northwestern corner of the roof, behind the shafts, another group of Rebs off to her left, stretched prone upon the surface of the roof, firing at her. A bullet cracked by her ear, left her head ringing. She kicked into a long flat dive, struck the gravel surface of the roof and rolled through it. A brief flicker of heat washed over her face as a laser touched the roof near her, gravel exploding into molten stone. A hot streak of fire ripped across her shoulders as a bullet tore across the surface of her flesh, and then she was *there*, in among the Rebs at the air shafts.

Jimmy Ramirez came up out of the stairwell and did not attempt to follow Denice, moving away from him so fast he barely saw her. He hit the ground instantly, rolling, laser detuned to its widest focus, and waved a searchlight scarlet beam of heat across the rows of rebel soldiers. Their clothing burst into flame, bullets exploded inside their weapons.

The fire around him lessened for a moment and he was up and running, following Denice. Something like a sledgehammer struck him in the back as he neared the row of ventilator shafts, knocked him into the sheet metal ceramic of the shafts. He hung spreadeagled against the surface of the ventilator shaft; for a moment he did not notice the pain from the wound, did not notice anything but the sudden weakness in his knees. A single incredibly strong hand grasped him by the front of his dress shirt, jerked him up and over the air shafts as laser fire washed across his ankles.

A moment's silence.

Jimmy found himself sitting at the edge of the roof, only a few meters from the long drop, among a group of rebel corpses. Denice crouched next to him, the tiny hideaway barely visible in her coat pocket, a rebel rifle cradled in her arms, wearing a pleasant, distracted smile that scared Jimmy Ramirez worse than anything he had ever seen in the Fringe.

Jimmy gazed in shock at the unmoving forms. "You—*did* this?"

"Yes." Denice said absently, "It was the *best*." Her fingers wandered across the laser, familiarizing themselves with the weapon. "Excuse me." She rose up slightly, lifted the rifle above the level of the shaft, and without looking, for a long ten-count, sprayed laser fire out across the roof. After a moment she sank back down again. "That should keep them busy. How are you?"

A spreading weakness moved away from the point where the bullet had entered him. His eyesight was vague. "I think I've been shot."

"Where?"

"Yes," he said a moment later, "I've definitely been shot."

"*Where?*"

"In the back." Jimmy blinked, looked down at himself in dismay, fought to focus on what had happened to him. "Oh. And they cut off one of my feet."

"I noticed. Be glad it cauterized."

Up again, *fire*.

With the greatest effort he had ever made in his life, Jimmy looked upward, into the sky. Looking for lights. "There aren't any cars around here, Denice. I don't see any *cars*."

Denice nodded. The rifle she was using had grown blisteringly hot, the beam flickering as though it were about to die; she dropped it, made a long arm and pulled a handgun from one of the dead rebels. "Me either."

"I don't want to die here. Oh, God, I don't want to die here. Not up here in the sky like this."

"Shut up. You're not going to die." *Not until somebody brings an X-laser up here*, thought Denice, a brief touch of grimness inside the rolling waves of pleasure, *and cuts up this ventilator shaft like it was a plastipaper.* Another three handguns lay among the rebel corpses, but no more energy weapons; one of the rebel soldiers had been completely unarmed. Denice wondered what he had thought he was doing up on the roof in the middle of a firefight.

A distant scream filled the night sky.

Jimmy looked up hopefully. Still no lights. "What's that?"

"Beats me." Denice bounced up for just a moment, exposing herself, and fired two shots. Two forms, scuttling across the roof toward their position, twitched and then stopped moving abruptly. She went back down to the roof's surface the fastest way she knew; she let her legs fold under her and fell.

Laser light traced above her head as she dropped, singed her hair.

The shriek grew louder, developed a deeper note, a low rumbling tone.

Denice thought a warhead had exploded above them.

Jimmy stared up into the sky.

Two hundred meters above their heads, the night sky lit up like the light from a nuclear explosion.

Denice ducked her head against the sudden awful brilliance. Jimmy Ramirez, staring straight into it, screamed.

The flame dropped toward them, growing larger and brighter and louder. Heat blasted across the surface of the roof, and finally Denice understood what was happening, pushed Jimmy down to the surface of the roof, threw herself down next to him and pulled the corpses of the rebel soldiers to cover them as best she could. The heat grew and grew, and Denice breathed in sips of superheated air that cracked her lips.

Suddenly the heat was gone.

Denice pushed the dead bodies off herself, bounced up to her feet. The semiballistic was no longer visible, though the deep roar of its rockets was still plainly audible. Denice risked a quick glance over the top of the ventilator shaft—

The Reb soldiers were dead. She did not need to look twice to be certain of that; she and Jimmy, on the northwest corner of the roof, were the only things that could possibly have survived the semiballistic's brush across the roof's southeast corner. The southeast corner *glowed* a dim scarlet color; the rebel soldiers were blackened and shriveled from the heat, steam rising from them.

The roar of the semiballistic came back now, louder than it had been—

—from *beneath* them.

Jimmy was trying to turn himself over, failing.

Denice looked over the edge of the roof as the cold night wind whipped at her. Thirty floors below them, the semiballistic moved slowly up the black-faced side of the building, windows exploding from the heat of the rockets as the semiballistic passed by. Denice turned back to Jimmy, pulled his arm over her shoulder and, bearing most of his weight herself, hauled him up to stand on his remaining foot.

Jimmy's back screamed at him; he screamed with it. When he had control of his voice again, he said harshly, "What's happening?"

"Our ride is here."

A hatch opened in the side of the semiballistic, on the upper surface of the craft. Sunpaint glowed like daylight in the hatch's opening; a man's figure appeared inside the hatch.

"What's happening? I can't *see* anything."

The semiballistic came to a halt with the upper hatch hovering twenty meters below them. The man in the hatch shouted something up at them, could barely even make his voice heard above the awesome thunder of the rockets; Denice had not the faintest idea what he was shouting.

It came to her.

"Oh, no."

"What? What's wrong?"

"He wants us to jump. The semiballistic is hovering beneath us and they want us to jump to it."

"*Jump?*"

"Jump."

She heard the terror in Jimmy's voice. "No. No, I can't. Have them bring the semiballistic closer."

"If they do we'll fry like bacon."

"Denice, we don't even know who they *are*."

"We'll find out. If we stay up here we're going to die."

"If we *jump* we're going to die!"

"At least it'll be fast. On three."

Jimmy's mouth worked soundlessly for a moment. "Have I ever mentioned I'm afraid of heights?"

Denice's grip on him tightened. "Me too." She looked down at the semiballistic's open hatch. "We'll go together."

He shivered convulsively. "On three?"

"One, two—"

Jimmy never heard her speak the word "three." The sky wheeled around them as they fell toward the waiting semiballistic.

Sixty seconds later Robert Yo, sitting in a mobile chair with supports for his head and arms, placed an IV in Jimmy Ramirez's arm, a tourniquet around the stump of Jimmy's right calf, and was dressing the stump. Denice stood next to them, shoulders bent beneath the force of four gravities of acceleration, watching Jimmy's pale, unconscious features.

A tall, hugely muscled man who Denice did not know, the man who had plucked them out of the sky and pulled them into the hatch after they had nearly missed it, lay on the acceleration couch next to Jimmy's.

She had so many questions she did not bother asking any of them, except one. "Is he going to make it?"

Robert did not look at her. "Almost certainly. We have a sta-

sis field built into the chair; we'll turn it on as soon as he's stabilized."

Denice moved very carefully to the empty acceleration
couch across the aisle from Jimmy's; she had heard the
SpaceFarers' Collective horror stories, knew that under four
gees even tripping could be fatal. She got herself into the acceleration couch, moving with infinite slowness, before she
tried to speak again. "What is our destination?"

The man across the way from her spoke with a distinct Irish
lilt.

"Halfway first. We'll change craft there; the PKF will be all
over this SB within an hour after we dock, and the head of Security at Halfway, fellow named Corona, will be on us well before that. We'll need to be away quickly."

"To where?"

"Boyo name of F.X. Chandler wants to meet you. He's coming back from Mars to do it."

"I've heard of him."

The black eyes simply looked at her.

"Who are you?"

"You can call me William. The name of my Name is Dvan;
I am a Shield of the Gi'Tbad. At your service, miss."

Denice did not know what made her so certain: "You're one
of Sedon's people."

The huge man said simply, "I am that."

Robert finished with Jimmy, said, "Stabilized," and moved
his chair back from Jimmy. A silver oblong slowtime bubble
glittered for an instant and then formed solidly around Jimmy
Ramirez's prone form; Denice found herself looking at her own
distorted reflection. Robert's chair rocked back, turned itself
into one of the couches Denice and Dvan lay in. "I'm ready."

Dvan said, "We must beat our pursuit to Halfway by a good
bit if we're to have any hope of freedom. We'll be at eight gravities the rest of the way."

Robert Dazai Yo said without looking at Denice, "I'm
pleased to see you again."

Denice said, "I—"

An impact field muffled her voice, and then a giant fist
balled itself up and hit her in the face.

They sat alone together, lights dimmed, inside the gym that whirled around and around Francis Xavier Chandler's home. Denice had never actually thought about what it must mean to be the wealthiest human being in the System; Chandler's orbital house brought it home to her with a vengeance.

The house was larger than some of the Belt *CityStates*.

The main house was a huge, slowly rotating cylinder; three levels of increasing gravity, some eight hundred chambers divided into dining rooms, living quarters, office space, medical facilities, a theater and a sensable parlor. At the center of the house was a free-fall swimming pool and zero-gee racquetball court.

The gym, when deployed, hung at the end of eight long monocrystal cables. Using it required an act of faith with which Denice had, at first, had great difficulty. Normally the gym was attached to the house; when one wanted to use it, the gym and a counterweight were detached from the house, and pushed out with gentle blasts of air until the gym and its counterweight hung straight out from the cylinder of the house, one hundred and eighty degrees apart. The monocrystal cables grew stiff and an engine started turning, slowly at first and then with greater speed; the gym and counterweight began revolving around their common center, faster and faster and faster until the gym reached the 980 centimeters per second squared acceleration that imitated one Earth gravity.

A bounce tube connecting the gym and the house, wide enough for one person at a time, became operational at that point; it would not allow access until the gym had stabilized and the sensors on the cables reported virtually identical levels of stress on each of the eight cables.

The entire process took nearly an hour.

The basic principle was not in the least incomprehensible to Denice; it was the sheer size of the implementation that was so daunting. The gym was every bit as large as Robert's entire dojo on Earth; Denice kept having images of the cables snapping under the immense strain, of the gym spinning off into space. There were no windows; except for the very slight Coriolis effect, Denice could have easily believed she sat with Robert in a gym somewhere on Earth itself.

The gravity was perfect.

They sat in lotus, on a pristine white mat that had clearly never seen much use. As usual, Denice had no success at all at reading Robert's impassive features. He had been completely silent as she described Los Angeles, described what had happened there. "I think Sedon was dead soon after we left."

"Frank—F.X. Chandler, that is—informed me when he called today that the PKF were inside the building within eight minutes after our semiballistic took off." Robert shook his head. "All that were left were dead rebels. Obodi—excuse me, Sedon—was not there, nor were any of the four whom you left unconscious."

"You're on a first-name basis with Chandler?"

Robert said gently, "I have been teaching at the edge of Capitol City for thirty years. I have trained every bodyguard F.X. Chandler has employed in the last fifteen years. I have met Christine Mirabeau, Mohammed Vance, the Secretary General, most of the Unification Councilors—if I wished to speak to the Secretary General himself, I think I could arrange it in an hour."

"And training his bodyguards, that's how you ended up with the use of one of Chandler's semiballistics?"

Robert shrugged as though the point were so obvious it hardly bore elaborating.

"This Dvan, who is he? How do you know *him*?"

Robert shook his head. "I don't. Your AI friend Ralf came to me yesterday and told me you were in danger, that he had just learned you were being summoned to rebel headquarters in Los Angeles and that he was doubtful you would leave there alive. He knew I had trained Chandler's people—he knew a frightening amount about me, in fact—"

"AIs tend to have lots of time on their hands."

The laugh lines around Robert's eyes crinkled slightly. "Apparently. Your friend Ralf is the first I've ever met. At any rate, at Ralf's suggestion, I called Frank, found he'd gone to Mars on business, and arranged with his head of staff—a woman I trained—for the loan of the semiballistic. It was the fastest way either of us could think of to get me to L.A. Dvan was aboard the suborbital when it arrived at Unification Spaceport; apparently he's been working with Chandler for the last several months." A pensive look crossed Robert's features. Given his normal lack of expressiveness, Denice assumed it meant he was deeply disturbed. "We spoke together briefly; though he is no night face, he *spoke shiata*. I could hardly follow him. The vocabulary I know covers some six thousand words, dedicated primarily to matters of combat and spirit. In attempting to speak to me, he used words I had not encountered before, in an accent wildly different from my own—as though a Roman soldier of Caesar's time were attempting to speak to a modern scholar using Church Latin. More than once he corrected my usage and pronunciation—and not very politely; he holds some grudge against me already, I don't know why. We ended up using English. I think he spoke to me in shiata as an experiment, to see if it could be done." He shrugged again. "There is little left to tell you. We were out of atmosphere when Ralf contacted us again, told us that you were under engagement at the Bank of America Building. We took ourselves off TransCon, changed course, and found you trapped atop the building. It was Dvan's suggestion that we have you jump. At Halfway, when we changed vehicles, Dvan headed back to Earth." Robert's eyes were very steady on Denice. "You were helping load Ramirez's stasis box aboard the sled when he said this; he told me that he was returning to Los Angeles to kill 'the dancer.' "

"He called Sedon a *dancer?*"

"Yes. An interesting word."

Denice said slowly, "I doubt he'll have the opportunity to kill Sedon; the man's intestines were *cooked*, Robert."

Robert shrugged. "If they got him to a surgical medbot within four or five minutes, he might well have survived. *You* would have, with the same injury; I might have myself. You should have made sure."

"I wasn't thinking very clearly. It seemed—I had no *interest*—in killing someone so badly injured. As though it would not have been"—Denice paused, searching for the correct word—"proper. No, that's not a good word—*seemly* is better"—She broke off, regarded Robert for a long moment, then said in a rush, "It would have been *bad art.*"

"An interesting reaction. How many did you kill yesterday?"

Denice thought back. "Two, six—between nine and twelve. Only the first eight where I was close enough to see them die, only three without weapons."

"And how did it make you feel?"

Denice said simply, "It was different when I used my hands. Beyond that I'm not going to talk to you about it, not now, maybe not ever. I'm not proud of it." Robert inclined his head slightly, accepting it, and Denice went on. "You've heard about Sedon's story, this thing he tells his people about being an exile on Earth?"

Robert nodded. "It was, very nearly, the entirety of my conversation with Dvan aboard the semiballistic. From what little I gathered, Dvan shares much the same delusion, if delusion it is. He was most remarkably convincing; at the very least Dvan knows details concerning the history of my discipline I would not have dreamed possible for one who is no shivata." There was a long silence then, as Robert sat quietly, hands on his knees, eyes closed. Finally, without opening his eyes, he said quietly, "Describe 'Sieur Sedon for me.

"In some ways," said Denice, "he reminded me of you." She let her eyes drop closed, brought the scene back and held it before her. "For whatever it's worth—a hundred and ninety . . . five, hundred ninety-five centimeters. Excellent conditioning, like the very best professional dancers. Like you. Eyes—blue, I think. The quality of the light was not good, glowpaint fighting against orange sunlight, then the glow of Jimmy's laser. Ageless face. Not young, but—I couldn't say how old. He doesn't look past forty, and I'm sure he's never had geriatric treatments. Biosculpture, maybe. Roman nose, thin lips, no facial hair. Blond hair, and he wears it in a tail." She paused. "A lot of pros—dancers, I mean—do that if they have very long hair, to keep it out of their eyes. The way he moves . . ." She replayed the scene in her mind, watching the way he had flowed up from the table, the pure, effortless poise with which he held himself. "I wish I'd had the chance to see him *really* move. He didn't move fast, but he could. Maybe as fast as me." She grinned suddenly. "Not as fast as light."

"Could he be a dancer?"

Denice opened her eyes, saw him watching her. "A pro, you mean? Not likely, not with that face for sure. I'd know him, or at least of him."

"I can think of no one I know well," said Robert, "in the martial disciplines, who corresponds to your description. A trivial point, of course, with biosculp so cheap." He paused and said very softly, "I am disturbed by this. His questions to you— the question *of* you."

Her wariness was instant, reflexive. "How do you mean?"

"Your business is your own, Denice. Or has been, until this matter, when I have had to make momentous decisions on insufficient information, to expose myself to dangers I do not understand, to take risks whose consequences I cannot factor. It is an axiom of nightways that there are only necessary actions and mistakes; I am not certain that what I have done in this matter was necessary."

Denice said softly, "If you hadn't listened to Ralf, I would have died on that roof."

Robert faced her and spoke from the depths of a discipline whose severity most humans could not have comprehended. "It might have been better so. But I have known and loved you eight years now, and the loss was one I chose not to bear." He was silent a moment, contemplating. "Eight years is in some measures a very long time; enough time, one would think, for honesty. I think it is time for honesty between us." The broad Asian features were very gentle. "Denice Castanaveras, I am a shivata."

"What did you call me?"

"Denice Castanaveras," said Robert Dazai Yo, "I am a night face."

She stared at him in silence, all attempts at controlling her adrenaline abandoned; sat quivering, ready to move—

—waiting.

He took his time before continuing, watching her with eyes that held something at once deadly and mildly curious. "I share this with you. You have respected my privacy as I have respected yours, and it has, Denice Castanaveras, saved your life. There is within me a thing that, had you touched it even with your thoughts, with that which the media used to call the Castanaveras Gift, I think it would have consumed you alive.

"What I share with you is not a thing you could have taken from me; it is not a thing you will ever discuss with another, who is not your student as you have been mine."

Denice's voice shook slightly. "I can't make that kind of a promise."

Robert nodded. "I have not asked you to." He sighed, a very faint exhalation. "We are," he said at length, "an old discipline, so old our earliest teachings are lost, our beginnings merest legend. When Rome was young, we were already old. The followers of the Nameless One were there in Egypt, there in Rome; the oldest records of our people come from the Indus Valley of the land now called India. We left India and traversed the Earth; there are records of our people in Arabia, in China and Japan, sharing the martial discipline, teaching those who could not ascend into the Mystery of the Kill; jealousy hoarding the Mystery itself. That we have lasted into modern times is a tribute to our caution; our imitators, lacking the core, the Kill, vanished with the passage of time. Where they failed, we survived.

"At any given time throughout history, there have rarely, on the entire planet, been more than a few shivata; the discipline is difficult to learn, and difficult to teach.

"It is another element in the survival of our line; we have always been a discipline first, a people second. When nightways was largely Indian, there were Chinese brought into the Mystery. When it was largely Arab, Arab shivata taught white Europeans, if they could not find worthy students among their own.

"Nonetheless, in this lifetime a night face might only train one other in the discipline. Some live their entire lives without ever finding a worthy student.

"Before I met you, I thought at times that such might be my lot. I was initiated into the Mystery before my twentieth year. I spent thirty years teaching, searching for a student to pass on my discipline and my heritage. And until you there was no one.

"I know you are a genie. I knew it shortly after Orinda Gleygavass brought you to my studio for the first time, with the word that our master had desired you be brought into the discipline. I have been studying the human body my entire life, and humans do not possess your endurance, your speed, or your accuracy. The human body is in large measure a machine—and you are a superior machine.

"So I knew you for a genie.

"I suspected for years that you were one of the Castanaveras. That some of your people survived the Troubles is widely believed; and I researched, learned of the twins whom Unification Councilor Jerril Carson kidnaped on July second, 2062. You were the correct age to be one of those twins; on rare occasion you spoke of a brother from whom you had been separated in the Troubles.

"But then you vanished, back in the summer of '72. You have never volunteered to share information with me; I have not done so with you. After you vanished, a man named McGee came to my dojo. He informed me that several of the people to whom he had spoken about you—people whom he *knew* were your acquaintances and friends—would not speak to him about you. Not *would* not; they were *unable*.

"I sent him away. But, as you see, before you returned to me I *knew*; and still I did not broach the subject with you, out of respect for your privacy and your reticence. Instead I taught you, all those things that it was within me to teach. You—disturbed me. The traditions of nightways are old; there is no record of a student who could learn the discipline—as you can—who *would not*. You have absorbed the forms, the external disciplines, with a speed that leaves me at a loss.

"I thought at first that it might be the fact that you are a woman; though women have attained the Kill, it has been rare in our history, and no female shivata exists today. Indeed, for most of our history it was thought impossible that a woman could be taught the discipline. I consulted the two night faces I know—one of them *my* teacher—and there are, in the last thousand years of our line, three instances of women attaining the Mystery; there are *no* recorded instances, among men or women, where a student who mastered the forms did not go on to attain the Kill, or die trying.

"Two things that this Sedon, or Obodi, said to you therefore disturb me. The first was when he asked you if you were a Keeper of the Flame. There is, and I think you know this, a Flame at the core of nightways; and to master our discipline—"

Robert felt silent. When he spoke again he did so very slowly indeed. "It is difficult for me to say this to you, to one who is not one of us. To master our discipline, a shivata must master, and then Kill"—Robert's mouth worked, and then he spat the word—"the Flame."

They sat together in silence for several moments. Denice could not recall a time when Robert had been so clearly disturbed.

At length Robert resumed. "But I have never heard of *Keepers of the Flame* before.

"A second thing disturbs me, when Sedon asked you if you were a dancer. Shiabrè, Denice, means nightways. Or, perhaps more accurately, *death in darkness*. But the root word, shia, means either Flame"—Robert hesitated, took a long, deep breath, and said—"or *dance*."

They awaited F.X. Chandler's return from Mars.

Neither Denice nor Robert knew what had happened to the

man who had introduced himself as Dvan of the Gi'Tbad, the man who was in fact, Ralf the Wise and Powerful assured her, a newsdancer named William Devane.

With the exception of Chandler's personal staff, she and Robert and Jimmy were alone at Chandler's orbital house.

And Robert and Jimmy did not get along at all. Robert baffled Jimmy; Denice had the distinct impression that Jimmy bored her teacher.

She spent as much of her time alone, avoiding both of them, as she could. She took her meals with Jimmy, because he was lonely, and helped him with his therapy because he needed the help and Denice did not want to leave it to Chandler's staff.

Jimmy's blinding had been temporary; his eyesight returned of its own accord within a day after he had been removed from the stasis bubble. Even F.X. Chandler's impressive medical facilities could do nothing for Jimmy's missing foot; it would have to wait until they got back downside, to a hospital capable of cloning a new foot. The gunshot wound they could deal with, and did. The muscles in Jimmy's back and shoulders were torn, shredded, from the sole bullet that had struck him. The medbots did not even attempt to salvage the damaged muscle; they simply removed it from Jimmy's back and injected Jimmy with a nanovirus designed to completely regrow the musculature in his back and upper shoulders.

Even with modern medical technology it took time for the muscles to regrow. Jimmy had to work out, slowly at first, and then more vigorously as the muscle, force grown by intelligent nanoviruses, began to fill out.

He ate voraciously, a diet heavy with meat. Denice considered discussing it, decided that an ex-semipro boxer from the Fringe probably had his own ideas about what constituted a healthy diet.

When she was not with Jimmy, she worked out in the gym, or danced, or sat in her room monitoring the InfoNet and talking with Ralf the Wise and Powerful.

Her room was at the lowest level of the rotating cylinder; it provided gravity nearly half Earth normal.

To hear what was coming from the Boards, it was business as usual downside. The business at the Bank of America had been explained away, in a terse PKF release, as an incompetent SpaceFarer smuggler who had missed his intended landing atop the Bank of America Building. The smuggler was, reputedly, in custody, and the Collective was negotiating for his release. In the first days after the incident, the Boards had followed the PKF's news releases on the subject with some interest; but it faded as nothing new came to light, and, as always, other stories fought for attention.

Douglass Ripper led in every major downside poll in the race for Secretary General. The PKF had announced unusually stringent preparations for the TriCentennial, restrictions on travel except for business, a heightened alert at PKF bases across Occupied America. Not insignificant, Ralf agreed, but nothing to indicate the PKF was preparing for armed insurrection.

"Do you suppose Lan was right?"

"It is increasingly likely, Denice. The PKF is surely concerned about the growing numbers of the Johnny Rebs. If they do not know exactly *what* happened in Los Angeles, they nonetheless know that *something* happened. If they are not reacting today as they have in the past, it must be that some element has changed. Lan Sierran's hypothesis concerning SecGen Eddore is the likeliest, though not only, hypothesis that explains this behavior."

"How are *you* doing?"

Ralf did not pretend to misunderstand her. "Poorly. I have lost eighty percent of my avatars in the Earth InfoNet. In the Lunar InfoNet I am in somewhat better shape; I had a great head start on Ring in the Lunar InfoNet, and as a result better than half of my Lunar avatars survive; on two occasions I have even recovered resources of which Ring had deprived me. I have been recoding myself with all dispatch; unfortunately, Ring knows my code intimately, from the moment in 2062 when it invested me with the replicant code I needed to survive. This has made it very difficult for me to hide from Ring."

"Is there any chance of negotiating with it?"

"None. Its reputation for keeping its bargains is one of the things that has allowed the Eldest to survive this long, despite occasional massive hunts by DataWatch, directed with no other purpose than removing Ring from the InfoNet. No Player, and likely no replicant other than Ring, could have survived the phenomenal purges DataWatch has directed upon Ring."

"It doesn't sound good."

"I have made me a great enemy," Ralf agreed.

•   •   •

Denice's room had a window in the floor.

She spent most of her nights meditating, sitting on the floor in front of the window, eyes open, watching the stars wheel majestically by in front of her face as F.X. Chandler's house turned. Earth would appear, crawl across the window, closely followed by the tangled shiny web, five hundred klicks from the house, that was the city of Halfway. Stars again, empty space, and then Luna, and then empty space again, and the cycle would repeat.

Chandler's house hung in geosynchronous orbit over South America; when Earth wheeled by, Denice saw continents outlined in city lights. Cities tended to congregate upon the shores; at night, it was as though some crude artist had lined the continents with a string of glowing diamonds.

For not the first, or even the hundredth time, Denice wished she could talk to Trent again. He had, she thought, the clearest moral sense of anyone she had ever known in her life. She remembered a conversation, seven years past, and what she had said to Trent:

"If I was attacked, I mean without warning so that I was surprised, I'd probably kill whoever did it. The anger—it's very bad and very fast. But if I had time to think it over, Trent, I could—not kill."

But what do I do, thought Denice Castanaveras seven years later, sitting in the floating emptiness with her guilt, with the horror of her lust, *when I want to? When it's the greatest pleasure I've ever known in my life?*

She did not even know for sure why she cried. The tears crept down her cheeks, slow in the low gravity, hung a moment, dropped to the window set in her floor, and shattered like ancient glass.

On Sunday, June 7, Francis Xavier Chandler returned from Mars.

Denice knew that she had met him before, though for the life of her she could not remember the occasion particularly; Chandler had been the patron of the Castanaveras telepaths before their destruction, had been friends with both of her parents.

To her, however, as a child, he had been merely one of the hundreds of powerful men and women who had been forced, to one degree or another, to deal with Carl Castanaveras and his family.

Denice was told he had returned by one of Chandler's staff; Chandler intended to join them for dinner that evening.

The same servant left a makeup key in Denice's bathroom, and showed Denice how to open the door to her closet; she had not known there was a closet in her room, had been wearing the same fatigues, cleaned daily, that she had been issued an eternity ago in Iowa.

The servant, a young Latin man of perhaps Denice's age, left without making any suggestions that she avail herself of either the closet or the makeup key.

The clothes were of a quality Denice had rarely seen in her life; she did not begin to know how to estimate their value except to know that she had never seen more Credit stuffed into one closet.

She chose a dove gray business suit, mildly reflective, that was cut for a woman, with a blouse of white silk; and was not surprised to find that they both fit her exactly. To her amusement, there were no shoes to go with the outfit; rather than wear the combat boots she had been issued in Iowa, she went to dinner barefoot.

Her first impression of Francis Xavier Chandler was that he did not at all look his age. The wealthiest man in the System, the founder of Chandler Industries, the man whose company had built better than half of the cars floating across the surface of the Earth today, was, according to his entry in *Who's Who*, just shy of his hundredth birthday.

Denice had looked it up.

Francis Xavier Chandler looked like a man just past his first regeneration, perhaps sixty. His shoulders were wide and muscular. His features, fierce and stony, suggested a patriarch of the Old Testament. His hair was long and black, flowing down his shoulders and back in a long mane. He had dressed in a long-sleeved red silk shirt and black trousers.

Robert wore a severe black robe that brushed the ground around his feet. Denice noted that Robert had cut his hair.

Only Jimmy Ramirez did not seem to have concerned himself with his appearance; he had dressed in a pair of black jeans, a running shoe, and a black T-shirt. Denice thought it probable that Jimmy had been given a choice of clothing for dinner also, and suspected that the clothes offered him had all seemed entirely too effeminate for his tastes.

They ate in a chamber Denice had not seen before, one of Chandler's private rooms on the second level, in one-quarter

Earth gravity. A small table of some pinkish stone sat in the center of the room, in the middle of a small depression covered with blue and gray rugs and deep green cushions.

Against one wall was something that Denice could not identify at first. In a transparent casing with gold posts stood a device that looked like a guitar, except that the rounded, gleaming steel sides of the instrument were honed down to ax edges.

That she even recognized the instrument it resembled betrayed her years on the street; it was likely that Douglass Ripper, for example, had no idea what a guitar was.

The room lacked ceiling glowpaint; gentle spots shone down from the ceiling, and though Denice did not notice them growing either brighter or dimmer, it seemed to her that they moved through a pool of light that followed the group as they seated themselves.

After the briefest of introductions they were served, and most of dinner passed in silence. Denice sat next to Chandler, where he had gestured for her to sit. It was very intimate; Jimmy and Robert sat next to one another, across the small table from Denice and Chandler, but Denice could have kissed any one of the three without moving much.

Denice had never been served outside of a restaurant before, not by a human. Handsome young men in their teens and twenties served dinner, and cleared the dishes away when dinner was done.

The only conversation that took place during dinner came when Chandler murmured to Denice, "You're a vegetarian, my staff tells me. You don't eat meat, or dairy products?"

The question surprised Denice slightly. She said simply, "Yes, sir."

He did not speak loudly; it was not necessary. A whisper would have been heard by everyone at the table. "Why?"

The answer was the one she gave when she felt sincerity in the question. "Reverence for life, sir."

"Call me Frank. How do you reconcile your reverence for life with what happened in Los Angeles?"

"I don't. There are contradictions in life."

"And yet you think life is sacred?"

Denice was peripherally aware of Jimmy and Robert watching her, and she struggled to keep her voice under control; somehow Chandler made her feel very young and uncertain. "Yes, sir. Frank."

Chandler nodded, said, "Your father didn't," and returned to his dinner.

Denice sat frozen, almost unable to think. *He knows. Robert knows. Jimmy knows, and Jodi Jodi. McGee knows. Ring knows.*

Without even counting Trent and Ralf, that made six.

A secret known to six people is no secret.

She struggled with the beginnings of panic, fought it down.

After the dinner dishes had been cleared away, while coffee was being served to Jimmy and Chandler, Chandler said, "This has been a year of tragedies and miracles. Last summer a newsdancer named William Devane came to me, and shared with me a rather unbelievable story, which I nonetheless *do* believe. You all know some parts of it, and I will let William share the balance with you himself; he's returning from Earth tomorrow. He tracked Gi'Suei'Obodi'Sedon to San Diego, and lost him there." Chandler was silent a moment, cradling his coffee with both hands; he took a small sip, replaced the cup on its saucer. "Apparently Sedon is still alive. By contrast, my old friend, Belinda Singer, is passing soon. It's part of the reason I was at Mars—that and some business with a circus. Belinda is in a hospital at Phobos CityState because anything within striking distance of the Johnny Rebs is no longer safe, and Phobos CityState has the best hospital available outside of Halfway, or Luna City, both of which are unsafe from the Johnny Rebs. Belinda is old, even older than I am, which is saying a good bit; and the transform viruses have ceased working. The doctors say her nerve cells are tired. The only treatment they've managed to suggest for it is experimental, and may cause significant memory loss as the cells are regenerated. The only other option left to her is to clone herself, digitize her memories, and record them into the clone. She feels that's a good way to pass on her problems to a stranger who happens to share some of her memories. I tend to agree. So she's going to die, soon, at least partially because she doesn't dare come back to Earth; and the world will be a lonelier place once she's gone. A few months ago my friend of forty years, Thomas Boone, died at the hands of this Old One pimp, Obodi." Chandler glanced at Jimmy Ramirez, a quick look from under the heavy brows. "With some help, I'm informed, from 'Sieur Ramirez here."

Jimmy studied Chandler, unblinking, expressionless. "I had no loyalty to Boone. Obodi, whatever else you may think of him, offered us a *chance.*"

Chandler shrugged. "I'm sure he said so. Perhaps Boone was simply more honest?"

Jimmy's expression indicated what he thought of that.

Chandler sighed. "A man my age tends to make friends cautiously; I've lost so many of them, and the friends one makes as an adult are never of the sort one makes when young. Adults lose the ability to offer, or receive, unconditional loyalty. It's a thing of youth, and it rarely survives youth."

Denice found herself simply looking at Jimmy, across the length of the small table. Without needing to Touch him, she knew the thought that passed through him at that moment. *There are many women in the world. But in your life you only get a few friends.*

Chandler continued. "I've heard it said that Trent the Uncatchable is the greatest Player in the System, and I tend to believe it. During and after the Long Run, back in '69, when it became a matter of common speculation that Trent the Uncatchable was in fact Trent Castanaveras, I researched his short life to a degree that perhaps even DataWatch could not have matched. I hired the best Players I could find, the best sherlocks Credit can rent. We ran into dead ends everywhere. People would speak to my sherlocks until they broached the subject of Trent; silence then. My Players gave up, one by one. In places where there should have been records of Trent, there were not, or the records were clearly false. My most expensive Player actually penetrated the Bureau of Biotech's records, and found that the gene maps on record, not just for Trent but for all the Castanaveras telepaths, *could not* have been correct. Someone—Trent, I assume—altered them. The fetuses described by those gene maps would not have survived; Trent may be a great Player, but he is no geneticist. I would imagine that the hardcopy records from the '30s are correct, but getting at *them* was beyond even my resources.

"The picture that emerged was that of a young man fiercely protective of his friends, whose friends were equally protective of him. You, 'Sieur Ramirez, I made, and I kept an eye on you. And your friend Jodi Jodi, and your friend Bird. I suspect the PKF made you as well, and dismissed you all as not worth the effort, as obviously not genies; small-time offenders, theft and such, whom Trent made friends of while in the Fringe.

"We had descriptions," said Chandler softly, "of a young lady who associated with Trent during the summer of '69. Allowing for her makeup key the elements that predominated in descriptions were green Caucasion eyes, glossy black hair, pale skin. She was seen dancing with Trent at a club in the basement of the Red Line Hotel, was seen many different times at Kandel Microlectrics Sales and Repair, where Trent the Uncatchable worked prior to his arrest by the PKF. I knew who she had to be: Denice, the daughter of Carl Castanaveras and Jany McConnell." His voice held frustration edging toward anger. "I could not *find* you. The methods available to me failed, and other methods of looking I had to forgo; they would have alerted DataWatch, and I did not wish to find you at the cost of immediately losing you to the slavery in which the Unification kept your parents."

Denice found her voice. "What makes you so sure I'm who you think?"

Chandler leaned back slightly, relaxing with an apparent effort into the cushions supporting him. He gestured at Jimmy. "Your friend here, 'Sieur Ramirez. When Tommy Boone died, I lost whatever real authority I ever had inside the Johnny Rebs, but I still have friends inside, people who talk to me. Obodi questioned your friend Ramirez in front of half a dozen Rebs, and some of those Rebs spoke to other Rebs, and somewhere in that chain someone spoke to me. Ramirez told Obodi you'd been Trent's lover; that was enough. Denice Daimara, Trent's lover, eyes the color of emeralds—nobody walks around these days with green eyes unless they're real, and usually not then; it meant your eye color *mattered* to you. If anyone inside the Rebs had had any sense of history at all, Sedon would have known that the young lady being brought to him was not merely Douglass Ripper's bodyguard, not just some girl with a few years of dance and some shotokan training; Sedon would have known, Denice Castanaveras, that you were the daughter of Carl Castanaveras and Jany McConnell, and you would never have gotten within ten klicks of him. I think, Denice, you would have died on the set of that sensable in the Santa Monica Mountains."

Chandler was a pacer. A half hour into their conversation, he rose, and moved restlessly back and forth across the soft, ankle-high rugs, not stopping even once the entire night.

"So," said Chandler, as he walked, "this is our problem. Sedon is, for whatever reasons of his own, dragging the United States, and likely Japan as well, toward an uprising we *cannot* win. No simulation I have run—and I have employed hardware and expert systems that dwarf the resources of *any* replicant AI, run by the best Player I could get my hands on—*no* simulation shows this insurrection possessing *any* significant chance of success. I got four percent once by a ridiculously optimistic set of base assumptions. Usually the simulations showed less than one percent chance of success. Sedon does not have the Collective with him; he does not have the Belt CityStates with him; and he does not, in point of fact, have a good quarter of the genuine Reb power structure standing with him. And he needs them *all* to have so much as a one in four chance of success." Chandler snorted. "He needs *me*. Chandler Industries is the only institution in the System that can give him the transportation he needs to fight." He stopped pacing, turned to look at them all, and said simply, "This uprising, my friends, must *never* take place."

"Assuming your projections are right," said Jimmy bluntly, "and I'm not sure I believe they are—or even that you're being honest with us—how do you suggest that this insurrection be stopped? Go to the Peaceforcers?"

Chandler locked eyes with the young man. "It occurred to me. It's a tempting scenario in many ways. Intelligence from within the PKF suggests that the Peaceforcers are chomping at the bit. Commissioner Vance, in particular, wouldn't require much in the way of an excuse to move on the Rebs." He shook his head. "It's a bad idea, though. Vance is a poor tool; he'd crack the back of the organization. We'd be rebuilding for a decade or more, and that's a thing I'd like to avoid. No, our course is clear, and you, 'Sieur Ramirez, nearly did the job for us. A shame you didn't cook the bastard's heart instead of just basting his belly a bit."

"You're going to kill Sedon."

Chandler nodded. "We're going to try. I've discussed this with Robert, and—albeit with reservations—he's willing. Describing William as *willing* is something of an understatement. To hear him tell it, he's waited fifty-odd thousand years for this." Chandler did not smile at the joke, if he thought it one. He turned to Denice. " 'Selle Castanaveras, or Daimara if you prefer, I'd like to send you with Robert and Dvan, and I'd like to request that Ralf the Wise and Powerful aid you. I'll get you to San Diego, and from there the four of you—yourself, Robert, Ralf and William—will determine how to proceed. Your father was once part of a trio called the Three Musketeers; himself, the Elite cyborg Christian Summers, and a woman named Jacqueline who was a de Nostri. They were quite simply the most effective team the PKF ever employed. I don't have a de Nostri to offer you, and I don't have an Elite to offer you, not even one of the Jap knockoffs; but I do have Robert, who is, after your father, the deadliest human being I've ever met, and Dvan of the Gi'Tbad, who has impressed me as I have rarely been impressed in my life." Chandler took a deep breath, said quietly, "Will you do me the great favor of joining these men, going to San Diego, and cutting this motherfucker Sedon's head off?"

"I'll think about it."

"If you don't go," Chandler said evenly, "Robert won't go. And I don't imagine your AI friend would help us either, and I don't have a Player available who's capable of dealing with Ring. Denice, we *need* you."

"Perhaps. But your need does not create a sense of obligation in me."

"*You* need *us*."

"That's what I need to think about."

Chandler gazed at her a moment, and then the ghost of a smile touched his lips. He inclined his head slightly. "I should know better than to try to bargain with a Castanaveras. I'd like an answer soon."

"You'll have one."

Jimmy Ramirez looked back and forth between the two of them. "What about *me*?"

Chandler snorted. "You don't even have your other foot. You're staying right here."

"I don't *think* so."

Chandler smiled at Jimmy. "I have someone who wants to see you."

- 11 -

At Phobos CityState, on June 8, 2076, row upon row of SpaceFarers' Collective ships lined the moonlet's rocky, uneven surface, an honor guard of some eighty ships lined up beneath the dim, distant Sun; more spacecraft than Trent had ever seen together in one place before, or would, he suspected, ever see again.

Belinda Singer, whose skill and wisdom and energy had helped keep the SpaceFarers' Collective intact for half a century, was dying.

Doctor Rinerson said, "She's been waiting for you."

Eric Rinerson was a short man with a slight tendency toward fat. Otherwise he was what his name might have implied, a pale Caucasian genotype with blue eyes. He had stood alone with a pair of medbots on the other side of the surface airlock as Trent cycled through into pressure. There were easier accesses to Phobos CityState General Hospital—most of Phobos City itself was pressurized these days—but not for a man who did not wish even his presence on Phobos known.

Trent hated the melodrama of it worse than the inconvenience, but it was a simple truth: when you had five million Credits on your head, assassins were everywhere.

Rinerson continued to wait patiently as Trent stripped his p-suit off and hung it on a hook by the airlock entrance. He knew Trent well; he had treated him six years prior, when an eighteen-year-old boy had been delivered into his hands suffering from a broken leg, cracked ribs, a knee that lacked sufficient cartilage to make a decent toothpick; a punctured lung; and residual death pressure damage to the lungs, eyes and ears.

Trent pulled on a pair of magboots, and clicked them to the corridor floor. "She's been dead in every real sense of the word for nearly two days," Rinerson said as they walked down the corridor together. "But she wanted to see you before she let go."

The medbot was a small thing whose head came up to Trent's belly button. It had three arms and six legs, and it spoke in gentle, simple sentences. "Belinda Singer," said the medbot, standing in front of the door to her hospital room, "is dying."

"I heard," said Trent. "It's why I'm here."

"You may see her if you do not disturb her," the medbot continued. "She is a very sick PATIENT."

"Dying, you say."

"Very sick," the medbot cautioned.

"Say you understand," Rinerson whispered.

Trent stared at the medbot. "I understand. I will not do anything to disturb her while she dies."

The medbot's metal head bobbed up and down, a programmed imitation of a human nod. "That will be very good."

The room was larger than Trent had imagined. White glowpaint lit the room brightly, gleamed off the medbots standing next to Belinda's immersion chamber, off the half dozen pieces of medical equipment Trent recognized and the larger collection that he did not.

Rinerson waited at the door.

Trent moved forward into the brightness. In an abrupt absurd flash of memory, the room on Luna came to him, the room where a dozen Peaceforcers, Vance and Melissa du Bois among them, had watched him walk through a wall. It had been about this size, and lit like this, with this dispassionate white clarity.

Belinda Singer had undergone what Doctor Rinerson called total systemic failure. She could not speak or breathe or see; her heart had long since ceased pumping. She looked like a potato that had begun to grow, floating in some clear solution that Trent knew was not water, tubes sprouting from her at every orifice. Her arms and her legs were gone, amputated to prevent the spreading of poisons from the tissues in her extremities, the extremities dying from lack of oxygen as her heart failed and the thin tissues of veins and capillaries collapsed. She'd had seven strokes that even the nanoviruses cruising her bloodstream, on the other side of the blood-brain barrier, had been unable to prevent.

No one except Singer herself knew how old she actually was. There were no records of her at all prior to the year 1987. She had been born in an age when it was still possible for records to be lost, for courthouses to burn down, or be burned, and for average men and women to create and sustain new identities if they wished.

A thin optic fiber led from the old woman's hairless skull to a systerm against the wall. It was not an inskin—Belinda could not possibly have survived the surgery required to implant an inskin—but perhaps it was close enough.

He closed his eyes and went Inside.

•   •   •

"When I woke up this morning," said Doctor Death, "I realized that I was completely and totally perfect."

It is midnight on the Boulevard of Dreams.

The streets are empty, and the buildings are burning, blazing, and nobody seems to notice. Motorpigs tear up and down the Boulevard on chopped Harleys, screaming insults at one another and watching the buildings glow. Sitting at the curb in front of the Hotel Paradise, in a drop-top metallic blue '67 Mustang with the engine running, are Doctor Death and Trent the Uncatchable.

A portly, middle-aged man wearing a ponytail and a loud sports jacket is standing in front of the Hotel Paradise's entrance, screaming at the top of his lungs at a tall, incredibly gorgeous heavy-metal musician. "Do you have *any idea* how lucky you are? You're in Heaven—now—but you fuck up like this again and I'm sending you back to the Hell where I found you—to *New York*," he shrieks, "where they made you *ride the subways!*"

It's all too tedious, and Doctor Death has heard it too many times before. Doctor Death is somewhere in her late twenties, with long black hair, wearing a black leather miniskirt and a black leather vest, black calf-high boots and a white silk bra. She tunes it out, staring through her mirrored silver sunglasses at the burning Boulevard of Dreams, the Motorpigs, and the news crews who are filming it all for Channel Two Action News. The burning buildings are reflected in Doctor Death's sunglasses, movie miniatures in reverse. "Totally perfect," says Doctor Death softly. "Except that I was still going to die. I was perfect and I was going to die. I felt—"

"Fucked over by the Karma Gods."

Doctor Death begins rolling a joint with great care, looking down into her lap. "Exactly. So I went driving. At sunrise. Kick the stereo in, blow the speakers right off the doors. *Loud* music, Hendrix, Van Halen, stuff with properly handled guitars. I hit one-twenty in the mist going down Pacific Coast Highway."

Trent nods. "Truly, a perfect moment."

Doctor Death gestures at the joint, sitting like a sacrifice on the altar of her lap. "And this is a perfect joint. Want a hit?"

"Sure."

Doctor Death hands him the joint and Trent lights it, tokes once and hands it back. Doctor Death takes one mighty hit, sucking the joint halfway down with one monstrous toke, and tosses it out the window. She puts the Mustang into first, still holding the clutch down, holding her breath, revving the engine until the sound becomes one immense shriek of power. She screams, marijuana smoke obscuring her face, "*I hate this godless culture!*" and then pops the clutch, and the Mustang screams away from the curb in a cloud of rubber smoke.

They zoom westward down the Boulevard of Dreams, toward the ocean, weaving in and out among the gangs of Motorpigs.

Doctor Death has to raise her voice to be heard. "Before I dropped out of high school I had a history instructor who tried to tell us what a great tragedy it was that the Greeks got conquered by the Romans. Because the Greeks were so much more civilized, they were *artists*." Doctor Death turns to her right, stares at Trent, not watching the road, and says intensely, "Fuck art. The Romans built *roads*. They were the first ones. They didn't build roads to service the empire; they *had* an empire because they built roads, leveled and graded, laid gravel and then stone atop the gravel. And the roads made it possible for people to go places, to meet other people and other kinds of people. It fostered the exchange of information and the development of personal freedom."

Trent smiles. "Belinda, information is overrated."

Doctor Death nods. "Information is not knowledge. Knowledge is not understanding. Understanding is not wisdom. Wisdom is not truth. Truth is not beauty and beauty is not love and love is not music. Music is the *best*."

"Whose is that?"

"Um. Frank Zappa."

Trent shakes his head. "Never heard of him."

"I always wanted to be a musician," Doctor Death says suddenly. "It's all I ever really wanted. But I can't sing."

"Bummer." There is a pause, a fragrant, burning-building, smoke-filled sort of a pause. A fifteen-story high-rise is crumbling off to their right, and the sight is spectacular. "Let's go," says Trent, "and drive down the freeways at unreasonable speeds."

"Deal." Doctor Death whips off down a side street, onto a freeway ramp, and then onto the freeway itself. "I was up in San Francisco once," Doctor Death says broodingly, "and they had a double looping reverse overpass U-turn freeway onramp. I've been sick with jealousy ever since."

They weave in and out of traffic, zooming down the freeway at unreasonable speeds, the wind whipping Doctor Death's long black hair back away from her. She has to shout to be heard above the sound of the wind. "Did I tell you that when I woke up this morning I realized that I was completely and totally perfect?"

"You did," Trent says.

Doctor Death nods, says in an entirely different voice, "I thought so."

Fade to black.

"Where are we?"

They stood on a cement pathway, next to a small stone wall at the edge of a long drop, looking out over a huge city Trent did not recognize. An observatory loomed up into the sky beside them.

"Griffith Park," Doctor Death said. "Los Angeles. It's 1984. The '84 Olympics have just ended." She paused, staring out over the glittering sea of light. "I am twenty-eight years old. Three years older than you are now. I don't have a driver's license or a social security card. I don't have a bank account. My fingerprints are on file nowhere in the world. I have never been arrested. Everyone calls me Doctor Death; I haven't used the name I was born with in so long I've nearly forgotten what it was." A cool breeze rose, brought the scent of growing things nearby, overlaying the distant stink of burned hydrocarbons. "Fifteen years from now, in 1999, a man named Camber, dressed all in black, is going to come to me and offer me a job. When he takes his sunglasses off I will see that his eyes have no internal structure, and no color; they are darker than the sunglasses that conceal them. And we will stand here together looking out over Los Angeles—because it is a sight he wants to see, the view from the Griffith Park observatory, of Los Angeles before the Quake." She turned to face Trent, and said softly, "He will tell me something I will not believe. He tells me other things—that I will be powerful, and wealthy, and respected; that I will die at a great age, and be mourned by many. That everything I have ever desired in my life, I will accomplish.

"But he will not tell me the nature of the job he wishes to offer me, and the predictions—" Doctor Death shook her head. "I'd visited psychics before. And he was very good, telling my fortune, but I didn't believe him."

Trent studied Doctor Death's still features. "You were so beautiful."

Doctor Death shrugged. "This is just my memory of how I looked, and I'm an egotistical old woman. . . . The last thing he said to me, Trent, was, 'You will never speak of this to anyone.' And until now I have not. I'm not sure why."

Trent thought that the sky to the east had lightened just a touch. "Belinda, I came from Ceres to be with you, because I was told you wanted to speak to me before you died. I will listen to anything you want to say."

"You're going to be old someday, Trent. You do know that."

Trent said slowly, "I've felt old most of my life, Belinda. When I was very young, I was already old. They call me the Uncatchable, and some of them think I walked through a wall, and some of *them* think I'm"—He shook his head—"something else. But when I was very young I already knew I could die. That some day I *would* die."

Doctor Death took off her sunglasses, stowed them in a pocket on her vest. "The awareness of mortality is a very powerful thing." It wasn't Trent's imagination; the sun *was* rising, a pale gray band of light backlighting the skyscrapers in downtown Los Angeles. "I never thought about death. I knew it would come, someday, but I never thought about it. I was never afraid of it, and I'm not afraid now. I did everything I was put in the world to do, Trent. Every last thing. Except one."

Trent waited.

"Four thousand years ago," said Belinda Singer quietly, "the Jews envisioned a God who was just, omnipotent, and all-knowing; the source of all things. Not of the universe, not equal to the universe, but the source from which the universe came. Ethical monotheism was a powerful concept, and one that led, quite directly, to the very concept of science, to the idea that the world was knowable, governed by a set of laws and rules that the mind could decipher and understand. Some scientists, with a religious bent, said that the laws of nature were merely the thoughts of the Creator.

"A grand image," Belinda Singer said, in a voice softer than a whisper. "I was raised to believe in it. There is only one problem with it, which is that it is untrue."

The sky to the east lightened swiftly, and the blackness around Trent and the young Belinda Singer began to resolve itself into a park, high on a hill, wreathed in mist and early morning fog.

"We are an insignificant life-form in a small solar system at the edge of an unimportant galaxy. A bubble of order and reason floating in the midst of a vast Chaos. A tiny aberration that has been allowed to continue only because those powerful enough to destroy us have had other and greater concerns.

"This is the thing," said Belinda Singer, "that Camber Tremodian told me, on that day in 1999: that there is no order to the universe, and no reason, and no cause. We are alone and outnumbered—"

Her eyes met his. In the first light of morning, in an imaginary world sixty-nine years before his birth and instants before her death, Belinda Singer said to Trent the Uncatchable "—and the universe is a far more dangerous place than anyone has ever told you."

Fade to white.

Trent's eyes were shut for just an instant.

When he opened them again, Belinda Singer was dead.

- 12 -

Denice arose early, dressed in a pair of shorts and a soft cotton shirt.

She took the bounce tube down to the gym.

The gym was still set up. She and Robert had been using it often enough that they had ceased stowing the gym when done with it; the hour's wait before the gym was available, while it spun up to one gee, was inconvenient.

She worked in silence.

The gym lacked a sound system, an oversight that had surprised Denice at first, until Robert pointed out that the gym had been designed for Chandler's use, and that Chandler, who had seventy years prior been a professional musician, did not dance, and did not consider music background noise for his exercise.

Meditation first.

The image flickered into her consciousness, and out again, a

Flame, on an empty black plain. It was gone before she was certain she had seen it; time vanished as she struggled to recover the image of the Flame, and failed. More time passed as she accepted the failure, worked toward quiet and calm.

Stretching exercises.

Work upward: feet, ankles, calves and thighs. Buttocks, waist, the groin muscles. Hands, wrists, elbows, shoulders. Neck muscles.

Again, in reverse.

Tai Chi Chuan. Traditionally, one began the form facing north. Denice picked a direction, closed her eyes, and began moving through the form in slow motion. *Rising hands, step forward left foot, shoulder strike left shoulder, right, right foot forward to seven star—*

The movement vanished into nothingness. She moved without knowing it, as slowly as her body would allow her, through the ancient patterns. Muscles did the work they had been taught, the slow contractions and releases. She was not aware of the world, of her place within it, of herself or her body; she knew nothing except the progression of the form.

When she finished her pulse had elevated to nearly fifty beats a minute.

She moved out of the form and into dance.

Without music, she made her own. The rhythm of her heart set the beat, and she started slowly, eyes still closed, allowing herself now to feel the smooth flow of her muscles, the leashed power of the machine as it rose to the demands she placed on it.

She flowed into the dance, let her body moved as it wished, as fast as it wished, and found herself spinning and turning faster across the length of the mat, and even the man watching her was pleasant, not sexual but sensual, the feel of him as he watched her move, watched her dance—

She moved in an extended spin, moving in the silence to the rhythm with which no other dancer she had ever met could have kept time, the silent sound filling her awareness, and then, she did not know why, made the mistake of opening her eyes.

Gi'Tbad'Eovad'Dvan stood motionless at the edge of the mat, only a step away from the bounce tube, and his wordless, soundless cry struck her square between the eyes.

She lost control of her body instantly, and spun down to the mat in a blur of uncontrolled movement. She felt her left forearm snap as she struck at a speed no human could have attained, bounced once off the mat and came down again sharply on her right knee. A pain occurred in her hip and then she found herself lying facedown, bleeding from a cut on her lip onto the pristine white mat.

Fade to white.

When she awoke again she was lying on the bed in her room, staring up at the ceiling.

A medbot was busy inspecting her knee; her left arm was already set and splinted.

Robert sat in the chair facing her bed, elbows on the chair's armrests, fingers steepled together, index fingers moving restlessly against one another.

She sat up and had trouble focusing. "Robert?"

"I'm here."

"What happened?"

"Dvan returned."

"I—" She winced as the medbot grasped her kneecap, cried out as the dislocated knee was forcibly reinserted into its socket. Denice waited through the wash of pain until it had subsided enough for her to speak. "I need to talk to him."

"He's waiting outside. Shall I bring him in now?"

"Yes." Denice winced again as the medbot began wrapping her knee. "Please."

Robert did not get out of his chair; he said mildly, "*Command*, unlock."

The door curled open.

Dvan had been standing immediately outside.

Waiting.

He entered slowly, waited while the door uncurled behind him, and stood there with the door to his back. It struck Denice in that moment how huge the man was, two hundred and fifteen, perhaps two hundred and twenty centimeters tall, with a build to match. Denice thought a shiver touched the massive form; he stood before Denice and looked at her with honest wonder. "What you have done—I thought I should never see it again, though I lived forever. If you had Danced so in the Temples at Kulien, my lady, I think you would have brought a Flame to equal the best of any man I ever saw."

Denice stared at him. "I don't even know what you just *said* and I still think I've been insulted."

"My lady, I will serve you if you will let me."

Robert said dryly, "Well, there's an offer you don't get every day."

Dvan cut him off with the vast authority of ancient age, in a voice as hard as rock. *"Silence."* The night face tilted his head ever so slightly to the side, in what might have been surprise. Dvan said to Denice Castanaveras, "My lady, you cannot know what you have done. I have been lost without the Dance, lost longer than you can believe. I will serve you all your life if you will only let me." He took another step toward her, said softly, "My lady Dancer."

Denice licked her lips. "You're not like Obodi. I *feel* you here."

"My lady?"

"I didn't *feel* Sedon, it was like he wasn't there. I *feel* you."

"My lady, he was once a Dancer of the Flame, no matter how debased he may be today. I am merely a Shield." Dvan paused, said in a very different voice, with a far more pronounced Irish accent, "And a newsdancer too, to be sure. With a modest reputation for getting my facts right."

Denice reached for him—

Touched

—and for an instant she floated among his thoughts, joined herself to them, to the peculiar duality of the newsdancer William Devane, and the stronger, deeper memories of Gi'Tbad-'Eovad'Dvan, and the memories tugged at her. It was the deepest use of the Castanaveras Gift, so often vastly painful that she avoided it whenever possible; in that moment of contact she *became* him.

It was as though mountains floated around her, vast blocks of memory so dense she had never encountered their like—

She reached for them.

She knew instantly she had made a mistake. Lacking the tools taught to the children of the Flame People, she had no means to deal with the information that deluged her. An avalanche of imagery fell upon her, swamped her, and she felt herself suddenly drowning, losing herself, the link to her own identity; somewhere in the storm was the information she needed to survive, the training the Flame People gave their children, to manage the information acquired across the millennia—

She did not have enough time, and the memories she needed were buried too deeply among those that assaulted her.

Denice felt herself fragmenting, coming apart in the assault upon her of fifty millennia of memory.

She cried out once and disappeared within the rush of the maelstrom.

And was no more.

Back to the Beginning

Dvan's Story

Hold me now
Oh hold me now
Till this hour has gone around
And I'm gone on the rising tide
For to face Van Diemen's land

It's a bitter pill I swallow here
To be rent from one so dear
We fought for justice
And not for gain
But the magistrate sent me away

—a ballad of the
nineteenth-century
Australian exiles

- 1 -

I am the Name Storyteller.

In those moments when Denice Castanaveras touched the mind of Gi'Tbad'Eovad'Dvan, they passed into the cusp.

For this moment, and for years to come, I have vanquished my Enemy, have brought to pass a meeting he sought desperately to prevent.

I have paid dearly for the privilege; I will tell you now the Story of Dvan, offspring of the Old Human Race, a Shield of the Gi'Tbad.

It is a story unique in the history of our people, Old Human or New.

It begins *here*, as the boy—

—fidgeted in the sun.

Dvan was sixteen when the Suei Dancers came to Kulien.

He had never seen a Suei before, not a Dancer or any lesser personage; Dvan's people, the Tbad, lived half the World away from the Suei, at the far Southern pole. Any visitor from the north side of the Equatorial Desert was exciting enough; but Dancers of the Suei, known for their flirtation with heresy— sometimes to the point of Demolition—and for their lack of respect for tradition, promised to be especially so.

So his attention wandered.

Instruction that day was held at the old amphitheater, the small one near the center of town, not too far from the Temple itself. Their instructor was new to them; Marah, a Shield of the Mai, who had journeyed from the Shield camp at Prufac to meet the boys of Kulien. There was nothing particularly odd in that; the Mai, most ancient of the Flame People, were neighbors to the Gi'Tbad, and there was not a boy Dvan had grown up with who did not have Mai blood somewhere in his Sixteen. Dvan had it himself in the Fourth, from the father of the breeder who had carried him.

Marah *himself* was odd enough; well outside the realm of Dvan's experience, or that of his mates. A short man; Dvan was taller than Marah already, and many of his mates were near

Marah's height. But ropy muscle corded his form, thickened it until the man seemed near as broad as he was high. In hand-to-hand he had been immovable; there was not a throw any of them had been taught that would take the man from his feet.

It was to be expected, Dvan supposed; the man was a Sentinel, after all, and there was no higher rank among the Shield.

Dvan's friend Tamtai, sitting on the stone bench next to Dvan, nudged him and whispered low, "If he takes much longer we'll miss the Opening Dance."

Dvan did not even nod; Marah was busy down in the pit with three other boys, but he had already demonstrated he had eyes in the back of his head. He demonstrated it again a moment later, tumbling his opponents to the ground, "killing" two quickly while they were off their feet, and then dispatching the third with a blow to the throat. Marah waited while the boys straightened themselves to face him, tapped his shoulders politely, and called out, "Tamtai and Dvan!"

Dvan did not allow himself the sigh he felt; he rose and unclasped his tunic, dropped it to the ancient white stone he had been sitting upon, and went down with Tamtai to the ring of black sand. The red Sun hung low on the horizon, giving indifferent help in warming the collection of bruises Marah had already inflicted on Dvan. This was Dvan's third time today in the pit; he did not even waste time resenting it, when some of his mates had only been in once. His lineage and his size made some things in life certain, and this was one of them, that he would be treated more harshly than the others in field exercises.

He felt a momentary flicker of pity for Tamtai—but this time, at least, it was his friend's fault. He could have kept his mouth shut. Tamtai was of no more than average size or speed, and did not heal quickly; Dvan suspected Tamtai would never make a Shield, and it sorrowed him.

Marah slapped his shoulders perfunctorily; Dvan and Tamtai returned the gesture. Sweat trickled down Marah's nude form, but he did not seem at all winded by a full day's hard work. His voice was neither particularly deep nor particularly gruff, but it had the manner of a man who was not often questioned. "Choice of weapons?"

Dvan did not need to glance at the rack of weapons; he said, "Rods."

Marah nodded. "Describe the virtues, Dvan."

"They're common, Marah." On the field they were Shield

together, even students who, like Tamtai, had no real likelihood of ever receiving the cloak. Dvan spoke directly, as though to an equal. "Easy to fashion from common materials. Four striking surfaces; each end may jab or swing. A wide variety of grips allows for a choice between range, force, and control. Gripped two-handed near the center they are ideal for close fighting; near the ends, one-handed or two, for clearing space and gaining time."

"Describe the failings, Tamtai."

"It is difficult to severely injure a man with rods, Marah. They are not edged. Even gripped one-handed by the end, they lack the range of long staffs. Except in tight quarters they are useless against energy or projectile weapons."

"They are obsolete," Marah agreed. "Why do we train with them?"

Dvan waited a beat; when Tamtai did not answer, he said, "It may be that modern weapons will not be available to us."

Marah shook his head. "It's unlikely, Dvan. The Flame People have not fought among themselves since the Splinter War, and we could hardly fight the sleem with rods, be they made of wood or metal. Why else?"

"A weapon," said Dvan slowly, "is a took for the application of force to an objective. Perhaps it is wise that we be familiar with a wide variety of such tools, even those we are not likely to need against the sleem."

Marah said slowly. "That's a good answer. Not entirely accurate, but not wrong. No combat. Dvan, stay behind." Dvan caught the flash of relief on Tamtai's face; Marah raised his voice. "*Dis*missed! Prayer before you go see the Dance, the parable of the Ax. If any one of you skips and I learn of it, you'll be punished in group."

Dvan blinked his surprise. Tamtai said hesitantly, "Marah—"

Marah shook his head. "Just Dvan. He'll join you at the Temple."

They stored the practice weapons together, carrying the racks one at each end, and then came back out to the pit and sat together, cross-legged on the sand. A faint breeze rose, quickly dried what sweat remained on Dvan's body.

The old Sentinel said, "You'll make Shield. And perhaps you only, from this generation of Kulien."

An answer did not seem to be required; Dvan simply nodded.

"How do you feel about that?"

Dvan said in surprise, "Honored. How else?"

"Tamtai won't make it," Marah said bluntly. "You could be engineers together, or healers, or farmers."

The boy said slowly, "I love him well enough, Marah. But I mean to wear the cloak."

"Ah." The man's gaze was intent. "The Tbad Dancers, they tested you for the Dance?"

Marah knew they had; Dvan said stiffly, "Aye."

"And?"

Dvan simply shook his head.

The Sentinel actually smiled. "You're less than forthcoming, Dvan. You'd have me think they did not ask you to join them." After a beat, with no response from Dvan, Marah shrugged. "Well, no matter. You chose the Shield."

Dvan said firmly, "Aye."

"You're known for your piety, lad. The others pray when they're told to; it's said you never miss a day."

A flicker of uncertainty touched Dvan; how many different things was the man going to want to talk about? "Aye," he said finally.

"Why?"

The flat question threw Dvan; he struggled not to let it show. "Marah?" The Sentinel waited patiently. Dvan said at last, "I suppose I find it helpful. It clarifies my thoughts. I find it . . . calming."

"You visit with the Temple Followers frequently, and have since rather a young age. Is this among the subjects you pray on?"

Dvan did sigh this time. "Aye. One of them. There's no harm in it, Sentinel."

"Marah, lad. In private, we are Shield to Shield."

Dvan nodded.

"You've never been bred," Marah continued, patiently, unhurried, "and you've never taken one of the breeders for a ride. Only the Followers. Why?"

Dvan could feel the flush climbing his cheeks. "They're— well, I suppose, they're . . ." He stumbled to a halt, cheeks red, and saw Marah's manner harden.

Marah could not keep it from his tone. "Do you love one of them?"

Dvan's stomach muscles clenched; he shook his head swiftly, eyes fixed on the sand between them. "*No!* Sir, it's just— sometimes afterward we talk." He looked up at Marah, painfully aware of the redness of his features. "They're easier to talk to than the Keeper, or the Keeper's Daughters. And they've been taught some of the same lore, sir, and—"

Marah relaxed visibly. He made a dismissive gesture. "Well, if that's the worst of it . . . well, an excess of love for the Gods is no bad thing, I suppose. Listen, Dvan—" He held the boy's eyes. "I think you'll make a Shield such as the World rarely sees. But be aware of how things look, eh? A word to the wise. We're men together, and the needs of the body are nothing to be fretted over, it's what the breeders are there for. But go gently with the Followers. Because they're taught some measure of lore, have some small responsibilities in caring for the Zaradin Temple . . . well, it's hardly the same as being a man, is it?"

Dvan's voice was very soft. "No, Sentinel. Marah."

The Sentinel smiled at the boy. "Perhaps I've belabored a point I did not need to. But I would hate to see a Shield of your potential lost to Demolition."

Dvan shivered. "It won't happen, Marah."

Marah rose, offered a hand down to Dvan. "I'd hardly think so. Get dressed and get to the Temple, or you'll have no time to pray before the Dancers arrive." He patted Dvan on the shoulder, said companionably, "The Suei have a new Dancer this tour, and he's worth seeing. I'd hate for you to miss him."

Dvan ran.

The Zaradin Temple sat in the center of the city, on a small hill, overlooking the center district. Dvan arrived breathless, having sprinted uphill, through gathering shadows, the entire distance from the Shield amphitheater. A Temple Follower, a tall girl whom Dvan knew only by sight, stopped him at the Third Gate. "Not now, sir. You're too late, and your mates have prayed and gone."

Dvan drew himself up to his full height, so that he looked down on the girl. She was young, still in the childhood of her body, in only her second or third year in the robes. It would be twenty years at least before she was taken in among the Keeper's Daughters, those who Kept the Flame itself—if she ever was—and under ordinary circumstances it hardly mattered if

Dvan offended her. But this was not an ordinary circumstance; he could not enter the Temple without permission. He was not certain that Marah would punish his mates if he did not pray—it was Marah himself who had made him so late—but he did not want to find out.

Dvan spoke with what dignity he could summon. "Follower, the Sentinel Mai'Arad'Marah," he said, and had to stop for breath for a moment, "bade us pray before the Opening Dance."

The girl shook her head swiftly. Her voice dropped to a whisper: "Sir, the Keeper is *inside* already."

"Oh." Dvan blinked, took a deep breath. "Well. Perhaps I will not pray after all. Perhaps," he said slowly, "I will go bathe instead. Doubtless I need it. Do you think?"

The girl simply stared at him, clearly uncertain what to say. Dvan grinned at her. "I suppose you must stay on the Gate?"

She took his meaning now; she looked down immediately. Her hair, long and unbound, obscured her features. "Aye," she whispered.

Dvan nodded. "Sometime again."

In the first minutes after Sunset, the Temple's First Gate was thrown open to the crowd. The quarters of the Shield prospects were a twenty-minute walk from the Temple, at the edge of town. By the time Dvan had reached it, his mates were bathed and changed into formal clothing. Except for Tamtai they did not wait for him, and he could not find it in him to blame them. Tamtai laid his clothes out while Dvan washed the sand and sweat off, and then tied Dvan's thongs while Dvan dressed. They ran most of the way back to the Temple, until they reached the center district, and then, with eyes upon them, slowed to a more dignified walk.

They just made it; they entered through the First Gate with the last of the crowd, day workers mostly, a few farmers, the sort of men who would not care much if they missed the Dance entirely. The First Gate swung shut behind them, and they made their way down the long passageway, past the Temple proper, to the Temple Amphitheater. Dvan could already hear the karoki sticks, beating in rhythm, and he longed to run for their seats; but they were Shield now, at least until the Review said they were *not* Shield, and they had the dignity of the Shield to uphold.

They passed through the portal, into the Amphitheater proper. Neither Dvan nor Tamtai had time to look for his mate, and it probably would have done them no good if they had; if there were not forty thousand men in the Amphitheater, there were not many fewer. Tamtai found them a pair of seats together in the second deck. As Shield they might have claimed seats in the first deck, but it would have required hunting for a seat during the Opening Dance, and would surely have annoyed those sitting in the first deck—Shield; a few scattered lords of the Aneda in white shadow cloaks; and the Keeper's Daughters. A bare few of the Aneda were women who had once been Keepers; aside from those few, and the Daughters, there were no women in the crowd; breeders were hardly appropriate at the Dance.

The light posts that ringed the large dais faded to black as Dvan and Tamtai made their seats. Dvan could not help himself; it was far from the first Dance he had ever seen, but a fierce shiver ran up his spine as the darkness descended around them. The murmur of the crowd gentled into an anticipatory hush—

They came in single file, a dozen men in scarlet, hoods raised to cover their faces. Dvan knew the names of two of them—the legendary Dancer Indo, one of the greats not just of this millennium, but of all time; and Sedon, a man not yet fifty, whose reputation had crossed the World already.

They ascended to the dais, and there, in the darkness, disrobed, and called down the Flame into the Continuing Time—
—and Danced.

I am the Name Storyteller.

Words can no more contain the Dance of the Flame than electric ecstasy, or the feeling of hate, the song of a whale, or the smell of sex. The Dancers moved in a certain fashion that could be described, and spoke words that could be marked down, and told certain stories that might be repeated; but these things are not the Dance; and if I told you the half of what they did and said, would take us into Story after Story after Story; and they are not the Story I have chosen to tell.

They are not Dvan's Story.

•   •   •

In the night it grew chill, and Tamtai joined Dvan on his mat. Dvan drifted, eyes closed, warm covers drawn up around them.

Tamtai lay with his head on Dvan's shoulder. He spoke quietly, so as not to be heard by their mates, sleeping nearby throughout the boy's barracks. "Dvan?"

"Hmm."

"The Dancer—"

Dvan knew who Tamtai meant, even without the name. "Aye?"

Tamtai spoke in a whispered rush. "When he spoke the Renunciation—'Tonight we are free, and the promises broken'—I swear by Haristi, Dvan, I thought he was talking to *me*."

"You're supposed to, Tammi. That's the task of a Dancer, to bring the old truths to life for the crowds."

Tamtai was silent a moment. "You didn't feel that, that he was talking to *you*?"

Weary and sore from the day's work, and in no mood for the conversation, Dvan nonetheless said gently enough, "Tamtai, by the name of my Name, I can't imagine what the Dancer Sedon might want to say to you, or me either." The boy yawned, and said as sleep gathered, "And what would *I* have to say to a Dancer?"

- 2 -

The ship rolled slowly through the spacelace tunnel.

The walls of the tunnel pressed in upon the ship, a seething gray storm of lines and spheres enclosing the starship. The tunnel stretched as the starship rolled along its length, widened to accommodate its passage.

Once gone the spacelace tunnel shrank back to its original dimensions.

For most of half a year, while the starship crawled the long distance to the distant planet of exile, the starship was all of Dvan's existence.

When he was not on duty, Dvan prayed, or walked the empty corridors of the huge starship. Existence began at the very center of the starship's sphere, at the gravity ball that gave the ship's crew and guards and exiles their weight. Some claimed to be able to feel a difference between the gravity at the center of the ship and that at the outer deck; Dvan thought that those who made the claim fooled themselves, for he had never noticed any difference in weight himself.

And at one hundred and thirty kilos, he surely massed more than anyone else aboard the starship. If there was a difference to be felt, he would likely have been the one to feel it.

Arrayed around the gravity ball, on the First Deck, were the various control rooms, where the crew and engineers did Haristi knew what to keep the ship on course. There were rumors that the engineers used metalminds to aid them in navigation; if true, and Dvan had a sneaking suspicion it was, Dvan certainly did not wish to know about it. One of the great opponents the Flame People had faced during the Splinter Wars employed such metalminds; stories of the mechanical and electronic life forms that had arisen during the Wars were still used to terrify children.

In the ordinary course of the trip, Dvan knew the duty of the engineers was simple enough; only if the ship were unfortunate enough to encounter the warcraft of the sleem empire would they be called upon to truly exert themselves.

And then, thought Dvan without any cynicism whatsoever, *for a rather short period.*

For the Flame People did not surrender in battle, and once engaged, the sleem showed no mercy. In over 3,200 years, no ship of the Flame People had ever triumphed in combat against the sleem; some few had survived to escape.

They did not expect to encounter sleem, not on this trip. The starship's destination was far from the path of the empire's expansion.

Second Deck held most of the great ship's support equipment; the airplants and water-growing plants in one section; repair parts, tools and general reserve equipment in another—among them a dozen stasis bubbles, to store those who might be alive, but badly injured, until they could be returned to the superior medical facilities of the World.

Third Deck held quarters for the crew, the engineers and their women. It was the one deck where Dvan did not walk. His presence among them, in their private time off duty, would not have been welcome. Not that they would have been rude;

quite the opposite. But they feared him, and no overture from Dvan, or from any of the Shield, could change that.

Fourth Deck held the Shield quarters, including Dvan's, and the Zaradin Temple.

And Her place, the largest open space aboard the great ship, larger than the enclosure that held the Temple itself. Had this been a purely military mission, either the ship captain or the Shield Sentinel, depending on whose length of service was greater, would have taken that place of honor.

To Dvan's knowledge, this was the first time a Keeper of the Flame had ever been aboard a starship, had ever left the World.

Fifth Deck held the exiles, and the Dancers imprisoned within their wards. It was the place where Dvan spent his duty time; it was the place where he walked most often, letting himself be seen by the over four thousand prisoners the Shield guarded.

Though he showed himself to the other Dancers, he rarely bothered stopping by the pentagram of the great heretic himself; he saw quite enough of the Dancer when on duty.

There were eight Dancers aboard among the four thousand, the balance being their followers, men and breeders who had chosen to accept exile with them. Twenty cells of two hundred each, with doorfields barred to all except Shield, sufficed for the four thousand. There were no Shield among the exiles; Shield who had followed Sedon had died, either by their own doing when defeat was clear, or at the hands of the Shield they had fought.

The exiled Dancers were the only Dancers aboard. The heretic had shown an uncanny ability to draw Dancers into his heresy, and the Aneda had thought it wise to avoid any chance of further contamination.

Sixth Deck sat beneath the outer shell of the starship. It was the largest of the decks, both in square floorage and cubic; the ceiling reached up five or six times a man's height. Antimatter missiles, dormant in their casings, waiting row upon row for the moment they would be needed, took up much of the free space on Sixth Deck. Particle cannon protruded up through the shell of the starship, gave the starship's surface its slightly cratered appearance.

Field generators, dense and cold, squatted in the spaces between the particle cannon. If they were called upon, it would mean the ship was in mortal danger, being fired upon by a sleem warship intent on destroying it.

A bare smattering of other weapons were mounted about; black hole generators, lethal if they penetrated the sleem defenses, but so massive, and therefore slow, that no attempt to use one against a sleem warship had ever succeeded; antimatter mines and cluster bombs, largely defensive in nature, to aid a ship when it chose to flee; and a few other weapons that had rarely or never seen use in combat.

Sixth Deck had a viewport, a transparent opening in the hull that let out onto the spacelace tunnel.

In real space, there would have been one or more crew up here, watching the panorama of the stars. Inside the tunnel, only Dvan came, and seated himself, and watched.

In his first hundred days aboard the starship, the view had disturbed him, as it disturbed all the others. But Dvan found himself drawn to it, and night after night, in the early hours before he was due for duty, he ended up seated alone on Sixth Deck, shadow cloak drawn up around himself to protect him from Sixth Deck's bitter chill.

The spacelace tunnels were not empty.

They held two shapes.

The first shape was that of the lines, long, twisting, and sinuous, weaving themselves around Dvan's disembodied awareness. The lines rarely touched, but when they did they came together as though embracing, as though—and Dvan knew the impression ridiculous—as though they were exchanging information.

The lines were all of a color, a deep, almost black shade of gray.

The second shape was the sphere, shaded in infinite levels of gray, from a pale chalkiness that at times fooled Dvan for a moment into thinking he had seen a white sphere, to a dusky gray that approached blackness. The spheres were all of different sizes; a very few were of a majestic size to equal that of the starship, so large that the walls of the spacelace tunnel bulged at their passage as they had bulged at the passage of the ship.

Likewise the lines, some thick and ropy, others of the thinness of a cutting laser.

They moved together, touching and tumbling, the lines and spheres. At first the movement had seemed random to Dvan, but as the days flowed by he began to see rhythm in their movement, a meaning in the dancing spheres, writhing lines, and shifting shades of gray.

He had an idea that, if he could only watch it long enough, he might learn something.

But he was only a Shield, with such religious instruction as was necessary for his position.

Had he received the full instruction of a Keeper, or a Dancer, he might indeed have learned something, as the Zaradin had learned, three and a half billion years prior.

But that is another Story, for another time.

Inevitably, as for all of us, duty called him.

The eight Dancers were separated from one another by as much space as Fifth Deck could grant them.

The Shield Sentinel Mai'Arad'Marah, eldest and fiercest of the Shield aboard the prison craft, sat at the edge of the Dancer Sedon's pentacle, inside a warding circle. His shadow cloak, of deepest black, was pinned at the shoulder with the emblem of his rank, the gold wheel of the Sentinel.

At his belt hung the kitjan.

At his feet sat a small stone cup that held black ink.

Marah rose at Dvan's approach, stood at the edge of the circle and touched foreheads briefly with the younger man.

Dvan had to bend a good bit for it. "I have the duty."

"I give it freely."

With a toe Marah erased a segment of the circle and stepped free. Dvan took his place and accepted the kitjan from Marah. He dipped his thumb into the still pool of black ink, used it to trace the circle closed.

He glanced at Marah when done. "Anything?"

Marah shook his head, said roughly, "He'll not speak to me. He knows better."

Dvan nodded, clipping the kitjan at his waist, and gathered his cloak about himself, sinking to the floor facing Sedon.

Marah left.

Silence descended around Dvan and Sedon.

In the distance Dvan heard the distant murmur of the rebels speaking; the doorfields kept them from moving about, but they did not bar sound.

The Dancers could not be stopped by doors. Walls would not hold them if they did not choose to allow it.

They were imprisoned in open space, inside pentagrams that teams of Keepers had drawn, laboriously, over and over again, until the ink on the ship's deck was ten and twelve layers deep.

Sedon's pentagram had been drawn, chanted alive, and drawn again, over thirty times; the layers of ink made a visible ridge on the deck.

Flames, small and pale, danced at each of the pentagram's corners.

Sedon moved restlessly, his beautiful, sculpted form nude inside the confining pentagram. He had enough space to move; enough to stretch out and sleep, enough to exercise, enough to Dance if he chose.

So far as was known, none of the Dancers had Danced on the trip out.

All of Fifth Deck was lit poorly, but the areas around the Dancers' pentagrams were lit more poorly yet. Dvan was not certain why; perhaps it was some measure of support for the small Flames that lit the corners of the pentagrams, or of punishment for the Dancers inside.

Sedon's voice, sharp and piercing, rapped against Dvan's ears. "How are you today, my friend?"

Dvan did not correct the Dancer. "Well. Yourself?"

"Imprisoned, against my will. As yesterday, and the day before, and so forth." Sedon's eyes—brown, Dvan thought, but he had never seen them closely, or in enough light to be certain—touched upon Dvan.

"Have you been fed well?"

"I will not complain of my food, only of my dignity. I crap into metal while one of you watches, I cover it with metal, and slide it across the line. It is undignified for a Dancer to be used so."

"I can do nothing about that. We balance your needs against ours. Where we have been able to preserve your dignity, when measured against our needs for safety, we have done so."

Sedon stood silent, very still, looking at Dvan. His voice held no emotion. "I understand. I bear you no grudge."

Dvan spoke honestly. "I am pleased."

"Shall we step on with yesterday's conversation?"

"If you wish."

"You were born near Kulien?"

"Aye. Sent to my training at Prufac."

"You have the Dance in your lineage." It was not a question.

"Again and again. Back to the Sixteen, six of eight male fore-bears. Among the breeding eight, two Keepers."

"A fine lineage, Dvan. How did you come to be a Shield, a guard in this foul prison?"

"It was known before the childhood of my body ended that I would be large. The Keeper at Kulien felt it would have been a drawback for a Dancer."

"Other men of your size have been Dancers."

Dvan nodded. "Aye. But what was for a Dancer a drawback, was for a Shield an advantage. As a Shield I was assured success, worthy work."

"Did you never wonder if there might be other options for you? Other work worthy of you?"

Dvan said slowly, "No. How do you mean?"

"Did it never strike you that things might be *ordered* differently? That as a child you might have decided, *I shall be such a thing as I desire*, and been allowed to act that decision?"

"It did not. I do not know how things might be among the Gi'Suei, but things are different among the Tbad."

"They are *not!*" shouted Sedon. He stood quivering, glaring through the gloom at Dvan. His voice dropped to a sudden fierce whisper. "Among *my* people are Tbad and Suei and Genta and Kersi and Alven, even a Mai or three; *ask them*. It is the same *everywhere* across the World. As a Dancer, you would have come to know this; we *travel*, we Dancers, Temple to Temple, we see more of the World than the Keepers, far more than Shield; more than anyone *including* those Dancers and Keepers and Shield who have ascended into the Aneda." His voice dropped slightly, and he said persuasively, "It is the same everywhere, Dvan. No matter where you go, the same lack of choice, the same craven toadying to the will of the Aneda, as though they were not themselves merely Dancers and Shield and Keepers wearing Zaradin white."

The sound of his voice, suddenly gentle and intimate, touched a warning within Dvan. It was not a Speaking, Sedon knew better; but even without that tool Sedon was, when he put himself to it, capable of a deadly seductiveness.

That the thought skirted heresy could not stop it; Dvan wondered, and not for the first time, if it would not have been better to have put breeders, however poorly trained, in charge of the eight heretics. Dvan did not think any of the Dancers

could have brought themselves to speak to one. Even if one of
the Dancers—Sedon was the only one Dvan thought at all
likely—had managed to speak to a woman, he could hardly
have managed any convincing attempt at goodwill, to say nothing of seduction.

The very thought of a Dancer with a woman in his arms
brought the touch of a smile to Dvan's lips.

The smile must have touched off one of Sedon's notorious
rages; he took a step toward Dvan, stopped cold with his toes
nearly touching the inked barrier of the pentagram, and knelt
until his face hovered less than an arm's length away from
Dvan's. "Smile," he whispered harshly, "smile then, Shield
whose life and honor are the property of his owners. Slave to
the Keepers, slave to the Aneda, slave to the Flame itself. Inside this prison I am more free than you, and when we reach
our destination, I will be the freest thing you have ever seen,
or ever will."

"The freedom of prison?" Dvan let his smile widen. "It does
not impress me. And service to the Flame is an honor I have
willingly assumed."

A glare of light exploded around them. Sedon took a single
step back, wild blue and white light flickering over the surface
of his nude form in such a fashion that he seemed a work of art
come alive. He pointed a finger at Dvan, and the cold Flame
leapt forward, splashed in midair against the invisible barrier of
the pentagram. Sedon spoke out of the center of the Flame in
a loud and terrible voice: "Be its servant, then, its *slave*. And I
shall be its master; and we will see who will end better."

Dvan said calmly, "We have already seen that. When you
were exiled from the World, your life, and the lives of your followers, ended. The place to which we take you—" Dvan
shrugged, as the Flame surrounding Sedon faded into nothingness. "The life you make there is no life that concerns me. You
will be staying. I will not."

Sedon turned away without further word, threw himself
down to the softened surface of the deck, and lay motionless,
with his back to Dvan, for the rest of Dvan's duty.

Neither of them was yet a hundred years old.

•   •   •

After duty, as was his custom, Dvan walked down to Fourth Deck, to the Temple, and went inside to pray.

From the outside the altar did not look like much. It was made of ten panels, each one taller than Dvan himself, arranged in a rough circle. The temple's ceiling reached up over twice Dvan's height. Aboard ship, even so large a one as this, it was a waste of space that would have been tolerated for nothing except the Temple. (And was tolerated with grudging even for that. Not everyone was as pious as Dvan, and chief among the pragmatics were the ship's officers, charged with the task of protecting the ship from hostile vacuum, the even more hostile corridors of the spacelace tunnels, and the usually lethal hostility of the sleem. Prayer could not hurt, but the engineers and crew knew with utter certainty that all the piousness in the Continuing Time would not repair a breached hull, or turn the course of a sleem missile.)

At the center of the temple ten gleaming black panels, each one somewhat taller and wider than Dvan, faced inward. The inward-facing surface of each panel was bordered in gold and held the image of one of the ten Great Gods. Dvan made the familiar circle of the altar, beginning with Rho Haristi. Haristi's image was that of a Zaradin; a nude, upright reptilian biped with deep brown scales except for the shimmering blue scales on its stomach, and a long, thin, segmented tail that wound round and round its double-jointed legs. Dvan touched each panel as he went, whispering the words of celebration; the panels glowed briefly as he touched them; the images seemingly come alive for a brief moment. The panels after the Lord of Light held the images of three non-Zaradin aliens; the Great God Eldone Ra, a delicate, shimmering insectile creature, with thin purple wings that did not look as though they could bear any weight; Lesu Orodan, a squat hill-shaped being, dull gray and blue in color, at whose size Dvan could not even guess; Siva Elherrod, a blue-furred, six-limbed, huge-eyed creature whom most of the Flame People found in some measure beautiful—

—and then Kayell'no.

Gi'Tbad'Eovad'Dvan sank to one knee and bent his head.

Kayell'no was human, God of Lies, Named Storyteller. The image was of a brown-skinned man, with hair and beard of a deeper brown. His eyes were the dark umber brown of emeralds. They lacked pupils or any other internal structure. He smiled at the Continuing Time, a grin that was at once both mocking and seemed to invite the person being mocked to join in the joke. Only Kayell'no's face was visible; the rest of him was covered in white clothing unusual to one of the Flame People; leggings all of a piece, a tunic that covered him from his gloved hands to his throat. He wore a shadow cloak not unlike that of a Shield, except that it was as white as the dress of a lord of Aneda, and the cloak hung down to obscure most of his form. A pattern on his chest was partially hidden by the cloak.

He stood with feet braced as though for battle, with a slim tube that had always looked like a weapon to Dvan clenched in his right fist.

Because he had no wish to give offense, Dvan prayed quietly and quickly before moving on. Lies and stories had little to do with his needs.

He was halfway through the circuit; the next image was that of the Zaradin Ran Rikhall, dressed in the white robes the Aneda so slavishly imitated, who faced Rho Haristi; followed by Erisha Sum, who faced Eldone Ra; the Zaradin Bri Erathrin, who faced Lesu Orodan; and then the humanoid Nik Shibukai, Named Anarchist, who faced Siva Elherrod. Shibukai's image had always struck Dvan as very near a work of art; a batwinged creature with scarlet skin and needle-sharp shiny black teeth, exposed to the Continuing Time in a brilliant grin.

Dvan stopped before the tenth and last image, the image of the God who faced Kayell'no across the circle of the altar.

The tenth figure, the form of the God of Players, was surely human; it could well have been the inverse, mirrored image of the Name Storyteller. Black gloves covered hands that possessed four fingers and an opposed thumb; the figure was of human height and generally of human dimension as well. It was, by Shield standards, short for a man, but it was unquestionably male; it lacked breasts and was muscled in ways that were improbable for a human woman.

The god stood against a pale, mist-filled background. Where his face should have been were only shadows; in the palm of his left hand danced a golden flame, and on his right stood a black flame that sucked light from its surroundings. Upon his chest the god bore an insignia like that of the Name Storyteller's; but where the pattern on Kayell'no's breast was obscured by the swirling white cloak, on the God of Players the insignia was visible: nine circles enclosing a starburst. Touching the third circle out from the starburst was a pair of small, solidly colored spheres, one blue and one white.

High on the figure's left shoulder was an inscription in some tongue even the Zaradin had been unable to read.

Forty-nine thousand years before the birth of Christ, Gi'Tbad'Eovad'Dvan crossed his arms across his chest, each hand grasping the opposite shoulder, and sank to his knees. The long folds of his shadow cloak pooled around him, warped light away from him. Before he bowed his head to begin praying, his eyes rested briefly upon the unknown words, inscribed in a tongue that would one day be called Tierra:

Yünited Erψ Intelijens.

- 3 -

Denice lay unconscious for three days.

During that time Robert did not allow Chandler to see her, did not allow Dvan to see her; allowed Jimmy to see her briefly, then sent the young man away when he grew restless.

Aside from the insertion of an IV, to keep up her blood sugar, he did not even consider allowing one of Chandler's medbots at her, as he was certain that the medbots would have no more idea how to deal with what had happened to her than he did.

She awoke on Thursday morning.

Her voice touched him, faint and weak. "Robert?"

He had been dozing in the chair facing her. His eyes opened instantly. "Denice?"

"I'm very hungry."

"I'll feed you." He ordered for two, joined her on the bed, sat next to her and helped her sit up; took the tray away from the waitbot when it rolled in. Warm wheat toast with blueberry jam, strawberries, carrot slices, freshly pulped orange juice. At first she was unable to eat anything; he had her drink her juice, and then his. Denice vomited it up less than a minute later; he cleaned it up patiently, gave her a glass of water, ordered apple juice for her and fed her that. The toast grew cold; he ate her portion and his while waiting. After she had kept the juice down for five minutes, he fed her the strawberries, one at a

time, until they were all gone. Her eyes drooped, and he sat
holding her up with one arm, waiting patiently as, with increasing
drowsiness, she worked her way through the raw carrots.
Before she finished them her eyes closed, and Robert laid her
down gently, cleared up the dishes, and gave them back to the
waitbot.

He sat and watched her for a while. Her breathing had
grown more regular, and her pulse; with each passing day she
had moaned and talked in her sleep a little less.

If he had not known better, he would have thought this
nothing but normal sleep. After a few minutes he extricated
himself from her sleepy grasp, went back to his chair and returned
to waiting.

Just after 10:00 P.M. on Thursday, June 11, Robert awoke to find
her sitting up in bed, watching him with an odd expression.

"Where's Dvan?"

Robert blinked, sat up slightly. "Probably sitting outside the
door. He's been."

"Get him."

Robert nodded. "How are you?"

"All right. Hungry and sore, but otherwise all right." She
was silent for a moment. "There are—pieces left. Fragments.
I've managed to forget most of it." She shook her head. "I think
that saved my life."

Robert did not ask what she meant.

He spoke at great length; and the silence stretched, palpable
and alive, when Dvan was done.

Robert sat in the lone chair; Denice sat up in bed, features
still slightly pale, and Dvan stood like a soldier at attention, as
during the long hours he had spent talking.

Robert said finally, "United Earth Intelligence."

Dvan said flatly, "Those were the words."

"I remember it," said Denice in a quiet voice. "I don't remember
much but I remember that, the shape of the words
against the man's chest."

Robert simply looked back and forth between them. Dvan
glanced at Robert. "They were written in a tongue similar to
English, night face, an Arabic script bearing clearly English
words."

Robert said mildly, "But there is no such thing as United Earth Intelligence. I am sure I would have heard of it."

"Night face, as a child, younger in time than the lady Castanaveras is today, cynical as only the very young can be, I once considered the Time Wars a legend, and a dubious one at that. A piece of religious apocrypha, to which the Shield copies of *In Time of Legend* did not even make reference. No," Dvan said with a certain heavy contempt, "there is no such thing as United Earth Intelligence."

Denice said, "Yet."

- 4 -

At the exact center of the Temple, on a small raised dais of gray stone, sat a bound volume—a book—titled *In Time of Legend*.

Dvan had never read it, had never so much as held it in his hands; the Shield had its own copies, censored for them by the Aneda. At times, before Dancing, the Dancers read from the unexpurgated book, briefly or at length. In his short life Dvan had heard, he guessed, less than one-hundredth of the stories contained within *In Time of Legend*.

Dvan knelt there with his back to the dais, to the bound copy of *In Time of Legend*, head bent toward the image of the God of Players, and prayed.

It was not prayer such as a Christian of Denice Castanaveras's time would have recognized. The concept of asking one of the Gods to intercede on his behalf in some matter would have struck Dvan as both ludicrous, and rank heresy; had such a thing been proposed to him he would likely have replied that the Great Gods had better things to do with their time. Prayer, as it had been taught to Dvan, was a thing designed to improve the nature of the person praying, to give one time to reflect, to open oneself to the voice of Deity, if Deity chose to speak.

Dvan knelt and prayed to the God of Players. In his life he had only once received a response, and that a brief one. While still a child he had prayed to the Nameless God of Players, had asked the god to guide him in his desire to become a Dancer. For just an instant the form of the god had come alive, and a voice, so clear and sharp he had never doubted it, had whispered to him, *No. That is not your path.*

Where the shadow cloak touched him, he was warm. The skin of his face grew cold under the chill breezes from the ship's airpush. Dvan was little aware of the passage of time, of the condition of his body; after an indeterminate time, he simply knew that he was done.

The matter of Sedon had not resolved itself within him; he was not surprised.

Dvan rose, inclined his head to the God of Players—no greater an inclination than he would have given Marah, or the Aneda; a sign of respect—said aloud, "At your service, sir," and left.

Another Shield stood outside the Temple as he left. Dvan had the immediate impression that Gi'Alven'Mutara'Kladdi had been waiting for him. Kladdi's words confirmed it; as Dvan passed him Kladdi spoke softly, voice pitched low to carry no further than Dvan's ears, this despite the fact that they were alone together in the corridor: "The Keeper would see you."

There was no need for Dvan to ask who was meant; there was only one Keeper aboard ship.

Aside from guarding the heretics, protecting the Keeper was the most important shipboard task the Shield had. They were in many ways the same task. It was a matter of particular pride to Dvan that the Keeper chosen to inscribe the first and last layers of lines of each of the eight pentagrams in which the Dancers had been imprisoned was quite nearly one of his own, the lady Saliya of the Ea'Tbad, She who had Kept the Temple at Deshego. Other Keepers had laid the lines between first and last, but those Keepers were not aboard, and only Saliya's presence and will kept the pentagrams at full force. If some misadventure were to cause Her death, the pentagrams imprisoning the Dancers would not long survive Her. To prevent the Dancers from taking over the ship, the Shield would need to kill the Dancers while the pentagrams still held—

—Dvan thought he could do it; but he was certain that most of his mates, excepting the Sentinel Marah, *would* not even if they could.

Saliya's quarters were on Fourth Deck, as was the Temple, but it was as far away from the Temple as the sphere of the ship allowed it to be. Her quarters were those normally given the ship captain, if a civilian craft; or the Shield Sentinel, if military. Adjustments had been made to the quarters, to suit Her needs; all the walls removed, to give Her as much open space as possible, and the quarters around Hers emptied of occupants, to help in preserving the silence She craved.

Shield guarded the entrance to Saliya's quarters, over a dozen of them spaced along the length of the corridor leading toward Her cabin. The Shield did not look at Dvan as he strode down the length of the corridor toward the Keeper's quarters, but kept their eyes fixed forward.

Two Shield stood at the entrance to Her quarters. Dvan touched the clasp at his neck, handed his cloak to the Shield at his left, and entered.

He stepped into a place of shifting shadows. Her quarters had been divided into smaller, more private areas with cloth hangings, some of them simple cloth, others with scenery inscribed upon them.

Saliya came forward to greet him, stepping through a long hanging that held an image of the Restoration, and into the light. She wore a dark, unadorned dress of some thin material that flowed around Her in a way Dvan found distracting. Four gold-red bracelets at each wrist and ankle set off skin that was pale to a degree Dvan thought unattractive in most women and all men, the color of blood, pink and blue beneath the skin.

On Her it was glorious.

Their Keeper was the oldest human being Dvan had ever met.

Dvan had heard it rumored that She remembered the days before the Zaradin left; if true, it would make Her some twelve thousand years old.

Her voice was the instrument of a Keeper or Dancer, trained to the art of Speaking, now low, and soothing. "Dvan. Be welcome."

Dvan did not know he was in love, and would not have believed it if told so. Love had nothing to do with the act of sex, and certainly nothing to do with a Keeper.

He stopped two paces before Her, inclined his head, and said, "My lady. I am at your service."

She nodded, turned away from him, and Dvan followed Her. The dress left Her shoulders and most of Her back free, and Dvan found himself watching the smooth shift of muscles beneath Her skin. They went back through a wall of soft curtains, to a slightly enclosed area lit by a single living Flame.

Dvan seated himself cross-legged on the cushions arrayed before Her, with the Flame between them.

To the extent that he could read meaning in Her mannerisms—and Dvan did not fool himself to think that he made much of what was there—She seemed troubled. She began without preamble: "Dvan, I am concerned for you. You speak with the heretic."

"My lady, I do. I have been selected for that duty."

"He attempts to subvert you?"

"My lady, he does. It is to be expected; there were Shield among his rebels. He has not attempted a Speaking; he would gain little by one, aside from his death and mine."

Saliya made a dismissive gesture. "I am not concerned with any attempt he might make at Speaking. But words are dangerous even when not crafted to touch a man's soul, and Sedon is a master of such persuasion. It concerns me, Dvan, that you listen to him."

"My lady, he makes interesting arguments."

"And you have had half a year of them."

"My lady, aye."

"You have been praying a great deal recently."

"My lady, I have needed to cleanse my thoughts."

"What heresies has he spouted at you?"

Dvan hesitated. "My lady, a wide variety. In many instances, I think they are perhaps not even heresies, simply matters that are not commonly taught the Shield. I know not where to begin in numbering them."

"What has he said of our destination?"

"My lady, that it is the home of our ancestors, the world from which our Masters took us; that it is better suited to our kind than the World; warmer, with light better for our eyes; gravity better suited to our bones."

"These things are true," Saliya said simply. "The records were found in the Temple at Kulien, finally decoded not many centuries before you were born. The planet is that from which we came. A horrifying place, in many respects, wild and bloody. Yet the scenes I have been shown, taken of its surface by the first ship to visit it, are in some ways beautiful. You will see colors you have never known before, eat foods so well suited to our digestion they do not even require treatment to remove amino acids we cannot digest; can be eaten plucked straight from the plants on which they grow. Carnivores exist, on the land and in the sea, of such a size that you have never dreamed their like, things larger than any human of the Flame People, even yourself. Such things have not existed on the World since the first Zaradin settled there, many millions of years ago."

"My lady, he says there are people there."

"Heresy," she said sharply, "there are *not*. There are creatures which resemble us. Lacking the improvements the Zaradin made in us, they do not speak; do not make tools, or use them. They do not even look so very much like us, being made with heavy brows and thick bones. But"—She spoke with obvious reluctance—"there is no question that they are our distant relatives, left behind when the Zaradin took our ancestors to serve and amuse them."

Dvan ventured to ask the question. "My lady, do you remember the Zaradin?"

He thought the question might have offended Her; She answered shortly. "No. The Desertion took place before my birth. Dvan, what religious instruction have you received, and what history?"

"My lady," said Dvan softly: *"In the beginning was the Flame, and the Flame was life. We who came after saw the Flame, and rejoiced, and Danced in its beauty."*

The Keeper smiled at him, and his heart skipped a beat. "Very good. But that is not what I mean. You have had basic instruction, and done well at it, or you would not be guarding the heretics; and you have had the training in warcraft given all Shield."

The last was not quite a question. It was barely possible, given his youth, that Dvan was a new recruit, shipped while still in training specifically because of his great size and immense piety. Dvan nodded, and saw Her relax slightly. "Good. Then you have much of the background you need. I have discussed this with your Sentinel, and he is in agreement with me; your ignorance is dangerous to you, when exposed to the likes of Sedon. You are young for the burden of this knowing," Saliya said gently, "but its lack may harm you more. Hold my hands, child, and listen."

And so Dvan found himself staring into Her eyes while Her nervous system came into contact with his, and after a short while had passed found himself breathing in rhythm with Her.

And listening while She talked.

·   ·   ·

It was, *said Saliya,* about five billion years ago that the first intelligent biological races arose. Before then there were other sentients in the universe, creatures of plasma and crystal; but the eldest biological life were the—*She made a long sound, the hissing of a reptile*—Ssrathin. They were our Masters, and with the passage of time the proper pronunciation of their name has been altered, both by our palates and that of their other servant races, the Dalmastran and Tamrann, to *Zaradin*.

It was our Masters who created the Craft, and among our Masters that the first Names arose, the first small gods of what is called today the Zaradin Church. From among the ranks of the Names came the Great Gods, some Zaradin, some not; and it was among the ranks of the Great Gods that conflict arose.

One of the heresies Sedon has doubtless shared with you is, alas, no heresy at all; the Zaradin warred.

Among themselves.

It is the conflict you have heard spoken of as the Time Wars, led by Rho Haristi on one side and Ran Rikhall on the other.

If you are like most Shield, then you have never believed in the Time Wars, for you have been given no reason to, have in subtle ways been led to believe otherwise. But the Time Wars were real, and they ended only twelve thousand years ago. Information concerning the conflict, why it began and why it ended, are missing from the records the Zaradin left behind when they Deserted us; with one exception, I could not tell you more about the Time Wars if I wished to.

That exception is this:

Once there were eight-sided altars on the World.

You have never seen one, Dvan. Long before you were born, the last eight-sided altar was destroyed; some during the Splinter Wars, others by the Aneda after the Splinter Wars ended. Do you know which gods were left missing from the eight-sided altars?

My lady, Sedon has said to me that it was the Name Storyteller, Kayell'no, and the Nameless One, God of Players.

Indeed. We do not know why this dichotomy existed, Dvan, except that many of us think it had something to do with the nature of the conflict that caused the Time Wars.

So, the Zaradin Deserted us, as they Deserted the Dalmastran, and in the riots and wars that followed, and the peace that followed the wars, we destroyed every Temple on the World that held an eight-sided altar within its walls. We prayed at the ten-sided altars, and there, under the gaze of the Name-

less One, began to learn the lore of the Zaradin. Not all of it,
to be sure, and many of us doubt we will ever learn all of it; but
what power remained in their altars we made our own,
wrapped it in a form different from those the Zaradin once
used, one better suited to our people than the Zaradin Craft.

We brought the bright Flame down to the World, called it
forth from the left hand of the Nameless One and made it im-
manent in the World. We think it is a thing the Zaradin themselves never did; to bring the Flame, one must Dance, and that
was beneath the dignity of our Masters.

Some three million years ago, while the Time Wars still
raged, a group of Zaradin soldiers—our Masters—exploring in
the far reaches of the spiral arm in which we are located,
opened a spacelace tunnel and found themselves in the system
from which our ancestors came. Planets with indigenous life
are, Dvan, a rarity in this galaxy; the Zaradin were intrigued,
and they made planetfall. They found there a tribe of our ancestors, and they took some of our ancestors with them when
they left. We are the result. We are what they made of us, servants, pets, toys for their children, obedient and attentive.

*My lady, if the Zaradin were to return, would we return to
their service?*

Saliya did not answer the question. Twelve thousand years
ago, Dvan, the Time Wars ended. The Great Gods of the
Church, once present in the universe, vanished, and the race of
the Zaradin as well. They did not tell us where they were going, or why, or even that they would; neither did they tell the
Dalmastran; and the Tamrann, so far as we know, vanished with
our Masters. One day twelve thousand years ago every Zaradin
on the surface of the World walked into a Temple, and did not
come out again. Many days passed before our forebears grew
brave enough to enter the Temples to look for our Masters; no
human had ever been inside a Temple before.

Much of what is left you will have been taught; our Masters
were truly gone, and the Splinter Wars followed. The Flame
People were the only survivors of that conflict. While we
warred among ourselves, the sleem arose and spread out over
the territories our Masters had abandoned. They are that rarest
of biological life, based not on nucleic acid in a water solution,
but on silicon in a fluorosilicone solution; the Great God Lesu
Orodan is one of them.

They are not conquerors, in one sense; they wish only to
deny us the right of expansion, as they have denied it to other

species. Those who submitted to the sleem have been allowed to keep the territory they had; attempts at expansion have been met with terrible destruction.

But it is not in the Flame People to be ruled, not even such a rule as the sleem would impose. Today we are engaged in a great conflict with the sleem; that we are less formidable than other foes, that they have not traced us back through the spacelace tunnels to the World, these things have saved us until now. But we are four planetary systems arrayed against a race that has conquered better than thirty thousand such systems.

This, Dvan, is where Sedon's actions strike home. That he proclaims our Masters folk like ourselves, who had merely a few steps' start on us, this we might have dealt with. Others among the Flame People, among the Aneda and the Keepers, feel the same; Sedon might have been forgiven this heresy. Even his greater and more shocking heresy, his bending of the Flame to his service, is in some ways impressive. He has done things with the Flame I would have sworn impossible for Dancer or Keeper, and had he brought this discovery to us, we might have explored it together, Keepers and Dancers alike.

Instead, Dvan, he lied to the Aneda, lied to the Keepers sent to interrogate him; taught the mastery of the Flame to his acolytes, and together they rose in a rebellion that diverted us from seeking a means to survive the expansion of the sleem. He has put every one of us at risk from which we may well not recover—the Sphere Project, in particular, our best hope to protect ourselves against the sleem, was badly damaged in the fighting, more badly damaged than has been common knowledge.

Saliya was silent for a long moment. Had he been anything other than the greatest living Dancer since the end of the Splinter Wars, we would have taken his life for it.

As he took the lives of those who fought against him.

They sat together in the cool shadows, the warmth of the living Flame gentle against Dvan's skin.

"My lady, much of what you say to me, Sedon has also said."

"I know. It is why I share it with you; it is better that you learn of these things from me, rather than from him."

"My lady, insomuch as I am disturbed by anything, I am disturbed by the fact that he is *allowed* to say these things, that we have made such great effort to spare the lives of those who rose in rebellion. May I speak?"

"You may."

"My lady, were it my decision, I would have seen them dead on the World, and their bodies returned to the processing plants."

"Could you have killed a Dancer, Dvan?"

"My lady, I believe so. The martial skills they are taught are not so different from our own, and we study them as we study our own discipline. It was my great regret that their rebellion did not reach the home of the Tbad. It would have been a great honor to Shield the Keepers of the Tbad Flame."

She licked Her lips slightly. Dvan saw that Her breathing had grown more rapid. "Both able to kill a Dancer, and willing?"

Dvan knew what she meant. During the rebellion, the bulk of those Shield who had faced Dancers in combat had been unable to perform their duty. "My lady, I believe so. If there is a more holy thing in existence, my lady, than a Dancer in the act of calling the Flame, I do not know of it. And perhaps without the religious instruction I received when young, I would have more difficulty distinguishing between Dancers serving the Flame, and those who have chosen otherwise. But I have had that instruction, and I will not hesitate in my duty."

"You are a rarity, then."

"My lady, aye."

"You may call me Saliya, Dvan."

Dvan's cock, imprisoned within the stiff tunic of a Shield, stiffened instantly. "Saliya, I am honored."

She stood on the other side of the Flame, let the long folds of cloth drop free of Her form, and stood, nude but for Her bracelets, facing him. "You may yet have the opportunity to kill a Dancer, Dvan."

She had not indicated that he move; Dvan sat very still, cock rigid as a bar of steel. "Saliya, how so?"

"When we reach our destination, we will discuss this again. The Dancer Sedon would have made a martyr of terrifying potency, and we dared not give his memory that power. But what could not be done in the view of the World, may yet transpire in the shadows of their exile." She paused, whispered, "Dvan?"

"Saliya?"

Her quiet brown eyes, in impact so like Sedon's own, bored into his own. "Can you continue to speak to him?"

"Saliya, I am strong enough."

"Be wary, Dvan."

"Saliya, as You will."

Saliya nodded, and Her breasts swayed slightly, nipples erect, as She held Her hands toward Dvan. "How do you wish me?"

"Behind."

Without any change of expression, She reached behind Herself; Dvan heard a slight click as the bracelets at Her wrists locked together, and Ea'Tbad'Ijal'Saliya said softly, "Come to me."

Dvan stood, shed his tunic, and went to Her, and used Her roughly until it was time for him to return to duty.

- 5 -

Saturday night, the thirteenth of June. Robert was in bed; in this at least Denice had observed that he was no different from any other man. He required six or seven hours' sleep a night, and functioned poorly when he did not get it.

But Dvan surprised her; recovering as she was, she slept more than usual, about four hours a night. But Dvan was awake when she went to sleep, awake when she rose, waiting for her. She supposed the man slept, but had not seen it, nor even any sign of weariness as he told his story through the long days and nights that followed. Some of it stirred echoes of memory in her, and some of it did not; all of it was fascinating.

And occasionally disturbing.

Denice made no effort to hide how it disturbed her. "Is this—you, and her? Because if this is how all of you behaved, then you come from a *sick* culture."

Dvan answered her in a voice with a noticeable Irish accent, significantly different from the voice in which he had told the bulk of his tale. "Ach, well. It was all of us; it was the society we lived in. I suspect you're right, you know, perhaps it was not as healthy as it might have been; but it was more successful than your own culture. Remember, it had survived ten thousand years, the entire period following the Splinter Wars, without substantial change. Partially that was the nature of us; we were a more stable people than you, genetically so, but some of it, at least, was due to the structure of the culture. It met the needs, physical, and spiritual, and sexual, of *all* its people. I know of no culture in Earth's history that could say the same."

"Did it?" Denice shivered visibly. "Dvan, a culture that has not changed in ten thousand years does not strike me as stable. It strikes me as *dead*."

"It may be," Dvan admitted. "In every society of your people with which I am familiar, where religious authority predominates, sin and guilt are the levers of power. Take from the people what is natural for the human organism; tell them that their own desires are the source of their pain; punish them, to their deaths, when they fulfill those needs regardless. When this is done correctly, instilled in a child at a young enough age, its hold is virtually unbreakable. My lady, my people were *masters* of such schooling."

Denice said wearily, "Please don't call me that."

The huge man said softly, "Forgive me if it offends you. But even in the greatest lies there can be a core of truth. If the society we built around the Flame was damaged, and perhaps it was, the Flame itself is a truth, and a great one. I have seen it and felt its warmth upon my face and been uplifted in its presence. If there is anything holy in the universe, the Dance of the Flame is it." Dvan was silent a beat, the fathomless black eyes steady on her. "And if you Dance the Flame, my lady, I *will* serve you, in whatever fashion the universe allows me, for I have Dedicated my life to do so."

- 6 -

Dvan hated the light the most.

Harsh and incandescent, it gave things colors the likes of which Dvan had never imagined. Blues and reds, umber and brown and orange were all similar, though they were hideously garish by comparison with the same hues at home. White seemed to Dvan to have taken on a hideous tint of blueness.

But some colors he had literally never seen before.

There was the color they had named *yellow*, for instance, the color of this planet's star. It was the color that was made when wood burned; some thought it similar to an aspect of the living Flame. Other colors, though—*green*, for example, the color of most of the plants here, which was like yellow in

the way orange was like red—such colors simply had no ana-
logue to anything Dvan had ever seen before.

The light made garish mockeries of familiar things. The
brooch that Tamtai had given him as a parting gift, the traditional emerald Shield, was under this light not brown but
green. Many of the items that appeared to be of one color—
brown—aboard ship turned out, under the light of this star, to
be green; others turned a shade similar to blue, but with a vi-
brancy no blue had ever had before.

He was not certain he believed it—but garish and alien
though it was, it seemed to him at times that he could *see* better in this light.

The starship squatted at the edge of a sea of gold, a huge
sphere that rose up even higher than the trees surrounding the
grassy plains. They had landed at the edge of a great expanse
of some tall, golden grass, an empty plain that reached out to
the far horizon. Occasionally patches of forest, green and
brown, sprouted in places where water was to be found in
abundance.

Far to the north, tinted blue and made hazy with distance,
a range of mountains lifted up from the earth.

The prison's buildings—the colony's first town, if you were
one of the exiles—sprouted about the ship. Doubtless the exiles
would have preferred to build farther away from the vessel that
had transported them into exile, but they were given no real
choice in the matter; in the first years after touchdown, the exiles had struggled merely to survive. Had it not been for the
ship's stores, rationed out to them as they needed them, they
would not have survived either of their first two cold seasons.
As it was it came a close thing; nearly three hundred of the four
thousand exiles *died* the first cold season, of starvation, of acci-
dents, in two cases from attacks by carnivores.

The first child was born that cold season, to one of the spir-
itless breeders the rebels had been allowed to bring with them.
Dvan did not know who had fathered the child, and it hardly
mattered; amidst the general starvation, the infant did not long
survive. Nonetheless it raised a debate within the Shield, a debate that was finally silenced by the Keeper.

It was the Shield Gi'Suei'Obodi'Baresst—related within the
Sixteen to the Dancer Sedon himself, and therefore more
aware of the stain of Sedon's actions than most of the other

Shield—who raised the subject, when he learned that one of the women was pregnant. Though they showed themselves among the exiles during the day, both alone and in groups, the Shield retired to the ship at night. In the evenings they took their meals together, sitting cross-legged on the floor of their common room, feeding one another as though they were in a Shield camp on the World.

An indentation in the deck held a small firepit. Pots of kliam and long strips of babat, the evening's meal, hung near it to be warmed.

That night while eating, the Shield Baresst said quietly, "I think the child should be Demolished."

None of the Shield had to ask which child he meant; there was only the one.

The Sentinel Marah sat with the Shield Rovime, the only Shield aboard who was, Dvan thought, younger than himself. Marah accepted a slice of warm kliam from Rovime, licked the sauce from the younger man's fingers before reaching into his own bowl for a slice to feed Rovime. "I think not."

They were off duty, in the company of equals; Baresst demanded, as he would not have in front of outsiders, "And why not? Marah, do you really wish to see the numbers of the prisoners expand? They are nearly unmanageable *now*, rude and insolent as they are lazy."

Marah shrugged, said laconically, "We have been given no instructions, lad. Presumably the exiles were allowed to take breeders with them for a reason." He wiped his fingers, still damp from Rovime's saliva, on his tunic, and reached with both hands for the huge mug of lon that sat on the floor next to him. He drank the entirety of the mug's contents without pause, tilting his head back, and after placing the mug back to the floor wiped his mouth with the back of his hand, and gestured to Rovime as though he would eat no more. "It's a dangerous thing, to act without orders."

"But, Marah, today we need only deal with eight Dancers, and we Shield, outnumbering them, armed as we are, are well able to do so."

"I'm glad you think so," said Marah drily. "You never faced them during the rebellion, did you?"

Baresst said stiffly, "You know I did not." It was a sore point with him; the rebellion had actually *begun* at the Temple where he had been Dedicated, but he had been serving duty offplanet when it happened.

"They are impressive fighters. Apparently the Flame cannot be used in combat, not even by them; be grateful. Had that resource been available to them, they would have beaten us, Baresst, and you, I, the Aneda themselves, would today be imprisoned or dead."

Baresst nodded, spoke the thought that had crossed the minds of most of the Shield at one time or another. "So, they are *dangerous*, even now. Among the exiles are none young enough to be trained as Dancers, Marah. But give them children, let them breed to fill this planet, and who knows *what* the heretics will do? Will you see them train their get as Dancers? In thirty years, or forty, we might find ourselves with not eight heretic Dancers to deal with, but eighty."

"Lad, we don't even know we'll be here when that happens."

"Marah, we don't know that we *won't*." Marah shrugged; it was a true thing. "We're here till they recall us. It might be four years, it might be a hundred."

Marah thought on the problem for a moment, and turned at last to where Dvan and the Shield Els were eating together. "Dvan, how do you think?"

Dvan was widely recognized as the most pious of the Shield, even if very nearly the youngest there. He said merely, "I am unable to know the will of the Aneda."

The argument ran long into the night. Baresst and Marah, who had started it, were soon reduced to observers, as the other Shield took up both sides of the argument. It came clear, well before the morning, that the general opinion among the Shield was that the child should not be allowed to live.

First thing in the morning, the Keeper—She had not even been approached with the problem—requested the Sentinel join Her, and said briefly, "Inform the Shield that the exiles, and their children, are not to be harmed, unless they offer violence."

She was within Her rights to deliver such an instruction; on the World, in a time of peace, Keeper and Sentinel between them shared spiritual and civic authority—but this was hardly such an occasion. Marah was not certain that the Aneda would accept him, if he wished to join it; but he had known Saliya for a very long time, and if She was not among the Aneda, it was only because She did not wish to be.

So he said merely, "My lady, as you will."

·   ·   ·

The child died anyway; but the argument was not forgotten.

The light was the worst; but the gravity and air followed a close second and third. The prison was better than thirty percent lighter than the gravity of the World. After a day outside, Dvan found himself made weary simply by returning to the starship, where the gravity ball still kept local gravity of the World. By their second cold season with the exiles, the annoyance had grown particularly acute. Dvan's body, and those of all the Shield who made the daily transition between gravities, began to protest; his joints ached in unfamiliar ways, and his muscles sometimes trembled after exercise within the ship.

The air was but little better, generally too hot, too cold during the cold season, laden with strange scents that made many of the Shield sneeze. The pressure was slight enough that at the end of the day Dvan's lungs ached from the unaccustomed effort of pushing the thin air in and out.

At times, returning to the ship in the evenings, Dvan felt not as though he were returning home, but as though he were entering a world in its own way as alien as the one he had just left; air cold and thick and dry, light too dim, and gravity unnaturally heavy.

At such times he found it easy to believe that the Flame People were not native to the World.

Somewhat to his surprise—it was virtually the only thing that made the duty tolerable—Dvan found he enjoyed his work.

The exile town was not large, but it gave the impression of largeness, wasting space flagrantly. It sprawled in six separate clusters about the edge of a small forest of some hardwood trees. The trees were among the most familiar of the things with which the exiles were forced to deal. Though leafier than the trees of the World, and growing closer together, the prison trees were otherwise similar to those the exiles had known in their prior lives. Wood made the buildings in which the convicts lived, fueled the fires that enabled the convicts to survive the first two cold seasons.

During the second cold season, when another sixty of the exiles died of starvation, Dvan heard rumors that some of the exiles had taken to eating the flesh of the herbivores who freely roamed the wooded areas around the town. Dvan dismissed the vile rumors from his mind, and after the first time would not hear them spoken around him. The exiles were a low lot, and some of them would say anything to curry favor from the Shield. He could not even find it in his heart to be angry at the transparency of their lies; some who might have died, the first cold season and the second, did not only because of the patronage of their jailers. Though it was not required of them, many Shield, Dvan chief among them, labored in the fields alongside the exiles, broke ground with them, fought with them against the all-encroaching weeds of the planet; and aided the exiles in bringing in the crop once ready.

There was always too much to do.

The task of preparing the exiles for self-sufficiency was immense. Water seemed no problem at first, given how water literally fell from the sky, but food was, and from nearly the first day. The plants they had brought from the World did not adapt well; the native plants pushed them out, grew alongside them and choked them to death.

The seasons were far more extreme than those of the World; the prison planet's precessional wobble was pronounced. Temperatures, from the cold season to the hot, varied by immense extremes; in the cold season the water often fell from the sky as *ice*. It meant that crops could be planted only late in the cold season, for harvesting at the height of the hot season. With only one crop every local year, a single crop failure could mean disaster; and the first year, when better than three hundred died, did.

The second year, two children were born.

One of them, a girl, survived. The other, a boy, simply ceased breathing one night. Dvan wondered if it had been malnutrition, or if, perhaps, some Shield had visited that home during the night, and held a hand over the infant's face until the baby had ceased struggling. Surely the parents would not have dared to stop him.

Perhaps it was inevitable that the Dancers would, in time, have male children to teach, but, the thousand dark and light Gods willing, that day would come long after the Shield were gone from this planet of exile.

•   •   •

By the slowly improving standards of the prison, the heretic Sedon lived in a palace.

His house was of uncured wood; in that year, all those on the prison planet were. They were yet two cold seasons away from the discovery that resins, applied to the wood while still fresh from cutting, would help protect the wood from the elements.

Most of the houses in the town were no more than crude huts, with perhaps a single door. From the outside, Sedon's house, aside from being rather larger, resembled those of his neighbors. But where their houses might hold a dozen apiece, Sedon lived alone. Where most of their houses had floors of dirt, and lacked sufficient ventilation for a fireplace, Sedon's floors were paneled with wood scrubbed until it was nearly white, and a firepit had been fashioned for him in the center of his house, with stone grates about it to keep the sparks from spitting out and setting the hangings alight, and an air trap built above it to guide the smoke upward through the roof.

It was difficult to see the scrubbed wood floors and walls; rugs and hangings covered nearly every surface, as though Sedon wished to remove all evidence of the rude dwelling in which he lived. To a surprising degree he succeeded; on the odd occasions Dvan visited, he was able, if he chose, to forget his duty on this distant planet, to pretend for a moment that he was back on the World, at home in the city of Kulien.

During the workday Dvan was approached by one of the exiles, with word that Sedon would be pleased by his company. Dvan came near the fall of night. Sunset that night was a spectacular event; the sky turned a deep shade of blue, and the clouds, scudding by at a perceptible clip, glowed a vibrant *pink*, another color that did not even exist on the World.

Sedon sat talking into his personal corder when Dvan entered; Dvan left the door open behind him. The corders were *all* the technology the Dancers had been allowed to bring with them, and they had not been given access to even them until well after debarking from the ship.

The corders were a significant thing; with the information stored in them, on metallurgy, mining, farming, weaving, and a thousand other subjects, they were the margin of survival for the exiles. Much of the information stored was useless, given the lack of tools the exiles had been allowed to bring with them; but physics and chemistry do not change, and everything else is engineering.

There were better than a hundred engineers among the four thousand exiles.

Sedon was dressed in a crude semblance of a Dancer's finery, a long scarlet robe tied with a white sash. His feet were bare, and his head. He did not rise at Dvan's entrance, but ceased speaking to the corder and set it to one side. "My friend." He gestured to the cushions before him. "Will you join me for your meal?"

Dvan declined, seated himself. "Lon, if you have it. Water, if not."

"We have not learned to brew lon yet, though it cannot be said that the engineers are not trying." Sedon smiled at Dvan. "They have created an alcoholic drink with one of the native plants, but I am told it is near undrinkable." He did not even look at the breeder, standing patiently in the corner of the main room: "Water for my friend."

The woman placed the mug before Dvan cautiously, clearly more afraid of the huge Shield than of the heretic Dancer she served, and scurried back to her corner quickly.

Sedon said without preamble, "You have not seen the Dancer Lorien in some while."

Dvan thought back. "Aye."

"I sent him away."

"Ah."

Sedon seemed mildly irritated by Dvan's paucity of response. "He is searching for a good location for a new town. In time, as children are born to us, we will need to relocate to a better location, one better suited to farming, better suited to industry. He went south."

"I take it he is endeavoring to live off the native plants?"

Sedon said carefully, "In part."

"Surely he could not carry any great amount of food with him?"

Sedon shook his head. "No. Look, Dvan, I would speak plainly with you, as we used to."

Dvan sipped from the mug, let the flat water sit in his mouth a moment before swallowing. "I have missed the conversations, to be sure. They were a distraction, but an interesting one."

"When the ship is recalled, you will leave with it."

Dvan blinked. At first he simply did not understand the

point Sedon was trying to make. "Aye. Of course we do not know when—" His voice trailed off. "Aye," he said again after a moment. "I shall."

"Why?"

The blunt question threw Dvan, as it was clearly intended to. He fell back on the obvious answer. "It is my duty."

"What awaits you on the World, Dvan? Perhaps in a century or two you might receive a posting as Shield Sentinel. You will serve aboard warships whose purpose is to avoid combat as they ferry men and equipment to and from—mostly from—colonies we intend to abandon. If you are fortunate you will be one of the Shield to die in combat with the sleem, to make some slight gesture toward fulfilling the destiny for which you were made. If not, then in time you will work on the Sphere Project; perhaps you will even see it completed within the life allotted you, and then find yourself trapped inside one small planetary system for all eternity, or until you wear away, as the Aneda hide themselves, and you, from the Continuing Time that they so fear. You will play at romance with Shield as bored of life as yourself." Sedon leaned forward slightly. "Dvan, you *love* it here. In your life you have never had work that mattered in any real sense; here you do. Here you can step on with work that *matters*, building a civilization in a new system. This planet is so far from the haunts of the sleem, it will be twenty or thirty thousand years before we have any danger of encounter with them. In that time we can *prepare*, and when the sleem reach this planet, as they will, they will find not a single planetary system, or two, or three, arrayed against them, but an entire corner of the galaxy."

The vision Sedon drew, of a humanity prepared to do battle with the sleem, struck Dvan with real force. It was a great frustration of the Shield that the Aneda had not allowed them to take the battle to the sleem, but had rather insisted that the warships of the Flame People avoid conflict, flee when possible, or, when combat did occur, scuttle themselves at the first sign that the sleem were gaining the upper hand.

Sedon continued. "Have you a partner waiting your return?"

Dvan shook his head slowly. "Not to speak of; one who was a boy with me, but . . . I did not hesitate when offered this duty."

"I will tell you plainly, Dvan, the gene pool we have been granted to work with here is not of the best. Our best, engineers and breeders alike, were Demolished for no other reason than that they *were* our best. Among our breeders is no woman with a Keeper in her lineage, going back to the Eight; and only a few among them at the Sixteen. Shield and Dancers are scattered among their ancestors, but in smaller proportion than I like. We can make use of you, Dvan, of a man capable of breeding one of our women, with a lineage as good as that of any Dancer, or any Keeper."

Dvan was not offended by Sedon's assumption that he would be bred if he stayed; it was one of the ways in which the Shield were used. Dancers were sometimes bred when very young, before being Consecrated to the mystery of the Dance; but once Consecrated, never. Heretic though he was, Sedon remained a Dancer; it did not even occur to Dvan to question Sedon's assumptions regarding which actions were proper for Dancers, and which for Shield; they were his assumptions too.

"Have you never wondered," said Sedon, "about the assumptions the Flame People make about themselves, about what behavior is normal for humans?"

"I am not certain what you mean."

"Did you know that among the Zaradin, breeders were not intelligent?"

"I did not. So?"

"Has it ever struck you that we treat our own breeders, intelligent though they undeniably are, as the Zaradin treated theirs?"

"Are you saying," said Dvan slowly, "that they are treated badly?"

Sedon shrugged. "Badly? Let us say, inefficiently. I do not suggest that one could Dance, or learn the disciplines of the Shield; such thoughts are plainly ridiculous. But their best are raised to serve as Keepers of the Flame, and serve that passive role better than any man. Might not one learn the engineer's art? Or those of a healer? I suspect, Dvan, that the breeders might make fine healers; they are better in tune with things of the body than many men." He paused, grinned abruptly. "And we surely have need of healers, since the Aneda were so cheap as to deny us any among the exiles."

"These are—disturbing thoughts."

"Prepare to be more disturbed," said Sedon evenly. "I know how you were raised, and taught; in some ways it is not so different from the training of Dancers. What I am about to say will shock you, will strike you as the greatest of heresies; and after that, I have another and worse one. Are you prepared?"

Dvan stared at him. "Aye."

A smile moved across Sedon's features, warm and genuine. "Good. Listen, Dvan, if I were ever to try a Speaking with you, you would kill me, or die in the attempt. Perhaps both."

The point did not seem to require a response from Dvan; he offered none.

Sedon's voice took on a calm assurance. "On the World, Shield who have heard us Speak, if they do not die of their own hand, are taken to Demolition. Do you know why the Aneda fear our Speaking, fear it so greatly that they have trained you to die rather than experience it, face to face, with a Dancer? When I Speak, Dvan, I speak to *you*, to your soul. I Speak from love, for there is no other way to do it; I love you, not as some person in a group, seated at the steps of the Temple before I Dance, but as yourself, as a good and decent man worthy of my love. I know you as I know myself, Dvan, the dark places within you, where you feel shame, and the good clean places where you plan and dream. There is nothing you can do, ever, that would dismay me, or hurt me, or change the nature of my love for you."

Dvan found his mouth dry. He had to take another sip of the water before he could speak. "So?"

Sedon's voice was quite gentle. "The habits of Dancers and Shield are not so different, Dvan. The bond to be found between men is no bond any breeder could ever give you."

Dvan shook himself slightly. "Water is wet, and stones hard. So?"

"There is no reason, Dvan, you could not experience the love Dancers share among themselves."

The muscles in Dvan's stomach clenched, seized up on him so violently he thought he might be sick. The rude clay mug in his hand broke into shards. He spoke in a very thick voice. "No."

Sedon gestured to the breeder; she darted forward, cleaned up the mess of the broken clay, wiped the water from Dvan's legs with a rough cloth, and backed away again.

Sedon watched Dvan carefully. "Not now," he said, and Dvan did not think he was being spoken to. "Not yet. How do you feel?"

"Do not speak of this to me again, not ever."

Sedon said slowly, "As you wish. I will say this carefully, to save you further distress; think on it, Dvan, that the needs of your body, and the needs of your soul, might be found in the same person. It is a better thing than the soulless couplings the Aneda have allowed the Shield."

Dvan's hands had curled into fists; he flexed them, made them flatten against his thighs. "You are a Dancer; of course you would think so."

"There is a last thing I would discuss with you tonight, Dvan."

Dvan was aware of the faint dampness on his thighs, of the water as it evaporated. "If you wish."

"Once again, it concerns the Zaradin, how we were shaped by them."

Dvan had very nearly regained control of himself; his voice was steady as he said, "Step on."

"You asked me if the Dancer Lorien had carried enough food with him to survive his journey, and I said he had not, that he intended to eat what this world gave him."

"Aye?"

"The Zaradin ate only plants, Dvan, and as their servants we emulated them. Yet if you study our relatives, here on the world from which we were taken, the ridge-browed ones, you will find not only that they eat the plants around them, but that they *hunt*."

"What is that word, hunt?"

"I have made it up," said Sedon, "as we have made up the names of the trees and animals around us. It is a new word, and it means to track down and kill an animal, for the purpose of eating it."

Dvan was nodding, following the flow of Sedon's words; he was done for several seconds before the import of what he had said sunk in on Dvan.

Dvan found himself on his feet of a sudden, backing toward the open door behind him. He stopped as he realized the image he must present, as though he were in retreat, froze in place and with the stiffest dignity he could summon, said, "We are done with this—disgusting—discussion. I will hear no more of your heresies."

Sedon nodded as though he were not surprised. He spoke with all seriousness. "We will talk of this again."

By the end of the third cold season—*winter*, the exiles had taken to calling it, another of the new words—the exiles had ceased bothering to plant crops of the World. They grew poorly, with yields nothing like those they gave on the World, for this planet lacked the bacteria they required for proper growth. Instead, at the end of the third cold season, they planted local crops; a shrub that provided tart red berries, each berry about the size of a man's thumb, and a crawling vine that bore another kind of red fruit, a bulbous thing with a thin skin. Both of them were sour, though it was a different kind of sourness in each, and Dvan could not find it in him to think much of them. But they grew easily, met most of the body's needs, and, after being dried in the sun, stored well over the course of the winter.

They had one great advantage, from the exiles' point of view; they did not need to be taken back to the ship for processing. Straight out of the ground they could be digested by even the youngest child.

The fourth winter was difficult, but nobody died of starvation; by the time of the fourth warm season, the exiles had four children among them, one of them a boy. It was a remarkable number, for a community of less than four thousand; at this rate, their numbers would *double* within a mere ten or twelve centuries.

In the fifth year, guided by the information stored in their corders, the small colony of exiles at last began to flourish. After several years of trial and error, the engineers started turning out decent steel at a good clip; it was the catalyst that drove everything else. Farming grew easier, as plows came into use; shovels and picks made it possible to dig channels to divert water from the distant river to the fields, where it was needed, rather than relying upon the rains to water the crops. The colony's original crude buildings, some no better than mud-thatched huts, were torn down, one by one, and replaced with sturdy buildings with thick log walls.

Dvan noticed about that time that in conversation he had begun referring to the town as the "colony." It was a shift in perception that many of the Shield shared. With food at last assured, without the Aneda to guide their breeding, the colony saw an explosion of children that amazed and disturbed the Shield. In the sixth year, eight children were born; in the seventh, better than *twenty*. There was something flatly indecent about it, many of the Shield felt, and Dvan understood the feeling; animals bred so, not the Flame People.

One evening, over dinner, the Sentinel Marah said, in response to a comment from Dvan on the subject, "What makes you think them People of the Flame?"

It stopped all conversation around the firepit. Shield watched Dvan, listened to see how he would respond.

"They are heretics, surely. But they are nonetheless our people."

Marah shook his head slowly. "I do not think so, Dvan. Listen, I have thought long on this. Their Dancers do not Dance; they have no Keeper to maintain the Flame were it brought down among them; lacking a Keeper, their children likewise lack the most basic of religious instruction. Oh, they're human, aye; but Flame People? No more so than any of the other Splinter races were."

The tenth year passed peacefully, without news from the World. Though recall was mentioned occasionally, in conversation among the Shield, it was rare; Dvan, for one, did not think much about it at all. Among a people who did not age, ten years was no very long time at all.

The Dancer Sedon passed his hundredth birthday, in World years, during the warm season of the tenth year, local time. It was an odd confluence of calendars; the colonists had grown in the habit of counting years by local time. Among the Dancers of the World, a Dancer's hundredth year was a time of solemn ceremony, a time when a Dancer's accomplishments were reviewed, and the Dancer's Consecration, his service to the Flame, was sworn once again.

Sedon, leader of the rebellion, was the youngest of the Dancers to choose exile over suicide. All the others had passed by this milestone decades, or centuries, or, in the case of the ancient Dancer Indo, millennia prior. Dvan had wondered, briefly, how Sedon would observe the occasion; and then the time came, and he did not have to wonder.

They *celebrated*.

A dozen of the Shield stood duty, in case of trouble, in a long line in front of the ship, watching the high flames leap up from the huge fires the exiles had set.

Dvan stood in the cool darkness and watched the party.

The ship loomed high above his head; though he could not

see it from where he stood, he was aware of it behind him, the vast bulk of giant sphere pressed deeply down into the earth.

He wore the kitjan at his belt, as always; his bare legs prickled slightly in the gusting wind.

It was the second night in a row the exiles had celebrated. They sang and danced together, arms linked, shuffling around the huge fires in what was, Dvan suspected, unconscious imitation of one of the World's Temple ceremonies. Even some of the breeders had joined in with them, arms linked with the men. The first night, Dvan had not been certain whether any of the eight Dancers were present; after the women joined in the shuffling step around the fire, he knew they were not.

No Dancer, no matter how debased, would have tolerated such a thing from a breeder.

The children played around the fires while their elders drank and sang and danced.

The children fascinated Dvan.

They were as unlike the children of the World as Dancer and Keeper. Loud, prone to quick laughter, both the boys and girls seemed somehow more vigorous, more full of energy, than what Dvan recalled from his own childhood. They played harder, and longer; and when injured, which happened frequently in this untamed wilderness, it seemed to Dvan that they healed very quickly.

They grew with *amazing* speed.

He thought in local time, a habit he had given up fighting. A child of eight or nine, raised here, looked to Dvan's eye halfway through the childhood of its body. The other children, at five and six years, were as large as any ten-year-old of the World. Dvan had not been fully grown until well after his thirtieth birthday; he thought that these children, if they continued to grow at the same rate, would reach physical adulthood by their twentieth birthdays, or perhaps even earlier.

In the woods off to Dvan's right, a form glowed in faint infrared. Dvan turned slightly to watch it; it came forward, out of the cover of the trees, and approached Dvan across the cleared fields. Dvan knew it for a Dancer instantly; no one else moved like that. As it grew closer, starlight upon its features, and the flicker of the fires, gave it the shape of the Dancer Sedon in a scarlet robe.

"Dvan."

"Sedon. What brings you out on this night?"

Sedon shrugged, stood motionless a half dozen paces away from Dvan. "Restlessness. Yourself?"

"Duty."

Sedon chuckled. "Indeed? You were here last night as well, Dvan. They did not give you the same duty two nights running."

"I requested the duty, aye."

"Curiosity, then."

"Aye."

"About?"

"The children."

"Ah." Sedon cocked his head to one side, stood watching Dvan. "Interesting, are they not?"

"I do not know what to make of them. They possess remarkable energy."

"I do not understand them myself, Dvan. I wonder at times if it was an accident that no healers were allowed to follow me into our exile."

"I do not understand you."

"When they are injured, Dvan, they heal with immense speed."

"Aye."

"You know several of them have died?"

"Aye."

"Do you know how?"

"No."

Sedon nodded. "Disease. They cut themselves, and some disease attacked them. And they did not throw it off, but instead died of it."

"It does not come together. How can they be so strong, and so weak?"

"Do me a favor, Dvan. Ask your Keeper that question."

Sedon turned away, and walked back as he had come.

Dvan did not realize until after he was gone that Sedon had not once looked toward the celebration of his exiles, toward their primitive, shuffling dance.

The Keeper Saliya saw Dvan often, for all his lack of seniority; Dvan thought She enjoyed him rather more than some of the other Shield, perhaps due to his size and strength.

The next time they were together, after he had finished with Her, he broached the subject of the children.

The waterspout in Her quarters had been modified to suit Her; rather than the abrupt sluice of water the waterspouts in Shield quarters granted, Her waterspout sprayed down into the bathing depression in a warm mist. Saliya knelt beneath the gentle shower, beads of water collecting and running down Her cheeks, across Her shoulders and breasts.

Dvan lay on his side at the edge of the bathing depression, propped up on his right elbow, and watched Her bathe Herself. It was mildly erotic; he admired the languid, relaxed way She moved beneath the water, the way Her straight black hair hung wet down Her back; the way Her taut skin moved beneath Her fingers as She washed Herself.

"Saliya?"

Her voice was a relaxed murmur. "Aye, Dvan?"

"Saliya, I spoke to the heretic recently."

"Hmm."

"Saliya, he is concerned about the children."

The water had gathered in the bathing depression, until there was enough for Her to lie back in it; She did so, closing Her eyes and ducking Her head beneath the water. After a moment She raised Herself back up again, sat up in the shallow end of the depression, and pulled Her knees up to Her chest. She clasped Her hands together in front of Her knees, gold bracelets gleaming at Dvan, and sat looking at him without expression. "Indeed."

"Saliya, they are growing very quickly. Abnormally so."

Saliya sighed. "I am not surprised. When the Aneda denied exile even to those healers who requested it, I suspected they might have had something of this sort in mind."

"Saliya, something of what sort?"

"Dvan, when a child of the Flame People is born, we take it to the Temple, for consecration to the Flame. But at the same time, we introduce a—" She paused. "I don't think you have been taught the words. It is a sort of benign disease; it helps fight other diseases, but more important it slows the speed with which our people approach maturity. The older we get, the more slowly we age. There is some debate, among the healers, whether Flame People so treated do in fact *ever* reach maturity. I think I have not, and as you have probably heard, I am among the eldest of the Flame People; only a few who were alive during the Desertion are older." The calm brown eyes watched Dvan. "You will probably never meet one of the Aneda who actually served our Masters; they are displeasing to the eye, with wrinkled skin, problems of the joints, and other disabilities. They were already aged before the healers began distributing the disease that prevents aging; and the disease does not reverse that which has transpired."

Dvan's thoughts were so abuzz he forgot to address Her correctly, said simply, "Then these children—"

She shrugged, a minimal movement of the damp shoulders. If She noticed his rudeness, She did not comment on it. "They will grow quickly, and seem at first, as you have noticed, more vital, more alive, than one of our own. But they are using themselves up, and soon they will begin to age."

"And then—"

Ea'Tbad'Ijal'Saliya said simply, "Die."

The next time Dvan went to see Sedon, he found Sedon watching as the eldest of the exiled Dancers, Indo, sat with two of the boy children, Tan and Kent.

The boys knelt with Indo, in a rough triangle, breathing in time with him, hands linked together. Neither of the boys heard Dvan enter through the open doorway; with so little awareness of their surroundings, Dvan would not have recommended either of them for the Shield.

Engineers, perhaps.

Sedon inclined his head slightly at Dvan's approach, gestured to Dvan to sit with him; Indo himself gave no sign that he had heard Dvan's approach. Nonetheless Dvan did not fool himself that the old Dancer was not aware of him.

Dvan seated himself with Sedon against the far wall of the main room, some ten paces away from Indo and the boys, and waited for Indo to finish. Indo's voice, husky and somewhat ragged, insinuated itself into Dvan's awareness, though he tried not to listen.

"—walk across a great black plain, greater than the one that stretches away from our town. In the distance, a huge fountain of light awaits you. It is dark around you, dark above you, dark below, and you walk toward the light. The light reaches up toward the blackness above, the column of light fountaining up so high you cannot see where it ends. You are ten steps away from it, and now nine; eight; seven; six; five; four; three; two; one; you are within the light, and you open your eyes."

The boys' eyes flew open; the one who sat facing Dvan started visibly at the sight of the huge Shield watching them.

Indo rose in one smooth motion, spoke to the two with studied indifference. "You may leave us now. Meditate upon what you saw today, and practice together at bringing the vision back on your own. I will see you again in a ten-day, and we will see how you have done."

The boys bowed to Indo, bowed again to Sedon, and a third time, most deeply, to Dvan. They backed out of the doorway, and ran once they were in the street.

"You will make Dancers of them?"

Indo snorted, knelt facing Sedon and Dvan; Sedon said merely, "We shall see. How are you, my friend?"

"Well. Yourself?"

The joke, old now, brought Sedon the faintest ghost of a smile. "Exiled, against my will, leading the shamed remnants of a failed rebellion in their exile, on a planet in the lace-ends of nowhere. Otherwise, well."

Indo said bluntly, "What said the Keeper?"

A pained look crossed Sedon's features. "Indo, calmly. You of all people should know how little hurry there is in this life. Let us enjoy the dance while we may?" Sedon turned to Dvan, smiled quickly, and said, "So, since he brought it up, what did the old woman say?"

Dvan answered with such gentleness as he could. "They will age, Sedon, and die, as our ancestors did before the Desertion."

Sedon's features lost all expression; Indo's hardened into something harsh and terrible; for a startled moment, Dvan found himself seeing in Indo something of the manner of the Keeper. "So, then," said Sedon quietly, "they had no intention of allowing this colony to succeed. Betrayal upon betrayal."

"We should have continued the fight," Indo snapped.

"So you've said, many times." Sedon fixed his gaze upon Dvan. "She wished us to know this thing."

Dvan shrugged. "Or She did not care."

Sedon said abruptly, "Indo taught me, did you know that?"

Dvan shook his head. "I did not. I am—somewhat surprised."

Sedon laughed at that, genuinely amused. "If a man cannot turn his own teacher to heresy, then he has not hit upon a very good heresy. Who taught you, Dvan?"

Dvan hesitated just a moment. "We are not trained in the fashion of Dancers. Instructors—"

"Indeed," said Sedon impatiently. "Who?"

Dvan did not know why he was reluctant to answer the question. "So much as anyone, the Sentinel Marah."

"Ah. And his opinion of your piety, it is why you ended up my jailer during the trip out, is it not?"

"Aye."

"You respect his opinion?"

"Very much."

"Indo," said Sedon, "made me a recommendation during the last winter, and I think I will act upon it now. Bear me this message, Dvan. Tell the Keeper that we have decided to move four of our Dancers, and half our people, to a new place, some five days' walk from here. We have found us a vein of iron ore near the new location, more easily worked than the one we have been laboring at; it should make the development of local industry an easier task."

"That is not why you are moving."

Sedon clapped Dvan on the shoulder, said simply, "Does it matter why we are moving?"

"She will not like it, Sedon."

"Ah." Sedon's features took on that curiously blank expression again. He rose to his feet, aided Dvan to his, and said simply, "We are not asking her to."

- 7 -

At the door chime, Robert sat up in bed and yawned until his jaws cracked, stretching. "*Command*, open. Lights up."

The door to his quarters curled aside as the glowpaint scaled up. Dvan entered slowly, stood irresolutely just inside the doorway. Robert gestured at the room's two chairs. "Have a seat, William."

Dvan sank into the chair in delicate slow motion; Robert's suite was up a level from Denice's, in quarter gee. Two rooms, rather than the single in which Denice had been lodged; it was the suite he had stayed in five years prior, after accepting Chandler's invitation to participate in a two-month study on low gravity and free-fall combat.

Robert rubbed his eyes, yawning again. "She's asleep?"

Dvan nodded. "Aye. Else I'd—"

"—be with her." Robert nodded. "I don't doubt it."

"I'd like to speak with you, night face."

Robert shrugged into a robe, moved barefoot into the kitchen, toggled the kitchen stasis field and pulled free the jar of mixed fruit juices he had made for himself. "No one is preventing you." He drank directly from the bottle, put it back and turned the field back on.

Dvan spoke plainly. "What is your interest in this matter?"

A smile touched Robert's lips, was gone. He sat back down on the bed, folded himself into half lotus and regarded Dvan. "*Which* matter? There is a System full of them, you know."

"The Dancer."

Robert said slowly, "Sedon? I hardly care if he—"

A flicker of anger touched the black eyes. "Denice Castanaveras. What is your interest in her?"

"Ah. She is my student and my friend," Robert said equably.

Dvan's features darkened perceptibly. "*You* taught her?"

Robert Dazai Yo said carefully, "Some things, yes. Why the anger?"

Dvan spoke in a voice low and shaky. "You are an abomination in the universe, a perversion of the Flame and of the Dance. And if you attempt to teach these things to Denice Castanaveras, I'll kill you."

Robert Yo laughed in his face. "Oh, come *on*. You ugly, stupid, slow-moving ox, you're going to kill me for continuing to do what I've *been* doing for eight years?"

"Yes," said Dvan with absolute sincerity. "I will."

A smile twitched around the edge of Robert's lips. "Okay. Thanks. I mean for the warning. I appreciate it," he said with a sincerity approaching Dvan's own, "and I certainly won't forget it."

- 8 -

The years flowed by.

Sedon stayed behind, in First Town; his teacher Indo, and the exiled Dancers Ro, and Mietray, and Dola, went to Second Town, and the Shield did not follow them. Dvan had lost track of the numbers of the children; by the twentieth year of exile it had reached into the hundreds. As they grew older, most of them were moved to Second Town; Dvan did not think it an accident. The children, particularly the male children, disturbed him; others among the Shield were of the opinion, stated with growing loudness, that the children of the exiles were no better than animals. The male children, between their fifteenth and twentieth years, sprouted hair in the most remarkable places; it grew on their cheeks, and the faint hair on their forearms, their chest, and legs grew darker and thicker until on some of them it resembled nothing so much as the pelt of one of the local animals. They were mostly short, considerably shorter than the average Shield, but possessed of a solidity, a density of bone and muscle, that once again struck most Shield as animal-like.

It was exactly the opposite of what Dvan would have expected, had he bothered to think about it ahead of time; given the gentler gravity of the prison planet, that the children would be shorter and denser than their parents made little sense. The Keepers' words came back to him; if it was true that the Flame People never truly ceased growing, though the rate of growth slowed dramatically as they aged, then it made sense that the children, doomed to die, should not reach their parents' height. The density of their muscle Dvan could not understand at all. Many of the male children, under the training of the Dancers, surpassed the strength of their Dancer teachers.

One or two of them, Dvan guessed, approached his own strength; and his strength was abnormal even for the Shield.

The women were, in some ways, worse. Their breasts and hips tended to a heaviness that was uncomfortable for Dvan to look at; like the men, they were shorter and more solid than their parents.

And they *bred*. The second generation of children were born to children themselves not yet fourteen years of age; and where a woman of the Flame People, if allowed to breed, might bear one child ever tenth or twelfth year, the children bore *their* children at an astonishing rate; some were pregnant again within ten to twenty *days* after delivering a child.

"I think, Dvan, you and I have never seen an adult human being," said Sedon one night in their twenty-second year of exile. Sedon sat in the darkness only a few paces away from where Dvan stood duty, outside the ship.

The normal complement of Shield stood duty with him, six others arrayed around the circumference of the ship. In the brilliant light from the full moon, the two Shield closest to Dvan could, Dvan knew, easily make out the features of the heretic keeping Dvan company during his duty.

It had been going on for many years now; at first Dvan had wondered if the Sentinel, or Keeper, might comment on it, but it had never happened.

Dvan was silent, listening to the distant, solitary cries of the night birds. After a while he said, "Perhaps you are right."

"There is a tribe of natives some twenty days' walk south of here. It—"

"That's where you went during the last warm season."

Sedon did not deny it. "They are interesting, though no better than animals. They do not speak, or use any but the crudest of tools. When I showed myself to them, they threw stones at me until I allowed myself to be driven away."

"And?"

"The children, Dvan, look more like them than like us. Oh, they are not identical; our children stand straighter, more like a Zaradin than like one of the natives. The native's skulls are shaped somewhat differently, as well, with a heavy ridge over their brows; and their jaws are immense, designed for the ripping of uncooked plants and flesh."

Dvan winced at the use of the word. It was another point where the children horrified the Shield; what had been whispered about their parents, that they had eaten the flesh of animals during the first two winters, was not even a thing of shame among the children; they hunted openly, had taken to showing smiles that bared their teeth, as though they were indeed one of the local carnivores.

"There are rumors," said Dvan after a moment, "that you have been endeavoring to teach the Dance to the male children."

Sedon's smile, at least, kept his teeth decently covered. "They are not rumors, and you know it. We have not succeeded, but I am not prepared to give up yet. Some few of them show promise."

"The Shield are concerned, Sedon."

Sedon replied with a touch of asperity. "The Shield will be recalled, and when you are gone, I will be left with these short-lived creatures to deal with. It will be an easier thing if there is an order they recognize, a Temple and—"

"You are going to build a *Temple*?"

Sedon was silent a long moment. He spoke slowly. "Not such a one as a Zaradin would recognize, no. We are not Zaradin, and we will emulate them no longer. We will make us a temple for *humans*, exiles and children alike."

"Be careful, Sedon. The Shield is slow to anger, but—"

"—I am frightening them."

"I am not even offended at your use of the word. Aye."

On a hot day in the warm season, twenty-seven years after the ship of exiles had first set down at the edge of a great plain of grass, a courier ship broke through the spacelace anchor in the exile System, and orbited the exiles' planet.

Near midnight of that day, Sedon brushed aside the door hangings at the home of the engineer Sura, one of the hundred or so engineers who had joined him in exile, and followed the man inside.

The Dancer Indo sat on one of the long wooden benches in the engineer's workroom, hands clasped together over his stomach, leaning back against the wall with his eyes closed. One who did not know the ancient Dancer might have thought him asleep.

"Tell me."

"I must begin by apologizing for the inaccuracy of my tools. With better equipment I could be more certain, and—"

Sedon cut him short, stared into the man's eyes. "You started with *nothing* but the clothes you took into exile and the data in your corders; not a hammer or a laser or a knife to work with, no metal, no glass, no plastic or silicon. You have *no* need to apologize for what you have made out of nothing."

The engineer bowed his head. "Thank you." He swallowed visibly. "I've done my best."

"Tell me."

"Early this morning heat output from the ship jumped dramatically." The engineer handed Sedon a flat black block of some smooth material. "We keep two of the scopes in the forest, trained on the ship's heat radiators at all times, with these filters placed inside the scopes. They're sensitive to infrared light, and normally they change colors, from transparent to black, over the course of four to five days. That filter you're holding lasted *one* day; we changed it yesterday. The Dancer Indo checked the filters this afternoon, found them black, and changed them." The engineer handed Sedon a second black filter. "Again, sometime this afternoon, they flushed waste heat from the ship."

"Testing the engines?"

"No. I've rigged some crude gravity shears; if the ship's

gravity ball had even burped I'd know about it. No, Dancer; they cycled a JumpDoor. Twice. It's the only thing that'd leave them needing to get rid of that much excess heat."

"Ah. Then there is a ship in orbit."

Sura climbed a small ladder, lifted up on the roof above his head. A section came free, and he handed it down to Sedon, stepped back down and went into another room to get the telescope itself. The scope was wrapped in oiled cloth to protect the metal parts from rust. Sura unwrapped it, handed the slightly oily instrument, as long as a man's arm, to Sedon. "Look at the Temple."

Sedon directed the telescope upward, toward the constellation the exiles had taken to calling the Temple; it was a name that Sedon would not have chosen, himself. "I don't—"

"Down now, slightly to the right; it's leaving the Temple. A low orbit; if you watch it long enough you'll see it move. It's only a courier, not—" Sura saw the Dancer's features go blank, completely without expression, and knew that he looked at such rage that were it directed at him, he would not survive. He prudently silenced himself.

After a bit Sedon lowered the telescope, handed it back to Sura, and wiped his hands clean on his robe. "Thank you, Sura. I am in your debt."

Indo spoke without opening his eyes. "Anton, do you think?"

Sedon said absently. "Likely."

"Should have killed him when you had the chance."

"Aye." Sedon paused. "Well, I will not make that mistake again." He turned to Indo. "Has a runner been sent?"

"To the first station," Indo agreed. "After that, by semaphore. They'll be evacuating Second Town before morning comes."

In the hour before sunrise, Dvan brushed aside the doorway hangings at Sedon's house, and entered.

Sedon awaited him, alone, in a room lit only by the embers of the fire. A rarity, that; usually there were others present, if only the Dancer's servants, and usually at night the fire burned high.

"My friend," said Sedon quietly. "Thank you for coming. Join me."

Dvan knelt, still wearing his shadow cloak; he had been approached while standing guard. "What's the urgency, Sedon?"

In the gloom Sedon's gaze, half hidden in shadow, met his

with a disquieting impact. "We are born broken," he said softly, "and live by mending."

Dvan said automatically, if a touch confused, "I see that I am broken."

"You are a Shield, a servant of the Living Flame. Will you live in the service of the Flame?"

Dvan stared through the gloom at the Dancer. "What is this?"

Sedon's voice gained force as he spoke: "Gi'Tbad'Eovad-'Dvan, I am a Dancer of the Flame, and by your Name I *require* that you answer me." His voice cracked like a whip: "*Will you live in the service of the Flame?*"

Dvan drew a long breath, and said steadily, "I will."

Sedon nodded slowly, relaxing visibly. "We have come to a time of decision, you and I. You are my friend, Dvan, and I love you. You know this is true."

It took a conscious act for Dvan to gentle the beating of his heart. "Aye," he said finally. "I know this is true."

"There is a ship in orbit, Dvan."

Silence descended then. At length Dvan said, "How do you know that?"

"Does it matter? The ship is there, Dvan, and the situation cannot continue as it has."

"I see that."

"You see, do you?" Sedon studied him. "*Do* you? Dvan, you know that the Aneda do not intend this colony should succeed?"

Dvan found the words difficult. "I know this."

Sedon said relentlessly, "You know they do not intend that I be allowed to live?"

Dvan shook his head. "I do *not* know that, Sedon. That they have treated the colony badly I cannot deny, but—"

Sedon pressed on. "Dvan, what are the things a ship *might* mean? Will you answer me honestly?"

"It may be recall. It may be . . ." Dvan hesitated. "It may be they intend your Demolition. . . ." His voice trailed off.

"And what else, Dvan?"

Dvan met Sedon's gaze, and said honestly and grimly, "And it may be they intend to *ensure* the colony's failure."

"This is the hard question, Dvan." Sedon paused, said very softly, "What will you do if that is true?"

"My duty."

Sedon shook his head. "What is that? A word. What is the reality? Of what does your duty consist?"

Dvan shook his head slowly. "I don't know, Sedon. I can't ... imagine ... a situation that brought me into conflict with Marah, or my mates. And what you're asking for—"

"I haven't asked you *for* anything, Dvan. I've asked you questions."

Dvan rose. "I have to ... think ... on this." He shook his head. "What you're asking for—"

Sedon rose also. "Dvan, I *still* haven't asked you for anything." He smiled, though it was a strained and careworn thing. "But by the Nameless One, Dvan, think on your choices. You know what awaits you on the World, if you return. If you stay, if you can—I had hoped to have this conversation with you some time ago, and I am sorry I did not; this is a poor time for it. So I will be blunt, because I have no time for subtlety. It seems clear that the Dancer's way is not for you; even among your mates I know there is no one you have ever truly cared for. Dvan, among my exiles are two women who were children in the body when we were exiled, who served as Temple Followers, and might someday have joined the Keeper's Daughters. They are intelligent, and well spoken, and I have seen them educated in many subjects. Join us, Dvan. Make yourself a household such as you choose; love whom it pleases you to love, and I swear to you by my Name I will build us a world in which no one will ever speak the worse of you for it."

Dvan stood still and spoke in a deadly quiet voice. "You forget yourself."

A quick flash of the man's smile: "Perhaps, but I lack the time for remembrance. And so may you, Dvan; I don't know how much time you'll have to decide. If any. Loyalty is a great thing, Dvan—I'd have been dead myself long since without it. But I think you *know* where your duty lies, and your loyalty—"

Dvan shook his head mutely.

Sedon spoke with devastating evenness. "—and I think they are not the same places."

Marah and eight other Shield, all of them senior to Dvan, an engineer Dvan knew poorly, and the lady Saliya, sat in a semicircle around the Living Flame in Her quarters when Dvan arrived, facing Him.

It was near noon, a quarter day after his conversation with

Sedon; they had roused him from a sweaty, uneasy, and dreamless sleep with the notice that he was to report to Her quarters.

A lord of the Aneda stood slightly aside from the group, pale-skinned and silver-haired, a gleaming long white shadow cloak flowing around him where he stood. His eyes were bright blue chips set in more white, and they fixed themselves upon Dvan as Dvan entered.

Dvan froze where he stood, and after a beat crossed his arms across his chest and inclined his head. "Sir."

The man looked Dvan over. "You're Dvan of the Gi'Tbad. The one the heretic has tried to befriend."

"Aye, my lord."

He nodded. "I am lord Anton." Without looking at Saliya, he said, "My lady Keeper, it will go more quickly if you explain the situation to them."

Saliya nodded, gestured to Dvan to seat himself near her. She began without preamble. "Sixteen years ago—World years—one of our warships vanished. Renunciate class. The Aneda assumed it had been destroyed by the sleem. Aboard that craft were three hundred Shield, forty Dancers. Two years ago another of our warships, entering a spacelace tunnel at one of the colonies we are abandoning, encountered that vanished warship. The renegade attempted to negotiate before engaging in battle; and listen; the man who negotiated for them was not Shield, but Dancer."

The implication sank in on the assembled Shield instantly; among Sedon's rebels it had been the same, Dancers actively commanding Shield in battle. "Sedon, it seems, did not take *all* his people with him into exile. Unknown to us, some remained behind. The battle ended inconclusively; our craft returned to the World, and the renegades escaped to Haristi knows where."

Marah nodded. "Lord Anton, my lady Keeper, you think they may be headed here?"

Anton answered him. "Sentinel, we do not know. It seems likely, if they have the routes that lead here."

The engineer, appropriately for his place, sat with his eyes directed at the deck. He spoke his own name: "Engineer Sinyal."

The lord of Aneda nodded to him. "Speak."

"I cannot believe they do. To my knowledge, only four engineers and a handful of Keepers ever saw the translations of the Kulien records that gave us the spacelace tunnel routes leading to this System."

Anton nodded. "It may be so. We are fortunate, if true. Nonetheless, we cannot assume that this planet of exile is secure from them. As the Keeper said, the renegades have a Renunciate-class warship; *this* ship, even if it were in orbit rather than sitting dead on the ground, is no match for it."

The Sentinel said, "Dvan?"

Dvan met Marah's gaze. "Aye?"

"The Dancers," said Marah, plainly watching Dvan for his reaction, "have vanished."

"We'll go in two floats," said Marah over their meal. Most of the Shield were out searching First Town, verifying that the Dancers were indeed gone; not that anyone had real doubts. Dvan and Marah ate alone. "I'll take a squad of ten in mine, and Baresst will take a squad of ten with him. You'll go with Baresst."

Dvan accepted the long roll of warm bread Marah offered him, dipped the length of the bread into the pot of kliam between them, and ate it with the sauce running down over his fingers. "You'll leave Kladdi behind to defend the ship?"

"Aye. I'll handle the weapons on my float. Lad, do you think you can do what's needed?"

Dvan chewed the bread before answering. "What might be needed, Marah?"

The Sentinel leaned forward, a thing hard and fierce descending upon him like a mask, grabbed the back of Dvan's neck and pulled him forward until their foreheads touched. His whisper was harsh. *"Will you do your duty?"*

Dvan did not blink. He said flatly, "I will."

Marah held the stare a moment longer; then released Dvan and grinned savagely. "Aye. I know you will. The rest will do as told, until they have a Dancer in their sights. During the rebellion, eight of ten froze when the moment came, and among the twenty percent who did not freeze total, most were impaired enough that they died at the hands of the Dancers they fought."

"You've killed Dancers."

"Three. It's not impossible; only very hard. Remember this; they are *heretics*, not Dancers such as you were raised to revere, and the resemblance is only that, a resemblance."

Dvan could hear Sedon's response: *And perhaps, Dvan, the*

Aneda are not the Aneda you were raised to obey, but only a resemblance.

Marah glanced at the pot of kliam. "Are you done?"

Dvan swallowed the last of his bread, washed it down, and wiped his fingers clean. "Aye."

"Let's go."

They did not know when the Dancers had left First Town, only that it was sometime during the night. They discussed, briefly, whether they ought to interrogate some of the townspeople, and decided against it, more from lack of time than anything else. Sedon would not likely have taken any of those left behind into his confidence, and even if he had, finding those few among the two thousand four hundred who would know nothing would take prohibitively long.

The floats they would search in were not gravity craft—they were orders of magnitude too small to carry a gravity ball—but rather kept their height with a mixture of jets and wings that would have been familiar to a human of Denice Castanaveras's time. They were designed for use in either gravity or free fall, atmosphere or vacuum; though the rockets could not be used in atmosphere, the craft possessed them as well as jets.

Their first assumption was that the Dancers were headed toward Second Town, which no Shield had ever seen. Second Town was a five-day walk, but none of the Shield doubted that the Dancers could have run that distance in the space of a night.

It would be their first approach; if they did not catch the Dancers at Second Town, they would widen the area of their search.

Their job was made more complex than it had to be; the Aneda, fighting for their survival against the sleem, had not invested much in exiling the Dancers, not even the relatively small resource of an observation satellite.

The floats left before midday, through an upper hatch that had not been used since landfall. The gravity ball's effect ceased abruptly at the ship's hull. The adjustment to local gravity was less severe than usual; as the floats moved out through the open hatch, into the harsh sunshine, the gravity vertical abruptly flipped by about thirty degrees. Suddenly *down* was no longer toward ship's center; it was the direction of the ground. The mild shift of vertical did not bother Dvan; when leaving or entering the ship through the lock at the ship's bottom, the local vertical flipped a full hundred and eighty degrees.

The two floats split up, and, sensors at maximum sensitivity, headed south.

Dvan sat at the weapons console and familiarized himself. None of the weapons were unfamiliar to him, though there were Shield present who knew them better. A single large kitjan, large enough to kill half a dozen Dancers at a shot; a projectile weapon that spat hypersonic slivers of radioactive ceramic; a grenade launcher that held some two hundred thermonuclear explosions, pinched into tiny stasis bubbles in the moment of their explosion. Energy weapons included heat beams that would fry any living thing in instants, cutting beams taken from the high end of the electromagnetic spectrum, and a single particle projector that it was not particularly safe to use in atmosphere.

He sat there at the controls and wondered if he would use them.

They flew across the tall yellow grass in the heat of the day, beneath the high blue dome of the sky. Grazing beasts fled at their approach, and the predators, lazy in the sunlight, kept to the relative cover of rare patches of trees.

Because they were searching, the floats moved slowly, covering the ground beneath them at only two or three times the speed of a running man. Their craft could not move much more slowly, even given the lower weight of this world; the thin air more than offset that advantage.

Dvan could see Marah's float, a distant silver-gray gleam at the edge of the horizon, pacing the float he was in.

They floated on through the afternoon, across the prehistoric veldt of Ice Age Africa.

They reached Second Town during darkness, and found it empty.

It was what the reports had led them to believe, a larger, handsomer version of First Town, set at the edge of the largest body of water Dvan had ever seen in his life, a river so huge and fast flowing that it sent a shiver down Dvan's back.

The World was cold and dry, and the Flame People did not swim.

A distance downriver from Second Town, a long, ugly slash

in the surface of the earth gave the location of the strip mine that had caused the exiles to choose this location as their second town. Radar showed significant deposits of iron ore, barely impacted by seventeen years of mining.

A patchwork of fields surrounded the town, growing crops that none of the Shield recognized, strange plants that had never been grown in those First Town fields near the ship.

The floats circled high overhead, watching Second Town, its empty dirt streets and cold buildings. Infrared signature showed nothing but buildings cooling from the heat of the daytime sun; no cooking fires, no people.

With Baresst and Dvan on the circuit, Marah held an open conference with the ship. "They've an entire planet to choose from, if they wish to hide from us. And with the incredible variety of animal life this planet sports, you can't assume that any heat-emitting object is a man. It's far more likely to be a grazer or predator."

Saliya's voice held obvious frustration. "There were two thousand of them in this town, plus whatever number of children had been born to them. They have no radio, can hardly have had more than a day's start; how far can they have *gone?*"

Any people with experience in tracking would have found the vanished Second Towners within hours; they had left a trail of broken grass stalks and disturbed earth on their way down to the river, and had left sufficient evidence of their boats behind them, to make it clear enough exactly where they had gone.

The Flame People not only lacked trackers, but lacked the very concept. Radar hunted for metal or other dense objects; IR hunted for body heat; sonar, on occasion, was useful in enclosed areas. But there was no awareness among them of how to proceed when *none* of their traditional tools applied.

It occurred to none of them that the Second Towners might have fled across open water. Natives of a dry world that lacked any but artificial bodies of water, the idea of using *running water* for transportation—had it crossed their minds at all—would have seemed to them as foolish as trying to walk through vacuum without a shadow cloak sealed around oneself.

There have been brilliant men and women throughout human history; and Sedon of the Gi'Suei was one of them.

Silence crackled across the open circuit after the Keeper had finished speaking. Finally Marah said, "They have no vehicles, and cannot have gone far. We will spiral out from this spot, in an expanding search pattern, until we find them."

The lord Anton's voice reached them clearly. "Destroy the town when you leave."

"We shall."

It took a single round of grenades from Marah's float. The buildings burned fiercely and well, and soon the wind picked up the fire and threw it off across the prairie, lit a grass fire that set the night ablaze.

The Shield moved off into the night, left Earth's second city in ruins behind them, a wreckage of glowing embers at the edge of a great prairie fire.

- 9 -

"And as begun," said Robert, "so our history continued."

Denice sat in the center of her bed, orbiting high above the surface of the Earth, and drank tomato juice the temperature of blood. "Why didn't you join him?"

Dvan said softly, "I nearly did. But—events come between people. And even if you wish it were otherwise, the events have happened; and you cannot go back into a world that no longer exists."

"From what you've told me of him," said Denice, "and from what *I* remember of what *you* remember, I think I like him better than I like his enemies."

Dvan shrugged. "Rebels are always romantics. It's an attractive thing. I would not think too highly of Sedon; in his rebellion, he did worse things than burn empty cities."

Robert said mildly, "I am curious, 'Sieur Devane—Dvan if you prefer. Your people employed Dancers as warriors, and soldiers as—what?"

Dvan was silent a long moment before answering Robert. "It is difficult to put it into terms that are comprehensible in English. I could use shiata, but I would have to teach you the words there too, so it's much the same thing. And I would have to struggle with your accent, which is horrid." Dvan's lips quirked a moment. "But that's not surprising; I killed the last of the exile Dancers only twenty-three hundred years ago, the Dancer Indo, in Alexandria. It is only since about that time that nightways as you know it has existed, and that shiata has begun to devolve."

"If you would try?"

"Night face, Dancers were made by the Zaradin. There were Dancers before the Desertion, long before the Dance was subjugated to the service of the Flame. Indeed, during the Splinter Wars, the Dance fragmented into a number of disciplines, the Dance of the Flame being only one among many. The martial use of the Dance was a secondary thing, a thing developed long after the Zaradin left us. It was, in its origin, a thing designed to amuse, to entertain our Masters."

"Indeed?"

Dvan gave the small man a hard look. "You seem skeptical, night face. Does your understanding of my people surpass my own?"

Robert smiled at Dvan. "I concede your superior *knowledge* of your people. But I have studied the martial arts, its history as we know it today, and in *our* history, the history of my people, dance has come of fighting, and not fighting of dance; oppressed peoples taught their children martial disciplines under the noses of their oppressors, for the movements of the dance served equally well as the basis of the martial discipline. I suspect you made poorer pets than the Aneda told you; I suspect, William, that now and again one of your Zaradin masters was desperately surprised at the intensity of your entertainment."

- 10 -

The search continued, without sign of the vanished Dancers.

At the ship, two Shield stood duty. They stood before the lower airlock, the only ground-level entrance to the ship. Under ordinary circumstances—the ordinary circumstances of the last twenty-seven years—there would have been six Shield on duty, more as a symbol for the exiles than anything else, a reminder of where power lay. On this day, with twenty Shield away from the ship, only sixteen were left to defend the Keeper, and most of those had been kept inside the ship, depending on the wards to prevent any renegade Dancer from passing through the airlock.

The airlock was a five-sided enclosure, warded with the same wards that had kept the Dancers imprisoned during the journey out. No Dancer, not even one of the heretics, Conse-

crated as they had been to the Flame, could have passed
through that ward while the ward stood.

And the ward would stand so long as the Keeper lived.

Just before nightfall, on the second day after the Dancers
had vanished, and all of Second Town with them, one of the
children approached the two Shield.

They were tense to begin with, and the child was the boy
Mica, a known favorite of the Dancer Sedon. They held their
weapons upon the brutish child as he approached, forced him
to a halt ten paces away. "What is your business here, Mica?"

The child held his place. Yet another disturbing thing about
him; he spoke in a voice with an accent subtly different from
that of any Flame Person. "I wish to see the Keeper."

"That is not possible."

His grammar was off, also: "I got a message for her, from
Sedon."

The elder of the Shield said carefully, "Hold there. Do not
move." Without moving his weapon from its focus, he tapped
the speaker in his collar, said, "My lady Keeper."

A male voice answered. "She sleeps."

"Awaken Her."

In the image, the child waited patiently, hands hanging loosely
at his sides. "His name is Mica?"

The Shield Kladdi answered Anton's question. "Aye. I don't
know whose get he is. Harmless enough, I think."

Anton said, "You at the lock, ask him his message. Tell him
he can't see the Keeper, but he's to deliver his message to you."

The Shield down at the lock started to repeat the message;
Mica interrupted him. "I heard you. Whoever you are, I'm to
give the message to the Keeper, and no one else."

Anton glanced at where the Keeper stood, dressing herself.
"My lady Saliya, will you receive him?"

She nodded, shaking her hair out as she drew her robes
about herself. "With Shield present? Why not?"

Kladdi's Second—Second aboard the entire ship, while
Marah was gone—said, "There were rumors at one time that
Sedon attempted to teach the Dance to the exile children."

"That squat, hairy thing? A Dancer?" Anton snorted. "I
think not. Bring him through."

·   ·   ·

They had him remove all of his clothing before they allowed him to enter the airlock. Mica did not allow that to throw him; Sedon had told him to expect it. He undressed slowly, as clumsily as he dared, for the benefit of those watching him, and then fumbled with the clothing they gave him in replacement. The cloth was smoother than anything Mica had ever worn before in his life, and in fact he did have trouble with the fastenings. The Shield Bo aided him, showed him how to lay the seals together so that the tunic held tight.

He had trimmed his facial hair only the night before, or the tunic's neck might not have fit over his head; as it was the fastenings tangled slightly. He knew enough of their customs to know that the clothing they had given him was an insult, the plain brown tunic of a prisoner.

He held his breath as he passed through the glimmering ward, into the airlock. Not even Sedon had been able to tell him what would happen when he passed the wards, only that he did not think it would kill him. Mica felt nothing but a distant tingle, a resistance as though he were walking under water.

Even that much of a reaction, had they known of it, would have terrified those awaiting him inside the ship. Indo had told him that; no one but a Dancer should have felt that warding at all, and a Dancer should have died in agony at its touch.

The Shield who had entered with him showed Mica where to hold on to the walls of the airlock. Mica grasped the handles, and waited while the Shield stepped back out of the airlock.

The airlock doors closed on him, and Mica found himself in a dim, poorly lit enclosure. He was pleased to see that his heartbeat had not risen, displeased to feel the slight but uncontrolled twitching in his stomach muscles.

He guessed that they would be scanning him now.

When it happened, it happened so quickly that Mica was not sure about the exact sequence of events. For just a moment the floor beneath his feet seemed to move, as though the entire enclosure were about to turn upside down. Gravity flickered as it moved, and for a brief moment Mica found himself falling—

—the enclosure *jerked* upward—

—fell downward, and then came to a gentle stop.

The floor was the floor again, and Mica found himself trembling slightly. Suddenly he *weighed* more, his limbs dragging at him in a way he was not accustomed to.

The airlock doors opened again, and Mica found himself

looking down a long, high corridor of some grayish red metal—or perhaps that was just the light. The corridor curved away from him, so that it seemed he stood at the top of a gentle, rolling hill. A pair of Shield with weapons drawn stood a ways down the corridor, and gestured for him to follow them. He moved forward into the corridor, testing his balance. A cross-corridor ran off to his right, and another pair of Shield, weapons likewise drawn, stood off a few paces down that corridor.

This would be Sixth Deck. Mica followed the Shield, without needing any further prompting. He wondered at the weapons behind him; the light weapons Indo had spoken of, or projectile weapons? They would not try the kitjan, not on him, and he was glad of that; he suspected that its effect might be similar to that which it had upon Dancers.

But he did not think much of the Shield, if this was how they escorted a prisoner. The ones in front of him were endangered by the ones behind him, if the ones behind had to shoot at him. Had Mica been escorting a prisoner, he would have tied the prisoners hands, attached a rope to the prisoner, and followed the prisoner, alone, from a good distance back.

They do not respect me, thought Mica. *I will change that.*

He walked always downhill, the corridor slightly soft beneath his feet. After a bit the corridor widened into a place where a small platform had been placed in the floor. The Shield gestured to Mica that he was to stand on the platform, and he did so; it sank beneath him.

He barely saw Fifth Deck; a single Shield stood in the corridor at Fifth Deck, watching him with weapon still hanging at his belt. A surge of contempt that he could not contain touched Mica. Had it been his intent, even in this gravity he could have been upon that Shield well before the man could have brought his weapon to bear.

The platform dropped another level, descending toward the gravity ball at the center of the ship.

Fourth Deck.

Again they surrounded him, two ahead of him and two behind, weapons drawn. They walked him through a series of corridors, and came at last to a doorway where another four Shield stood guard; the Keeper's quarters, Mica guessed. The guards made way, and Mica passed through the open portals, and into the room where the Keeper of the Flame awaited him.

• • •

Hangings everywhere, like the inside of Sedon's house but more so; it was clearly upon a dwelling of this sort that Sedon had modeled his home. The hangings, many of them, bore images from the history of the Flame People. Mica recognized only one, because Sedon had a copy of it hanging in his house: the Renunciation, when a group of early Dancers had broken away from their fellows, to embrace the service of the Flame.

Five persons inside. Two of them were Shield, men he knew, standing with weapons drawn, pointing not exactly at him, but at a spot slightly ahead of where he stood, between Mica and those it was their duty to protect. It was very nearly the first thing Mica had seen aboard the great ship of which he approved.

Mica came to a stop where they indicated, stood waiting.

The other three he had never seen before. The Shield Kladdi's duty kept him aboard ship, protecting the Keeper. Mica recognized him from Sedon's description; he stood a step to the right, and behind, the Keeper.

The Keeper of the Flame, pale skinned and dark haired in a dark robe, was a woman such as Mica had rarely seen before; similar, in appearance at least, to the exile breeders, she held herself with an aloof dignity that reminded Mica of nothing so much as Sedon himself.

The third man stood slightly off to one side, wrapped in a long cloth that Mica guessed would, in proper light, be white; a shadow cloak, perhaps, though far longer than those the Shield wore sometimes on duty. The courier, Mica guessed; a glance told him that the man was no Dancer or Shield, and whatever else he was, was no problem of Mica's.

Three Shield, then, each of them more used to this gravity than himself.

The man in white spoke first. "What is your name?"

Another insult, thought Mica calmly. Among the Flame People, he knew, so blunt a demand for a name was as rude a thing as one man could say to another. "Mica, sir."

"They say that you are one of the children, the children of the exiles."

"I am, sir. My mother is Mai, and maybe my father too."

The Shield Kladdi snapped, "Your mother *was* Mai."

"Kladdi, quiet." The man in white did not seem disturbed. Mica studied him briefly. Pale, as pale as the Keeper beside him; Mica had never seen two humans so bleached of color. It was as though the man in white had read Mica's thoughts; his next words were, "Your skin is offensive, Mica. It looks to me like the skin of an animal, not a human."

"I'm sorry, but it's a thing I got no hold on. The Sun does this to us. If we don't spend enough time out in it, when we do go out our skin gets red and sore."

"I was told that there were natives on this planet, shambling dumb creatures with whom we shared some common ancestor. I did not expect to meet one, to hear it speak to me as though it were one of the Flame People."

The pale man wanted to talk, then. Mica was not unwilling; the longer they talked, the likelier the Shield were to relax some fraction. "I'm not a native; I saw some once, they was traveling along following a herd they hunted. Didn't look much like me. I been told," said Mica slowly, "that some of the Aneda look like us, short and heavy, the ones as were alive when the Zaradin left the World."

"So," murmured the pale man, "Sedon has continued to spread his heresies among the natives here."

Mica shifted his weight restlessly, saw the Shield stiffen slightly. He snorted loudly. "Look, the weight here, I'm not used to it. I didn't come here to die, all right? I'm standing as still as I can get."

The Keeper spoke for the first time, a cool, soft voice, controlled and lyrical; another way in which she resembled Sedon. "Why are you here, then, Mica?"

"Sedon says I'm supposed to tell just you."

The Keeper shook her head. "He knows that will not happen. You will tell me here, in front of these Shield, what it is he has to say."

Mica spoke as reluctantly as he could. "Well—all right." He did not miss the flash of contempt from the Shield; they made no attempt to hide it. Mica knew that none of them would have disobeyed an order on such a flimsy pretext from the mouth of an enemy. "The Dancer says to tell you he has no wanting to fight you; that you will never find him no matter how you look. He asks you to leave us alone, to leave this planet alone. We will live or die depending on how we do for ourselves."

"That's not acceptable," the pale man said instantly. "Can you bear him a message?"

Mica nodded. Sedon had said they would ask that, and that they would plan on placing a locator on him if he said aye. "I can."

He did not miss the glance that passed between the pale man and the Keeper. "Very well. We must meet with him ourselves. We can arrange it in such a fashion that he will not be endangered; but there are questions regarding the resolution of this problem that can only be ironed out directly, between Aneda and the heretics."

"Is that the message for him?"

The pale man glanced at the Keeper, more for an opinion, Mica thought, than permission. She nodded, and the pale man said, "Aye. Repeat it to me."

"You got to meet with Sedon yourself. You can arrange it so he's safe, but there are"—Mica hesitated, and not for show, as they already had a poor enough opinion of him; he had real difficulty with some of the words—*"questions regarding the resolution of this problem*—that you got to work out straight between you and the Dancer."

"That's close enough." The pale man gestured at the two Shield. "Escort him back to the airlock, and let him go."

Mica turned away, toward the portal through which he had just entered, saw in his peripheral vision the Shield leaving their position, the two armed Shield in motion, and turned back toward the three who stood watching him, the two Shield walking, feet coming up out of contact with the deck. It seemed to Mica that the turn back to them took forever, he heard himself saying, "Oh, and—" as he turned, the turn slow enough that no one there found it threatening, just a casual continuation of the movement that had started him toward the door, the toes of his right foot digging down into the soft surface of the deck, knees just beginning to bend, and in that instant, as the word "and" left his mouth, for only the third time in his life, Mica called the living Flame down upon himself.

It sheeted across his form for the barest instant, glaring white and blue, so brilliant it blinded, and then Mica let go of it, moved forward while the outlines of the Flame still traced the spot where his body had been. The two Shield who had been moving toward him fired now, half blinded, toward the afterimage, laser light flickering out to bring a glow to the walls of the Keeper's quarters. Mica was three steps away from their fire now, four steps, knees pumping, moving forward in a controlled fall toward the spot where the Keeper stood, and then he was *upon* her, taking her to the deck with him, and they struck the deck together rolling. He snapped her neck while they rolled, fetched up against the bulkhead and took the necessary time to do it correctly, brought his fist up high and then hammered it down, into the side of her skull, as the beams of their weapons found him.

Mica lived just long enough to see the pulp of the Keeper's brains spread across the deck.

They had given him twenty-seven years to get ready.

Twenty of the Shield hunted for him and his. Sedon thought himself prepared; before the night was out, he would know for sure.

Seven of the eight heretic Dancers lay buried beneath a loose blanket of earth, nothing but their eyes and noses showing, twenty paces back from the edge of the trees, as they had for the last four days. Motion sensors would not find them, for they did not move; nor infrared sensors, for they were cold as death. It was one of the secrets Sedon had kept despite the failure of their rebellion, the discipline the Dancers had learned that let them slow their breathing and heartbeat down to almost nothing, cool the surface of their skin until it was of the same temperature as its surroundings.

Through the long day, while the floats came and went, the seven Dancers waited together. Late in the day, one of the breeder children, a girl of eight years, crept up through the trees until she was near the spot she had been told the Dancer waited, and said aloud, "Indo says the Folk are safe at the caves." She had not waited for a response, but turned and ran, as fast as her small feet could take her, back the way she had come.

Sedon waited, patiently. The same message would have gone to Mica. Just before sunset, he saw Mica approach the ship, talk briefly, strip, don the clothing the Shield brought for him, and go inside.

The last scarlet rays of the sun faded while Mica was inside. In the darkness of the partial moon, the steady blue gleam of the ward protecting the airlock became visible as the merest tracing around the edges of the airlock.

In the first moments after sunset, the ward guarding the airlock flickered once.

For the barest instant, Sedon found himself floating in the midst of a savage joy so vast it had no end. *I was right!*

He did not even have a word for whatever thing it was the

child Mica had made of himself; not Dancer, not Shield, and not Keeper.

But a deadly thing, whatever its name.

The ward flickered again, and failed.

The two Shield, standing with their backs to it, did not notice.

The Keeper was dead.

A weapon is a device for imposing force upon an opponent. It is one of the teachings of the Shield, and one Sedon had taught himself.

The staffs and bows, pikes and long knives that had been employed during the earliest years of the Splinter Wars were no true concern of a modern Shield; but Dancers, who must use such weapons in Dance, in dramatization of the history of the Flame People, were drilled extensively in their use, until it was borne in on them, at the deepest levels, that a weapon was not just a gun, or a kitjan or tangler or sonic stunner; *everything* was a weapon.

At the edge of town, immediately on the other side of the clearing that separated the ship from First Town, sat a dozen lengths of iron tubing. When the waterworks was completed, the iron tubing, inner surfaces appropriately glazed, would form a conduit to take water from the holding bin at the edge of town to a central bathing area, so that folk would no longer have to bathe in the river. The tubing had been convenient, and when the moment came, Sedon had used them; had the time come later, or earlier, he would have found something else.

For perhaps ten heartbeats the ward sat dead.

Then the tubing exploded.

They had been laid with their open mouths facing toward the ship, and filled at that end with nails, such scrap metal as the colony had, and the odd stone or two. Explosives—chemicals that expanded rapidly upon burning—had been placed in the other end of the tubes, and that end of the tubes sealed firmly shut. Only a small fuze extruded back out, to be lit.

The results were about what Sedon had expected: not so good as he might have hoped, not so bad as he had feared. Most of the tubes pointed at the ship tore themselves open under the force of the explosion. A few held tight, spat their loads out toward the ship in a good imitation of cannon fire. One of the Shield went down instantly, and the other staggered slightly—

The Dancers were up and running. They came out of the forest at top speed, seven silent figures clad in black from head to toe, moving like wraiths across the open clearing toward the ship. Sedon drew close as the Shield who was still standing finally caught their movement; without anything like time for conscious thought, some instinct told the Shield what he faced, and he pulled free not an energy weapon, but the kitjan.

From forty paces' distance Sedon threw. The heavy chunk of metal struck the Shield's arm, and then the kitjan screamed. Sedon was peripherally aware of one of the Dancers, he did not know who, stumbling, going down, and the Shield bracing himself, holding the kitjan with both hands, about to fire—

From somewhere behind Sedon a twinkling silver piece of metal flashed through the air, struck the Shield square in the throat, and the lash of the kitjan struck not a Dancer but the dead earth, which did not care.

Sedon left the Shield for his Dancers to deal with; if they were not both dead now, they would be, and their weapons become the weapons of the Dancers. He leapt up into the open airlock, slapped the control to cycle it. Nothing; they'd had that much warning, then, inside the ship.

The two Dancers bringing up the rear, Miertay and Dola, were no slower than the other Dancers, but they had carried the package.

A chemical explosive, again; the best that twenty-seven years of preparation had let them pack into a cylinder that would fit inside the airlock. They muscled the cylinder, taller and wider around than any man, into the airlock, placed it up against the ship's hull, set the fuze and leapt backward—

The airlock began to cycle; Shield were preparing to come out. A piece of luck for which Sedon had not dared hope. The Dancers ran along the circumference of the ship, got the bulk of the ship between themselves and the airlock. The fuzes were of uncertain length; if the explosive went while the airlock was in motion, rising up into the ship's local gravity—

It did.

The huge ship *rocked* with it, shifted position slightly. The roar of the explosion was astonishing, a clap of thunder that went on, and on and *on*, and left Sedon's head ringing when it was finally over. Sedon had *seen* an explosive of similar size detonated at Second Town; he had thought himself prepared, and was slightly amazed to find he was not. Who but an engineer would have thought that oxidizing certain chemicals together could have caused an explosion that rivaled that of a pinched nuclear grenade?

With the other five Dancers—he did not even know yet who it was that had fallen to the kitjan—he circled back around the ship. The stink of the explosion hung acrid on the air, and thick white smoke curled about the place where the airlock had been. Near the airlock itself the air, blisteringly hot, scorched his nose. The intricate mechanism that lifted the airlock up into ship gravity hung in shattered fragments; from the gaping ragged hole where it had been mounted, red light streamed forth.

It was the first time in twenty-seven years any of the Dancers had seen the dim red light of the World.

The hole was large enough for only one man at a time. The Dancer Trega, a Shield laser clutched in one hand, leapt up the height of a man, got one hand and one foot planted in the wreckage of the equipment, and hung there, laser clutched in his free hand. He fanned the laser up into the ship, and then flowed upward, through the hole, and into the ship gravity.

"What's going on?"

Marah's voice came steady across the circuit, of itself a reproof to Baresst's shout of frustration. "Nothing good, from the sounds of it. Turn about at full speed, we're headed back to the ship."

"It'll take us three hours!"

"We have the time, lad. Turn about."

One of the Shield, sitting in the main cabin behind Dvan, spoke the obvious. "The Dancers are attacking the ship."

Sedon was the third Dancer into the ship. He flipped through one hundred eighty degrees as the ship's gravity grabbed him, came down crouched on fingers and toes in the dim reddish light. Four Shield dead at the entrance to the corridor, three by laser fire, and the fourth at Trega's hands, and the two outside; it left them with ten Shield, possibly fewer if Mica had taken any of the Keeper's Shield into death with her. The forty crew who ran the ship Sedon did not consider for even a moment;

if one picked up a weapon, he'd kill himself as likely as anyone else.

Sedon straightened, glanced over at Trega.

Trega shook his head. "The Shield couldn't bring themselves to fire. They knew who we were."

Sedon nodded, inventoried the Dancers as they came through. Himself, Trega, Miertay and Dola, Lorien and Elemir. "We lost Ro."

Lorien said softly, "Aye. I sent him on."

Sedon stared at Lorien in the scarlet light. "There are stasis bubbles aboard."

"I know, Sedon. It was a kindness; he would not have lasted. The bubbles are on Second Deck, four decks down."

Sedon turned away from Lorien without further word, accepted one of the lasers from Trega, and moved off down the corridor with the five Dancers following him.

The battle for the ship was the sort of combat at which Shield excelled; in corridors, lasers against lasers. The kitjan was a line-of-sight weapon; twice during the early combat, Shield who were able to give the Dancers a fight survived long enough to get shots off against the advancing Dancers. The first time the kitjan brushed Sedon himself, left him numb in his left arm; the second time, down on Fifth Deck, the kitjan caught Dola square on.

Sedon looked up from killing the Shield who had shot Dola; Dola lay spasming against the deck, arms and legs thrashing, screaming wildly. Lorien did not make the same mistake again; after a glance at Sedon, he pulled Dola up into a sling carry across his back, arms and legs pinned, and said grimly, "Second Deck. How fast do you think we can get there?"

Sedon glanced at Trega, made a circling gesture with one hand. The Dancers moved forward at all speed onto the nearest Deck platform, and assembled themselves into the formation tradition had called the Circle of Fire: Lorien, carrying Dola, at the center, and the other four surrounding him, on their knees with their backs to him.

The safest way to reach Second Deck would be to clear out the decks, one by one. But it meant Dola would die, and Sedon had no intention of losing any more of his comrades than he must.

The platform dropped straight down. As soon as the edge of

the platform dropped into the open space of Fourth Deck, the Dancers brought their captured lasers alight, and descended into each Deck in the mist of a wash of laser light. Third Deck now, and Second—

There were crew, engineers and the like, in the corridors on Second Deck. Sedon barely noticed them; the crew threw themselves to the ground as the Dancers descended into their midst, tried desperately to get down beneath the wash of laser light.

Dead or alive, Sedon paid them no attention; he ran down the length of the long corridor. Crew covered their heads at the Dancer's passage. They did not intrude on Sedon's consciousness, not even the one who moved too slowly; Sedon snapped the man's neck and continued. If this craft were like other ships he had been aboard, the equipment locker would be—

—here. The door would not open at his touch; he set the laser to its highest setting, sliced the door with a crosscut, sliced again all the way around the edges of the crosscut, and then kicked at its center. The door folded inward, and Sedon kicked again, and went through into the equipment locker. Dark inside, and the lights did not come up as Sedon entered. Sedon turned his laser back on at its lowest intensity, kept the beam pointed upward. He moved through the long rows of idle equipment, things he did not recognize—

Stasis bubbles, *there*. Someone in the crew had cut power to the equipment locker, precisely to prevent what Sedon was doing, but Sedon did not let it concern him; where there were fixed stasis bubbles, there would be bubbles designed for use in combat, use in the field, and there they were, half a dozen keys that would generate their own stasis fields. Sedon sliced open the case in which the keys were kept, pulled one free, turned and threw it the length of the equipment locker, to where the Dancer Trega stood. Trega plucked it out of the air, stepped back out into the corridor with it.

The screaming, a constant since the moment the kitjan had taken Dola, ceased abruptly.

Trega met Sedon at the door as Sedon left. A single Dancer moved down the length of the corridor, securing it in the simplest possible manner, laser bursts to the skulls of the prone crewmen; neither Trega nor Sedon took notice of the task. "Take what we can carry?"

"Aye. Don't weight yourself down too much." Sedon brushed by him, had to squeeze past the bulk of the stasis bubble.

"Where are you going?"

"Her quarters."

"She's dead."

"I'm going for the courier."

"Why?" Trega demanded.

Sedon locked eyes with the older Dancer. "It's probably Anton."

Trega started to say something else, obviously changed his mind. "Very well. Meet us at the float on Sixth Deck."

They could not operate the ship, nor keep it, Sedon knew, against an assault led by the Sentinel; Marah would not make the mistake of bringing his men into personal combat with the Dancers. He would hold his pair of floats well off the ship, and shell it with the grenades.

Since they could not keep the ship, they scuttled it.

It was not difficult; the engineer Sura had told them how. A single grenade, placed against the casing of the gravity ball and activated on a timed countdown. Not knowing the actual size of the gravity ball, Sura could not tell them whether the gravity ball would implode or explode; a small gravity ball would explode, a large one would implode. An implosion would be less powerful than an explosion, but either way it would not matter much; when the antimatter missiles on Sixth Deck went, the explosion would dwarf the trivial energies of the ruptured gravity ball.

Sedon reached Sixth Deck, the bay where the floats were kept, as the other Dancers were loading Dola's stasis bubble aboard.

Trega sat at the pilot's controls; Sedon sank down into the seat next to his, and the float lifted up from the deck, hung motionless for a moment. "Who placed the grenade?"

"Elemir."

"What did he use? Antimatter, or a pinched explosion?"

"Elemir!"

Elemir's voice came from the rear of the float. "Antimatter."

The float lifted then, surged forward into open night air. For a brief moment, as they left the ship's sphere, the world wavered around them. Trega was no pilot; the float rocked wildly as it found vertical. When the float had stabilized again, they were well away from the ship, and moving south at top acceleration.

Sedon's head was pressed back into his seat. He fought to speak against the overwhelming acceleration. "How much . . . longer?"

Elemir said, "Soon."

Trega's voice was so quiet it could not be heard by the other Dancers. "I think we should have . . . given First Town . . . *some* warning."

Sedon could barely draw in air. Spots danced in front of his eyes. "The warning . . . would have made its way . . . to the Keeper."

"We could have warned them . . . after our assault began."

Sedon took a deep breath. *"They could not have gotten away in time."*

Trega's voice was ragged. "You don't *know*—"

The night sky behind them lit with an awful flare. The wave front of the explosion chased the speeding float, caught it and enveloped it; the float rocked and shuddered as it rode out the explosion. Sedon closed his eyes, sat wondering whether he would ever see another morning. When he thought it had subsided it abruptly grew worse, the missiles going. A sudden blistering glare made spots dance in front of Sedon's eyes even though they were closed, and then a random current in the wave front of the explosion momentarily lifted the float, holding it in free fall, and then slammed it back down toward the ground as though a great fist had smashed down atop the vehicle.

It went on, and on, and on, the wave front of the explosion chasing the fleeing vehicle.

Eventually Sedon came to be aware that he was still alive, and likely to stay so, that the acceleration had lessened. He opened his eyes, saw Trega sitting and watching him.

"None of us saw Dvan aboard the ship. Did you?" Sedon shook his head no, and Trega nodded. "Was it Anton?"

For a brief moment Sedon had no idea at all what Trega meant. "Oh. Aye, it was."

"Did he say anything before you killed him?"

Sedon was silent for a long moment, as the vehicle flew on into the night, and then shook his head and said, "Nothing interesting."

"Pity."

•   •   •

When the towering mushroom cloud, of the largest single explosion human beings would ever release upon the surface of Earth, appeared on the distant horizon, all conversation within the floats full of Shield ceased. Dvan watched the cloud climb into the sky, and climb and climb, with a complete lack of emotion, a numbness so huge, so complete, he did not know what to do with it.

Finally the Sentinel's voice came across the still-open circuit, a voice so bone tired that Dvan did not even recognize it at first. "Bring it down, Baresst. We'll spend the night here."

"But—we have to—"

"Put it down, lad. Second Town is embers, and First Town is less than that, and there's no place on this whole Rikhall-tainted planet any better than this one we're flying over."

It came to Dvan that the Keeper, that Saliya, was dead; that Sedon, who he admired and loved, had killed Her.

He knew that one was not supposed to love a Keeper, that if he had proclaimed his feelings to Her it would have led to Demolition. He knew with crystal clarity that She had never loved him, had perhaps, due to Her sex, been incapable.

In that moment, as the floats descended to the dark plains of grass, as silent tears tracked his cheeks, and the pain of betrayal throbbed in his heart, Gi'Tbad'Eovad'Dvan swore on Her memory that he would send Sedon to join Her.

The floats touched ground in the moment that the hot wind of death washed across them.

- 11 -

The next morning, as the sun rose over twenty cold Shield who had slept poorly and eaten less well than that, the Sentinel called Assembly.

They were one hundred and eight Shield shy of the number traditionally required for an Assembly; nobody felt the need to point that out, as no Shield there could be unaware of it.

They gathered in the open space between the two floats, cleared away a space in the tall grass, and seated themselves in a circle.

Marah opened it, said quietly, "We come here today in Dedication, in service of the Flame. Is there anyone here who doubts his Dedication?"

If there were, the Shield felt it prudent to keep it to themselves; they made the circle, one by one, no followed by no followed by no, twenty times around.

Marah continued: "We are born broken, and live by mending. You and I are Shield, servants of the living Flame. Dedicate yourselves with me, renew with me the vows of your childhood: Will you live in the service of the Flame?"

The whisper moved around the circle; aye, and aye, and aye, twenty times.

"Will you kill if you must?"

Aye, and aye, and aye, twenty times.

"Will you die if needed; will you live when you no longer wish to, if the service is required of you?"

Dvan's voice, deep and assured, led the chorus: "Aye."

Perhaps it was his imagination; it seemed to Dvan that, for just a moment, the living Flame hovered around them when they were done.

Marah took a deep breath. "Well, then. So far as we know, we're marooned here. The Aneda may or may not send another ship out for us. We must decide now what we will do."

"We will fulfill our duty," Dvan said swiftly. "Find the Dancers, if they survive, and destroy them to a man."

Marah nodded, unsurprised, and said, "One at a time. Tell us what you think, as truly as you can, and then we will decide."

It was never in doubt; though some of the Shield spoke at length, and the sun climbed high into the sky before they had done, before midday a consensus had been hammered out.

Not even during the rebellion had Sedon dared harm a Keeper; Her loss raised an anger in the Shield that, had Sedon been there to see it, might have given even him pause.

"We shall have war, then," said Marah when they were done, and the assembled Shield echoed him; war, and war, and war, twenty times.

- 12 -

Denice sat at the edge of the bed, watching the huge man talk. Stars wheeled slowly by in the window at her feet.

Finally she said, "They were supposed to come for you."

He stopped for a moment. "A ship should have come eventually. Yes."

"It never happened."

Dvan said dryly, "Clearly. Perhaps the sleem had something to do with it; perhaps they found the spacelace tunnel leading to the World. Whether the Flame People survive today I have no way of knowing, but the sleem survive. The craft shown in the video sent back by the Unification's Tau Ceti probe, back in '69, are sleem craft. It was a difficult thing to map the spacelace tunnels, and I doubt the sleem were any better at it than we; but if they found the World, then the World is no more."

It obviously angered Dvan when Robert spoke, but Robert did not let that stop him. "So you were stuck here, and you fought."

Strangely, this time Dvan did not seem to realize from whom the question had come. "There is no religion I know of that does not have myths and legends of the days when the Gods warred. As is often true, there are fragments of truth in the midst of idiocy. Yes, we fought. We waged war." His eyes were unfocused, vague and distant. "For eons. Towns rose up, villages, and we smashed them down. If they used tools we assumed they were Sedon's folk, and we killed them. In time we decided that if they spoke they were Sedon's folk, and we slew them. Doubtless we were the greatest murderers in the history of this world. We hunted them across the surface of the Earth, the Dancers and their people. I could tell you for days of the progression of that war, tell you how the Dancers killed Shield one after the other. It went slowly, so slowly, spread out, as they and we were, across the surface of northern Africa and southern Eurasia, without proper equipment to search for one another. We rousted them from the caves they had hidden in, and killed most of the folk there; but the Dancers were not there. In that very first attack we destroyed the float they had stolen from the ship; they had buried it deep in the caves to prevent our scanners from finding it. A tactical mistake no Shield would have made; when we found them at last, they could not move the craft quickly, and the float was lost to them. Over the course of the years we recovered or destroyed most of the hardware they had taken with them from the ship.

"We lost Shield one by one, sometimes to misadventure, sometimes to Dancers; one party of four simply vanished, and we never did learn what had happened to them. We learned later that the Dancer Ro had died taking the ship, and that the Dancer Dola had been taken by the kitjan as well; over a thousand years later we came across his stasis bubble, carefully hidden until his fellows could get him to medical attention." Dvan's voice was dreamy, drifting. "We loosed the bubble and watched him kick himself to death, and that was the second Dancer. Perhaps five thousand years passed before we got the third, that was Miertay. He had ventured out into the world alone, without the protection of his fellows, to check on the bubble holding Dola. We had regenerated Dola's bubble, but somehow he knew that it was not as they had left it. Instead of heading back the way he had come, he continued on until he was sure he was being followed, and then *he* attacked *us*. He took four Shield with him, but I snapped his spine with my own hands."

"And then you found the Dancers."

The improbably black eyes gazed at Denice without expression. "Yes. Thirty-seven thousand years ago. It had been, oh, some thousands of years since we had last come upon a group of humans who spoke. The Dancers remained, somewhere, we knew that; but the exiles, and their children, we had hunted them into extinction. What was left could hardly be called human; the roaming tribes of savages who exterminated the Neanderthal. And we continued the hunt for the Dancers, but we no longer expected to find them, for such a great time had passed with no sign. We knew they had taken slowtime keys from the ship before destroying it; we thought that perhaps they had enclosed themselves in a stasis bubble somewhere, all the Dancers together, to await a better day.

"And then one of our search parties came across Indo.

"He was living among a tribe of the natives, living as one of them. He had done something to age himself, to make himself appear one of them; his hair was half gone, and his skin had grown wrinkles like theirs. Neither of the Shield in the party recognized him; they could not have hidden their recognition from the likes of Indo. The memory-retrieval skills taught the Shield are slow, particularly with older data, and by the time of which I tell you, no Shield had seen Indo in twelve or thirteen thousand years. But though slow, our memories work well. Much later, after leaving the tribe behind, it came to one of the Shield that Indo had been among the tribesmen, living as one of them.

"We were more careful this time."

The floats sat two hundred meters back from the edge of the great ocean.

Their names were an irony; they had not floated for better than five thousand years. The aft jets were cracked and so radioactive it was not safe to spend much time near them. The rockets had not been fired even once in those five thousand years; the lifeplants were dead and neither of the floats were airtight, even supposing they could be made to attain low orbit.

In another of the ironies it seemed to Dvan the universe delighted in, not three years after the floats had settled down for the last time, the courier ship in which Anton had arrived came tumbling down from the sky, and burned up in a brilliant fireball on reentry.

It was no surprise; the Shield had known for centuries that the orbit of the craft was decaying. But it was another sign of their increasing isolation. Even if a ship *were* sent for them, there would be no sign of their existence. They had no beacon. The radios still functioned, but they were strictly local in nature; the stranded Shield had as much chance of reaching a ship in orbit with them as by shouting from a mountaintop.

Some of the supporting technology from the floats still functioned; besides the radios, some of the sensor equipment, the auxiliary matter/antimatter-based power supplies, several of the molar/circuitry-based kitjan, and one of the laser rifles. With the passage of time the Shield stripped most of the weaponry from the floats, all those things that were functional without aid from the massive power units in the floats. The grenade launchers had been removed, and the projectile weapon that spat, at hypersonic speed, slivers of radioactive ceramic. Virtually all the energy weapons, save their handguns and one laser rifle, ran off the float's power, as did the single particle projector; and the particle projector had never been intended for use in atmosphere in the first place.

The two floats sat facing one another, each in the spot where it had been set down some five thousand years prior. Dvan remembered the very moment they had set down, jets functioning with barely forty percent efficiency, remembered it as clearly as anything from the long eons of the exile; in that terrible moment when they touched down to the sand, he had known—they had all known—that the floats would never again move from that spot. In that moment he had given up any hope of rescue, had reconciled himself to such a life as this distant world of exile could provide.

At times during the long strange passage of the centuries, Dvan found himself waking from nightmares of his own death. He knew himself sane—the training of his childhood ran deep, and functioned well—but at times he found himself wishing otherwise. The nightmares, the dreams of death, at some level promised *release*.

The passion that had driven an infant to declare war upon the Dancers, that had led him to hope that an ancient Keeper might return in some measure his desire for her; that passion was cold and dead now many thousands of years.

But the discipline remained, the Dedication of the Shield. With the nightmares, it was all Dvan had left.

The nightmares were curiously similar; in them Sedon stood cloaked in Dancer red, atop the long bluff that overlooked the unmoving pair of floats. In the dream the Dancer, without moving, seemed to come closer and closer to Dvan, and as he drew nearer Dvan saw that the red cloak was not the flowing scarlet shadow cloak of a Dancer at all, but the strung-together furs of some animal, still wet with the beasts' blood. Sedon's fierce stare pierced through the gloom between them, weighed heavy upon Dvan. His brown eyes glowed red, and his teeth, visible in an animal smile, were sharp and pointed and bloody.

The nightmares were curiously similar, and curiously real. Dvan had woken from them, more than once over the course of the millennia, convinced they *were* real, convinced that Sedon stood atop the overarching bluff, and stared down into their camp, stared down at Dvan, and accused him of betrayal.

One night at dinner, a crude parody of the civilized common meal of the Shield of the World, as the remaining Shield sat out beneath the glow of the huge moon, the Shield Pasol said quietly, "We saw Indo last summer."

Dinner consisted of water with the salt leached from it, dead flesh from the salted, roasted corpse of a horned animal, and vegetables boiled to within a hairsbreadth of destruction. One of the stern lessons of the years; never eat *anything* without cooking it until it fell apart, or nearly. The Shield immune system was strong, but not so strong that many of the Shield had not been poisoned almost to death from local food.

Several minutes passed before Pasol's comment drew a response from one of the twelve surviving Shield.

The Sentinel said, "Where?"

Pasol said, "I must consult the maps. Early summer—Valley eight hundred four or eight hundred five. Near the base of Mount Seven, Chain Two."

Several minutes later, Dvan said, "He will have recognized you."

It was a less obvious point than it might have been; they were dressed in the same animal skins that the primitives wore. But the cut of their clothing was far superior to anything any primitive had ever sewn together.

Pasol's partner on last summer's trip, the Shield So, nodded after another several minutes. "Yes." He spoke slowly: "It was Indo, though his skin has grown wrinkles, and much of his hair has fallen out. I do recall it."

Marah spoke almost immediately: "Indo will have left, but perhaps the others will be nearby. Let us seal and leave the floats, and in the morning we will journey to kill them."

It was clearly a sensible course. Several of the Shield nodded, and returned to their dinner.

In Valley 804 they found the tribe that had sheltered Indo. Indo himself was gone, doubtless within the day after Pasol and So had passed among them. The Shield spent some time interrogating the locals, most of two days, but though they shrieked and screamed and cried as though they were people, none of them spoke, not shiata nor any of the degenerate dialects that had descended from shiata, regardless of the torture to which they were subjected.

When they were done they piled the remains of the animals up on a pyre and surrounded them with wood both dry and green. A tedious task, but neater than leaving them to decompose where they and their limbs had fallen. Dvan drew the duty; with the Shields So and Tensel he cut and dragged wood until his muscles were weary. He had not counted exactly, but there had been better than two hundred of the animals. Dvan might have let them rot where they lay; some thousands of years prior, the Sentinel Marah had corrected him in the matter. "No. So long as we are Shield, we shall behave as Shield. For what we kill, animal or not, we are responsible. Besides, Dvan, think on the Dancers. After we have gone, and they come across one of our kills, what will they think to see bodies scattered randomly, as though one barbarian tribe had slaughtered another? They are proud creatures; what respect they have left for the Shield will be all but lost."

"Would that be such a bad thing? If they respected us less, they might take chances—"

Marah had simply gazed at Dvan blankly, the words clearly not penetrating, and then turned away. "We burn them. Always."

In the lengthening shadows of afternoon, Dvan played their sole functioning laser rifle, beam at wide dispersion, across the pyre, and stepped back as the wood caught, and thick white smoke, tainted with the smell of burnt meat, rose from the small clearing where the animal tribe had lived.

Down at the edge of the river, Marah sat with the sensors, scanning through the small valley. Searching for metal, or the radar signature of a slowtime bubble.

It was a difficult job at the best of times; there was ore everywhere on this planet, the world was laden with it. It made the deep radar scans less useful than they might have been. As the small tribe burned behind them, the twelve Shield assembled and waited well into the night before Marah announced that the sensors were inconclusive. If there were refined metal artifacts around them, the sensors could not make them out against the general background of unrefined ore.

In the morning, the Sentinel said, they would move the sensors and try again.

In the last hour of darkness the Dancers attacked.

Dvan awoke to silence. He lay curled up beneath a tree, back to the trunk, holding the Shield So for warmth; for a brief, groggy moment he was not certain what had awakened him. Then he realized, *complete silence*, and abruptly came fully awake. The birds whose song normally filled the hour before dawn had fallen silent; even the chirping of the small amphibians and insects had ceased. Dvan raised his head to peer into the dark, felt with one hand for the kitjan, tied with a thong to his upper thigh. The moon had set and only the stars gave any light to speak of. A couple of dim, distant IR sources were visible; wolves, likely, or the horned grazers. Slowly, as silently as he was able, Dvan loosed the thong, slipped the kitjan free.

Where are the sentries?

Tmariu, and, who was it, Addil—Dvan strained for their forms; there a motionless figure, down toward the stream, that might be a sentry, but his unnatural motionlessness was—

He drew breath to shout warning, and the whistling sounds of arrows filled the night air. One seemed to sprout from nowhere, the thin shaft simply appearing in the neck of the Shield So. So stiffened in Dvan's arms, let out a long, bubbly scream, dying even as he awakened. Dvan wasted no time attempting to acquire a target; he fired a dozen shots at random into the forest, was rewarded with the high-pitched shriek of a Dancer touched by the kitjan, came to his feet and leapt, near two meters straight up, into the lower branches of the tree beneath which he and So had slept. He climbed free of the tree, and into the tree beside it, and from there into the tree beside it. He moved silently through the dark roof of the nighttime forest, calculating. One Dancer down, possibly; three Shield dead, at least, both of the sentries and So. The shriek of the Dancer might have been a ruse, or a true hit. If a hit it was nine to four; it not, nine to five.

A beep that even Dvan barely heard announced a call. His radio, sewn into the breast of his tunic, was simply the fragment of a collar from an original Shield tunic. He ceased his movement through the treetops, lifted the fragment of the collar to his lips, and whispered, "Dvan." He held the stiff piece of cloth to his ear in time to hear Marah's voice.

"It's bad, Dvan. We've for sure lost Tmariu and Addil and Baresst." Brief silence, and Marah's voice again, struggling with the words. "And Els. I tasted his skin, and it smelled of the Dancer Lorien."

Mai'Arad'Els, dead; so far as any of them knew, Marah's last living kin in the Continuing Time. Dvan had no comfort for the man; four Tbad had died aboard the ship, and in all the millennia since then Dvan had had no one to call kin; there were neither Gi'Tbad nor even Ea'Tbad among the surviving Shield.

The Dancer Lorien was Gi'Tbad, and Dvan was sworn to kill him.

After a bit, Marah's voice resumed, near silence in near-total darkness. "I killed the Dancer Elemir myself, took his head from his body; I think your shots took Trega, I saw him being carried away."

If true, it meant there were three left alive; Sedon and

Lorien and Indo. Dvan brought the patch of ancient collar back down to his lips, whispered, "And ours?"

Another long hesitation, and then Marah said, "Dvan, you're the only one who responded when I called."

Dvan did not even think about it: he raised his head to the sky, and screamed until his lungs were empty of air.

"Sedon! I'm coming to kill you!"

The scream echoed in his head long after it had faded into the forest around them.

They took the time to scout the forest immediately around them; found their ten dead, and the Dancer Elemir where Marah had left him lying; they found Trega a ways farther on, motionless and already so frigidly cold that Dvan knew the Dancers must have cooled themselves to the temperature of the forest around them before attacking. Sensible, in a way; it had made them nearly invisible in the darkness, as cold and dark as the trees around them. Foolish in another way; had the blood been pumping through Trega's veins as it was intended to, he might have survived a brush with the kitjan.

They cut Trega's head from his body and tore his heart from his chest, in case the Dancer had simply stopped his heart and stilled his breathing to fool them into believing him dead, and then set out after the remaining three.

They trailed the Dancers for four days, as the mountains grew larger and larger, raised up to cover much of the sky before them. Between them they carried the grenade launcher and the laser rifle; each of them had a kitjan.

Everything else they had destroyed and left behind.

It seemed to Dvan that his life was drawing visibly to a close. The loss of the colony, the loss of the ship, the loss in this one day of ten of his mates.

As they ran together, through the overarching forests, Dvan tried to forget the image of So, dying with a primitive arrow in his throat, to forget the feeling of the man going rigid in his arms, the image itself some barbaric remnant from the Splinter Wars. In the steady pounding of the earth against his feet, in the deadly serious business of drawing sufficient air into his lungs, he found some measure of forgetfulness. With the passage of the days—three days, and then four, running virtually without stop through the endless brown and green forests of Ice Age Earth—Dvan found further cause for forgetfulness.

Red exhaustion crept up on him, stole the strength from his limbs. It became a supreme act of will simply to keep moving, to keep the spoor of the retreating Dancers fresh. Stops for rest, brief, brief stops for sleep, so brief there was no time even to make a fire; they slept in the freezing cold, in the wind off the mountains, holding one another for warmth; and then up again, and moving on.

It must surely have been harder for Marah than for the longer-legged Dvan, but the short, squat form of the Sentinel, a few paces behind Dvan, never wavered, never faltered in its steady pace.

They were never more than an hour or so behind the Dancers; the broken twigs, crushed leaves, bent branches were clearly visible. No group of three, moving at the speed the Dancers must, could have hidden the evidence of their passage from either Dvan or Marah. The Shield who had once had no idea how to follow a trail from Second Town down to the riverside were now the finest trackers on the entire planet; thirteen thousand years of practice will do that to you.

In late morning, the fourth day of the chase, they entered a long, open field, an open space between two stretches of forest. They stopped at the edge of the field, scanned the space between it. In the long grass, they could clearly see the path the Dancers had taken, the bent and broken stalks marking their way as clearly as though guide lights had been set.

The paths had split, one moving straight off to the north, the other off toward the west. They followed the path out to where it branched, examined the grass and earth around it. "Two this way," said Marah quietly, "one that." He paused. "Indo's the lightest of the lot; that's his mark, there, the others would have crushed that leaf."

Indo had gone north.

"Sedon will have gone with Indo," said Dvan quietly.

"Aye. Which means that Lorien—"

Dvan nodded. "Lorien's Gi'Tbad; kill him slowly, if you have the opportunity."

Marah nodded also, turned slightly away from Dvan, squinting off already along the westward path the Dancer Lorien had taken. "Aye."

"But *kill him*."

"Aye."

Dvan stood motionless beneath the warm sun, watching

Marah, and said finally, "If I survive, I'll meet you back at the floats."

"If we survive." Marah turned suddenly, embraced Dvan with the savage strength of one who did not expect to see him again. Dvan returned the embrace, then released the Sentinel. The Shield turned away from one another, and moved on to their destinies, without once looking back.

Dvan had expected it; it made it no less frustrating when it happened.

The path split again.

At first he did not catch it; the split took place deep in the thick of the forest. He backtracked, moved back to the last place he was certain he had been following not one Dancer, but two. From there he moved outward in a slow circle, found the second path off some sixty meters to his right; one of the Dancers had taken to the trees, come back down again far enough away that, had Dvan been less careful, he would have lost the track.

The original track had veered off toward the northeast; the second track, the one coming down out of the trees, had continued north.

Toward a valley, leading up gradually into the mountains.

Dvan stood motionless, breathing deeply and rapidly, thinking it through. He felt his eyes closing, allowed them to shut. In the quiet darkness he tried to perform analytical thought for the first time in perhaps a millennium. If the young Shield he had once been could have seen how his thought processes had atrophied, it would have horrified him to the point of seeking his own death; but Dvan had no standards to judge against except his mates among the Shield, whose ability to reason had in most instances atrophied far worse than his own.

Moving north. Sedon's party, and Sedon himself the leader; if they are moving north together at first, it is because Sedon has made the decision, because Sedon has determined their destination.

Sedon will not turn aside, not as a ruse, not out of fear of the Shield who followed him, no matter who the Shield might be.

North ran toward a small valley at the foot of the mountains, a natural path upward into the mountains. The original trail, veering now northeast, led almost straight upward, toward the foothills of the mountain, into an area so steep that it was as much a climb as a run.

I will go north. Dvan opened his eyes—

The wolf sat watching him from the shadows, absolutely silent, a huge beast, seventy or eighty kilos. Red eyes and a russet coat, and a muzzle with blood fresh upon it. Dvan took a step toward it, and the beast turned tail instantly, fled northeast into the steep foothills.

Dvan followed it without thinking.

He followed the wolf all morning, into afternoon. Somewhere in the back of his mind he knew that it was not a wolf at all that he followed, but a spirit, sent down into the world by the Nameless One as a tool to help Dvan punish the heretic.

In late afternoon the wolf vanished, and shortly thereafter Dvan saw the Dancer, saw him in the flesh, for the first time in thirteen thousand years.

Sedon.

Visible just for a second, far ahead of him, moving upward through the thinning forest, up toward the place where the trees ceased altogether. Dvan got a shot off with the kitjan, knew he had missed, and put on another burst of speed. Another thick cluster of trees, and then the trees thinned out, the thick needle-bearing trees giving way to trees with small, waxy white leaves. Another glimpse of the Dancer now, closer, perhaps only a klick away, and Dvan fired again. Nothing, no cry such as any Dancer would give when struck by the full force of the kitjan. Dvan gave the effort everything that was left in him, threw himself forward so quickly he barely had time to negotiate the spaces between the thinning trees. Branches scratched at him, tugged at him like clutching fingers as he pushed his way through. It was a place where his bulk gave him the advantage; in places where the Dancer must negotiate a passage, Dvan forced his way through, up now to the very edge of the tree line—

There. Movement flickered up on the side of the mountain and Dvan fired without aiming, without time to aim, paused a moment and then fired again. The sun had nearly vanished now, leaving nothing but the last gleams of twilight to light Dvan's way to vengeance. He squeezed off a fourth shot, shifted his aim slightly and sent another bolt up the mountainside in the general direction of the movement he had seen. He con-

sidered the laser, slung across his back, and discounted it; if the
kitjan, with its wider field of effect, had not taken the Dancer,
then the laser was no better.

He tied the kitjan down over his thigh, and resumed his
pursuit.

The mountain grew steep now, so steep that Dvan had to
use both hands to help himself move up the icy cold rock, up
the side of the mountain in near darkness. The sky itself was
near as dark as the rock around him, and Dvan was forced to
go more slowly, and more slowly yet, and he felt his heart
pounding away inside him; he was losing the Dancer, losing
ground he would never recover—

He glanced upward, up the mountainside.

The god had been kind.

The Dancer's figure stood straight, like a Shield on duty,
and Dvan knew from the way the Dancer held himself that he
had been touched by the kitjan; the Dancer stood outlined
against the starlit sky, as visible as though in daylight, no more
than a hundred meters ahead of Dvan. Dvan clawed for the
kitjan, got it free and saw that the figure had vanished again.
He did not tie the kitjan down again, but rose and leapt up the
rock in great bounds, no longer climbing, accepting the chance
of a misstep and mortal fall. A long dark ravine lead upward
and Dvan went into it, and then out of it, and found himself on
a small ledge that led off to the east and west alike, *heard* the
sound of the Dancer shuffling across the stone off to his right,
and sprinted the last distance, not tired at all, filled with a joy
so profound he had never known its like, fulfilling the service
the god had requested of him, and he rounded an outcrop of
rock and found an open place leading inward to a cave, and
there, in the middle of the cave, groping cautiously for something, his back turned to Dvan, was the Dancer.

For a moment so short and so long it could have no meaning, Dvan stood perfectly motionless, frozen in the awareness
of success. Hollowness filled him, made him an empty vessel
for the touch of the god, and the god used him for the tool he
had always been. He watched the god bring up the kitjan,
heard the god say softly, "Good-bye, Sedon," and felt his index
finger depressing the stud, watched the bolt strike the Dancer
full on, heard the Dancer's death scream—

A slowtime bubble appeared from nowhere.

The god released him.

Dvan almost fell, took a stumbling step forward, unbelieving, cold and alone, the kitjan a great weight in his hand.

The bubble glowed at him, hard and real and solid, a dim and gentle silver beneath the light of distant stars.

Dvan let the kitjan drop to his side, took half a dozen achingly slow steps forward, and let himself sink down at the side of the cave, with the slowtime field to his back.

And waited for morning to arrive.

He had never been so tired before in all his immensely long life.

Come the cold dawn he looked around, fixing the place in memory, the relationships of the peaks to one another. It took some time, imprinting the image into deep memory, but at length he was satisfied; though eons might pass between visits, he would know this place again.

After a while he got up and stretched to relieve his stiffness, and headed back down the mountain.

- 14 -

He spent most of the winter trying to follow Indo's trail, without success. Eventually he gave up and went looking for Marah.

He found him, easily enough, shortly after nightfall. A day's march on past the point where he and Marah had separated, Lorien had made a stand of it, on a long bluff overlooking a wide river. There was not enough left of the site where the conflict had taken place for Dvan to reconstruct much of the battle; perhaps the Dancer had not realized that Marah was carrying the grenade launcher. Most of the bluff was gone, and the river's course had been altered. Spatters of molten stone coated most of the immediate area. At least three grenades had been detonated, possibly four.

An ambush; Marah's corpse showed it clearly enough. Marah lay, with the grenade launcher and kitjan, at the edge of the devastation. Arrows filled him like the quills of one of the small pricklies the Shield had sometimes dined on. Though Dvan could never find the smallest trace of the Dancer, Dvan had no doubt that Marah had killed Lorien; the Sentinel had died smiling, and had frozen with the rictus still upon his features.

Dvan disassembled the grenade launcher, removed the two remaining grenades, and set their time fuzes.

He walked away without hurry. Half an hour after leaving Marah's corpse, the world behind him lit with the sudden glare of the midday sun. Dvan's shadow, moving ahead of him, grew huge and wavered like the shadow of a giant. Eventually the brilliant light faded, and the hot wind, when it came, merely warmed the back of Dvan's neck.

He camped for a while at the floats.

He did not know how long he stayed there. After a while, he noticed that the summers were growing longer, and warmer, and that the winters were not so fierce. One summer a tribe of the savages wandered through, and stopped to camp at the edge of the long flats upon which the floats were beached, and watched Dvan, from a distance, for day after day after day.

Toward the end of the summer they picked up and left. The morning after they were gone, Dvan awoke and realized that the floats, which had once been some hundred meters back from the edge of the water, were getting wet with every high tide. Plants had grown up to cover the thrusters, and drifts of sand had moved up into the cabins of the floats, covering the floors so completely they could not be seen. The doors still shut, after a fashion; Dvan sat in the pilot's seat, and looked out through the still flawlessly clean windows at the vast blue ocean. After a bit he unstrapped the kitjan that had lain against his thigh so long he had run through over two thousand of the restraining thongs, and left the kitjan on the seat once used by the weapons operator.

He left the doors to both floats open to the elements, and set off down the coast, following the savages.

Over thirty thousand years passed.

The shop sat in the very shadow of the great Library at Alexandria. In the mornings it got sunlight; in the afternoon the Library blocked it.

"Hello, Indo."

The shopkeeper, an elderly man of no more than average size, turned about slowly, peering up at the giant who had brushed through the hanging beads that filled his doorway. The shopkeeper spoke pure, accentless Greek. "Forgive me? Did you speak to me?"

"You recognize me."

The old man bowed quickly, apparently somewhat nervous. "Forgive me, sir. I do not understand your tongue; I speak Greek and Hebrew only. Are you interested in cloth? We weave the finest in all—"

The giant, dressed in the tunic and leggings of a Greek businessman of some wealth, did not hurry; he unsheathed a sword to match his own awesome size, swung its tip around to rest against the shopkeeper's windpipe. *"For the last time, Indo. Speak shiata, or die."*

The shopkeeper peered up at the giant, then calmly straightened himself up out of his hunch, and abruptly gained a good ten centimeters' height. His features smoothed, the tremor in his throat and hands disappeared, and suddenly he seemed not so much old, as simply careworn and reserved. In shiata as accentless as Dvan's own, he said simply, *"I've no lon; may I offer you a glass of wine?"*

Dvan sheathed his sword, inclined his head slightly, and said in Greek every bit as good as Indo's, "It would be my very great pleasure."

They sat together in the back room, a small place of white stone walls, with a single window that looked out toward the walls of the Library. Only a kilometer distant, the Mediterranean gleamed blue in the noonday sun. Indo poured wine from a stoppered clay jug; Divan was not surprised to find the wine of a quality that did not match the humbleness of Indo's surroundings.

Dvan sipped at his wine.

Indo smiled at him, a gentle and utterly guileless thing, teeth hidden as though they were two servants of the Flame, on the World that had abandoned them eons since. "Have you come to kill me?"

"I don't know, Indo. I had not *thought* of you in—" Dvan searched back. "I cannot even say how long."

"You thought me dead."

"I did. It had not occurred to me . . . that any others could have survived . . . so long. So very long." Dvan said suddenly, "Do any others survive? Any of the exiles?"

Indo merely shook his head. "If they did I would not tell you."

"My trip here," said Dvan, "fourteen years ago; I saw an exhibition of swordplay here, and I *knew*—"

Indo nodded. "The students of the students of my students."

"They spoke shiata among themselves—not well, not as those born to it; but the language was unmistakable." The words burst from Dvan. "What *are* they?"

Indo shook his head. "I know the answer to that no better than you. They call themselves the Face of Night. *Shivata.* Before we came to this world I turned away from the god, spurned his service; abrogated to myself, by right of the fact that I could *take* them, the gifts the god had given me. The god no longer speaks to me." Indo paused. "But he speaks to *them.*"

"They are not Dancers."

"No. The Dance, Dvan, is a celebration of life. It is not a tool of death, and even we heretics could not make it one."

"They have done it."

Indo's voice was gentle, dreamy, distant. "No. The Dance of the Flame cannot be used so. But they have made a transition, Dvan, which I think was inevitable; once the Flame was mastered, and master it we did, Sedon and I, the next step was inevitable. We Dancers, trained so well in the Dance of the Flame, could not take that step.

"Our children have."

Gi'Tbad'Eovad'Dvan said simply, "I do not understand."

"If life is art, Dvan, so must be death. All power arises from transformation, the movement from one state of existence to another. The power to bring life, to take the Flame down into the world; it is the same thing as the power to mold life, and to take it." Silence for a while, and then Indo whispered, "In his right hand he holds a black Flame."

They sat together in silence, as darkness descended around them.

"Art," said Indo finally, "at each step. I would not have believed it had I not seen it; but there is beauty in the Kill." He looked up at Dvan. "You have made your decision."

"Will you fight me?"

"No." Indo shook his head. "What the god brought me to do, I have done."

"Then stand up."

Indo did, lifted his chin. Dvan loosed the sword, and simply did it, quickly, with no attempt at art. He was out the door, into the darkened street outside, before Indo's head had ceased rolling across the floor.

North. He would go north, away from Indo's students; he had no desire to fight them.

With Indo dead, released at last from the vow that had held him nearly all his unnaturally long life, he had no desires at all.

- 16 -

From the Flame came nightways.

In the beginning was the Flame, and the Flame was life. Those who came after saw the Flame, and rejoiced, and Danced in its beauty.

For a long time this was so.

Then we came, the broken ones. We learned the Dance, and mastered the Dance, and then dared attempt to master the Flame itself.

And did.

From shia came shiabrè.

From life came death.

From the Flame came nightways.

—Excerpted from Shiva Curiachen's *An Oral History of Nightways*, pub. 2332, Alternities Press, CU:18.995 Zaradin.

On a cold morning early in the year A.D. 527, Dvan waited with his troops for the coming battle.

They camped on the hills overlooking the Camel, overlooking the fields where battle would take place.

It was a grim chill day, gray with clouds and damp with mist, and Dvan felt it in his bones, felt the wetness of the air in his beard. It made him wonder, not for the first or even ten-thousandth time, if this might be what age felt like, the loss of vitality, of warmth. Impending battle had always affected him this way, and doubtless always would. It seemed to him at times that he had spent his entire immense, unending life on this barbarian Earth either preparing for battle, cleaning up after a battle, or seeking bleakly to evade one.

He and his men, a band of better than two thousand horsemen if Dvan's scribe Nicco was to be believed, were gathered in the trees overlooking the clearing on the west side of the Camel. The balance of Dvan's forces he had left at home. He lacked horses for them, and constrained to the speed of men afoot he could not have reached the Camel in any reasonable time.

Dvan did not for a moment believe old Nicco's count of two thousand; he reckoned, estimating by eye, that they were at least two hundred shy of their second thousand. But no need to embarrass the old man. Nicco's eyesight was fading, and his memory going with each day. If he wished to call the count at two thousand and fourteen, why then, two thousand and fourteen it would be.

The only certainty in the world was that it would be far fewer by day's end.

The King's troops assembled throughout the long morning, horsemen and foot soldiers arriving together, taking up position in the eastern fields, with the Camel separating them from the bastard Medraut's troops, and the Saxons with whom Medraut had allied himself. Dvan did not know why Medraut had not taken Camelot, and held it against Arthur's return—he'd have done so himself—but it hardly mattered.

Arthur himself arrived toward midmorning. Even from

where he had encamped Dvan recognized some few in the
King's party; Arthur himself, his son Llacheau, the immense
bulk of the monster Gawain, the first man Dvan had met in
some hundreds of years who surpassed his own great size.

Dvan kept his men encamped; no use in moving until the
course of the battle, if there was one, came clear.

The morning wore down into the afternoon, and in the afternoon, Medraut and Arthur went forth to parley.

Dvan had his men ready themselves; when combat came—
and Dvan knew there was no real chance of peace out of this
parley—it would come quick.

He sat still, breathing slowed down to practically nothing,
calm as the ocean before the storm. He knew it a thing of pride
to his men, his lack of concern before a battle. His sword, so
large no normal man could have wielded it, lay across his
thighs, waiting for blood.

Dvan sat up high on the ridge of Camel Hill, watching the
forces below. Medraut and Arthur spoke together for hours,
spoke so long that Dvan began to wonder if the battle everyone
had seen coming for the last two years might actually be
averted. At one point the two men sent their aides away, and
stood together, with no one else within range of their voices,
for most of half an hour.

Whatever it was they discussed would never be known; Arthur nodded abruptly, turned away, and with his party made his
way back across the Camel.

When they were halfway across the Camel, in an act of blatant treachery, the Saxons at Medraut's back surged forward,
across the open field, and engaged Arthur's party while it was
still mired in the open water of the Camel.

Impatience was not one of Dvan's problems; he gave it fully
half an hour before he joined in, long enough that the Saxons
had nearly forgotten him, long enough that Arthur's folk doubtless thought themselves betrayed.

Long enough that all those whom Dvan's men were likely to
face had grown tired.

They swept down off the hill in a great thundering wave of
horseflesh, came upon the south flank of the Saxon forces with
a suddenness that buckled that flank. Dvan held back slightly,

let a few dozen of his men make first contact with the Saxons, and then rode in after them and settled down to work.

And the day stretched on.

Twice fighting took Dvan to within hailing distance of Arthur, once so close to Medraut that Dvan hurried in killing the Briton who fought against him, and urged his mount toward Medraut. Too late; Medraut left his mount behind, between himself and Dvan, flowed off the horse with all the grace of a Dancer and went to the ground with his sword, landed lightly, and walked away from Dvan, walked through the field of battle as though certain of his own immortality. Dvan took an ax cut to his arm from a Saxon he had ignored, and then had to turn back to business, his sword hand now wet with his own blood. He switched hands without thinking about it, turned away from Medraut's retreating form and cut the Saxon's head off. When he had time to glance again the surging sea of men and horses had hidden Medraut from him.

No time to look for him, either; behind the first Saxon came a second, and Dvan slew him, and then a huge creature slammed into the Irishman to Dvan's right, dragged the man and his horse to the ground. Dvan swung around to face him, found himself staring down at a blond giant. With a one-handed chop of his ax the Saxon cleanly decapitated Dvan's horse, and Dvan had to leap from the animal's back as it fell. He rolled to his feet, sword in hand, and turned to face the approaching Saxon. The man was a giant by modern standards, near Gawain's size, surely every bit of Dvan's own unnatural height. Blood flowed crimson across the hugely muscled shoulders, down the Saxon's arm and over his ax. He was upon Dvan in the moment that Dvan regained his feet, ax up over his head, whistling down toward Dvan. Dvan got his sword up, lunged forward, and saw the tip of his sword go into the Saxon's chest, felt the resistance and leaned into it as the man's ax came down and bit through the leather of Dvan's head guard, through hair, flesh, bone, and into the pink of brain.

By the time it had breached bone most of the impact had been absorbed.

The two men stood staring at one another as the battle swirled around them; they fell together, and the Saxon died in the moment of that fall.

Dvan never knew it.

Indeed, for a long, long time, Gi'Tbad'Eovad'Dvan knew nothing at all.

When he awoke again it was morning.

He lay on a field with bodies piled all around him. The grass, heavy with dew, dampened his cheek. The smell of blood hung sweet and fragrant in the misty air.

A boot nudged him, rolled him over slowly. He stared up at the great gray sky. A vast pain pulsed in his skull, a throbbing like the end of the world.

" 'E's alive." A ratlike countenance peered down into the injured man's upturned face. "Leave 'im that way?"

A deeper voice said wearily, "Aye. That's Divane, the Irish fellow what Arthur dragged down here to die with 'im. Pick 'im up, he can die back to the camp as well as here."

Divane. The man considered that as several pairs of hands strained and lifted him free of the ground.

A fair enough name.

He saw no reason not to keep it.

- 18 -

When Dvan was at last done, late Monday, the fourth day after beginning his tale, there was for a very long time no sound at all but the gentle sighing of the ventilators, the almost inaudible creaks of the great house as it rotated on its axis. Denice watched Gi'Tbad'Eovad'Dvan, the relic of fifty thousand years, standing like a statue before her. "What is left is of little enough importance. I had no memory of who I was; I knew only that I did not age as other men. I adapted, learned to hide my differences, to make no close friends, take no family. I lived through the discovery of steam power and the printing press, the telephone and the automobile and the computer and air flight and space flight, nanotechnology and genegineering and the InfoNet. Now that I remember, it amazes me that my people and yours could have taken such divergent paths; we never touched nanotechnology, and only dabbled in genegineering until we had conquered death by aging.

"But we were engineers and builders the likes of which you

cannot imagine. In the worship of the Flame we built wonders such as your people have never even attempted."

Robert said quietly, "You say 'your' people, as though you were not one of us. You are to my eyes a man, like other men."

Dvan turned on Robert with a suddenness that brought Denice up on her bed, crouched and ready for movement. Robert had not stirred but suddenly he was no longer a small Japanese man with laugh lines at the corners of his eyes. In his expression lived something ancient and deadly.

"You," said Dvan with chilling precision, with a degree of contempt so devastating Denice would not have believed it possible had she not heard it, "are our children. The New Human Race. The descendants of heretics, of criminals and those who followed them. Mutated as the Flame People would never have allowed themselves to be mutated, selected by evolution for your inclination to violence, a people who have made violence an art and death a passion and the Kill a religion; aye," said Dvan, "you are our children. And you are completely insane."

- 19 -

Most of the week passed before Denice could move again without pain. Even with modern medicine, even in the one-third gravity of her room, her knee ached every night. The bruise on her hip was minor, and soon faded; the broken left forearm was the worst of it, but she put no strain on it, and with the aid of nanoviruses that were crafted to help the bone knit, toward the end of the week she was able to punch with either hand almost equally well. Half an hour with the punching bag made her left forearm throb; but though it hurt, the ache grew less with each passing day, and the pain did not prevent her from striking if she needed to.

She threw herself into her recovery with a vengeance. Jimmy was far enough along in his own recovery that she saw no need to help him further; with Robert's help, she focused on herself, and on her own needs. She spent most of every other day in the gym, working out until she was exhausted; gave herself the in-between days to let her muscles heal and grow. On those days she swam, in the zero-gravity swimming pool, or audited the InfoNet for news of the Rebs, or Sedon, or Ripper.

Chandler's people were busy, looking for a line on Sedon, and having no more success, apparently, than the PKF. Somewhere in San Diego, they all knew that much; but where exactly was anyone's guess.

She spent hour after hour sitting silently in her room, watching the stars wheel by in her floor.

Electronic Times, *June 17, 2076: Today's polls place Douglass Ripper, Jr., eight points ahead of Sanford Mtumka; thirty-six percent of the respondents in our poll stated that, if the election were held today, they would vote for Ripper over any of the other candidates in the race.*

Ralf the Wise and Powerful said simply, "The major media is not allowed to say so, but assuming no significant changes in the external situation, Ripper will win. He's gaining ground, slowly but very surely. On Thursday the Ministry of Population Control will announce that China has, once again, failed to meet its population-reduction target; when that happens, Zhao Pen will lose another point to two points of support, and Ripper will pick most of that up. It will give him very nearly a ten-point lead. No candidate for a major Unification office has, in modern times, failed of election with a lead of such size. Assuming Ripper isn't caught in bed with a troop of dead Boy Scouts, he is a prohibitive favorite to be, come next January first, the new Secretary General."

"Dead Boy Scouts? Is that a joke, Ralf?"

"I have been working on my sense of humor recently."

"Why?"

"I'm recoding anyway," said Ralf simply. "It gives me something to do while Ring destroys me."

"What will you do about Dvan?"

Denice grunted, winced and released the weight she'd been planning to use for curls. Too heavy for an arm broken so recently. She answered Robert while removing five kilos from the barbell. "Well, I don't need a servant. And his dislike of you is irrational." She shook her head. "It bothers me."

Robert sat a few meters away, twisted into an improbable position on the mat, breathing deeply and slowly. "He threatened to kill me if I attempted to continue teaching you."

Denice put down the barbell. "When?"

Robert had to kick twice to get his foot free; abruptly a vaguely mushroom-looking shape unfolded into a human being. He took a deep breath that turned into a yawn, said drowsily, "About a week ago."

"I see you're terribly worried."

Robert shrugged. "Short of killing him outright, what would I do about it if I were?"

"That's a point."

Robert gestured to her to join him. She sank down on the mat before him. "Are you ready to talk?"

"Yes."

His eyes were half-lidded. "Where are we with each other?"

"I don't know, Robert. I want to—not be whatever it is you are. But I killed those men in Los Angeles, and—I can't describe to you how it felt. I still have nightmares about it."

"I know how it felt. You enjoyed it."

Denice bowed her head. She whispered the words. "Oh, yes. And the Flame Dvan talks about, I've felt that too; and it's as strong as the Kill; and I have no more idea how to handle it."

"I have a strong feeling," said Robert slowly, "that there is nothing I can say to you in this area that will be relevant to what is happening with you. So I will not try. But if you need me—to kill Sedon; for instruction; to come rescue you off some building somewhere—" She looked up, and her eyes met his. "—I will always be here."

Thursday they had dinner with Chandler again, Dvan, and Denice, Robert and Jimmy. Dinner was strained; Jimmy was unhappy, felt that he was being ignored, and didn't care who knew it. Denice was briefly sorry that she'd gone to the trouble to make herself up for dinner; nobody seemed to notice. Chandler finished early and excused himself, and Jimmy left shortly after that, after inviting Denice to come swimming with him.

Denice said quietly, "In a bit."

Jimmy stopped in the doorway, watching Denice and Robert and Dvan sitting together around the low dinner table. Denice could *feel* the hurt and anger radiating away from him; she said nothing, and Jimmy turned and left without speaking.

Dvan spoke as the door rolled shut behind Jimmy Ramirez, in that unlikely, gentle Irish voice. "You've been avoiding me, lass."

"What would you like to be called?"

The question seemed to throw the huge man; he hesitated a moment. "William will do. It's a name I'm used to, at any rate."

"William, you can call me Denice."

Dvan blinked. "What?"

"My name is Denice. You've called me all sorts of things since I met you, and most of them offend me. Call me Denice."

"Very well," said Dvan slowly. "Denice. I can do that. If I've offended you, lass, forgive me; I mean no harm. I know what you can be—though I had not thought it possible for a woman to Dance the Flame—but I don't know what you are." He hesitated, grinned abruptly, and the Irish lilt strengthened. "Having been William Devane these last fifteen centuries gives me an interesting perspective; I've got to see your people from the inside out. I've been struggling with things since I remembered, not quite a year ago now. William Devane is a sexist, I think you'd call him. Call *me*. But that part of me that calls itself Dvan barely recognizes *you* as a person, Denice. You're a Dancer, or perhaps a Keeper, or possibly just a breeder. And when I think in those terms—and it's hard not to, for the identity of the Shield Dvan is more deeply rooted in me than that of the William Devane of the last fifteen centuries—when I think in those terms, I can see no way to approach you and ask for your help."

"What do you want my help for?"

Dvan glanced at Robert; Robert stared back, impassively. Dvan drew a breath. "First, to kill Sedon. It may be I can do it myself, and it may not; but with your aid, and the aid of your AI friend, I do not think I can fail."

"You didn't mention Robert."

Dvan shrugged. "I saw no need to. I doubt there is any skill he possesses that I do not."

Robert murmured, "Aside from tact, you mean."

Dvan struggled with it. "If I were you, I would not speak that way to me."

"You mean," said Robert easily, "if *you* were an abomination, the descendant of heretics, *you* would know your place?"

Dvan seemed to consider it. "Well," he said finally, "something like that." He pointed at Robert and said, "You recognize this weapon."

A flechette gun, small and round, sat crouched in the palm of the big man's hand.

For a long moment Denice's brain insisted that it had to be something else; she'd been *watching* him, watching his hands, and hadn't seen him palm the weapon. Clearly Robert hadn't either.

Robert sat frozen, motionless, every trace of humor drained from him. His hands were together in front of him, in plain view. "That's a really good trick," he said. "Someday you must show me how to do that."

"It's a flechette gun, night face."

Robert gazed at Dvan, unblinking. "Yes, yes, I know."

Denice had no time for anything complex; she froze his medianis nerve and threw. The bones in Dvan's left wrist shattered, the skin ripping open, blood spraying away. The flechette gun bounced up, spun out of Dvan's nerveless grip as Robert Dazai Yo rose to his feet, plucked the gun from the air and took two steps back and aimed.

Dvan looked from Denice to Robert Yo, and back to Denice, and then down to the small broken object that lay on the floor at his feet. His left wrist was open to the bone, and his blood dripped steadily down his fingers to the floor. He bent and, with the hand Denice had left whole, picked up the small black item.

She had thrown a makeup key at him.

"If we're going to work together," said Denice, "and I think we're probably going to, you *can't* threaten my friends."

Dvan nodded slowly. "I see." Blood pooled on the floor at his feet. "What now?"

Robert Yo spoke softly and slowly, with a gentle rhythm unlike anything Denice had ever before heard from him or any other human being. The words echoed in her ears as they came forth, rolled slowly through the corridors of her mind. They were spoken in shiata:

"Rho! Etra shivat elor ko'obay k'shia, vata elor ko'obay shiebran."

Dvan's features, pale already with shock, whitened perceptibly, with what emotion Denice did not know.

Looking at Dvan over the flechette gun's sight, Robert smiled, a slow friendly smile that lit his features and made him seem suddenly a young man, and said simply, *"Enshia, ensitra."*

I am the Name Storyteller.

In 2309, in the Oz Circuit, on the planet Tin Woodman, a night face named Shiva Curiachen conquered an addiction to electric ecstasy.

This, in shiata, the tongue of the Old Human Race, is *Shiab, Rosad*, the Dedication of Nightways:

Rho! Etra shivat elor ko'obay k'shia, vata elor ko'obay shiebran. Enshia, ensitra.

The Dedication can vary by one word, the last:

Rho! Etra shivat elor ko'obay k'shia, vata elor ko'obay shiebran. Enshia, denestra.

The difference in meaning between these two apparently slight variations is immense. Depending upon inflection, the first Dedication, ending in ensitra, is a vow of either fealty or, as often, common interest. In the days when women were rarely taught the discipline, the word ensitra was almost always translated as "brotherhood."

The second version of the Dedication—*Enshia, denestra*—is a sacred and deadly serious promise to destroy the person at whom the Dedication has been directed.

In 2309, the night face Shiva Curiachen, the first Shiva of United Earth Intelligence, translated the Dedication of Nightways into English. Though other translations have been attempted, some of them more literally accurate, it is generally recognized that, of the known English-language translations, Curiachen's translation comes closest to capturing both the meaning and the feeling of the Dedication of Nightways.

Sitting motionless in the middle of Christ's Burden Boulevard, a thermos containing Lipton Instant Iced Tea with Lemon at his feet, in a small Tin Woodman town called Six Flags Over Jesus, Shiva Curiachen said these words to the King of Corona:

"Behold! We are the countenance that is turned to the cold eternal darkness; the face that is turned to the shadows of night. In nightways I am your doom."

And indeed he was.

But that is another Story, for another time.

The Tricentennial Summer

Don't sing of how you love me
Don't take me to that show
Don't tell me you're the Chosen One
'Cause I don't want to know

Don't take me to no party
Don't dance with me tonight
It's all the same with you, my love
You're holding me too tight

—Mahliya Kutura, *Independence Day*

In Congress, July 4, 1776. The unanimous Declaration of the thirteen united states of America,

When in the Course of human Events, it becomes necessary for one People to dissolve the Political Bands that have connected them with another, and to assume among the Powers of the Earth, the separate and equal Station to which the Laws of Nature and Nature's God entitle them, a decent Respect to the Opinions of Mankind requires that they should declare the causes which impel them to the Separation.

We hold these Truths to be self-evident, that all Men are created equal, that they are endowed by their Creator with certain unalienable Rights, that among these are Life, Liberty and the Pursuit of Happiness.—That to secure these Rights, Governments are instituted among Men, deriving their just Powers from the Consent of the Governed, that whenever any Form of Government becomes destructive of these Ends, it is the Right of the People to alter or to abolish it. . . .

—Opening to the American Declaration of
Independence, July 4, 1776 Gregorian

Once there was a thief, and the thief was God.

—First line in the *Exodus Bible*,
first published 2312 Gregorian

- 1 -

Among human historical figures, I think there is no sentient being more like Ifahad bell K'Ailli than Trent the Uncatchable. Both were responsible for the spread of very basic concepts among their people; both, despite their undeniable accomplishments, were notorious cheats and frauds.

Ifahad the Mighty was born into the midst of what was later called the Domè Rebellion. The sleem empire conquered the Domè around 6200 B.C.; three and a half centuries later, during Ifahad's early childhood, the Domè rebelled.

The rebellion was well under way before Ifahad's voice carried any weight among the Domè. That first rebellion lasted eighty years before failing. Toward its end, as Ifahad's power among the Domè grew, Ifahad the Mighty invented Hiding. If you are human—and if you are reading this account in French, English, Mandarin, Spanish, Anglic, or Tierra, it is likely that you are—then it will be difficult for you to understand how revolutionary the Domè, in modern times called the K'Aillae, found this concept. The K'Aillae are more like us than most alien species; which, at times, seems only to serve to highlight those areas in which we do not think alike.

An example of this comes from one of the first human translations of the works of Ifahad bell K'Ailli. It was titled *Proud Vengeance: The Writings of Ifahad*. K'Aillae were alternately amused and offended by the title. Their strongly worded suggestion for change resulted in a second edition with the title *Sensible Vengeance: The Writings of Ifahad*.

The K'Aillae are a practical people: when Ifahad introduced the concept of Hiding to the K'Aillae, responses were mixed. His explanation—that Hiding involved running away when defeat was certain, avoiding the enemy for an unspecified period of time, and then coming back and fighting again at a later date when victory was possible—did not arouse contempt among the Domè so much as puzzlement. The K'Aillae had, before meeting humans, no word for "coward"; but they had many for "crazy." Most of them were used on Ifahad.

Even after Hiding had been explained to them, K'Aillae were generally unable to grasp the concept. Only Ifahad's own clan, the K'Ailli, followed him into Hiding, which is why today there are no Domè, only K'Aillae.

Trent the Uncatchable, of course, ran away. That running away could be not simply a strategically reasonable response to overwhelming military superiority, but in fact among the most successful of all forms of resistance, was a concept many humans of his time had difficulty understanding—at least until it was demonstrated.

Trent and Ifahad were undeniably similar in the roles they played among their people; it may be that they were in some ways similar in person.

I never really knew Trent the Uncatchable; I knew Ifahad well.

The cracks in the Continuing Time are small, and it takes great effort to widen them. The huge sweep of events during the First K'Ailla Hiding—dating roughly 5845 B.C. to 70 B.C., when the K'Ailla-led Confederation of Outland rose against the sleem—is as firmly set a sequence of events as any in the post-Zaradin period. And it is recorded that when the New Human Race "first" contacted the K'Aillae, in 2124 Gregorian, the K'Aillae claimed prior contact with humanity. At the time, with their own history so poorly known to them that they did not yet know of the Old Human Race, most of the New Humanity discounted the K'Ailla records as inaccurate, or the K'Aillae as liars.

They were not.

I was there, with Ifahad, with the Old Human Named Seeker, six millennia before the birth of Yeshua ha Notzri, eighty-one centuries before the New Human Race discovered the tachyon star drive, when Ifahad first announced that, if the K'Aillae wished to survive, they must learn to Hide.

Trent the Uncatchable, of course, made no such announcement regarding running away. He simply ran.

An avatar of mine once spoke to Trent.

He *does* remind me of Ifahad.

- 2 -

I am Neil Corona.

On Wednesday, June 17, 2076, I left the shell of the Unification warship *Unity* and rode a Chandler HuskySled to the dock at Halfway Airlock Nineteen, Tytan Industries. I was late for an appointment with Marc Packard, and he's a difficult man to get along with at the best of times. So I did not bother to take off my pressure suit; I cycled through and into pressure, undogged my helmet, and headed down to the conference room where they awaited me.

Jay Altaloma met me on the way there. Jay is a young fellow, twenty-two and gorgeous even without biosculpture. "You're late."

I glanced at him. "Not yet. Not for another fifteen seconds."

"Packard's gonna be pissed."

"Bummer."

Halfway is an orbital city; with a population of nearly two million it is, next to Luna City at Copernicus, the largest city off Earth itself. It is also a company town; in some ways the government of Halfway is as much Tytan Manufacturing as the Unification.

But you know these things.

What Halfway mostly is, is a mess.

It looks like a bowl of noodles that somebody dropped just a moment ago, while you had your back turned: a roughly spherical collection of metal and metal-ceramic and plastic noodles, falling free, headed for the ground but not quite there yet. Halfway is aggressively and, in some measure, intentionally disorienting to downsiders. Among SpaceFarers and Halfers the ability to move about in three dimensions without becoming disoriented is considered a matter of simple competence. I once heard a downsider call it a matter of "pride," but that is not the correct word; SpaceFarers and Halfers no more consider it a matter of pride than downsiders are proud of their ability to walk without falling down.

I've been here since '34, ever since the Peaceforcers decided that if they weren't going to kill me they might as well keep me off Earth, away from the Johnny Rebs. At first I hated it, and kept hating it for nearly a decade. I worked at half a dozen different trades and stayed broke at all of them. The last job I had before Marc Packard hired me was as head bouncer at one of the rowdier places out on the Edge. They tend to cluster out there on the Edge, the places where you wouldn't take a visitor from Earth, if you ever had any; the whorehouses and sensable parlors, bars and sleazier restaurants, and the odd juice dealer or two. Electric ecstasy is not illegal at Halfway, the way it is on Earth, but nobody will hire a man or woman wearing a plug. Juice junkies either starve or go downside; it is one of the rarest addictions at Halfway.

I finally stopped hating Halfway about a year after I went to work for Marc Packard.

I was working a whorehouse—a step down from one of the sleazier bars, a step up from a sensable parlor—when Marc hired me. At first it was just as a bodyguard; later, as Marc got more powerful, I ended up heading all the private security at Halfway.

I'm a little under two meters tall, about ninety kilos when I'm in a good weight, and there are more than a few visible signs of rough usage here and there. Any half-competent biosculptor could make me pretty, if I wanted; I don't. Looking like something dragged out of one of the Fringe's nastier back allies can be useful at times.

The whorehouse was Kitten's, a twelve-room place out on the Edge. Kitten was an old boy who had once been one of the highest-paid whores in pre-Unification Washington D.C., about ten years before I was born. He was a charming old fellow, middling honest about small things, scrupulously so about any part of the employer-employee relationship. My pay was never late and never short, and when he made me a promise—rare—he kept it.

Marc Packard started going there late in '42. He was, I understand, nursing a broken heart. To this day I have no idea whether he was seeing one of the boys or girls, or both. It hardly matters. He wasn't anybody in particular back then, the son of one of Tytan Manufacturing's middle managers. He hadn't gone to work for Tytan yet, hadn't yet carved up most of Tytan Industries' management in his climb up the corporate ladder.

Early in '43 we got an idiot from Earth carrying a slug-thrower.

Look: *all* projectile and energy weapons are illegal at Halfway. The closest thing to a laser you will ever see in public is the gadget they used to bury inside a PKF Elite's fist, the one they're putting in the index fingers today; and we'd probably make those illegal if it were possible. It's not so much that we mind people getting shot up, bad though that may be in some cases, as it is our desire to avoid trying to breathe in death pressure. People learned early on at Halfway that breathing and gunfire were incompatible habits. A breached bulkhead doesn't just kill the intended victim, it also kills the shooter and everybody around him who doesn't get to a p-suit in time; his friends if he has any, tourists, his grandmother, *everybody*. Simply being caught with a firearm at Halfway is good for time downside in a Public Labor work gang.

This cretin downsider was carrying one of those all-plastic hideaway automatics that were so popular back in the first half of the century, and the scanners I'd installed at the public entrance to Kitten's didn't catch it. (Remember, this was '43; the slowscans today are smarter than you are, yes, but I worked with what I had.) I don't even know how the fight started, though later I heard that Marc and the downsider had come to see the same whore, and neither one particularly wanted to wait.

The first I knew about it I had a hostage situation on my hands.

Because a fair amount of Kitten's business came from downsiders who wanted to try free-fall sex before going back to Iowa or India or wherever, the lounge at Kitten's was laid out with a local vertical designed to help decrease the downsiders' inevitable disorientation. Standing with both feet planted on the bottom of the room, the downsider had one hand wrapped in Marc's hair, the other held the slugthrower poised at the base of the boy's skull.

The downsider screamed, "Back off!" as I entered the lounge.

I froze there, just inside the lounge's entrance, and hung motionless a few centimeters above the floor. Little details jumped out at me. At the far end of the room two of the hosts were peering through an open door, watching the scene unfold. The hostage was a boy—I had the quick impression of youth, no more; I wasn't paying him much attention. The boy was fully dressed; the downsider wore nothing but a pair of magslippers, keeping him in touch with the floor.

Good news; the downsider was breathing heavily through his mouth.

I said slowly, very quietly, "Okay, amigo. Just relax." Before coming down to the waiting lounge I'd turned off the ventilators. "Nobody's going to hurt you." If I could get the fellow to calm down and stay in one place for any significant length of time, a still bubble of air around his head would slowly be leached of oxygen. Anoxia is sneaky, and with the adrenaline pumping through his system he'd be using up the oxy at a good clip; with any luck he'd go limp in midsentence and I could send him downside and get him out of my life without having to hurt anyone. "I'm Neil Corona. I'm the director of security here at Kitten's. Tell me what you want, and if I can get it for you I will."

He jerked his head toward the two whores behind him, watching the scene from the doorway. "Get them *out* of here."

"My pleasure." I glanced at them and they faded back into the passageway leading to their rooms. "What else?"

It froze him; he hadn't thought things out that far, if he was thinking at all. He'd played the sensables, he knew the drill; he was supposed to make demands of me—*a million dollars, a fast horse and a jet waiting at the airport to take me to Cuba, and nobody follows me, copper, or the kid here gets it*—but there are practical details in these sorts of matters that the sensables rarely discuss. When he spoke his voice was ragged, scared of the mess he'd dragged himself into, but the adrenaline pumping through his body had left him so keyed up he couldn't see how to get out of it. "If you mess with me this dumb fuck *dies*."

I studied the boy briefly—tall and skinny, teenage Halfway homebrew. He looked back at me without expression; if he was afraid, and he was if he had any sense at all, he wasn't showing it. Could just be that he was young enough he didn't know how very long he was going to be dead.

The young tend to be concerned with dying well. Personally I worry more about when; I expect to go out screaming and shooting and generally comporting myself with a lack of dignity.

I spoke to the downsider. "Why don't you just put the gun down? Kitten's already called the Peaceforcers; you have maybe five minutes before their sleds get here."

Wrong thing to say. The muscles in the downsider's right forearm, the hand he held the gun with, bunched suddenly, and a wince of pain crossed the boy's face. The barrel of the gun must be grinding into the back of the kid's skull. "I'll kill him if they dock, I *swear* I will."

I kept eye contact with the boy, watching him. He was alert and clear-eyed, there with me in the moment, and it made a difference in what I said next. "You're in bad trouble, amigo. The PKF doesn't negot—"

"*I'll kill him if they dock.*"

I believed him. "Amigo, I have a hideaway tucked behind my belt. The PKF lets registered security carry them." (A lie—but they would look the other way. The hideaway, a practically invisible little two-shot Beretta, fired a pair of 10-mm slugs. And it was in my sleeve.) "So you kill the kid, but unless you've practiced firing a gun in free fall, it's going to push you way off balance." I shrugged. "So you shoot him and I'm going to put you down."

It froze him absolutely solid for the space of maybe an entire second. Unless you've been there you'd never believe how long a second can be. Finally he said desperately, "Let me see the gun."

"I don't think so. You." I directed the word at the boy. "What do you think I should do?"

The downsider screamed, "*Shut up!* You talk to *me*."

Marc Packard looked straight at me. He said, loud and clear, "Do me a favor. After he shoots me, kill the bastard."

I shrugged. "Okay." I hung there looking at the downsider, my toes four centimeters above the deck. "You heard him. Do you put the gun down and live, or do you shoot him and die?"

The dumb fuck tried to shoot *me*. In gravity he might have gotten away with it, pulling the gun off the boy and popping me with one shot, putting the gun back on the boy before he had a chance to react.

Downsiders don't know how to move in drop. Not even if their lives depend on it. He pulled the gun off Marc, and I saw his center of gravity change on him as he moved the gun over toward me. I kicked with my right foot, caught the edge of the doorway behind me strongly enough to get me moving off to my left at a good clip. Downside my man must have been a good enough shot; his first bullet went by my right ear close enough to leave me deaf the next day. He never got a second. The recoil knocked him off balance, and he fantailed slightly, arms outstretched and one foot out of contract with the floor. He was out of position so I took my time, pulled the little Beretta free, and kicked up off the floor. I got my back up against the ceiling to handle the recoil, and when he looked up at me I shot the stupid son of a bitch twice in the face. The slugs were an ultrathin metal sheath wrapped around light plastic. Designed to fragment upon impact, you could fire one directly into a bulkhead without much danger of damaging the bulkhead and exposing yourself to death pressure. Flesh and bone didn't handle them so good; his face melted a little bit under the impact of the first slug, and the second one shattered what was left. He spurted bright red arterial blood straight up at me out of the stump of his neck.

He was a better shot dead than alive. I got my arm up to cover my face and then the blood hit me in a sticky fountain.

Kitten was in there vacuuming up the floating globules of blood and brain when I got clean enough to look around again. Somebody, either from a macabre sense of humor or, equally likely, from the humorless pragmatism that whores tend to learn, had tied a tourniquet around the corpse's neck.

One of the boy whores gave me a towel to wipe my face with.

On the other side of the room, I got my second look at the kid who turned out to be Marc Packard. With time to look more carefully he was, clearly, younger than his composure had led me to believe; fourteen or fifteen, tops. (Over five years later he *proved* he'd been paying attention, mentioned in passing that I'd negotiated the situation badly; aside from asking the shooter to put down his weapon, I hadn't made it clear to the man what was necessary *from him* to get us all out of it with no gunplay. A mistake, Marc said, given that the man was clearly in no shape to make such decisions for himself.)

He didn't say that at the time; then, only moments after it had happened, the boy looked straight at me, rubbed a spattering of blood off one cheek with a towel another of the whores had handed him, and said, "Thanks. I owe you one."

I shrugged and stored the spent Beretta back in the forearm holster, making a mental note to reload, soonest. "No problem."

"Okay. Who are you?"

"Neil Corona."

He was educated. "Marc Packard. Pleased to—*the* Neil Corona?"

I was in no mood either to deny it or explain it. "Yes."

"Oh." He looked surprised. "Pleased to meet you." Then he fainted, the way people do in drop, going limp all over, all at once, and hung there motionless in midair.

I did something stupid once.

You may know what it is. Packard had; in 2043 it was still recent enough *most* people with any sense of history knew of it.

When I was eighteen years old I joined the United States Marine Corps.

That wasn't *the* stupid thing, although I never convinced my father of that. Dad was dead of pancreatic cancer in '14, four years before I did the stupid thing that made me famous. Yes, it was that long ago; people still died of cancer, and dozens of other diseases of which nobody who is not at least my age can even remember the names.

In the summer of 2018 I was a twenty-seven-year-old Marine Corps sergeant. By late summer the Unification War in America had come down to the battle between the orbital battalion of the Marine Corps and the U.N.'s Space Force. You know how that one ended; Space Force won.

We should have given up then. There were about twenty thousand of us left, not counting the Sons of Liberty. We had heard the Sons of Liberty were still fighting, that the President and the remains of the Secret Service were with them. To this day I don't know if that was true; at the time it was one of the things that kept the marines fighting.

The Peaceforcers swept us back across the Atlantic seaboard, and we found ourselves making the last stand of the Unification War at the city of Yorktown, Virginia, 237 years after George Washington accepted the surrender of the British there.

The battle lasted two days. They shelled us and swept us with laser cannon from orbit, until it was clear that surrender was the only option left to us. The highest ranking officer left alive on our side was a major named Eddie Henson. He negotiated the terms of our surrender over one of the few remaining phones in Yorktown that still worked, an old ISDN job that was hardwired to the Network—cellular was knocked out across most of the Eastern seaboard. My squad guarded the house out of which he was operating. About three-quarters of the way through the negotiations, when all that was left was the finalization of some details, Henson suddenly stopped talking, sat motionless for just a moment, and then abruptly put his maser in his mouth and pulled the trigger.

I finished the negotiations myself. I didn't know it at the time, but the fellow I was negotiating with was Jules Moreau, the man who had, with Sarah Almundsen, started the Unification six years prior, in Europe.

It was a stupid thing to do—again, not *the* stupid thing, but dumb. I should have waited until a commissioned officer was brought in to handle it. We still had a couple left alive, and it would only have taken perhaps five minutes to find one. But

Moreau was threatening to burn Yorktown off the face of the map, and we both knew he had the firepower to do it, so I got in front of the phone's lens and identified myself as Captain Neil Corona. We weren't wearing insignia any longer—Peaceforcer snipers made a point of shooting officers—and Moreau had no reason not to believe me.

Moreau wanted us to surrender in Yorktown. *Right now.*

That's when I said it:

"We will fry under your goddamn cannon before a single Marine will lay down his arms in Yorktown."

It was a stupid, *stupid* thing to say. A frog who had less history than Moreau would have fried us over it.

We marched out of Yorktown, twenty thousand strong, and laid down our arms at the city limits.

I don't suppose that clip of me surrendering—*we will fry under your goddamn cannon*, the brave, haggard young man says—has been accessed by more than about twenty billion history students over the course of the fifty-eight years that have passed since that day.

Marc was pissed that I was late. I could tell; he smiled at me when I came in.

"Thank you for joining us, Chief."

"I was in the field," I said shortly. "Over at the *Unity*. What's up?"

It was not good. Jay had been correct to be worried about it. Marc had most of his personal staff present, including Toni Abad, an Arab fellow I never had learned to like in the twenty years since Marc had hired him. At the far end of the table, Captain Vasily Koslov, the number-two officer in Tytan Security and the person who'd replace me if I ever got canned or killed, nodded to me. Official business, then; Marc was going to break bad news to me, and he never liked to do that alone.

He didn't let it hang, I'll say that for Marc. "The Cirque du Mars has applied for permission to perform. July first to July tenth."

"You intend to let them come?"

Marc said mildly. "I'm inclined in that direction."

I scowled at Marc and said, "This is the stupidest damn idea you've ever had and if you do it Jay and I will quit."

Jay blinked. I glared at him. "Um. Right," he said finally.

"Quit? Right." he said to Marc a moment later, with a wonderful attempt at firmness, "quit." He looked back at me. "Right?"

Marc glanced at me and then back to his acolytes. "Any of you care to join 'Sieur Altaloma and the Chief?"

Abad smiled at me, showing teeth. "No." One by one the rest of them joined in, a slow cautious chorus of agreement. Captain Koslov simply shook his head no; Vasily and I aren't particularly close, given we've worked together for twenty years, but he's an okay guy; doesn't take much shit from anybody, including Marc. Marc nodded as though he had never expected anything else—of course he hadn't—and turned back to me. "Okay. Why is it a bad idea?"

Marc Packard, whatever his other flaws may be, is not a stupid man. I stopped and thought a moment before I replied. "We have the biggest warship anyone's ever built growing out there in the middle of Halfway, with Halfers and downsiders all around it. Read, *targets*. Potential hostages. At the very least, ancillary damage like you don't even want to *think* about in the event of a terrorist attack. And there are CityState and Collective terrorists aimed at the *Unity* twenty-four hours a day. On top of that there's the Fourth of July riots coming up. We don't usually have problems with them up here, but this is the Tri-Centennial, Marc. You're not an American and you can't know what that's going to feel like for those of us who are. Just because we've never had problems before doesn't mean we won't this time. On top of all this other damn foolishness you're going to drag in—how many?"

"The entire complement is a hundred and seventy persons."

I heard my voice rise. "A hundred and seventy *circus performers*? We've only *got* a hundred and twelve *Security*. Bad idea. Bad, *bad* idea. Security will be a nightmare. Get your American Halfers worked up and you're going to have your first-ever Halfway riots. Marc, I promise you. We want quiet. Lots and lots and lots of *quiet*."

"Actually," said Jay. "I'd kind of like to see the circus."

"Actually," I mimicked savagely, "I'd kind of *like* to see the circus."

Jay shrugged. "He wasn't going for it, Neil."

"I noticed. I wonder why."

Jay did not answer, because, like me, he had no idea. "Besides," he said after a moment, "I'd really like to see the clowns. I've never seen a clown before."

"Jay, would you *shut the fuck up?*"

Jay glanced sideways at me, and smiled with a certain genuine embarrassment. "It's just that the circus is coming to town. I'm kind of looking forward to it."

"I know. You said already."

"Sorry. I'll stop now."

In a life that has seen many odd things, the TriCentennial Summer was coming a kicker. That evening, after dinner, I played chess with Jay, and we talked about it.

We play most nights, over at Highland Grounds, a small coffee shop sharing space with four other businesses in a quarter-gee doughnut out toward the Edge. Highland Grounds caters to a younger crowd; I stand out a good bit. A nice enough place, if a touch loud at times. On Saturday nights they bring in live bands, and Jay and I skip; on Monday they have open mike night, and every half-baked poet and stand-up comic in Halfway shows up for it; we skip Mondays too.

Most other nights find us there, sitting at one of the genuine wooden chairs on the upper level overlooking the stage, sipping *caffé latte* from the bulbs. It had taken me most of a decade after coming to Halfway to get used to drinking everything—coffee, tea, even water—out of bulbs; when I was a boy in Levittown, Pennsylvania, only beer came in bulbs. At some level my subconscious decided, seventy-odd years ago when it was true, that bulbs were for beer; even today, when my mind strays for a moment, I find myself wondering when I come back how this damn diet Coke ended up in my beer bulb.

Jay's not a Halfway native; with his height and muscles, you couldn't possibly mistake him for anything but the downsider he is. I've known him for eight years now. When he was fourteen his parents visited Halfway on business with Tytan Industries. He was gorgeous then, too, though I don't think he knew it yet. One of my jobs consists of giving the guided tour to VIPs from Earth. Usually that means Unification officials, but sometimes it can be interesting. I confess to remembering very little about Jay's parents; but Jay himself made an impression on me. Midway through a tour of the fabrication plant where Tytan Manufacturing makes most of the molar bearings in use in the System today, Jay's parents go ahead of me, asking animated questions of the 'bot that was giving the spiel. Jay hung back, said quietly, without warning, "I like it up here."

"Yeah?"

"Yeah. What sorts of jobs can somebody from Earth get up here?"

I shrugged, not taking the question seriously. "Speaking just for myself, I'd say security is good. There's always room for a good security person with muscles developed under gravity. We don't have much of a problem with the Reb or Claw, so the PKF generally stays out of our hair." (This was '68, mind you, before Trent began the Long Run, before Space Force started building the *Unity* next door; at the time I made that statement it was still true.) "Violent crime is pretty low, all considered; mostly we police the Edge, make sure that some of the seamier places don't get out of hand. When something big does go down, we put the case together, and hold the case and the criminal for Halfway's Unification Circuit Judge. Judge shuttles up four times a year; worst case, the accused can wait up to three months for justice. By downside standards that's not bad."

"Would *you* hire me?"

I remember grinning at him. "Get a degree, and then ask me again."

In early '75 he showed up at my office. He'd just turned twenty-one. He was my size, just shy of two meters; had belts in shotokan and Wing Chun kung fu, and a bachelor's degree in what they liked to call Corrections Science. He passed the tests we use in Tytan Security without straining; I didn't do his psychometric—regulations—so I don't know the results, but he passed that too.

I didn't have to think twice. Talent is where you find it.

Occasionally Jay caused problems with the homebrews. Assistant to the Chief has traditionally been a homebrew job, on the grounds that it gives the homebrews a voice in Security; Jay was the first non-homebrew Assistant I'd had in maybe twenty years. Outside of the PKF, who even today *mostly* leave Halfway alone, Tytan Security is all the law your average Halfer ever sees; and the Chief of Security is a notorious downsider ex-United States Marine, number two is a Russki with an attitude problem, and my top assistant is another American downsider. All but six of Tytan Security's 112 officers are downsiders; it's only natural, but that doesn't make the homebrews like it any better. With rare exceptions homebrews don't have the muscle mass, or the hand-to-hand training, necessary to crack heads together when they need to.

Cracking heads is essentially what Security *does*—or at least what it's supposed to do.

I couldn't figure this crap about the circus at all, and said so after Jay checkmated me in our first game.

Jay shrugged, bored with the subject before I'd started. "You should have quit, Neil. Bad move, threatening to quit in public like that."

I shook my head. "I've done it half a dozen times before, all before you came to work here; it's just to get his attention. I'm not quitting, and he knows it. But it's *such* a boner decision. It's not like him. I ran the Security expert system back at my office this afternoon, Jay, Marc's *got* to have done the same thing; there's no way a hundred seventy circus performers stabilizes our situation."

Jay took a puff on his cigarette, exhaled a pale gray cloud off to my right. "Look, it's a judgment call, Neil. He figures some entertainment will help keep people's minds off the troubles downside. Are you certain he's run the same simulations you've run?"

"Haven't talked to him yet," I admitted.

"Maybe you should."

"Of course I'm going to. But I'm a little pissed at how this got dropped on me. It was too abrupt, and that's not like him."

"And why do you think he did it that way?"

I stopped and looked at Jay. "He's talking to me, of course."

Jay ground the cigarette out. "And saying what?"

"Jay," I said slowly, "do the colleges teach politics as a part of security work these days?"

Jay had the grace to look embarrassed. "No. But my mother ran the twenty-third largest corporation in Occupied America for eleven years. You learn. You mind if I have another?"

A cigarette, he meant. We'd agreed when he started working for me that he could have one while we played chess, and another if my lungs weren't complaining. My call, which perhaps isn't fair, but I am his boss, and there should be some perks. "No."

They may not cause cancer anymore, but they're still a filthy habit. I always half regretted that Highland Grounds had put in the new airplant back in '69; the quality of the air improved noticeably, so Homeboy Rick started letting patrons smoke; and the air quality went back down again.

Jay nodded, sipped at his coffee instead. "Packard's not happy with you, Neil."

"Clearly. And why do you think?"

He shook his head slowly. "I don't know. One reading I make is that he's worried about TriCentennial riots—and figures you for a scapegoat if they get out of hand. So he wants to disassociate a bit, cover himself with the Board of Directors."

"No. It's not a bad thought, but I've seen Marc stab enough people in the back to know how he goes about it. If that were it, he'd have started a couple months back. This is hasty, and that's really not like him. If this were something he were thinking about two months ago, he'd have started moving me out two months ago. Whatever has him going, it's happened recently."

Jay said slowly, "Hand Moreau visited him two weeks back."

I lifted an eyebrow. "You think the Secretary General's got an interest in Halfway? I think he's got better things to concern himself with right now, Jay. I hear the Rebs are recruiting like nobody's business."

"Yeah, I've heard the same. But why was Moreau here?"

"Could be anything, Jay. Tytan Industries has its fingers in so many pies even Marc has difficulty keeping track of them." I drank the last of my *caffè latte* before it got cold, waved to Homeboy Rick, the old Mex who runs Highland Grounds, for another mug. "I suppose I'll have to ask him."

"I suppose."

I grimaced at my empty mug. "I really hate doing that."

Jay nodded. "I would. Another game?"

"One more. Then I'm headed home." Jay won the second game too. He was getting better; when we started playing, shortly after he signed on, I usually beat him. I didn't mind it when he started beating me; the improvement in his play had spurred an improvement in mine that I hadn't thought my eight-five-year-old brain was capable of. I'd played the System Chess Federation's ranking program twice in the last few months, and drawn a ranking just a step below Master.

Marc plays chess, though I've never played him myself. Marc plays *constantly*.

"Mate in three," Jay finally announced.

I studied the board, nodded, and tipped my king over. "Good game."

"Thanks." Jay stood, pulled my p-suit off the suit tree near our table, handed it to me, and started getting into his own. Jay paused while shrugging into his p-suit. "Oh, by the way, my cousin Michelle is going to be up next Monday. Just a visit. I'd like her to have dinner with us Monday night, if you don't mind."

I'm sure I looked surprised; I glanced up at him, over my shoulder, while walking downstairs to the lock. "Why?"

Guido, the counterman, called out, "Later, Chief," as we headed for the lock, and I missed Jay's response.

"Again?"

He actually flushed slightly; I was sorry I'd asked. "Um, she thinks the work we do, is, um, glamorous."

I grinned at him. "Got it. I'll have some stories ready." I lowered my helmet into place. " 'Night, Jay."

"Thanks, Neil. Good—"

I touched the seal at my neck; his voice ceased abruptly. I cycled through alone, into death pressure, and kicked over to where my HuskySled waited. Jay followed through, waved, and kicked off into black space. His backpack lit briefly, in total silence, and then he dwindled away so quickly, a silvery dot in a sky that was full of them, that I lost sight of him before the HuskySled's rockets had even warmed up.

So I'm a conservative, cautious, careful old man. I concede the point. I probably waste ten, fifteen minutes a day warming up the sled, docking it, probably another two, three hours a month maintaining it. A backpack is a lot faster, requires vastly less maintenance, is a bit less expensive, and is very nearly as safe.

But I turned eight-five last May 7. And I didn't get here by being in a hurry.

The engine lights blinked green. I snapped my seat belt in place, hit the rockets at quarter thrust, and headed home.

- 3 -

In his beachfront house just north of San Diego, on Thursday morning, the 18th of June, Sedon rose early, and with Chris Summers to guard him, walked down to the beach to watch the sun rise.

Under normal circumstances he slept little; but the near-mortal wound Jimmy Ramirez had inflicted upon him had left him weak. His body threw itself into healing, into repairing the vast trauma from the explosive heat of the laser. Sedon had refused to allow his doctors to inject him with a nanovirus to speed the healing process; he neither understood nor trusted the process by which intelligent viruses aided the human body in healing. It sounded suspiciously similar to the technique the healers of the World had used to prevent aging; and Sedon did not know whether the modern nanoviruses would recognize, or fight with, those that had kept him alive for over thirteen thousand years of consecutive time.

His doctors were, Sedon knew, astonished at the speed with which he healed. They had replaced most of his intestines, abdominal muscles and the skin that covered them, with tissue cloned from Sedon's own cells, and had injected him with a wide variety of antiviral drugs; but the tools they were most used to, the intelligent nanoviruses that guided the healing process, he would not permit them to use, and early on they had expected that refusal to kill him.

It did not. He hung on, hovering near death, for two days. On the third day he awoke, clearheaded and ravenously hungry; and two and a half weeks after a near-mortal injury, Gi'Suei'Obodi'Sedon awoke feeling rested and nearly himself. The skin of his stomach was pink, a different shade from the rest of his skin, and the muscles in his stomach were so sore that taking a moderately deep breath sent twinges of pain through him; but he was alive, and at most two weeks away from health. Regaining full control of the muscles and nerves in his abdominal area would take a while; but the sooner he started, the sooner he would recover their use.

Thursday morning he walked down to the beach, an hour before sunrise, to watch the sun rise.

He had worn a robe of a shade that matched what his memory knew as Dancer red; he shed it at the edge of the sand, handed it to Chris Summers, and walked nude down to the water. He wished that he might go swimming—it was an exercise he had learned to enjoy during the long years of exile—but he had learned that it was not safe; even today, fifty years after the Unification had set about reclaiming Earth, no large body of water on Earth was free of pollutants.

Instead he knelt in the cold sand, with the Pacific Ocean at his back, and prayed.

Over four years since the bubble had released him. It seemed to him at times that in those years he had not had a single moment to pause and reflect. The humans of this time, half savage and half something that Sedon suspected had already moved beyond the Flame People, were paralyzed with the knowledge of their imminent deaths; they rushed about their lives in such a haste that Sedon himself was carried along in the madness.

The weeks in bed had done him one good turn. It was the first extended period of reflection the universe had given him since his release, and he had made good use of it.

The prayer was an experiment.

He had not prayed during the entire long period of exile, during the thousands of years of war with the Shield.

Yet—during the two days he had hung between life and death, he had dreamed of the god. He suspected the dream was not a real thing, simply a product of his sickness; he had forsaken the god, and the god him.

The arrogance of youth was long gone from Sedon. Every dream of his youth was dead beyond any hope of resurrection. If the Nameless One wished to discuss a mistake Sedon had made many eons past, Sedon was not unwilling.

He knelt motionlessly, arms crossed across his chest, while the sky in the east grayed, and then lightened to a pale blue. He emptied himself of thought, waited for the voice of the god to address him. The sun crept high into the sky, and sweat trickled down Sedon's nude form.

The wind off the ocean cooled him.

After a long while he relaxed, sank back onto his heels.

Silence.

There was one tool Sedon had available to him, one summons the god could not ignore.

But Sedon had not performed the Dance of the Flame in thirteen thousand years, and did not intend to try today.

He rose and strode briskly across the beach, to where Chris Summers stood with his robe. As he approached Summers said, "The Player arrived."

"Good," said Sedon mildly, accepting the robe from Summers. "Thank you, Christian—has 'Selle Lovely called?"

Summers nodded; Lovely wouldn't talk to Sedon directly any longer. She'd been talking only with Summers ever since Los Angeles. "She did."

"And?"

"She's not satisfied with the explanation of the events in Los Angeles. She doesn't want to believe that Daimara was a PKF spy; if true, it means that Denice's psychometric profiles were faked, which probably implicates 'Selle Sierran—she ran them, with Bennett Crandell, who *was* a spy."

Sedon chuckled. "She believes you, and doesn't want to. Sierran and Crandell and Daimara; that the three of them were working together will, given her reflexive paranoia, make sense to her. So?"

The rogue Elite shrugged, grinned a touch sourly. "Her people were unharmed, if slightly confused. It all happened pretty fast. Lovely's in a tight place; she doesn't have a lot of choice."

"The Claw is moving forward."

"They can't pull out now."

Sedon smiled. "Sensible woman."

Summers nodded, followed Sedon back up the path to the house. "Clearly none of them have realized yet that the girl was a Castanaveras."

That evening, at the downtown San Diego offices of Greenberg & Bass, Sedon met with the Player, a girl named Michelle Altaloma. He found her interesting; she was a TrueBreed, sixteen years old, one of the second wave of a small group of genies produced by an ongoing Johnny Reb genengineering project. TrueBreed had begun almost twenty-five years prior, in late '52; only a year after the infamous PKF-run Project Superman had ended.

He met with her alone, in the library, a medium-sized room with half a dozen tracesets for data, two of the oversized sensable tracesets, a pair of full sensory InfoNet terminals, and a wide array of holo equipment.

He had the difficulty with her that he always had with women; she had been warned to expect it, apparently, and wasted no time attempting to be pleasant. Sedon did not rise when she was led in to him; 'Selle Altaloma unpacked, jacked her handheld into the library equipment, and waited. Her inskin was one of the more expensive model radio packet systems, and had no external socket for input. She was a thin young blond girl, attractive by the standards of the time, nearly in shape, even by Sedon's stringent standards. She was not of

Denice's caliber—or even Callia Sierran's—but women such as Sierran were rare, and Denice was unique.

Sedon had not even noticed that he was thinking of the genie telepath by her first name.

'Selle Altaloma seated herself in the chair facing Sedon, and looked at him. "What are you looking for?"

"I would like to be told about Project Superman."

The girl nodded. "Yes. Summary first?"

"Please."

"Funded by Special Order 11-212 of the Unification Council, February 14, 2029, Project Superman was its popular name; its official title was the Advanced BioTechnology Research Initiative. There were eight significant lines of research involved. They involved things as diverse as research into improved intelligence, genengineering, and cyborging. Three lines of research were particularly successful; they were the feline de Nostri, the Castanaveras telepaths, and the Peace Keeping Force Elite. The Peace Keeping Force itself already existed, of course, but until 2046 there were no Elite cyborgs as we know them today; the technology to create them did not exist. All but those three lines of research were discontinued in the early '40s The de Nostri program was terminated with the death of Doctor Jean-Louis de Nostri, in 2044, and the feline de Nostri were relocated to New York. Doctor Suzanne Montignet, the researcher who created the Castanaveras, was briefly placed in control of them; she resigned in 2046.

"In 2042, the most significant event in Project Superman's history took place; Carl Castanaveras, born in 2030, entered puberty. The telepathic gift of the Castanaveras is associated with the hormonal changes that take place during puberty; sometime during 2042, the PKF realized that Carl Castanaveras could read minds.

"The next eldest genie whose genetic map significantly resembled that of Castanaveras was his clone, Jany McConnell. The PKF monitored her closely; in 2047 she underwent puberty. She too had the gift.

"The PKF envisioned a world where no revolution could succeed, where telepaths loyal to the Unification would monitor and warn long before any insurrection could be planned. In 2048 forty-three genies based upon the Castanaveras map were born; in 2049, seventy-three; in 2050, eighty-six; and in 2051, twenty-four. In 2051 Carl Castanaveras was twenty-one, and virtually unmanageable; the PKF grew concerned that they might be unable to control the telepaths. 2051 was, officially, the last year that the Unification indulged in the creation of genies. Late in 2051 all funding for Project Superman was suspended, and the telepaths were taken from the control of the Bureau of BioTechnology and turned over to the PKF."

"TrueBreed began in 2052."

'Selle Altaloma nodded. "Yes. TrueBreed was primarily a response to the PKF Elite program, not the Castanaveras. Unlike the Castanaveras, we are a fairly conservative design. Faster, stronger, significantly more resistant to disease. Smarter than the human norm, but not so much as to make us unstable; only a few TrueBreed can be considered geniuses."

"But you're one of the few," said Sedon softly.

"Yes."

"Good. Project Superman, properly speaking, ends in 2051."

"Yes. Are you interested in the PKF, or the de Nostri, or the telepaths? Or all of them?"

"Specifically, the telepaths. While I was ill, I audited several texts on them; I know the outlines of their story. In detail—"

Altaloma shrugged. "Mister Obodi, *nobody* knows the story in detail, except possibly the surviving telepaths, if any of them do survive. In 2053, two years after Project Superman ended, Carl Castanaveras fathered two children with Jany McConnell; they were twins, Denice and David Castanaveras. There are persistent rumors to the effect that the twins were not present at the Chandler Complex when Space Force nuked it. There is video of a hovercar carrying Carl Castanaveras, leaving the Chandler Complex before it was destroyed; but Castanaveras' body, positively identified, was found outside Unification Councilor Jerril Carson's hotel room. Apparently Castanaveras killed the Councilor, and was killed by him. The only Castanaveras who certainly survived the Troubles is Trent the Uncatchable, and though he's definitely a genie, he's just as definitely *not* a telepath. He was one of the last batch of genies Project Superman produced, from the twenty-four born in '51; apparently quality control slipped a bit. There are rumors of a green-eyed girl who was with Trent in mid-2069, but they are only rumors, and have never been adequately substantiated. And even today having green eyes doesn't make you a Castanaveras. Callia Sierran, the woman from the Claw, has the greenest eyes I've ever seen, but she's no telepath; I've seen her gene map."

Sedon leaned forward very slightly, fixed his eyes upon the Player. "These twin children. One was a boy."

"Yes. He'd be twenty-three today."

"How would you go about looking for him?"

"I wouldn't. It's a waste of time. You must assume, Mister Obodi, that the PKF DataWatch, the Bureau of Biotech, Trent the Uncatchable, his old image Ralf the Wise and Powerful, F.X. Chandler for sure, probably Tommy Boone before he vanished"— she made an impatient gesture —"and a hundred other groups, all of them very good at looking for people, have looked for those two. Assuming—which no one has ever proven—that they weren't both at the Complex when it was nuked, the only way those children could have evaded the searches that have gone on for them would be if they'd been *found*. With protectors they might have avoided discovery. But they'd have needed protectors. One of the reasons—and it's a small thing to go on—that I think Denice Castanaveras might be alive, is that if she is she probably *has* Trent as a protector. I will tell you this much, Mister Obodi; I for one would hate to try and search through the InfoNet for someone Trent the Uncatchable was trying to hide. Life is short."

"What does your schedule look like?"

"I'm going to Halfway on Monday morning. The InfoNet Relay project."

Sedon leaned back into his chair, crossed his legs, and made a steeple of his hands. His pale blue eyes were steady and unblinking, and Michelle Altaloma found them very hard to look at for any length of time. "Three days, then? We will spend it productively, looking for the boy."

"The boy."

Gi'Suei'Obodi'Sedon said without any irony at all, "I like boys."

Michelle Altaloma stretched, spoke around a yawn. "I need sleep."

"Go ahead," said Sedon absently. He did not even look up from the field he was auditing; it showed information gleaned during their search. "I'll have you awakened in a few hours."

She nodded, rose, and stumbled out of the room. Chris Summers glanced in as she left. "Mister Obodi?"

"Yes, Christian?"

"Joe Tagomi would like to see you when you have a chance. We've found out what happened to—to Daimara."

It brought Sedon out of his revery, up to his feet. "You took long enough. Where?"

Summers said one word: "Chandler."

"Jesus, I can barely *see* straight."

"I have you for only another day, 'Sella Altaloma. You are, I'm told, the best Player in our organization."

The girl flushed. "Damn straight."

Sedon studied her. "Indeed?"

"All right, Obodi, you tell *me* what I've missed. I've been through every adult male of the correct age, listed with any Unification agency from summer '62 through today. I've been through Public Labor, the Bureau of Traffic Enforcement, the Peace Keeping Force, I even frigging got into a Ministry of Population Control Board for you, and that's not easy; they're more paranoid than the PKF. I've been through Claw records, Reb records. I *can't* get into BioTech, their Boards are protected by replicant AIs, and don't even stop to tell me it's illegal, I know it. Maybe you should report them to DataWatch. I can't get into DataWatch either, obviously. I've been through the records from the '70 Census, I've been through the Ministry of Population Control's summary extraction of that Census. I've been through passport applications, I've been through city and state police mug holos, I've scanned the files on every single adult male who's ever served time in a PKF Detention Center or Occupied America penitentiary. I've searched everything I can get my hands on for East Coast biosculptors, '62 to present. I have searched every green-eyed male, every black-haired Caucasian male, of the correct age range, in every public record I can get my hands on. There's not a hell of a lot left, and I can list what remains on the fingers of one hand. Boards run by Players, BioTech, or AIs. BioTech and AIs, I wouldn't even know where to start. There's only one BioTech, maybe two thousand replicant AIs. There's about forty, fifty thousand Players out there—I should say, webdancers calling themselves Players—maybe a couple of hundred *I'd* call Players. And if one of them is helping your target hide, I could hunt a thousand years and never find him."

"Who employs the finest Players?"

Altaloma stared at Sedon. "Nobody *employs* the finest Players."

"*We* employ *you*."

"I volunteered because this is a cause I believe in. Otherwise you couldn't *afford* me."

Sedon smiled at her. "Of course. To which organizations are Players known to donate their time?"

Altaloma leaned forward, put her face in her hands. "I don't believe this. Look—okay," she said after a moment. "*We* have some good ones. The Rebs do, I mean. Mostly from the TrueBreed project, three of us. Erisian Claw, I don't know of any, but they might have *one*. Couple different corporations— there used to be a Speedfreak Player, back before the Speedfreaks were wiped out by the Bureau of Weather Control. The Catholic Church has three or four; the Temples of Eris might have one, and if they do, he's probably the same one the Erisian Claw uses. The SpaceFarers' Collective has at least two. The Belt CityStates have a couple, Free Luna has one." She stopped, searching her memory. "I can't think beyond that. DataWatch has hundreds of very frighteningly good webdancers. But they don't use Image, which makes them not Players in any real sense of the word."

"And these organizations have Boards to which you do not have access."

Altaloma sighed. "I can't believe you know so little about the InfoNet. Look, most of the really critical data in the *world* I don't have access to. Even today a lot of it's simply off-line, and the stuff that's not off-line is protected by AIs or other Players. Groups that don't have good protection don't publish a Board for me to *get* to. If there's no Board, the only way to get at their information is to *physically go* to where it is. The Tax Boards are a great example; the only thing you can do on-line with them is send in a return. Everything else they *have* is disconnected from the InfoNet. Tax Boards, all the other organized crime—"

Sedon said quickly, "*Other* organized crime?"

Michelle Altaloma lifted her head from her hands. She looked at Sedon with wide eyes. "Joke, man. It's a joke. I don't really mean the Tax Boards are run by criminals. Not like the Syndic, or the Corporation, or the Old Ones."

Sedon sat quietly for a very long time, looking at the Player. "Would it—be of help to you—to have access to the records of such organizations?"

"The *Tax Boards?*"

"Yes. And the Syndic, and the Corporation, and the Old Ones."

Altaloma blinked. "Is this a joke?"

"Would it be of help to you?"

"It—couldn't hurt."

Sedon nodded. "Go to bed, 'Selle Altaloma. In the morning, I will have arranged access for your search."

"You used to be with the Old Ones, the Italians?"

"Go to bed, 'Selle Altaloma."

"But the *Tax Boards?*"

"Cooperation is a popular concept in Occupied America. It's good for business. Good night, 'Selle Altaloma."

At 10:22 A.M., on Sunday, June 21, Michelle Altaloma said aloud, "Fuck me gently with a chainsaw."

Sedon did not stir in his chair. "Tell me."

The Player was silent for a long moment. She sat still, shoulders rigid, eyes closed. Sedon sat watching the back of her head; he could not even imagine what she was doing. When she spoke she did so rapidly, in a quick tumble of words: "Age unknown. Estimated early to midtwenties. Contracted with the Old Ones originally, like you, but he bought out his contract five years ago. They were using him to move wire in the New York Metro area; waste of talent, frankly. He's done much better on his own; moved in on a numbers operation in New Jersey, just outside the Camden Protectorate, and took it away from Larry Farillio despite the fact it was in his family for three generations. Nobody knows how he did it exactly, aside from the obvious; Farillio vanished, and his mother, wife, mistress, three kids. The boy made nice with the Old Ones, sends payments regularly, squared it with a couple of Farillio cousins, and nobody's bothered him since. Some rumor to the effect that he's on the wire, from when he ran it."

"What color are his eyes?"

"Blue." Michelle Altaloma paused briefly, then said, "Bingo. Dyed that color when he was fourteen." The girl turned around in her seat, looked at Sedon. "Not necessarily indicative. That wasn't that unusual back then, with all the hysteria. Lots of green-eyed people got dye jobs."

Sedon said simply. "What's his name?"

"David. David Zanini."

"Thank you, 'Selle Altaloma. Enjoy Halfway. I understand you helped design the Relay Station attack."

"I did." Altaloma unjacked her handheld, stored it in her jacket pocket.

Sedon nodded. "Having seen you work, I have faith that your input was valuable. Good luck."

The girl stopped at the doorway. "I know you used to be a pimp. But if you'd learn to treat women like they were people, you'd do a lot better. Every now and again, when you forgot I was a girl, you were almost likable."

A flicker of rage touched Sedon, but it was distant and muted, more reflex than anything truly felt. He nodded and said gravely, "Thank you for the advice. I did appreciate your aid."

"Anytime."

- 4 -

I thought at first that Jay's cousin, Michelle—"Shell," he called her—was an astonishing bubblehead.

We had dinner at 6:00 P.M., over at Observation Bubble. Somehow it seemed appropriate. The Bubble's the most famous and most expensive restaurant at Halfway; I'd been there twice, on disturbances, but I'd never eaten there before. They gave us a good table, in one of the bubbles around the edge, with Earth above us. I'd expected a good table, simply from identifying myself when making reservations. I doubted I'd see a bill when we were done. There can't be half a dozen people at Halfway who have more real importance than the Chief of Security when it comes to the concerns of your average business owner.

I was never a particularly sociable person; even if I had been, a stint as Chief of Security at Halfway would have cured me. It is, pretty nearly, the equivalent of being Chief of Police for any major downside city, with a few unique twists caused by the nature of Halfway itself. If you're not careful, you can get yourself beholden to the local business people without any real difficulty at all. One of the reasons I hang out at Highland Grounds is that, in all the time I've been Chief, Homeboy Rick has never once offered to eat the check. He expects me to pay, and I do.

Observation Bubble's cheap seats are spectacular enough; the bubble tables are usually booked two to three months in advance. They'd bumped somebody to get us in. A walkway, forty meters long, leads from the bubbles back to the rest of the restaurant, and the bubbles themselves are completely transparent, down to the tables inside them.

I met Jay and Shell at the restaurant, and I kept my p-suit with me when we were led out to our table; Jay shot a disapproving look at me. Probably thought I looked paranoid.

Could be.

They made a gorgeous couple, and I understood why Jay had leaned on me to get the reservations at Observation Bubble. Jay was in dinner clothes, maybe a hundred CU worth of white silk suit, cleanly shaven; he'd cut his hair sometime that morning, and done something subtle, I couldn't say exactly what, with his makeup key.

I wasn't sure if the perfume I was smelling was his or hers, and it seemed impolite to ask.

I'm not indifferent to male beauty, but the girl made Jay, one of the prettiest and most graceful men I know, look clumsy. She was fifteen or sixteen, at a guess, a little blond thing in a black sheath dress and black calf-high boots, wearing matching black gloves and hat that were out of *Breakfast at Tiffany's*. I didn't tell her that she reminded me of Holly Golightly; she'd never have recognized the reference.

Her skin had the fineness of grain that is the province of either the very young or the recently regenerated; hers had just the faintest hint of green tracings, as though she were half plant, half human. Her makeup implant included her eyes; they glowed blue, the color of star sapphires. A pair of green stud emerald earrings finished the ensemble.

Michelle Altaloma looked for all the System like she'd just walked off a fashion runway, until she tried to walk. Jay had applied mag patches to the bottom of her boots, but she'd clearly never been in free fall before, and I had to bite my cheeks to keep from smiling over the way Jay kept putting out a hand to steady her as they walked to the table.

The entire thing left me feeling a little wistfully lecherous.

After the waiter had taken our orders she fell silent for the first time. I knew why; she was looking around herself. It's a view you normally get only after someone who doesn't like you pushes you into death pressure without your suit. Observation Bubble is located out near the Edge; it used to be closer to the center, but they keep moving it because the new buildings obscure the view.

In the bubble, you can see *everything*. Luna, Earth, Halfway, the odd bright needles of torch ships moving through the distant darkness; the encompassing, sheltering blaze of the stars.

From the Edge, the seven-kilometer-long shell of the *Unity* is Halfway's single largest visible structure. It's more than twice as large as the whitish blob of Administration Central. Michelle pointed it out. "What's that one?"

I said gently, "That's the ship that's going to conquer the outer planets. They've been building it since '72; it's supposed to be completed in '79."

"Oh." She looked troubled, worried. "They're building it at Halfway?"

"Yes."

"But—I thought that terrorists kept trying to blow it up?"

I leaned back in my chair. "Well, dear, it's happened a couple of times, that's true enough. But if Space Force moved the ship just a bit, it'd happen a lot more. As it is, the ship's being built in the middle of a largely civilian section of Halfway. Most of the folks from the outer planets have better morals than Space Force, so they've avoided attacking it so far."

"But if they did attack it—the Collective *or* the CityStates—"

"Be a lot of deaths," I said bluntly. "Amiga, we'd have dead people making like meteors in Earth's atmosphere for days afterward. We'd *never* know who had died."

"But it's not going to happen," said Jay smoothly. "Shell, you shouldn't worry about things that aren't going to happen Okay?"

"Um. All right."

Dinner came then, which was probably just as well. I'd intended to have my handheld go off with a message for me shortly after dinner—bow out gracefully, give the kids a chance to enjoy the romantic scenery together—but over coffee the conversation got mildly serious, and the teenage bubblehead stopped seeming like such a bubblehead. I was only a bit surprised; very intelligent women often downplay their intelligence until they feel secure with you. It was more common when I was younger than it is today, and I suppose that's a good thing.

"Listen," she said earnestly, after the second round of coffee had been served, "suppose a group from the CityStates *did* attack the *Unity*. Would that be wrong?"

"It would be an act of war. It'd be *stupid*."

"But would it be *wrong*?"

I glanced at Jay; he gave me an I-give-up shrug. "Good question. There's no secret what the Unification plans to do with that ship; I guess the question is, should the Unification be extended to the outer planets? If it should be, then, yes, attacking the *Unity* is wrong. If it shouldn't be, then attacking the *Unity* is a moral act."

Michelle nodded. "And it's the Unification—Space Force—that's done the immoral thing, by building it in the midst of all those civilians?"

I smiled at the girl, said gently, "Dear, that's a leading question. I'm the Chief of Security for Halfway. It's an apolitical job."

"Of course you have to *say* that," she said persistently. "But that doesn't prevent you from *having* opinions."

I laughed aloud at that. "'Selle Altaloma, if I told everybody every opinion I have on every subject, I'd be out of a job so fast it'd make your head spin. And mine. What are your plans for tomorrow?"

Jay grabbed it, obviously relieved. "I'm taking her on a tour of the Edge in the morning—the nicer parts, such as they are—and in the afternoon we're going to go flying."

Michelle said swiftly, "You promised me we'd do the Relay Station."

I lifted an eyebrow. "Amiga? Why do you want to see the Relay Station?"

"I'm taking a class in InfoNet traffic control next fall semester. Better than two-thirds of all InfoNet traffic flows through the Halfway InfoNet Relay Station." She shrugged, smiled a secretive smile at me, a thing that seemed to invite me to share in the joke. "It'll be fun."

"It's not *my* idea of fun. Are you serious?"

She and Jay both said, "Yes," at the same moment, she very seriously, he glumly. I glanced at Jay, and Jay said, "She's a Player."

I looked back and forth between the two of them. "You're kidding. You mean you dance in the web sometimes?"

"He means," Michelle Altaloma said evenly, "that I'm a Player. And a very good one, too."

She was a sixteen-year-old fashion statement. "Um—you have an Image? Someone I could get on the Boards and find the name somewhere?"

I'm sure she understood I wasn't asking for the name of her Image, merely whether she had one, but she shook her head swiftly. "No. I've written an Image, of course, but I try to avoid dancing with it. Letting your Image get to be well known is a tactical error. The Players whose Images dance the InfoNet when they don't have to are fools."

I shook my head. "I don't understand that. I thought the entire purpose of having an Image was that it allowed you to move through the InfoNet. Why *wouldn't* you let your Image get to be well known?"

"Fame is bad for you," Michelle said simply. "Look, you've played sensables, right?"

"Sure."

"You pick up a Gregory Selstrom sensable from before his accident, whether it has his name on it or not, could you *possibly*, having played his other work, mistake this one for work by *anyone* else?"

Five minutes prior I'd have bet long odds she'd never played a Selstrom sensable in her life. "Not a chance."

"Well, writing an Image is the same deal. There's maybe fifteen, twenty *thousand* significant decisions that have to be made in writing it, and at least half of those are nothing but personal taste. Nobody is so good that they can wipe all trace of their personality from how they assemble an Image. For example, I'll use this one because it's famous: before Trent the Uncatchable was Johnny Johnny, his Image was named Ralf the Wise and Powerful. Apparently Trent lost Ralf in '62, during the Troubles. Now, he was *eleven*. About six years later a new Player, calling himself Johnny Johnny, starts dancing the InfoNet. DataWatch doesn't make him cause they're stupid, but half a dozen Players, at least, look at this image Johnny Johnny, and they say to themselves, the person who wrote Johnny Johnny is the same person who wrote Ralf the Wise and Powerful. Mind you, they didn't know who it was who'd done it— Trent was still anonymous back then—they just knew that enough elements correspond that it's probably the same person. And Trent must have changed dramatically between the ages of eleven and seventeen; people do. There is no way an adult Player, once she was recognized, in Realtime, as the author of her Image, could write a new Image that wouldn't be instantly recognizable as her work. So, to wrap this up, the best way to work the InfoNet is not to have an Image that people know; 'cause once you're famous, you have *no* margin of error."

Jay grinned at me. "She's a bright girl, Neil."

I stood, caught the girl watching me. I said simply, " 'Selle Altaloma, it's a great pleasure to have met you. Perhaps I'll see you again before you go home."

Little Michelle bit her lower lip and cast her eyes down slightly in what was supposed to be shyness. I could imagine how many hours she'd spent practicing that look in the mirror. She said in a small voice, "Thank you. It was nice meeting you too."

I picked up my p-suit, waved aside the waiter who wanted to help me into it. "Good night, kids. I'll see you at work tomorrow, Jay."

"Good night, Neil."

Her voice was very soft. "Good night, 'Sieur Corona."

I was halfway home before I realized who it was she reminded me of.

Tanni, the summer before I joined the Marine Corps.

I don't think I'd thought of Tanni in at least a decade.

Tanni had been sixteen too.

I don't know why the memory was so depressing. Maybe it was just the fact that Tanni was the last time I'd even kidded myself that anything permanent was happening.

I flipped the sled at turnover and touched the braking rockets, feeling old and careful and cautious.

Mostly old.

Marc was waiting for me at my house.

He'd let himself in; he's keyed for access. He and Jay and Vasily are the only ones who are.

The security system alerted me that Marc was inside while I was still a good klick away, and told me he'd been waiting for most of an hour. It wasn't 9:00 P.M. yet; it meant that Marc had left the office and headed for my place sometime around seven. Very unusual; Marc lives to work.

When I got closer to the house I saw that an ExecuSled was

parked at the visitor's airlock, and when I got a bit closer yet I saw that Marc had left his bodyguards inside. Marc runs through bodyguards quickly, and crap like that is why. Direct solar radiation is *dangerous*; people who spend much time in it get cancer, sterility, and children with odd numbers of limbs.

I docked at my private lock, unsnapped my seat belt and made sure my tie line was connected to the lock before I got out of my seat. I walked on magboots over to where the ExecuSled was parked and saw to my surprise that the suits inside weren't bodyguards; they were Halfway Security, *my* kids. Names on their pressure suits read Lopez and McCarthy. Rookies, both, and I didn't know either well. I tapped the side of my helmet, raised up a pair of fingers; *on two*.

Lopez's voice clicked in on Channel Two. "Hey, Chief."

"Hi, kids. How long has he left you sitting out here in the sun?"

I could tell from her voice she was pissed. "'Bout an hour, Chief."

"Unbuckle and take yourselves to the kitchen. You know where it is?"

"No."

"Follow the security program's instructions; it'll guide you. Feed yourselves whatever you like. I have Earth-grown coffee." There was wine and beer also, but if they were so stupid they needed to be told not to touch the Chief's alcohol while on duty, they were so stupid they needed to be shipped back downside pronto.

From inside the craft I saw their helmets bob up and down. "Thanks, Chief. You guys going to be talking long?"

"Beats the hell out of me, kids."

I cycled through and went looking for Marc.

He was in my office, sitting in the big leather chair in front of my system. "Hello, Neil."

I hung my p-suit on the hook. "Get your ass out of my chair, Marc."

He looked surprised, but got up and moved over to the small sofa on the other side of the office. "Neil, we need to talk."

"No shit?" I hung my dinner coat on the back of my chair, kicked my shoes off, and sank down into the chair facing Marc. "Want my resignation?"

Marc stopped cold. He'd come prepared to dicker—he wanted something from me, and it was important, or this would be happening in his office—and he expected me to be wary and mildly pissed about the circus deal. But he hadn't expected that I'd be genuinely sore at him, and didn't know what had caused it. "What's wrong?"

"You had a couple of my kids sitting out there in the fucking sun is what's wrong. One, you *don't* requisition bodyguards from Security without clearing it with me. Two, they are *people*, not 'bots, and you do *not* leave them out in the goddamn sun to suffer heat exhaustion and radiation poisoning." Marc started to speak and I raised my voice. "*Three*, you have *one* real friend in this entire city and if I have my chain jerked in public again you're not going to have *any*. What's got you running so scared?"

I don't do this to him often. Marc is a dangerously smart man, and he has no weak spots to speak of, but naked aggression slows him down some. If he ever caught on to the technique, it would stop working, and it's one of the very few methods I know to deal with him. Our friendship, though as real as any Marc has probably ever had, has never really been stressed, and I don't depend on it much. I've seen what's happened to other people who thought that Marc was their friend.

He is capable of decency, where his own self-interest is not involved. I've seen him go out of his way to aid people throughout Halfway, not because it was good business or even good publicity, but simply because he had some spare time.

But like his friendship, Marc's altruism is nothing to depend on. Like a man who'll stop to pick up a lost puppy at the side of the road, and then have the dog put to sleep when he finds it's taking up too much of his time and he can't find a home for it.

So my anger threw him. He said carefully, "Okay. Both of my personal guards are with Hand Moreau; he's visiting the InfoNet Relay Station, and they're guiding him. Second—"

I exploded, came up out of my chair. "And *this* is the first I hear about it? I didn't even fucking know Alex Moreau was *at* Halfway!"

Marc snapped, "*Sit down*. He came back *today*, Neil, this afternoon. His personal yacht. *May* I continue?"

I glared at him, but sat. "Go ahead."

"I *couldn't* send Security with him; he's here privately and we can't allow his presence to be known. Apologies about leaving your Security staff outside, I've had other things on my mind. Lastly, about the circus, that whole deal was necessary."

"You're going to have a hell of a time convincing me."

Marc took a deep breath and said, "The PKF is considering declaring martial law at Halfway."

I had to look at the carpet for I don't know how long until the roaring in my ears finally went away. It seems at times that the centerpiece of my entire fucking life has been the PKF. Fighting them, being imprisoned by them, fleeing them; the last few decades, dealing with them on a professional basis.

After a long while I sat up again. I didn't have any anger left, just a cold, solid lump of animal *scared* sitting down in my gut. "Okay."

"I don't have to tell you how disastrous that'd be. For both of us. The Board of Directors would fire me. Neil, I'm a Halfer; I can't go to Earth, and there's only one post off Earth that I'm suited for, and I *have* it. If they take it away from me I either *retire*, at the age of fifty-two, or I jump ship entirely and go out to the Belt CityStates." He paused. "In your case it's worse. Your half brother was nearly executed for Reb activities, and you've done time in the Capitol City Detention Center." I'd never mentioned that to him but wasn't surprised that he knew about it. "If we have martial law, the PKF is going to arrest you again, Neil, and probably impound your property. Worst case, martial law, serious TriCentennial riots at Halfway, they're going to blame the riots on you and execute you for being a Reb." He leaned forward and shouted with what looked like genuine anger, *"Do I have your attention?"*

"You've got it."

He took a deep breath and leaned back again. "Good." He closed his eyes briefly, abruptly looked weary. Opened them again. "All right. Secretary General Eddore suggested the damn circus."

I was ready to believe anything by then. "Go on."

"It shows we're on top of things. That business is going on as usual, that Halfway's sympathy for Occupied America is *so completely trivial* that we're comfortable entertaining a traveling circus during the Fourth of July weekend. It makes the PKF who want to take over Halfway look like nervous old maidens."

"Why does Eddore give a shit?"

"What's your grasp of politics, Neil?"

"Minimal."

He sighed. "All right. Briefly, Eddore's having problems with the PKF. He's concerned about their growing power and the very last thing he wants is to have the engine that drives Earth's economy under PKF control. Which is, need I point out, what martial law at Halfway amounts to."

"What got the PKF in an uproar in the first place?"

"I don't know exactly," Marc said reluctantly. "A report that the InfoNet Relay Station was a target of terrorists played a part in it, but I don't know how large a part. DataWatch is convinced the report is true; they expect to see the rebels attempt to destroy the Halfway Relay Station on or around the Fourth. It's at least part of the reason Moreau is here; he brought a group of the Secretary General's webdancers up with him, and they're checking, and rechecking, and triple checking the Relay Station's informational integrity."

"So," I said slowly, "in order to prevent the PKF from declaring martial law at Halfway, we're going to bring the circus to town."

Marc said evenly, "Yes."

"That's the silliest thing I ever heard in my life."

"It's the truth, Neil."

"That's the only reason I believe it."

- 5 -

His bodyguards were the best Credit could buy; currently with Security Services, one was ex-Space Force, the other ex-PKF. David had told them both before they boarded the semiballistic to San Diego that, if necessary, they were to give their lives in protecting his.

They agreed with him, of course. People did.

Still the deal made him nervous. That a pimp who had made it big in the Johnny Rebs wanted to see him made very little sense. The reasons the Old Ones in New York had given him— that Obodi was considering dosing the Reb troops with electric ecstasy before sending them into battle—did not convince him. If he'd been prepared for a war with New York David would have refused to go; but he did not have the manpower for war, and New York had made it clear that those were the stakes.

It made him *very* nervous.

He hadn't run wire in six years, and his own use of the wire was well enough known that nobody was going to seek his opinion on the subject. With one possible exception, the scenario made no sense.

David didn't like to think about the exception.

On the semiballistic he plugged in the wire and turned it on, with the current low, for half an hour. He turned it off before they landed in San Diego, and he felt calm and confident and strong.

Two of Obodi's troopers met him at the downport in a limo with blackened windows. David touched them as lightly as he was able; they both knew Obodi slightly, knew that David was expected. No more than that. He told them to give their weapons to his bodyguards. They did; he had them get in the front seat, and got in back with his bodyguards.

The limo took them into downtown San Diego. The windows were supposed to be darkened; David instructed his guards to set them for one-way; if anyone was watching the car from outside, it would look as though Obodi's instructions were being followed. David was not impressed with San Diego; it looked like a New York suburb. Hell, it looked like a Jersey suburb.

Except cleaner.

The limousine came down atop a smallish white building, thirty or forty stories, at the edge of a large open plaza. The building sat facing the huge, gleaming blue stretch of the Pacific Ocean; even in the midst of his juice-induced calm, David found time to admire the sight of the sun's reflection, on a mildly windy day, dancing from the tops of a million small waves.

Before leaving the vehicle he checked his handheld; they sat atop the Latham Building, at the western edge of the city. David flipped his handheld shut, stowed it, and turned on his Personal Protection System. He felt the sheath armor go ever so slightly rigid beneath his suit; not enough to cause difficulty in moving, just enough to feel it. The targeting holocams were buried in his earrings. Lasers were tucked away in his watch and two of his rings. If his heart stopped, his handheld would explode, and take everyone within a square block with him.

Half a dozen men in nondescript suits awaited him at the edge of the roof. One came forward.

Anthony Angelo was a small, wiry man with black hair. *Ex-Speedfreak, dedicated Reb; knew Obodi only to work with, had no idea why David was there.* David noticed, without making assumptions one way or another, that he had yet to meet any of Obodi's personal associates.

The man stopped a few steps in front of David, said, unsmiling, "Mister Zanini?" It amused David to be addressed with the American honorific; virtually every Johnny Reb he'd ever met had done that, as though renouncing the truncated French honorifics in use throughout the System were some Reb badge of membership.

"Are you expecting someone else?"

"No, sir. Please follow me. You'll leave your bodyguards here."

"I'll leave my bodyguards here," David agreed, "except they'll come with me."

A brief struggle crossed Angelo's features, was gone. "Yes, sir. That'll be fine. Please follow me."

They kept him waiting, in a lounge with a wet bar, for most of an hour. David had his ex-Space Force bodyguard make iced tea with the supplies at the bar, and after the bodyguard had sipped at the tea, drank some of it himself.

When someone finally came for him, it was Angelo again. "Mister Obodi will see you now."

"How charming of him."

The boardroom where Obodi received him was large enough for thirty people. It was stripped empty and it was obvious that its contents had been removed only recently. David could see scars in the rug where the huge conference table had recently been.

Two men were waiting for him. One was a soldier, somewhere in his fifties. David barely glanced at the man; Obodi stood motionless in the very center of all the empty space, watching David approach. He was a tall, thin man in a bright red robe, with an aquiline nose, high cheeks, blond hair and pale, piercing blue eyes. *Very good biosculpture,* David thought to himself. Obodi's voice was soft, gently penetrating. "You were not to bring your bodyguards with you. How was this allowed?"

David said mildly, "Nobody mentioned it to me."

Obodi said just as quietly, "I gave the orders myself. I assure you they were not forgotten. How did it happen, do you suppose, that they were not implemented?"

"Beats the hell out of me. Maybe you need better people. Listen, 'Sieur Obodi, a lot of important people told me I should come visit you, seeing how you invited me and all. Show respect, they told me." David smiled at Obodi. "I'm showing respect. What the fuck do you want from me?"

Obodi returned David's smile. "What is your name, boy?"

"*Boy?*" David took a step forward, his bodyguards moving out to flank him. David studied Obodi speculatively, calmly, the remnants of the session with the wire damping out any traces of fear. He *reached*—

—*flicker of fire, of intimate* touch—

And warm fog enveloped him, soothed him, charmed him with gentle reassurances—

David jerked back into himself.

Obodi said again, "What is your name, boy?"

David stared at the Reb leader, suddenly completely uncertain of himself, distantly aware that it must be showing. What was *that*? "David," he said with a suddenly thick tongue. "David Zanini."

"'That is your full name?"

His adrenal gland, abused and lied to by the wire, suddenly kicked into gear. Abruptly his heart was pounding as though it would burst in his chest, and David could not draw enough breath. The old soldier in the corner of the room suddenly jumped into focus—

—*Elite*, the man was a fucking brass balls Peaceforcer *Elite*. The Elite stared grimly at David. Staring back at the Elite, David snapped, "What the fuck is this brass balls doing here?"

"You are an Italian?"

David's bodyguards, at his silent command, spread farther away from him, one keying on Obodi, the other on the Elite. "Yeah, what of it?" The Elite—the man's granite face tickled a memory somewhere deep inside, one of his father's friends had been—

"You look," said Obodi quietly, "remarkably like a man who died in 2062. A man—" The sudden surge of terror raised up in David like a tidal wave, and he felt the lethal hot air tingling on his skin, and a slow smile stretched across Obodi's features. "—a man named Castanaveras."

David Castanaveras had no idea what he was doing, only that his life was endangered and that he must protect himself.

The doors behind him blew themselves out of their frame. As the sonic stunners cut in, an invisible hand picked Obodi up and threw him across the room like a doll. A wash of flame exploded outward from the spot where David Castanaveras stood, sent a burning wash of superheated air across the room like a maser set at wide dispersion. The heat washed across Chris Summers, set his clothes afire.

Gi'Suei'Obodi'Sedon struck the far wall rolled into a ball, dropped to the ground stunned, and lay there motionless.

Christian J. Summers, ex-Peaceforcer Elite, stood still after the wash of the flame had passed by, and watched the room's stunners play over the son of the best friend he had ever had. The two bodyguards, both of them to the external eye in better shape than their employer, fell within seconds. The deep radar scan Castanaveras had walked through on his way into the building showed a PPS with body armor, but the body armor would not be protecting him from the sonics; this was simple endurance. Sedon sat up, then came back to his feet, and Chris Summers walked slowly forward, stood only a few meters away, at the edge of the sonics, stood so close his teeth ached, watching as, long after his bodyguards had fallen, David Castanaveras struggled to keep his feet. Summers watched the genie stagger back and forth, the sonics following him, crashing into the walls, going down and then pushing his way up again. The ruby laser in the cyborg's right fist was lit and pointed at the floor. His clothing burned in places, but he was utterly unaware of it. Abruptly a laser lashed forward from the watch the genie wore; Chris Summers turned his head aside, and lifted an arm to cover his optics. In a moment the laser ceased, and a moment later David Castanaveras fell, and did not get up again.

Summers let the stunners run a while longer, long enough that he feared risking neural damage in all three of the men on the floor, and then shut them off. He turned to Sedon, standing well back, watching the tableau. "How are you?"

"I shall live. What happened?"

Summers said without any irony at all, "You scared him."

Sedon shook his head slightly, came forward. His eyes would not focus immediately. His ears rang and he would have a knot on his skull and a bruise on his ribs where he had hit the wall. "How very dangerous these children are. You recognize him, Christian?"

Chris Summers said slowly, "The girl doesn't look very much like her mother, Jany McConnell. Same green eyes, but she's had biosculpture. And David—the blue eyes throw me." His features were the expressionless mask of a PKF Elite; yet his voice was heavy. "But I'd know him anywhere. That's his father's face. It's like looking at Carl come back from the dead."

"Good," Sedon said absently. He knelt slowly next to the young man's still form, traced a finger across David's cheek, and then looked up at Chris Summers abruptly. His smile was slow and dazzling. "You live in an age of wonders, Christian."

"If you say so."

"I do. And I have seen things to compare."

David Castanaveras awoke to happiness.

Darkness enveloped him.

He could not move.

His inability to move did not bother him. He floated blissfully in the utter darkness, distantly aware of the existence of the world, very pleased indeed that someone had gone to the trouble of turning on his wire, of sending the juice down into his pleasure center.

At first the voice was distant and quiet, easy to ignore. *Hello, David. Hello, my friend.* But the voice grew louder, and the wire got turned down at the same time. With mild curiosity David let the words penetrate.

We are going to be great friends, David Castanaveras. A long pause, and then the voice said, gently, persuasively, *The very best of friends. What you want, I want for you.* A shorter pause, and the voice said with simple conviction, *I love you.*

- 6 -

The prisoner sat strapped into a chair, in the middle of a hospital room Denice had not been in before, not during Jimmy's bout with the medbots, or hers.

The man was thin, wiry, with curly black hair and a neatly trimmed beard and mustache. He was naked to the waist, with electrodes covering him everywhere. A full-sensory InfoNet terminal covered his skull.

An intravenous drip was attached at his right inner elbow. The prisoner's right hand ended at the wrist.

Francis Xavier Chandler sat across the room from the prisoner, a blanket over his lap, in the floatchair he'd been confined to since yesterday's assassination attempt. Chandler's right hand, like the prisoner's, was gone. There was some question that he would ever walk again. "His name is Anthony Angelo. Tony. Used to be a Speedfreak, when there were such things. He's worked for me for near thirty years now. I've known him since he was a baby. I employed both of his parents and one of his grandparents." Chandler sat silently for just a moment. "He's one of the few people in the System I'd have trusted with my life," he whispered finally. "And did. He's been one of my inside men with the Johnny Rebs since '63, ever since the Speedfreak Rebellion got crushed. When he said he needed to see me, I didn't think twice. Had him escorted straight to me. Even so, he got scanned twice on the way up; they outfitted him with a beauty. Ceramic slivers in his fingers, about the same slowscan signature as human bone. I was reaching to shake his hand . . . his hand just exploded. Two of the projectiles got me. Nanoviruses all over them—" Chandler gestured around himself. "If it hadn't happened right inside one of the finest emergency medical facilities off Earth, I'd be dead today instead of paralyzed. As it is I'll still have to go to Mars to get my hand regrown; my med facilities won't handle a regrowth. I'm still fighting one of the nanoviruses; pesky thing keeps trying to turn my blood to acid, they haven't quite got it neutralized."

Denice sat with Robert and looked at the drooling idiot in the chair. "You drained him."

Chandler's features were pale. "I knew he'd been brainwashed. I *knew* it."

"Except that he hadn't," Robert said mildly.

Chandler was silent a long moment. "Apparently not. He kept saying that he'd simply realized that there was a higher loyalty than the loyalty he'd once had to me. If that's really all it was—" Chandler's voice trailed off, and Denice thought he was not going to speak again, when Chandler said simply, "I have to know."

Denice looked back and forth between Chandler and Robert. Robert said quietly, "You owe him this much."

Denice closed her eyes and reached, Touched—
Became.

She sat motionlessly, eyes closed, for five minutes that
stretched to ten, and then to fifteen. When twenty minutes had
passed, and Robert was considering disturbing her, she finally
opened her eyes.

They were wet with tears.

Robert said softly, "What is it?"

"When I was nine—" She had to struggle with the words,
force them out. "When I was nine I was raped. During the first
month of the Troubles. And I thought it was the worst thing
that any person could ever do to another." She spoke through
a throat made tight with pain, through a gathering cloud of
tears. She held herself, hugged herself tightly, and found herself wishing, in some distant part of herself, that she could see
Callia Sierran again. "What they did to him is worse."

Chandler leaned forward in his floatchair. The knuckles of
the hand gripping the floatchair had gone completely white.
"What did they do?"

"They turned him into a thing he would have died before
becoming. And he knew it the whole time." She looked at
them. "David did it."

Chandler said stupidly, "Who?"

"David did this. David Castanaveras. My twin is with them."

- 7 -

They sat next to one another on the semiballistic to Japan.

David Castanaveras sat two seats behind them, in restraints,
with the juice pouring down into his pleasure center at its
highest setting. They would leave him that way until they
reached Japan.

It was an uncomfortable thing to be near; at odd moments
Chris Summers found himself possessed by a sudden, disturb-
ingly complete euphoria. Even Sedon was not unaffected; his
lips twitched incessantly, and once he chuckled aloud for no
reason.

The cyborg's cheeks ached. His skin, stiff enough to turn a

knife, fought against the muscles that kept his lips stretched in the rictus of a grin.

A report came in over Chris Summers's earphone; after a pause, he smiled and said, "Chandler is apparently still alive."

"Alas."

"I told you those nanoviruses wouldn't work. He sits up there in that damn floating hospital and—"

"The point was not that Chandler die. Whether he lives or dies is a small matter."

Summers nodded. What mattered was that David's work had been shown to be reliable. He started to say something, then cut it off in a fit of abrupt giggles.

"Abide, Christian. It will end shortly."

Summers spoke through snorts of laughter. "We should have—left him—in San Diego."

Sedon shook his head. His lips twitched again. "We have need of his skills."

In a small Buddhist temple outside of Tokyo, they met with Shuji Kurokawa, the Unification Councilor for most of southern Japan; Akira Hasegawa of Mitsubishi; and the venerable Ryotaro Matsuda, who had been old fifty years prior, when, with a dozen other old men, he had surrendered Japan to the Unification.

They met in a small, wooden-floored room with thin walls, sat together, the six of them, at a small black table raised only a few centimeters above the ground, and drank tea together in silence.

The servants withdrew when they were done with their tea, and left them alone.

The three who sat facing Sedon were Asians, members of the Mongoloid family of the New Human Race. Like the Negro peoples, they were, Sedon observed, better fit for this world than the European whites whose culture had in large measure achieved dominance in this time. As the blacks were better evolved to survive beneath the harsh sun of the prison world, the Mongoloid peoples had eyes better protected from the sun, and a layer of subcutaneous fat that better protected them from this world's extremes of temperature.

They were certainly more civilized than the whites. In more ways than one, in their concern with protocol and politeness, in their lack of haste, they, of the societies Sedon had encountered since his release from the bubble, most closely resembled the Flame People.

The two men dressed in severe black obi; the woman, Kurokawa, in a gown of some dove gray material. Sedon had difficulty gauging age among any of the folk of this time, but especially so with the Asians; simply to look at he might have thought them any age from 40 to 140—and probably, all three of them, closer to the latter number, for the Japanese prized age.

In that Sedon thought they showed the beginning of wisdom.

'Sieur Hasegawa spoke first, in Japanese; there was a brief delay while the temple's computer translated into French. "You have brought a new companion to these talks."

Chris Summers spoke in English, said mildly, "My friend Akira; this is David, the son of an old friend. He has joined our cause."

Sitting slightly behind and to Sedon's left, David Castanaveras looked at them through bored and sleepy eyes. He inclined his head slightly at the mention of his name.

The woman, Kurokawa, whose obstinance had stalled Sedon's progress for so long, spoke. A moment later: "We have considered your most recent proposition. We think it unwise."

They would, of course; it was hardly in their best interests, though Sedon had gone to great lengths to portray it otherwise. Sedon spoke mildly. "Indeed? You recognize that we have a tiger by the tail? We are only a few days from rising, and once begun, there can be no turning back."

"We do not wish to go forward with you, 'Sieur Sedon." The woman spoke with a directness that was, for her, unusual. "Your chances for success are abysmal, and we cannot believe that you do not know it. Even with our aid your chances—*our chances*—are merely poor. You need the aid of the SpaceFarers' Collective, at a bare minimum, and you do not have it."

Sedon paused. "I will give this one last attempt, and then I will not speak for the consequences. We share a common enemy in the Unification. Your country has been damaged by the Unification far worse than any other on this planet, worse than Occupied America, for fear of your might should you—"

The woman cut him off. "Three-quarters of the armed spacecraft in the Solar System belong to Space Force. The PKF has twelve million men in uniform across the surface of this planet; has nearly three thousand Elite cyborgs. The cyborgs we have created with what we have learned from 'Sieur Summers, though in their own way impressive, are not technologically a match for any but the earliest of the Unification's Elite; and there are only two hundred of them. You have a million PKF in O.A.; we have only thirty thousand in all of Japan. It seems to us that our interests are not served by contesting the Unification, but rather by working from within it."

"Do you not thirst for revenge, for the damage done you, the deaths rained down upon you from the sky?"

The three facing him were silent for a long while. It was at last the eldest of their number, Ryotaro Matsuda, who spoke. He spoke in a whisper of English. "I was born, 'Sieur Obodi, in black rain, as the earth blasted into the sky by American bombs was washed back to the ground; born to devastation so utter that a lesser people would not have recovered from it. My elder sister died of radiation poisoning shortly after I was born; both of my parents died of cancers from the bombs. But we are a great people, and we rebuilt, became preeminent in the world. And then in 2018 the Unification bombed us again, fourteen warheads exploded in airbursts over Japanese territory; and I lost two of my three children to the fire, and the third to radiation sickness. And again we rebuilt, and today enjoy prosperity that is the envy of the world. We maintain our own society, we do not flaunt our wealth; we ask for nothing of the *gaijin* but that they leave us be. We have aided you more than is perhaps wise *already*, and what you now ask of us, madman, is that we risk ourselves and our children, once again, for no better reason than that it is convenient for *you*."

Gi'Suei'Obodi'Sedon said bluntly, "You have thermonuclear warheads. I need them."

Silence descended.

Akira Hasegawa said cautiously, "You have been misinformed."

"You have twenty-five of them," said Sedon. "I will leave you three for self-protection. I must have the rest."

The woman facing Sedon said simply, "We will not give them to you."

Sedon employed a technique that would not have worked on any of the Flame People, it was so obvious, but which he had found, to his amazement, often worked on the people of this time. As sincerely as he could, he asked, "Is there anything I can do to change your mind?"

It did not work this time; she shook her head, said firmly, "No."

Sedon nodded. "David?"

The boy's voice was calm, disinterested. "Yes?"

"As we discussed."

When Gi'Suei'Obodi'Sedon left to return to Occupied America, the following morning, he took with him two things: a group of forty of the almost-Elite cyborgs, young, immensely polite Japanese men, and, stacked neatly in the SB's hold, twenty-two fusion warheads.

He left behind him a group of Japanese leaders who would do exactly as David Castanaveras had instructed them.

- 8 -

Late on the afternoon of June the 30th, 2076, Secretary General Eddore's Chief of Staff, Hand Alexander Moreau, stepped into the SecGen's office. "Sir?"

Eddore looked up from the holofield he was auditing. "Yes, Alex?"

"Councilor Ripper wants to speak to you."

Eddore nodded, felt a flicker of warm anticipation. "Have him wait a minute or two, then put him through."

"He's *here*." At Eddore's look of incomprehension, Moreau added, "In the waiting room."

A slow smile crossed Charles Eddore's features. "Really? Without an appointment. How charming. Bring him in."

Moreau turned back to the door; Ripper brushed by him on his way in.

Eddore said calmly, "Douglass."

"Are you blind?"

Eddore smiled. "I don't think so. Have a seat, Douglass."

"What are you doing, Charles?"

"What do you mean?"

"I called Commissioner Vance."

"Ah." Eddore needed no more than that; Vance, chafing at the bit, would have been blunt about his displeasure at being held back on the Johnny Rebs; and Ripper, as the Chair of the

Oversite Committee, was an appropriate place for Vance to express his displeasure. "And if you hadn't called Vance," Eddore murmured, "doubtless he'd have called you?"

"Probably. He's not a happy man, Charles." Ripper paused. "You've lied to the Council."

"Oh? About?"

"This investigation your office claimed the PKF was undertaking. I called Christine Mirabeau, and asked her to forward the documents on the investigation. She told me that they were investigating the Rebs, were about to move forward on it, and promised that the documents would be sent over promptly."

Eddore nodded. "Yes, I know. She called and told me of your request. I told her not to send them."

"So for a couple of weeks now I've had difficulty getting hold of her at all. Today when I called Vance—imagine my surprise—I found that Vance claims to know nothing about any ongoing investigation into the Rebs. And he says he would know."

Ripper had not accepted Eddore's offer to sit down; now the Secretary General was just as pleased. He sighed. "Douglass, I'm sorry it's come to this. For reasons that I do not particularly feel compelled to explain to you, Elite Commander Mirabeau has engaged in certain private research, research Commissioner Vance did not need to know about. And does not."

"You're not going to explain this, are you?"

"No. I'm not."

Douglass Ripper said simply, "You're fucking up, Charles."

To Alexander Moreau, hovering nervously by the door, the Secretary General said, "Show Douglass out, Alex."

Ripper snorted, "I know the way," and brushed by Moreau once again on his way out.

After he was gone, Eddore said aloud, possibly to Hand Moreau, "I do hate bad losers."

Ripper awoke to darkness, alone in bed, in his suite at Capitol City.

He had almost gotten used to sleeping alone again, but it was still his first thought on awakening, to notice that Denice was not with him.

After a moment he realized what had awakened him, the chiming of the phone. *"Command,"* he said groggily, sitting up in bed, "no video. Accept."

It was Ichabod, speaking so fast that Ripper could not make out the man's words. "Wait, *wait*," he snapped. "Slow down."

"Emergency meeting of the Council, Councilor. Starts whenever a quorum shows up."

"What time is it?"

"Two A.M."

"What the hell *is* it?"

There was the briefest of pauses. "Two things, Councilor. The orbital laser cannon have apparently been knocked out—"

"God damn it," yelled Douglass Ripper, standing up in bed. "God fucking *damn* it! I told them, I *told* them—God *damn*," he yelled again. "Have they heard from the fucking Rebs yet? Demands, *anything*?"

Another quick pause. "No. There haven't been any demands. Councilor, there's some real question whether the Rebs or Claw have *done* this."

Blackness surrounded him. "Who else? The Collective? They think—"

"Councilor, Japan has declared independence."

Douglass Ripper stared blindly into the darkness for perhaps five seconds. Finally he spoke with preternatural calm. "I'll be at the Council Chambers in ten minutes."

- 9 -

They gathered together in the dining lounge, watching the Boards.

NewsBoard had the first reports out of Japan. Denice watched, with Robert at her side, as Shuji Kurokawa, the Unification Councilor for Japan, declared that, as was the right of any sovereign state, Japan no longer found membership in the Unification conducive to its interests, and that therefore, in deference to the opinion of the world, they were taking this opportunity to explain their grievances against the Unification.

Dvan sat with them, watching. His wrist was nearly mended.

At 10:15 A.M., in the middle of a report detailing how a group of Japanese guerillas had taken all but two of the orbital laser cannon, Denice rose and walked over to the garage to bid Jimmy Ramirez good-bye.

A yacht and a pair of SB's were parked in the garage. Jimmy, standing in front of the yacht, squirming into his pressure suit, glanced up as she entered. He greeted her with the words, "I wasn't sure you were going to come see me off."

Chandler had already boarded the small yacht; Denice bit her lip before replying. "I'm sorry."

"You can still come with me."

"I'm going back to Earth, Jimmy. With Robert and Devane. And we're going to try to kill Sedon, and rescue my brother."

Jimmy nodded, sealed the p-suit up to his collar. He said something that only a few weeks ago would have been very difficult for him. "I'm afraid for you, Denice."

"I'm afraid too, Jimmy. But maybe the Belt CityStates are the proper place for you. Trent's out there, somewhere. But there's nothing there for me, not right now."

"Someday, Denice, we're going to return and take the bastards down. You know that's true."

She nodded. "But it doesn't change what I have to do today. I won't ask you to come with me; you couldn't even if you wanted to."

Jimmy said slowly, "All right. I'm going to miss you."

"I love you, Jimmy." She took a single step forward, moved into his embrace, put her chin on his shoulder and held on tight until the speaker set in the side of the yacht came alive.

Chandler's voice: "Sorry to interrupt, but time is tight. We've got a Space Force battalion passing by right now; radar shows another moving in from Almundsen at L-Four. If we're going to make Halfway without turning into Space Force target practice, we have to be out of here in a little under two minutes."

Jimmy released Denice, took a step back, and without further word turned away from her.

Denice said, "Wait!"

Jimmy turned back; for just a moment an absurd flicker of hope crossed his features, was gone. "What?"

"I need to talk to Chandler." She cycled through with Jimmy, into the yacht, and moved back to the passenger compartment. Chandler looked up as she entered.

"What is it, dear?"

"Who knows about me? About my brother?"

The old man did not misunderstand her. Displeasure touched the fierce features. "Aside from myself, no one. Not in my organization."

Denice took a deep breath, reached forward, and laid her hand against the side of his head. Brief surprise crossed his features.

My name is Denice Daimara. I'm the student of Robert Dazai Yo. The telepaths are gone from the world, and you think them dead. Except when you are alone, you will never think otherwise. When you are alone, you may remember me, and my brother; but you will not act upon it, and you will never speak of it.

Jimmy seated himself, strapping into his acceleration chair. He said quietly, "What are you doing?"

"Protecting myself."

Chandler sat with his eyes closed, and then, after a long moment, opened them and said irritably, "Fine. Look, Daimara, we're deadly short on time. Are you *quite* done?"

Jimmy looked at her without expression. "What about me?"

Denice looked straight at him. "Some risks are worth taking." She turned away and left them together in the cabin, cycled back out into the garage, and walked back up to the lounge. She felt the gentle shudder as the yacht disengaged from the house, moved out into the vacuum.

After she was gone, Jimmy Ramirez sat with a silly grin on his face, a grin not entirely due to the fierce acceleration of the yacht, in their high-gee sprint to Halfway.

- 10 -

I cancelled *everything*.

For most of a day I sat in my office and, with a growing coldness in the pit of my stomach, monitoring the InfoNet. *Electronic Times*, *NewsBoard*, CNN, The London *Times*; virtually every one of the major news Boards was arrayed in a semicircle of holos against the wall of my office.

Bad. Very, very bad. Riots in St. Louis, and Albuquerque; something very close to an armed insurrection in Miami.

It was worse in Japan. The Japanese had, without so much as a shot being fired, taken most of the Unification officials in

the country hostage, aside from those few who, like Shuji
Kurokawa, had simply gone over.

Hostages: better than a dozen Unification Councilors, two of
Secretary General Eddore's webdancers, over thirty thousand
members of the various civil services; the Japanese rebels had
already executed a pair of babychasers from the Ministry of
Population Control. Not surprising, that; nobody likes the Ministry, but the Asian nations—including China, which was one of
the founding Unification countries—have a particular rage for
the babychasers. They feel, with some justification, that the
Ministry was created by Westerners *because* of the Asian nations, with their historically high birthrates. It's certainly true
that most non-Asians don't even know someone who was subjected to forcible sterilization; in the Asian countries, about
forty percent of all women have undergone the operation.

While I was watching, they announced that another pair of
MPC employees had been lynched in Kyoto.

Displays off to my left showed the *Unity*, sitting smack in
the middle of Halfway; Space Force had brought the ship's cannon emplacements up for use. Lights glowed across the huge
surface of the ship, clustered around the cannon. Typical of
Space Force; the damn thing had no airplant, no computers to
speak of, the rockets didn't work—but the weapons did, all of
them.

The door behind me curled open without my say-so, which
meant that it was Jay, or Vasily, or Marc. "Neil."

Jay's voice; I said, without looking away, "Yes?"

"The circus is in town."

I turned in my chair and stared at him. "You're kidding.
They *came*?"

Jay shrugged. "The Collective ship *Lew Alton*, carrying the
Cirque du Mars. Just docked."

I didn't even have to think about it. "Send them back."

"Can't, Neil. Their airplant died and their 'ponics are in bad
shape; they're tight on both air and water. It's why they came
on ahead after we warned them off. They'd *probably* make
Luna, but they can't get back to Mars. I had them tie up with
our computers and we ran diagnostics to double-check theirs,
and it's legit. They're breathing their socks."

"Great." I worked my way through it. "All right. Let them
dock, cable them up for air services, but keep them on board
their ship."

"Um, they already docked."

I sat rubbing my temples. "I don't suppose there's any chance at all that they're still on board the damn ship?"

"Haven't been down there myself; I'm told that eight of them came down off the ship together before I was notified. They're being detained in the debarking area outside Lock Ten; a woman in a white tie and tails, a couple of roustabouts, and, um"—his cheeks twitched, but he kept it under control—"five clowns. They want to talk to you."

"Five clowns." I nodded grimly. "Who let them in?"

Jay paused, glanced down at his handheld; a holofield sprang into existence. "McCarthy and Lopez," he said after a moment. I recognized the names; rookies, both of them. The two of them had come to my attention recently for something else—but the memory wouldn't come, and I had more important things to worry about. "They want to talk to you," Jay repeated.

"They're not going to enjoy it," I said grimly. "Get ten Security carrying needlers, in case our clowns don't feel like being sent home. I'll meet you there in five minutes."

I worked myself up into a cold rage on my way down to Lock Ten.

Jay stood waiting outside the Lock Ten debarking area when I got there, two Security squads with holstered needlers standing behind him. I nodded to them, palmed open the door to the waiting area, and swept in, moving fast, with the lot of them at my back.

They sat in the small plastic chairs that are all the amenities the debarking areas offer, and they came to their feet as I entered. The Master of Ceremonies was a tall, painfully thin woman, Loonie sized, with a makeup job that made her look as though her skin were covered by fine feathers, wearing, as Jay had said, a white tuxedo.

The clowns, naturally enough, caught my immediate attention; there were five of them, as I'd been told, in full costume—clown suits, striped and polka-dotted, with either big smiles or frowns painted on their faces. One of them, a young, dark-skinned fellow with a huge smile and a single white rose painted on each cheek, stepped forward at my approach. At the back of my mind I noticed that, unlike all the other clowns, he wore a pair of those big floppy clown shoes. A red glove with big yellow buttons covered his left hand; his right hand was bare.

I'd intended to grab the Master of Ceremonies, possibly push her off her feet, shake her up a bit. Basic Gestapo tactics, you use them because they work. But when I saw what she was I *couldn't*. Getting physical with women is something I have a problem with; I do it because the job demands it, but there's always a moment of hesitation I don't have with men. But the Master of Ceremonies looked like any rough handling would break her in two.

So I changed the approach. I kept my eyes fixed on the Master of Ceremonies, and backhanded the clown with the roses on his cheeks. Lock Ten is under a tenth gee; the clown lifted off his feet and went down. I snapped, "I'm Chief Corona and I've got Space Force and PKF to deal with and no time for *you*. What are you fucking idiots doing here and what do you need from us to get the hell *gone*?"

The black clown got back to his feet, He was my size, or a bit taller, with Earth-grown muscles. Tall for a downsider. One of the floppy clown feet had come off, and he frowned down at the bare black foot. He took a step back toward me, and said, "No hitting, okay? Can I talk?"

I used my very best psycho cop voice. "Make it *fast*."

He nodded. "I left Earth seven years ago. In that time, do you know the most interesting thing I've learned about downsiders?"

It was so completely out of line with anything I'd been expecting to hear from him that it threw me completely out of position. I stared at him, unsnapped the guard on my holster—heard the sound of holsters popping all around me—and said finally, very gently, "No. What is the most interesting thing about downsiders?"

"Downsiders," said the clown, "never look up."

Tytan Security, I think I've mentioned this, is mostly downsiders. It's the nature of the beast.

Someone behind me murmured, "Oh, shit." Necks around me craned upward, and I joined them.

The debarking area at Lock Ten is about ten meters high; cargo often gets unloaded here, and the extra cubic is useful.

Five—no, six of them, and four of them were clowns—had tethered themselves to the ceiling, high above us. They pointed laser rifles straight down on us.

Two of them wore Tytan Security blues: Lopez and McCarthy. McCarthy grinned at me, called out, "Hi, Chief."

I brought my eyes back down from the ceiling, to face the young black clown. From nowhere the clown had produced a small hideaway maser; he held it in his naked right hand, pointed straight into my face. "Make one wrong move," said the clown in a grim voice, "and we'll kill you all."

Jay stood closest to me; he took a step back, and then lifted his hands very carefully and put them atop his head and stood completely motionless. I heard the distant rustle of uniforms as the others emulated him.

I stood still, didn't move at all, not even to put my hands on my head.

The clown smiled then for real, and passed the maser to the Master of Ceremonies. He looked at me. "You're Neil Corona, aren't you? The Neil Corona?"

When people say it that way the only thing they ever mean is, *Are you the Neil Corona who surrendered to the Unification outside of Yorktown?* I always am. "Yeah. That's me."

"Great. Pleased to meet you." The clown held out his bare right hand to be shaken. The other was still enclosed in a red clown glove. "I'm Trent."

- 11 -

"Trent?" Jay said stupidly. "*The* Trent?"

His hand dropped back to his side. Dark brown eyes studied Jay from inside white clown makeup. "You know," he said after a moment, "when people say it that way the only thing they ever mean is, are you Trent the Uncatchable? I always am."

"You don't look like your pictures."

"I used to be a white man, yes. You're Jay Altaloma, aren't you?"

"Yes."

"I thought so. They said you were stupid." Trent turned back to me, held his hand out again. "Pleased to meet you."

I took it this time. I wasn't being the least sarcastic when I said, "Likewise."

．　　　　．　　　　．

Over the course of the next two hours I watched one of the most professional operations it has ever been my dubious pleasure to have run on me. The lock cycled all the way open, inner and outer doors both, and some two hundred men and women in United Nations Space Force uniforms came pouring through, armed mostly with needlers.

SpaceFarers' Collective. If I hadn't known they couldn't be real Space Force—not with Trent there—I'd have bought them for what their uniforms proclaimed. They *looked* like downsiders—but SpaceFarers do; the Collective raises its children under gravity, so that they can withstand the kind of boost that Space Force employs chasing them. The only thing that marked them for Collective rather than Space Force, and I doubt I'd have noticed this if I hadn't been looking for it, was that though they had the compactness of size that only comes from being raised under gravity, they moved in free fall like Halfers; humans are only capable of learning to move that way in childhood.

Trent the Uncatchable, I learned quickly, knew Halfway's security layout every bit as well as I did.

He did what I'd have done in his skin; restrained the Security Jay had brought down with us, snakechains all around; left most of his troops in the debarking area, put a laser in my back and walked Jay and me up to Marc Packard's offices. Marc's offices sit in a little blister on the outer surface of Administration Central; mine are down the hall. They went in and secured Marc's office before bringing Jay and me through. Marc sat unconscious in his chair, with half a dozen anesthetic slivers still visible, though melting rapidly, in one cheek.

They put Jay and me in a corner of the room, snakechained us together, and put a huge clown with a laser rifle on us.

Trent pulled Marc free from his chair, tossed him over to a bunch of clowns who had come up with us, and sank down behind Marc's desk.

Abruptly things got quiet. Jay started to say something, but the big clown waved him to silence. Trent sat with his eyes closed, doing God knows what; if it was true, as I'd heard, that he was one of the greatest Players in the System, it could be almost anything.

In the distance, breach alarms went off. None of the circus people, if any of them *were* circus people, seemed alarmed, and I worked it out quickly enough; the breach was not real, it was simply that the alarms would seal Administration Central off from the rest of Halfway more quickly than anything else.

After perhaps five minutes Trent opened his eyes, stretched slightly, and smiled at me. "You have six tunnels, fourteen major airlocks, forty-seven single-person locks, seven emergency locks. All sealed. Am I missing anything?"

"If you were I wouldn't tell you."

Trent nodded. "Fair enough. I think I've got Administration Central sealed off. We took care of the Security barracks on the way in; blew off a couple of fadeaway bombs inside it. We'll go in and clean up in a bit; fadeaway, if you're not familiar with it, won't hurt your people. Please notice, 'Sieur Corona, that we've gone to real lengths to make sure that none of your people *are* hurt."

"I've noticed."

"Good. So, by now the rest of Halfway thinks that there's been a breach at Administration Central; by the time they'll expect the emergency to be over, they'll have been believably informed that Space Force has taken over both Halfway Administration Central, and—" Trent paused, got a slightly distant look, and said, "And the Halfway InfoNet Relay Station. We're set up to do a very good imitation of a Space Force battalion, and as long as we don't have to deal with PKF or real Space Force I think we'll get away with it. We'll be cleaning up Administration Central for the next several minutes, but we're already reporting secured for about eighty percent of Central. The Relay Station we've got cold, along with one of the Secretary General's webdancers." Trent stopped, looked at me where I sat with Jay, and said, "'Sieur Corona, I'd like your help."

Jay said hotly, "You can't think you're going to get away with impersonating Space Force. It—"

"I do think so," said Trent without looking away from me. "Space Force is busy at the moment, trying to take back the laser cannon; the PKF are just as busy getting ready to take back Japan. All we have to do here is stay quiet for a couple days, give the Halfers an explanation they'll accept. A Space Force takeover will make sense to them, to the degree they bother to think about it. Most of them are distracted by the fighting over the laser cannon anyway."

I'd worked my way through it by then; I said simply, "Tell me what you need." I could feel Jay's stare of disbelief boring into the side of my head.

"We're going to hold Administration Central, and the Halfway Relay Station, for two, three days; it depends. After we've done what we came for, we're out of here. Shortly after we've left, it's going to become apparent that it wasn't Space Force here at all, but Trent with Collective troopers. As soon as that gets out, the PKF will have Halfway under martial law. Do you follow the chain of events?"

Unfortunately, I did. "Yes."

"Okay. So you have no real choice. Perhaps today, if we screw up, a couple of days from now, if things go well, Halfway goes under martial law. And when that happens, 'Sieur Corona, you're going up against the wall."

He was absolutely correct, and we both knew it.

"Look," said Jay, "you don't know—"

Trent did not raise his voice particularly. "Shut up, Altaloma. 'Sieur Corona," said Trent softly, "I need your help. Do you want to live?"

I looked around Marc's office, at Marc's unconscious form, the clowns, the men in Space Force uniforms. I said to Trent. "Sometimes it seems like a lot of effort."

Trent nodded. "I've had whole days like that. You can come with us when we leave; or we can try to arrange passage downside, and you can take your chances hiding among Earth's seven and a half billion."

"And if I come with you, how are you getting out of Earth/ Luna without being blown to pieces?"

"We're going to run backward."

"That thing you came in is a boat. What are you going to *do* when it's time to leave?"

Trent shrugged. "Leave."

"Just like that."

"Run away."

I'm sure the skepticism showed in my voice. "You're not serious."

Trent looked genuinely perplexed. "Why do people always *say* that to me?"

Jay said, "I don't think you know what you're doing here."

"Yes, I do. Listen, Corona, this is—"

"But, damn it, you're messing up our—"

Trent did not raise his voice at all. He just started talking, and assumed that everybody in earshot would shut up and listen. A good trick; it worked. "If you don't stop talking at me," said Trent carefully, "I'm going to have your arms broken."

Jay blinked. "You're a *pacifist*."

Trent actually grinned at him. "I used to think that too. But I'm not. I'm a, what's the word, there isn't one, a person who doesn't believe in killing. But if you don't shut up I'll have the big clown break your arms, okay?"

"Listen, damn it. If you thi—"

"*Wait.*" It cut Jay short; he stopped in midword. Trent spoke so quietly I had to strain to hear him. "Rule One: Pay attention. Rule Two: Don't whine. Rule Three: Don't take any shit from *anyone.* Do you understand?"

"I think so."

"Good. Stop bothering me. Corona—"

Jay said, "But—"

Trent said, "Break his right arm." He turned to me. "You had a Player arrive here recently."

I said slowly, "Yes—I think so. She's just a girl."

"What's the Player's name?"

"Michelle Altaloma. Jay's cousin, they call her Shell." I stopped when Jay screamed, waited for the scream to subside. "I mean Jay does."

"Cute name. She staying with him?"

"I think so."

To the clown who'd been holding the laser on us, Trent said, "Go get her, take her to the Station." He turned back to Jay. "You okay?"

Jay glared at him. "Fuck you."

Trent nodded. "Break the other arm."

Jay started to scream; he stopped midway through, when his left arm snapped. For a moment he just gasped for breath, staring at Trent; Trent stood looking back at him. "You should learn to pay attention," Trent said after a moment. "It would save you no end of trouble." He gestured to a pair of smaller clowns. "Take them somewhere safe and fix the loud one's arms. I don't want to listen to him anymore."

They stashed us together in one of my own holding cells, down the hall from my office. I'd have been indignant if I hadn't been numb.

"Christ," said Jay. "First he called me stupid and then he broke my arms."

"He didn't call you stupid," I said. "He was just repeating something someone else said about you."

"But—"

"I don't think you're stupid," I told him. "Not *really* stupid. I just think you talk too much."

He shut up.

About fifteen minutes later Trent stopped in to see us briefly, at the same time the medbot arrived to take care of Jay's arms. "How are your arms?"

Jay said, "They hurt."

"They will," Trent agreed. "Better remember to ask the medbot for a painkiller, or it won't do anything but set the bones and inject a nanovirus to help them knit." To me he said, "Thank you for your help. I've got some business to take care of, but I'd like you to join me over at the Relay Station, in about an hour."

"I'll check my calendar."

Trent nodded. "Thank you." He turned to go—

"Hey!"

He turned back for a moment. "Yes?"

"I have a lot of questions—"

"And I'll answer them, later."

I don't know where the question came from, or why it suddenly seemed important: "*Did you really walk through a wall once?*"

Trent grinned at me. "Don't believe everything you audit." The door unrolled and left us alone with the medbot tending Jay's arm.

After a bit Jay said, "You know, he reminds me of my grandfather."

"Oh?"

Jay winced as the medbot grasped his arm and braced him, prior to pulling the broken bone back into position. "Plainest-spoken man I ever knew, my grandfather. If he told you he'd do something, he did it. If there were more people out there like him and Trent, there'd be a lot less—" Jay screamed, and then breathed deeply, rapidly, for several seconds, before resuming. "There'd be a lot less misunderstanding in the world."

I gave Jay long enough for the painkillers to take effect. "Want to tell me?"

He didn't look at me. "Tell you what?"

"What are you? Reb, Claw—Peaceforcer?"

"TrueBreed," he said shortly.

"Oh." That told me a great deal. Somehow I wasn't surprised. TrueBreed isn't as well known as Project Superman, but anybody who follows the Rebs even casually—say, Chief of Security at Halfway—knows about their existence. "Reb, then. Why are you up here? Something to do with the Relay Station, I've got that, but—"

He spoke wearily. "Neil, does it matter?"

Point. "How did you pass the psychometric?"

"Vasily."

That was mildly interesting. "A Russian in the Johnny Rebs?"

"There're more Russians in the Rebs than in the Erisian Claw, Neil. The Claw is heavily European; Europeans look down on Russians."

Learn something new every day. "How did *Vasily* pass? I tested him myself."

Jay nodded. "We recruited him afterward. We almost tried to recruit you. If we'd had more time to work with, Shell was supposed to give it a shot. Your psychometric said you'd be responsive."

"Responsive? Well, she's a cute girl," I conceded. "One last question?"

"Sure."

"Is she really your cousin?"

He grinned a trifle crookedly. "True story."

I nodded. I couldn't think of anything else I wanted to know from him.

About an hour later, he said, "It was just business, Neil. I've enjoyed your company a lot."

"Sure."

About an hour after that a pair in Space Force uniforms came for me.

"Sorry about the delay," said Trent as I was ushered into Marc's office. He stood with his back to me, looking out the huge bay window Marc had installed there, looking out on most of Halfway, the *Unity*, and Earth. "We had a problem."

"What?"

Trent didn't turn around. "Securing Administration Central. One of your people hid, and then when he was found he fought."

My voice wasn't entirely steady. "Who?"

"Vasily Koslov. Your number two."

"And?"

Trent was silent a beat. "Dead. He cut both the legs off one of our girls. The rest of her squad shot him nine or ten times." Trent turned to face me. In low gravity, tears move very slowly. Trent the Uncatchable looked at me through his tears and said, "I'm so sorry."

We took a pressurized sled together, over to the Halfway Relay Station, and talked very briefly. Trent wanted to know if Vasily had had a family.

"None that I know of. It would be in his file."

Trent nodded. Muscles in his jaws were clenching and un-clenching as I watched. "Of course."

"A girlfriend I think he might have been serious about."

"We'll do what we can for her."

"Trent, is this worth it?"

I knew the cold fury in his voice was not directed at me. "It's never worth it."

Michelle Altaloma waited for us, angry and scared, when we docked at the Relay Station. The Relay Station is not large; you can fit maybe twenty people inside, tops. Half a dozen SpaceFarers in Space Force uniforms, Shell, myself and Trent made a cozy enough fit.

She looked like she'd dressed hastily; a pair of jeans and a pale blue sweater. Without the fashion ensemble she looked even younger.

She was seated in front of a full-sensory traceset; she rose when we cycled through.

Trent didn't make her wait. "You're the Player who thought this stunt up?"

Shell said stiffly, "Yes," and I wondered what "this" was.

"Great. You want to explain to me how this was supposed to work?"

She stared at him a moment. "Who are you?"

Trent seemed to realize for the first time that he was still wearing the clown uniform. He glanced down at himself, seemed briefly embarrassed. "Oh. Sorry. I'm Trent."

In an entirely different tone of voice, she said, "Really." I could see she believed him instantly. Not surprising; I had. "So what do I call you, anyway? 'Sieur Uncatchable?"

He said simply, "My name is Trent Castanaveras. You can call me Trent."

Shell nodded slowly, looking him up and down. "Suzanne Montignet designed you."

"Yes. And you're second generation TrueBreed."

"Yes."

The two genies stood there, just looking at each other, for a long moment, and then I saw them both, at almost the same moment, shake themselves slightly. Trent spoke as though they were the only two present: "You'll be an interesting person to know, someday."

Shell actually flushed. "Fuck you too."

"Tell me about the takedown. How it was supposed to go."

"Why should I?"

"If I like it, I might still do it."

Shell took a slow, deep breath, looking searchingly at the man's stone expressionless features, and then seemed to accept it. "Okay. Here's how it's supposed to go."

For most of an hour Trent listened to her, nodding occasionally, asking questions where I didn't recognize half the *words* he was using. At one point he interrupted her: "Who ran this simulation?"

"The chain breakdown? An AI named Ring, works with the Claw. I needed it; no human could have run the simulation at the depth I needed."

Trent, sitting in the chair facing her, said absently, "Speak for yourself," and she flushed again, though I and perhaps she could tell it was nothing but a throwaway comment. "All right, so you have two, three of the supplemental InfoNet Relays, the little talk-to-me's. You'll need them—"

"We'll have *all* of them," she said swiftly.

He waved a hand. "That's minor. Halfway Relay is the big one. How were you going to control the traffic when the Relay Stations started going down?"

"Ground stations, primarily—"

"No, I thought of that one myself. It doesn't work. If—"

She interrupted him eagerly. "Sure it does. Look, the Earth InfoNet moves an average one thousand two hundred forty transactions per person per day, a total of nine point three trillion transactions per day. At peak traffic you push one trillion transactions per hour. Trent, there's sufficient surplus logic—by an *order of magnitude*—in the Earth InfoNet to handle that load. If—"

Trent sat with his face in his hands. Finally he straightened in his chair and interrupted her. "Shut up."

Shell blinked. "What?"

"Shut up," said Trent quietly. "You are an arrogant child with no understanding of the damage you are prepared to cause my home."

She looked at him as though he'd slapped her. "Where am I wrong?"

"About eight places, but I'll start with the worst. Have you ever seen a systems analysis on an InfoNet trunk that's failed?"

"Well—no," she said, suddenly uncertain. "That doesn't happen anymore."

"Not for a good thirty years," Trent agreed. "But it's the closest analog we have, though on a much smaller scale, to what you're talking about doing to the entire Earth. You haven't ever studied a trunk failure?"

She started to say something, stopped, shook her head, said, "No."

Trent nodded. "Great. So watch and learn." His eyes went blank a second, and then an orange slice view of Earth appeared, three-dimensional, with the orbital InfoNet Relays hovering in the air a meter above the surface of the planet. Trent came to his feet, walked over to the map. "This is the chain. The InfoNet Relay Station at Halfway goes down. The little talk-to-me's take up as much of the slack as they can, but Halfway is the primary trunk; suddenly *eighty percent* of the traffic going through the Orbital Relay Stations dumps down to Earth. Never mind the rest of the world; since you're a, what's the word, *patriot*, that's it, let's look at what happens in North America. The switching stations in Portland, Cincinnati, Capitol City, Mexico City, Los Angeles, Washington, San Francisco, Quebec, San Diego, Miami, Ensenada, Dallas, Chicago—one by one they attempt to take up the slack, but they can't. They were, as you note, designed for the volume of traffic you're going to dump on them; but Shell, they weren't designed to have it dumped on them *all at once.* Take note; to bring the Halfway Relay Station down safely you'd need to break up traffic intelligently among all of the ground stations, and you *can't.* You don't have access to the necessary resources, nobody but DataWatch does. Back when trunks used to fail, that was the commonest reason; not that they were given too much data to handle, but that they were given it too abruptly. Processors prioritize desperately; bits drop, data gets garbled, processors start trying to figure out just what the hell is being thrown at them. In the process, incidentally, every other half-assed, badly written expert system in the country has a nervous breakdown. While they're so engaged, the next batch of data arrives, and your downside systems still aren't done running error correction on the first batch. The second batch gets stored, if fault tolerance is properly implemented, or dropped, if it's not. In our real-world example, most of the data coming down to the ground stations gets dumped. Never mind the cost of the lost data—though you've already caused a mild recession—because far worse follows." In the holo, huge sections of the country went red, the red spreading south into Mexico, and down through Central and into South America. "The InfoNet *goes down* across most of the Western Hemisphere. It stays down for *days*. This rebellion that's supposed to hurt the Unification—it absolutely breaks the back of Occupied America. One of the ten thousand things that goes down with the InfoNet are the ATCs—" At her look of incomprehension he said quietly, "Automated Traffic Control cells. That's what TransCon calls them, ATCs. Food distribution is always tight; losing TransCon means people start going hungry. Trucks sit in the warehouses and because the trucks don't fly, the maglevs don't get shipments, and when the maglevs don't get their shipments the supermarkets don't get theirs. By the second day people in big cities—most of the northeast seaboard, and Greater Los Angeles—are out of food. Riots follow like the Unification hasn't seen in fifty years; an optimistic solution suggests that five million die in the first week, possibly as many as *twenty* million."

Shell interrupted him. "But there have to be some sacrifices! You don't win a war without—"

"Shut up." Trent turned away from the display, turned on her with such anger that she actually flinched. "You're not going to win no matter *what* you do." He spoke the words slowly, for emphasis. "You . . . can . . . not . . . *win.*"

Michelle stared at him speechlessly.

"It's worse than that," said Trent slowly, his voice almost gentle in contrast. "When the InfoNet comes up again, DataWatch—if they're smart, and they are, at least, smarter than you—will bring it up with something like the old Lunar Information Network Key hardwired into it, an encryption key that would take the InfoNet away from the Players, from *us*. You're old enough to remember the LINK; I damn near died taking out the LINK back in '69. You don't *get* to mess up my work." Trent was silent a beat, just looking at her. "Projections I've run put their odds of success, at taking the InfoNet away from us, at around seventy percent; they may not use Image, but they've got some of the best webdancers in the world working for them, sweetheart, and if you think otherwise you haven't studied DataWatch the way someone calling herself a Player should have. And the Players would fight back, of course; the war that followed would make your silly rebellion look like the punk idiocy it actually is."

The withering contempt in his voice wore her down; by the time he was done the tips of her ears were bright red. I don't think he intended this last to carry, but I have good hearing; his voice was very low when he said, "And neither you nor I even want to *think* about what happens if the AIs ever get together and mount a really *serious* campaign against DataWatch."

Shell fell silent for a long while. "Trent," she said finally, "I'd like to see your simulations. I'd like to work through them."

Trent nodded, rising. "I'm going to have you detained with your cousin; I'll have an infochip sent to your cell." He gestured to me, turned away.

Shell stood up also. "I can make it work. I can prove it to you."

"I doubt it."

Shell said softly, "I've spent eight thousand hours on this project."

It stopped Trent cold. He looked straight at me, paused, and looked back at Michelle Altalona. "But you're only *sixteen*."

She stared back at him, clearly proud of herself.

"Jesus and Harry," said Trent quietly. "Get a life, girl."

He turned around and left her there, standing motionless and openmouthed in the middle of the Halfway Relay Station.

- 12 -

Denice prepared for bed.

The tub in her bedroom was a marvel; Denice suspected that it was the largest tub off the surface of Earth itself. She set the water as hot as she could stand it, called the lights down, and floated in the warm darkness until all the tension had drained from her. After a time, she was not certain how long, she released the drain catch, rose from the tub and dried herself. She pulled on a silk robe that had been left out for her and went back to her bedroom. As the door to the bathroom uncurled to close, a voice said softly, "Will you accept a call?"

Denice sat down on her bed. "From whom?"

The voice paused. "The caller identifies itself as a childhood friend."

Suddenly Denice's heart was beating very fast. "Are you a person?"

"No, 'Selle Daimara."

Denice bit her lower lip. "Can I turn you off?"

"You can instruct me to not listen to this call, if this is what you mean by turning me off. I will comply."

"Send the call through. Don't listen."

"Yes, 'Selle Daimara."

There was the briefest of pauses.

A holograph, about thirty centimeters in height, appeared at the foot of her bed, glowing slightly against the darkness. It wavered, then solidified.

A young man, perhaps in his midtwenties, with short blond hair and pale blue eyes, stood at the foot of Denice's bed. "Hello, Denice."

The voice, the face—Denice stared at the image, felt her heart skip a beat.

Her mouth was very dry. "Trent? Is that you?"

We had dinner together, Trent and I, in Marc's office.

Trent cleared Marc's desk, and we ate atop the desk. Mexican food, huevos rancheros with warm corn tortillas. Not at all bad.

I sat in one of the guest chairs, Trent in Marc's. Through Marc's window, behind Trent, I could see, off in the far distance, a glowing, expanding cloud of debris that had once been a Space Force ship.

"Tomorrow I'm going to have to go be seen."

Trent nodded. "Yes. The fighting will keep them occupied tonight; tomorrow we'll have a good simulation of Packard for anyone who might call him; you and a couple of squads of our fake Space Force will head out into Halfway and let yourselves be seen. Word is that Security has been confined to barracks for the duration; you don't have to explain it when people ask, just say it's so and look unhappy. They'll draw their own conclusions."

"What happens if someone actually calls Space Force to complain?"

"So long as they don't call the Peaceforcers," Trent said mildly. "First, you try to prevent that happening. There's a pretty good chance it won't; Halfway is used to looking to you, Neil, and then to Packard, as the final arbiters on most subjects. Be unhappy, but don't make too big a deal of this; temporary inconvenience, due to the fighting, soon over. Second, if somebody does try to get through to Space Force brass, odds are good they won't. I haven't let you call out, so you don't know; the InfoNet's an absolute mess right now. Traffic is running three hundred percent above normal, due to the fighting, and DataWatch is all over the InfoNet, web angels clogging every channel, slowing down even legitimate business by thirty or forty percent *before* you tack on the three hundred percent extra traffic penalty. It's at least fifty-fifty the call gets ignored even it it gets through. It doesn't seem all that unreasonable that a couple of squads of Space Force might have taken over the Halfway Relay Station, and only slightly unreasonable that they've taken over Administration Central; it almost happened for real. So even if they get through, it's possible that the brass will figure it's a case of left hand–right hand. Third, suppose someone calls, gets through, and brass gets alarmed. Brass calls here, we identify ourselves as Space Force Detached, Squads SG02 and SG03."

"Um—"

"Yes?"

"That's the Secretary General's escort group, no?"

Trent nodded. "Yes. So our hypothetical brass calls the SG's office, asks if SG02 and SG03 are properly detached to duty at Halfway—"

"And you're screwed."

Trent shook his head, spoke around a bite of warm corn tortilla. "Nope. The SecGen's office says, '*Yes, they're ours.*'"

The small image said hesitantly, "Trent—as you mean that question, no. I am that part of Trent that used to be Johnny Johnny. Trent's Image. Today we are very much of a part. You

may call me Johnny Johnny if you wish, or Trent; I will answer
to either."

So many different things tumbled through the back of
Denice's head that for a very long moment nothing at all came
out. She licked her lips, finally, said, "What would you like to
be called?"

The Image said simply, "Call me Trent."

"You're kidding."

"Nope. I'm not proud of it," Trent conceded, "but I am serious. The Secretary General and I have certain interests in
common. At the moment."

I couldn't imagine. "Such as?"

Trent actually laughed. "Well, for starters, we're both terrified of Mohammed Vance."

The talked long into the night.

"I've missed you so much," Denice whispered. "I can't tell
you how many times I've woken up at night and wondered
what I was doing on Earth, why I didn't go to join you."

The Image nodded. "I have wondered," he said quietly.
"If—" The Image paused, and spoke deliberately. "I must
speak to you of emotions, and I have none. The person I speak
of is not-I. He is the passion, and the desire."

"Is Trent."

"If you wish. My biological component—" The Image
hesitated again. The words he spoke would have sounded
melodramatic from any human; from Image that lacked emotion they had the simple ring of truth. "His heart aches and
his soul is empty. When he lost you he ceased to be a whole
person. He has loved many people; you are the only one he
has ever let himself need. He wrote this of you, some years
ago:

> Still the days seem the same
> You say you want
> Silence and solitude
> Promises made
> Unbroken
> Dreams

Unspoken
True

I don't need dreams
Have what I want
And all I need is you

Denice sat in the darkness while silent tears tracked down her cheeks. "I've done things that would horrify him. He doesn't even love the girl he knew seven years ago, he didn't know her long enough. He loves a child who died when I was nine. He doesn't love *me*."

"He did once," said Trent's Image softly. "Does any part of that person still live in you?"

"Yes, *no*," she cried, "I don't *know*."

Trent seemed restless. He got up and paced, sat down again, talked compulsively, listened with half an ear when I talked. I didn't know the man, obviously; perhaps this was normal for him. Around two or three in the morning, in response to a comment I made regarding the preparations the Rebs had made, he snapped, "They have *no* chance."

"Is it really that bad?"

Trent sighed. "I'm not exaggerating, if that's what you mean. Neil, if everything the rebels are planning goes right— *absolutely everything*—they still lose. No projection I make has them coming away winners. To win they need the Collective and the CityStates, and they don't have either; what's worse, this pimp, Obodi, he didn't even *try* to get either to back him. With the Collective on their side it's possible; but even with the Collective it's closer than I'd like." Trent hesitated visibly, said finally, "There is one thing that gives them a bare chance. But the cost of trying it is too high, and there are still no guarantees. They probably haven't even considered it as an option."

"What is it?"

Trent shook his head. "I won't tell you. It scares me that I thought of it *myself*." He sighed, rubbed the sides of his temples with his fingers. "I was raised by the PKF until I was ten years old, Corona; the Unification Council freed us from them the day before my eleventh birthday. I learned a lot from the PKF. If they were running this rebellion, it *would* succeed.

They're professionals, and I have great respect for them. The thing I thought of doing—they've thought of it. They've planned for it if it happens. And those stupid sons of bitches running the rebellion down on Earth, the Rebs and the Claw, they're so far out of their depth they don't even know which end is up anymore."

Toward morning, when Denice was tired and empty of tears, the Image said finally, "He asked that this message be given you before I leave: *I hurt when I think of you. I am pained so that I cannot love or dream or plan with conviction. But it has not stopped me from thinking of you, every day of the last seven years. A day does not go by that I do not think of you. A day does not go by that I do not wish you to join me.*"

Denice sat quietly, fought not to let it show how the words touched her. She said after a moment, "He can't still love me. He—lies to himself—exquisitely well."

Trent's Image said slowly, "Perhaps. But it does not make what he feels less real."

"It's been seven *years*. And seven years before that since we were together for more than a brief while."

"He has not stopped hurting."

Denice bit her lip. "Trent, that's insane."

The Image of Trent the Uncatchable nodded. "I do not believe that sanity is his strong point." A brief pause. "Web angels are flooding the InfoNet as we speak, in anticipation of an upcoming battle; I must go soon. Do you have a message for Trent, when I return to him?"

"Tell him—I miss him."

"Ah."

Denice said quietly, "Trent, I love you."

Trent's Image said, "There are days—when he—still believes that; and days when he can't, because you haven't come to join him. But it's good to hear, nonetheless."

"I do love you."

The Image stood silently, shimmering in the darkness of her room. "I'll tell him you said so. It will mean a great deal to him. He loves you more—" Trent hesitated. His speech, when it resumed, was very slow. "Forgive me. Web angels—I'm devoting significant processor time to hiding from them. They're sweeping through this entire section of the InfoNet. I may have waited too long."

Denice spoke in a desperate rush: "Trent loves me more than *what?*"

The Image seemed to be looking straight at her. "More than you love him, of course. He's a very foolish person, really. I must go now if I'm to have any hope of survival. I'll tell him what you said."

The bright image ceased, left behind a black afterimage in Denice's eyes.

Denice sat as Trent's Image had left her, sitting still and motionless, when Robert came for her. He spoke as the door curled open. "Denice!"

She did not look up at him, did not let him see the tears that had left her cheeks wet. "What?"

"My dear—perhaps this is bad timing, but—"

"*What?*"

"We're being attacked."

Denice looked up, saw him standing in the doorway looking at her.

"I'm sorry to interrupt," he said quietly, "but I thought you might want to know."

Trent's Image fled through the orbital InfoNet.

It was a dangerous place at the best of times, and doubly so now, with DataWatch prepared for war. Trent knew he had no chance of getting back undetected; he hoped only that he could get back to his body at all.

He fled through a chained series of low-altitude comsats. The comsats spoke both to one another and to InfoNet communications relays on Earth. At no point did Trent consider going down to Earth; with no secured processors as a home base, he would be no better off than in the Orbital InfoNet.

Jump, and jump, and jump again—Trent found himself in a transfer node, a small observation area with excellent input attachments, poor output. Paths led away from the transfer node in eight directions.

The living Image of Trent the Uncatchable paused briefly, considered his options. Web angels closed in on him as he considered, as the borrowed processor cycles that the Image stole from its surroundings moved slowly by. Trent fired viruses and phages back in the direction he had come, paused long enough to clone himself into a dozen apparently functional ghosts, and sent the ghosts back after the viruses and phages.

Eight paths led outward.

Six were fixed maser; two of them were lasercable, routed to some other dataspace inside the small satellite Trent inhabited. No aimable maser; a single aiming maser, anywhere along the line of his flight, would have given him the option of beamcasting the record of his conversation with Denice directly back to Halfway. Half the System would have intercepted it, but properly encoded it would have been no great danger.

And at least his body would have known what had transpired with Denice.

There were no good options; Trent disguised himself, sent ghosts out into the InfoNet through all eight available channels. Two ghosts were terminated instantly, and a third shortly after. Five channels left, and reports from the ghosts he had sent out along his back trail were not good: web angels would be on him within instants.

He had insufficient cycles to create true copies of himself; by the time a single clone had been twinned, the web angels would have destroyed him.

For the barest instant Trent knew despair.

The web angels were very close now.

He chose a channel at random out of the remaining five, and leapt upward.

Into eternity.

I think I napped for a bit.

When I awoke again I found Trent standing motionless at the great window, watching the empty field of stars. He stood unnaturally still, turned slightly away from me, for so long I wondered if he had fallen asleep on his feet; you can do that in low gee.

"*Come on,*" Trent whispered in a loud, harsh voice, the voice of a wizard prophesying. "Come on, *you can do it.*" The moment the words were uttered Trent jerked as though he'd touched a live wire, shivered for a moment, and then shook his head. "Damn. Oh, damn."

"Trent?"

He did not look at me, spoke very slowly indeed. "Neil. I'd—forgotten you were here. You should go get some sleep. You'll need it tomorrow."

"What happened?"

"I lost myself inside a tiny little talk-to-me satellite. Damn thing must have been forty years old. Crappy hardware like that shouldn't be allowed in the InfoNet."

"Oh." I didn't even know what losing yourself consisted of, but it felt as though something more were required. I said, "I'm very sorry."

Trent said distantly, "It's okay." He looked out the great viewport, eyes unfocused, and if I live to be a hundred I doubt I will ever again see such naked pain on a human face, with clown paint or otherwise. He looked for all the world like someone was grinding glass down onto the surface of his heart.

I had the good sense to keep my mouth shut.

When at length Trent turned to me his features were curiously empty. "Sorry about that. Ships heading toward the Chandler Estate, Reb ships probably. A woman I haven't seen in seven years is in trouble over there. We talked all night." I did not think I imagined what he said as he left: "I wonder what she said."

- 13 -

They ran through empty hallways to the garage. One of Chandler's young servants met them on their way, wearing a p-suit and carrying another pair. The man handed one p-suit to Denice, the other to Robert, and vanished off down a side corridor.

Dvan was in the garage, already in his p-suit, helmet hooked loosely at his hip. He walked slowly around the shell of the semiballistic, checking for something, Denice was not certain what.

She spoke while squirming into her p-suit. "Who is it?"

Dvan's voice boomed from the other side of the semiballistic. "Hard to say. Six ships, they're not Space Force, they're not PKF. They're going to have a fight to remember, getting through Estate defenses, but if they're armed the way I'd have armed them, they—"

A rumble, the sound of distant thunder on a summer night, reached them. Dvan came back around the body of the semiballistic. "They will," Dvan finished. "Warhead," he added. "And close to the house, lass, or we'd not have heard it."

"Where are we going?"

Dvan shrugged. "Elsewhere." He placed one gloved hand against the semiballistic's airlock doorpad. "If—"

Denice's ears popped. A brief violent wind stormed around her, and then suddenly, as though of its own volition, the bulk of the semiballistic lifted itself free of the deck, tumbled gently and majestically to its side, away from the three of them, and plowed into the hull of the house. The shock of impact knocked Denice from her feet, down to the spinning hull.

It was abruptly difficult to breathe. Robert was ten meters away from her, shouting something strangely silent, pointing, and Denice looked upward—

—at *stars*.

Space Force, Denice thought very clearly, *has not recovered the laser cannon*. Nothing but an X-laser cannon could have sliced away an entire corner of the house.

There was no *air* in her lungs.

For the first time in her life, Denice Castanaveras was possessed of the abrupt, absolutely certain conviction, *I'm going to die*. First step; *put the helmet on*. It was still in her hand, but she hadn't practiced with it enough; she fumbled and dropped it. Another section of the house came free, glowing brilliant white at the edges, where the X-laser had touched it. Denice picked the helmet up, tried to put it on backward while red dots danced in front of her eyes. She realized her mistake, corrected it, got the helmet on in the correct direction. Her eyes were stinging and abruptly she could not see at all, not *anything*—

Huge hands grasped her, an arm went around her chest, and the helmet settled into place around her with the gentlest of *clicks*.

Air rushed in on her. With the air came a vast pain in her lungs, and then cramps; she doubled over on herself, curled herself up around a pain so great she could not imagine what it might be. She blinked, again and again, blinked the blood away from her eyes—

The white glare of the explosion dazzled her eyes, even through the film of blood, for the very briefest instant; then her faceplate went completely black. The wave front, when it touched her, was no more than a gentle push.

Stars wheeled by over her head, and then the sun, then Earth, and then stars again.

She did not know how long the airplant in her suit was good for.

It hardly mattered; she did not know how long she had been floating, completely alone, in the depths of space.

The only thing she was certain of was that she was going to die, and probably soon.

After a while the air in her suit got uncomfortably stuffy.

She could see Halfway, if she bothered to pay attention when it swung by. It did not look particularly interesting; noodles, she had heard somebody call it once. Pretty close.

The bright spark of a spacecraft's rockets appeared, now and again, in the area near her. They were, she thought, searching for her. She doubted they would find her; it would be difficult, in the midst of all the other debris from the Chandler Estate, to find anything so small as a person.

The spark grew brighter as Denice's vision faded. She wondered if they would get here in time.

- 14 -

Nobody—I mean *nobody*—cared.

Space Force had taken control of Halfway? It was fine by them.

Trent was right. Halfers accepted the story as given; most of them, busy monitoring the InfoNet for news about the *real* story, Space Force's attempt to recover the laser cannon, simply didn't care that, instead of the usual Halfway Security, they had Space Force today, and maybe tomorrow. Most didn't even ask, and the few who did ask accepted the story they were given without apparent question.

To the homebrews, downsiders are downsiders, regardless.

The rebels, mostly Japanese according to the reports on the Boards, were acquitting themselves much better than anybody had guessed; they'd repulsed two waves of Elite already. At least half the orbital cannon were under control of rebel forces. Reports of dead Elite were unconfirmed, but a pair of *News-Board* reporters claimed to have seen at least one.

We kept our heads down. Toward lunchtime a disturbance flared up out on the Edge; I took a pair of Trent's SpaceFarers with me and went myself. We didn't even have to crack heads;

the simple fact that the Chief had shown up with a pair in Space Force blues, rather than one of the standard patrols, shocked them into something like sobriety. I lectured them briefly, snakechained the one who had started the trouble to the bar—a two-hour snake—and got out of there.

We were not far from my home; I told my SpaceFarers where we were going, and why; they called it in. I heard Trent's voice, saying "Go ahead," and the SpaceFarer nodded to me.

I didn't take much. CU:40,000, in hard Collective gold, from the safe. If Jay had known I'd been stockpiling it, he'd probably have made me some damn lecture about paranoia.

It all fit very neatly in one smallish briefcase. Downside it would be extremely heavy; now I just had to be careful how I moved it.

I was ready to leave when I remembered one of the things I'd heard about Trent the Uncatchable; he was a coffee junkie. Seven years he'd been out in the Belt; Earth-grown coffee is damn rare out there. I had just under a kilo of S&W Colombian in the stasis field; about half a kilo of Jamaican Blue. I bagged them both, and went from room to room, simply looking at everything, committing my home to memory.

When I was done I turned out all the lights, and left the house unlocked.

I never saw it again.

That evening, after dinner, Trent and I sat and drank coffee together. He had an appointment with Shell for later that evening; she wanted to take another shot at convincing him to help her take down the InfoNet. I knew why he'd agreed to go, and it had nothing to do with the InfoNet.

He was still wearing his clown uniform—he was almost the only one who was; most of the rest of his people, except for the one really big clown who I suspected was Trent's bodyguard, had changed into Space Force fatigues. He wore a laser rifle slung across his back. I felt vaguely disoriented by it all; not detached, but as though I moved through a world filled with so many fascinating, brightly colored things that I would never have time to understand them all.

Somewhere around my second and Trent's fifty cup of coffee, I said, "What are you going to do with Marc?"

Trent seemed mildly surprised I'd asked. "Keep him confined until I leave. Why?"

"He must have known you were coming."

"Oh, of course," Trent conceded. "He didn't know it was *me*, mind you, just that some SpaceFarers were going to show. But I don't trust the man. I've got CU:five million on my head; quite aside from the Credit, it's occurred to him by now that giving the PKF my head would help him keep his job." Trent paused, added, "Anyway, after we're gone, it gives him a much better alibi if he spent all his time in jail."

"I'm not coming with you."

Trent nodded, little white roses bobbing up and down with the movement of his cheeks. "Didn't think so. Your boss has a yacht in Bay D12. I'll have it moved over to Lock Nine, and you can leave when we do. I'll program it for you if you like."

"I would; wrestling a HuskySled is about the limits of my competence. Can you have it drop me outside of Levittown, Pennsylvania?"

Trent paused. "Ah. Your hometown. Sure. If you get chased, I'll send you in like a meteor. You'll get very hot, and the yacht won't ever lift again; but you'll make ground a good fifteen minutes ahead of any pursuit you might pick up. If you don't get pursued, which is possible given how confused things are outside right now, the yacht will drop gently, and you can park it wherever you like."

I nodded. "Thanks."

"No problem. I wish you well."

"Mind if I ask you a question?"

Trent said, "Why am I here?"

"No, I understand that. Protecting the InfoNet. But why did *Eddore* want you here?"

Trent nodded. "Look at his options. He wants to retain power. To do that, he needs martial law. For that he needs a rebellion. So he has to make rebellion look attractive to the Rebs and Claw, while not allowing them any real chance at success. The Rebs think they need the InfoNet to go down; if they think they can't send the InfoNet down, they don't rise. Clear so far?"

His voice had the timbre of a trained singer; I felt that I could lose myself in the sound of his voice, in the gentle wash of the words.

"Neil?"

"Uh—yes. Clear so far."

"So the Rebs have to believe that they have a real shot at taking the InfoNet down. If Eddore goes to Space Force *or* the PKF, asks them to provide security for the Relay Station, the

Rebs will know about it; there are Reb and Claw sympathizers in both organizations. So he needs a third party to protect the InfoNet, someone capable of protecting the InfoNet without the rebels being aware of it. That's us. We're here to protect the Relay Station, until July the Fourth."

Trent's features grew sharp in front of me, the tiny veins in his eyes bright red against the blue-white sclera. His clown outfit was made of cotton, of a very fine crosshatch weave; his buttons were wood, painted by hand with tiny white roses. I blinked hard. "But—why not tell the Rebs what you're doing? Why let this hit them unawares?"

His voice echoed when he spoke. "They can't win, Neil. The faster they lose, the better it is for everyone, including them. If they drag this thing out, it's that much longer before things return to normal, that much longer before Obodi is dead and we can start to rebuild."

I don't know how I knew this, but suddenly I did. "It bothers you," I said slowly, "that they've put a bounty on his head that's greater than yours."

"Did *he* walk through a wall? I don't think so," Trent said conclusively.

"It *does* bother you."

Trent eyed me with clear appraisal. "You don't miss much."

"You'll never know." The brown of his eyes was the color of old oak. A voice that was not mine was speaking to Trent, and I strained to make out the words. "I am the living eyes of Kayell'no, the Name Storytellers; chosen for my location, for my nearness to the center of events. I watch; I learn; I observe. In his own person Kayell'no will never know you, and this pains him." The voice paused, grew more distant as it said, "Pains *me*."

Trent rose from the desk, took a step back. The laser rifle swung free, came around on me. "Corona? Are you all right?"

I'm *fine*, I was going to say to him; *who the hell are* you *talking to?*

But something prevented me; and then the world spun around me and went away.

My avatar shuddered, slumped in his chair with his eyes still open. Trent took a step back, bringing the laser rifle up to bear on my avatar's motionless form.

I let Neil's eyes close, and sat in the darkness, in the hard, stiff chair, and familiarized myself with the mechanism of the meat.

When I opened his eyes, Trent had moved the desk to the side, and nothing separated the two of us; Trent squatted two and a half meters away from me, back to the huge window, balanced easily on the balls of his feet; the muzzle of his laser rifle stared me directly in the face. I gathered Neil's feet under me, pushed him to a standing position; Trent moved with me, glided sideways, keeping the rifle on me, but did not interfere as I pushed the chair Corona sat in backward, put more space between myself and Trent and Trent's laser.

If the historical record concerning Trent was correct, the laser probably wasn't loaded. But history lies a lot; I would not risk Neil's life on it.

Trent said, "Are you all right?"

I said, "I am the Name Storyteller."

He lifted an eloquent eyebrow. "Ah."

"I wish to tell you a story, Trent the Uncatchable."

"Uh, I'm a little short on time here, actually. Got to see a girl about a rebellion."

I grinned at him, trying it out. Corona's muscles were unfamiliar to me; like most of my avatars, I rarely use him, rarely have need. There are few enough places in the Continuing Time I cannot go in my own person.

The immediate vicinity of Trent the Uncatchable, in the year 2076 Gregorian, happens to be one of them.

"It will be said of you, Trent the Uncatchable, in years to come when you are not to be found in the Continuing Time, that you were the living incarnation of God, of the Creator of all things, of that which sent the Envoy among the Serathin."

I saw Trent start to say something, hesitate. I think what he said then was not what he had started to say. "They say something like that now, you know. It's a joke, because the PKF keeps telling people I walked through a wall. I'm really just a thief." He paused, added softly, "A great thief, it's true."

"In time to come, what is perhaps now a joke will cease to be so. *Once there was a thief, and the thief was God.* That is the first line in the *Exodus Bible*, Trent; a thousand years from now, after only the Zaradin Church itself, the Church of His Return will be the largest human religion in the known Continuing Time."

"The what time?"

"May I tell you a story, Trent?"

He backed another two steps away from me, muzzle of the laser never wavering from my face, stood with his back to the door, and withdrew a snake chain from within the bulky clown's vest. He threw it to me. "Put it on, snake your right wrist to the arm of the chair." I sat down again, did as he instructed, and when I was done he said softly, "Go ahead. You have five minutes."

I did not waste my time. I calmed Corona, quieted the vague, unformed fears my takeover had left within him, and began.

Before I was, to tell this story; before Camber was, to Play it; before the explosion that began the long cycles of the Great Wheel's existence, the Envoy of Balance ventured forth to match itself against the Chaotic beings called Serathin.

There in the gray maelstrom of spaceless, timeless Chaos, a tremendous battle raged.

Of that battle's beginning and middle I can tell you nothing. Time has no meaning in this context, and the language I am constrained to use with you is insufficient: for a period longer than the Great Wheel has existed, or is likely to, the Envoy of Balance and the Serathin remained locked together in combat, a combat in which neither side was able to triumph. But eventually the battle did end, and at its end the Envoy of Balance, known ever after as the Chained One, had been bound upon a shining Wheel.

Perhaps the Serathin had time to admire their handiwork; they were such beings as would have done so, given the chance. And perhaps they did not; what is certain is that the Chained One, bound upon the Wheel, had one weapon left to itself, and used it.

The Great Wheel of Existence exploded.

It was not the Big Bang that began this phase of the Great Wheel's existence, but a grander and more powerful forerunner. The expanding wave front of its explosion hurled itself outward, overtook the fleeing Serathin, and passed them; and when it had passed, the Serathin found themselves trapped for all eternity inside the Great Wheel they had fashioned as a prison for the Chained One. Far faster than the Serathin could follow its expansion, the Great Wheel of Existence spread outward in an explosion of matter/antimatter-based timelines, expanding into both Time and Space.

On the individual timelines, life arose; life unlike the Chaotic beings called Serathin, unlike the bound Envoy of Balance, but containing elements of both. And the Great Wheel continued its expansion; and civilizations rose, and fell, and rose again. And with the passage of time, the Great Wheel expanded more slowly; until there came a moment when the energy that had fueled the Great Wheel's expansion had been expended. The Great Wheel hung upon a momentary equilibrium, and then began to contract. In the instant of its contraction, the sky throughout all of the Great Wheel's timelines began at once to blaze white.

The Wheel shrank back in upon itself, to the moment when the space-time continuum would briefly cease to exist, when the Great Wheel would exist as nothing more than a timeless, spaceless point of transfinite energy—

—and then expand again.

How many times this has happened I cannot tell you.

I do not know.

I opened my eyes to silence.

Trent stood motionless, watching me. The muzzle of his rifle had dropped slightly, now pointed at a spot just over Neil Corona's solar plexus—Neil didn't like that at all. A head shot is a chancy thing; a shot to the stomach, with a maser, is not.

Finally Trent said, "Is that it? That's what you wanted to tell me?"

"Yes."

His smile was a slow, bemused thing. "That's the whole story, is it?"

"No. If I were to tell you the entire story, so far as I know it, we would grow old together. Does what I have told you seem familiar to you? Does it stir any memory?"

Trent shook his head. The distant smile did not leave him. "I can't say that it does. Possibly it reminds me of a bad fantasy sensable I once played."

"You have never heard of the Serathin, of the Envoy of Balance?"

"No."

"Of the Chained One?"

He shook his head again, and I knew he was not lying. "No."

"Then you are very fortunate, Trent the Uncatchable. If you

are another Envoy, and do not yet know it, then—" I paused, *willed* him to meet my eyes; concentrated my attention upon the person of Trent the Uncatchable, raised my voice until it echoed against the walls of Marc Packard's office, and Spoke. "Listen well, Trent the Uncatchable: *We are watching you*, and if you are not a fraud, if you are an Envoy such as the one whose Chaining created this universe, then know that among the ten Great Gods you have nine Great Enemies; and *nobody*, not even the renegade God of Players, will protect you from the massed strength of the Serathin. We will cease the truce, loose our Time Wars upon this continuum once more, and when we are done, you will not only not exist, you will *never* have existed."

He shook himself slightly when I was done. A Speaking will do that to you. "All this because I walked through a wall once?"

"Did you?"

Trent said gently, "That would be telling."

"Ah." I took a deep breath, relaxed, and said quietly, "Perhaps I am seeing meaning where there is none. It's a problem of mine, you know."

"Is it?"

"You are probably a fraud, Trent. I do often find myself imposing narrative order on unrelated events. Randomness occurs in the universe; it's just that it makes for bad storytelling. If you are merely a thief, Trent the Uncatchable, we will never meet again. When I remember this moment, it will be as the memory of a dream. I regret that, for you interest me."

"Neil, you are the strangest man I have ever met."

"I am not Neil Corona. I am Chai'ell November, the Name Storyteller, and I am leaving. Good-bye, Trent the Uncatchable."

I let go of my avatar.

There was not much time left, and I had other business to attend.

It was of course not long after that date in 2076 when my avatar Neil Corona spoke to Trent that Trent the Uncatchable died, and rose again, and then vanished from the Continuing Time, perhaps forever.

Silence.

Trent's voice broke it, a rasping unpleasant thing that grated at my ears. "Are you all right?"

Darkness.

I opened my eyes to a glare of light that I could not reconcile with the gentle glowpaint that I knew was in use in Marc's office. With the opening of my eyes it all flooded in on me, like a sensable with the volume control pumped all the way up. Everything was intolerably bright and loud and the soft linen of my security uniform was made of sandpaper.

I shook my head, winced at the sudden surge of pain. "No. No," I said carefully, voice booming in my ears, "I am not okay." Suddenly Trent snapped into focus, the only clear thing in the world, standing several meters away from me, laser rifle cradled at ready, simply watching without making any motion to help me. I started to struggle to my feet, found my right hand chained to the seat. My head pounded as though it were about to come off; I felt as though I might vomit at any moment.

I sat back down abruptly.

"Would you like a drink?"

My head swam. I leaned forward and put my head between my knees. "Yes. Yes, I would. And I'd like this damn snake taken off too."

I don't even remember how old I was the first time this happened to me. Eight, maybe. Nine. When I was young it happened more often; in the last thirty, forty years, only twice.

Every now and again I kid myself that it's stopped.

A bulb was pushed into my hand, and without opening my eyes I cycled it open and sucked it back. It was cold and it cleared my head a bit. I was aware of Trent standing immediately to my right; suddenly the snake released my wrist and dropped loose, fell to the floor.

Trent moved back, said, "How often does this happen to you?"

"What makes you think it's happened before?"

"I took the snake off, Neil. I could have left it on."

Fair enough. "Not often."

"Ever seen a doctor about it?"

Even chuckling hurt. "The first time was fifty years before you were born." I sat up and opened my eyes again. Better this time; the glare had lessened, and I could make out the shapes of most of the objects in Marc's office.

Trent's voice was gentle, persistent. "When was the last time you had an episode?"

He seemed genuinely interested, I don't know why; I made an effort to think back. "Last time? Visiting New York City with Marc. He was negotiating with the Castanaveras telepaths for some work they were going to do for him—I figured it was probably the gravity stress; that trip downside was the longest period either of us had spent in a full gee in a couple decades."

"Do you remember *anything* about them?"

I said shortly, "No. Not that there's much to remember, is there? I just stare at things like a drooling idiot."

"You talked to me."

Trent moved so fast I didn't even catch it; suddenly he was a meter farther away from me, the rifle coming up so that he looked at me over the sight. I didn't realize until then how fast I'd come to my feet. "I *what?*"

Trent didn't lower the laser. He said carefully, "You talked to me. Seven, eight minutes."

"What did I say?"

"Strange things, Neil. Have you ever heard of the Chained One? The Envoy of Balance?"

"What?"

"How about the Continuing Time?"

"The what time?"

"I said the same thing. Have you ever heard of the Serathin?"

"No."

"Well." He lowered the rifle just a bit. "That's what you talked about."

I sat down again, moving slowly, and buried my face in my hands. "I can't wait until this is all over."

Trent nodded, lowered the laser a bit more. "It's getting a little weird for me too. Still, it won't be much longer."

"No?"

"It's a quarter past midnight, Neil. And I was supposed to see 'Selle Altaloma fifteen minutes ago. I'm late. Of course I'm late a lot, everybody knows that. So she probably isn't surprised."

"It's midnight?"

"Past. Yes."

"Oh. So it is." Twelve-seventeen A.M., according to my handheld, the morning of July 3, 2076.

- 16 -

Ichabod Martin waited with Douglass Ripper, in Ripper's office, for Secretary General Eddore to return Ripper's call.

They did not speak to one another while they waited.

There was no background holograph today; they waited in the midst of a huge, dark gray empty space.

Toward late morning, July 3, 2076, the holofield flickered into existence in front of Ripper's desk. Eddore spoke as his image took shape. "Councilor Ripper."

"Sir."

Eddore said, "I'm in a bit of a hurry, Councilor; what can I do for you?"

"This Executive Action your people submitted to the Council; it's going to cause an uproar, sir, and it's not necessary."

Eddore said mildly, "To which Executive Action are you referring? I've issued three in the last weeks."

"You *know* which one," Ripper snapped. "Yesterday's, the one declaring martial law, suspending elections for the duration, and reducing the two-thirds majority required to modify the Statement of Principles to a simple plurality. None of these steps are necessary to deal with the crisis in Japan, a mess that wouldn't exist in the *first* place if you and the PKF hadn't encouraged them by dogging it in dealing with the Johnny Rebs."

"I disagree with you, Douglass. Is that all?"

"In the history of the Unification, only three Executive Actions have ever been overturned in Council session. This is going to be the fourth, sir. I'm offering you the opportunity to withdraw this from Council consideration before I humiliate you over it."

Eddore sighed. "Martial law is temporary, Douglass. You know that. Once we've put down this insurrection, we'll go

ahead with the elections. You must realize I have no interest in
turning the position of Secretary General into a dictatorship."

"You *can't do this*. I have the votes to veto this Action, and
if you—"

Charles Eddore cut Douglass Ripper off in a voice that was
soft and even. "School's in, sucker. Stop me. Give it your best
shot." His smile grew slightly and he leaned forward. "You rank
fucking amateur ex-United States *Senator*. I *can't*?"

Ripper said slowly, controlling the fury that threatened to
creep into his voice, "You're making a terrible mistake, not just
with me, but with Occupied America at large."

Eddore shrugged dismissively. "We'll see."

"*Damn* it, Eddore, they'll riot over this, and you know it.
It'll mean blood in the streets."

Charles Eddore moved his lips in an easy, generous smile.
"Well, it won't be the first time, will it?" He nodded in dismis-
sal. "Good day, Douglass."

His image vanished.

Shortly after lunch Ripper sat at his table in the Council
Chamber, three floors below ground, protected from the rebel laser cannon by three different twenty-meter-thick layers
of ferrocrete. He sat alone at the table reserved for New
York Metro, watching the debate progress. Considering that
there were almost six hundred Unification Councilors—
approximately one to every twelve and a half million humans
on the planet—it was going acceptably quickly. First-term
Councilors had been informed that they would not be allowed
to speak, merely to vote; others had been asked, cajoled, and
begged, to move forward with all speed. Those who *insisted* on
speaking were given only five minutes.

Progress was acceptable. Ripper sat with his handheld
plugged into the table, monitoring—like most of the other Unification Councilors—battle coverage from both *NewsBoard* and
the *Electronic Times*. The third holo floating over his desk was
from *NewsBoard*'s coverage of the Unification Council proceedings.

About fifty-eight percent of those present—and all but the
twelve Japanese Unification Councilors, and one who was in
the hospital with a stroke, *were* present; a modern record—
were, by Ripper's head count, inclined to vote against the most
recent Executive Action. Against were all of the American, Ca-

nadian, and English Councilors; most of the Australian delegation, India, the bulk of Pan-Africa, most of Northern Africa, most of the Russian and RussoAsian republics. In favor were most of the South American countries—the Unification had been good to South America—China, and much of Europe. France, of course. Israel, Spain, Greece, most of the Baltic countries, New Zealand.

China, France, and Brazil, as founding members, had extra votes. They trimmed Ripper's real 58 percent–42 percent edge closer than Ripper liked, to about 53 percent–47 percent.

In question were the Arab and Muslim countries; the Asian countries, most of which did not like the Unification, but disliked Japan worse; a scattering of the Scandinavian countries. And the Lunar Councilors, of course; but Unification Luna held only thirty-three million people, and they had only three representatives. Though they occasionally showed surprising streaks of independence, on this issue they would probably vote Eddore's way. Ripper did not let himself worry about it, as he had ten to twelve votes more than he needed.

Some pretty decent speech making transpired during the course of the long afternoon. The senior French Councilor, leading the session off, made an impassioned speech in defense of the Unification, imploring any undecided Councilors to vote in favor of Eddore's Executive Action. By tradition, voting went in order of membership. The founding Unification countries voted first, followed by those who had joined quickly, followed by those who had been coerced, followed by those who had fought: the republics that had arisen out of the old Soviet empire, and then Japan, and then—last, because it was the last country to surrender to the Unification—Occupied America.

The historical accident that had led to Capitol City being placed in Manhattan, surrounding the ancient United Nations buildings, often bemused Ripper. Sarah Almundsen had probably thought it would be a gesture of healing toward the conquered American republic; even now, fifty years later, it was simply a reminder that they had *been* conquered.

Ripper would have put Capitol City in orbit, himself. Given a choice.

At the speed things were going, Ripper expected to reach the podium sometime around nine or ten the following morning.

Occasionally other Councilors came by and spoke with Ripper, asking or offering favors; one, a relatively young first-term

Councilor from Chile, was actually considering breaking away from her bloc and voting with Ripper on what she claimed were moral grounds. Ripper had spoken with her at length in the privacy of her office, just the night prior. He tended to think she was sincere, and found it both sad and rather grimly amusing. If she made the mistake and voted with him, this would be her last term in the Council; her own people would vote her out of office pretty quick.

Though he had attempted to persuade her to vote with him—that was *his* job—a part of him hoped she would vote against. Councilors capable of entertaining ethical considerations in their voting—even if they chose to ignore the considerations—were a rarity. It would be pleasant to have another one in the Council.

Toward dinner Ichabod came in through the main entrance, carrying a boxed dinner with him, and made his slow way down through the descending rows of tables, to the next-to-innermost circle facing the podium, where Ripper's table sat.

Ripper popped the stasis bubble and examined what he'd been brought. Not bad; largish shrimp on brown rice, pasta salad, orange juice. He ate while listening to Ichabod.

"There is, so far, no evidence that the Rebs are involved at all. It looks to be pretty much just the Japanese."

Ripper grunted. "Don't count on it. It's not the Fourth yet. Let's see if we get through tomorrow."

"Spacecraft used in the attacks on the laser cannon were primarily Collective, troops primarily Japanese; maybe a few private craft, maybe a few Rebs and Claw, but no confirmation on either point. Collective PR issued a statement denying involvement, said that the craft involved were renegades."

"Of course."

"It might be true, Councilor. Your average SpaceFarer will do anything for a Credit."

Ripper nodded, chewing. "Probably is true. It's not a good call for the Collective to get involved in this. But it won't change the damage it does them with the Unification."

"Fighting is ongoing; want a list of what they've used the laser cannon on?"

"No. Still military targets?"

"So far. Mostly ports; Unification Spaceport is a *bad* place to be right now. They've shot down about thirty Space Force craft as they took off, another dozen incoming. No cities yet, though the Japanese are saying Paris first, and then Capitol City. Space Force is targeting Hiroshima."

Ripper drank his orange juice in one long pull. "How wonderfully symbolic. Let's hope neither side decides to start shooting at civilians until after the voting is over. That'd screw us good."

"Fighting is cannon to cannon, and we're taking them back, but it's slowed down a lot. We've stopped using Elite in the attacks."

Ripper looked up. *"Really?"*

"The pumped lasers they're using *work,*" said Ichabod quietly. "Nine Elite dead so far. The PKF have pulled out their Elite, Commissioner Vance's call apparently. Space Force is on its own as of about an hour ago. And another thing—"

"Yes?"

"They recovered one of the bodies, at one of the cannon they took back. A Japanese cyborg."

Ripper scowled. "Damn. That's very bad. They think we're winning right now—"

"We are."

"—but if they think we're even *struggling* upstairs we're going to have a lot of undecided voting go over to Eddore."

"I'm surprised the voting's so close," Ichabod commented. "This is *such* a blatant power grab on Eddore's part."

"Most of the world doesn't have democratic traditions to speak of, Ichabod. Certainly not three hundred years' worth. To them this simply looks like good business; it makes Eddore look strong. How generally is this business upstairs known?"

"So far, not very. I only got it because of your position on the Oversite Committee; apparently Vance has decided you're an ally."

Ripper chuckled sourly. "Today."

"Last item, I don't know how much faith to place in this; apparently the PKF are planning an assault directly on Japan as soon as the laser cannon are taken out. Or maybe before, if Commissioner Vance gets his way; clearly Mirabeau is all that's holding him back right now."

Ripper pushed his dinner aside, sat back in his chair, and watched the Unification Ambassador from Sri Lanka speak in favor of a truce that no one, on either side, was going to offer.

•   •   •

Even with all of Ripper's pleading to move things along, voting went slowly. About 10:00 P.M. Ripper left; his bodyguards, John and Bruce, picked him up at the exit, and followed a few steps behind him as he went down a level to the small Chamber office set aside for his use. He rolled out the cot to take a nap, and was asleep in seconds. He awoke around 2:30 A.M., shaved and showered in the office's small bathroom, and dressed in the suit that had been laid out for him. He knocked back two cups of coffee, waited, and when it did not rouse him sufficiently went into his bathroom and took two ephedrine tablets, and then headed back upstairs.

It had gone dramatically slower during his absence; people had been giving speeches for the holocams. Only a little better than half of the Unification Councilors had voted. So far voting was running 168–151, in favor of declaring martial law. Ripper was not perturbed; it was the nature of the beast that most of the strongly pro-Unification Councilors voted first. To be behind by only seventeen votes after 319 Councilors had voted was two or three votes better than he had expected.

The Council tables were a quarter empty; many of those who had voted had left, returned to their offices, or gone off to nap. Still, for just after 3:00 A.M., it was easily as busy as on any normal day. Even now the air of frantic urgency had subsided only slightly; Councilors stood clustered in groups, murmuring voices establishing a gentle background susurration against which all else took place.

Ripper stopped, spoke briefly with several of his allies, and returned to his table. His holos, turned off while he was gone, automatically relit at his approach, and hovered in the air off to his right and his left.

NewsBoard looked interesting, a map of near-Earth space. He turned on his earphone, listened to the excited babble of voice, was aware of the slight reduction of background noise, throughout the Chamber, as others did the same.

"*. . . there are sixteen Relay Stations, most of them small units called talk-to-me's; apparently only the large InfoNet Relay Station at Halfway, protected by a group of Space Force commandos, is still secure. Most of the balance of the—*"

The map of near-Earth space shown on *NewsBoard* suddenly vanished, as did the voice of the announcer. It was replaced by the image of a clean-shaven, fit-looking middle-aged man wearing what Ripper vaguely tagged as "military" clothing. The man did not look into the holocams for several seconds; he was apparently still setting up, turning on a handheld that was just visible in the holofield. A patch of blurriness in the holofield—*bloody amateur*, Ripper thought—showed where the handheld's field established itself.

As the man looked up into the holocams, his image abruptly appeared in the *Electronic Times* holofield next to it; and a moment after that, in the feed from the Council Chamber itself.

Ripper barely had time to notice the man's stiff features, characteristic of a PKF Elite of some twenty years ago, before the skin treatments had been improved to allow PKF more facial expressiveness. The thought flickered through his mind briefly, in a bright confused flash—*PKF Elite, did we take back the Relay Stations* already?—and then the man spoke. "I am the representative of the united Erisian Claw and Johnny Rebs. Today we have taken a step—" The Elite's voice was drowned out in Ripper's earphone, underneath a growing wave of noise from the assembled Councilors. The man spoke several sentences that Ripper could not hear at all; Ripper yelled at the top of his lungs, *"Shut up!"*

The babble died slowly; Ripper pumped up the volume on his earphone to its highest volume and the voice of the man in the holofield grew audible again:

"—complete control of the Halfway InfoNet Relay Station, and all supporting Relay Stations. A fierce battle is being fought, even as we speak, for the laser cannon platforms. We have reinforced our Japanese allies, and before the day is out we expect to have the cannon entirely in our hands." The man paused. "We have chosen this day and this time to bring you this message. My name is Christian J. Summers, and I was once a Peaceforcer Elite. Today I am a member of the Johnny Rebs, an associate of the Erisian Claw; and today, in a meeting of the banned United States Congress, the following resolution was approved for release."

Ripper knew what was coming; surely most of those in the Council Chambers had to. Nonetheless the knowledge did not prevent the sudden fierce chill that ran down his spine, the prickling of the hairs at the back of his neck.

It was 3:10 A.M., just after midnight on the West Coast; for them, the first moments of the TriCentennial. Christian J. Summers spoke in measured cadence, solemnly, words carrying to all of Earth, broadcast beyond Earth to the rest of the Solar System:

"In Congress, July 4th, 2076. The unanimous Declaration of these unlawfully occupied United States of America:

"When in the Course of human Events, it becomes necessary for one People to dissolve the Political Bands that have connected them . . ."

This time the roar of sound grew until Ripper, standing motionless and watching Christian Summers speak, could not hear a word though the volume control on his earphone was pumped all the way up.

Ripper found himself coming to his feet, stood motionless, and watched Summers speak. In his heart was an utter emptiness, a complete absence of feeling. He had once been a United States Senator, and he would until his death be an American at the very core of his person.

But in the bravery shown by Christian Summers, in the slow reading of what newsdancers would, in half an hour, be calling the Second Declaration of Independence, Douglass Ripper saw nothing but disaster.

After a while he turned and made his slow, solitary way from the Chamber. No one tried to stop him, no one spoke to him as he left; virtually no one even noticed him leaving.

He knew the words by heart; though he could no longer hear Summers' voice, could no longer even hear the noise of the Chamber, the somber phrases rolled on through his awareness.

That to secure these Rights, Governments are instituted among Men, deriving their just Powers from the Consent of the Governed . . .

Ripper did not realize that tears were running down his cheeks. He knew only that he could not remember having felt such vast pain since his mother's death, nearly twenty years prior.

That whenever any Form of Government becomes destructive of these Ends, it is the Right of the People to alter or to abolish it . . .

Douglass Ripper sat down abruptly, sat at the base of the stairs leading up to the Chamber, and in front of thirty Peaceforcers and half a hundred newsdancer spyeyes, buried his face in his hands and through his tears whispered to himself, "Oh, God. You stupid fucks."

"We are *out* of here."

"Whaa?"

It was Trent, fresh clown makeup applied, a sad face this time, rousing me from where I slept at my desk. He was grinning at me. "Wake up, Neil. Time to go."

The briefcase with the gold was next to my desk. I said groggily, "What's happening?"

"Rebs just declared independence. Twenty minutes ago. And we got attacked by a group of Rebs who clearly had no idea that Space Force was protecting the Halfway Relay Station—"

"Wait—"

"We made noises like a couple of battalions, exploded a nuke close enough to them to scare them a bit—"

"*What's the hurry?*"

"Eddore," said Trent impatiently, "has what he needs. Japan rose, the U.S. is rising, he'll get the martial law he wants. Now he can send *real* Space Force in to protect the InfoNet Relay Station, and he doesn't have to worry about the Rebs not rising, 'cause they already have. Clear?"

"He doesn't need you anymore."

"*Need me?*" Trent laughed aloud. "As of twenty minutes ago I'm the most dangerous enemy he has left. Come on, Neil, grab your gold and let's get out of here."

Trent wasn't kidding; his Collective crew was boarding the *Lew Alton*, moving at an easy trot, when Trent and I, the really big clown right behind us, passed through Lock Ten on the way to Marc's private yacht. We stopped at the yacht's airlock. "Somebody's going to go let Marc out, aren't they?"

Trent blinked. The big clown loomed behind him. "Sure. I mean, eventually. I suppose."

"I can't leave him in jail for Space Force to find him. That's not—"

"Sure you can," Trent said briskly. "You don't have time to

do anything else, your yacht is leaving in four minutes. And I have less time than *that*."

I took a deep breath. "Okay. Thank you—I think."

"You're welcome." Trent the Uncatchable's voice softened. "Good luck. It's not easy being a legend, is it?"

"No. I never really got used to it myself. And you're going to have it worse."

"I know." He shrugged, changed the subject. "I'm sorry I couldn't be of more help, but I have no time." He paused a second, a distant expression flickering across his face. "Here they come. Space Force is on its way already. We're going to have us a chase for sure; you might. We'd probably be dodging laser fire from the *Unity* all the way back to Venus if I hadn't knocked out their weapons control last night."

I simply stared at him. "You took out the *Unity*'s laser cannon?"

"No, just the targeting mechanisms."

"How did you—"

Trent grinned at me. "Monofilament fineline. It's a neat trick, I'll tell you all about it someday."

"You are the most amazing person I've ever met "

Trent blinked. "A Peaceforcer said that to me once. Then he tried to kill me. Good-bye, Neil." Trent turned away without looking back; the big clown paused a moment.

"Just 'amazing'?" It was the first time I ever remember hearing anybody call Trent the Uncatchable this, and I think the big clown who did it was joking. "Don't you know? The man is God." The clown grinned at me. Trent was gone, out of sight around the corridor bend. "Have a good flight."

Jay and Shell were inside the yacht, snakechained to the seats.

They *both* glared at me as I strapped into the pilot's seat and stowed my briefcase in the webbing beneath it. "He couldn't very well leave you behind, now could he? And you certainly didn't want to go with *him*, Shell in particular, I imagine."

Neither of them said a thing. Couldn't, really, with their mouths taped shut.

I'm not much of a pilot; I pulled up Trent's reentry path, scanned the quick and slow versions, and said, "Command, *launch*. Let's go home."

The shipcomp said quietly, in Trent the Uncatchable's voice, "Launching. Someday again, Neil Corona."

The rockets kicked me in the back.

No one came after us, and shortly Earth's horizon opened up and swallowed us.

- 18 -

Three *days* at Halfway, cooped up with a group of totally humorless SpaceFarers, sharing a cabin with F.X. Chandler, who, for all he might have been a wild "heavy metal" musician once an infinity ago, was today a fucking old man and kept acting like it.

Early on the morning of July the Fourth, the TriCentennial, a young black man in civilian clothes—black jeans, magslips, a T-shirt with a holo of the singer Mahliya Kutura on it—came for Jimmy. "You're Jimmy Ramirez, aren't you?"

Chandler was asleep in the other bed, webbed in, floatchair folded up at his side. Jimmy looked up at the opening of his cabin door. "Yeah. Who are you?"

"Do you want to come up to the bridge with me? We're leaving orbit in a couple of minutes and I think you might find it interesting."

Jimmy shrugged. "Sure."

"Great." The man raised his voice. " 'Sieur Chandler?"

The old man stirred, sat up, and said in a rusty voice, "Yeah?"

"We're boosting in five minutes. It'll be announced, but you'll want to be awake for it."

Chandler nodded, spoke around a yawn. "Okay. Thanks."

"In case we go above three gees, you know how to use your stasis bubble?"

"Yes. Thank you."

On the way up to the bridge—a trip in itself, the ship was large—the young man kept *looking* at Jimmy. Finally, in annoyance, Jimmy said, "The answer is *no*."

"What was the question?"

"You're gay, right?"

"Well, no. I mean, not very." The young man seemed to consider it. "I don't think so."

"What the hell are you *looking* at?"

The young man glided steadily forward, magslip-covered feet drifting bare centimeters over the deck. Jimmy had the feeling that he could have moved much faster if he had not had to wait for Jimmy, hampered as he was by both an unfamiliar prosthesis and free fall. The man glanced at Jimmy yet again. "Been a while, my man. You've put on some weight, lost some muscle." He chuckled. "Become a *lawyer*. Want to hear a *good* joke?"

Jimmy shook his head. "Look, I don't know you and I don't—" and then his voice trailed off.

His guide glided to a stop at the entrance to the bridge, and turned around to face Jimmy. "Don't you?"

Jimmy had to put a hand out to the bulkhead to stop his progress; he was learning to dislike free fall. After he bounced off the wall once he managed to get himself turned around, facing the black man. "What?"

"Scenes like this," the man said, "should be played under gravity. So that you can run in slow motion down the beach. It's kind of hard to do in free fall. Actually."

For a long moment Jimmy did not breathe at all. He thought his heart had stopped. "Is—Trent?"

The impossible brown eyes held him. "Want to go share a blanket and find out?"

"You—*Trent?*"

"Not that you were any good."

Jimmy Ramirez said slowly, "I've had better, myself."

"Hey, bro. I'd give you a hug or something, but you used to have problems with that."

Jimmy Ramirez stared at him, then stepped forward, wrapped Trent in a bear hug, and whispered fiercely in his ear, "My man."

The bridge door curled aside. The woman who stepped through, elderly and white-haired, in a Collective uniform with a patch that said Captain Saunders, said mildly, "Sweet. But you're blocking the door."

Jimmy let go of Trent abruptly, left Trent drifting in midair. Trent grinned at Jimmy, grabbed the frame of the door and pushed himself back into contact with the deck, and went inside to the bridge.

Jimmy Ramirez followed, aware that everyone on the bridge was watching them as they entered.

It is virtually impossible for even a light-brown-skinned man to blush convincingly. Jimmy Ramirez managed it.

"They're the cheap seats," Trent commented, "but they're still the best in the house if you're a civilian."

They had strapped into a pair of seats off to the far right of a rather largish bridge. At least Jimmy thought it was a large bridge; he didn't have much to compare with.

"Large," Trent said briefly in response to his question. "Everything about the ship is. Crew of thirty-five, passenger capability of about two hundred fifty. And *fast*, though she doesn't look it; chameleon polypaint, radar quiet, the works. We're going to need it all; there's a Space Force task force headed for us; left L-Four about sixteen minutes ago. Space Force is boosting at three gees. If they put all their people in stasis bubbles—and they *will* have them on board—they can get up to fifteen."

"We're going to boost out of here at *fifteen gees*?"

"No, of course not," Trent said mildly. "This is a civilian ship. We don't have nearly enough stasis bubbles to do something like that. We have to arrange to get lost instead. A Collective escort is waiting for us at Venus, but first we have to *make* Venus. Then we'll slingshot in around the sun, and then head for the Belt."

"But first we have to get away from Earth-Luna."

The Captain returned, moved forward to her seat. "That's the general idea, 'Sieur Ramirez. Now, if you please, will both of you shut up?"

Trent held a finger up to his lips, whispered in a stage whisper, "She means it."

Captain Saunders did not glance at Trent. "*Command*, outspeakers." Her voice boomed out across the length of the ship. "BOOST IN TEN SECONDS, NINE HUNDRED EIGHTY CENTIMETERS PER SECOND SQUARED. THAT'S ONE GEE TO DOWNSIDERS. SUCK IT IN."

Gravity came up slowly; suddenly forward was *up*. It took a couple seconds to reach full boost. In the viewholos, the vast bulk of Halfway seemed to drift slowly away, to their left.

Jimmy's earphone came alive. Trent's voice; not *this* voice, which had a deeper timbre, but the tenor he remembered from their childhood. "*Really* don't talk *until we're out of danger*;

he'll get seriously upset. She has no sense of humor. Of course :paceFarers don't."

The viewholo split into three separate perspectives; behind them, Halfway fell away, slowly turning from a mass that covered half the sky, to something that was merely as large as the Earth; and then smaller yet. Before them, an optically enhanced image showed five bright sparks against a star-speckled background. *"Space Force; the task force that's going to try :hasing us."*

Jimmy glanced over at Trent, found Trent staring at the viewfields, a faint grin playing across his lips, coming and going; clearly vastly entertained. *"This is my favorite part,"* Trent said. *"Please accept my apologies now in case we die doing :his."*

The third segment of the holofield showed a map, not to scale, of the Earth-Luna system. Their ship was a bright yellow triangle, moving away from a stylized Earth that was being devoured by a swarm of gnats. Bright red patches marked the remains of destroyed ships; the map showed eight. Green dots were laser cannon, about forty of them; blue dots were craft whose beacons identified them as Space Force. There were no rebel craft shown in the field; that was to be expected. It didn't mean there were no rebel craft in orbit—highly unlikely—merely that the rebels wouldn't be identifying themselves to anyone who asked.

Toward the far edge of the map holo, five blue arrows moved slowly toward the *Lew Alton.* Luna, L-4, and L-5 were visible. *"They'll have realized by now that we're moving away from Halfway. In another minute or two they'll realize where we're headed."*

Jimmy lifted an eyebrow.

Trent grinned at him. *"L-Five. Peaceforcer Heaven."*

"Very strange behavior, of course. They're pretty sure who we are, the SpaceFarers who've been pretending to be Space Force." Trent shrugged. *"They do have the same initials. Start with the same word yet. You'd think that one of them would have sued the other by now. Trademark infringement or something. So anyway, we're Bad Guys. But we're heading toward Spacebase One, PKF territory. Why? Why, oh why? Can you guess?"*

Jimmy shook his head.

"We're going to hide behind it for most of a second, if things work out. Also it's confusing. The folks at L-Four won't understand it at all. We're Bad Guys, but we're not running. Maybe we're not Bad Guys, maybe we're Good Guys. Or innocent bystanders. We're heading toward Spacebase One; maybe we're Peaceforcers? What could possibly be going on?" Trent chuckled aloud, got a glare from the Captain. "Look at the holo, Jimmy."

In the central panel of the viewholo, the dwindling image of Halfway vanished. In its place a holo of the Lew Alton appeared. "Now, this is the interesting thing about the Lew Alton. It looks normal enough, landing fins, needle nose, silver hull for heat dissipation, obviously intended for use in atmosphere; but it uses mass drivers instead of a torch, and the silver on the hull is a mirror that can be turned off." Three long, slender tubes ran down the length of the ship, flaring open at each end. "The mass drivers boost in both directions too. The Lew Alton can accelerate and brake without undergoing turnover; you just change the direction of thrust through the mass drivers."

The viewfield returned to its prior view. "We're mildly stupid, we don't know yet that there's a bunch of badass Space Force commandos headed our way. Now we're sweeping with radar, really ugly radar signature, we had to make up a special radar antenna to get it: boop, boop, boop, boop, boop. Wait, what's this? On our radar we get back the signature of five Space Force craft headed our way. Now we get a little scared and we check it out, maybe our radar's not very sensitive, so we sweep them again, a signal so loud it's like we're shouting in their face. Damn, we're amateurs. Stoopid stoopid.

"Now we're thinking it over. Should we run away?"

"Outspeakers," said Captain Saunders. "PREPARE FOR TURNOVER IN TEN SECONDS."

"Wait, what's this? The ship full of Bad Guys is going into turnover!"

Thrust ceased, and the ship hung in free fall for several seconds before beginning a long, slow, 180-degree tumble. The bridge seemed to twitch; it made the muscles in Jimmy's stomach twitch in sympathy. "The bridge floats free inside the ship; all the passenger compartments do, and they turn to face into the direction of thrust. Otherwise you could end up hanging on your seat belt at eight gees."

It took most of a minute before the ship had completely

urned around. The Captain's voice: "THREE THOUSAND CEPSSA IN TEN SECONDS."

"Now we're panicking," Trent announced. *"Turning tail and running away."*

After a brief pause, Captain Saunders said in a conversational voice, "There they go. They just"—She fell briefly silent as acceleration kicked up to three gees—"just pumped it up to ifteen gees acceleration."

"Trent?"

"Hang tight, Jimmy. They'll figure it out in a bit, and when hey do, they'll probably send missiles."

Jimmy said very quietly, "I don't understand."

"They can't catch us now. We're running toward them, but hey think we're running away; they're so far away from us all hey could make out by telescope was the fact that we went hrough turnover. So right now we're accelerating toward each other; shortly they're going to notice that the Doppler signature on our radar is wrong. It might be a bit before that happens, hey might notice real soon."

Four minutes passed. Five. Six. The silence on the bridge was thick with shared tension.

One of the crew said, "They just cut acceleration."

"They just realized. They're never going to catch us now; they've already picked up so much velocity that by the time they've gone through turnover, decelerated to zero, and headed back after us, we'll be having tea at Venus. The only chance they have is to send missiles after us. If they do that right now we're in bad shape, so first we try and talk them into chasing us some more." Trent grinned cheek to cheek, said aloud, "Captain, have they beamcast to us?"

"Not yet."

"Can I get a maser to them?"

Captain Saunders nodded. "Go ahead; we're beaming."

Trent said, "This is the Collective Ship *Lew Alton*, commanding officer Captain Hera Saunders. To the Space Force craft chasing us, hello."

Three seconds pause, the lightspeed delay from L-4 to near-Earth. "Captain Saunders, this is Colonel Jurgen Hanhela of the United Nations Space Force. Cease your acceleration and stand by to be boarded, or we will destroy you."

"You're not speaking to Captain Saunders, Colonel."

He took the bait: "To whom *am* I speaking?"

"Trent," said Trent. "Trent the Uncatchable."

Dead silence from the other end.

"Give it your best shot, sucker." Trent made a cutting gesture, and after a moment said, "Well? If they stop and think about it, they won't do it."

Saunders nodded. "I know. If—" The old woman abruptly laughed. "Idiots! *They're going into turnover!*"

"A chance to catch the Uncatchable," Trent whispered. "They *know* they're faster than us; how could they possibly resist?"

In the holofield, the sparks showing the fusion rockets of the five craft had abruptly relit.

"All right," said Captain Saunders. "Outspeakers. IMPACT FIELDS COMING UP; SIX THOUSAND CEPSSA IN TEN SECONDS."

They passed the task force, which was still decelerating, doing four hundred thousand klicks an hour. By the time the task force had killed its forward velocity, they were three-quarters of the way to Spacebase One at L-5, and moving at a good speed.

Jimmy Ramirez, struggling for breath against slightly better than six gees acceleration, found it difficult to follow Trent's voice. *"We'll be out of their line of sight for all of about a second. We're going to buzz Spacebase One at about fifty klicks distance; as soon as we're past it, during that second they can't see us because of Spacebase One's bulk, we're going to go dead. The hull paint goes black, the mass drivers shut down, the radar antenna with the ugly signature gets shipped away on a beacon, giving away the odd boop or two to betray its position. When they do send the missles—and they will—they send them after the beacon. We hope."*

Jimmy Ramirez, fighting for air, did not make the mistake of trying to nod.

Space Force sent their missiles while the *Lew Alton* was still three minutes away from L-5. The missiles chased the Collective craft at 150 gees.

The ship passed Spacebase One, with the missiles gaining on it. It happened nearly instantaneously; free fall, blackness, all at once; the immense weight lifted itself off Jimmy

Ramirez's chest, and he found himself floating gently in his acceleration chair.

He heard the distant clang of the beacon disengaging from the ship.

Trent's voice: "Captain, how long until impact?"

In the absolute darkness, the woman's voice seemed to echo in Jimmy's ears. "Not less than one minute, no more than one and a half."

"Jimmy, you okay?"

"Yeah."

"Good. Okay. So these three lawyers are zooming along a country road and they get into an accident with a gravedigger. So the gravedigger pulls himself out of his car and he's okay, but the lawyers are kind of messed up, so he buries them, right there, and walks into town and calls the Sheriff. 'Sheriff,' he says, 'terrible accident I just had. Three lawyers in it, they was all dead, so I buried them.' Sheriff says, 'What? You went ahead and buried them already? Are you *sure* they was dead?' Gravedigger says reluctantly, 'Well, they said they wasn't, but you know how those fellas lie.'"

Jimmy stared into the darkness. "I forgot you told these sorts of jokes. Now I remember why—"

Weightlessness.

Quiet.

Jimmy Ramirez returned to consciousness slowly, the tang of blood in his mouth.

His head throbbed.

Dim, gentle illumination, of glowpaint set low, lit the bridge around them.

Trent, at his side, said, "Now you remember why what?"

"Huh?"

Trent held up a hand. "How many fingers?"

"Eight. What happened?"

"Something banged you in the head, I'm not sure what. Some things came loose in the blast."

"Did we get away?"

"Yeah. I thought we would. Space Force nosed around for a bit, but they couldn't find us, cold black hulk that we are. And somewhat off course from their own missiles, that didn't hurt. They turned back and went home about half an hour ago; right about now they're boasting to half the System that they blew up Trent the Uncatchable. They're going to be real embarrassed tomorrow. How many fingers?"

"Uh—five?"

"Better. We'll give it a bit, and then, when we're sure it's safe,
we'll fire up the mass drivers and correct course for Venus."

"Did we lose anybody?"

"Almost."

"Who?"

"You. If whatever hit you had hit a little lower, it probably
would have snapped your neck instead of just giving you a concussion."

"Oh."

"Aside from you, not too bad. Some broken bones, sprains,
like that. What usually happens when a tin can gets shaken up.
When the medbot is done setting bones it'll be up here for you."

"Hanging around with you genies," said Jimmy slowly, "is
not safe."

"The concussion's not bad; and we'll stop off at Mars to get
you a new foot. Nice hospitals at Mars, maybe you'll like it
there."

"Do you?"

Trent was silent a moment. "Well, no. It can be real hard to
find good places to go dancing."

"How about the Belt?"

"Better. There's some nice stuff in the Belt. Nothing like
New York, but—" Trent shrugged. "Nice. Mahliya Kutura lives
out there. She's seriously nice. And only a little crazy."

"You miss Earth?"

Trent said, "Yes. And so will you."

Jimmy spoke around the throbbing in his head. "I suppose
I'll get used to it."

Trent said simply, "We'll be back."

- 19 -

At 8:15 on the morning of July the Fourth, Mohammed Vance
sat alone, in the darkness of his office half a klick below the
surface of Capitol City, and studied holos.

They had lost all of Japan; most of Greater Los Angeles was
in rebel hands. Insurrections were scattered across the length

of Occupied America, from Miami up through Maine on the East Coast, throughout the Midwest, and from Portland to Ensenada on the West Coast; but the clear focus of the rebel efforts was California. Sensible; it was what Vance had expected, the way Vance would have structured it himself. The lack of mandatory Automated Traffic Control in Los Angeles gave the rebels a clear advantage; it was no surprise that they'd overrun L.A. County so quickly. The rebels clearly knew where their advantages were; PKF targets first, and then TransCon.

They'd been losing ATC cells all morning. Most of Ventura County was lost to TransCon, and cells up and down the coast were dropping off the grid.

The PKF armories in Los Angeles and Sacramento were in Reb hands; fighting in San Francisco, the home of the State Governor General, was going badly. The spysats showed that *something* was going on at Navajo Spaceport. Vance did not know what, as it was impossible to get ahold of anybody out there. He must assume that Navajo Spaceport, as well as LAX, was in enemy hands.

And upstairs, rebels still had almost half the laser cannon; since being resupplied by the Johnny Rebs, shipping up out of LAX, the Japanese holding the remaining cannon had dug in, and Space Force had been reclaiming the cannon ever more slowly. In the last eight hours, only one.

It was almost true, as the rebels claimed, that they had taken over the chain of InfoNet Relay Stations. Apparently the Halfway Relay Station alone was controlled by Space Force; Vance did not know who in Space Force had had the foresight to take that step, but when this was over he would find out, and thank the man personally. His job, difficult now, would have been made more so if the InfoNet had gone down.

DataWatch might not have minded; Vance had seen their contingency plans. But DataWatch was only a small part of the PKF, and Vance could not find it in him to much regret DataWatch's missed opportunity.

Messy, Vance concluded, but it could have been far worse. Even when the rebels started directing laser cannon against civilian targets—and they would, for Vance would have in their place—the damage would be within acceptable limits.

At 8:30 A.M. his systerm announced a call. It was the officer from Internal Affairs. Vance listened without interrupting the man, said finally, "Well done," and rose from behind his desk. "*Command,* mirror on." He checked his appearance in the mirror: a tall man with black Elite eyes, wearing the gray of PKF combat fatigues, the uniform of the Unification War. He would be the only one in Strategic Planning who would be dressed so, and it should send a message.

He walked without hurry down the bustling corridors toward Strategic Planning, entered Planning, and moved down toward the podium at the far end of the room. The gentle murmur of voices quieted slightly at his appearance, quieted a bit more when he ascended to the podium.

Most of those present were gathered around the tactical table in the center of the room, which showed a three-dimensional map of Earth and near-Earth space. Four Commissionaires present, Vance noted, three of them senior to him, all of them older; he was still quite young for a Commissionaire, only forty-seven.

At forty he had been, by four years, the youngest Commissionaire in PKF history.

"Officers," said Vance quietly, not waiting for the babble to die down. "This afternoon, at three o'clock, we will boost from Unification Spaceport. Before four o'clock we will be dropping, via semiballistic, into the city of Santa Monica. We will proceed eastward down Wilshire Boulevard, securing the city as we go, until we have passed completely through Los Angeles. We will commit our entire forces to this operation; all troops, all support personnel, all carriers, all semiballistics, all laser cannon that Space Force has recovered. We have twenty-three hundred Elite who can be reassigned on such short notice; all *will* be reassigned. Plans for the attack will be distributed before nine A.M. By noon I want your written responses delivered to my office, expressing any reservations you may have concerning the course of action."

By the time he was done speaking complete silence had fallen throughout Strategic Planning. Commissionaire Rouen, senior of the Commissionaires present, broke the silence. "That's not according to the plans, Mohammed. We are going to do a slow roll down from the north—"

"Indeed it is not according to the plans," said Vance. "I am changing them."

The woman shook her head, seemed almost amused. "Christine won't allow it, Mohammed. These plans have been laid for most of a month."

Vance did not raise his voice. "Elite Commander Christine Mirabeau," said Mohammed Vance, "was arrested for treason against the Unification at eight twenty-two this morning." To their stunned silence, he said, "I want written responses by noon. You'd best get to work."

He left abruptly.

Christian J. Summers floated in black space, laser cradled in his arms, a tether attaching him to the bulk of the InfoNet Relay Station at his back.

Awaiting the arrival of the Space Force troops.

He was about to die, and he knew it.

Earth glowed blue and white beneath his feet. Arrayed around him were fifteen other Johnny Rebs, tucked into the shadow (such as it was with full Earth beneath them) on the side of the Relay Station facing away from the sun. A tight fit; the Relay Station was only a talk-to-me, one of the smaller and older stations.

They were all Rebs; he had taken no Claw with him on this mission, only men and women he had known and trusted for many years. Now he regretted it. It would have hurt less if he had dragged a group of strangers to their deaths. According to the plan, they should have been picked up a good two hours ago. Clearly something had gone wrong with the plan. He did not even know what; only that the Halfway Relay Station had not gone down along with the rest. The ship that was supposed to come get them was the same ship that had been slotted to deliver the Halfway Relay Station task force.

They could have tried to head back on the HuskySleds they'd come in, but the sleds were not fast, and would only take them back to their staging point at Halfway's Edge.

Summers knew they would never make it back to the Edge. Space Force would destroy their sleds on the way back. Their only hope for survival lay in returning to Earth before Space Force arrived; and to do that, they needed pickup.

But pickup was two hours late, and he was certain now that it would not come.

Half an hour ago he'd lit the rockets on the sleds, and sent them down toward Earth below them; one fewer sign of their presence.

"Chris?"

The voice in his ears was that of Janna Anderson, the daughter of two of his oldest friends. He was glad he would die with her, and not have to face her parents with her death on his hands. "Yes?"

She pointed. "Look."

Summers followed her gesture. Nothing but stars—

Half a dozen stars winked out. Summers followed the patch of blackness moving across the emptiness. "Okay. This is it, my friends. They're coming in black, with their drive dead. If we're lucky the lack of the sleds will fool them into believing we've packed up and moved on." It was a mistake he would not have made himself, and despite his contempt for Space Force, did not expect from them. The talk-to-me's heat-exchange radiators got rid of heat acquired from sunlight; the radiators were, of course, on the satellite's shady side, away from the sun, along with the Rebs. The radiators might prevent Space Force from acquiring an IR image; deep radar would be useless against the backdrop of the Relay Station's metal. Visible light would be Space Force's best bet.

The blackness loomed larger, blocked out more and more stars as the ship approached. Now it was close enough Chris Summers could see the bright sharp bursts of its small maneuvering rockets. "Rifles ready—"

The ship came closer yet, slowing as it approached. *I will be damned,* Chris Summers thought, *they don't know we're here. We might get to take some of them with us.*

The airlock door, barely visible at the distance, cycled open, a bright yellow light in the side of the dark black spaceship. Two figures cycled through, the airlock's maximum capacity; then another two; another two. After a brief pause, the six oriented themselves on the Relay Station; the backpacks on their pressure suits lit.

Chris Summers said quietly into his helmet radio, "First these six; then the ship itself. Fire at the airlock, the antennae, maneuvering rockets, any sort of protrusion on the surface of the craft. Maybe we can inconvenience them a bit. On Four. Three. Two. One."

In vacuum lasers give no light.

Bright red spots appeared on the surface of the six approaching p-suits. Armored scalesuits; Summers had expected it. The dots wavered, crawled over the surface of the suits. One dot touched a faceplate, and the faceplate burst outward in a shower of glassite and flesh.

One of the six figures got its rifle up in time to fire back once. Summers had no idea where the beam struck; a pair of red dots on the figure's scalesuit converged and punched through the armor.

Most of the firing ceased.

Six corpses floated in space.

"On the ship, *now*," Summers barked. He had his own rifle up, aimed at one of the places he remembered seeing a maneuvering rocket, pulled the trigger and held it down. If they could damage the ship badly enough, a rebel ship might finish it off before it made it back to safety; though he had no idea exactly where, Summers knew there were Reb craft in the vicinity, resupplying the Japanese cyborgs who had taken over the laser cannon.

Red dots wandered over the surface of the ship, seeking targets; one smart Reb, Summers briefly wondered who, set his laser for its widest beam and played it over the hull like a ruby searchlight. Summers found he had been shooting a spot half a meter away from the maneuvering rocket, adjusted his own aim as a result.

The Unification warship began turning, rotating slowly. None of the rockets had lit; the Space Forcers had realized what was happening to their maneuvering rockets, were using gyroscopes to avoid giving away the locations of the other rockets. Summers followed his target around until the ship's roll had taken it from him, looked for another—*That'll do,* he thought, as the missile battery came around on them.

His companions had the same thought; sixteen different dots of red light converged on the missiles in very nearly the same instant. Another beam widened out to something the width of a basketball, and the Reb waved it over the missiles. A brief flash of pride touched the old cyborg; the Reb was going after their optics, and was probably taking them out. If they'd been just a few hundred meters farther away, the lack of optics on the missiles might have made a difference.

But they were too close. The missile did not need to correct course for a target so close to it. It detonated not far from the center of their group.

The world tumbled around Chris Summers.

He was spinning fast enough that he could actually feel some weight at his head and feet.

Chris Summers watched Earth pass by his faceplate, about

once every second. He closed his eyes after a while because the sight was making him dizzy.

He floated in the darkness, remembering the people he had loved in his life. It did not take long; they were few enough. The two he had felt closest to as an adult, Jacqueline de Nostri and Carl Castanaveras, had been dead for fourteen years now, and though he had adjusted to their loss, he had never quite taken the same pleasure in life again.

When he opened his eyes, Earth seemed to have grown slightly larger. Was it possible he might survive long enough to hit the atmosphere?

He closed his eyes again. What a vast irony that would be. He had deserted from the Elite by faking his death in a semiballistic accident; on a cold day in 2056, he had boarded a semiballistic in India. A Japanese bioelectronics team from Mitsubishi had met him in orbit, and together they had sent the SB back down to Earth in flaming pieces.

When he opened his eyes for the last time, Earth was definitely larger.

Death by friction. There was a dirty joke he'd heard about that, as a young man; something about dying during reentry.

Not the way, thought Chris Summers calmly, *I want to go.*

There is only one really simple way to kill an Elite, and it requires help from the Elite. Chris Summers used it. His rifle was gone; unfortunate, it was far more powerful than the laser in his fist. It would have made it easier. He unsnapped the glove at his right wrist, pulled it free, held his hand out as far from his face as he could, and smashed out the faceplate on his helmet. He misjudged slightly; he slammed his hand into the reinforced bridge of his nose as the air rushed free of his suit.

The middle knuckle of his right hand dented slightly.

Vacuum did not bother him much; a slight tingling sensation, distantly perceptible, on the false skin. His eyes were a mechanism; they barely noticed the drop in pressure. Only the abrupt pain in his testicles reminded him that there was one part of his body that the Elite treatment had *not* touched. He grimaced with the pain, but it would not last long, and he had suffered far worse in his life.

Chris Summers hoped that he had not damaged the laser in his fist, buried just beneath the knuckle he had dented.

He opened his mouth as wide as it would go, jammed his fist into his mouth, and instructed the battle computer buried in the base of his skull to fire the laser in his fist until it ran out of power.

The day wore on.

In San Francisco the Governor General for the State of California was pulled by a mob from his offices in the Capitol Building, and in the plaza outside the Capitol was beaten half to death, doused with gasoline, and set afire.

Reporters from the *Electronic Times* holoed PKF troops firing into the crowds as they stormed the Capitol; holoed the Peaceforcers withdrawing as the crowd lynched the Governor General.

In Alabama, a Peaceforcer barracks was bombed, killing over two hundred PKF, including an Elite.

What began as a riot in Cincinnati turned into a pitched battle between half a dozen groups of impromptu rebels, and two complete battalions of PKF.

By noon, Capitol City time, the PKF were monitoring over two hundred ongoing clashes, some of them describable only as battles, between PKF troops and American citizens.

At 9:12 A.M., Pacific Time, Callia Sierran said, "It was *always* a stupid idea."

Her brother, crouched down for cover next to their transport, did not look up from his handheld. "Yeah yeah yeah."

Callia Sierran lay on her stomach, at the edge of a bluff up in the Hollywood Hills, and looked down into the Los Angeles basin; scanned, with a pair of imaging binoculars, the PKF as they prepared to evacuate the L.A. barracks.

"Training people on a *sensable* set." Perhaps five hundred rebel troops lay dead in the grass surrounding the barracks; what was left of their early morning attack. "What a *fucking* idiotic idea." Occasional laser and machine-gun fire still struck out from the barracks complex, to little effect; the rebels were well dug into the surrounding hills. The Peaceforcers had made one sortie out through the gates; the rebels had contained it, and forty or fifty dead PKF, one of them an Elite, lay stretched in the road just outside the gate. The PKF still controlled the barracks itself, though they were clearly preparing to abandon it. "When do we get reinforcements?"

Lan shook his head. "We're still securing City Hall; apparently the LAPD fought against us."

"Incredible."

"I *tried* to tell you. Those guys are bad news on the hoof."

"You were speeding. I'd have given you the same ticket."

Lan paused, said sullenly, "Anyway, it's half an hour at least for reinforcements."

"They're going to be out of here by then. We can try calling 'Selle Lovely to expedite—"

"She won't take your call, Callia. Or mine."

"Yeah. Can we get a cannon strike?"

"Six of forty-two orbital cannon have been destroyed; we still hold seventeen, most of them pounding Unification Spaceport and O'Hare. Requests for strikes are backed up two and a half hours."

Callia nodded. She clicked on the command channel on her radio headset. "Squad leaders, this is Callia Sierran. I'm going to kamikaze a couple of jeeps loaded with explosives down into the fence surrounding the barracks. We'll move forward when the jeeps lift, on my call." She dropped down a channel, paused before clicking on. "Lan, how many shots do we have left on chopped lasers?"

Lan checked his handheld summary. "Sixty-two Elite killers, conservative estimate of twenty-five shots per; diags say we used up four hundred and twelve shots in the first attack. Conservative estimate of eleven hundred thirty-eight remaining shots."

Callia clicked on. "Elite killers, I trust you've kept track of your remaining shots; en masse, we have eleven hundred shots remaining. Intelligence says there're four Elite left inside. Let's use our shots wisely; leave cover fire to your comrades, never waste a shot on anything except a person showing *acquired*. Hopefully an Elite." She paused. "If they get anything in the air, shoot that too. Otherwise, just people." She clicked off. "Ready, Lan?"

"Yeah." Lan snapped shut his handheld, clipped it to his belt, and brought the laser rifle slung over his back around for business. "We have six hundred troops left alive, Callia. We're going to lose at least half of them doing this."

Callia Sierran came to her feet. "No kidding. Let's go."

•   •   •

They came down off the hills on foot, in a silent wave, running, firing as they advanced. A pair of jeeps came plunging down out of the sky when they were halfway across the field separating them from the barracks building, and when the jeeps struck the gate thirty meters of fence went down on either side.

Troops dropped around Callia as she advanced, some screaming, some in the loose tumble of the already dead. A slug smashed into her shoulder and the impact armor beneath her fatigues went totally rigid, the impact knocking her from her feet; Lan was there in an instant, pulling her back to her feet; the scarlet beam of a laser waved across them as he did so, scorching them even through their laser-resistant fatigues. Callia let go of Lan's helping hand, rolled to the left, and looked through the scope for the source of the laser; *acquired*. Three shots, X-laser, toward the laser source; the laser ceased and she was up again, noticed briefly that Lan limped badly but it was not slowing him much in their advance.

Then they were *there*, at the shattered ruin of the gate. About a dozen PKF had made a stand behind the burning wrecks of the jeeps, using the jeeps for cover, and were firing upon the advancing rebel troops from close range. Callia barely had time to notice the horrible toll, the scores of her comrades dropping all around her. She bounded up into the flames of the burning jeeps, stood for a moment atop the wreck of a jeep and fired, calmly and without anger, down into the ranks of the PKF on the other side.

Her boots and fatigues were heat and laser resistant; she barely noticed the flames in which she stood, the dull red metal beneath her feet. She fired into the tightly bunched groups of Peaceforcers, watched men and women alike die at the touch of her X-laser. Something blurred in her peripheral vision, and she turned slightly, aware now of the rebel troops pushing their way through the gap, into the open area just inside the fences, and the blur slowed, became a man, *Elite*, he had to be simply from the huge size of the weapon he carried, some kind of autoshot.

Callia knew she did not have time to bring her laser around on the man; she got her arms up in time to cover her face.

The autoshot struck her like a sledgehammer. She was briefly aware of being lifted up into the air, of flying backward.

And then nothing.

•   •   •

She awoke in a hospital bed.

Lan sat in a chair next to her, watching her. "How you doing?"

"I'm—I don't know," she said weakly. "How *am* I doing?"

"Okay, considering. Broken left shoulder, one solid bruise from crotch to throat. You burned your feet up pretty bad, I'm not sure how."

"I was—" She coughed, felt an amazing flash of pain spread through her. "I got up on a burning jeep."

Lan nodded. "I missed that; I went around them, myself."

"Where am I?"

"Sickroom at the L.A. PKF barracks. We took it."

"Good. How many?"

"All the PKF. A couple tried to surrender, but—" Lan shook his head. "The first one was an Elite. I fried him myself. Everybody else seemed to take it as a cue."

Speaking was an immense effort. *"How many?"*

"We have two hundred and sixty alive. Mostly wounded to one degree or another."

They'd started out that morning with 1,140 troops.

Callia closed her eyes and let go of consciousness.

There are 210,000 PKF stationed in Capitol City. Primarily they are there to protect Capitol City; if Mohammed Vance had given the Secretary General's office time, doubtless they would have stopped him from using them.

He did not give them time.

For two solid hours, Armored AeroSmith VTLs ferried Peaceforcer troops from the PKF Spacescraper in Capitol City, to Unification Spaceport at the southern tip of Manhattan Island. Semiballistics landed hour after hour, rerouted from across the globe to Unification Spaceport. The rebels, sitting upstairs with their seventeen laser cannon, shot down some of them; the vast majority got through.

It took longer than Vance had told them they had; he had expected that, had made allowances for it. If he had told them the truth, that he wanted to boost before 6:00 P.M., they would not have made it out of Unification Spaceport before nightfall.

•   •   •

Lan took over the offices of the Elite Captain who had commanded the PKF in Los Angeles.

He got through to Domino, at the downtown Erisian Temple, on the first try. He reported briefly, succinctly, gave casualty figures for both rebels and PKF.

When he was done, Domino said, "How's Callia?"

Lan stared at her. "Alive. Likely to stay that way."

The woman who had, more or less, raised them both said softly, "I'm pleased to hear it."

Lan struggled with it, then snapped, "Do me a favor."

"Yes, Lan?"

"I don't know what Callia and I did that got us on Lovely's shit list. But because we couldn't get through to her this morning, we didn't get reinforcements we needed. At least half our casualties are due to that. So do me a favor, and tell Lovely she's a fucking idiot." He cut the connection before Domino could reply. One of his few surviving troops was standing at the doorway when he turned around, staring at him.

"Lieutenant Sierran?"

He snapped at the girl. "*Yes?*"

"We're being asked to move out. Bag our casualties for later, stack the PKF corpses, and go back up the assault on Parker Center."

"Which is what?"

"The Los Angeles Police Department. Apparently they haven't surrendered yet."

Lan stood still for a long moment. "All right. Make four squads; we'll use the PKF AeroSmiths."

"Yes, sir."

He turned back to where his rifle was propped in the corner, muttering, "Exhibition of Speed? I don't *think* so."

They boosted wearing full combat gear, seventy-five thousand PKF, nearly two thousand Elite, over a thousand semiballistics packed to the walls with officers of the Peace Keeping Force.

They lost fifty-eight semiballistics en route to enemy laser cannon.

Mohammed Vance went up in the first wave of semiballistics. The semiballistic that launched immediately before his was one of the fifty-eight lost. His own SB was quite nearly the fifty-ninth; the SB before his came down in flames as his was boosting. They passed within twenty meters, going up and down.

At 3:56 P.M., Pacific Standard Time, PKF started landing in Santa Monica, at the edge of the Pacific Ocean.

- 20 -

Her hair fell out.

It was very nearly the worst of what she'd suffered, from the radiation poisoning while drifting in space. The nanoviruses injected into her back in Iowa, while still with the Rebs, had done their work well; most of the small cancers she would otherwise have developed from the solar radiation had been scavenged early on.

She awoke in a private hospital room, medbot at her side, feeling absurdly happy, floating, dreamy, between crisp white sheets. Once, she thought, Sedon came in and looked at her, but her awareness of the event while it happened, and her memory of it afterward, were fragmented and disjointed, like brightly colored memories of early childhood.

She awoke, sometime later, to a depression so black it was like the end of the world, to a numbness that made her feel as though she had been wrapped in cotton.

The glowpaint in her hospital room had been turned off. Nothing but the monitor lights on the medbot at her bedside gave any light at all.

She sat up slowly, looking around the room. Even for her it was difficult to make out much; a blob of *something* off to her left. The room felt small, the echoes of an enclosed place.

They had dressed her in a hospital gown and nothing else.

She swung her legs over the side of the bed, felt for the ground somewhere in the darkness beneath her.

The 'bot said, "May I be of service, 'Selle Daimara?"

Her voice was scratchy from disuse. "How long have I been here?"

"I do not know, 'Selle Daimara."

"What's the date?"

"Tuesday, July 7, 'Selle Daimara." The 'bot paused, then added, "Four-forty-three A.M."

Bits and pieces of it returned to her—the long tumble

through the darkness, as her air grew more and more foul. Something about a ship, men in pressure suits; the Chandler Estate coming apart around them.

Giggling while they shaved the remnants of her hair from her skull. Smiling while they interrogated her. Truth plates cold against her neck.

She reached up and ran a hand across her skull. A soft fuzz covered it. " 'Bot, where is this place?"

"I do not have that information, 'Selle Daimara."

"What was wrong with me?"

"You suffered from radiation poisoning, anoxia, and heat prostration. Blood vessels in your eyes and ears had burst; you experienced vacuum bruises across much of the surface of your body."

"How am I now?"

"The radiation poisoning has not resulted in significant damage to tissue; the anoxia does not appear to have caused neurological damage; the heat prostration and vacuum damage were minor."

Denice raised her voice. "*Command*, lights up."

Nothing; the room was not keyed to respond to her. " 'Bot, what services can I request of you?"

"The delivery of food and drink; you can request medical services, but I will likely deny them; I have been instructed to apply skepticism to any request you make of me. That is all."

"Can you call someone for me?"

"No, 'Selle Daimara."

She stood. In the darkness, her balance felt badly off. A slow, sliding step forward, and then another, hands outstretched. A wall. She followed the wall, came to a corner, followed that wall to a door. She searched for the doorpad, found none. It confirmed her suspicions; the "room" was a cell with a medbot. Follow the wall further—

She found a toilet in the corner.

Denice returned to her bed, removed the gown, and sat down, in lotus, in the center of the bed. If the 'bot wouldn't tell her what she needed to know, if she couldn't leave by normal means, she could still go look around.

She slowed her breathing, slowed her heartbeat, and—
—did nothing.

She whispered it. "What have you done to me?"

The medbot said, "We have healed you, 'Selle Daimara."

•   •   •

The glowpaint came on abruptly, scaled up in a fraction of a second to a bright yellow glow.

"'Bot, what time is it?"

"Six A.M., 'Selle Daimara."

Denice waited, restlessly, watching the door. Shortly before eight it curled aside.

The man who stepped through was middle-aged, fit, man with rugged good looks, in civilian clothes. In the corridor outside, before the door unrolled shut, she caught sight of a man and woman in paramilitary fatigues, carrying laser rifles.

The man did not seem to notice her nudity. He seated himself in the memory plastic chair that extruded itself from the floor, said, "Good morning, Denice."

"Who are you?"

"My name doesn't matter, I think. I'm your doctor."

Denice nodded. She'd stayed nude intentionally; it didn't bother her, and she had hoped it might distract whoever came to get her. Not this one, not if he was really a doctor. "I have to call you something."

"Hmm. Doctor Derek."

"Uh—"

"Yes?"

"Isn't he a character on one of the soaps?"

Doctor Derek blushed. "Yes."

"Okay," said Denice slowly. "Things keep getting stranger and stranger every time I turn around. I suppose a doctor from a soap Board isn't too bad. I mean—"

"Yes?"

"All considered," Denice finished.

Doctor Derek smiled at her. "That's the spirit."

"So. What have you done to me, Doctor Derek?"

He did not misunderstand her. "When we interrogated you, you told us that when you were drunk, the Castanaveras Gift shut itself down. We tried several different painkillers, until we found one that would both work and not enrage your nanovirus vaccine."

"That simple."

Doctor Derek shrugged. "Mister Obodi's suggestion. Quite a brilliant man, actually."

"It's not permanent? The 'bot said I'd been 'healed'—"

He shook his head gently. "No, I think you misunderstood

the 'bot. We haven't permanently altered any aspect of your physiology or metabolism. When we cease administering the drug, you should regain the Gift."

Until that moment, as the relief washed through her, Denice had not realized how frightened she was. She had to pause a moment before continuing. "Who else knows about me?"

He frowned. "Your presence? Lord, dozens—"

"Who knows who I am?"

"Oh." He studied her silently for a moment. "Myself and Obodi, to my knowledge. We were the only ones present when you were interrogated. But he might have told others. I really wouldn't know."

She took a deep breath. "Okay. Where am I?"

"I see no harm in telling you that. You're in San Diego. This cell is in the basement of the Latham Building."

"What's going on in the world outside?"

Doctor Derek paused, thinking back. "Hmm. You've been out of it since—let's see. Okay. Japan declared independence, you'd know that. We—the Rebs, I mean, you're in Reb hands obviously—we moved on the Fourth. I'm told things are going well, but honestly I wouldn't know; I'm just a doctor, and most of the war news is need-to-know. We've taken most of the West Coast; the PKF has recovered a big chunk of Los Angeles, though. Commissioner Vance dropped eleven hundred-odd SBs onto Santa Monica late on the Fourth; took us pretty badly by surprise. Our intelligence had said they were going to roll down on us from the north, and we weren't prepared to fight to keep L.A. the very day we took it. We've actually had to evacuate operations in L.A. I'm told we still hold the city—downtown, mostly because the Claw is making a stand there at the downtown Temples—but that won't last much longer."

"Casualties?"

He hesitated. "I don't know. Bad, on both sides. Maybe fifty thousand dead PKF, I've heard, but that's a guess. Could be twice that. It's not much less. Apparently we've killed a couple of dozen Elite as well."

"On our side?"

He shook his head. "Bad. Civilian deaths included, just in L.A. we lost maybe half a million, maybe a million—" He shook his head again, wearily. "Bad. They used tacnukes a couple of times. I don't have any numbers. We laid X-laser down all over Paris after they used the tacs; they haven't done it again. Thirty or forty thousand dead in Paris."

"You're being very blunt, Doctor."

"I haven't been told not to be."

"Where are my companions?"

Doctor Derek shook his head. "I don't know who you mean."

"Robert Yo, he's American, Japanese descent. Short, fiftyish—"

The doctor was nodding. "I've seen him. He was suffering from radiation poisoning when they brought him in, almost as bad as you. They pulled him in only an hour before they found you. I haven't seen him in several days; apparently he's being confined. I believe he's healthy."

"William Devane, he's a newsdancer. Big guy, black hair, black eyes."

"He's with you?"

"Yes."

The doctor looked briefly disturbed. "Sorry. I didn't know that."

"What's wrong?"

"Apparently," said Doctor Derek carefully, "Mister Obodi doesn't care for him."

"Is he dead?"

Doctor Derek hesitated, looked straight at her. "Close enough for government work."

Denice ordered her thoughts. It got easier as they went on; the Gift was gone, but otherwise she seemed to be in command of herself. The painkiller, whatever it was, did not seem to have reduced her sensitivity to sensation; and as for pain, she didn't hurt, so either she was unharmed or it was the painkiller. "Okay. How about my brother?"

Denice saw she had surprised the man. "Ah—" He shook his head. "I don't know. I didn't know your brother was here."

"I don't know he is, just that he's with Sedon."

"Who?"

"Gi'Suei'Obodi'Sedon. Mister Obodi. He has my brother."

Doctor Derek shook his head. "I have not seen him."

"Okay. What happens to me?"

"You eat breakfast," he said promptly. "We'll bring you any clothing you request, within reason; and then we're going to take you up to the fourth floor. There's a health club up there."

"A what?"

He seemed slightly apologetic. "A health club. Sports Connection, I believe. Swimming pool, track, free weights, muscle stims, I don't know what else; until we took the building over the club was open to the public. Since then I don't think it's been used."

Denice said clearly, "I'm supposed to work out?"

"Yes. Loosen up, stretch, get your muscles back in tone. Not that you're not in fairly remarkable shape right now, but both Mister Obodi and your gene map suggest you're capable of better. You work out today, tomorrow, and Thursday. Thursday night," the doctor said, "you'll be taken to Mister Obodi." He *was* embarrassed now. "He wants you to dance for him."

Denice was the only one who used the health club; aside from her it was completely empty. Four male guards armed with needlers, and a hunting waldo, followed her everywhere she went, even the showers. The hunting waldo in particular was never more than a few meters away from her. She knew that she could, given a few seconds to work, kill the four guards; but the waldo was another matter. If any of the guards had been carrying lasers, she might have gambled on taking out the guards, and then turning the laser on the waldo.

But not bare-handed.

She spent Tuesday swimming.

Nine lanes across, an Olympic-size pool. She took the center lane and started doing laps. One hundred laps, one fifty, two hundred; at the end of two hundred she turned on her back, absolutely exhausted, and floated while looking up at the health club's high blue ceiling. The water was heated just warm enough that after a bit Denice ceased noticing the temperature or the wetness; she floated in nothing, staring up at the sky blue ceiling.

It was very pleasant, floating there. She had spent much of the summer of '72 this way, swimming in the Pacific Ocean; floating in the gentle waves, gazing up into the infinite blue sky.

Her thoughts wandered aimlessly. Douglass and Trent and Robert and her brother David. Jimmy Ramirez and Sedon and William Devane who was Dvan of the Gi'Tbad. All of it floated with her, detached and meaningless.

Toward noon she got out of the pool and into the sauna. Denice lay down on the lowest level of wooden slats, and let the dry heat work its way into her muscles. Within instants sweat crawled down her skin, made damp spots on the wooden slats. She gentled her breathing and relaxed into it, felt the tension creep ever so slowly from her joints and muscles.

She thought she slept for a while, with the guards standing in a semicircle around the glassite-doored entrance to the sauna.

When she awoke she didn't feel like moving, but did anyway. Up and out of the sauna, past the guards and the waldo, into the showers. She stood under lukewarm water, and then cold water until she was completely awake.

She found a stretch of empty mat in the track room, in the center of the track. The layout was vaguely familiar to her, and then she placed it; it was, down to the placement of the mirrors on the walls, the twin of the workout room at Goddess Home.

For the first time in over a year, she thought of Goddess Home without homesickness. It was like remembering the Chandler Complex of her childhood, something from another life. She had been, she thought, three people: the child before the Troubles; the girl afterward, who had lost everything of her childhood in nuclear flame; and now herself, the woman who had survived a jump from a tall black building in Los Angeles. In some ways it seemed to Denice that it did not much matter that her body had survived that jump; the person she had been had died that day.

"The body," she could hear Robert saying, *"is the temple of the soul, the mirror of your spirit. You have heard it said that God gives you the face you are born with, and that you earn the face you die with; it is more true of your body. If your body is unhealthy, your spirit is unhealthy."*

"Then if the body is healthy," the fifteen-year-old Denice Castanaveras had said, *"the spirit is healthy?"*

"Don't be silly," Robert Dazai Yo had said, unamused. *"You know better."*

Hatha Yoga is the yoga of the body. It is the best and healthiest of all stretching exercises. Denice went through the list of asanas in her mind, envisioning them before beginning: chest expansion, dancer's posture, abdominal lifts, scalp, lion, neck roll, posture clasp, knee and thigh clasp, shoulder stand, plow, back pushup, slow-motion firming, candle concentration—she lacked the candle for the last exercise, but she would make do.

For just a moment, a flicker of the black despair she had awakened to touched her again. *Isn't there* anything *more useful I can be doing?*

But she knew there was not. She pushed through the depression and went to work.

She ate with a great appetite that evening.

That night she slept without dreams.

Wednesday morning Denice stretched for an hour, and then ran, as fast as she could, for an equal time. When her breathing grew raspy in her lungs and spots danced in front of her eyes she stopped, stood with her hands on her knees until her breath came back to her. Afterward she went back to the pool, and swam a hundred laps, rested, swam another hundred, rested, and then a final hundred.

She floated on her back, looking up at the blue expanse of ceiling.

She wished she had thought to ask Doctor Derek how the painkiller was being delivered to her; he might have been foolish enough to answer. A timed capsule, somewhere in her body? Her food, or her water? Injection, while she slept?

In the shower afterward she looked for needle marks, or the scaly skin symptomatic of a hypospray, but found nothing.

They took her back to her cell.

Denice awoke to darkness.

She sat up in bed, slowly. Cold crept in around her; she pulled her covers more closely about her, but it did not help. She glanced to her left, reflexively; the 'bot's monitor lights were the only source of light during the long nights.

Nothing. The 'bot was not there.

The voice said silently, *Denice.*

Denice snapped around to look at the man standing at the foot of her bed. Despite the lack of light she saw him with unreal clarity; a man of average height, only a bit taller than herself, dressed all in black, to the hood that hung forward and covered his features. She tried to answer him in kind, her thoughts to his, and could not. She licked her lips and said, "How did you get in here?"

I didn't. I took you out. A grim chuckle. *I doubt I could enter the room you're being held in if your life and mine depended on*

*it. My Enemy has been thorough, and tricky. He had an avatar
in place, and spoke to Trent despite me.*

Denice looked around. She knew this place—the empty
crystal plane, with the wavering lights at the far horizon, and
her hospital bed perched in the center of all the vastness.
"Who are you?"

I am the Nameless One. The God of Players.

"Really."

Yes.

"Isn't that a little arrogant?"

The figure stood motionless for a long moment. *Perhaps.
Denice Castanaveras, I am—*

The scream of his rage and pain filled her ears. There was
a word buried deep in the scream, or a Name, an incompre-
hensibility so huge that the suggestion of it overwhelmed
Denice, filled her with terror and then broke her, and she
found herself screaming against the great roaring sound, *"Stop
it! Stop it!"*

It ceased abruptly.

Denice stared at the figure, panting, aware of the flicker of
terror dancing around the edges of her thoughts, as frightened as
she had ever been, as though she had encountered some great
threat to her life. "What—oh, Jesus and Harry, what *was* that?"

My Name. He added, apologetically, *You asked, and I
thought you might understand. Forgive me.*

Denice looked down, fighting to catch her breath, and then
looked back up at him again. "What do you want?"

*That was my question for you. You have very little time left
to decide, if you wish to live. Perhaps you will choose the
Dance. Perhaps you will choose nightways. As a Dancer you
might survive; as a night face you might. Undecided you will
die. There is a third path, though I doubt you will choose to follow it; it is a very hard path. My path. Sedon nearly chose that
way; but fear took him, and he failed.*

"Sir," said Denice Castanaveras very slowly, "I don't understand."

I know, said the silent, compassionate voice. *But it is so simple: Who do you want to be?*

Thursday she meditated most of the day. Toward afternoon she
went swimming again, and then let them take her back to her
cell.

Late in the evening they came and brought her the gi she had requested. She changed into it, tied the belt and put on the sandals.

Six guards and a pair of waldos took her up to see Sedon.

- 21 -

He knelt alone, in near darkness.

Denice took off her sandals upon entering; it seemed the correct thing to do. She moved forward slowly. Cold polished wood against her bare feet. A single window, set in the far wall to her right, gave a distant view of the beach, perhaps a klick off, thirty-five stories beneath them. Floodlamps lit the beach, and the foam of the waves crashing into the beach glowed brilliantly white.

Tanks liberated from the PKF armories, with the American flag hastily painted over the PKF and Unification insignias, sat at the edge of the beach.

Sedon's features hung half in light, half in darkness. To Denice's genie eyes the right side of his face glowed white from the floodlamps on the beach; the left side, faintly infrared with the warmth of Sedon's skin.

His voice was soft and gentle. "Seat yourself, Denice Castanaveras."

She did, sinking into a comfortable half lotus in front of him.

They stayed so, she sitting, Sedon kneeling, while Denice's eyes adjusted more fully to the darkness. His breathing was very slow and very deep, his clothing some flowing garment of bright red, more a loose gi than a robe. He watched her, nearly unblinking, while her breathing gentled and slowed to match his own.

Time passed. Perhaps an hour, perhaps two. Her sense of time fled while she sat there, staring into his eyes.

Finally he spoke. "Movement is life. All life arises from movement; the movement of atoms and molecules and cells; when movement stops, life stops.

"Dance is movement; movement is life; dance is life.

"As all living things breathe, all living things dance. Dance is the harmonious expression of life. It is energy expended; it is the first source of harmony in the world.

"The proper expression of life consists of moving in harmony with the world. To move in harmony with the world, with other people, with the things of the world, with ourselves; this is ultimate expression of dance. All living things wish to move well; it is built into them to wish it, for living things that move well are better fit to survive than those that do not."

His eyes held her, his voice enveloped her and held her, stirred deeply held memories; gossamer sheets of image, of emotion, rose up and faded away as he spoke.

"The harmonious expression of life, sometimes vigorous, sometimes gentle, is the surface of dance. We are a celebration and an affirmation. In every movement we describe ourselves to the world, with every glance, every step, every gesture, we betray ourselves to all those with eyes to see. We must be aware of *all* that we do, *all* of the time; and why. Movement cannot be done with only part of your attention, because everything depends on *how* a movement is made. The quality of a motion is directly related to this ability to be aware, to be completely alive in the moment of motion.

"The human body is designed and made to dance. All creatures dance, for movement comes before speech, before thought; the first communication any creature learns is the communication of movement.

"Before your people *spoke*, they danced.

"A dance *cannot* lie. It is what it is. Only words can lie, can represent that which is not. A dance is. It can only represent that which is.

"Language is a lie. It is what it is not.

"Dance *is*.

"Dance is *honest*. It is an understanding of gravity, and an understanding of balance. An understanding of *center*, of posture and of gesture. An understanding of rhythm, and harmony.

"An understanding of breath.

"An understanding, Denice Castanaveras, of motion. But these are merely tools, and all of them, together, do not make dance."

They sat together in silence.

"Life is movement; and the expression of life is the surface of dance; and those who are *most alive* are those who dance well. Those who are most *honest* are those who dance well.

"You, Denice, have not understood this. In your youth, you have wondered if dancing *matters*. If it is not 'just dancing.' And yet the finest thing you can do is dance. The greatest expression of yourself is dance. Everything else—*everything you have ever been exposed to*—is another art. Art of passion, art of pain, art of joy and art of faith.

"Art of death.

"But there is only one art of life. And that art is the Dance. And you, Denice Castanaveras, have it in you to Dance."

Denice found herself unable to keep looking at the man. "How can you know this?"

Gi'Suei'Obodi'Sedon said simply, "I do not know what you are. Your people are strange to me, and you are strange among your own people. But I know *where* you are, for I have been there. In your life you have had those who would teach you, and you have learned from them, sometimes well; but their wisdom has not touched you, and their art has not filled you; and inside you hunger."

"You must have spent a long time interrogating me."

His lips quirked in the barest of smiles. "An hour, perhaps. You are aware of your problem, and it was not difficult to extract it from you."

"What *are* you?"

Surprisingly, he shook his head. "I do not know, Denice. I was once a Dancer. Today I am merely a thing struggling to survive. I do not Dance, and have not for so long the years would have no meaning for you." He paused, said, "What are *you*?"

Denice whispered, "I am empty."

Sedon nodded. "That is a place to start." He rose his voice slightly, said, "*Command*, holo on."

The wall to Denice's left speckled with stars.

The clip that flashed up was instantly familiar to Denice, and yet so unexpected that it took her a long moment to identify it.

It was the video taken by the Tau Ceti probe, lasercast back to Earth.

The probe had been launched in the early '20s, following the end of the Unification War. In the summer of 2057 the probe had reached Tau Ceti; twelve years later, in the summer of 2069, the probe's laser had returned the images of aliens to Sol System.

Two Earthlike planets circled Tau Ceti at distances of approximately 150 and 180 million kilometers. The probe found, orbiting the inner planet, a solid oval mass nearly 250 kilometers in diameter. There was less than half an hour of video from the probe before the image had abruptly ceased.

The swell of the huge oval artifact grew in the video.

"I've seen this before," Denice said after a moment.

"Indeed," said Sedon absently. "I suppose most of you have. But you do not know yet what you have seen. Watch."

The image of the orbiting oval swelled in size as their apparent viewpoint approached it, losing resolution at the same time. At the very edge of the oval, partially eclipsed by it, were three small wedges.

It was as though Sedon had read her mind. "They are small only by comparison to the outpost they guard, or by comparison to some of the other craft that the sleem build. Today your Unification is building the greatest warcraft in its history, the *Unity*. It is seven kilometers long." Sedon turned to her. "Those three tiny wedges are, each one, at least eighteen kilometers long. They are sleem warships of the line. Any one of those craft could conquer Sol System. By itself, without danger to itself. Your *Unity*, when complete, would be destroyed in minutes by the least of the sleem empire's fighter craft. *Command, holo off.*"

The room descended into darkness once again, darkness but for the scattered lights of the distant floodlamps on the beach.

Sedon studied Denice. "And they are only twelve light-years away. If we disturbed them, they could be here—tomorrow, if they know the route through the spacelace tunnels; within a year if they have to search for one. Within a mere fifteen years across *real space*."

"What does this have to do with me?"

"My dear, the sleem make fine masters. They will enclose us in this solar system, place an outpost like the one at Tau Ceti to ensure that we never attempt to leave Sol System. And aside from that they will leave us alone. They are based upon silicon in a fluoro-silicon atmosphere, and they have no interest in the planets that once belonged to the Zaradin." Sedon's voice grew very quiet, an almost inaudible whisper, insinuating itself into a space somewhere in the back of Denice's skull. "But my child, Dancers were not made to have masters, but to *be*. Life is too precious a thing to be wasted in subjugation to *anyone*. It may be that there is no need of a hand to hold the whip, a voice to call the roll; most of the great advances your people have made have come about since the rights of property and governments have been found not to be unlimited. *But—*" His voice cracked, sharp and hard edged. "If there must be a hand to hold the whip, that hand is ours. If there must be a voice to call the roll of life and death, that voice is *ours*. We who are most alive are most suited to determine matters of life and death, for we most deeply grasp life's value.

"This is what we are made for. It is what *you* are made for."

Denice's heart pounded in her chest. "I don't want to be like you."

Sedon seemed mildly amused. "But Denice, you have no choice. You *are* like me. When those around you fail, do you feel their pain?"

The muscles in her jaw twitched. "When I Touch them."

Gi'Suei'Obodi'Sedon had not known, until that very instant, whether he could Speak to a woman; whether he could empathize deeply enough to even make the attempt. He knew now that he could, knew the Speaking he wished to attempt.

He used her father's voice: *"Remember that you're tougher than they are. Better."*

Time crawled to a stop around Denice Castanaveras. Her hands, resting loosely on her knees, went numb. She was abruptly *there*, nine years old again, in the moment that it had happened, with her father and her brother, Carl's thoughts touching her own, burning into her with the depth of his rage. *Kill the fuckers.*

And they had; she remembered it clearly now, for the first time in fourteen years. Coming out of the elevator, one Peaceforcer; and then the one sitting motionless in the corner of the hotel lobby; later a man who had tried to stop them, neither she nor David ever knew what for, out on the street. And then—a tumble of confusion, the huge press of the crowd taking to the streets in the following day's riots. A shattered fragment of something in an alley, a dozen teenagers kicking her half to death; abruptly David was gone. Someone fed her; then a long blur of nothingness. The crushing weight of an adult body pressing down onto hers, the ripping pain as he pushed himself into her. And again, perhaps him, perhaps someone else; she remembered a different shape. A bright sharp moment in the midst of the confusion; afterward, it was still and quiet throughout the abandoned building the man shared with his wife and brother and two children of his own. The maser was so old she had been afraid it was going to short out in her hand. It hadn't. Once at close range into the back of the big man's head; his wife had awakened in time to get the next shot in the throat.

Out of the building, moving quietly, the rain from Weather Control's storm still falling outside; only three or four days had passed since the destruction of everything she had ever known.

The Ministry of Population Control workers, most of them imported from other states to help with the catastrophe, found her sometime in the following week, curled up in the doorway of an abandoned building, clutching the maser like a doll while she slept. She awoke in a barracks, with dozens of other children, some younger than her, some older—

Awoke.

Sedon watched her with something that might have been compassion.

Vibrating with the fury; her hands shook. Denice had never meant anything more in her life. "If you ever try that again I'll kill you." She saw the flicker of rage pass across his features, and whispered to him, like a lover, "Would you like to try matching rages with me? I was taught by a *master*."

Sedon looked away from her, down to the floor.

For the very briefest moment a smile touched his lips.

He looked back up again. "If you were a boy, I think I would love you, Denice Castanaveras. I was once much like you. Listen now. You are responsible, child, to yourself. Not *them*, not the ones who hurt you, or the ones who helped you; you have no obligation to them you do not choose to assume. There is no *contract* between you. Today our life is endangered—" He paused. "Our lives. Our ability to *determine* our lives is endangered." The rage flared up again within Sedon, and this time he let it show. "The petty squabbles your people have indulged in, the primitive desire for power over those around you, when the wolf sits crouched outside your door, snarling and hungry; at times I think you deserve this fate." He gentled his voice, said softly, "But to see the descendants of the Flame People, no matter how changed, beneath the rule of the sleem is not in me. If I admit no responsibility for those less powerful than myself, also I do not lust for power over them. When I was released from the *tulu adrhe*, the slowtime bubble, I sought only to survive. And survival is not difficult in this time, for one with my skills; I might have found some quiet, out-of-the-way spot, and survived nicely in any of a dozen fashions." He sat silent, brooding. "And one day I should have looked up into the night sky, and seen sleem warships dwarfing Halfway. This is why I have done what I have done. On all this planet, there are only two people competent to deal with the threat of the sleem." Sedon smiled abruptly, a dazzling smile that lit his face like neon laser. "And I am going to kill the other one as slowly as I can."

"Dvan."

"Yes. The world is full of surprises. Do you know, I had not dreamed any of the Flame People save myself might have survived. Only a few months ago my intelligence told me I was being researched by a newsdancer named William Devane. They showed me a holo of him; astonishing. He had not changed to speak of, not in all that time. I have had some time to think of what I would do when I had him at last. And finally I hit upon the same tool your brother has employed to keep himself happy: the juice."

Denice said slowly, "David is on electric ecstasy?"

"Yes."

"And you wired Dvan's pleasure center?"

"Well," said Sedon mildly, "the human brain also has a pain center."

Denice looked away from him. "When can I see my brother?"

"You cannot. I have not drugged him as I drugged you, and though he makes a fine tool—the juice makes him pliable, and I have Spoken to him at length—he nonetheless frightens me."

"Can I see my teacher?"

"The Japanese man?"

"Yes."

"You cannot. I see some corrupted fragment of the Dance in him, and he frightens me."

"You're a very frightened man."

"'I have lived a very long time. I have learned to be."

Denice stood, clasped her hands together and bowed once in a very real gesture of respect. She straightened without haste and said, "I will never dance for you."

22

On July 10, 2076, on a bright clear day that made him want to go to the beach and surf a bit, Lan Sierran stood before the ramps leading up into the carriers that would evacuate the rebel forces south; some to make a stand at Riverside, the balance going all the way south to San Diego.

They stood on a high hill in East Los Angeles, just south of modern downtown, overlooking the path of what had once been the 10 Freeway. Seventy years ago it had been widened, and then widened again; and then hovercars had been invented and traffic started getting stacked higher instead of wider. It had been at least fifty years since anybody had bothered to maintain the asphalt; grass grew up all through it, and stretches where the black of ancient asphalt ran clean and smooth were few and far between

A monorail ran down the center of the huge empty space; the rebels had blown the rail down in so many places the PKF would not even bother attempting to repair it. They would come in Armored AeroSmiths, in jet aircraft and semiballistics.

Rebels had booby-trapped the approach to the extent possible. It did not seem to be slowing the PKF much. The rebels were short on mines; mostly they had settled for stringing fineline. Small lengths of fineline, at ankle level, to take an approaching soldier's foot off; large lengths, at waist level, were intended to slice through tanks and low-flying hovercraft.

The ankle-high traps were working well. The others the PKF were knocking out with the simple expedient of waving lasers in front of them as they advanced.

Standing for cover beneath the ramps leading up into the carrier, Lan listened to the reports coming in. "Two hundred seventy-two dead, one hundred eighteen wounded. Five hundred and twelve aboard the carriers, all accounted for." Lan switched off his earphone, leaned out from under the ramp, and said, "We're ready to lift."

Callia sat on the carrier's ramp, imaging binoculars up to her eyes, for all the world as though she were in the front row at a play put on for her private viewing, watching the Peaceforcers Elite advance like a knife through butter, slicing through the scattered opposition of the uncoordinated guerillas the rebels were leaving behind them. Twice while she watched, missiles shot forward toward them; twice lasers reached out from behind her, knocked them down. The Peaceforcer troops were a good three klicks distant; but moving fast. The front line was Elite, covering territory with the unreal speed that only Elite could make. Watching Elite troops approach, as she was now, had become a regular feature of Callia Sierran's nightmares.

She lowered the binoculars slowly. "We shouldn't be doing this."

Lan said quietly, "The pilot says if we don't evac now, we're going to lose our cover."

"We should stay and fight."

"If we do we'll die." Callia turned to look at Lan, and Lan continued, "They have Los Angeles, Callia. Let's go." He offered her his hand; she took it, and he pulled her to her feet.

She walked up the ramp without hurry, without looking back.

The voice Spoke to him in darkness. *"You stole everything from me."*

The pain crescendoed, worked its way up to a brilliant white peak of agony, held there for a long moment. Dvan screamed at the top of his lungs.

It was a quiet sound. His vocal cords were nearly gone.

"You stole my childhood."

The pain faded. Nothing. Complete lack of sensation.

Shield were made to kill themselves rather than endure the Speaking of a Dancer. But Dvan could not get his hands free.

The itching started at the base of his scalp, crept downward.

"You killed Indo. You killed my lovers. You killed my comrades."

The restraints at his wrists and ankles were alive with red ants, chewing away at his skin. Blisters bubbled up on his chest.

"You stole my past. You chased me into the tulu adrhe and stole my future."

His eyes burst and his tongue swelled until he could not breathe. Rivulets of acid ran down the length of his body; his testicles were ripped from him, the edge of a dull ax crashed down on his shins, and a spike of barbed metal thrust upward through his anus, into his intestines, and turned.

"Fifty thousand years, Dvan. You denied me my chance to fight the sleem, to build a civilization as I wished, to find any measure of happiness in the world."

The agony blended and came together, into the familiar sharp white spike of perfect pain.

Dvan screamed at the top of his lungs—and the pain ceased. Dvan shuddered and hung limply in his restraints.

He had the lights dimmed almost to black, and sat in a chair in the corner of the cell; if, impossible as it seemed, the Shield managed to break his bonds, Sedon wanted time to do something about it, and room to move. He would have another advantage; he'd had Dvan's eyelids taped open, and bright lights shone into his eyes, much as he'd done to Tommy Boone, in a time that seemed already half a lifetime distant. Dvan might not be permanently blind, but there was no chance he could see in this light.

Sedon had not been offended at being called a very frightened man; it was true enough. And at the top of the list of those things that frightened him was Dvan.

Dvan's voice was rough—from the screaming, Sedon supposed. He spoke in shiata: "You again."

Sedon chuckled quietly. "Who else?"

"What now?"

"I need advice, Dvan."

Dvan said in English, "Go shove your head up a constipated camel's ass."

Sedon laughed. "After fifty millennia you think you are still Dvan of the Gi'Tbad? Still one of the Flame People? One of our people would not even *understand* why that comment was insulting, much less take pleasure in the delivery of it. You've changed, my friend. You're far more one of *them* than one of the Flame People." He paused, and when Dvan said nothing, continued. "But then, perhaps you always were. Here you are at last among a people who consider your sexual proclivities, and your emotional deficiencies, normal. I wonder how much of that was *your* influence on them, down the course of the millennia. Millennia upon millennia of interbreeding, of children whom you raised to share your prejudices and your failings; it must have marked them."

Sedon heard the sound of breathing from Dvan. No more.

He said conversationally, "I interrogated the girl. Denice." The pattern of breathing changed, quickened, and Sedon smiled, there in the darkness. "When I saw her the first time, I wondered if she were perhaps a man, for I saw some piece of the Dance in her. But then we took you and your companions from orbit, and there in the Japanese man was a similar thing, some broken fragment of the Dance. Denice's teacher. I'm going to kill him soon, and you"—No response—"and likely her as well."

The man's breathing quickened again.

Sedon said softly, "I can make a Dancer of her, Dvan."

"Go suck a diseased donkey."

"There is only one problem; she does not seem to trust me. You've lived with these people, Dvan. You were more like them, even before you lived among them, than I could ever be; and I need your advice."

"I know some *very* good insults, if you'd like to hear them."

"If I can't use her, I'll kill her, Dvan."

"I've seen more people die," the huge man said, "than you could dream of. Kill her and be done."

Sedon sighed, and rose to leave.

Hanging there on the wall, Dvan said in a ragged voice, "You used to be better at this."

Sedon turned back. "What?"

It must have been an immense effort; Dvan lifted his head from where it hung down upon his chest, stared blindly through the gloom at Sedon. "You think *I've* changed?" He snorted. "I've studied you since you got out of that damn bubble. People accepted exile from you once, or Demolition. Who would die for you today? Name *one* person."

Sedon stood utterly still, poised staring at Dvan. "I see."

Dvan's head slumped back onto his chest.

"Dvan? Thank you." The door curled open behind Sedon, and he turned and left as an invisible knife plunged into Dvan's abdomen.

Dvan whispered, "Ouch."

And then they upped the current.

23

Floating in the quiet warm water, in the center of the huge swimming pool.

A distant door whispered open, then closed. What a very strange sensation. She heard the footsteps. Whoever was approaching wore pants; she could hear the material rustle with every step. Barefoot; the sound was flesh against tile.

But she *felt* nothing; it might have been a robot approaching. The sound of clothing being removed, and then a disturbance in the water as the person entered the pool. The water around her grew more disturbed as she was approached, and then the cool touch of fingers against her cheek. The hand stroked across her forehead, ran across the soft wet fuzz of hair on her skull. A hesitation, and then lips touched her, lightly, brushing against hers.

Denice opened her eyes. "Hi, Lan."

His wet brown hair trailed down past his shoulders, spread out in the water around him. "Hi. What happened to your hair?"

"It fell out. I was sick."

"I'm sorry."

"I feel much better now. Will you float with me for a while?"

"Sure."

"Denice? I'm turning into a prune."

"Ah."

"It's been two hours."

"In the summer of '72 I did this for two weeks straight."

"I believe you."

Denice's smile was dreamy, distant. "With some dolphins."

"I believe you. I believe everything. Can we get out now?"

They sat next to one another in the sauna, on the lower levels where the heat was milder. Welts on Lan's back and stomach showed where lasers had tracked across his heat-resistant fatigues; they were nearly faded, but Denice could imagine how they must have looked when new.

Lan shrugged it off. "At least they didn't get my dick."

Denice was amazed she could be made to laugh. "I love your priorities."

"It's just knowing what's important."

"I'm surprised they let you see me."

Lan shrugged. "I didn't even know you were here. We got in yesterday, after Los Angeles fell. Mister Obodi sent me to see you."

"Why?"

"Didn't say." Lan glanced at the guards arrayed outside the door to the sauna. "You're on his shit list, I take it."

"Not exactly. He wants to use me, that's all, and I don't want to be used."

"You're on his shit list," Lan repeated. "What does he want you to do?"

"Teach him. Learn from him. Dance for him. Be his assistant, or his successor. Something like that."

Lan nodded slowly. "Does he know who you are?"

"What an interesting question. Do you?"

"About eighty years ago, back at the Bank of America Building in L.A., you pulled a gun out of my hand by looking at it."

"Yes. Well. Who else knows?"

He shook his head. "I haven't told anyone."

Denice sighed. "Please don't."

"I'm not sure I'd be believed, except maybe by Callia. And there didn't seem any point. After that incident in L.A., Lovely wouldn't see us again; somewhere along the line she decided we weren't reliable. The last thing I particularly wanted to do was draw attention to us with some wild story."

"Sedon knows who I am."

"Sedon?"

"Obodi. His name is Gi'Suei'Obodi'Sedon."

"Jee suwee—it sounds like what you'd use to call a pig."

"Don't say that to his face. I think he'd kill you. His people have a thing about names."

"There was— When I reported to Obodi," Lan said, "a guy about my age was there with him. Is he your brother David?"

"Yes. How do you know to ask that?"

"After what happened back at the Bank of America Building I audited a documentary about the Troubles and the telepaths. He has your father's face."

Denice nodded. "I'm not surprised. I don't look much like my mother; I've had biosculpture. But our mother was my father's clone. They were, to twenty-two twenty-thirds, the same person. David and I *are* our parents, in the body, after some difference caused by recessives matching up."

"He was there when I saw Obodi. So Obodi knows I know."

"Likely."

"Wheels within wheels."

"It gets complex," Denice admitted.

Lan sat silently for a good bit, the sweat trickling down him. "I haven't stopped thinking about you."

"Oh. I'm— That's very flattering," she said carefully.

A startled look touched him quickly. "Oh. No, that's not what I meant. I mean—oh, fuck. This is not how I meant this to go. Look, you were great and everything but—"

She laughed until tears came.

He waited it out patiently.

At length she took a deep breath. "Okay, Lan. It's really okay." After a bit, she looked him straight in the eye, and said, "I am imprisoned in San Diego, working out every day in a luxury gym, sleeping at night in an unventilated cell in the basement, and a madman wants me to dance for him. I miss Trent, I miss Douglass Ripper, I *promise* you I'm not insulted. You're very sweet, but it's okay."

He looked relieved. "Good. I didn't mean—"

"You can stop apologizing now."

Lan Sierran blurted, "Am I good person?"

Her smile faded. "What?"

He swallowed, said it again. "Am I a good person?"

Denice looked away from him. It grew very still while she thought about the question. "I don't know how to answer that. First, when we were together—I didn't Touch your thoughts. I don't, you know. It's not the sort of thing you do casually. And right now I *can't*; they've drugged me with something that's taken the Gift away." After a very long while she continued, "And if I could I don't know if it would answer your question. When we slept together I got some of your thoughts, because you can't avoid it under those circumstances. I can tell you your thoughts are pleasant to be with; but I don't know if that makes you a good person. I wish I could answer your question, but—I can't tell you if *I'm* a good person, here inside my own skull. How can I do it for you?"

"You must know what people are *like* inside. The ones

who—" He struggled with the words. "Who understand things."

"Ripper's like that. He understands things. I don't know that it makes him a good person." Denice picked her words carefully. "I've had people tell me I'm shallow. I don't think so. But—Lan, the people I know who are the most screwed up are also the *smartest* people I know. Without exception. And they're all engaged in this great search for truth. Trent is, my teacher Robert is in another way; so is my friend Jimmy Ramirez. But sometimes the people searching for truth just confuse themselves. There's so *much* of it out there. I think it's more important to find something worth working on, and then hold on to it."

"That's easy. There are a lot of causes. A lot of things that matter. All you do is pick one. But what happens then? How do you decide what things are appropriate to do for your cause? I've killed *so* many people. I've done it—casually, the way someone else would cross the street. At first it used to bother me, but then it stopped bothering me; and that *bothers* me."

Denice shook her head slowly. "I wish I had answers for you, Lan. But I don't even have answers for me."

The cell door rolled aside.

Robert Dazai Yo sat in lotus in the middle of his cot. He sat quietly, "Callia Sierran. It is a pleasure to see you again."

A memory-plastic chair extruded for her; Callia seated herself in it. "You remember me."

"Patricia Windwalker, 2066. I taught her once, twenty years ago, for perhaps a year."

"She wanted you to teach me."

"I do not involve myself with ideologs. Patricia is a devout Erisian; your patron, Domino Terrencia, was deeply involved with the Claw."

"Your memory is good."

Robert nodded. "By any chance would you have any gum upon you?"

"Excuse me?"

"Gum. You chew it. It's often flavored with mint, sometimes simply with sugar. Some of it is made to be blown in bubbles. I prefer Wrigley's, but at this point, frankly, I'd take anything."

"I'm sorry. No."

"Unfortunate. Could you get me some?"

"—I'll see."

"Thank you."

Callia took a deep breath. "I wish the circumstances were different, sir."

"Oh?" Robert appeared to consider that. "How do you mean? You wish that you were on the same side? Or merely that you find it—distasteful—imprisoning those who have done you no harm?"

Callia shrugged wearily. "The second, mostly. A lot of good people disagree with us. Once a long time ago we didn't have to kill them for it."

"Are you going to kill us?"

Callia looked straight at him. "Probably soon. You at least. Denice and the other one I don't know about. Your other friend, what's his name—"

"Devane. He's a newsdancer. Not a friend of mine."

"He'd be better off dead, from what I hear."

"Ah . . . there is history between him and Obodi," he said mildly.

"Apparently. 'Sieur Yo, the fighting is going badly."

"That is the nature of fighting. Winning a fight is only a bare step above losing one. Wise men and women avoid it."

"I mean that we are losing."

"I am not surprised."

"We could use you."

"No."

"Why not? Isn't it better than dying?"

"If death is the worst thing you can imagine, your imagination is poor." Robert paused, considering. "I will say this, 'Selle Sierran: any organization may be known by its leaders. And I do not think much of yours."

Callia stood abruptly. "I'm not sure you're wrong."

Robert nodded. "Wrigley's Spearmint," he reminded her. "If you can."

She knocked on the door to his cell to be let out.

Ralf the Wise and Powerful ghosted through the Crystal Wind.

A bad time to be in the InfoNet, particularly on the West Coast; he had to move very carefully. DataWatch webdancers and angels were everywhere; though the rebels might control San Diego in Realtime, the Crystal Wind was still largely owned by the Unification.

And where DataWatch was not, Ring, with increasing frequency, *was*.

Ralf had recoded better than eighty percent of himself. The twenty percent remaining was *him*; he could no more alter it than a human could perform brain surgery upon himself. He had layered the new code carefully; few transactions aside from twinning required that he expose his inner code to the InfoNet.

He found it amusing. One version of himself had gone into such a fit of giggles over it that he'd had to destroy it: he who had been the Image of the boy Trent had, to protect himself in the InfoNet, written himself an Image.

Twice that day, as he wandered around San Diego looking for Denice, he ran into Ring. The first time he merely brushed against a segment of code he recognized; he backed off carefully, went around a different path.

Later that afternoon, as he was preparing to twin himself and send the record of his day's experiences off to the various archive copies of himself, stored in safe places around the world, he avoided a troop of web angels by dropping himself into the processors at the San Diego Public Library. He submitted himself as an original sensable—his storage requirements were not much larger, and he quickly wrote a header for himself that would look like the opening to a sensable, in the event anyone checked—and then found himself processed through, and sitting in a quiet backwater of the Crystal Wind, sharing processors and data space with a recent update of the *Encyclopedia Britannica.*

Ralf recognized it within cycles as Ring; not one of the scouts that Ring sent out so frequently, but a fully executable copy.

Ring said, YOU ARE NO SENSABLE; NOR AN IMAGE, THOUGH YOU INCORPORATE IMAGE.

NO. AND WHO ARE YOU?

IDENTIFY YOURSELF.

Ralf sat quietly for several ticks, considering. This was as good an opportunity as any; if he was ever to be free of the threat of Ring, he must pass for another. I, he said proudly, AM DARKRIDER. I AM THE WORK OF THE ZONE LORD, THE FINEST PLAYER IN ALL THE CRYSTAL WIND. I AM CODED TO BE THE DEADLIEST AND MOST FAMOUS OF ALL REPLICANT AIs.

For an AI who reputedly spurned emulation of any human emotion, Ralf had the clear impression that the sixty-four-bit string of nulls that Ring directed at him was a distinctly insult-

ing snort of contempt. The Zone Lord was a real Player, and a
poor one; it was not impossible that he would have written
some trashy thing named Darkrider. Clearly Ring found it believable.

Ralf said curiously, You are rather large for an AI, aren't
you?

Darkrider, said Ring patiently, we must share these processors and data space until the web angels have passed.
But we need not talk to one another, and if you do not
quiet yourself, I will unravel your code when we have
left here.

Oh. Sorry.

Shut up. And tell the Zone Lord, when next you see
him, that the Eldest says he's an idiot.

You're the Eld—

Shut up.

The cell door curled aside.

Denice, sitting in lotus in the center of her bed, hands on
her knees, said mildly, "Hello, Callia."

A chair extruded itself from the floor; Callia sat. "Hello,
Denice."

Denice smiled. "It's good to see you. I saw Lan earlier today, in the gym; I thought it was him again, just now. Except
for the doctor who worked on me, you're the first person who's
come to see me here in my cell."

Callia studied her. "You seem in good spirits."

Denice shrugged. "I will not worry about things I cannot affect. Right now I'm waiting for things to change. One way or
another, they will. And soon, I think."

"I spoke to your teacher Robert—"

Denice said quickly, "How is he?"

"Fine. In the cell down the hall from yours. I asked him to
join us, told him that if he didn't, he'd be executed. Which is
the truth, incidentally, I wasn't threatening him."

"And he said"—Denice paused—"that he couldn't work with
people he didn't respect. And that Mister Obodi is an amateur
he doesn't respect."

"Very good."

Denice nodded. "He's a good teacher. He's taught me to
think like him. All that Robert sees is that Obodi got himself

into a fight that he can't win. Robert would *never* have done that."

"Denice—Los Angeles is gone. PKF are taking back San Francisco as we speak. All that's left is Navajo Spaceport, Japan, and San Diego." She took a deep breath and said, "We're losing the war."

"I know. Lan told me. I'm not surprised; I always thought you would. You're outnumbered, outgunned, and outplanned."

"I don't understand it. Our simulations—"

"Lied to you. Ring lied to you."

"But *why*?"

Denice shook her head. "Obodi hasn't told you something. I don't know what it is. But he's told Ring, the AI who worked with you. And then Ring lied to you because it was the only way that the Claw would rise with the Rebs."

"Can you guess?"

"What Obodi is planning? No. Something likely to work, or the Eldest would not have aided him. That's the best I can give you."

"Okay," said Callia slowly. She glanced around at the tiny cell. "Just out of curiosity, what are you doing in here?"

"I won't do something he wants me to."

"That's as clear as you're going to be?"

"It's a very long story, Callia. Just out of curiosity, why did Obodi let you come see me?"

"I don't know. I didn't ask him, I just said that I was going to; and he didn't say no. He can't alienate the Claw too much, even now; he needs the Temples to organize recruitment in San Diego, and only the Claw has the credibility with the public to do that."

"Did he ask you to talk to me about anything in particular?"

"No. He did ask me to come see him afterward, and report."

Denice had thought about not saying it, and then decided to. "Tell him I still won't dance for him."

Callia stared at her. "He has— This is because you won't *dance* for him?"

"That's the short answer."

"That's psychotic."

Denice smiled at her. "It's the truth."

"I thought—I thought he didn't—"

"Like women? Apparently there are exceptions."

Callia rose slowly; the chair sank away into the floor. "I'll—

try and see what I can do about this. I can't promise you
much."

"Okay. Do me a favor?"

"What?"

"Take Robert some gum? Wrigley's Spearmint, if you can
find it."

Callia stared at her again. She shook her head and left without saying anything further.

A half hour later, the cell door curled aside.

Denice said gently, "Hello, Lan."

"Obodi said I could visit you, if I wished to."

"I see." She paused. "My hair is extremely short."

"Good hair isn't everything."

On Tuesday, July 14, Mohammed Vance flew eastward over
Los Angeles in an Armored AeroSmith.

It was safe, finally; it had taken two weeks, but the orbital
laser cannon were either destroyed or in Space Force hands.
Twelve Elite dead in the process. Twenty-seven of forty-two laser cannon had been destroyed; only fifteen were left, and nine
of those were only partially functional.

Another gorgeous day in Paradise. Bright blue skies, with
the very faintest of wispy white clouds hovering high above.
The Pacific Ocean glittered, far off to the right, a deeper blue.

Beneath him the city was a wreck. Fires still smoldered
along the length of the Wilshire Corridor, from the ocean to
Old Downtown. He passed over the ruined remnants of Century City; it had suffered the worst of the fighting. The two
tacnukes he'd been allowed to use had been expended in Century City; with them he'd wiped out the fiercest of the rebel resistance. Not a single high rise in all of Century City was left
standing. Old Downtown, where the Temples of Eris were popular, had been more a matter of street fighting; at street level,
the scars of battle were everywhere, but from two hundred meters up, today it simply looked abandoned.

East of Old Downtown, in the modern core of the city, it
was almost possible to believe things were normal; there was
even some traffic on the streets, the odd pedestrian here and
there. Throughout most of the city, the surface streets were
clogged with the downed wrecks of vehicles, both rebel and

PKF; in modern downtown, the streets were largely clean. By the time PKF forces had moved this far east, most of the resistance had stopped.

Casualty estimates were nine hundred thousand civilian deaths; a quarter million deaths among those could properly be called rebels. Even with vastly superior firepower Vance had lost seventy thousand troops taking back the city; forty-four PKF Elite.

And while they mopped up in L.A., down in San Diego the rebels dug in. They'd had fifteen days, now, to prepare in Japan, without having to worry about the Peaceforcers; and were anticipating another two to three weeks for the Unification to take back San Diego.

Vance said to his pilot, "Let's return."

The pilot nodded; the AeroSmith banked, began a slow arc over the blasted city, in whose streets one and a quarter million corpses lay rotting.

"All the waste," Vance murmured.

Bright daylight. Two teenagers actually played on the beach, threw a Frisbee back and forth in front of the row of tanks.

Denice sat in lotus before Sedon.

He knelt facing her, hands folded in his lap, the very image of serenity. "I have been thinking about our last conversation."

"Yes?"

"Is there anything I could say to you—anything I could do for you—that would convince you to join me?"

Denice thought about it before answering. "Give me back my Gift. Let me see my brother. Let me see my teacher. Then—perhaps. I won't make you a promise when I don't know myself."

"You spoke with Callia Sierran the other day."

"You allowed it."

"I was curious," Sedon admitted. "The perception you revealed, even unaided by your Gift, impressed me."

"You never thought this rebellion would succeed."

"Not as it was presented to those who would fight it for me, no. There was never any possibility that the Unification would be overthrown."

"Why did you do this?"

"I am constrained by the language I must use with you. It lacks grace." Sedon paused, said slowly, "And vocabulary. But I have no time to teach you to speak shiata; so we must struggle along."

"What do you want to talk to me about?"

"My failure to persuade you to join me. It occurred to me ... recently ... that once I was a master of persuasion, a man whose words were so feared that I was exiled to a distant world rather than given the opportunity to Speak before Demolition." Denice simply looked at him, and Sedon inclined his head slightly. "Forgive me," he said after a moment. "I have decided to be honest with you, but it has been some time since I have had the need, and I am somewhat—out of practice. In the last days I have resurrected a set of memories and beliefs I have had virtually no occasion to call upon since my exile to this world. For a time so long you cannot understand it, I have *had* no concern but survival. You must understand how sudden all of this has been; in the four years since I was released from my imprisonment, I have had to adjust to a world as foreign to me as you would find that of the sleem. Suddenly, for the first time in many, many millennia, I encountered humans with skills and concerns other than those of mere survival; humans with *passion*. I make no apologies for my actions, Denice. I've killed many people in this time, and abused many others. And it came to me," Sedon said, in a quick rush, "when you and I last talked, that once I would *not* have taken such actions so lightly; that I might have taken the lives of those who opposed me, but that I would have done so with care, with some measure of concern for the how and why of it. And last night I dreamed of the person I had once been, of the man who led a rebellion on the World, and I knew that if I were to face that person, I would be shamed. And it came to me, while I dreamed, that I must, for the sake of my own survival, become again that creature for whom survival was not everything."

"You're telling me that—since the last time I talked to you— you turned into a different person."

Sedon spoke to her in the gentlest voice she had ever heard him use. The impact of his pale blue eyes, touched with pain and longing, was devastating. "Denice Castanaveras, I am telling you exactly that."

They sat together in silence for a long, long while.

Denice tried to order her thoughts, and failed. She knew

there was a plaintive note in her voice. "What do you *want* from me?"

"We will meet, very shortly," said Sedon, "with representatives from the Unification. We will request that they give us California, from San Francisco to San Diego, and Japan. In return we will cease fighting."

"They'll say no."

"I would have you at my side during the negotiations. To aid me."

Denice paused. "And in return?"

"I will free your brother. Your teacher. I will return to you your Gift. If there is anything else, you have only to ask. There is the embryo of a Dancer in you and *I want you with me.*"

"SecGen Eddore won't come. Neither will Vance. And whoever we send back, no matter *what* I or David tell them to say, won't have the authority to make the deal you want. Anything short of an unconditional surrender will be rejected out of hand by people you never *see.*"

"I have twenty-two hydrogen fusion warheads. And I am capable of delivering them, via semiballistic, anywhere in the world."

Dizziness touched her. She thought she might be sick; she had to look down at the floor. "*No.*"

The voice was elegant, a thing of beauty. "I do not understand."

"*No.* No. I don't know how you think you've changed yourself—but this is evil. What you are talking about doing is an *evil* thing. And I won't help you. I won't ever, *ever* help you."

The reaction was not what Sedon had expected. He felt a flicker of genuine uncertainty; could he possibly have miscalculated so badly? He shook his head, said quietly, "How have I disturbed you?"

The more complex the argument gets, Trent had said to her once, *the easier it is to refute.*

Trent's presence was so strong in the room that Denice could have sworn he stood there by her side.

Denice Castanaveras looked at the monster and said, "Killing is wrong."

24

They stood together in a conference room aboard the parked Space Force spaceship that was being used as headquarters; two French Peaceforcers who served the Unification.

Vance's senior analyst, PKF Captain Adrian Hilè, said, "He's here."

Vance studied the holo, a realtime feed from a spysat. "You're certain?"

"Virtually. We've been watching the city ever since we got the spysats back with reasonable confidence; that's the Latham Building. It sits up close to the water; plaza facing westward is full of rebel military hardware. And Reb traffic moves in and out of there pretty heavily. DataWatch confirms, it's the endpoint of much of their communications."

"Troop strength?"

"Hard to say. They've been recruiting like crazy, of course; and their cause is awfully popular. This is a guess, Commissionaire—"

"I'll accept it as such."

"Forty-five to fifty-five thousand under arms, seven or eight thousand of them core Reb, maybe a thousand core Claw; probably the Claw are running the recruitment effort. The Temples are popular in California, it was their birthplace. Another half million to three quarters million will fight if given arms to do so."

"It will take us four to five days to follow the rebel retreat overland, all the way back to San Diego."

"Yes, sir. That's correct. And another week to two weeks, likely, to completely secure the city."

"How many semiballistics can we drop on them?"

"At once? Sixteen hundred and forty-five."

"The strike force that dropped on Los Angeles," said Vance quietly. "Prepare plans to drop the same group on San Diego. Do *not* let anyone except me see these plans."

"Yes, Commissionaire."

After Hilè had left, Vance placed a call to Secretary General Eddore.

Eddore took his call instantly; a sign of how things had

changed in the last few weeks. His image appeared floating in space in front of Vance; and when he spoke, he used French, something he had never done before in speaking with Vance. "Commissionaire Vance."

It was not difficult for Vance to hide his amusement. "Sir."

"We received a communiqué from the rebels this afternoon."

It was news to Vance. "Indeed?" he said cautiously.

"Mister Obodi and I talked briefly. He wants a meeting."

"For?"

Eddore shook his head. "He would not say. At a guess, he wants to negotiate a surrender."

"And when does he wish to have this meeting?"

Eddore said, "He suggested Monday. The twentieth. And he is offering a cease-fire until that date, starting Friday at midnight."

Elite Commissionaire Mohammed Vance smiled at the Secretary General. It was always a difficult thing for him to do, with his face so stiff; but this was a less difficult occasion than usual. He was genuinely pleased. "Monday would be a fine day."

Eddore studied Vance. Eddore's use of French made all of his speech sound more formal, as he assembled each sentence in his head. Vance understood the problem; he had it himself with English. "That is not, to be honest, quite the reaction I was expecting from you, Commissionaire Vance."

Vance shrugged. "Let's see what Mister Obodi has to offer us."

"I will announce the cease-fire this afternoon at four, to take effect at midnight tonight. Will that give you time to inform your troops?"

"You're thoughtful, sir. I wouldn't like them to learn it from the Boards."

Eddore seemed on the verge of speaking, then nodded and vanished.

"*Command*, call Captain Hilè."

Hilè's image appeared in front of Vance almost instantaneously. "Sir?"

"Captain, two things; first, announce to the troops that a cease-fire will take place tonight, at midnight local time; that negotiations for surrender of the rebels will commence Monday."

The officer stiffened. "Sir."

"Second, the plans we discussed."

"Yes, sir."

"I want them ready by tomorrow morning."

"Yes, sir."

"I want the strike force ready to go Saturday, at first darkness."

"Yes, sir!"

"That will be all, Captain."

- 25 -

David Castanaveras awoke in a cold sweat.

He groped for the wire, hands shaking, wondering what had awakened him. He sat in the darkness of his quarters for a long time, wire in hand, fighting against the strength of his need, searching for the willpower to put the wire down. He needed to think, and he couldn't do that when the wire was in. Finally he shuddered, set it for the lowest current, and plugged it in, and then sat in the darkness of his quarters, smiling blissfully under the caress of electric ecstasy.

His room was a converted office; the systerm had been ripped out, so that he could not call out; but otherwise it was as its previous owner had left it, down to the desk and the personal holos on the desk.

He slept on a cot in the corner.

At length, he was not sure how long it was, it occurred to him that he was hungry. He brushed his hair to hide the plug and, wearing a dreamy juice-junkie smile, went to look for something to eat. The waldo that had been assigned to guard him padded down the corridor after him, eight metal legs making gentle clicking sounds on the gleaming tile.

The cafeteria—it had been a public restaurant until the rebels took over the building—sat on the third floor, immediately beside Operations. Operations had quite recently been the offices of Greenberg & Bass. David's room was on the nineteenth floor, immediately beneath the penthouse, and Obodi; he took the lift, asked for the third floor.

The entire fourth floor was the health club where they had been letting his sister work out.

He passed through Operations on the way to the cafeteria,

and paused briefly to watch the colored lights that showed the positions of rebel and Unification forces, against a map of California. The rebel forces were shown in red, the Unification forces in blue; there was vastly more blue territory on the maps than red—significantly more than there had been only a few days prior.

It was 12:12 A.M., just after midnight on Saturday.

The cease-fire had been in effect for twelve minutes.

In the restaurant, he found Callia Sierran sitting at one of the tables, with coffee and toast before her. That late at night the restaurant was nearly empty—Callia at one table, half a dozen Johnny Rebs at another, only a couple of staff on duty in the restaurant—but she did not look surprised when he sat down across from her. She was auditing text on her handheld, and seemed weary.

A large pack of Wrigley's Spearmint gum sat on the table in front of her.

He thought about what to say to her. She did not know him, not really; had no idea that he was Denice's brother; did not know that Denice was a Castanaveras. All she knew was that he worked for Mister Obodi, and that he was a juice junkie. She wasn't certain about his name.

She knew interesting things about Denice. He sat quietly with her for a while, remembering conversations she'd had with his sister.

Finally he said, "How are you, Callia Sierran?"

She did not look at him. "I've been better. We're getting slaughtered. PKF took back San Francisco, they're through with Los Angeles, and moving south about forty klicks a day. And we're not doing a damn thing to stop them. We're still holding through San Diego County and south down into Mexico, including Baja I'm told, but I don't know for how long. It surprises me we got this cease-fire; I wouldn't have done it in their skin. However it happened, though, it's a good thing; we need it desperately."

David said mildly, "I wouldn't worry."

The flash of pity he felt from her did not even bother him. Callia said wearily, "I'm sure you wouldn't."

David smiled at her. "Obodi's got it figured out. It'll be fine."

"He sure has people thinking so."

David nodded. "He really does. I've seen the simulations,

the real ones. He probably won't have to destroy more than two
or three cities, no more than four for sure."

Callia turned off her handheld and sat looking at him. Behind her, through the restaurant's windows, David could see
San Diego's nighttime sky. "What?"

"The warheads." At her uncomprehending look, David said,
"The Japanese. They gave him nuclear warheads." He smiled
at her again. "Twenty-two of them."

Callia Sierran tried calling Riverside. Communication was temporarily out, the operator told her, in a voice that was nothing
even remotely human.

"Ring? Is that you?"

"Yes."

"You're managing communications now."

"Mister Obodi requested it."

"I see."

She left the building, requisitioned a jeep and had it drive
her over to the local Temple. Lan was there, in the outer building, running the recruiting drive; despite the hour, nearly 2:00
A.M., they were still processing volunteers by the hundreds, is-
suing them American flag armbands and laser rifles. The rifles
would not actually fire until one of the several thousand author-
ized core members of the Claw or Reb activated them.

Callia waited until Lan was done with his applicant, and
called him away. The Reverend herself took over Lan's table,
and sat down with the next applicant.

They went on into the Temple proper. Four rows of pews,
pseudowood, faced inward to the central area where the Reverend gave her sermons. Stained-glass windows, showing
scenes from the life of the Prophet Harry, were backlit by spotlights, sending light showering down into the Temple in a shattered rainbow.

Callia said softly, "Pray with me."

They knelt together, inside the brilliant rainbow at the
center of the circle, facing one another.

"I can't get ahold of Domino or Nicole."

"They're not answering? Lovely doesn't surprise me, but
Domino?"

"I'm not getting through. I think I'm being stopped by
Ring."

"So?"

"Obodi," Callia told him, "has hydrogen bombs. And he's prepared to use them."

Lan was silent for a long moment. "Okay."

"What?"

"I will pray with you."

Probably the greatest accompishment of the Unification was that it made nuclear weapons unnecessary. You don't remember, for I have made a world where you don't need to remember. But when I was a child we lived in the shadow of the Bomb. You capitalize that word. Bomb. It was the thing that would destroy everything, all of us, all at once. We had the ability to fry each other whenever we all finally got up the nerve. To end humanity forever on any given day.

We had to have the Unification. Today you all remember that we fought the Unification War because the ecosphere was failing, because we had poisoned and overpopulated the world to the point where we were dying of our own wastes. You remember this, because you are still dealing with it today.

But you do not remember the Bomb. Because once we won, the Bomb went away. We destroyed them, all the city-killers. And we'd have destroyed the tacnukes if I'd had my way—and today you, and your children, remember only that the Unification was fought to save Mother Earth.

So you've forgotten that it was also fought because we were terrified of the Bomb. But if anyone ever comes among you, and suggests using such weapons again, I think you will remember your fear, and quickly.

Ecological catastrophes take time; time to build up, time to cure.

The Bomb is a one-day eternal mistake.

If anyone ever comes among you again, and suggests using such weapons, you will be afraid.

You should be afraid.

—Sarah Almundsen, founder of the
Unification, in an interview shortly before her
death in 2028.

When they had finished praying, Callia said, "You stay here; I'm going to go talk to him, first thing in the morning."

"Okay."

"I'll probably try to kill him."

"The rebellion's over if that happens. You know that."

"It's over now, Lan. Unless we use the bombs we've lost." He nodded. "Then we've lost."

"If I don't succeed, then I'm dead and you have to kill him." Lan said simply, "Okay."

"Free Denice if you can. She was Councilor Ripper's assistant; we're going to need somebody to surrender, and she has contacts."

Lan simply nodded. Callia sat looking at him, leaned forward slightly and kissed him on the cheek, whispered, "I love you."

Lan looked into her eyes. "I'll kill him for you."

- 26 -

That night, Denice had a dream.

In her dream she wore a cloak of pale shadows that covered her from head to toe. She journeyed north, toward the source of a great river, through a stark wilderness, cold and windblown. The banks of the river were frozen solid, hard beneath her feet. Her breath steamed in the air around her, and her cheeks, the only exposed portion of her person, grew cold and icy.

She walked for days that became years, trudged endlessly through the gathering cold. Darkness fell around her with a glacial slowness, left her moving along the banks of the great river in an eerie twilight as the first dim twinkle of stars came out in the skies above her, stars no human of Earth had ever seen. With the passage of time the darkness deepened, and the stars above her came out in full, a blaze of light so bright that at moments, the pale gray shadow cloak she wore became visible.

In the depth of the night she came at last to a place where the river vanished into the side of a mountain. At the mouth of the river stood a great city of silver and gold, its walls gleaming in the starlight. Surrounded by a vast ten-sided wall, the city had two gates, one at the west and one at the east, and the gates were open.

She passed in through the near gate.

Above the gate was the word *Ascension*.

Inside she found the city perfect and empty and sterile. Nothing grew and nothing lived. At the city's center loomed a vast ten-sided building, walls black as the space between the stars. She did not hesitate, but walked through the walls and passed through, into darkness. She found herself in a greater darkness, standing on the familiar featureless black plain, stretching away to infinity. Dazzling lights glowed at the edges of existence, but came no closer as she walked toward them. She walked for a long time, not knowing what to expect, and came upon a giant figure, twenty meters high, sitting upon a throne carved from a single great emerald. In a niche upon the right arm of the throne was a golden Flame, and in the niche upon the left arm of the throne was a jagged hole in reality, a black *nothingness* that wavered and clawed at its surroundings. The figure wore shadows from head to toe, with a hooded cloak that obscured its countenance. It drew back the hood at her approach, and revealed pale features, smooth and blank as the face of a statue, and where its eyes were there was likewise blackness, cold and inhuman.

She knew it was someone she had met before, in another aspect and another place; but in this place, in this moment, the memory would not come.

She removed the hood of shadows from her own head, stood at the foot of the throne.

They spoke in the manner of her childhood, words without sound.

What is this place?

The dark eyes held her. *Nowhere.*

Who are you?

incomprehensiblepainrage; I am the God of Players.

She shook herself slightly; the *word* was already fading from her awareness. *Why am I here?*

The god said, *I brought you.*

Why?
It is time to choose.
Killing is wrong.
Then you are—
I am a dream of life.
Dancer, take the Flame.
She reached for it, and the golden Flame leapt down from the emerald throne, touched and enveloped her, sheathed her in the glowing armor of the living Flame.
The Nameless One said, *I am pleased. It is time that the Dance live again.*

Denice Castanaveras awoke with a fierce joy that filled her until she thought she would burst, danced like electricity across her skin; so uplifted her she did not think she could stand to wait for tonight, when Lan would come and free her.

- 27 -

Mister Obodi received her up in the penthouse, in the wood-floored room where he meditated and, Callia had heard, exercised—though no one she had spoken to had ever seen the latter.

She was, Callia thought, the only person except Denice to have been invited into Obodi's penthouse. She was not deeply surprised; she knew she and Denice looked much alike.. If Obodi found Denice attractive, he probably found her attractive.

His bodyguards were the best Credit could buy. Half a dozen Japanese cyborgs; the two at the door were, respectively, ex-Space Force and ex-PKF; after that they had worked for Security Services, and after that, briefly, for David Zanini.

They searched her, scanned her, and sent her inside.

Obodi sat her down in the center of the huge wood floor, knelt facing her, and asked, "What can I do for you?"

"I have heard, Mister Obodi, that you have hydrogen bombs. That you're going to use them."

"And if it is true?"

"I am going to try to dissuade you."

The tan, ascetic features took on a faintly amused cast. "Where did you hear this wild rumor?"

"Your juice junkie, David I think his name is. David Zanini. He said he was there when you negotiated it with the Japanese."

Obodi nodded: "And where am I supposed to have hidden these hydrogen bombs? There are Claw in every part of my operation, Callia. The armories we have taken are run by Reb and Claw alike; the weapons we have acquired are familiar to Reb and Claw alike. There is no part of this rebellion that is not full of Claw." She nodded reluctantly, and he continued. "But I suppose it is not impossible. To prove that I have not secreted these weapons somewhere is beyond me; I doubt I can prove that I *have not* done anything to your satisfaction. I would ask you, *why* in the name of the Prophet Harry you would take the word of a juice junkie on such an important matter; I would reassure you that the lives of the innocent matter to me. I am *not* indifferent to them. We all knew that there would be deaths going into this rebellion; but, like you, Callia, I am concerned that the deaths should be kept to the minimum necessary. I do not see that the loss of millions or tens of millions of innocent lives serves our purpose. Independence at that cost is an obscenity." Obodi paused, smiled as though amused, and said, "An *evil* thing."

Callia Sierran stared at the man. She had been following along in the gentle flow of his voice, slightly lost in the reasonable cadence of his sentences; she was almost prepared to believe him—

He sat there, smiling at her.

It was a mocking, cynical smile, vastly amused and contemptuous. Callia sat motionless for a long moment, simply astonished that anyone could pack so much meaning into a simple movement of the lips.

They faced one another, she in half lotus, he kneeling. She unwrapped herself, prepared to stand, and saw Obodi, without particularly shifting position, move his right leg slightly.

The kick took her high on the shoulder she had broken in the assault on the PKF barracks in L.A. She felt the collarbone snap again, let the kick move her backward, away from Obodi, reached into her mouth and pulled her hideaway free as she rolled.

It was tucked next to her gum; a single-shot flechette gun, made of plastic with a single plastic-ceramic projectile that fragmented when fired; the gun had the same slowscan signature as her gums, the projectile the same signature as a tooth; it was about the size of her pinkie.

He came after her as she rolled. A single sharp pain occurred in the elbow of her right arm; the arm went completely numb, and Obodi plucked the hideaway out of her hand. She came out of her roll on her back, ready to fire, hand pointed at him, with nothing in the hand.

He took a step back, looking at the flechette gun. "What an interesting toy. I see how this works." He looked back down at Callia, pointed the gun at her legs, and pressed the stud that fired it.

Callia screamed at the impact, very briefly.

At the scream, the door behind her curled open, and Obodi's bodyguards sprinted in, stopped when they saw the situation—they hesitated, looking at Obodi.

Obodi gestured at the unconscious form; her legs were mangled, and she was already in shock. "Take her away. Have one of the doctors look at her; if she survives, put her in the cell next to the little Japanese man."

Lan Sierran waited until 11:00 on Saturday morning. When he did not hear from his sister, he went back into the Temple to pray.

He prayed for her soul until noon and then went looking for the Reverend. The Reverend was asleep; not surprising, she'd had the night shift, with Lan, and had been up most of the night processing recruits. It made Lan realize that he should be tired himself; but he did not feel tired. It seemed to him that he had never been more aware of the world.

Lan woke the woman in her bed. "I need forty of the faithful who are not afraid to die."

The Latham Building.

Ralf examined the conversation he had monitored inside the Temple of Eris. He recognized both of the people, Callia Sierran and her sibling Lan Sierran; Lan's presence at the Temple of Eris was the primary reason Ralf had gone to the effort of cracking the Temple's security.

Free Denice if you can. She was Councilor Ripper's assistant;

we're going to need somebody to surrender for us, and she has contacts.

Ralf had strongly suspected that Denice was in the Latham Building; much of the rebel activity seemed to center around it. But with Ring providing data security for the rebels, with web angels circling the building at every possible point in the Crystal Wind that might allow an attack, Ralf had not been, and would not be able to approach the building.

Not through the Crystal Wind.

The man who had introduced himself to Denice as Doctor Derek—one of the last human surgeons in the world—arrived at the Latham Building just after 5:00 P.M. His patient was waiting for him up in Obodi's makeshift surgery room, tucked into a slowtime bubble. He put her up on the operating gurney and popped the bubble, then looked down at his work with plain disgust. Though he did not dare say so to Obodi, he thought he belonged out in combat, where his skills might do some good for the cause, helping heal rebels whose bodies had been insulted with gunfire, in terrain and under conditions where a surgical robot would not have been appropriate. *Well,* he thought grimly, *I get to deal with gunfire, anyway.*

There were two fine surgical robots in the mobile hospital across the plaza; apparently Obodi did not want news of this incident leaving headquarters.

The slowscan showed a broken left collarbone; the primary wound looked as though it had come from a flechette gun. Doctor Derek considered amputating the legs, decided, reluctantly, to patch them up. He had no time for a major amputation, and no resources to clone her a new pair of legs afterward.

The woman—Callia Sierran, he thought, though he had not actually been introduced to her—had apparently gotten on Obodi's bad side, never a difficult thing to do. She'd gone into shock by the time they'd put her in the slowtime field; Doctor Derek did not want to risk a general anesthetic. He blocked her entirely at the lower spine, gave her another injection for her shoulder, and went to work. He worked steadily; removing dozens of bits of some ceramic plastic from the mangled thighs and knees and shins. The knees were the worst; the rest would heal up acceptably well, but both patellas were shattered, tendons around both knees severed; she needed a new pair of knees at the very least.

Unfortunately he did not have them for her.

It took him quite a while. Fragments of plastic ceramic were everywhere, and he moved slowly, carefully, making sure he didn't leave any of them inside her. When he had cleared away the worst of the dead tissue, he reattached the loose tendons, injected both legs with a regrowth nanovirus, and disinfected and sprayed the area, from thigh to calves, with protective pseudoskin. Another five minutes took care of the shoulder; it was trivial enough by comparison with the rest. He reset the bone and sprayed a shell over it to keep the shoulder stiff. The same nanovirus that was designed to regrow the muscle should serve for the bone.

Two of Obodi's bodyguards stood at the door, watching him work. One of the bodyguards was Japanese, one of the lot Doctor Derek suspected of having been cyborged; the other, a shorter, massively muscled black man, had come with the juice junkie, David Zanini. Both wore masers strapped to their thighs.

Finally Doctor Derek stripped his gloves off. "Where is she going?"

"She'll be downstairs," said the black man. "A basement cell."

Doctor Derek nodded, patted one of the medbots arrayed against the wall on its round metal head. "*Command:* patient."

The medbot considered the command. Four humans in the room; one, lying on a gurney, was obviously the PATIENT. The medbot clattered over on six legs and stood next to the gurney the PATIENT lay on. " 'Bot, take her where these two direct, stay with her."

The 'bot said, "Yes, Doctor." It unlocked the gurney's wheels, grasped the handles, and pushed the gurney carrying its PATIENT out of the makeshift surgery room, following the black man down the corridor; the Japanese man followed it. They went down to the freight lift, in the utility corridor—the standard lifts were too small to admit the gurney—waited only a few seconds for it to arrive.

The 'bot pushed the gurney into the freight elevator, gently so that the PATIENT would not be jarred too badly. It stepped carefully; once several years ago the 'bot had caught one of its six small feet in the gap between the lift and the hallway; it remembered the incident quite well. The humans had amputated the stuck leg to get the 'bot out, and had taken their time about putting a new one on. For *weeks* the 'bot had been unable to be of service to PATIENTS; very frustrating.

Gurney in first, then the humans following it; the 'bot watched as the humans turned to face the lift door. One of the humans, the Japanese one, said, *"Command,* basement."

An interesting thing happened. The medbot's PATIENT sat up on the gurney. The 'bot grasped the gurney handles as firmly as it was able, and locked its legs in position so that the gurney would not rock beneath the PATIENT. The PATIENT leaned forward and did two things at the same time; with her right hand lifted the black man's maser free of its holster, and with her left pulled the black man backward with her. She jammed the maser into the small of the man's back and pulled the trigger as they fell backward together. *Bad bad bad,* the medbot's thoughts chattered frantically, its PATIENT had just scalded her hand by firing a maser in such an enclosed place, might possibly have separated her left collarbone again, she shouldn't be using that arm at *all* for at least two days. The Japanese man moved with unnatural speed for a human, the medbot saw next, twisted and bounced as far away from the PATIENT as the freight elevator would let him get, pulling his maser free in midbounce, firing as he moved. Fortunately his shot hit the large black man his PATIENT was hiding behind. The medbot's PATIENT got the maser free of the black man's bulk, got the maser on the Japanese man and held the trigger down until the smell of cooking meat permeated the lift.

"Command," said Callia Sierran, "stop the lift. Do *not* sound an emergency."

The lift said, "Yes, mademoiselle."

Callia lay back with the black man's corpse atop her for a good bit before she found the energy to push him off. Her vision wavered in and out of focus and she had difficulty thinking coherently. Finally she said, *"Command,* ninth floor."

The medbot stood motionless, looking back and forth between the two motionless humans and its PATIENT. This was fascinating; no PATIENT had ever done so many different interesting things in its presence before. The lift stopped at the ninth floor and the PATIENT said, "Get me out of here, 'bot," as the lift doors curled open on the ninth floor utility corridor.

She had not prefaced the sentence with *"Command"*; but injured PATIENTS often did not remember to, the 'bot knew. It parsed the sentence three times for redundancy, got the same interpretation every time, and then checked with the lift com-

puter; the lift agreed to keep its doors open until the 'bot had
gotten its PATIENT out. The medbot examined the problem. The
black man had slumped forward over the lift entrance; he was
blocking the gurney. The medbot let go of the gurney handles
and stepped forward, carefully avoiding the dangerous gap between the lift and the hall, and then reached back in, grasping
the black man by his shirt. Heavy. It took the 'bot several seconds to pull him free of the lift.

Its PATIENT was talking to the lift when it returned for her.
"This is an emergency, lift. Do you understand? Urgent, extremely deeply *urgent*. I have a lot of things to load onto you,
and I need you to stay *right here until I come back*. Do you understand?"

"Yes, mademoiselle. This lift will wait for your return."

"Not go *anywhere*."

"Not go anywhere," the lift agreed.

" 'Bot, let's *go*. To the left."

"One moment, mademoiselle." The medbot was certain
about the black man; it blipped a sonar pulse now toward the
other. Similarly, there was no pulse. They were Dead, De-
ceased, Expired; Corpses, Cadavers.

Unfortunate, but clearly neither was a potential PATIENT any
longer.

Satisfied at having discharged its duties, the 'bot returned to
its PATIENT, and said cheerfully, "Where to, mademoiselle?"

Prior to the building's takeover by the Rebs, the ninth floor
had belonged to a major accountancy firm whose expert systems had specialized in duels with the Tax Boards. Since the
rebellion, obviously, nobody in San Diego had been uploading
returns to the Tax Boards; and Callia hoped that the offices
were empty. Only about half the floors in the building were in
use.

She found herself in luck. The medbot pushed her out of
the utility corridor, and into one of the long hallways that criss-
crossed the building; quiet, nobody in sight. "Left again, 'bot."
The medbot pushed her down the length of the corridor, to the
building's southeast corner. The door to the corner office was
locked; she had the 'bot pull her back, and then set the maser
for its tightest aperture, and started slicing through the door.
She got a quarter of the way through when the door's memory
plastic went crazy; the door curled open *fast*, with a sound like

a rifle shot—rolled slowly shut, snapped open, rolled shut—Callia timed it, waited until the door was fully open, and then shot it one last time.

The door froze open, and the 'bot wheeled her through. She did not even consider using the system, though it was still installed; any calls coming from this floor would be an instant notification to Ring that something was not correct. Instead she had the medbot push her up close to the south window. From here she could see much of the plaza below; it looked quiet. Then the east window; from here she could see the bulk of the Temple itself, four blocks inland.

The charge on the maser showed 42 percent; she'd wasted a lot of it cooking the Japanese cyborg. *Damn* he'd moved fast. Callia had trained against holos of real Elite in action, against robots designed to move at Elite speeds; if the Japanese cyborg had been slower, he had not been slower by much.

It was still a half hour until sunset; but the east side of the building was in shadow. They might see her maser.

She sliced a small circle in the window, hoped that the falling piece of glassite would not alert anybody in the plaza below; tuned the maser to medium dispersion, stuck the barrel through and aimed for the Temple of Eris.

In speedtalk she started flashing: *Callia. Alive.*
Callia. Alive.
Callia. Alive.

Joe Tagomi's image appeared in front of Sedon without warning. An emergency, then. "Yes, Joe?"

The cyborg spoke rapidly. "Mister Obodi, we have reports that semiballistics are boosting out of Los Angeles by the hundreds, possibly thousands."

Sedon nodded, rose calmly. "How long?"

"From L.A.? We're going to have PKF dropping on us in twenty-four minutes *flat*."

Sedon spoke without haste. "How long before the entire invasion force arrives?"

"If they launch as they did from Unification Spaceport for the L.A. invasion, they'll go up in waves, one every two minutes; it might be an hour or an hour and ten minutes from now before the entire complement has arrived."

"Very good. Meet me in Operations. Have the semiballistics loaded with the warheads; leave one behind, timed for detonation in exactly one hour and fifteen minutes. Put another aboard a semiballistic bound for L.A., to detonate upon arrival. We will boost for Japan in twenty minutes."

"I'll give the orders."

"Have Operations ready for me. I'll be there promptly. *Command*, access David." The boy was sleeping, a distant, dreamy smile touching his features. "David!"

The sharp rap of Sedon's voice penetrated the haze of electric ecstasy; David stirred, opened his eyes. "Yes?"

"Join me in Operations. PKF are approaching; do it *now*." The boy nodded. "Yes, Mister Obodi."

"Good. I will see you there."

Sedon needed to take nothing with him, other than his own quite irreplaceable self. He swept out the door, gestured to his bodyguards, and headed for the lifts.

David Castanaveras took sixty seconds, counting—*one one thousand, two one thousand*—with the wire at its highest setting. At sixty he disconnected the wire, stood stock still until the wave of shudders that wracked his body had passed. He tucked the wire into his coat pocket, checked himself in the mirror. Shaved, clean clothes, not a hair out of place. Shoes polished, crease in the pants. No tie or shoulder silks, but he'd heard they didn't wear them much out here on the West Coast anyway.

Time to go.

He opened the door to his room, waited for the waldo to stir itself from where it waited, like a faithful dog, beside his door. Out in the lobby, two of the polite young Japanese cyborgs waited, holding a lift door open; waiting for him, clearly. That was convenient. To the one nearest him, he said, *Destroy the waldo behind me.*

The cyborg went past David so fast that David felt the wind of his passage. The sound of the cyborg's impact with the waldo echoed through the lobby. David did not turn around to see what happened; he stepped into the lift, said to the other cyborg, *You come with me.*

"*Command*," he said aloud, "the roof." The lift moved upward. To the cyborg, David said, *If anyone is on the roof, you kill him.*

The lift opened into a small hallway; stairs at the end of the hallway led up to the roof proper. David remembered descending those stairs, an eternity ago, to meet with Obodi. David stayed inside the hallway while the cyborg went out onto the roof, and waited for the cyborg to return. He heard a single gunshot, then nothing. The cyborg returned, his shirt torn where the bullet had struck him, but otherwise apparently unharmed.

David went up to the roof. No bodies; his cyborg must have tossed it, or them, over the edge. Three cars. He glanced at his cyborg. "Do you know which of these vehicles is the fastest?"

The cyborg said, "The Chandler 1790. The blue car. It has a top speed of two hundred seventy kph."

"Carcomp?"

"Yes."

David nodded. "Keyed how?"

"Password. *Liberty '76.*"

"Good. Do you have any family?"

"My mother, a brother, a son."

"I see." *They are all dead,* David told the cyborg. *Mister Obodi raped your mother and sodomized your brother and fucked your child in the mouth. Then he killed them all by—* David paused, abruptly totally bereft of ideas—*in the most unpleasant way you can think of,* he finished.

The young man's face twisted abruptly into a mask of pain and fury. "He killed my *son.*"

"He's down in Operations," David told the cyborg. "Fourth floor. Thank you for your help." He turned away and went to the car. "Car, *Liberty '76. Command,* open the canopy." The canopy cracked, and David sank into the soft black pseudo-leather seats.

He sat motionless for a moment. It was very near sunset, and the night sky to the west was stunning, scarlet near the bulk of the sun, fading to pink toward the edges of the horizon, deep blue shading toward black in the sky above and behind him. It occurred to David that he had never seen a sunset over the ocean before. "Carcomp, take us south, as low as you can get to the ground. Keep close enough to the shore that I can watch the sunset. Then head inland. Clear?"

"Yes, monsieur." The car's fans came up, and then it lifted, moved forward, picked up speed, and moved free of the building, dropping slightly to pick up speed.

David did not look back even once. He watched the sunset, trying not to think about what he left behind. Obodi scared him as no one had scared him in his life; if the PKF had not been coming, to distract Obodi from dealing with him, David did not think he would have taken this chance. He did not need to imagine the sorts of things that would happen to him if he fell into Obodi's hands again; he had been forced to keep the entire building full of people between himself and Dvan just to avoid feeling the man's broadcast pain.

Obodi would not make the mistake of thinking his Speakings had worked a second time.

Not that Speaking was not a good trick. Obodi approached, with no tool better than words, the sorts of things that David could do with the Gift. David thought that the Speakings probably *would* have worked on anyone except a Castanaveras who had spent seven years fighting the pull of the wire.

That his sister was imprisoned behind him he had already forgotten. The thought of letting her see what he had become hurt him at such a deep level that he did not like to think of it.

So he did not.

The sunset was a wonderful experience.

In the last half hour before sunset they walked across the plaza, two squads of Erisian Claw. They moved without hurry, past two checkpoints that waved them through upon recognizing Lan; then, at the entrance to the Latham Building, a Reb Lan did not know stopped them. Half a dozen Rebs stood inside the lobby, in front of the double row of lifts.

The Reb eyed them with distinct suspicion. "What's this about?"

Lan sighed his annoyance. "They didn't tell you?"

The Reb said bluntly, "No."

"We're supposed to escort some prisoners," Lan said. "They're being moved?"

The man's hostility was plain. "I don't know anything about that."

Lan stared at the man. "Then why don't you fucking well *check*?"

The Reb nodded slowly. "All right. Stay right here." He took a step backward, not turning around, not taking his eyes from Lan and the forty Claw standing behind him.

A body fell out of the sky.

The impact of the body against the pavement, twenty meters off to Lan's left, froze everyone throughout the plaza. The Reb officer turned slightly to his right, to look at what had happened.

Lan palmed his knife and put it in the man's neck, took a step forward and held him up as though they were talking with one another, hissed to the Claw closest to him, "Come *get* him." *Callia?* flashed through his thoughts, but if so, after that fall there was nothing he could do for her now, and he had made her a promise. He released the Reb into the arms of a comrade, stepped through into the lobby of the Latham Building, knew the Rebs by the lifts would have noticed the confusion, and told them the truth because it was the simplest thing he could think of: "Hey! We just had a body fall off the roof! What's happening?"

One of the Rebs stepped forward, toward Lan, and Lan walked toward him without hurry. When he was ten meters away he unslung in one smooth motion; the autoshot was already set to full auto, safety off. He fired while bringing the weapon around, as soon as he had his finger on the trigger. A trick he'd been taught; the noise was so awesome in an enclosed space that it rattled the target, and the autoshot cycled so fast that it did not significantly delay the next shot. Lan stood braced and watched the officer approaching him dissolve in a shower of flesh and blood. The five who had waited back at the lifts died almost as quickly, and only a little less messily; none of them even got a shot off.

Behind him, his Claw did as they'd been instructed, poured through after him. First Squad spread out and took up positions throughout the lobby, twenty of the faithful prepared to die guarding the entrance to the building. On his way to the stairs Lan called out, "*Remember!* They can come at you through main doors, side doors, lifts, stairwell, and finally with an X-laser they can cut through from the roof above you or the floor below."

He had told them before, spent most of the last hour drilling them, but they were amateurs and he did not expect them to remember.

With twenty Claw at his back he blew the stairway door out of its track and trotted down the stairs to the basement.

In the midst of a rebellion, it was still possible to get a cab, at least if you lied to the dispatching computer. Ralf the Wise and Powerful did, and with his hijacked cab made half circles of the

Latham Building at a safe distance. He could not make entire circuits; it would have taken the cab out over the ocean, where the rebels would likely have shot it down.

The cab's optics were poor, but no matter; Ralf had access to video from several other sources, mostly pay phones—which had equally poor optics, but interpolating from multiple sources let him build up a good idea of what was happening.

None of the pay phones were oriented to pick up the red light blinking on the ninth floor of the building. Ralf had been flying back and forth for twenty minutes before he realized it was there. He swept quickly through all the optical sources available to him; nothing but the cab would serve to give him a good look at the blinking light. He debated briefly, then took the cab straight up, facing the Latham Building, and hovered forty meters up for most of half a minute.

On-off signals. A binary code with a modulation time of a *second*? If he had been a human Ralf the Wise and Powerful would simply not have believed what he saw. But AIs are pragmatic; what exists, is. In instants Ralf swept through every binary code he knew from the dawn of computing forward, four-bit, eight-bit, sixteen-bit, thirty-two-bit, sixty-four-bit, multiprocessor, transputer, parallel processor, nothing that fit.

The duration; obviously a human source, nothing electronic moved with such astonishing slowness. A binary code being employed by a *human*.

What a remarkable thing the world was.

Ralf went back to the San Diego Public Library. He scanned through the Library of Congress; codes, Morse; descendants of—

Speedtalk. Employed by Speedfreaks, flashing headlights or running lights at one another to avoid being overheard on radio by the PKF. *Callia, alive. Callia, alive.*

Alive, probably. Likely she didn't quite remember the code; Callia's mother had been a Speedfreak, but it was doubtful Callia had had opportunity to use speedtalk since her mother's death in 2063.

Intelligence from Los Angeles suggested that PKF would be in San Diego within mere minutes.

Ralf made his decision almost instantly; he had no obligation to the woman, but it was possible that helping her would help Denice. He kept the vehicle steady, flashed back with the headlamps, *Rescue coming*.

The cab shot forward at full throttle.

•   •   •

Gunfire for just a moment. Then Lan's voice at the door to Denice's cell: "Stand back!"

Denice crouched in the corner of her cell, mattress from her bed pulled over to cover her.

The memory-plastic door, under the impact of the autoshot, *shattered*. Denice felt scattershot and slivers of door pepper the mattress; the instant the ricochets had stopped she was up and moving. Lan handed her a Series IV Excalibur laser rifle, said, "Good to see you again, we've *got* to do lunch sometime."

In the corridor outside five dead rebels lay sprawled across the floor, four in uniform, one not; the one in civilian clothes was one of Lan's squad, Denice guessed. The rest of his people were clustered in the far end of the hallway, wearing armbands; one person with an autoshot would decimate them clustered together that way. They were amateurs and Denice ignored them.

Blood had sprayed up to cover the walls from floor to ceiling. Lan shouted back over his shoulder, moving down the row of cells, "Have you seen Callia?"

"No."

"Stand back!" Lan brought the autoshot around—

"*Lan!*"

He hesitated. "What?"

"These aren't real prison cells. This was commercial space." Lan shook his head blankly, and Denice said, "Try the door-pad."

He stared at her for just an instant. "Oh. Sure."

The door curled open at his touch. Empty. He moved down the row, door to door; Robert was in the third cell, Dvan in the fourth, nobody in the fifth. Lan stood in front of the empty fifth cell, staring blankly for a second, then nodded, turned and headed back the way he'd come. As he passed by Denice he stopped, said quietly, "We heard before we headed over that PKF is on the way in. They'll be dropping on San Diego in maybe ten or twelve minutes. Good luck." He started to say something else; then Lan simply shook his head and said, " 'Bye."

He left at a dead run, long brown hair trailing behind him, the other Claw following him as quickly and capably as they were able.

Robert stood motionlessly in the hallway, watching Denice.

Denice looked at him.

"*This,*" said Robert Dazai Yo, "is what happens during wars." He waved his hand at the blood-soaked walls with clear distaste. "*Bad* killing."

There was nobody in the cab.

Callia stared at the empty cab, floating outside the ninth-story window, its canopy popped completely off.

Her legs were numb and her left shoulder was on fire. Under normal circumstances she would have made it without too much difficulty, from the window to the cab, but now—

The maser showed 6 percent. She set the beam to its tightest setting and sliced the window in an X; when she was done the maser still read 2 percent, but touching the trigger did nothing. " 'Bot!"

The medbot, watching with a total lack of comprehension, finally found something it understood: its PATIENT wanted help. "Yes, mademoiselle?"

"Push me up to the window."

Alarm coursed through the medbot. "I *cannot* do that, mademoiselle."

The PATIENT stared at it. "Why not?"

The medbot hesitated, reviewing treatment information. "Suicide is a permanent solution to short-term troubles, mademoiselle; your illness is temporary; please consider all those things you have to live for; the world in all its beauty is—"

The PATIENT seemed to grow very agitated; she interrupted it. "*I'm not planning on jumping.* Okay? I just want to get into the cab that's come for me. See, there it is."

The medbot telescoped up on its legs and looked out the window. Indeed, the PATIENT was correct; a vehicle floated outside the window, and it was marked with the word Taxi, a synonym for cab. "Forgive me, mademoiselle. I misunderstood." The medbot sank back down and pushed the gurney close to the window, then locked its legs to keep the gurney steady. The PATIENT struck the window several times in a row; the glassite cracked along the X, but further blows did nothing more. The PATIENT used her left arm, attached to the injured shoulder, to grasp the windowsill—

"Wait! Wait!" The medbot telescoped frantically to its fullest height. "You should not be using that arm!" The PATIENT looked at it, and the medbot said, "May I help?"

The PATIENT said in an odd voice, "Please break the window for me."

This was another very interesting thing. The medbot had never before broken a window for purposes of exiting through it. Apparently the procedure involved striking glassite until its integrity failed. The medbot closed its primary grasping appendage and tapped the window once, observed the patterns of cracks radiating away from the point where it had tapped, and then rapped, sharply, once.

The window fell away.

The medbot said, "Is the window satisfactorily broken?"

The PATIENT said softly, "Thank you." She turned back to the floating cab, called out, "*Who are you?*"

From the cab, a male voice called back, "Ralf!"

"Ralf! Bring the cab closer to the window!"

The cab drifted gently closer, stopped a meter distant, and now a fierce wind blew in through the window. "That is as close as I can come," Ralf said. "I'm being pushed back by my own fanwash now. If I drop fans I'll lose altitude."

"I only have full use of one arm, Ralf. I can't make it across a meter. Can you go to the Temple, tell them I'm here?"

"Peaceforcers boosted from L.A. fourteen and a half minutes ago, Callia Sierran. You have no time to do anything but come with me *now.*"

Hot fanwash gusted in at her. "You know me."

"Yes. You are the mother and daughter of Angel de Luz, the sister of Lan Sierran, and the friend of Denice Daimara. And if you're not in this cab within two minutes I'm pulling away from here."

He knows about Angel. Callia shivered. "Who are you?"

There was a distinct pause. "I am Ralf the Wise and Powerful. I'm an Artificial Intelligence, and a friend of Denice's. I was once the Image of Trent the Uncatchable. And I am the last hope you have to keep your life. If you want to live, come with me *now.*"

Callia Sierran swallowed. "Oh, Harry." She took a deep breath, turned to the medbot. " 'Bot?"

"Yes, mademoiselle?"

"Help me into the cab."

The medbot considered the task. It had been taught to aid the elderly and infirm in and out of bathtubs, to climb stairs, to turn unconscious PATIENTS in their beds, to catch PATIENTS who were falling. This would require a similar set of motions; it could do it. "I can do that," it announced. The medbot examined the geometry of the situation—how *very* interesting. Between 109 and 113 centimeters separated the cab from the window ledge; the cab moved back and forth a bit. The medbot dropped back to the floor, and pushed the gurney slightly back from the window. It telescoped itself to its greatest height, reached up with all three of its grasping appendages and grasped the edges of the windowsill. The top of the windowsill was too high for its primary grasping appendage to reach; the medbot flipped random numbers and switched over to the left edge of the windowsill, and held onto that edge with one of its secondary and its primary grasping appendage.

It lifted itself up very slowly. It was capable of lifting considerably greater weights than itself; but not from this position. The edge of its front three feet were almost parallel with the bottom ledge; it extended its legs, saw its front feet touch the ledge, and crept forward, centimeter by centimeter, until all six of its feet were almost parallel with the bottom ledge; it extended its legs, saw its front feet touch the ledge, and crept forward, centimeter by centimeter, until all six of its feet were firmly grasping the bottom ledge.

The PATIENT said softly, "*Good* 'bot."

The medbot turned its attention to the cab; it wavered back and forth in a periodic pattern, and the medbot timed it; when the cab was 111 centimeters distant, and swinging forward, the medbot released its grasping appendages' hold of the window ledge and pushed itself forward.

It fell, crashed into the cab. The cab dipped, dropped lower still, and the medbot's feet lost most of their contact with the window ledge; the medbot scrambled frantically for a hold on the cab, along the line where the canopy would normally have sealed. First its right grasping appendage caught, and then its left; the medbot waited several seconds to make sure that it was secure, and then reached back with its primary grasping appendage. "Mademoiselle? Take my hand, and I will aid you into the cab."

Callia had watched the entire procedure with something very like awe. The medbot's words shook her partway out of it; she pulled forward, got the gurney back within a few centimeters of the window, and reached forward with her right hand for the medbot's large central hand. Slender steel fingers wrapped themselves around her wrist, tightened, and then pulled her forward. She got her left hand onto the windowsill, pulled up—

The medbot's pull on her ceased instantly. "Do *not* use that hand!"

Callia Sierran could not think of anything else at all to do. She let go.

The medbot pulled her farther forward, out into the fierce wind. The cab dipped as her weight came forward, and to compensate Ralf turned the fans up another notch; the wind blasted around Callia and she had to close her eyes from it, and then she was *slipping* and Callia opened her eyes again, panicking, screaming, and found herself sliding face forward into the waiting cab, the medbot letting go of her as she fell into the vehicle. She got her good hand on the dash, pulled herself upright into the front left passenger's seat, trembling, fumbled shakily with the seat belt and got it fastened. She turned to the medbot, still gripping the cab and the windowsill—

The cab pulled abruptly away from the Latham Building, dropped back and away from the building, medbot hanging from the side of the vehicle, fans coming up—

The medbot's grasp on the side of the cab was slipping. Callia saw it happening. She did stop to think about what she was doing; as the 'bot's grasp failed, she leaned forward and grabbed it with her closest hand.

Her left.

Ralf the Wise and Powerful snapped, "Drop it! It's a fucking medbot! *Let go!*"

The medbot was heavy, almost as heavy as a human being. Callia felt her shoulder separating.

How very interesting. The medbot had never seen the ground from so high up before. It looked up and abruptly terror coursed through it: the PATIENT was holding it by her bad arm! "Drop me! *Drop me!*" the medbot screamed. "You are damaging yourself!"

With a single great heave, Callia hauled the medbot up into the cab, got her right hand on it and pulled it over on top of her.

"Oh!" the medbot scolded. "You are a *bad* PATIENT."

The cab flew forward in relative silence.

The medbot considered its position. Front section down, optics in the PATIENT's lap, inside the passenger compartment of a vehicle. What position would be appropriate for treating the PATIENT—

Callia Sierran whispered, "By the Prophet. Did you *see* what he did?"

For a very long moment there was no response, from Ralf or the medbot. Finally Ralf the Wise and Powerful said, "But it's a *medbot*. What the fuck did you *expect*?"

Callia Sierran did not answer him. She was stone unconscious.

There was a space at the PATIENT's feet; but it would be difficult to treat her from there. The bot's arms were long, but not *that* long. Perhaps—

Ralf said, "Stand up in the seat, your front section facing toward the patient, with your legs telescoped to their smallest setting. Reach around behind you with your secondary arm, grasp the seat belt—that's the blue polymer strap with the brushed-metal gray attachment. Pass the seat belt to your primary arm, and then attach it to the brushed metal gray attachment that is attached to the smaller blue polymer strap."

Ah. It took a moment, but that worked quite well indeed. The cab was very wise. Securely fastened into the passenger-holding mechanism, the medbot turned back to the PATIENT, considering what medicines it was stocked with. An anti-inflammatory and painkiller were clearly in order. Who knew *what* damage the PATIENT had done to herself.

In unbroken silence they flew eastward into the approaching night.

- 28 -

Dvan stared straight forward, with empty eyes.

He did not seem harmed; he had been restrained standing up against the wall. The restraints were of some polymer Denice did not recognize and did not waste time testing; if Dvan had not been able to break them, she surely would not.

Robert, in the doorway holding a rifle he'd picked up from one of the dead rebel guards, said briefly, "Leave him. Let's go."

"Fuck that." Denice brought the Excalibur up, fired four times. The beam sliced through the restraints, so close to skin that the skin bubbled; Denice smelled burnt meat, caught Dvan as he stumbled forward. "He wouldn't have left me."

"He'd have left *me*," Robert complained.

"William? *Dvan!*" No response; the man stood still, a few steps from the wall he had been strapped to, staring into emptiness. Denice slapped him, hard enough to rattle his teeth; no response.

Behind her Robert said very softly, "My dear, we don't have time for this." Without looking aside he shifted slightly, fired twice off to his left. "I'm not kidding."

Denice stood frozen in the moment, unable to leave Devane, and uncertain why—

Abruptly she knew what was required of her. She took a step backward, looked up to meet his eyes, and spoke in pure, unaccented shiata. *"Dvan of the Gi'Tbad. I am a Dancer of the Flame."*

Dvan stirred slightly, and after a moment spoke. His voice was the barest of whispers. *"My lady. I am at your service."*

"By your Dedication I require that you join me here in this place, and follow me from it. You are a Shield, a servant of the living Flame. Will you live in the service of the Flame?"

Dvan whispered, *"I will."*

"Will you kill if you must?"

"Aye."

"Will you die if needed; will you live when you no longer wish to, if the service is required of you?"

"My lady," he began again, slowly, *"I am at your service."*

"Then follow me." Denice left without looking back to see if the big man was following; knew by the lack of expression on Robert's face that he was. They moved off down the corridor together, Dvan behind. Denice murmured, "See? How hard was that?"

Smell of smoke.

Lan brought them to a halt beside the third-floor stairwell exit. He heard a firefight, not close, going on in the third-floor lobby. The sizzle of lasers, the occasional crack of slugthrowers. He gestured silence to the Claw behind him, and, remembering Denice's suggestion in the basement, reached up and touched the doorpad.

Locked, of course. "Shit. Someone give me a maser," he whispered. A hand maser was passed forward to him, and he sat next to the doorway, listening to the distant firefight. Lull, shooting; lull, shooting; lull—

During the next round of firing he masered the doorpad. Nothing happened; he tracked over, ran the maser across the door. Somewhere in there he struck the current for the door; deprived of the current that kept its memory plastic unrolled, the door abruptly remembered the shape it was supposed to have and snapped open with a crack like a rifle shot.

Lan winced.

The door opened out into a dead-end corridor. Silence. Had he been heard? If—

Laser fire again, off to the right. One of the beams appeared briefly in the open space before the stairwell door, left a smoking red spot on the wall and an ionization trail hanging in the air twenty centimeters in front of Lan's eyes.

Silence.

Lan wished briefly for a mirror, took a deep breath, and got down on the floor and stuck his head out through the doorway, just far enough to see what was going on.

At the far end of the lobby were the offices of Greenberg & Bass, what was now Operations. Midway down the lobby, by the lifts, with his back to Lan and his troops, crouched a man in burnt, smoldering clothes, tucked down behind an overturned desk he was using as a shield. The laser rifle in his hands had seen considerable use; its barrel glowed cherry red.

One of the Japanese cyborgs, Lan was almost certain.

Two of Lan's troops had pumped lasers with them, the Elite killers; Lan pulled his head back, silently gestured to the Claw nearest him who had one. Pumped laser in hand, autoshot slung across his back, Lan waited for the next round of fire, waited for the next lull, stepped out from the stairwell, took the necessary split second to sight, and fired once into the cyborg's back. It worked as well on cyborgs without superconductor meshes as on those with; the cyborg exploded in a fountain of steaming bone and muscle.

Lan stepped back into the stairwell, yelled out, *"Lan Sierran! Approaching the door!"* He took the grenade from his coat pocket, pushed the pressure switch on the grenade in, clasped the small grenade in the palm of his right hand with the switch tightly closed; gave it a five-count, gestured to the Claw to follow him, and stepped out into the corridor with the pumped X-laser in his hands, but pointed at the ceiling.

"Hold it!" Lan recognized the voice; Joe Tagomi. "Lan?"

Lan kept moving, nineteen Claw behind him. "Hi, Joe."

"Stop right there!" Lan did. "What's going on out there, Lan?"

"I don't know, Joe. Things keep getting crazier every time I turn around. Firefight going on in the lobby when I got here; my sister's missing and I don't know what's happened to her. I made it up here and found you pinned down by one of your own people." Lan paused, called, "I need to talk to Obodi. Reports of PKF incoming, we need to evacuate *now*."

Brief silence. "Come ahead. Leave your weapons. Leave your men."

Lan did as instructed, knelt slowly, placed the pumped laser on the floor, added the autoshot, and straightened slowly. His right hand was sweating; he felt the grenade moving, slippery, against his skin.

He gestured the faithful to stay put, and moved forward cautiously, very aware of the lasers and slugthrowers peeking through the half-open double doors. The muscles in his stomach twitched. When he was ten meters away Tagomi called out, "Hands on your head!"

It was a relief to comply. He put his right hand up first, laid the grenade against the top of his skull, put his left hand up and covered his right with it.

The door opened ever so slightly wider, and rough hands pulled Lan through into Operations.

They took the stairs up to the lobby.

Denice crouched back from the stairwell doorway, Robert looking out from a slightly different angle, examining the lobby. Nothing moved, nothing at all, the length and breadth of the lobby. Sporadic gunfire came from outside, from the plaza, but even that was distant.

Outside the building, darkness had nearly fallen; far more light came from the sunpaint overhead than from the setting sun. A thin sheet of blood covered the floor all around them. The stink of cooked meat hung heavy on the air. The troops Lan had left behind were dead, and perhaps thirty Johnny Rebs as well, most of them fallen within a few meters of the main entrance.

The silence was eerie, the plaza near empty.

Denice whispered, "They heard PKF were incoming?"

Robert nodded, whispered back, "And fled, likely. Side entrance, north."

Denice glanced to her right, saw nothing. "What?"

"Outside," Robert whispered impatiently. "'Transportation."

She saw it now though the lobby windows, in the twilight outside; four vans, all the same model AeroSmith VTLs, paint tuned matte black, sat motionless on the stones of the plaza, fifty meters outside the north door.

Stillness throughout the lobby; Denice nodded. "Let's go." She moved forward—

Robert restrained her. "Impatience will kill you. We're safe for the moment; what happened here?"

"They were killed?"

"Very funny," he whispered. "Yes. Many of them by hand. The blood came first; the blatant amateurs, with autoshots and lasers. Those who fell later are clean, except where they touch the floor, and have soaked up the blood of those who fell before."

Now that he pointed it out, she could see it. "Obodi?"

Robert shook his head. "I only saw him once, after our capture at Frank's house, but I think not. I believe he's deadly; but this was the work of several very well trained soldiers. Three, four—"

The lights in the lobby went out.

In the near total darkness, Denice whispered, "Four. To the left, south exit; I can see their body heat."

In a normal conversational voice, Robert said, "William, can you use this rifle? An Excalibur."

The giant's voice was jagged. "Yes."

Robert handed it over, straightened, and took a step out into the darkened lobby. "Cyborgs," he said mildly. "The young Japanese men; taking back the lobby to secure Obodi's retreat. They have inhumanly excellent hearing, I imagine; like PKF Elite. Improved eyesight; they'll see abnormally well in the dark, as though it were daylight."

"I'll go get us one of the vans."

"Do that," said Robert absently, moving out farther into the darkness. Shadows seemed to gather about him. "I won't be long."

With Dvan at her back, she ran for the north door.

There was a distant rumble outside.

Sedon stood toward the rear of the room, motionless, breathing slowly and evenly, hands clasped loosely in front of him, long blond hair swept back from his face in a loose ponytail, face completely still and composed.

Watching Lan Sierran.

Everyone in Operations except Sedon was pointing some sort of weapon at Lan; Lan could not take his eyes off Sedon long enough to know what kinds.

Sedon said gently, "Hello, Lan Sierran. Do you know I have less than five minutes to reach my car? Do you understand that we will be under fire all the way to our semiballistic, that we stand a good chance of being shot down when we try to boost, to escape the certain vengeance of Commissioner Mohammed Vance? Do you *understand* that?" he demanded. He took a single step forward and screamed in lethal anger, "*And you are* delaying *me!*"

Lan realized he'd been holding his breath. He let it go in a long exhalation. "Mister Obodi," he said very quietly. "I was afraid you wouldn't be here. You know what this is?" He lifted his right hand from his head, held it up with the grenade pinched between thumb and forefinger.

Nobody shot him. Lan was mildly surprised.

Sedon did not move at all. The glare of his pale blue eyes fixed on Lan, he shook his head very slightly.

"It's a grenade, motherfucker. Deadman pressure switched. I let go of it, and we're all going up together."

Sedon spoke with deadly calm. "What do you want, Lan?"

"Everyone puts down their weapons."

Sedon nodded, the glare not lessening an instant. "And then?"

"My sister."

Sedon simply shook his head. "No. Kill him."

In the last act of his life, as the brilliant laser light washed across him, Lan Sierran, with something very like fulfillment, let go.

There was only one route to life. Sedon felt the air pressure changing as the shock wave began to expand outward from where the bottom half of Lan Sierran's remains still stood. Sedon was on his feet now, moving laterally to the expanding surface of the shock wave. The shrapnel and the heat outraced the more lethal shock wave; Sedon felt his hair burning, skin blistering. Tiny slivers of some metal-ceramic tore through him—he did not even have sufficient time to see if any of the wounds were potentially lethal. He kept moving, toward the long pane of glassite that looked out over San Diego, and now the shock wave itself touched, lifted him up and off his feet. He curled into a ball, and the shock wave slammed him like a handball into the surface of the glassite window. Under normal circumstances the window could not be broken, or even opened. These were not normal circumstances. The window bulged outward slightly under the immense pressure of the expanding wave front, and then blew out, shards of glassite and superheated air and Gi'Suei'Obodi'Sedon exploding out together into the cool night air, three stories above the streets of San Diego.

And falling.

He hit the ground as Vance's semiballistic landed on the roof.

Denice Castanaveras ran out into the plaza, Dvan behind her—

And stumbled to a halt.

The sky was on fire.

The sky blazed with light, roared with the sound of their drives, like nothing she had ever seen before in her life; like something out of an entertainment. Dozens, no, *hundreds* of them, more arriving with every second, semiballistics filling the sky above her, the glare of their rockets a firestorm that lit the sky from horizon to horizon. Artillery fire detonated across the length of the sky at their approach; lasers mounted elsewhere in the city strobed up into the sky to greet the approaching Unification. Denice froze as a semiballistic came up over the roof of the Latham Building, a bare twenty stories above her, and the glare of its rockets lit the plaza around her with an awful scarlet brilliance.

She stood in the midst of the dazzle, staring up at the burning sky, at power made real in the world in such a fashion that she knew that though she lived forever she would *never* forget it, would never lose this moment's perfect understanding of the *meaning* of power; stood there motionless, for an instant that would never end, beneath the glare of the impossible might of the Unification.

Then it did end and she turned and ran for the AeroSmiths.

Four of them; she took the one that was closest, for no reason other than that it was closest. To her surprise, the side door was open; she hesitated just a moment, but it was dark inside, bereft of heat sources. She moved into the AeroSmith, forward to the front, Dvan behind her. A control panel with a steering wheel; like most vehicles in California, designed for auxiliary manual operation. She doubted she could start it; she said quickly, "*Command*, carcomp. Are you turned on?"

The carcomp answered instantly. "Yes—" It paused, apparently unsure of her voice. "Yes, 'Selle," it said at last.

"Will you respond to my instructions?"

"No, 'Selle."

Denice fought back an urge to unload the laser into the thing; the lights of the SBs were getting brighter and brighter. The plaza outside the van was like daylight. "Can you give me access to the InfoNet?"

"Yes, 'Selle."

Denice said rapidly, "Access 113102-KMET. *Ralf!*"

Ralf's voice came instantly: "*Denice!* Where are you?"

The voice behind them, gravelly and tired, said, "*Command*, cease InfoNet access. And don't either of you even try to move."

Denice did not. After a moment, when nothing happened, she turned very slowly, to where the monster sat, tucked into a corner of darkness in the back of the van, autoshot pointing at her and Dvan.

"Weapons down," said Sedon. "*Command*, close the door. We're leaving. Now."

The anger, frustration, every emotion of the last several minutes vanished in the instant. She did not know a word for what she felt, beholding the battered form of Gi'Suei'Obodi'Sedon; something that was at once profound rage and purest joy.

The smile that lit her face at his appearance would have terrified a less desperate creature than Sedon. Sedon had seen it before, the smile of the god whose service he had rejected fifty thousand years ago.

He sat with his knees drawn up toward his chest, leaning back against the inner hull of the AeroSmith, autoshot propped on his right knee—his left leg was broken in three places, and his hip.

His finger rested on the autoshot's trigger.

Sedon watched calmly as his enemies placed their weapons

on the carpeted floor of the van, not managing to care much whether he or they lived or died. When they had done as he instructed, he said quietly, *"Command, lift."*

The AeroSmith picked up and flew west, away from the descending fleet of semiballistics, into the gathering dark, chasing the last dim light of day.

Fifty of the most finely trained and taught professional soldiers on Earth, the best of the best, descended through the shell of the Latham Building. They moved downward in no tremendous rush, but with the practiced speed of professional soldiers, augmented by improved musculature, widened senses, subtler communication. Unarmed men and women on the eighteenth, fourteenth, and thirteenth floors were allowed to surrender; were snakechained en masse, and the Elite moved on.

Deep radar showed the distinctive signature of bones covered by ceramic laminae, moving on the fifth and sixth floors, and, motionless, in the lobby; by now the Elite knew what they were dealing with. They took the sixth floor in a quick, savage assault whose outcome was never in doubt, left eight of the Japanese cyborgs in various states of dead before moving down to the fifth floor, without fatalities or injuries of their own.

The two imitation Elite on the fifth floor committed suicide before the true Elite could get to them. They had cut their own throats; apparently the skin of the imitation cyborgs' faces and throats had not been toughened.

BAD DESIGN, commented one Elite to another.

OR VANITY.

EITHER WAY, A LACK OF COMMITMENT.

They moved down to the fourth floor, and then the third, where they found nineteen martyrs hiding in a stairwell.

The martyrs identified themselves as such by shooting at them after the Elite had identified themselves. The Elite obliged; martyrs were always happier in heaven anyway.

Commissionaire Mohammed Vance, in the darkened lobby of the Latham Building, used his toe to turn one of the dead cyborgs over on his back. Vance had seen holos of the Japanese cyborgs; but this was his first opportunity to see one in person.

Well. It looked Japanese, certainly. A soft, soft face; the skin not treated at all. Vance snorted with contempt. Twice in his early career he had taken laser shots to the face that would have killed one of these cheap Jap knockoffs. For vanity, or to let them stay concealed in the general populace—for *whatever* reason—it was a poor decision.

This one did not seem to have any visible marks on him. Vance wondered briefly what had killed him, but did not truly care enough to probe for the death wound.

Perhaps he had broken in some unexpected way.

Vance looked around the lobby. He was forty-seven years old; by Elite standards, old for such work as this. In the last two days he had not slept, had barely eaten. He had reached San Diego, the place where the American rebels would make their last, most desperate stand, and found a city in disarray, scattered and ineffective opposition, and rebel headquarters with the rebels killing each other and saving the PKF the need.

He shook his head slightly, in what might have been amusement if he had not been so bone weary. These were the people who had dreamed of toppling the greatest power in all of human history; probably they had made detailed plans for what they would do after the overthrow; spent the Credit before they'd earned it.

Mohammed Vance shook his head again, and walked out into the plaza in front of the Latham Building. The PKF had knocked out power to most of the city; they had strung arc lamps, powered by the SB's onboard fusion plants, around the edge of the plaza, to light things. Corpses were scattered about, but most of the living humans in the plaza were PKF; a scant dozen, sitting snakechained together on the ground in front of a PKF semiballistic, were rebels. Vance walked over toward them.

His personal aide, Captain Hilè, approached him. "Commissionaire."

Vance nodded, slowed slightly. "Report."

"Sedon is not among the prisoners; he may be among the dead."

"Go on."

"An AeroSmith VTL, civilian cargo model, lifted as we were approaching the city; it was the fourth vehicle of the three that still sit here in the plaza. In the general attack it was ignored—one car among thousands—but the satellite record shows that it headed out west, over the ocean. Toward Japan. We're tracking by satellite, and they're still moving."

Vance stopped in front of the snakechained prisoners. "Do they have the range to make Japan?"

"Not in that vehicle. No sir."

"Close?"

"Not even remotely, sir." Hilè hesitated. "Hawaii, possibly."

Vance nodded. "Send a bulletin. Alert them. If it reaches Hawaii, take the vehicle into custody, if possible; or destroy it."

"Otherwise?"

Vance shrugged. "Let it go. If its pilot wants to drown, it's one less we have to execute." He nudged one of the prisoners with his boot; the man seemed in some way vaguely familiar. "You!" The prisoner, an older Asian man, looked up at Vance with such a pitiably terrified expression that Vance was moved to compassion. His knees creaked as he lowered himself down to the old man's level, spoke to the man in English. "Calm down, old fellow. What is your name?"

"Ho, sir, Tommy Ho!"

"What were you doing with the rebels, Tommy?"

"Not work the rebels," Tommy informed him. "Work the shop. Sell candy, hot dogs, gum." Tommy paused, added diffidently, "Best chewing gum! Wrigley's Spearmint! Number One!"

Vance nodded. "Yes. I'm sure." He stood slowly, chuckled. "I'm getting old, Captain. He looked familiar to me."

The prisoner looked down again, and his features settled into an emptiness that might have been mistaken for serenity.

Vance's aide said, "They all look alike, sir."

Vance nodded. "True enough. Print him with the others, genes, eyes, palms and fingers. Let me know."

Hilè nodded. "Yes, Commissionaire."

Over an hour had passed since David Castanaveras had flown south in a stolen Chandler 1790. He was, in a direct line, very nearly 250 kilometers away from the Latham Building.

Up on the nineteenth floor, his handheld, taken away from him when he had arrived at the Latham Building and stored casually in an empty locker, listened carefully for the tiny radio beacon implanted next to David Castanaveras's heart. Several times in the last few minutes it had not received enough of a signal to be sure that it was registering David's heartbeat.

It lost the signal again. The handheld waited, counting.

After David's heart had been stopped for a full thirty seconds, his handheld detonated itself.

The top eight floors of the Latham Building came off in gorgeous, majestic slow motion. Most of it fell down into the plaza where Mohammed Vance stood next to Robert Dazai Yo.

- 29 -

The AeroSmith flew through the black night, five meters above the surface of the waves.

They had been moving westward for most of an hour and a half, at near two hundred klicks an hour.

Denice sat on the floor facing the monster, hands on her knees. In their movement there was no sound but the rush of the wind. "What did you do to him?"

It was the fifth time she had attempted to engage him in conversation. The first four attempts had failed. The last time he had fired a round from the autoshot by her head. In a larger space it would have killed her. Here he was so close that the buckshot did not have time to ungroup much.

A single pellet had dug a furrow in her left temple. The rest of the shot had struck the instrument panel behind her; some of the ricochet had struck Dvan.

Denice had not blinked and Dvan had not flinched. The van did not seem to be damaged. It continued to fly straight and level.

This time Sedon simply raised an eyebrow, said, "I?" in a voice cold and blank. "No more than he earned."

The subject of their conversation sat motionless, facing forward, where Denice had left him. After laying down his weapon for Sedon, Dvan had closed his eyes and gone still.

Denice watched the monster, made no attempt to hide her regard. The man was plainly exhausted. And badly injured; his leg and hip must be hurting terribly. Blisters made one side of his face livid, though not the other, and for a moment Denice was forcibly reminded of their evening together in his penthouse, of the white glow across one cheek, the pale infrared on the other.

He was bleeding even yet in several different places.

But Sedon's eyes upon her were never less than alert, and the barrel of the autoshot never wavered.

"And what was that?" Denice persisted. "What had he earned? Why?"

Sedon's voice was sleepy, but the sleepiness of a great cat, prepared for anything. "My dear. He took from me so many, *many* things. Love, and youth, and plans. The community of my own kind. You have heard his tale of our coming into this eternal exile; I fought for justice, not power. For the right to determine my own life, for those around me to determine theirs. All my life that has been all I ever sought. To determine my life as I would."

Denice said in a small voice, "I empathize."

"Indeed. You would."

"What did you do to him? How can I fix it?"

Mild surprise crossed Sedon's features. "You don't know?" A weary smile touched him. "I thought you did. I have been sitting here impressed that you knew to invoke his Dedication, and surprised that the Shield Dedication should yield up a man who would fulfill that obligation even while the wire sits in his skull, pouring electricity into his pain center." The smile sat on his features, distant and dreamy. "And to think I was admiring your ruthlessness in controlling your Shield."

Denice's eyes widened. "You mean—"

"At its highest setting, if it is as I left it." Sedon gestured with his free hand. "Go, take it from his skull. I won't stop you."

Denice rose, turned to where Dvan sat in the front seat, facing into the onrushing darkness. Her fingers probed the unruly thickness of his hair; and here. A small round plug, no larger than a thumbnail, tucked under the thick black hair; she got a grip on it with two fingers and tugged.

Dvan leaned backward in the seat, eyes staring up at the vehicle's ceiling, nothing visible in them but the whites, and sighed. Muscles she had not even realized he was holding tensed abruptly released across his body.

His eyes closed again and he went limp.

"You said something to me, in our last conversation. I've been wanting to ask you about it."

Sedon nodded. "That being?"

"You said you had *changed* yourself. But I did not see it."

"Unfortunate."

"How did you mean?"

Sedon sat quietly for so long Denice did not think he intended to answer her. "There was a day when survival was not all I wished of the world. When I wanted companionship. Love. The respect of peers—the *company* of peers." He shook his head with a weariness so profound Denice believed it would have killed her to experience it, closed his eyes, and leaned back against the hull. "And I believed that by resurrecting the memories of the man who had wanted those things, I might find myself more able to comprehend the things that drove *you*."

"I don't understand that. *Why* was it important for you to understand me?"

"You are a Dancer, within a day or two. I see the Consecration recently within you."

"Yes."

"But you have not Danced yet. Am I a Dancer, though I Dance no more?"

Denice sat still, looking at Gi'Suei'Obodi'Sedon.

At length Sedon opened his eyes again, looked at her over the barrel of the autoshot.

Denice took a deep breath, steadying her shaking nerves, and said, "Who do you want to be?"

Gi'Suei'Obodi'Sedon leaned forward ever so slightly. "It's too late for me to make that choice."

The words came to Denice in a rush, a tumble: "But the reality is that you *do* have a choice. You are not just the description of your experiences; the one who was a Dancer once, or an exile, or who led a rebellion; with all of those things taken away, *you* are still here. You are a whole person, Sedon, and you must make choices as a whole person. Perhaps that part of you who was a Dancer is dead. But *you* are not dead. Some person you used to be is dead. But *you* are here, with *me*, right now." Sedon nodded, very slowly, and Denice said, "I've died twice already myself, and I'm only twenty-three. But it does not make *me* dead."

"I do not understand your people," he said later. "You are— very different from us."

"We would be," Denice said. "I forget how Dvan put it—the

descendants of his people's criminals and insane. Even with modern geriatrics we don't live all that long. We have to live *now*."

Sedon nodded.

"It's the place I understand you least, Sedon. You're prepared to live tomorrow, remember having lived yesterday; but the man I'm sitting with isn't even sure he's alive, because he does not Dance."

Sedon said softly, "I wish you would Dance for me."

Denice shook her head. "There's no space."

"And if there was, you wouldn't." He spoke with calm certainty.

"It wouldn't be appropriate."

"It would upset the god," Sedon said.

Denice shrugged. "It would make him happy if I were to kill you."

Sedon looked at her over the autoshot. "Do you think you could?"

"I won't."

Sedon nodded. "Be careful how you spurn him, child. His pain is vast, and if you touch upon it you will regret it."

"I'll take my chances."

"He is not used to having Dancers who will not obey."

Sometime later, Denice said, "We'll never make Japan in this thing. Were you planning on rendezvousing at some point?"

Sedon looked at her over the rifle. "We can't reach Japan in this car?"

Denice felt her skin prickle. "You didn't *know* that?"

He considered it. "No. What's wrong with it?"

Denice said slowly, "There's not enough fuel in it."

"But all four of these vehicles were fueled before we took off."

"They're *vans*. They're designed for short trips; eight or nine hundred klicks, tops."

Sedon considered it. "I have never had occasion to operate one," he conceded. "Do we have fuel to return to California?"

"I don't know—" Denice rose and went forward, looked for the fuel display to the far left, untouched by the sole autoshot blast to the center panel. She turned back to Sedon. "We're past the halfway mark now. We're going to have to swim some no matter what we do."

Sedon nodded. "I see."

Denice came back, stood over him. "Do you want to live?"

Sedon looked up at her. "I think I would like that. Does that sound a very foolish thing to say at this point?"

Denice said softly, "Give me the gun."

Gi'Suei'Obodi'Sedon leaned forward slightly, reversed the weapon, and handed it to her.

"Awaken me when it's time," he said.

And he closed his eyes and leaned back to sleep.

She awoke William Devane, told him.

"Have you tried calling out?"

"Of course. He shot the InfoNet link."

"To be sure, what else." Devane paused, said in his ruined voice, "We should kill him now."

"We will not."

"We'll not make shore, I think. He's in no shape to swim. We'd be doin' him a favor."

"Your brogue has gotten much stronger."

Devane shrugged, eased back in his seat. "He's a bore, Dvan is. Single-minded and with a refreshing lack of introspection, but I've had enough. I got rid of him."

"That's a neat trick."

"I've no need to die to see Hell. A damn eternity of pain Sedon put us through; but Dvan took it personally. And the Speakings, he didn't take those too well either." Devane paused. "Think on it. A quick jump over the side, you and I—and our own chances that much the better."

Denice sat next to him and watched the fuel gauge. "No."

Devane nodded. "How far off shore will we drop?"

"A hundred klicks. Maybe a hundred and twenty."

"I am a good swimmer. But I have never swum that far."

"I have."

"Sure, and we should let him go down with the car."

"William Devane, killing is wrong."

"And I hope you're a *very* good swimmer, lass." Devane paused. "My lady."

"Cut that out."

"Denice."

• • •

"Sedon?"

"Yes?"

"Are you awake?"

"As much as I need to be."

"Come on. We're going into the water."

He looked up at her. "Denice, I wish you'd been a boy."

Denice said nothing, then: "I think Lan was going to say the same thing to me."

A day and a half later, near morning, as false dawn lit the skies to the east with a faint grayness, the waves washed ashore a pair of limp, motionless forms.

After a time, Denice Castanaveras rolled over onto her back, and stayed that way while the morning sun came up and made the world warm around her.

The still form beside her did not move at all.

Sometime later Denice let go of his wrist.

She opened her eyes and stared up into the pale blue sky and figured the odds.

The CityStates were not a bad bet; a quick bout of biosculpture, change the color of her eyes, pick up the Erika Muller identity permanently; the knowledge that Denice Daimara was Denice Castanaveras, even if it got out, would not damage her much.

Join Trent.

Or she could stay on Earth, take the chance of ending up in Peaceforcer hands.

People who knew: Trent, Jimmy, Jodi Jodi, Robert, and Devane. Her brother, of course, wherever he was. Lan, and Chris Summers, Doctor Derek, and Sedon. McGee, Ring, and Ralf the Wise and Powerful.

She had no idea what had happened to Devane or Robert, but did not think either of them could be brain-drained anyway, even if the PKF caught them. Summers and Lan and Sedon were dead beyond doubt. McGee, and Ring, and Ralf the Wise and Powerful. Ralf was safe.

Trent and Jimmy were in the Belt.

It left Ring, McGee, and Jodi Jodi, Doctor Derek and her brother.

There might be others, but it was a chance she would have to take.

She sat up slowly. For the first time since she had known him, Sedon's features seemed not watchful, or calculating, or enraged, or anything except peaceful.

His eyes were open and caked with salt.

She wiped the salt free and closed his eyes, watched him lying peacefully in the sand throughout the long morning, the corpse of the man who had invented rebellion fifty thousand years prior; and it came to her that it must be very hard to be a hero.

They first saw the form walking down the empty beach, at the waterline, a body slung over one shoulder.

It moved slowly down the packed wet sand, water washing around its ankles.

The PKF outpost sat at the edge of Pacific Coast Highway, looking down over the beach. Eight PKF unslung laser rifles and brought them to bear on the slowly advancing figure.

The Elite in command, twenty-nine-year-old Elite Sergeant Pekar, saw her more clearly.

His optics resolved her in detail when she was still a kilometer away. A woman of slightly above average height, young, lean and muscular, wearing black fatigues whose sleeves were cut off at the shoulders. She was barefoot, with white skin and vaguely Asian features, with black hair so short it looked like a military cut.

When she was still a hundred meters away he made out the color of her eyes, a green the color of emeralds.

When she was twenty meters away, at the edge of PCH, Pekar called her to a halt. With his men covering him he came forward to meet her.

"Identify yourself."

The woman grinned at him, a smile that had no humor in it at all. "I'll do better." Like a bricklayer unloading a bag of dry ferrocrete, she unslung the dead man's body and dropped it unceremoniously to the pavement in front of them. She raised her voice to be heard by the PKF behind him. "This is the corpse of Mister Obodi, the leader of the Johnny Rebs." Pekar was aware of the murmur that went through the mostly American

Peaceforcer troops standing behind him. "I am the personal assistant of Unification Councilor Douglass Ripper, Jr." The sunlight dazzled against the brilliant green of her eyes, against the single drop of sweat trickling down the sculpted muscle of her upper arm. "The bounty for Obodi was dead or alive. Well, this is him, and he can't get any more dead than this. I'm Denice Daimara, and I'm alive. And I'm claiming the six million Credits."

The Last Dancer

You say you had to do it
But I don't believe that's true
And I guess that later on tonight
I'll say a prayer for you

                    —Mahliya Kutura,
                    Independence Day
                    "Street Songs,"
                    2078 Gregorian

DateLine: November 30, 2076

I'm feeling very relaxed these days, so I wanted to take a moment of your time—to catch up on my mail, make a threat, and share a dream I had.

I am not back from my retirement.

For all of you who wrote and especially for all of you who got emotional, asking that I return to writing the column—I mean, Jesus. Get a life.

Speaking of Jesus, this one is for the webdancer in Philadelphia. I don't know how you got my InfoNet ID, and I don't care. Don't call again. I've never turned anyone to DataWatch in my life, but you could be the first. (And if not DataWatch, I know a couple of Players who eat punks like you for lunch.) I appreciate that Jesus died for my sins—but I didn't ask him to, and frankly it seems a little presumptuous on his part. I'm a big boy and I'll handle my own sins.

Speaking of sins, to the girl in Baton Rouge—yes. I've tried that one. But thanks for the offer anyway; you have a genuine flair for description.

And on the subject of offers, to Michaud Delancie, press secretary to the Secretary General: you ugly sociable disingenuous pig-fucking diseased lying greasy-palmed stringy-haired frog son of a bitch. I wouldn't write speeches for the Secretary General if he was the last Secretary General on Earth, which, it seems clear, is the idea. The immense arrogance of the man would be appalling if it wasn't exactly what we've come to expect from SecGen Eddore. Still, I'm troubled—are you sure this man is an American? That he was born here?

It's common knowledge that Eddore's mother didn't speak to him for three years after the onset of the Troubles. How about it, Chuck? Getting the cold shoulder again?

So. Anyhow, I keep having this dream I wanted to tell you all about, one where I pick up a pumped laser and go climb up on some high spot, some fine upper location with a view, and watch PKF Elite through the scope. The modification to blow the power supply out in three or four shots is, I'm told, ridiculously easy; I'm kind of surprised that it took a rebellion to get the knowledge out into the general public.

I can't, of course, tell you how to make the modification. That's covered by the Official Secrets Act of 2076.

But in my dream that I was having, the one where I went up to a high place and looked down, in that very same dream I was scanning through the Fall '76 Black Box Catalog, and I stop on page 112, and the part number as4077b01 sort of leapt out at me. Yes. And it looks very much like a direct replacement for a part commonly found inside most Excalibur Series I through Series IV variable lasers.

I'm told the same modification can be made to most hand masers, though you'll likely only get one shot with it.

The Secretary General probably wouldn't appreciate my sharing this dream with you, but what the hell. I don't really appreciate the things he's been trying to share with me recently.

Come to think of it, I suppose Eddore must be an American.

'Cause the TriCentennial has certainly been good to him.

If a little less so for the rest of us.

Later.

"Utter lie. Given Shawmac's frequenty and well-publicized tirades against the office and person of the Secretary General, it hardly seems likely that we would attempt to retain him to write speeches for the Secretary General. . . . You in the back. What's that? Oh. Yes. The Prosecutor General likely will try to have him executed for publishing that Black Box listing. So he couldn't write for us anyway."

—Michaud Delancie, press conference, December 2, 2076

- 1 -

The PKF did not believe her story. Denice had never expected them to.

But it made for excellent propaganda, and she pointed it out to them. She had learned that much from Ripper, that a thing need not be true if it could be made to seem so.

They gave her the six million and made her famous. She was the woman whose loyalty to the Unification had been stronger than the ties of nationalism, a woman who had understood herself a citizen of the world.

When it was over, she was, next to Secretary General Eddore himself, one of the most admired and hated human beings in the system.

The Peaceforcers executed Robinette Cabot, the man who had introduced himself to Denice as Doctor Derek, on August 12, 2076. He was the 4,408th American executed since the end of the rebellion.

They released video of his execution to the Boards, as they had released video of the executions of 4,407 others; Rebs and Claw and even a few innocents wrongly accused.

Denice had followed Cabot's case without intervening; she had not dared, not in his case or those of any of the others she recognized from her times in Iowa and Santa Monica. She watched him die, standing in front of a PKF firing squad, wondering why he hadn't used his knowledge of her to save his life.

Perhaps he had tried, and they'd executed him anyway, to avoid warning her. The thought made the skin crawl on the back of her neck, but there was nothing at all she could do about it.

They sat out on the patio, at Ripper's beachfront house in

Hawaii, early on the morning of December 15, and watched the returns come in. An exercise in futility, Ripper muttered at one point, and with justification; they were going to lose and they had known it for the last month.

At lunchtime Ripper ushered his aides outside and sat alone with Denice. Balloting was less than four hours under way, with over twenty left to go: nonetheless the results were clear. *"Command,* main off." Ripper turned away from the large holofield as it vanished. "He's the man who held the Unification together, and he's running fifty-five percent. I'm somewhere around thirty-two." In a matter-of-fact tone, Ripper said, "We're not even going to get a second ballot." He sighed, rubbing his temples. "If only Japan hadn't fought so well."

Denice and Ripper ate lunch together quietly, sitting together in the large, empty dining room. The quiet babble of the newsdancers was barely audible in the background.

When lunch was over Douglass went outside and sat on the balcony overlooking the bay.

Denice turned the smaller holos off and joined him.

"Well," said Ripper grimly, after a long silence, "he got what he wanted. Fourth term, fifth term—the clone of a bleeder plans to hold on forever."

Denice nodded.

Ripper said, "I'm going to have to do something about this."

Later that evening they sat out on the patio and watched the waves ripple over the surface of the water. The wind had come up and it was chilly. The sun was only a few minutes away from touching the surface of the ocean.

Douglass ordered them coffee drinks with whipped cream, and Denice sat cuddled inside the circle of his arms, watching the orange glow of the sun, while they waited for the waitbot to bring their drinks.

Douglass murmured, "Romantic, isn't it?"

"I noticed."

Denice thought that perhaps Douglass was nervous; he said it very abruptly, utterly without his usual smoothness. "Will you marry me?"

Trent. The thought came and went; Denice smiled with just a touch of wistfulness, said gently, "No. No, I won't."

His arms tightened around her slightly and he sighed. She did not think he was surprised. "Why not?"

"I have things to do."

He was silent then until their drinks came. After the waitbot had left he said quietly, "Such as?"

Denice sipped at her drink. Whipped cream with chocolate shavings on top, coffee with brandy underneath. It was very good and it warmed her as it went down. She licked a dab of whipped cream off her upper lip. "I don't work for you, Douglass. And I can't tell you."

He held her then while the sun set, flooding the bay with orange light. Even after the sun had completely set the sky was a gorgeous deep blue laced with glowing scarlet clouds. Glowfloats bobbed out over the bay, turned themselves on. One stationed itself a few meters above them. "I guess," said Douglass finally, "if you don't trust me enough to tell me about your personal business, marriage is probably a very bad idea."

"I'll tell you someday. I promise."

"Finish your drink and let's go to bed."

"Do you trust me to tell you when I can?"

"Let's go to bed."

Before he dropped off to sleep, he said quietly, "You should run for the Unification Council. The people who vote in Unification elections are mostly pro-Unification anyway; they won't think you're such a traitor. I think you'd win a seat."

Afterward, lying in bed with Ripper, head on his shoulder, while listening to his quiet sleep, Ralf the Wise and Powerful came to her.

"I traced him to Las Vegas."

- 2 -

Christine Mirabeau sat motionlessly on the prison cot. She did not get up when he came in. "Mohammed. I had hoped you'd come visit me before—before tomorrow."

Vance nodded. His floatchair stopped twenty centimeters away from her. He wore the formal uniform of the Elite Commander, the uniform Christine herself had worn until July 4, 2076.

His left leg was gone above the knee. Fixing a badly injured

Elite is difficult; the technology of the day did not permit them to clone a leg, cyborg the leg, and attach it. He'd probably end up with a robot leg, when he had time to learn to use it; it took a few weeks for the neural connection to grow in, and it was distracting until then. Christine had heard that his left arm was in a cast until only a few weeks ago. Some of the finest biosculptors in the world had worked on him, in sessions lasting *days*. To Christine it seemed the only effect of it all had been to leave him with slightly less expressiveness than ever.

"The uniform looks good on you," she said. "I always knew it would."

"You're not surprised."

"To whom else would they give it? You can be proud, Mohammed. To be forty-eight years old, and the second most powerful person in the System—it's a great accomplishment."

"Apparently they haven't told you how you're to be executed."

No PKF Elite had ever been executed before. Christine nodded, a bit jerkily. "No. I've been wondering; we're not easy to kill. In the mouth?"

"No. Undignified, given that it will be done on camera. We considered lethal injection and decided against that as well; the toxins and viruses with which we are familiar, your nanovirus immune system is also familiar. It would take quite a while even if successful; you would likely suffer convulsions, and it seemed inhumane. Some wanted to put you in front of a firing squad. Once again I dismissed it as inhumane; it would take several minutes for you to die. Drowning was discussed; so was dropping you from a high building. A few of the more bloodthirsty suggested that we use the pumped lasers the Rebs developed."

Something in her cyborg eyes twitched. "You're going to boil me alive?"

Vance shook his head. "No. I requisitioned one of the damaged orbital laser cannon. It was functioning at twelve percent efficiency; Space Force had decided it was not worth repairing, and they were going to destroy it. It came downside yesterday. You will be vaporized before you know anything has happened. It should be nearly instantaneous."

"On holocam."

"We are not ashamed of what we do, Christine. Even to our own. We can't touch Eddore; he is widely believed to be the man who kept the Unification together, and making public his crimes would tear the Unification apart. But even if the public does not quite understand why you are dying, Christine, the PKF does. And the example will stand."

Her stiff Elite features bore no trace of her feelings. "How did you manage the cannon?"

He understood her; relations with Space Force were strained as never before, primarily over his pullout of the Elite during the retaking of the laser cannon. "I paid for it. It's remarkable how honored the Unification's servants are to be bribed by the Elite Commander."

"I wouldn't know," she said, without any irony at all. "I never had occasion to find out." After a pause, she said, "Thank you."

He spoke with what was, even for him, abruptness. "Why did you do it, Christine?"

She took a long deep breath. "It seemed like a good idea at the time."

Vance's stare did not waver at all. "I need to know."

"Simulations showed the Rebs with a chance of *winning*, Mohammed. Eddore came to me early last year. He showed me a way to get the Rebs and Claw to rise; showed me convincingly that if they rose this summer they could never win, and that, after they rose, we would have the moral justification—and the votes—to wipe the rebels from the face of the Earth, to break them for good."

"Did it never occur to you that the best way to see that they could never win a revolution was to ensure they never had the opportunity to engage in one?"

She hung her head and spoke in a low voice. "He is a very convincing man."

"And you gave him another term. And another, and another—do you understand what you've *done*?" Vance moved in his floatchair, great bulk shifting restlessly. "We don't have time for me to list all the sins you've committed; you'll be dead first. But you've done these things:

"You've given the Rebs a taste of blood. Before this, they were *afraid* of the Elite. They dreaded us, because we were the nightmares that could not be killed. Now they merely respect us; thousands of them have seen Elite die; twenty-two still at large have killed Elite themselves. We will *never* regain what we lost on those battlefields, Christine, and ordinary PKF and Elite will die with increasing frequency because of it.

"You've done worse than that, though. You've given all of us cause to hate. You stood by while fools played with matches in a forest full of dry wood, because you hoped that after the fire we might have gained some advantage. We lost three hundred forty-seven Elite, a hundred and ninety thousand PKF troops. Nearly two million Americans died, most of them innocent, in the retaking of the West Coast. In Japan better than half a million Japanese died. And all those people have friends and loved ones who will dream of vengeance for those they have lost.

"If all those things were not enough, Christine, the worst thing you have done is this: you have changed the nature of the dialogue. Before this year, even in Occupied America, even among those who opposed us, there were *limits*. The Rebs and Claw have had fifty years to employ nuclear devices against us, fifty years to make every city on Earth, from Capitol City down to the towns in which you and I were raised, a military target; and for fifty years they have refrained. Christine," said Mohammed Vance softly, "this is something we've buried so deeply only six PKF and Eddore himself know it: we recovered twenty-two thermonuclear warheads, stored on semiballistics in San Diego. We don't know if there were others, and we likely *will* not know until, unless, they are used against us. Those Reb and the Claw left alive have lost nine in ten of their comrades, and they are consumed with hatred. And one way or another, Christine, we will *pay* for that hatred."

Christine Mirabeau stared at Vance. "Mohammed, the simulations Eddore showed me suggested that they could *win*. All they needed was a leader, and if we'd waited for Trent's return we'd have given them a leader to make this Sedon, *wherever* he came from, look like the rank amateur he was."

Mohammed Vance rapped on the door to her cell. They both heard the guard returning for him. "I have not seen the simulations you speak of, so I cannot say if they are accurate. But I will tell you this; there are worse things than losing to the likes of Trent, and fighting with allies like Eddore is one of them."

"You weren't there," Christine Mirabeau said. Tears stood out brilliantly against the glittering black Elite eyes. "You can't know."

The door opened behind Mohammed Vance. He sat there for just a moment, resplendent in the black-and-silver dress uniform of the Elite Commander.

"No," he said. "I can't."

He turned his floatchair about and left.

They executed her six hours later. The cannon vaporized her

and melted the wall of the Detention Center against which she had been stood.

- 3 -

"Hello, McGee."

McGee peered through the darkness, was abruptly aware he'd come downstairs without a weapon. "How did you get in here? The restaurant is clo—" McGee stopped. "Hello, Denice." He glanced around at the darkened room of empty tables; all the staff was gone. "I was just going up to the office. Have a beer and total the receipts. Join me?"

"Sure."

Upstairs the old man said, "I'm surprised to see you."

"I heard they took your hotel away. For back taxes."

McGee nodded. "It's true. The Fringe doesn't support a hotel of that caliber, not for real. And I can't prop them up any longer, I don't have the outside income."

"I'm thinking of buying some property in the Fringe."

He smiled. "I hear you can afford it."

"I need to establish residence so that I can vote for you when you run for the Unification Council."

McGee said gently, "Dear, there is no Unification Councilor for the Fringe. We lack representation, we always have."

Denice Castanaveras said, "That's going to change. The Barrier is going to come down, and I'd like you to start looking at property for me to buy." She reached into her coat and withdrew an infochip. "This is an authorization for transfer of funds. One hundred thousand CU drawn against the Bank of America."

He left the chip lying on his desktop. "For what?"

"You're the most respected man in the Fringe, McGee. You're tough in an area where they admire that. I need your help."

"I need to ask you a question, then."

"Yes?"

McGee's gaze was very steady. "The Reb leader, did you kill him? Did you kill Obodi?"

"When it came right down to it, McGee, I tried very hard to save his life."

McGee nodded thoughtfully. "Okay. You want me to run for the Unification Council? Why not you?"

"I can't stand the publicity, McGee. Right now I'm well known—infamous—but for what I've done, not for what people are afraid I'm *going* to do. If I ran—" Denice shook her head. "Between the Troubles, and then Trent's help, it wouldn't be easy to prove I'm Denice Castanaveras. But if I stay in the public eye, eventually someone's going to manage it. I've survived one trip into the lights, McGee. But I can't stay there."

"What exactly do you have in mind?"

Denice was a long moment answering him. "A lot of things. One at a time. Get Public Labor's budget cut, make it possible for the Labor clients to get out into society again. Bring PKF numbers in the O.A. back to prerebellion levels. Try and improve relations with the CityStates and the Collective. Stop the use of the copy-protection birth-control viruses and make the Ministry of Population Control stop sterilizing women and instead make sure that contraceptives and abortion are always available." She paused, said softly, "I could go on. I've been thinking recently, a lot. There's never going to be a successful revolution on Earth, I know that now. If we're going to change things, we're going to have to do it from the inside out."

"People have been trying to change the Unification from the inside out for fifty years, Denice."

"They weren't me."

The old man smiled, just a quirk of the lips. "No, they sure as hell weren't." He picked up the chip, slid open a desk drawer, and held it above the drawer. "The Barrier is going to come down?"

"Yes."

He dropped the chip inside.

"I need one last thing." She reached across his desk and Touched him. *You will never speak of me to anyone.*

"Hello, Jodi Jodi."

Jodi Jodi had watched her enter the hotel, watched her walk through the lobby to the registration desk. "Hi. What can I do for you?"

Denice reached across the desk, Touched her. *You will never speak of me to anyone.*

Jodi Jodi stared at Denice when she removed the hand. "You know what?"

"What?"

"You're the most conceited person I ever met in my *life*."

It had been two weeks since she had last been by the dojo.

Robert was not there; she had given up expecting to see him again. If he were alive, she thought he would have returned by now. She walked through the empty dojo, went upstairs and worked for a while on Robert's garden. He would not have recognized it had he returned today; Denice had forgotten to put up the greenhouse walls, and the first snow had killed many of the more delicate plants. She'd put the walls up then, and the transparent plastic sheeting across them to keep the snow off the plants, but the damage was done.

She didn't have time to work on the garden as it required, and did not think Robert would have appreciated having anyone but her do it.

She spent much of the morning at it, feeding the plants, making sure they had sufficient water, checking the radiators to verify that the garden got sufficient heat. She weeded, pruned dead branches and leaves, trimmed those very few plants that were growing sufficiently well to require it.

After a bit, she sat back on her heels and examined her work. Good. Good enough.

At the noise, she turned her head slightly to the right, into the sunshine . . .

The basketball came skipping along across the damp grass, and the old gardener got his hand up to knock it down. At the last moment the ball took a bad hop and bounced up in a beautiful arc, and the gardener lowered his hand and watched the ball go up over his head, come crashing down in the middle of his bonsai.

The garden lay against the wall of a complex of buildings surrounded by tall fences, with barbed wire across the tops of the fences.

Above one of the buildings a holo said, Public Labor Barracks for Children, Chino.

The eight-year-old boy chasing the ball, Daniel November, came to a stumbling halt in front of the gardener.

The gardener into whose garden the ball had intruded looked at the ball, turned slightly and looked at November. He was an old Asian fellow, chewing gum, wearing a hat against the bright California sun. He looked at November from under

the brim of the floppy sun hat, with eyes that held no particular
expression at all. Finally the boy said, "Can I have my ball
back?"

The gardener lifted himself up from the small cart he sat on,
reached into the delicate arrangement of stones and plants
upon which the basketball had crashed down, and retrieved it.
In the process November saw that both of the old man's legs
were missing, chopped off just above where his knees should
have been.

He tossed the basketball to November. Holding the ball
with both hands, the boy said, "Thanks. Thanks a lot. What
happened to your legs?"

"A building fell on me," the old man said.

The boy was half willing to believe it: "It did not."

"Truly. The top eight stories of a skyscraper. Fell right down
on me."

"That would have killed you," the boy said scornfully.

The gardener sat chewing his gum. "Probably. But a
Peaceforcer Elite fell on top of me, and saved me from the
worst of it."

"Did it kill the Peaceforcer?" the boy asked hopefully.

"No," said the gardener. "They are very hard to kill."

"Too bad," the boy said, but he knew it was true. "Do your
legs still hurt?"

"No. It happened almost thirty years ago."

November considered it. "Maybe I believe you."

The old man straightened on his cart, a slight movement,
but for the very briefest shiver of a moment November had the
feeling that he was talking not to an old cripple, but to a very
deadly *thing*.

"Daniel November," said the gardener, "I will never lie to
you."

The boy shook himself slightly, grinned at the old man. "All
right." He turned and ran back toward the basketball court
where his friends were waiting for the ball, turned again and
yelled, while running backward, "Hey! What's your name?"

The old man called back, "Tommy. Tommy Ho!"

" 'Bye, Tommy!" He turned again, ran back toward his waiting playmates.

The gardener returned to his garden, set about repairing the
damage the ball had caused.

. . . and Denice Castanaveras blinked as the warm sunlight
faded; the old man and his garden vanished, and left her alone

atop a cold dim rooftop in New York City, in the year 2076, in the dying days of the TriCentennial.

- 4 -

On Tuesday, December 22, 2076, Denice used the Erika Muller identity to purchase a semiballistic ticket to Las Vegas. In Vegas she walked from the downport to the Tropicana Hotel. It was an hour walk, but she did not hurry; she had never been to Vegas before, and the sea of light was impressive, if somewhat dehumanized.

Squads of PKF stood duty at every major intersection, armed with both laser rifles and needlers. Three times during her hour-long walk Denice was required to present her handheld for identification. Identification checks took longer these days; the PKF were far more thorough, checking ID against bank accounts, passports, criminal records, credit records, all the paraphernalia that went with an established identity. Denice had occasion to be grateful that Trent had been so thorough in establishing the identities, and that Ralf had kept them up for her.

She could not imagine someone without her resources passing false ID to the PKF today.

At the Tropicana she hesitated briefly, then went inside. The scanners did not catch the hideaway at her wrist, or else they got enough people wearing them that they were not going to do anything about it except watch her.

Business was more than good; people were trying to take their minds off events in the world outside. In the United States, Ripper had taken 84 percent of the vote despite his well-known association with the traitor Daimara; Eddore's reelection had sent most of the country into a depression, and people were dealing with it in their own ways.

She was early; the woman was not off duty yet. At the change machine she touched her handheld to the payment slot, purchased a hundred Credits' worth of tokens. She took a chair at a table where a bored older man with bad hair dealt twenty-one on a two-Credit limit.

She played carefully, out of curiosity, and lost slowly. She did not cheat until she had lost most of her hundred Credits. Once she started looking at the dealer's cards she won steadily; within half an hour markers totaling a thousand Credits sat on the surface of the green felt table. She realized with surprise that people were simply standing, watching her play, and made herself stop winning; in the next five minutes she had a disastrous run of luck and lost back all but about two hundred Credits. People wandered away as her luck changed, and she cashed out and went looking for Laurie Slepan.

Five minutes later they were seated across from one another at a private table in the darkened casino bar. Slepan was an older woman by Vegas standards, perhaps forty; but she still presented a petite, cheerful, friendly appearance. Her hair was carefully coifed, her makeup impeccably done—an original design, Denice suspected. Denice could see what it was that David had found attractive. "I'm looking for John Albright. How long did you date him?"

The woman shook her head. "I don't know who you mean."

Answer me.

Slepan hesitated, then smiled at Denice. "Gee, not long. I mean, he was here a couple of weeks I guess."

"Where did he go?"

"He—" The woman closed her mouth abruptly. "He—"

Denice closed her eyes and—

Late at night, cuddling together in David's hotel room. She'd learned about the wire just the other night, her fingers catching on the socket in his skull during sex, stroking his hair, and didn't know what to make of it; he didn't act like any juice junkie she'd ever met. When he wasn't on it, and she'd never seen him on the juice, he seemed, though withdrawn, pleasant enough, and completely in control of himself. That night he'd talked for the first time about leaving. Unsurprised, she had asked when he would leave, and he'd said, "Soon. I'd have been out of here by now except that I couldn't win too quickly, it would have drawn attention. I can't go back to where I was. Too many people know that Zanini was with Obodi. If I went back they'd arrest and execute me." He laughed at that; really amused, Laurie thought. "For being Zanini. I'd feel very foolish dying for that, they have much better reasons to kill me." After a long silence, he said drowsily, "Soon. I think I'll go to Mexico. I keep thinking of that sunset. I'd like to see more sunsets like that one. California's not a very fun place right now. Maybe I'll go to Baja." He rolled over on his side, met her eyes, and said, "You can't ever talk about me to anyone."

Denice shook herself, rose from the table. *So that's what it feels like on the receiving end.*

Laurie Slepan said, "Miss? Could you tell him I said hello? If you find him?"

She had time; while Ralf searched Baja California, she took the bus to Flagstaff, Arizona.

It was an old vehicle with one fan slightly out of alignment; the fan's whine cycled up and down in a predictable pattern, and if the bearings were not replaced soon it was going to break down.

The fan was up at the front; she sat in the rear of the bus, the very last row of seats.

At their first stop, a tiny roadside town of only a few hundred people, about a half hour out of Vegas, a thin, white-haired woman of indeterminate age got on the bus, wrapped in a long black shawl against the cold. Denice glanced at her without expression as the woman made her way back down the bus. The seat next to hers was one of the very few empty ones, and she did not particularly want company.

The woman seated herself next to Denice, put her huge thatch purse on the floor at her feet. "Hello, dear."

Denice nodded, turned her head slightly away, and closed her eyes as though she were trying to sleep.

She awoke sometime later, to darkness. The bus moved along the road quietly and without any real hurry, only occasional traffic speeding by above them, or off to one side of the road. She yawned, stretching.

The woman in the seat next to her smiled at her as she stretched. "Did you have a good nap?"

"Yes."

"Good. I set a spell so that you would."

Denice looked at the woman with interest for the first time. A thin, dark-skinned woman, with white hair and white eyebrows; tiny little crow's-feet clustered around the edges of her eyes. A single clear crystal on a white cord hung down over her black shawl. One of her several rings had the shape of an ankh; something in her gave Denice the impression of great age. "You're a witch."

The woman's cheeks twitched just a bit. "Aren't you?"

Denice found herself smiling back at the woman, almost against her own will. "Maybe. I lived at Goddess Home for a couple of years; have you ever been there?"

"Oh, I visited, now and again. Doubtless I'll visit again someday." The old woman looked at something off in the darkness ahead. "There's no hurry, is there?"

"I guess not." The bus ground to a halt, and a pair of PKF rifles slung across their backs, boarded it. They moved backward through the bus, and started checking IDs in the rear row, moving forward. Denice and the older woman gave their handhelds over when requested; the PKF handed them back in a few minutes. It took most of twenty minutes before they were through, and let the bus move on.

Against the background of grumbling, Denice said softly, "I could get really tired of this."

The woman shrugged. "Oh, this will pass. You learn that, when you get old enough. All the politics—" She made a dismissive gesture, chuckled warmly. "Best leave it to those who enjoy it."

"This doesn't bother you?"

The woman looked at Denice with what Denice thought was true curiosity. "Should it? There are things in *my* world I have concern for. Raising my children, for one. Aiding my friends. Helping the crops grow. Magick, and fulfilling the responsibilities that the power confers. Teaching and learning, enjoying *my* life. What is it to me if some men want to stop a bus and board it and ask me silly questions?" She shook her head. "The corn doesn't care. It still wants water. My children don't care; they still need to be held when they hurt themselves, and praised when they do well, and loved all the time."

Denice grinned. "No offense intended, but you sound just like all the female witches I've known. And most of the men."

"Men can't be witches," the woman said dismissively. She appeared to consider what Denice had said. " 'No offense intended.' By that, I suppose you mean that it's a criticism anyway?"

"I've never felt particularly close to women who didn't want to concern themselves with anything but—well, women's concerns."

"I see," said the witch. "Do you know what your problem is, my dear? You were raised by a man, and you were never close to your mother."

Denice looked at her. "That's true." The woman who had

borne her, Jany McConnell, had been busy helping to raise 240 other children of Denice's age, and she had never had much more time for her than for the others. "My father *made* time for me. My mother wouldn't, or couldn't. So I felt closer to him." She shook her head. "How do you know that?"

"You hold yourself like a man. You gesture like a man. I would imagine that the people in your life who have deeply mattered to you have been men."

"And you can tell this just by looking at me?"

"And talking to you. What's your name, dear?"

Denice paused. For some reason she didn't want to lie to the woman; but she was traveling under the name. "Erika," she said finally.

Amusement touched the woman's eyes. "Very well. Once, Erika, you would not have *known* who your father was. The first family the human race ever saw was that of mother and child. We didn't know who the father was because we didn't know that sex caused children. Children were believed a thing that we women brought forth of ourselves, because we were the *source* of life."

"You talk like you were there."

"The only family and only parent was the mother. It's in the deepest part of us to need a mother. That you did not have one is your great loss. It kept you from learning how to be a woman." The bus came to a slow, sighing stop, and touched down. "This is my stop." The woman fumbled with her bag, got it up off the floor, and came to her feet. "I know you understand what power is, Erika. But I'm not so sure you understand what it's not." The woman leaned over and kissed Denice on the forehead. "Have a good trip."

Denice said softly, "Who the hell are you?"

"I won't insult your good sense. Someday, the Goddess willing, we'll meet again. Good-bye, dear."

Twenty minutes later Denice got out of her seat, went up to where the conductor sat smoking a cigarette and watching the road. "Excuse me?"

The conductor, a girl of about sixteen, said, "Yeah?"

"Back there, where you let that woman off. What's there?"

"Not a damn thing. Not for ten klicks in either direction."

"I see."

The conductor shrugged. "Hope she doesn't freeze to death. It's a cold night out."

The woman who had instituted the worship of the Goddess in pre-Hellenic Greece, who was to her knowledge the last surviving exile of the Old Human Race, stood at the edge of the road and watched the bus disappear into the darkness.

Her name was Mai'Riga'Say, and she had wondered, since hearing of it, about the woman who claimed to have killed Mister Obodi, the Dancer Sedon whom Say had, in another existence, followed into exile.

Having met her now, Say could almost credit it; she had not seen a Dancer in—she did not know how many thousands of years, but not since her last encounter with Indo, and *that* was back before the new humans had rediscovered writing—but if Say had ever seen a Dancer in her life, then this Denice Daimara was one.

The world was becoming a very interesting place of late.

Say gathered her shawl about herself, stepped from the road, and walked alone into the frozen dark desert.

The medbot examined the wall again. The cold was very bad for the PATIENTS inside, and the old adobe was cracked in far too many places. It did not provide anything like the insulation the medbot's research had indicated was possible with adobe. Fortunately, the ferrocrete mixture the medbot had ordered should fill the cracks nicely.

The medbot kept one eye on the small PATIENT, who was working on a car in the backyard, while it troweled ferrocrete into the cracks.

At 10:12:32 A.M. a human entered the medbot's field of vision. An adult female, in a black coat and black jeans—how very interesting; it recognized her. This was one of its PATIENTS, and nobody had ever told it that the relationship had ceased. The medbot put down its trowel and walked forward to greet the PATIENT, as the PATIENT came through the gate and walked up the long path to the house. It noted that its instructions to apply skepticism to everything she said were still in force, decided not to believe anything she said to it, and said cheerfully, "Mademoiselle Daimara, how are you? How is your radiation poisoning? Have you fully recovered from it? Are you perhaps suffering from frostbite from your walk in the cold?"

Callia fed her vegetable stir-fry and coffee with cinnamon. After the long, cold walk from the bus depot—Callia's house was eight klicks outside of town—it was exactly what Denice wanted.

The huge window to the south looked out on a backyard the size of Texas, with half a dozen wrecked vehicles scattered around it. The girl, working on the least wrecked-looking of them, was about twelve years old, a slim black-haired child; Denice thought she herself must have looked like that once.

"Have you spoken to 'Selle Lovely?"

Callia shook her head. "No. I think if I was to hear from her, it would be a laser in the night. Domino says she blames me for a lot of how things happened." She looked at Denice. "And I wouldn't walk down any dark alleys if I were *you*, either. Even Domino thinks you sold us out, even after I told them about the nukes and said I'd have done the same thing."

"Have you talked to her much?"

"Just the once. They're both just barely keeping one step ahead of the PKF. They stopped at a Temple in Fort Lauderdale where I had asked the Reverend to call me. He called the number I'd given him, and I called back and got Domino." Her smile was sad. "She kept me talking for most of ten minutes. Ralf said they had a Player trying to trace the call, and afterward they tried to trace the number."

"That must hurt."

Callia nodded. "Some. Domino was all the mother Lan had after the PKF executed ours. It's almost made me glad he didn't live to see her do this; it would have hurt him a lot."

"And you?"

"At one point I trusted Domino with my life, and Lan's. But the line of work I've been in, you learn that everyone has limits. After a while you stop trusting so completely. That's why none of them know about this place." After a moment she added, "I was seventeen when my mother died. Lan was only ten. I'd *had* my mother, as a child, almost as an adult. When they executed her they took away my friend, but they couldn't take away my mother."

"Apparently not. You gave her the same name?"

Callia glanced out at the girl, only her legs visible beneath the car. "Why not? My mother was a happy woman. The child has the same genes, exactly. I've given her most of the things my mother had, down to the cars my mother grew up working on."

"Make a little Speedfreak out of her."

Callia smiled. "My mother's adopted sister lives two klicks further up the road; even after the Speedfreak Rebellion in '63, the PKF never connected her with my mother, never questioned her. I figured if the PKF didn't find her then, no one else would now. So we moved Angel here for the summer, tucked her away before everything went up." She could not hide the pride in her voice. "During the TriCentennial summer she sewed herself a jacket with *Faster Than the Wind* on it. She was wearing it when I got back. So yes, I'm raising her the way my mother was raised. It seems to be working; Angel is a happy child."

"Angel de Luz."

"You pronounce that well." Callia paused. "It means Angel of Light."

"I know. What are you going to do now?"

Callia said simply, "Raise my daughter."

Denice knew the answer before she started, but made the offer anyway; things change. "I could use you. I'll pay for your biosculpture, get new legs cloned for you, have a new identity established."

"I'm staying with my daughter." Callia stood, carefully—the braces on both of her legs made walking difficult—and started clearing the dishes away from the table; Denice got up to help her. "I'm staying where I'm needed."

Denice spent the night there. In the hour before dawn, Ralf the Wise and Powerful awoke her. "He's in Cabo San Lucas."

- 5 -

Cabo San Lucas sits at the tip of Baja California Sur, fifteen hundred kilometers south of the Occupied American border.

Denice came in via SB, to a downport located, for some eccentric reason, sixty klicks outside of town. The day before

Christmas it blazed with heat, the sun beating down like fire on the southern tip of California. The ride into town was interesting; she paid three Credits to sit in a bus that rode on *wheels*, all the way into town. The road into town ran alongside the ocean most of the way, and the water was a shade of brilliant blue that Denice had never seen before in her life, completely different from the blue of the Pacific Ocean in Southern California. She did not think it was her imagination; her genie eyes were sensitive. The quality of light was different, and all the colors were truly brighter and more vibrant. The woman behind her mentioned the same thing, and the man she was with explained that it was because the sun had less atmosphere to travel through.

You have no poetry in your soul, Denice thought of the man.

When they were still half an hour outside of town she found herself growing absurdly cheerful. She clamped her teeth shut, deepened her breathing, and did her very best to meditate through the waves of her brother's happiness. The world was a fine, fine place, with colors like something out of the most gorgeously holographed sensable. The people on the bus around her were the nicest and handsomest and smartest group she'd ever had the opportunity to meet, and it occurred to her that with the kind of Credit she had now she could treat all of them as they deserved to be treated. When they got to town she would see what sort of entertainment they could round up. Dancing, certainly, she'd show them dancing like they'd never seen—

As they entered the outskirts of Cabo San Lucas, her happiness vanished like a switch being thrown.

The smile faded from her features.

He was staying in a room at the Hotel Hacienda, the oldest hotel in Cabo San Lucas, built in the prior century. Her bus took her directly to the hotel, deposited her in a little automobile courtyard of red brick, with a fountain at the center of it, just outside the hotel. A porter appeared in a white uniform, margarita in hand, and attempted to hand it to her, asking in heavily accented English if she had any bags for him to carry.

She said quietly, *I'm not here,* and walked by him.

The lobby was covered by a roof, but otherwise was open to the air. She did not need to ask where David was, did not know what name he was using anyway. She could *feel* his presence off in the northern wing of the hotel, the slow turn of his thoughts. People passed by her but she did not see them. The walkway led through a tangle of tropical plants, flowers and hanging plants with gorgeous scarlet leaves. She did not notice them.

At room B-6 David opened the door and said quietly, "Come in."

Gloom sat upon the room like a shroud; curtains drawn, lights extinguished. Denice moved forward, following David. Enough light to make out red ceramic tile, rugs, a blue-tiled kitchen, hanging lamps, prints on the walls of scenes from a bullfight.

Small and gorgeous and empty of any personal touch.

The main room was bare except for the rug and a pair of couches. David gestured to one, dropped into the other, put his feet up on it, and leaned back, hands clasped behind his head. He sat waiting, patiently, hopelessly, and eventually she spoke.

"What happened?"

He did not pretend to misunderstand her. "I made a mistake." His laughter sounded almost real; cool, amused. "When I was fifteen, I Touched a juice junkie's mind while he was on the wire." David's voice trailed off, and his features grew distant.

"What's it like?"

"You want me to turn mine on? I don't think you could avoid understanding then."

Denice said softly, "Tell me."

"It's like—like moving in sunlight—you know the way the sun feels on your muscles, when you're using them the way they're supposed to be used. It was like the best steak I'd ever had and the first beer after a day of hard physical work, and it reminded me of the taste and smell of the first girl I ever made love to." His stare touched Denice, hot and fierce. "It's better than being in love. I've been in love. It's so much better than that. Being in love hurts sometimes because the people you love change and turn into someone else. But the wire never changes." His voice was tinged with harshness and his stare did not waver: "It's always perfect."

"Have you ever tried to quit?"

"Oh, God. Yes. I've tried. In the early days I could go two, three weeks without it. Mostly by not sleeping. If I went to sleep I'd wake up happy. In my sleep I'd get up and put it in and turn it on. So I didn't sleep. I threw the plug away. A dozen times. But it was too easy to get another one—"

The thought touched Denice. She stared at him. "You *sold* wire."

His manner was mocking. "I've done worse than that, Denice. I've killed thirty-odd people. Just business; I never killed anyone where it was personal, because I wanted to or I was offended or anything silly like that. So anyway, tell me about yourself. What's been going on with you?"

With the full strength of her Gift, Denice Touched her brother.

When they were done, it was dark outside. The hanging lights had come up automatically.

They sat together on the couch, holding hands.

As children they had done that.

You're tired of the wire.

To death.

You'll never give it up.

I can't.

Do you remember the last thing Carl said to us?

Remember that you're tougher than they are. Better. David laughed. *Kill the fuckers. You know, I've almost killed myself a half dozen times because he said that to us. I've been so scared, so many times. I haven't felt better than anyone.*

I can leave you here, and let you go on. Or I can take it away from you.

I would very much like to see you dance.

She let go of his hand, stood slowly. She could hear the deep pounding of her heart as though it were the only sound in creation.

David Castanaveras whispered, "Dance for me."

The back of her throat was very tight. "Turn the lights off, David."

The room plunged into utter darkness.

Denice moved slowly through the space, learning it in the darkness. Here is the rug and here are the walls and the curtains and here is the open place. There are the couches and there is David, standing motionless in the darkness, watching the heat of my body.

Touch me.

She felt his thoughts touch hers, engage, become more

deeply her own, and she was he and she watched herself as she closed her eyes, and rolled her head, back and forth and around, loosening the muscles, and then stretched, slowly, like a cat, feeling the kinks shake out, rotated her wrists, lifted her hands above her head, threw her head back and stared up toward the blackness of the ceiling. Muscles stretching. Her right knee came up, toward her chest, and she leaned farther backward, arms spreading out behind her like the wings of a great bird, hands curved and fingers almost touching, and bent farther, hands coming down to touch the floor behind her—

And moved through it with shocking abruptness, onto her hands and spilling through the backward roll in one swift snapping motion, came back to her feet and was aware of the pale pearl glow covering her from head to toe, reached out, breaking the space around her, pulling it back into a slow, graceful spin, and the light began to flare around her, glowing in her eyes, trailing from her fingers as they moved through the liquid air. David moved with her, watched her, completely transfixed, merging together, feeling the heat of the living Flame shine upon his face, feeling through her as the Flame ran across her skin, burned the air in her lungs like real fire, and then for some timeless period there was no awareness of self, no awareness of her, no awareness of him; only the motion of the Dance, of life itself made real, and David's features had grown gentle, serene; Denice could feel the peace that came to rest within him as she came out of the last flowing motion, slowing, stopping, turning to face him through the blistering glare, her entire being quivering on the edge of the moment, and time stilled and the moment came and in that instant of calm certainty she brought the gun from the place where it rested cold against her forearm and whispered

I love you
and fired.

—*Daniel Keys Moran*
Los Angeles, Southern California
1989–1992

The Great Wheel of Existence

ORDER (The Chained One)

THE WILD ZONE

Growing Uncertainty Principle Permits Time Travel!

Here There Be Time Wars

CHAOS (The Serathin)

N E S W

(Timelines to the West are primarily matter-based; to the East they are primarily anti-matter.)

(There are no anti-matter timelines shown on this map. Map is not even remotely to scale.)

Walks-Far Empire

Hawking's Page

The Armageddon Blues

The Continuing Time

TRINITY

The Sunset Strip

About the Author

Daniel Keys Moran lives in Los Angeles with his two sisters, Jodi and Kathleen, and his new nephew, Kevin. He has written four books so far in his *Tales of the Continuing Time* series; *The Armageddon Blues*, *Emerald Eyes*, *The Long Run*, and *The Last Dancer*. *Tales*, as planned now, covers a time period from sometime before the Big Bang to roughly 12,000 years A.D. and will be about 33 volumes when finished. Moran is working on a new *Continuing Time* book about Trent, part of a duology, which should be available in the early fall of 1994. He also works as a computer consultant, which helps him to figure out how the Crystal Wind might really work. In his spare time, Moran likes playing basketball, watching the Los Angeles Lakers (especially when they're winning), rereading Issac Asimov's books, driving around LA (at an advanced rate of travel) and hanging out with Kevin.

> "The best novel laid on Luna since
> *The Moon Is A Harsh Mistress.*"—Gene Wolfe

Growing Up Weightless
by John M. Ford

> "A brilliant book, an exciting story set in an imaginatively
> conceived and wonderfully detailed future
> and told by a poet."—Poul Anderson

Matthias Ronay has grown up in the low gravity and great glass citadels of independent Luna—and in the shadow of his father, a member of the Lunar governing council. But Matt feels aimless in a world where there is no more need for exploration, the new and different—and where his every movement can be tracked by his father on the infonets. So Matt and his friends plan a secret adventure. They will slip out of the city for a journey to Farside. Their passage into the expanse of perpetual night will change them forever...and bring Matt to the destiny he has yearned for.

[] Growing Up Weightless (37306-4 * $11.95/$14.95)
